The Staging of Drama
in the Medieval Church

Cathedral of Rouen. Nave toward the east choir, xiii century.

The Staging of Drama
in the Medieval Church

Dunbar H. Ogden

Newark: University of Delaware Press
London: Associated University Presses

© 2002 Dunbar H. Ogden

Associated University Presses
440 Forsgate Drive
Cranbury, NJ 08512

Associated University Presses
16 Barter Street
London WC1A 2AH, England

Associated University Presses
P.O. Box 338, Port Credit
Mississauga, Ontario
Canada L5G 4L8

The paper used in this publication meets the requirements of the
American National Standard for Permanence of Paper for Printed Library Materials
Z39.48-1984.

Library of Congress Cataloging-in-Publication Data

Ogden, Dunbar H.
    The staging of drama in the medieval church / Dunbar H. Ogden
        p.   cm.
    Includes bibliographical references and index.
    ISBN 0-87413-709-8 (alk. paper)
        1. Drama, Medieval—History and criticism. 2. Liturgical drama. 3. Theater—Europe—History—Medieval, 500–1500. I. Title.

PN1761 .O38 2002
809.2'516'00902—dc21   00-048819

PRINTED IN THE UNITED STATES OF AMERICA

To the memory of my brother David

Contents

Chapter 4. The Costumes

Chapter 5. Acting

Chapter 6. The Music

Source Notes for Illustrations

Note. In the keys on the architectural ground plans with performers' movement patterns, entries in parentheses ( ) refer to *probable* positions of persons or features; entries in angled brackets < > refer to features *not* mentioned in the dramatic text.

Frontispiece. Jacket. Cathedral of Rouen: Nave toward east choir (xiii century), High altar in east choir (xiii century). Anne-Marie Carment-Lanfry, *La Cathédrale de Rouen* (Colmar: Saep, 1973).

Figure 1. William St. John Hope, "The Plan and Arrangement of the First Cathedral Church of Canterbury," *Proceedings of the Society of Antiquaries of London,* 2nd ser., 30 (1917–18): figure 5, facing p. 152.

Figure 2. Heritage Museum, The Canterbury Archaeological Trust, Canterbury. See also *Canterbury's Archaeology 1992-1993: 17th Annual Report* (Canterbury Archaeological Trust, 1993).

Figure 3. Martin Biddle, *Excavations Near Winchester Cathedral, 1961–1968* (Winchester: Wykeham Press, 1969), figure 2, p. 72.

Figure 4. Detail of Figure 3.

Figure 5. Carol Heitz, *Recherches sur les rapports entre architecture et liturgie à l'époque carolingienne* (Paris: S.E.V.P.E.N., 1963), plate xl; from the Bavarian National Museum, Munich.

Figure 6. British Library Additional MS 49598, fol. 51v.

Figure 7. Hartker, *Liber responsalis,* St. Gall, Stiftsbibliothek MS 391, p. 33. Reproduced from the fronstispiece of Karl Young, *The Drama of the Medieval Church* (Oxford: Clarendon Press, 1955), vol. 1.

Figure 8. Nikolaus Irsch, *Der Dom zu Trier* (Düsseldorf: L. Schwann, 1931), figure 56, p. 102.

Figure 9. Nikolaus Irsch, *Der Dom zu Trier* (Düsseldorf: L. Schwann, 1931), figure 85, p. 132.

Figure 10. Carol Heitz, *Recherches sur les rapports entre architecture et liturgie à l'époque carolingienne* (Paris: S.E.V.P.E.N., 1963), 194; "d'après F. Arens."

Figure 11. Carol Heitz, *Recherches sur les rapports entre architecture et liturgie à l'époque carolingienne* (Paris: S.E.V.P.E.N., 1963), plate xviii.

Figure 12. Adapted from Norbert Koch, "Der Innenraum des Braunschweiger Domes," in *Stadt im Wandel* 4, ed. Cord Meckseper (Stuttgart: Cantz, 1985), 501.

Figure 13. Adapted from Norbert Koch, "Der Innenraum des Braunschweiger Domes," in *Stadt im Wandel* 4, ed. Cord Meckseper (Stuttgart: Cantz, 1985), 501.

Figure 14. D. Gustaf Dalman, *Das Grab Christi in Deutschland* (Leipzig: Dieterisch'sche Verlagsbuchhandlung, 1922), Tafel 5. In the nineteenth century the sixteen-sided structure was moved into a side chapel. Early in this century it was returned to its original position.

Figure 15. Clemens, Mellin, Rosenthal, *Der Dom zu Magdeburg* (Magdeburg: Creutz'sche Buchhandlung, [1852]), I Lieferung, Tafel 1. By the time of Clemens et al., the baptismal font had been moved to the third bay of the nave. Subsequent excavations revealed what was more probably its original position in the second bay, where it stands today. I have altered the Clemens drawing accordingly. The greater distance from the sepulchre makes for greater theatrical effect.

Figure 16. Giuseppe Vale, "Storia della Basilica doppo il secolo IX," *La basilica di Aquileia* (Bologna: N. Zanichelli, 1933), 56.

Figure 17. Karl Young, *The Drama of the Medieval Church* (Oxford: Clarendon Press, 1955), vol. 1, opposite p. 302.

Figure 18. Hans K. Schulze, *Das Stift Gernrode* (Cologne: Böhlau, 1965), 93.

Figure 19. Hans K. Schulze, *Das Stift Gernrode* (Cologne: Böhlau, 1965), 113.

Figure 20. Adapted from Klaus Voigtländer, *Die Stiftskirche zu Gernrode und ihre Restaurierung, 1858–1872* (Berlin: Akademie Verlag, 1980), 28.

Figure 21. Klaus Voigtländer, *Die Stiftskirche zu Gernrode und ihre Restaurierung, 1858–1872* (Berlin: Akademie Verlag, 1980), figure 124.

Figure 22. Klaus Voigtländer, *Die Stiftskirche zu Gernrode und ihre Restaurierung, 1858–1872* (Berlin: Akademie Verlag, 1980), figure 125.

Figure 23. Peter Jezler, "Gab es in Konstanz ein ottonisches Osterspiel?" in *Variorum munera florum, Latinität als prägende Kraft mittelalterlicher Kultur, Festschrift für Hans F. Haefele,* ed. Adolf Reinle, Ludwig Schmugge, Peter Stotz (Sigmaringen: Jan Thorbecke Verlag, [1985?]), figure 2, p. 97.

Figure 24. Peter Jezler, "Gab es in Konstanz ein ottonisches Osterspiel?" in *Variorum munera florum, Latinität als prägende Kraft mittelalterlicher Kultur, Festschrift für Hans F. Haefele,* ed. Adolf Reinle, Ludwig Schmugge, Peter Stotz (Sigmaringen: Jan Thorbecke Verlag, [1985?]), figure 1, p. 96.

Figure 25. Georg Dehio, *Der Bamberger Dom* (Munich: Piper, 1939), figures 6–7.

Figure 26. Friedrich Adolf Ebert, *Der Dom zu Meissen* (Meissen, 1835), facing p. 152.

Figure 27. Georg Dehio, *Der Bamberger Dom* (Munich: Piper, 1939), figures 2–3.

Figure 28. René Tournier, *Les Églises comtoises* (Paris: A. et J. Picard, 1954), 67.

Figure 29. Armand Loisel, *La Cathédrale de Rouen* (Paris: Henri Laurens, [1913]), frontispiece.

Figure 30. Marcel Aubert, "Saint-Benoît-sur-Loire," *Congrès archéologique de France* 93 (1930): facing p. 620.

Figure 31. Georges Chenesseau, *L'Abbaye de Fleury à Saint-Benoît-sur-Loire* (Paris: G. van Oest, 1931), 201.

Figure 32. "Mort de l'escuyer dans l'église des Cordelliers [Friars Minor] à Avignon le 16 Octobre 1791," in *Collection complète des tableaux historiques de la révolution française,* 4th ed., vol. 1 (Paris: Auber, 1804), figure 58, facing p. 233; engraving by Pierre-Gabriel Berthault after a drawing by Jean-Louis Prieur.

Figure 33. Karl Young, "Philippe de Mézières' Dramatic Office for the Presentation of the Virgin," *PMLA* 26 (1911): 228-9. Young's "schematic" drawing is not meant to approximate the plan of the church of the Friars Minor, Avignon (which was not cruciform in shape). The sizes of the platforms are obviously disproportionate to the size of the church. The words "pars occidentalis," "pars septentrionalis," "pars orientalis," and "pars australis" do not appear in Mézières' text.

Figure 34. Joseph Girard, *Évocation du vieil Avignon* (Paris: Les Éditions de Minuit, 1958), between pp. 294–5. Detail of a map of Avignon (1618) by Marco Antonio Gandolfo and Théodore Hoochstraten. The western façade of the church was added in the fifteenth century.

Figure 35. Wolfgang Michael, *Frühformen der deutschen Bühne* (Berlin: Selbstverlag der Gesellschaft für Theatergeschichte, 1963), 39.

Figure 36. Wolfgang Michael, *Frühformen der deutschen Bühne* (Berlin: Selbstverlag der Gesellschaft für Theatergeschichte, 1963), 41.

Figure 37. A reconstruction of Brunelleschi's apparatus, by Piero Turchetti, in *Enciclopedia dello spettacolo* (Rome: Casa editrice Le Maschere, 1954), 2:1198.

Figure 38. Feo Belcari, *La Festa della annuntiatione di nostra donna* (Florence: Bartolomeo de Libri, ca. 1500); composed by Belcari ca. 1450; reproduced from Alfredo Cioni, *Bibliografia delle sacre rappresentazioni* (Florence: Sansoni antiquariato, 1961), 231.

Figure 39. Adapted from Millia Davenport, *The Book of Costume*, vol. 1 (New York: Crown, 1948), 102.

Figure 40. Wolfgang Michael, *Frühformen der deutschen Bühne* (Berlin: Selbstverlag der Gesellschaft für Theatergeschichte, 1963), 16–17.

Acknowledgements

I wish to thank the following people for their professional assistance with the book: Ben Albach, Eric Alexander, Gordon Armstrong, Christopher Balme, Franz Bäuml, Jonas Barish, Melissa Beck, Clyde Brockett, Amelia Carr, Mike Clover, Fletcher Collins, Hans Croiset, René Devisch, Joseph Duggan, Robert L. Erenstein, Marianne Fennema, Paul Fitisoff, Andrew Galloway, Wim Gerritsen, Wim van Gerven, Julie Goda, Stephanie Green, Christian Günther, Ashok Gurung, Cyrus Hamlin, George House, Tatsuji Iwabuchi, Dirk van de Kaa, Bruce Kapferer, Saskia Kersenboom, Dragan Klaiç, Arnold Klukas, Ortwin Knorr, Dorothy Koenig, Desirée Koslin, Stan Lai, Ralf Långbacka, Lars Olof Larsson, Wolfgang Lederer, Shimon Levy, Peter Lichtmann, Hanns-Rudolf Lipphardt, Elizabeth Lipsmeyer, Nancy Lundigan, Richard McCall, Sam McDaniel, Hans Man in't Veld, Piero Matthey, Daniel Meyer-Dinkgräfe, Kathy Moon, Pamela Morgan, Alan Nelson, John Neubauer, Giselle de Nie, Michael Norton, Paul W. Ogden, Melody Owens, Alan Pearlman, Giselher Quast, Ruthild Redeker, Virginia Reh, Hugh and Velma Richmond, Marvin and Mary Rosenberg, Martha Dana Rust, Steven Scher, Bernhard Scholz, Piet Schrijvers, Hinrich Seeba, Paul-André and Madeleine Siegenthaler, James and Sue Stinson, Shireen Strooker, Roger Travis, Ronald Vince, Eugene Waith, Paul Werlen, Gemma Whalen, Bart White, Agaath Witteman, Georgia Wright, Jason Wu, Sabrina Klein Yanosky, Margarita Yanson.

I owe a particular debt of gratitude to the following people. Each is an internationally respected expert on the subject of one of the chapters. Nils Holger Petersen on Winchester and the *Regularis Concordia,* Chapter 1. David Bevington on staging space and set pieces, Chapter 3. Mireille Madou on costume, Chapter 4. Kees Vellekoop on voice and gesture, Chapter 5. Richard Crocker and John Stevens on music, Chapter 6. Each gave me a detailed critique of that chapter. Any errors in fact and judgment are mine, not theirs.

The privilege of collaborating as stage director with members of the Nova Schola Cantorum, Amsterdam, and their Music Director, Marcel Zijlstra, has provided an otherwise unattainable understanding of the liturgical drama. One must play it to know it. We have performed the *Visitatio Marie Magdalene* at the Abbey of Egmond, where the fifteenth-century manuscript originated, and the twelfth-century *Play of Daniel* at the Little Church Around the Corner in New York City and, during the Musica Sacra Festival, at the Church of Our Lady in Maastricht. I am grateful to Marcel Zijlstra and the Amsterdam Schola for making possible the day-to-day and week-to-week process of evolving a production. A dramatic text and a piece of music find their complete form not on a page but on a stage. With each church rehearsal, I gained fresh comprehension of text and music, and of the stage directions over which I had spent hundreds of library hours.

Alois Nagler, director of my doctoral studies at Yale, set me on my pilgrimage into the Middle Ages. Then for nearly a quarter of a century Clifford Davidson has invited, edited, published my research. Both have been my professional guides in medieval theatre, together with Richard Crocker in music. The steady friendship of Douglas McDermott and Robert K. Sarlós has resulted in radical reshaping of the manuscript. During the two-year process of preparing text and illustrations for publication, the manuscript has also been in the hands of Travis D. Williams. An inspired young scholar, he has served as a true research assistant. And then Patricia Deminna with her indexing skills made a key that opens the book.

Grants from the American Council of Learned Societies and the University of California's Committee on Research have allowed for two years in the Library of the British Museum, the collections of the Victoria and Albert Museum, and the Parisian Musée de l'Hôtel de Cluny—and for work with students as research assistants. I have regarded this collaboration with students, both undergraduate and graduate, as an ongoing process of teaching. At the same time, their questioning has pushed my efforts toward clarity.

I am happy to have had such a congenial and careful team at the Associated University Presses. An anonymous reader gave invaluable advice. Jay Halio shepherded the manuscript to the publisher. There Julien Yoseloff held his hand over the work of managing editor Christine A. Retz, and the meticulous pencil of copyeditor Tawny Schlieski.

My wife, Annegret, thought through nearly every idea in the book with me. Finally her study of Old French had some use, she says.

I am grateful to the following for granting permission to duplicate copyrighted material: Akademie Verlag (figs. 20, 21, 22), Art Resource (fig. 17), Bayerisches National Museum (fig. 5), Böhlau Verlag (figs. 18, 19), Canterbury Archaeological Trust (fig. 2), Dieterisch'sche Verlagsbuchhandlung (fig. 14), Gesellschaft für Theatergeschichte (figs. 35, 36, 40), H. Cantz Verlag (figs. 12, 13), Modern Language Association of America (fig. 33), Oxford University Press (fig. 7), Société Française d' Archéologie (fig. 30), Society of Antiquaries (London) (fig. 1), Stiftsbibliothek (St. Gallen, Switzerland) (fig. 7), Zanichelli Editore (fig. 16).

Figure 6: Folio 51v from the Benedictional of Saint Ethelwold (B.L. Add. MS 49598) is reproduced by permission of The British Library.

Figure 34: The map of Avignon is reprinted by permission of Les Éditions de Minuit.

Frontispiece and jacket photographs by permission of Éditions SAEP, Colmar, France.

The *Lament of Rachel* is reprinted from *Anthology of Medieval Music,* edited by Richard Hoppin. Copyright © 1978. Used by permission of W. W. Norton & Company, Inc.

The lament of *Judaeus* is reprinted with permission of the University Press of Virginia.

Musical examples 90, 91, 92, 93, and 94 from Susan Rankin, "Liturgical Drama," in *The New Oxford History of Music,* vol. 2: *Early Middle Ages to 1300,* ed. Richard L. Crocker and David Hiley, Oxford: OUP, 1990, are reprinted by permission of Oxford University Press. © Oxford University Press 1990.

Every effort was made to acquire reproduction permission for the following figures: 3, 4, 8, 9, 10, 11, 15, 23, 24, 25, 26, 27, 28, 29, 31, 32, 37, 38, 39. The author and publisher would be happy to acknowledge in future editions the holders of copyright for these figures should such information be brought to their attention.

Introduction

By the year 1000 A.D. the coming of the Marys to the Sepulchre of Christ was dramatized in sanctuaries throughout Europe. It happened during the liturgical celebrations of Easter. In the eleventh century the playing out of episodes from the Christmas story—the journey of the shepherds and of the Magi to Bethlehem—began to unfold within the rites and services of the church, and in the twelfth century not only were scenes added to the *Visitatio Sepulchri,* but a period of great theatrical experiment occurred with dramatization of subject matter also drawn from the Old Testament, hagiology, and eschatology. Records of this kind of theatre continue into the era of the Reformation, at which time the ceremonies of the church were "purified" and these little plays, with a few exceptions, ceased to be performed.

All students of theatre are aware of the fact that we find here a second birth of drama, a phenomenon and a process much more fully documented than the early phases of tragedy in sixth-century Athens. The plays of the medieval church and their origins have been subjected to rather extensive literary and philological scrutiny, made possible by collections of texts published by Carl Lange in 1887, Karl Young in 1933, and Walther Lipphardt in 1975–90. In 1972, Fletcher Collins published a book about sixteen examples of the music-drama based on his experiences in staging it. But as yet no major attempt has been made to gather the body of primary evidence for the mise-en-scène and to examine it from a theatrical point of view.[1]

The present undertaking represents an endeavor to set forth staging principles and document practices in a kind of theatrical performance engendered from European life during a period of roughly seven hundred years and which reflected significant aspects of that life. I believe that the study of a play must be accompanied by a conception, as accurate as possible, of the conditions of staging for which it was intended and that any important dramatic production can be regarded as the hub of a social-cultural wheel, joining the arts and contemporary society. The acting of the drama in the medieval church exemplifies this thesis and must be considered first of all in its own right and on its own terms, not merely as a sort of stepping stone to more exalted ground.

This study is based on the conviction that the *dynamis* in the Aristotelian sense—the personal, central, generating force—of medieval church drama is profound spiritual faith. Herein lies our greatest obstacle to understanding and interpreting it. Time and again we shall note the participation of the worshippers in the drama of the medieval church—in singing, in presenting offerings, in witnessing directly the evidence for the Resurrection. A clear dividing line between theatre and worship cannot be drawn at this point. Located intimately within liturgical observance, the representations were not only didactic in intent but also constituted in and of themselves acts of worship.[2]

I believe that true representational drama occurs here when an action (an Aristotelian *praxis*) is imitated by speakers or singers of dialogue who impersonate Biblical-historical figures. Furthermore, the action must be sustained, not merely a moment of a few seconds' duration, and the performers and audience must be aware, however dimly, that they are participating in the imitation of an action. During the *Visitatio Sepulchri* these are not really Hebrew women walking to a cave-tomb; the priest who steps from behind the high altar is not Jesus himself. In other words, to have a play one must have the sustained imitation of an action and the attitude on the part of the participants—performers and audience—that this is a play. A play always contains an element of make-believe. But let us repeat: These dramas are heard, seen, and felt in the context and spirit of the liturgical experience.[3]

Principles of Organization

Young arranged *The Drama of the Medieval Church* according to types of plays, following Lange's organization, and based his discussions of each play type on the assumption that the simplest text represents the earliest form out of which the given drama then evolved to a more complex state. For instance, Young grouped *Visitatio Sepulchri* texts as belonging to the "first stage" (the simplest texts), "second stage," and "third stage." This "Darwinian" principle is erroneous. Our earliest manuscript of a play type is often not the most rudimentary, and although a gathering of plays by type is a matter of convenience, it precludes an overview of what actually appears in each century and what occurs over time among multiple manuscripts from the same church. Young's method often leads him to ignore important chronology. To some extent, Walther Lipphardt's organization of Easter plays by date and conjectured or established provenance counteracts the Darwinian classification that Young imposed, although Lipphardt's organization retains the concept of three "stages" (Stufen) of dramatic complexity proposed in 1880 by Gustav Milchsack.[4]

It is my purpose in this study to consider the major theatrical elements which constituted the dramatic performances given within the church during the Middle Ages: playing area, set pieces, special effects, costumes, acting, and music. In his preface to *The Drama of the Medieval Church*, Karl Young noted: "The final comprehensive study of mise-en-scène in liturgical drama, indeed, has not yet been made. For such an undertaking this treatise, and the monographs mentioned incidentally throughout, may perhaps serve as a convenient point of departure."[5] Young's collection, together with Lipphardt's, does just that. The subject makes a whole and significant story in and of itself. From a theatrical point of view it allows the intensive examination of a special kind of performance, one limited to particulars of mise-en-scène, within the bounds of the church building.

In order to preserve a picture of single productions and onstage moments, and at the same time to set these in the context of widespread recorded detail, I have focused each of four chapters (3, 4, 5, 6) on a specific aspect of staging, attempting to select significant examples and to arrange them with surveys of related material. Within each chapter I have endeavored to retain a clear sense of chronology, having dealt with the problems of origins and the beginning principles of ecclesiastical theatre in Chapter 1, and having sketched in Chapter 2 an overall summary of available texts, kinds of plays and their rubrical information, and characteristics of the drama from each century.

Those dramatic manuscripts which can be assigned with some assurance to a given church at a specific period immediately invite us to seek information about the physical structure where the plays were acted: the church was the real stage. Therefore we shall turn to the data on these playing areas provided by historians of architecture, and, in some cases, by archeologists.

Young makes no apology "for having treated these pieces from an exclusively literary point of view," adding, however, that "the adequate editing and exposition of the music associated with the dramatic texts might well require a separate treatise equal to the present one in extent."[6] That treatise is being written in our own time. Quite recently musicologists have achieved major breakthroughs toward full, comprehensive analysis of the music. And in that a number of the available texts do contain notation, to shut out the sound of the music and to disregard its fundamental role in these performances would be as aesthetically unsatisfactory as an examination of an operatic libretto deprived of its score.

As this brief résumé indicates, the present investigation should be considered a second step following the publication of texts edited by Young and Lipphardt. Assignment of additional dramatic manuscripts to specific churches and an increase in available data on architectural form and decoration of these structures at the time of performance will permit more and abler reconstructions. The pictorial arts, especially manuscript illumination, must still be made to yield up precious secrets about dramatic art. Only the first pages in the whole story of medieval acting have been written. A few hints in the rubrics tantalize us to learn more about the composition of various audiences, the impact of performance both on performer and on audience, and the dynamics of performer-audience relationships. Beginning perhaps with textual genealogies, the growth and cross-fertilization of theatrical traditions in ecclesiastical communities remains to be fully studied. And in the extant music of church drama lie some keys to its origin and to these relationships. But I hope that this compilation and assessment of information on staging contained primarily in the plays themselves, along with the attempted reconstructions, will serve as a valuable next step toward a richer understanding of a significant genre of theatre. It developed in its own right over a period of seven centuries—a genre which reflected and gave expression to the mind and spirit of the Middle Ages, and which provided a major heritage of the Renaissance.

Chapter 1

Winchester and the *Visitatio Sepulchri* in the Tenth Century

Bishop Ethelwold's Text of the *Visitatio Sepulchri*

The oldest full play of the medieval church which we possess—the visit to the Easter Sepulchre—was set down in Winchester sometime during the latter part of the tenth century, and it is not until the twelfth century that we again find rubrics so rich in detail as to matters of performance. Between the years 965 and 975 a special ecclesiastical council was called at Winchester, the capital city of England, in order to draw up a code intended to supplement the *Rule of St. Benedict* in Benedictine monasteries throughout the country. The leading spirits of this movement were Dunstan, then Archbishop of Canterbury, and his close friend Ethelwold, from 963 to 984 Bishop of Winchester; the mind behind the document was probably Dunstan while Ethelwold was largely responsible for the execution of the work.[1] The resulting *Regularis Concordia* contains a series of special notes on customs of monastic life and worship. Its fifth chapter is devoted to Easter observances and includes the following lines referring to Matins, the first service on Easter Sunday:

> While the third lesson is being read, four of the brethren shall vest, one of whom, wearing an alb as though for some different purpose, shall enter and go stealthily to the place of the "sepulchre" and sit there quietly, holding a palm in his hand. Then, while the third respond is being sung, the other three brethren, vested in copes and holding thuribles in their hands, shall enter in their turn and go to [before, ante] the place of the "sepulchre," step by step, as though searching for something. Now these things are done in imitation of the angel seated on [in, at] the tomb [in monumento] and of the women coming with perfumes to anoint the body of Jesus. When, therefore, he that is seated shall see these three draw nigh, wandering about as it were and seeking something, he

> shall begin to sing softly and sweetly, *Quem quaeritis* [Whom seek ye]. As soon as this has been sung right through, the three shall answer together, *Ihesum Nazarenum* [Jesus of Nazareth]. Then he that is seated shall say [sing] *Non est hic. Surrexit sicut praedixerat. Ite, nuntiate quia surrexit a mortuis.* [He is not here. He is risen as He foretold. Go and announce that He is risen from the dead.] At this command the three shall turn to the choir saying [singing] *Alleluia. Resurrexit Dominus.* [Alleluia. The Lord is risen.] When this has been sung he that is seated, as though calling them back, shall say [sing] the antiphon *Venite et videte locum* [Come and see the place], and then, rising and lifting up the veil, he shall show them the place void of the Cross with only the linen in which the Cross had been wrapped. Seeing this the three shall lay down their thuribles in that same "sepulchre" and, taking the linen, shall hold it up before the clergy; and, as though showing that the Lord was risen and was no longer wrapped in it, they shall sing this antiphon: *Surrexit Dominus de sepulchro* [The Lord is risen from the Sepulchre]. They shall then lay the linen on the altar.

> When the antiphon is finished the prior, rejoicing in the triumph of our King in that He had conquered death and was risen, shall give out the hymn *Te Deum laudamus* [We praise Thee, O God], and thereupon all the bells shall peal.[2]

The second service then commences.

Two extant manuscripts reproduce this passage almost identically, attesting to use at least until about 1100.

The Position of the *Visitatio Sepulchri* in Ecclesiastical Observances

The monastic day was marked by eight devotional services, called the Canonical Office or Hours—Matins, Lauds, Prime, Terce, Sext, None, Vespers, and Compline—while Mass, distinguished by use or consecration of the Host and the Sacrament of Communion, was celebrated after Terce on Sundays and on special feast days. Matins ended near dawn, the traditional time on Easter Sunday morning at which the Marys came to the Sepulchre, and it is at the close of Matins, just prior to the singing of the *Te Deum laudamus,* that the *Visitatio Sepulchri* was usually performed.

It was no accident that the new birth of drama occurred right at the very fulcrum of the whole church year—a calendar meticulously measured with rites to commemorate the earthly life of Christ and to elaborate the spiritual life of man, leading up to the climactic Resurrection, discovered and witnessed to here by the women at the tomb together with the community of medieval Christendom. Such sanctity surrounded the very act of the Resurrection that the depiction of *Christus resurgens* at the Resurrection moment did not begin to appear in the visual arts until the twelfth century, and only toward the latter part of the Middle Ages did the emphasis in church ritual shift from the glorious conquest of death to the agony of death itself.[3]

The Question of Origins

By the year 1000 the Easter dialogue *Quem quaeritis* was sung all over Europe, either as a trope or as a little play.

There are two beginning points for the *Quem quaeritis* piece, originally composed in the artistic surge of the Carolingian Renaissance. It originated as a trope. A trope is an addition to the regular liturgy: one or more extra-liturgical lines inserted in and sung during a regular church rite. The *Quem quaeritis* trope was in dialogue form beginning with the question, "Whom do you seek in the Sepulchre," and the answer, "Jesus of Nazareth." One version of the *Quem quaeritis* dialogue precedes the Introit to the Easter Mass. It concludes with "Alleluia resurrexit dominus." It first occurs in southern French and northern Italian monasteries, the earliest manuscript dated 923–34 A.D., from St. Martial of Limoges: Example 1.[4]

The other version was sung just before the final hymn, the *Te Deum,* of Easter Matins. It concludes not with the "Alleluia" but with the familiar antiphon "Surrexit dominus de sepulchro" (The Lord is risen from the Sepulchre). It first occurs in northern French, English, and German monasteries. Example 2, from a tenth-century manuscript, comes from Prüm monastery.[5]

Quem queritis in sepulchro o christicole?
Ihesum nazarenum querimus crucifixum o celicole.
Non est hic surrexit sicut predixerat;
ite nunciate quia surrexit dicentes:

Antiphona:
Surrexit Dominus [de sepulchro
qui pro nobis pependit in ligno alleluia]
Te Deum laudamus

Which version and which placement of the *Quem quaeritis* trope came first we do not know.

As time went on, the pre-Introit version tended to remain ceremonial in form and performance, whereas the Easter Matins version tended to be dramatized, with numerous variations in the tenth and eleventh centuries. For instance, an eleventh-century pre-Introit version from Novalesa simply has two deacons behind the altar sing the *Quem quaeritis* lines with two "cantores" in the choir singing the "Ihesum Nazarenum" lines. On the other hand, an eleventh-century Easter Matins version from Melk has rubrics instructing two priests dressed in white as angels to sit by the altar as sepulchre, and two deacons representing the Marys to approach. The deacons wear dalmatics, have their heads covered "in the manner of women," and carry thuribles with incense. They are bringing spices to anoint Jesus' body in the tomb. After the angels have sung "Non est hic," the women uncover the altar-sepulchre, perhaps symbolizing a gravecloth. The rubrics also stipulate qualities of voice: the women at first with low or humble voices, the angels exulting as they sing "Non est hic," and finally the women turning to their fellow monastics (ad fratres) and singing "Surrexit Dominus" with bright, clear voices. As in this pair of contrasting examples, the pre-Introit version was not acted out, whereas the Easter Matins version often was.[6]

In the *Regularis Concordia,* Bishop Ethelwold combined the two versions into two episodes, one from French and the other from German monastic sources, and he introduced two newly composed antiphons, "Venite et videte locum" (Come and see the place) immediately followed by "Cito euntes, dicite discipulis" (Going quickly, tell the disciples). He created this music-play by shaping the *Quem quaeritis* lines into an episodic piece and by emphasizing narrative rather than the older ceremonial announcement of the Resurrection. The *Regularis Concordia* contains only the written text, but a second tenth-century document contains the music: the Winchester Troper. Example 3 is the text with music of the "Quem quaeritis" play from the Winchester Troper.[7]

Example 1. *Quem quaeritis* trope from St. Martial, at Limoges (923–934 A.D.), for the Easter Mass Introit.

This new composition by Ethelwold and his associates was not widely influential. But its principle of creation became the engine that engendered the liturgical drama for the ensuing six hundred years: the combining of available liturgical materials, the composing of new music and poetry, and the addition of explicitly representational elements all within the framework of the liturgy.

With their *Regularis Concordia*, Ethelwold, Dunstan, and the young Oswald were leading a monastic

Example 2. *Quem quaeritis* trope from Prüm monastery (x century), for Easter Matins.

Example 3. *Quem quaeritis* play *(Visitatio Sepulchri)* from the Winchester Troper (x century).

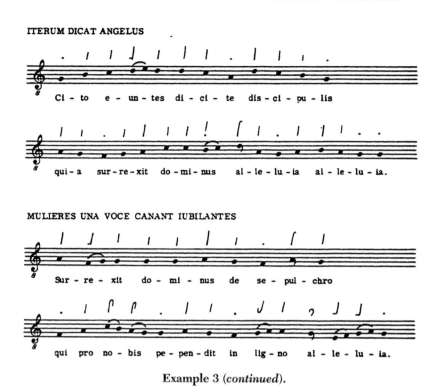

Example 3 (*continued*).

reform movement in England, following Benedictine propensity for modest experiments with the liturgy and for teaching within their ranks. As background for their devising of this full-fledged play one can cite Ethelwold's ongoing literary interests, his contacts with new movements in music and liturgy on the Continent such as the use of tropes, and the direct patronage of an enlightened king, Edgar. As background for the express teaching purpose of the *Visitatio Sepulchri*, one can cite Ethelwold's unique position as abbot and bishop of Winchester, where his church combined the liturgical functions of both monastery and the secular cathedral.

Furthermore, the thrust of the *Depositio* (ceremonial burial of a cross or the Host on Good Friday) and the *Visitatio Sepulchri* as stated by Ethelwold was not necessarily to teach the general laity but more especially members of the monastic community, and specifically those training to become priests or monks. Ethelwold writes that the *Depositio* is "for strengthening the faith of uninformed and uninstructed people and neophytes in particular" (ad fidem indocti vulgi ac neophytorum corroborandam). Ethelwold chose carefully the word *vulgus*, meaning at this time "uninformed people," rather than *vulgaris*, meaning "common people." *Indocti* means "uninstructed." Perhaps Ethelwold was thinking of 2 Peter 3:16, where with *indocti* the New Testament writer refers to people who do not understand St. Paul's letters. And *ac neophytorum* lays special emphasis—*ac* (and

in particular)—on those training for priesthood or monkhood, rather than referring to converts.[8]

By the same token, of the eight tenth-century "Quem quaeritis" texts possibly performed at Matins, only those from Winchester and the one from Verdun reveal signs of stepping outside the boundaries of liturgy toward an audience, toward drama, and toward teaching. In fact, as we shall see, the greater the distance between play and liturgical observance, the greater the inventive freedom in the dramatic composition.

The Sources of the *Regularis Concordia* and the Origins of the *Visitatio Sepulchri*

When we begin to ask ourselves where Dunstan and Ethelwold obtained their notion of the *Visitatio Sepulchri*, the *Regularis Concordia* directs us immediately to the Low Countries and to France, to the Abbey of St. Peter (Blandinium) at Ghent and to the Abbey of St. Benoît-sur-Loire at Fleury, from which monasteries the men at Winchester had summoned delegations in order to inform themselves as to monastic customs on the Continent.[9] While serving earlier as Abbot of Abingdon, Ethelwold had brought monks from Corbie to instruct the community in the chant, and later he sent one of his monks to study the observance of Fleury. In the late 950s Dunstan had spent a year or more in exile at the monastery of St. Peter in Ghent. It is quite probable that Ethelwold's drama was influenced in some way from the Continent—or even taken over from continental forms—but we have no proof.[10] Unfortunately no manuscripts relevant to liturgical observance at Ghent survive, but at Fleury is preserved a late twelfth-century collection of some of the most sophisticated plays performed within the medieval church—evidence of what we suspect to have been a strong dramatic tradition in that vicinity.

The Structure of the *Visitatio Sepulchri* and the Hand of the Director

The action of our first medieval play embodies a quest which comes to a successful conclusion in discovery. Lack of knowledge serves as the impetus for verbal exchange followed by a discovery, a jubilant reaction, and a public proclamation of the new knowledge. The structure we may call comic in that the play moves from complication to happy resolution, turning climactically on the two-phase revelation: the angel says, "He is risen," the women reacting with an *Alleluia*, and then the angel calls the women back to give them physical proof.

All of the elements of theatrical production exist in this performance. The playing space is a part of the church itself, here at the high altar, where a sepulchre has been set up with a veil in front. This set piece had contained within it a cross, which was removed before Matins, and now only the linen wrappings of that cross remain. Brothers from the monastery, who are dressed in vestments and carry hand properties, act the four roles: the angel is costumed in an alb—the basic, usually white, sleeved tunic of ecclesiastical garb—and holds a palm in one hand; the women wear copes—cape-like apparel, often highly ornate, worn by priests on festive occasions when they do not themselves celebrate Mass—and bear thuribles, probably containing incense, indicative of their intent to anoint the body of Christ with spices and ointments. The visual effect would impress the viewer with a sense of that same ancient sanctity which marked regular liturgical observance, endowing the actors with a rich timeless quality.

For the theatre historian perhaps the most remarkable single feature of the text lies in the attention to acting, with indications as to gesture, facial expression, and method of line delivery. The angel sits "quietly" at the tomb; when he sees the approaching women, he sings his first line "softly and sweetly"; he intones *Venite et videte* "as though calling them [the Marys] back" to the sepulchre; and he rises and lifts the veil in showing the place now empty. The women, probably making their entrance from the sacristy or from an area east of the high altar, move toward the sepulchre "step by step, as though searching for something"; the rubrics repeat the direction, for the angel sees them "wandering about as it were and seeking something"; the women answer his question in unison; when the angel exhorts them to tell the others of the Resurrection, they turn to the chorus for their *Alleluia* before the angel calls them back; on being shown the empty tomb, the Marys lay their thuribles within, take up the linen, and "hold it up before the clergy" while singing *Surrexit Dominus*; finally they "lay the linen on the altar." At the very outset the formal, symbolic action is touched with verisimilar elements.

Out of the accoutrements, the color and perfume and sound of liturgical celebration, Bishop Ethelwold devised the mise-en-scène of a production based on already traditional work of poets and composers. The lines in the early *Visitatio* texts derive largely from a liturgy that had evolved over a millennium, and the newly written music of the "Quem quaeritis" lines mingled with familiar melody, wherein the necessity for structuring the scene and the opportunity for the future dramatic author were self-evident. Although the manuscripts of the *Regularis Concordia* contain no score, we know something of Ethelwold's keen interest in music, and the neum-notation in the version of the *Visitatio* contained in the tenth-century Winchester Troper reveals the role of that plainchant attributed, along with the crystallization of the Roman rite, to Pope Gregory the Great (ca. 600).[11]

At the conclusion of the play, the Marys extend the gravecloths not only for the clergy to witness, but, as later texts will tell us specifically, also for the congregation as the symbolic apostles of Christ. The fact that this is a cathedral, with Ethelwold both bishop as well as abbot of the monastery, may well suggest the presence of a lay audience at Easter in Winchester. It is then that the populace enters into the discovery and often joins in the singing of a final, joyous hymn.

The Concept and Staging Principles of the Early *Visitatio Sepulchri*

The presentation within the church reveals an adoption of concepts basic to the symbolic and allegorical interpretation of the Mass by writers such as Amalarius of Metz (780–850) and carried on by Honorius of Autun (or of Augsburg?), Sicardus of Cremona, and Thomas Aquinas, who defined the Mass as a kind of reenactment of the life of Christ, with the celebrant as the chief, protean actor, and who conceived of the church year with its complex liturgies and festivals as an extension of this rememorative reenactment. This conception of Christian rite came into vogue at the time of this birth of drama, and the *Regularis Concordia* even cites a passage from Amalarius.[12]

That opponents of Amalarius complained about a tendency toward theatricality on the part of some celebrants in the Mass, whose form of delivery and gestures apparently became rather lively, is for us an indication of the solemn, measured nature of liturgical conduct, where the voice was raised in recitation, chant, and song.[13] Conscious attitudes toward these first plays did not differ essentially from attitudes toward other parts of the worship service in these early years.[14] Continued in the mode of Easter Matins, the acting was highly ceremonial, yet from the very outset we begin to find attempts at more approximate imitations of familiar, human deportment than generally permitted in the execution of the stricter ritual; here, for example, the Marys move "step by step [pedetemptim], as though searching for something." And the climactic display of the left-over shroud, the intimate and now suddenly useless wrapping of death, presents a strikingly realistic piece of theatricality.

The Sepulchre and the Playing Space

What did the sepulchre look like, and where was it positioned in the church? In order to address ourselves to the problems of the playing space and its use, these questions need to be answered as fully as possible, and here the *Regularis Concordia* leads us to three other Easter ceremonies. These rituals—the Adoration of the Cross, and the Deposition and Elevation of the Cross and/or Host—not only antedate the Easter play but after the tenth century they often exist independent of the *Visitatio*. One or more are frequently referred to or described in later texts which have no *Visitatio Sepulchri*.

During the service of None on Good Friday evening occurred the Adoration (*Adoratio*) and Deposition (*Depositio*) of the Cross, the latter specifically symbolic of the death of Christ. According to the *Regularis Concordia*, at one point in the Friday Office two deacons, "like thieves . . . shall strip from the altar the cloth." Two days later on Sunday at the conclusion of the *Visitatio* the three Marys will place the linen from the sepulchre "on the altar," doubtless references here to the main altar.

The *Adoratio* commences with singing as the veiled cross is borne before the altar, where it is eventually placed on a cushion. Every one in the church from the abbot to the congregation participates in the act of veneration, which includes prostration, the saying of psalms and prayers, and kissing the cross—a custom stemming from the earliest days of the Christian era. There then follows immediately the *Depositio* (it is optional here) with the somewhat ambiguous description of the imitation sepulchre:

> . . . on that part of the altar where there is space for it there shall be a representation as it were of a sepulchre, hung about with a curtain [sit autem in una parte altaris, qua uacuum fuerit, quaedam assimilatio sepulchri uelamenque quoddam in gyro tensum], in which the holy Cross, when it has been venerated, shall be placed in the following manner: the deacons who carried the Cross before shall come forward and, having wrapped the Cross in a napkin [sindone] there where it was venerated, they shall bear it thence, singing the antiphons *In pace in idipsum, Habitabit* and *Caro mea requiescet in spe,* to the place of the sepulchre. When they have laid the cross therein, in imitation as it were of the burial of the Body of our Lord Jesus Christ, they shall sing the antiphon *Sepulto Domino.* . . . In that same place the holy Cross shall be guarded with all reverence until the night of the Lord's Resurrection.[15]

The third ceremony, the Elevation (*Elevatio*) of the Cross, takes place just prior to Easter Matins and often in a rather secretive manner. Only one line from the *Regularis Concordia* mentions it: "On that same night [Easter], before the bells are rung for Matins, the sacrists shall take the Cross and set it in its proper place." An earlier note indicates that this "proper place" was in the eastern end of the church.[16]

Throughout the whole *Regularis Concordia* reference is always made, with but one exception, to "the altar," and so it seems that the representation of the veiled sepulchre is intended as being either on, at, or within the main altar, which often had one or more hollowed out portions, sometimes contained relics, and was frequently associated with the idea of a tomb.[17] The phrase *uelamenque quoddam in gyro tensum* describes a space curtained off on more than one side, while the words *in una parte altaris, qua uacuum fuerit* appear to indicate its position upon or at one side of the altar. The Anglo-Saxon gloss from the eleventh century would support the reading of "on that part of the altar" (si soþlice on anum dæles þæs weofdes).[18]

Since almost all churches of this period, and throughout the high Middle Ages, were "oriented"—

that is, constructed with the nave running east-west and the main altar at the eastern end—the staging area would have been in the east choir if the action took place in the vicinity of the main altar. Bishop Ethelwold had the angel "stealthily" take his place, sitting at the sepulchre as the reading of the third lesson came to an end. During the singing of the third respond, the three Marys probably entered from the sacristy, where they had dressed, from either the north or south side of the main altar. They would have wandered then in the east portion of the nave, and, after the angel's command *Ite,* they would have turned toward the choir, located in stalls a short distance in front (to the west) or on either flank of the altar. The Marys would have then repeated the turn from this position when showing the gravecloth to the clergy, before moving back up to lay the linen on the altar.

The *Regularis Concordia* indicates that the monastic clergy as well as the boy singers sat in two banks of stalls along the north and south sides near the altar, and because areas for public worship in churches of this period were built in the open, basilica form, the sightlines for the congregation, in the nave to the west of the clergy, would have been clear and unobstructed.[19] It was only in the high Middle Ages that structures such as rood-screens were introduced, at a time when the worshippers were placed at some distance from the miracle of the Mass and when the wine of Communion was frequently reserved only for the clergy.[20] In most European churches of the ninth, tenth, eleventh, and twelfth centuries, the relationship between the people and the rituals at the high altar was quite direct by the very nature of the architectural space, and the original purpose of the *Visitatio Sepulchri* at Winchester lay in making the entire community witness to the discovery of the Resurrection.

The Tenth-Century Churches at Winchester and Canterbury

We can be rather certain that the *Visitatio Sepulchri* as found in the *Regularis Concordia* was performed from ca. 970 to at least ca. 1100 in two churches: in the Old Minster of Winchester, considerably enlarged by Ethelwold, and in Christ Church Canterbury, where Dunstan served as Archbishop. The *Regularis Concordia* was drawn up for Benedictine monasteries throughout England, but nowhere else can we locate a production of this text with assurance. In fact, when Aelfric wrote a letter to the monks of Eynsham, about

the year 1005, sending them an abridgement of the *Regularis Concordia,* he omitted the *Depositio* and the *Visitatio Sepulchri.*[21]

The association with the Old Minster at Winchester appears obvious when we note Bishop Ethelwold's significant roles in writing down the *Regularis Concordia* and in building on that church, while a connection with Canterbury can be confidently posited because of Archbishop Dunstan's function there and in the Winchester Council and, equally important, because both early manuscripts of the *Regularis Concordia* have an association with Canterbury. Dom Thomas Symons says that the tenth-century manuscript was "written for, or at least adapted to, the use of Christ Church Canterbury," and that the eleventh-century manuscript, not a copy of the former, is part of a volume intimately connected with that cathedral. The evidence is less conclusive as to whether the *Depositio* and the *Visitatio Sepulchri* were also performed in the churches of a third, younger member of the monastic reformers, Oswald. Given Dunstan's apparent mentorship of Oswald, as well as evidence of similarities in architectural changes made to churches associated with all three reformers, it seems plausible that they were.[22]

Augustine's church in Canterbury, apparently erected on Roman foundations, burned in 1067. A hasty but too small reconstruction by Archbishop Lanfranc ca. 1070 then led to the building of a structure, begun in 1096, with nearly twice the area of the original. A reconstruction by William Hope, based on a contemporaneous description and on some archeological evidence as to Lanfranc's structure, furnishes us grounds for speculation as to the staging area of the *Visitatio Sepulchri* in the cathedral prior to 1067.[23]

The church had a double apse. It was oriented, that is, its nave ran east-west with the high altar to the east. Its main altar was located beneath the arch of the raised, eastern apse, near steps which led up to this area elevated over a crypt. Entrances to the crypt may have opened on either side of the steps. From these steps, according to the contemporaneous description, "towards the west the quire of the singers extended into the body [nave] of the church, shut off by a seemly enclosure from the resort of the crowd."[24] No mention is made of a transept. The church in Hope's drawing is about 65 feet wide and the nave is about 150 feet long. Excavations in the 1990s reveal approximately the same dimensions. Towers on the north and south aisles are recorded.

Since we have no evidence for a sacristy, we might posit the entrance of the Marys from the north tower,

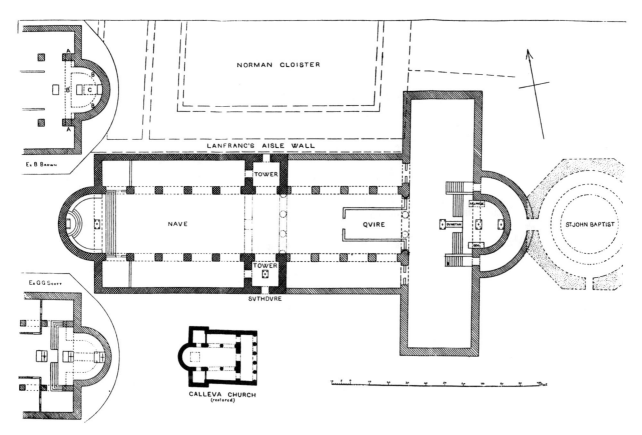

Figure 1. Conjectural plan of the Saxon Cathedral Church of Canterbury, prior to 1067.

adjacent to the monastery complex and normally used for instruction of "the younger brethren." This arrangement would have allowed the women to wander some one hundred feet through the worshippers and up to the steps of the main altar. The angel could have then addressed his question to them from above; they could have ascended, turned to go to the choir, returned, and finally displayed the linen from that high position to the choir, monastic community and laity (if present) below. Although we can imagine the congregation crowding toward the front, it is difficult to assess the matter of sightlines since we do not know the height of the enclosure about the choir.

Thanks to archeological excavation now completed at Winchester under the direction of Martin Biddle, dimensions of Ethelwold's building have been recovered.[25] The Old Minster, dedicated anew in 980 and destroyed in 1092 to make way for the present cathedral, consisted of an edifice some 225 feet long which incorporated a seventh-to-eighth-century church, forming a structure that, in Biddle's view, "may thus rank among the greatest churches of its time north of the Alps."[26] The high altar was placed either about 140 feet or 180 feet from the western entrance (near either position

four or six on the ground plan) to Ethelwold's nave. East of the main altar extended the older portion of the complex, perhaps in the latter tenth and eleventh centuries reserved for less public, more strictly monastic observances. The Old Minster presents our most direct documentation of the kind of interior architectural space which Ethelwold had in mind when he set down the *Visitatio Sepulchri.*

We have already cited evidence from the *Regularis Concordia* as to rows of choir stalls either flanking the high altar or, as at Canterbury, arranged somewhat westward of that altar. Because of the various eastern rooms, the existence of apses north and south of the juncture with the ancient church, and the probability of the baptismal area located off the north side of the ancient church (position eight on the ground plan), one is tempted to envision the Marys as entering the view of the spectators from somewhere beside or behind the high altar and circling into the nave before approaching the sepulchre.

Striking architectural parallels between Canterbury and Winchester in this period reflect a transition at the birth of ecclesiastical drama from a processional liturgy which moved along a series of smaller structures to a

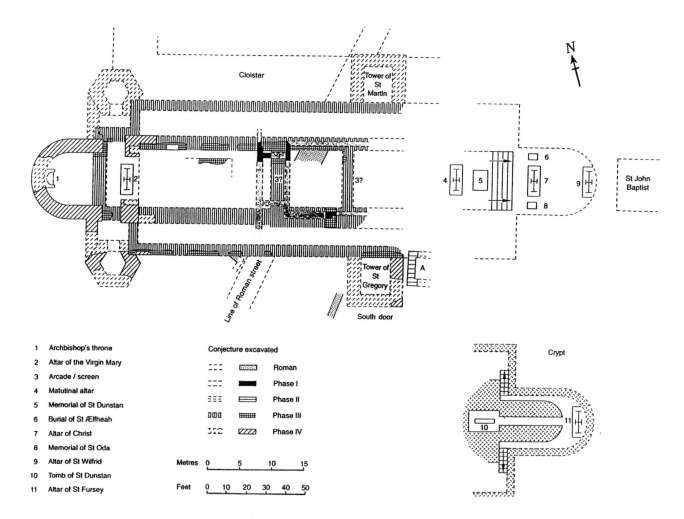

Figure 2. Ground plan of the Cathedral Church of Canterbury, 1990s excavations.

liturgy celebrated within a single church building. St. Augustine's complex at Canterbury consisted of a separate western chapel, a central church, and a smaller church to the east; the latter two edifices were connected via a great octagon in the eleventh century. This kind of three-part arrangement also stood at Winchester, with the ancient church to the east, joined to the central structure by Ethelwold, and a freestanding tower to the west.

The Problem of the Westwork

In excavations undertaken from 1966 to 1969, Martin Biddle and his associates uncovered evidence of a rather extensive westwork attached by Ethelwold to the western end of the Saxon church. Written documents reveal that in 971 Ethelwold had the relics of St. Swithin (d. 862) moved from outside the west door eventually to a reliquary at the high altar and to a kind of chamber behind that altar. This transfer probably occurred at the time of the westwork construction.[27]

Some scholars have envisioned performances of the *Visitatio Sepulchri* in the westwork. However, nowhere in the whole of the *Regularis Concordia* is there any hint of usage in a western area, while descriptions of these customs always refer to "the altar." In addition, we have every reason to believe that the performance in Canterbury would have taken place at the main altar, dedicated to the Savior, and not in the western (apse) chapel, dedicated to the Virgin. Until some other evidence is brought to light, we must conclude from the foregoing texts and from archeological data that at the writing of the *Regularis Concordia* Bishop Ethelwold conceived of the play as set in the east.

WINCHESTER, THE OLD MINSTER
INTERPRETATION, 1969

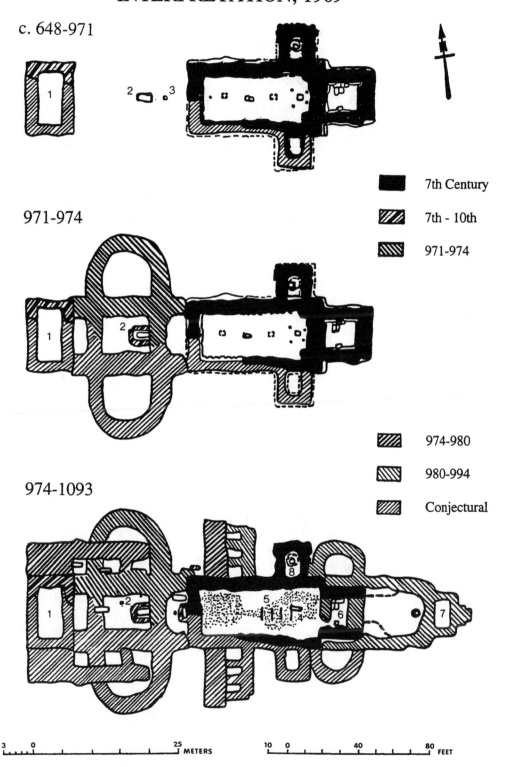

c. 648-971

971-974

974-1093

7th Century

7th - 10th

971-974

974-980

980-994

Conjectural

3 0   25 METERS   10 0   40   80 FEET

Figure 3. Winchester, the Old Minster: the plan and sequence of construction as interpreted from documentary and archeological evidence up to 1969. (1.) St. Martin tower, (2.) St. Swithin tomb, (3.) Stone cross, (4.) Main altar (?); chamber for St. Swithin's relics, (5.) vii–viii century church, (6–7.) Crypts, (8.) Baptismal area (?).

WINCHESTER, THE OLD MINSTER
INTERPRETATION 1969

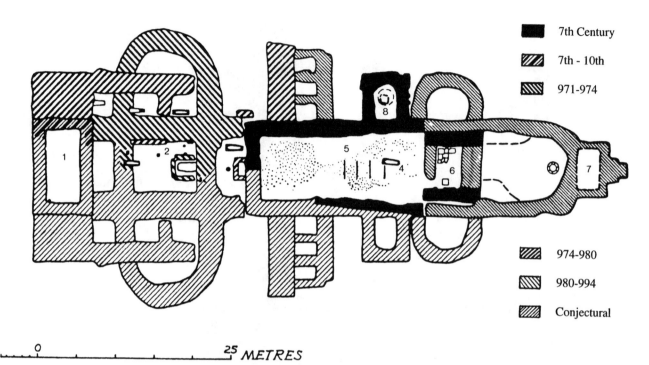

Figure 4. Winchester, the Old Minster, 974–1093.

Pictorial Evidence

What could the sepulchre in the drama have looked like? The earliest pictorial representation known to me of the visit to the sepulchre by the Marys is a carved ivory bas-relief from the fourth or fifth century. In it I can perceive a no more or less "theatrical" portrayal of the scene than in those miniatures, sculptures, and frescoes of subsequent medieval periods, governed by rules and modes of pictorial art, which often do furnish significant clues as to aspects of ecclesiastical architecture and contemporary concepts of the sepulchre and of the characters, but which never provide us with an immediate record of staging within the church.

The closest that we can come to the Winchester play in this respect is with an illuminated page of Ethelwold's *Benedictional,* which stems from the so-called school of Winchester—executed either at Winchester or at Ely—during the latter half of the tenth century. It illustrates quite well our difficulties with iconographic materials.[28] The three women wear chasuble-like mantles with scarves (not mentioned in the *Regularis Concordia*) pulled up over their heads; two at least carry unguent pots, one of whom also has

a thurible. The barefoot angel, who addresses them, sits on what looks like a sarcophagus—clearly not an altar—and raises his right hand with the first two fingers extended, a sign of blessing. He wears a gold tunic or alb and a blue, toga-like overgarment, holds a staff in his left hand, and is furnished with a nimbus and a very fanciful pair of wings (first noted in some *Visitatio* texts of the thirteenth century). The *Regularis Concordia* calls for an alb and a palm branch, while rare are mentions in later texts of any color other than white for angels.

The structure behind the angel presents us with apparently insoluble problems: Is it a tomb or a church? Could it have more than a vague relationship to any architectural feature of Winchester? G. F. Warner and H. A. Wilson, in their facsimile edition of the Benedictional, say that the angel "is seated on a large hewn stone"—not on a sarcophagus—and that behind the angel is the sepulchre, with two towers on the far side of the building.[29]

On the other hand, a number of contemporary depictions of this scene show us a kind of composite where gravecloths are revealed within what seems to be the open west end of a church, with the angel seated on a sarcophagus, a slab, a tomb house, or on a

Figure 5. Ivory (iv or v century) showing the Marys at the Easter Sepulchre.

Figure 6. Title page, Benedictional of Bishop Ethelwold (x century). B.L. Add. MS 49598, fol. 51ᵛ. Reproduced by permission of The British Library.

stone before the entrance.[30] It is possible, then, to interpret the central item in this miniature as a church building with a view from above of the open tomb within containing the linen.

Beyond the structure are depicted four soldiers, with spears and shields, in an attitude of sleep, having been rendered unconscious by the sight of the angel according to the Gospel of Matthew. They will not appear in Easter play texts until the thirteenth century.

The moment portrayed is probably either the angel's first question, "Quem quaeritis in sepulchro," or his statement, "Non est hic," for the women have not yet taken up the linen.

Yet the more we press for significant detail, the more we become aware of the distance that separates this scene from its staging. The general, contemporary concept of the moment corroborates what we know about it from our texts, particularly in the positioning and appearance of the major figures. In that regard we may have before us evidence of what was in the minds of the monks at Winchester when they went about constructing a sepulchre, although it is thought that miniatures of this kind usually show non-specific architectural features.

The examination of a second illumination, from a tenth-century manuscript with possible dramatic associations, seems relevant at this point: a miniature from Hartker's *Liber responsalis*, prepared in St. Gall and contemporary with the earliest *Quem quaeritis* texts from that monastery. In Bishop Hartker's collection of antiphons and responses, to be sung at various points in the Offices (the liturgical services), is a short piece which contains some lines of the *Quem quaeritis* dialogue:

In Die Resurrectionis ad Processionem

Antiphona: In die resurrectionis meae dicit Dominus, aeuia: Congregabo gentes, *et* colligam regna, *et* effundam super uos aquam mundam, aeuia.

Antiphona: Vidi aquam egredientem de templo a latere dextro, aeuia, *et* omnes ad quos *per*uenit aqua ista salui facti sunt *et* dicent aeuia, aeuia.

Interrogatio: Quem queritis in sepulchro, Xρicticole?

Responsio: Ihesum nazarenum crucifixum, o celicolae?

   Non est hic, surrexit sicut predixerat; ite, nuntiate quia surrexit de sepulchro.

Antiphona: Surrexit enim sicut dixit Dominus: Ecce praece*det* uos in Galileam; ibi eum uidebitis, aeuia, aeuia.

Antiphona: Sedit angelus ad sepulchrum Domini

stola claritatis coopertus; uidentes eum mulieres nimio terrore perterrite substiterunt a longe. Tunc locutus est angelus *et* dixit eis: Nolite m*et*uere, dico uobis quia illum quem queritis mortuum, iam uiuit, *et* uita hominum cum eo surrexit, alleluia. V*ersus:* Recordamini quomodo predixit, quia oport*et* Filium hominis crucifigi *et* tertia die morte suscitari. Nolite metuere.

Antiphona: Et recordate sunt uerborum eius, *et* regresse a monumento nuntiauerunt hec omnia illis undecim *et* ceteris omni*bus,* aeuia. V*ersus:* Crucifixum Dominum laudate, *et* sepultum propter uos glorificate, resurgentem*que* a morte adorate, alleluia.[31]

The brief lines occur amidst descriptive and jubilant antiphons, and we have no indication that this formed any sort of play.

But the illumination in Hartker's *Liber responsalis* presents us with a vivid depiction of the Marys at the sepulchre, striking in some similarity of detail to that in Ethelwold's *Benedictional*. From the right the three women approach the sepulchre; they wear mantles with raised headdresses, two carry unguent vessels, while the one in the center swings a thurible. At the left an angel sits on the now removed lid of the sarcophagus, or on a hewn stone, and gestures with his right hand, the first two fingers extended. The moment might be at his line "Quem quaeritis," or at "Non est hic." Like the angel in the Winchester illumination, he is barefoot, wears an alb under a toga-like garment, holds a staff in his left hand, and is furnished with a nimbus and a pair of wings; he has no headband. Two soldiers, in contemporary military dress with spears and shields, crouch above the tomb in attitudes of sleep.

This drawing shows us a single, open sarcophagus, viewed from above so as to reveal here two parts of the gravecloths—the *sudarium,* for the head, and the *linteamina,* the winding-sheet.[32] It is located within the arch of a towered structure which may represent either the (west?) facade of a church, or a separate mausoleum, possibly even in imitation of the Holy Sepulchre at Jerusalem. Whether the design of the architecture is fanciful or modelled on a real edifice in or near St. Gall, we cannot say. I believe that Hartker's illustration retains essentially the same relationship to the performance of the *Visitatio Sepulchri* as the Winchester miniature: a prevalent, visual idea of the event, disclosing generally valid information about the appearance of the characters and perhaps of the sepulchre, but adhering to the dictates of contemporary pictorial style.

Figure 7. The Three Marys at the Tomb, from Hartker's *Liber responsalis* (x century).

Chapter 2
Plays of the Medieval Church: The Texts

Some twelve hundred texts of the medieval music-drama have been discovered and published. The manuscripts range in date from the tenth century to ca. 1600. About a thousand of them are versions of the *Visitatio Sepulchri*, deriving from seven hundred different monasteries and churches. By 1600 the new polyphonic music had become the official music of the liturgy and the old plainchant was either augmented or discarded, together with the little music-plays. The Council of Trent (1545–63) banned these dramas as one of its reforms, thus also contributing to their end after seven centuries of performance.[1]

For the most part these music-dramas were produced within the framework of the liturgy, or quite close to it, and partook of the spirit of the liturgy. They were sung in Latin, as distinct from the later outdoor religious plays, where the dialogue was in the vernacular and was spoken. The staging occurred within the architectural church structure, as contrasted with the chiefly outdoor productions of the vernacular drama. As a very distinct art form this indoor music-drama did not evolve into an outdoor spoken drama—into mystery, miracle, and Passion plays—although along the way there were many links between the two genres. They adhered to their own processes of change and expansion, often in contrast to processes of change in vernacular plays.

The music-dramas are neither simply music nor simply drama, but could be compared to miniature operas akin to the celebration of the liturgy. Obviously the relationship between ceremonial ritual here and drama is a close one, and the difference, as we have discovered, can be blurred, even imperceptible. However, from the original rubrics—stage directions—in even the simplest of the plays we can see that the singers are representing the "characters" of angels and other Biblical figures.

Earlier scholars were misled into thinking that the

Latin church plays evolved into the later vernacular plays primarily because they studied the texts without taking into account the full experience of singing and mise-en-scène, a bit like substituting the experience of reading a libretto for that of attending an opera. When witnessing an operatic performance, a spectator realizes quickly that each, a play staged and an opera staged, is an organic artistic whole unto itself. Of course there are many connections between the two, but they are essentially separate entities. In no sense was the medieval music-drama replaced by spoken plays based on Biblical and hagiographical material. It remained within the liturgical context and continued to be performed for some seven hundred years, at times in the later centuries side-by-side with the outdoor religious drama.

From the outset it is possible to characterize different related "strains" or geographical groupings of music-drama texts as well as of music. As musicologist Susan Rankin points out, ". . . even when they had absorbed the same new ideas, no two versions of the play turned out the same, either in their dramatic structure or their sequence of sung texts. For no institution merely accepted another's version of the play without making alterations and improvements, in order to create an ensemble effective in a different architectural environment, or to conform to the requirements and potential liturgical practice there, or just to suit local dramatic, textual, and musical taste."[2] Extant stage directions reveal the same enormous variety. For just as each ecclesiastical community put its own mark on text and music, so the staging was fit to the singular features and associations of each individual church.

Most of the extant texts derive from monastic communities, a few from cathedral libraries, chiefly from France and Germany, with a smattering from Spain and Italy and a smaller handful from England and from Eastern Europe. With few exceptions the *Visitatio*

Sepulchri was performed at the end of Matins, the first service, on Easter Sunday morning. As we have seen in our study of Winchester, it required a sepulchre as central set piece: an adaptation of the high altar or even in some churches a special, fully enterable structure. Occasionally texts of two preceding Easter ceremonies reveal information about the sepulchre: the *Depositio Crucis*, when on Good Friday a cross was buried in it, and the *Elevatio Crucis*, when the cross was removed rather secretly on Saturday night or very early Sunday morning. Sometimes the Host was buried and then removed together with the cross.

The *Visitatio Sepulchri* appears most commonly as one dramatic episode or scene; there are also versions with two scenes, and even versions with three. The Marys meet an angel (or angels) at the Tomb, learn of the Resurrection, and proclaim it publicly. Or, in other texts, first this meeting occurs, then the women bring the news to the assembled community (usually the choir), and in a second scene Peter and John race from the assembly to the Tomb and make the discovery and the public proclamation. Or, in a few texts, a third scene is added where Mary Magdalen stays behind, meets Jesus, whom she thinks is a gardener, and finally recognizes him as the Risen Christ. The latter two- and three-scene versions are much rarer than the simple *Visitatio Sepulchri;* they first appear in the eleventh century. As already noted, in the simplest of the texts only the presence of rubrics with stage directions, such as those written by Bishop Ethelwold at Winchester, tell us that we have before us a play and not a piece of dialogue sung in the liturgy, such as the famous "Quem quaeritis" trope sung by a pair of single singers, or sung antiphonally by the choir divided into two groups.

The *Peregrinus* (The Wayfarer, or The Pilgrim) play also came to be produced in the Easter season. There are thirteen extant texts, from eight different localities. After the Resurrection, Jesus appears to two disciples, Cleophas and Luke, as they walk—through the church—toward the village of Emmaus. Disheartened, they talk of the Crucifixion. Eventually Jesus, still unknown to them, breaks bread with them at a table (sometimes up on a platform) and then mysteriously vanishes, and in that moment they recognize him. In some versions a second scene takes place after the two disciples have arrived in Jerusalem; Jesus appears to the gathered followers, and proves his Resurrection by showing his hands and feet.

As to the question of the "development" of the drama, Susan Rankin—who has done by far the most

extensive study of this music in recent times—shows in her comparative analysis of musical and textual transmission that rather than a so-called gradual evolution, the simple *Visitatio Sepulchri* developed in several waves or layers of composition and that these layers are identified by changes in the music, or isolated lines of text, and not by story line. In the first, earliest layers (represented by the *Regularis Concordia* of Winchester), "liturgical office antiphons based on the biblical narrative fill out the story of the Marys' visit to the sepulchre." By the early twelfth century the second layer was being composed: new narritive material and laments. Some early examples are texts from Palermo, Laon, Limoges, and Reims. A distinguishing factor here is the difference between the source material for the music used for the first and second layers; in the first, as in Winchester, the melody for the line "Venite et videte" originated from a chant; at Palermo, a new melody was composed for that line. The compositions of the thirteenth century added more, already extant liturgical material to the "Quem quaeritis" dialogue; however, rather than prose, these texts were written in metrical verse. The important point here is that these layers do not build upon each other, and Rankin has found in her research that "the many different texts added around the QQ ["Quem quaeritis"] dialogue show a great variety of narrative plans."[3]

We have already noted that medieval manuscripts preserve three major forms of the *Visitatio Sepulchri* drama: the single scene with the Marys at the Tomb, the two-scene version that includes Peter and John, and the three-scene version that includes Mary Magdalen. Susan Rankin has discovered that the three forms developed in two separate strains. The first is "the simple *Visitatio* idea presented in the 'Quem quaeritis' dialogue composed in the early tenth century or earlier." The second, with Peter and John, originated in Normandy, and, she hypothesizes, might well have been part of the repercussions of the Norman invasions of the eleventh century, leading to "several new and elaborate" ceremonies or plays including the *Visitatio* with Mary Magdalen, an Easter play called *Peregrinus* (The Wayfarer) where the Risen Christ appears to two disciples on the road to Emmaus, and a Christmas play with shepherds called the *Officium Pastorum*. Rankin concludes that these two traditions coexisted and paralleled rather than led to each other: the simple *Visitatio*, and this body of more complicated dramas.[4]

The *Peregrinus* play, mentioned above as part of the second strain of development, also came to be produced in the Easter season, at Vespers on Easter Day, or the first or second day thereafter. Unlike the "Quem quaeritis" dialogue, which was not based verbatim on the Gospels, these plays were taken directly from the Biblical (Vulgate) accounts.

To the Easter season also belong seven longer works called by Young and Lipphardt the *Ludus Paschalis:* a Catalonian text from Vich, two Netherlands texts from Maastricht and Egmond, a text from Klosterneuburg, one from Tours, one from Origny-Sainte-Benoîte (near St. Quentin), and one from Benediktbeuern. The incomplete Tours manuscript (thirteenth century), the largest of these in scope, includes a scene between Pilate and the Roman soldiers, a scene between the Marys and two merchant-spice sellers, the appearance of Christ to the disciples, and the incident of doubting Thomas.

Of all the Easter plays the most complex are four Passion plays: two in the *Carmina Burana* from Benediktbeuern, one from Sulmona, and one from the original Benedictine house at Monte Cassino. They too were almost entirely sung in Latin, but they have no direct tie to the liturgy, and their subject (Christ's Passion) is outside of the ritual celebration which characterizes the other liturgical dramas. They would have been performed on Good Friday, a day on which as yet no other known liturgical play was presented, but we do not know exactly where they fit in the liturgy.

It is important to realize that until the thirteenth century, the emphasis at Easter time was on the event of the Resurrection. The liturgical celebrations, including the plays, comprised joyous occasions and thus set the intrinsic tone of the music-dramas. Only as of the thirteenth century did the focus begin to shift to the human suffering of the Crucifixion, and that new focus, so readily visible in details of agony depicted in the visual arts of the period, became apparent in the staging of the outdoor religious drama as it emerged in the thirteenth and fourteenth centuries.

The second great season for liturgical rejoicing occurred at Christmas. Some twenty manuscripts of Christmas plays can already be dated to the eleventh century. They are of three kinds: the *Officium Pastorum* (The Play of the Shepherds), the *Officium Stellae* (The Office of the Star, or The Play of the Magi), and the *Ordo Prophetarum* (The Play of the Prophets). When the shepherds approach the manger, the midwives there sing "Quem quaeritis in praesepe" (Whom do you seek in the manger?), a reminder of the Easter event, and on rare occasions in that moment they even

quote the Easter music. We hear similar echoes though more distant in the Magi plays. Dramaturgically the shepherd and Magi plays are constructed like the Easter plays as they move toward an experience of discovery and revelation, but now with the manger instead of the sepulchre as central set piece. Musically, however, they abound with new verse forms and fresh, original compositions. Indeed, as John Stevens notes, "the documents do not support any theory of gradual evolution or of regular imitation by 'Christmas playwrights' of Easter successes."

The *Officium Pastorum* originated on Christmas Day, while the *Officium Stellae* was produced on Epiphany (Twelfth Night, 6 January). As of the eleventh century, the latter also began to include the episode of Herod, who soon became a dominant figure, as in the vivid twelfth-century *Ordo ad representandum Herodem* in the Fleury manuscript. Also in the so-called Fleury Playbook (a collection of ten plays) is a play about the murder of the Innocents, called the *Ordo Rachelis* and based on the *planctus* (lament) of Rachel over the children. In a sense these Christmas plays are rather more free from formal contraints of ritual than most of the Easter plays, and as a result one discovers greater inventiveness in them.

The *Ordo Prophetarum*, on the other hand, appears to have remained close to a simple, rigid homiletic form. It presents a series of Old Testament prophets—with the Roman Sybil, and even Virgil—each of whom rises and sings a passage predicting the coming of the Christ Child. There are two great texts with very full stage directions as to costumes and hand properties: from Laon (thirteenth century) and from Rouen (fourteenth century). The *Ordo Prophetarum* seems to derive from a sermon by St. Augustine, although there is some evidence here of Byzantine influence.

To these two seasonal centers of dramatic activity we can add a tiny handful of separate and very remarkable compositions: *The Play of Daniel* (twelfth century) from the cathedral school of Beauvais and a Daniel play by the wandering scholar Hilarius (twelfth century); *The Raising of Lazarus* (twelfth century) and *The Conversion of St. Paul* (twelfth century) in the Fleury Playbook; the *Sponsus* (eleventh-twelfth century) from Limoges on the Wise and Foolish Virgins; the Tegernsee *Antichrist* (twelfth-thirteenth century); and several St. Nicholas plays, four in particular from the Fleury Playbook (twelfth century). Finally, we have some dramas devoted to the Virgin: of especial interest, two Annunciation plays from Padua and Cividale (northern Italy, fourteenth century), and the elaborate *Presentation of the Blessed Virgin* by Philippe de Mézières (Avignon, 1372).

The dates of these latter music-dramas point to a general observation: the great period of creative ferment reached from the inception in the tenth century into the thirteenth century, and in fact this drama came suddenly into full bloom in the eleventh and twelfth centuries. Moreover, many of the bursts of dramatic activity occurred in vibrant cultural centers: for example, in Limoges, Rouen, and in or linked with Fleury. Side-by-side with the drama there we find major achievements in music, writing, the visual arts, architecture, and history. Indeed, the creativity of the music-dramas emerged as much because of the composition of new musical material as new textual material. It seems that the late eleventh- and early twelfth-century Norman precedent—"that new material could be composed for the presentation of a chosen story"—led to further development and more and more elaborate productions.[5] Many of the surviving manuscripts also preserve musical notation, and in Chapter 6 we shall deal specifically with dramatic qualities of the scores available to us.

In recent years we have entered an important era of new musicological research where a number of breakthroughs have been made, and nowadays major work on the music of the medieval music-dramas stimulates a lively interest in staging them, at times even in the monastic churches and cathedrals where they were originally performed. As their extant medieval musical scores, beginning in the tenth century, often make it possible to sing them, so their surprisingly extensive rubrics often make it possible to stage them. Moreover, when examined together the entire corpus of stage directions in the original texts tells us a great deal about mise-en-scène, about the use of architectural space, light, set pieces, props, costume, and voice and gesture, about not only how a line was sung but how it was played.

Chapter 3

Staging Space and Patterns of Movement— with Set Pieces and Special Effects

Staging Space and Patterns of Movement

The *Visitatio Sepulchri:* Introduction

The focal point of the action in the *Visitatio Sepulchri* is the tomb itself, indicated in play rubrics as the main altar, usually a veiled vessel on the main altar, a coffer, a coffer or altar surrounded by curtains, a temporary construction large enough to be entered, or a chapel with a receptacle and sometimes a sarcophagus and an altar. Inside churches at Aquileia, Gernrode, and Magdeburg permanent stone structures still survive which may well have been employed in dramatic observances of Easter. Holy Sepulchre chapels with dramatic associations stand just outside churches in Constance and Laon.

The location of the set piece determined essentially the pattern of the actors' movements and thus the theatrical employment of the church space. In France we usually find the sepulchre—either the main altar or a separate structure near it—in the east chancel or choir area. Occasionally it is located in a special chapel. In Germany, however, ninety percent of our definite examples reveal placement in the vicinity of the nave of the church, affording a more extensive playing area and bringing the action closer to the congregation. The few extant Italian texts also indicate the sepulchre in the nave. However, the situation in the British Isles differs as to documentation, where we possess only five indisputable examples of the *Visitatio Sepulchri:* two from Winchester, one from Dublin, one from Barking, and one from Wilton. Over a hundred English churches contain a permanent Easter sepulchre, recessed in the north wall of the chancel, but we cannot conclude that the existence of such a tomb necessarily indicates the performance of a play.[1]

Of the about one thousand now published examples of the *Visitatio Sepulchri*, less than half include stage directions with some information as to the sepulchre or as to the blocking pattern of the performance. As we have seen in the *Regularis Concordia,* that pattern for the first phase of the drama is quite simple: the Marys move to the sepulchre and then away from it to display the gravecloth(s). The sense of a short journey is inherent. With the addition of the race to the tomb, Peter and John repeat the movement at a different pace and sometimes they meet one or more of the women for a brief exchange before exhibiting the gravecloth(s). The introduction of the spice seller indicates a short detour on the part of the Marys, who sometimes also visit other altars before coming to the tomb. Finally the entrance of the Risen Christ to Mary Magdalen demands a singling out of Magdalen, the other women remaining at a distance, and the dramatic innovation of a sudden appearance. These two basic elements of dramaturgy make for one of the most important recognition scenes in all literature. Here Christ often shows himself near the main altar, especially if the sepulchre is in the east choir.

The sepulchre then constitutes our first physical set piece, which when large enough to be entered can be called a mansion of the sort which adorned the outdoor medieval polyscenic stage of juxtaposition, Shakespeare's Globe, and many court productions in the early Renaissance. Inherent in it is the sense of specific locality simultaneously visible with other defined places such as the main altar or the assembly of clergy and laity representing the community which receives the news of the Resurrection. Spaces between these points function as neutral playing areas, through which journeys are made and where meetings may occur.

It would be misleading to assert a general, gradual process by which the mise-en-scène expanded from choir to nave to the western doors. The earliest extant forms of the *Visitatio* from the tenth century centered about the high altar as the sepulchre; so did late forms, particularly in France. But at Verdun in the tenth century, the sepulchre was located in the crypt. As of the late eleventh or early twelfth century we also find the placement of the action in the nave, and in several works of the thirteenth century the whole interior is incorporated in the play, just as the entirety of the church was used in the processionals and stations of worship. The process from this kind of theatre to that of the Renaissance is largely a process of confinement, of separation between actor and audience, of formal physical restrictions on distinct playing space versus distinct viewing space. And when the Easter drama was put back into the church by Vigil Raber in Bozen in 1514, those divisions became quite evident.

Two eleventh-century texts from Monte Cassino imply a change in the presentation of the "Quem quaeritis" trope to incorporate the main altar as the sepulchre. The first begins as follows:

> . . . let a priest go before the altar, dressed in an alb, and toward the choir let him say in an intense voice:
> *Quem queritis?*
> And let two other clergy standing in mid-choir respond:
> *Jesum Nazarenum.*

The second text begins:

> When [the procession] is completed, let a priest go behind the altar, and toward the choir let him say in an intense voice:
> *Quem queritis?*
> And let two other clergy standing in mid-choir respond:
> *Jesum Nazarenum.*[2]

Each constitutes only a preparatory moment just before the Mass, but we find here evidence for a fundamental concept of the central set piece, defined by the position of the speakers.

Beginning in the thirteenth century rood-screens and rood-lofts (pulpitum) often separated the main choir from the remainder of the church, in many cases obscuring the view of the chancel area from the nave. However, the few *Visitatio* texts which we can positively associate with particular churches whose medieval architectural features are known to us do not reveal a change in the position of the sepulchre: most in Germany were and remained in the nave; most in

France were and remained in the choir. Generalizations of this kind about other plays must be more tentative since they are based on a considerably smaller sampling of texts, but it seems that otherwise the nave and especially the crossing served as the major playing area, with the striking exception of Rouen, where the manger for the *Officium Pastorum* was located in the choir, for the monastics gathered there, while the manger for the *Officium Stellae* was in the nave, for the townspeople as well as monastics. The Holy Sepulchre represented a secret place containing a mystery, the act of discovery of which by *dramatis personae* was much less theatrical than the subsequent testimonials of witnesses to the empty tomb, often publicly questioned by one or more members of the chorus, and the climactic exhibitions of the gravecloth(s).

The thirteenth century was a period in which the Mass became increasingly reserved to the clergy, and the canonical hours were observances by and essentially for a monastic community. In different churches the *Visitatio Sepulchri* was performed for different groups of worshippers: for the monastery and its *schola cantorum*, or an extended monastic community, or cathedral celebrants and their congregations, or clergy and townspeople (clerus et populus). The facts, then, that the Easter play continued to the end of the Middle Ages in close connection with the liturgy, that the interchange between the Marys and the angel(s) at the tomb was the beginning and not the theatrical climax of the drama, and that the sepulchre was sometimes conceived of as being in a secluded place, explain to some degree the varying view of the proceedings afforded different congregations, the degree of congregational participation, and even proximity to the church. The entire church could, for example, become the sacred space of the playing area for a *Visitatio*. A fourteenth-century *Visitatio* from St. Gall instructs the rector first to expel the populace from the church. Then at the head of a procession he must walk outside the church doors and beat thrice on the portal, whereupon a priest by the sepulchre inside must ask, "Quem quaeritis in sepulchro . . . ?". Changes in congregational participation may also at times reflect the church's attempt to purge the Easter plays of secular elements. A late fifteenth-century monastic scribe of a *Visitatio* in Regensburg displays a certain historical sensitivity when he remarks on the deletion of a vernacular section from the play: "Formerly the people here sang 'Crist ist erstanden. . . .' But this has been abolished in our times. Rather, let the choir boys sing three or four verses from the hymn and let the chorus respond." Just the reverse of this segregational tendency was true for most other plays, which were loosely if at all tied to the liturgy and where there was little ambiguity as to the public nature of the major set pieces.[3]

The chief productions which we shall examine in the following sections of this chapter represent a selection of texts which are rare indeed because each can be assigned on internal evidence to a particular church whose medieval architectural details are known and because the rubrics name such identifiable features as altars, tombs, or chapels, thus furnishing us clues for reconstructing the performance. We possess about two dozen such plays in all; those selected exemplify various uses of church space.

The Easter Sepulchre Outside the East Choir: Trier, Essen, Magdeburg, Meissen

Cathedral of Trier—the Sepulchre in the Crypt

This *Visitatio Sepulchri*, recorded in a manuscript dated 1305–7, represents the one-episode version of the play.[4] The famous cathedral where it was performed is essentially a Romanesque structure from the eleventh and twelfth centuries, built on Roman foundations, with a deep east choir raised over two crypts, only the easternmost of which was used in the thirteenth century, where a cross was buried in a sepulchre (in Monumento) during the ceremonies of Good Friday and a sudary was left at the *Elevatio* just prior to Easter Matins.

At the close of Matins the three actors in the roles of the Marys, carrying lighted candles, are given thuribles with incense before proceeding to the sepulchre, a suggestion of a scene in which elsewhere they will make a detour in order to obtain ointments from a spice seller.[5] No doubt their exit from the choir was via the central steps leading into the nave and thus wholly visible to the congregation. There were entrances with steps down into the crypt from the aisles to the north and south of the east choir. The Marys probably descend the northern steps to the crypt because later they ascend the southern steps. The foregoing *Depositio* and *Elevatio* ceremonies also maintained this same symmetry, the *Depositio* procession down on the north side, the *Elevatio* procession up on the south side. Meanwhile the chorus with lighted candles descends singing from the east choir into the church and stands in mid-nave. Perhaps after their

procession they turn and face back toward the east, toward the steps leading down into the crypt.

The "Quem quaeritis" exchange occurs between the women and two angels seated at the head and foot of the sepulchre, while chorus and congregation wait above. Taking the sudary, the three women then go "ad gradus cripte," where they sing part of the *Victimae paschali*. They sing no doubt at the head of the crypt steps, probably at the south steps since eventually they will exhibit the sudary from that side.[6] Standing in mid-nave the chorus hears and apparently sees them, and sings "Dic nobis, Maria, quid vidisti in via?" For their reply the three Marys move forward to the tomb of Archbishop Theodoric, at the south corner of the choir wall and rood-screen (near the Altar of St. Katherine). There they respond "Sepulchrum Christi," and raise the sudary. With an antiphon all pass into the choir for the final *Te Deum laudamus*, extinguishing their candles immediately thereafter. A slightly later text (1345) adds three theatrical details: the Marys sing the first three stanzas of the *Victimae paschali on their way* from the crypt steps to the Altar of St. Katherine, that is, *while moving* toward the chorus and congregation; then they not only display the sudary but in so doing they also point toward the sepulchre; and before the chorus returns to the east choir for the *Te Deum laudamus* the Marys make their final exit into the sacristy.

Striking here is the rather unusual location of the sepulchre in the crypt, where the "Quem quaeritis" dialogue occurs wholly out of sight of clergy and laity, and then the brilliant step-by-step progress to a climactic revelation. In the church proper one saw the Marys depart—dressed in purple copes—one listened expectantly, and then heard their voices from the subterranean area before they emerged to bring the news and the physical evidence of the Resurrection. We find here a pronounced example of a general tendency to underscore by theatrical means the public proclamation of the miraculous event, the literal carrying out of the angels' injunction "Cito euntes, dictate discipulis . . . ," rather than the moment of the Marys' discovery.[7]

In Chapter 6, with a discussion of congregation-audience, we will examine more in detail the astonishing secrecy of this hidden scene.

Collegiate Church of Canonesses and Canons at Essen—the Sepulchre in the West

Some of the most detailed rubrics of any text describe the ceremony, which included the race to the tomb,

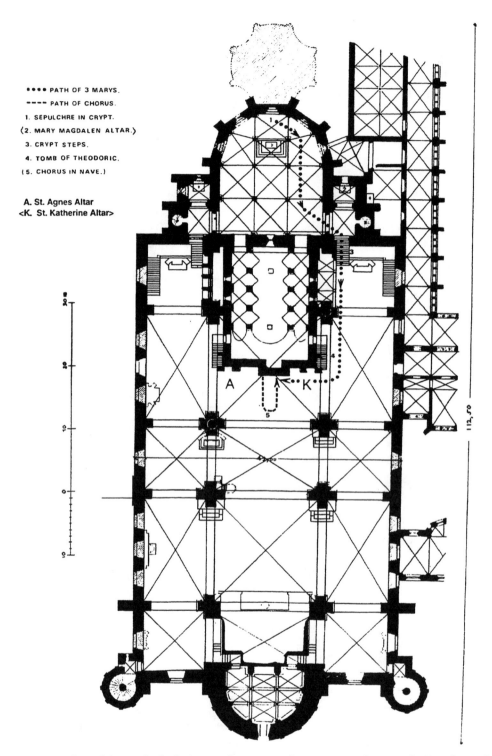

●●●● PATH OF 3 MARYS.

---- PATH OF CHORUS.

1. SEPULCHRE IN CRYPT.

⟨2. MARY MAGDALEN ALTAR.⟩

3. CRYPT STEPS.

4. TOMB OF THEODORIC.

⟨5. CHORUS IN NAVE.⟩

A. St. Agnes Altar
⟨K. St. Katherine Altar⟩

Figure 8. Plan of the Cathedral of Trier showing its three crypts. The east choir is above the two eastern crypts. *Visitatio Sepulchri*, **1305–7.**

in the minster at Essen in the second half of the four-teenth century.[8] The eleventh-century, oriented, Romanesque basilica became a Gothic hall church after the great fire of 1275, but the western end and the north and south walls survived. A raised gallery runs the length of each wall, that on the north side connecting with the raised choir of the canonesses in the north transept, close to the chancel entrance. At

Figure 9. Cathedral of Trier. Reconstruction facing east choir.

the west two towers (to the north and south) contain interior steps which lead up on either side to a second-level balcony and to a third-level organ-loft, both overlooking the nave from this westwork. The distance from this western apse to the chancel area is about thirty-five meters.

The representation of the sepulchre stood on the first balcony: there a large tent (tentorium) was erected in front of the Altar of St. Michael and within it was placed a coffer (archa), the sepulchre proper, into which during the *Depositio* were put the Host, reliquaries, and an ancient missal, and upon the lid of which was laid a gold cross with linen cloths. The chest or shrine must have been of fair size because two angels were later to sit on it. As many as a dozen people may then have entered the tent at the *Elevatio* in order to remove all objects save the linen; the cross was

replaced at the Altar of the Holy Cross, probably just in front of the chancel entrance.

After the third respond of Easter Matins, as usual, the *Visitatio Sepulchri* begins. Canonesses, canons, and children form a group in mid-nave before the great seven-branched candelabrum: the canonesses toward the north side, the canons and children (scolares) toward the south side. Two canons as angels, wearing white dalmatics, go via the canonesses' choir and along the raised north gallery to the St. Michael balcony, enter the tent, and sit on the sepulchre. They are furnished with a book and a light so as to be certain of their lines (et habeant librum, in quo contineatur cantus, quem cantaturi erunt, si exterius nesciunt et lumen, ut videre possint).

Three canonesses portray the Marys. They approach the sepulchre along the south gallery while the

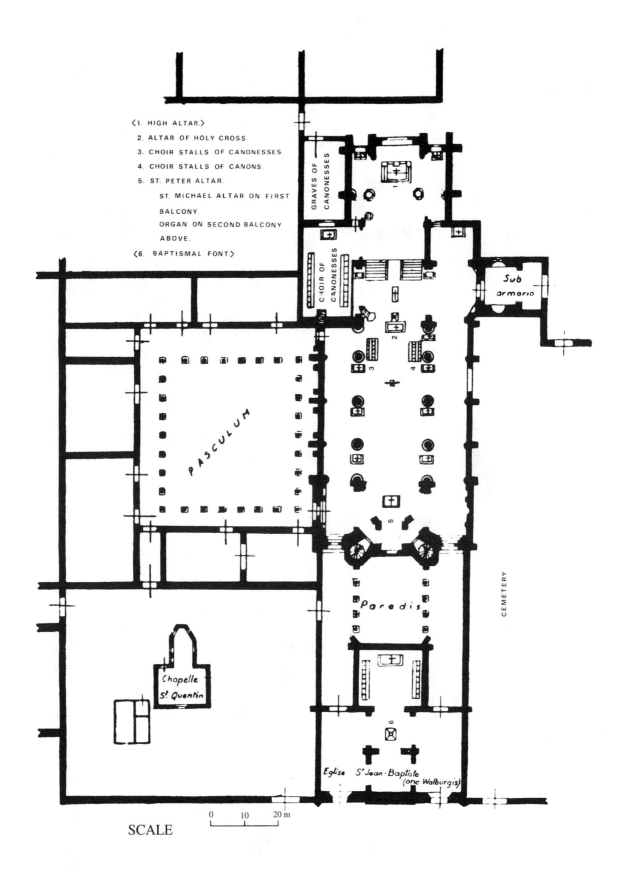

1. HIGH ALTAR.
2. ALTAR OF HOLY CROSS.
3. CHOIR STALLS OF CANONESSES.
4. CHOIR STALLS OF CANONS.
5. ST. PETER ALTAR.
   ST. MICHAEL ALTAR ON FIRST
   BALCONY.
   ORGAN ON SECOND BALCONY
   ABOVE.
6. BAPTISMAL FONT.

GRAVES OF CANONESSES

CHOIR OF CANONESSES

Sub armorio

PASCULUM

CEMETERY

Paradis

Chapelle St. Quentin

SCALE

0   10   20 m

Eglise St Jean-Baptiste (onc Walburgis)

Figure 10. Plan of the Collegiate Church of Canonesses and Canons, Essen.

canonesses in mid-nave sing the antiphon "Maria Magdalena et alia Maria." The three Marys, singing "Quis revolvet," stand at a little distance from the sepulchre, whereupon the "Quem quaeritis" exchange is carried on with the angels within the tent. When the angels sing "Non est hic," each of the women in turn moves to the tent, looks in, and asks, "Ubi est Jhesus?" (Where is Jesus?), and the rubrics add "vel similia verba" (or similar words). The angels reply "Surrexit, non est hic" (He is risen, he is not here), the rubrics adding "vel etiam similia verba" (or also similar words). These lines are spoken, not sung (et dicendo ad Angelos). Thereupon the women ascend to the organ-loft above in order to sing out "Ad monumentum venimus."

As the canons sing "Currebant duo," an older and a younger canon leave the group and hasten toward the sepulchre via the canonesses' choir and along the north gallery (the path of the angels). John, the younger, arrives first but waits; Peter then enters the tent, followed by John. The two angels hold up the linen and sing the antiphon "Cernitis, o socii, ecce linteamina et sudarium."

One of the disciples then ascends to the organ-loft and proclaims three times in an increasingly high or strong voice (primo in gravibus, secundo altius, et tertio bene alte), "Christus Dominus surrexit," the canonesses at their station responding "Deo gratias," with the same build in vocal quality. The congregation sings a Resurrection hymn in German (probably "Christ ist erstanden"), and the canonesses and canons sing alternate verses of "Te Deum laudamus."

The disciples followed by the angels return to the community, via the south gallery (originally the path of the women), while the Marys go back along the north gallery. The angels and disciples stand in a line between the canons and canonesses, the angels in the center. They bow together toward the east, and take their places with the canons.

The placement of the sepulchre at the western end of the church establishes here extreme physical polarity between the occurrences at the tomb and the apostolic representatives in the east. The widely juxtaposed stations are connected at the outset and at the end by journeys along the side galleries, while at the center of the drama the Marys announce their experience and one of the disciples proclaims the fact of the Resurrection from the organ-loft out across the whole of the church. Now at the crossroads of the action, as it were, stands the populace, looking both to the east and to the west. They are the earthly community of humankind for whom these events transpire in the present and who, singing a vernacular hymn, join in the celebration.

That the Marys are played by women here and, further, that Peter and John are specifically noted as being older and younger would perhaps lead us to expect a more marked tone of realism in the staging, but in fact the whole retains a rather strict, ceremonial formality within the expansive space. Also less is made here of the sudary, only shown by the angels to the two disciples, whereas movement to and from the distant sepulchre and vivid vocal effects characterize in particular this performance. It is in truth a celebration of the cross, a celebration especially composed for this church. Tantalizing is the thought that the author may have been a woman. As in cases where the sepulchre is in a crypt, so here the hidden "Quem quaeritis" exchange creates the impulse for an ensuing crescendo of spectacular public announcement with response from the opposite end of the church, and then processional compassing the entire interior space.

But while the position for the sepulchre in the west end of the church is quite rare, there are several examples of extended east-west movement patterns. In the Cathedral of Braunschweig it was part of the westwork. There the three Marys go all the way from the east choir to the western extreme of the nave. The (fourteenth-century) manuscript contains an alternative staging for the scene between Mary Magdalen and Salvator. Both the fact of an alternative mise-en-scène and the alternative itself are unique. In the staging given first in the manuscript, she is to remain at the sepulchre, where she sings her *planctus* and eventually Salvator appears to her. In the appended alternative, however, the rubrics call for her to make a little tour, while singing her lament—no words or music are changed. She goes in search of Jesus: first to the north church door that leads to the town, then eastward to the St. Bartholomew Altar in the middle of the nave (the other two Marys have withdrawn to that position), and then back westward to the great pillar opposite the tower of the westwork, where she proceeds "a little farther" and Salvator appears to her. Earlier Braunschweig texts do not indicate such a movement pattern. Taken together they provide a graphic illustration of the shift from earlier emphasis on the chorus to emphasis on single characters, they witness to a slight nuance from represented figure toward individual experience, they reveal for a few moments a departure from ritual toward narrative, they document the way in which the staging of the play could expand throughout the architectural space, and they

Figure 11. Collegiate Church, Essen. Interior of the western end (restored 1952), showing the second and third (organ-loft) levels.

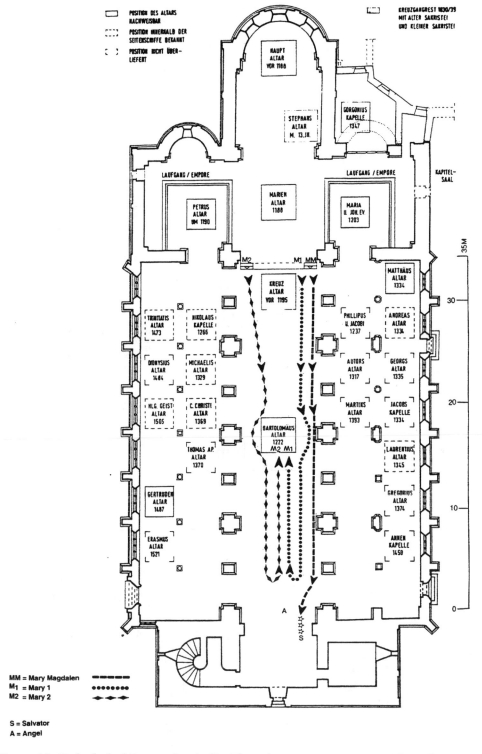

POSITION DES ALTARS NACHWEISBAR
POSITION INNERHALB DER SEITENSCHIFFE BEKANNT
POSITION NICHT ÜBERLIEFERT

KREUZGANGREST 1030/39 MIT ALTER SAKRISTEI UND KLEINER SAKRISTEI

HAUPT ALTAR VOR 1188

STEPHANS ALTAR M. 13.JH.

GORGONIUS KAPELLE 1347

LAUFGANG / EMPORE   LAUFGANG / EMPORE

KAPITEL-SAAL

PETRUS ALTAR UM 1190

MARIEN ALTAR 1188

MARIA U. JOH. EV. 1203

35M

M2   M1 MM

MATTHÄUS ALTAR 1334

KREUZ ALTAR VOR 1195

30

TRINITATIS ALTAR 1473

NIKOLAUS KAPELLE 1266

PHILLIPUS U. JACOBI 1237

ANDREAS ALTAR 1334

DIONYSIUS ALTAR 1484

MICHAELIS ALTAR 1329

AUTORS ALTAR 1317

GEORGS ALTAR 1335

HLG. GEIST ALTAR 1505

C. CHRISTI ALTAR 1369

MARTINS ALTAR 1393

JACOBS KAPELLE 1334

20

BARTOLOMÄUS ALTAR 1272
M2 M1

THOMAS AP. ALTAR 1370

LAURENTIUS ALTAR 1345

GREGORIUS ALTAR 1374

10

GERTRUDEN ALTAR 1487

ERASMUS ALTAR 1521

ANNEN KAPELLE 1450

0

A

☆☆☆S

MM = Mary Magdalen
M1 = Mary 1
M2 = Mary 2

S = Salvator
A = Angel

Figure 12. Cathedral of Braunschweig (St. Blasius) ca. 1200. First staging from the manuscript. *Visitatio Sepulchri*, xiv century.

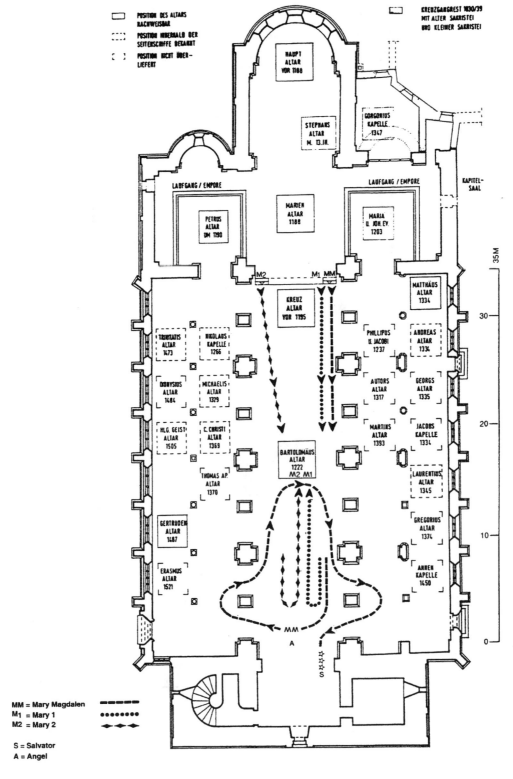

Figure 13. Cathedral of Braunschweig (St. Blasius) ca. 1200. Alternative staging from the manuscript. *Visitatio Sepulchri,* xiv century.

Figure 14. Cathedral at Magdeburg. Easter Sepulchre ("Otto I Chapel"), moved from the nave in the xix century.

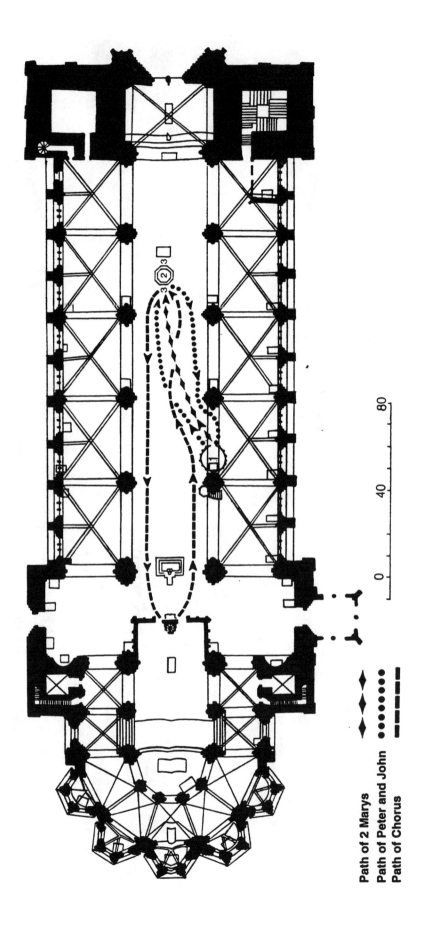

Path of 2 Marys ◆◆◆◆

Path of Peter and John ●●●●●

Path of Chorus ▬ ▬ ▬

1. Sepulchre = "Otto I Chapel"
2. Baptismal Font
3. Chorus et al.

Figure 15. Plan of the Cathedral at Magdeburg. *Visitatio Sepulchri*, xv century.

hint at a performer-audience relationship that differs from a celebrant-congregation relationship.[9]

At Essen, as far as we can tell, the sustained use of the entire church interior from high altar to nave to galleries to westwork for the *Visitatio Sepulchri* is quite rare. However, other kinds of plays, for example plays of the Christmas season, often do extend to the western doors.

Cathedral of Magdeburg—the (Permanent) Sepulchre in the Nave—and Other Permanent Sepulchres

A fifteenth-century text from the Cathedral of Magdeburg, a play that includes the scene with Peter and John, was acted in the nave of that church and may well have incorporated what is apparently a permanent stone replica of the Holy Sepulchre which stands in the fourth bay on the north side of the nave.[10]

This curious, sixteen-sided structure with a conical roof has a diameter of 3.75 meters, a height of 3.02 meters without the roof, and, judging by its style, dates from ca. 1240, the period of the present Gothic cathedral. It opens toward the west and contains an altar. By the end of the sixteenth century its original purpose appears to have been forgotten at Magdeburg, where our earliest written reference calls it a chapel in honor of Kaiser Otto I and where a seventeenth-century guide to the cathedral surmises that it was a model of Otto's original church.[11]

The language of the fifteenth-century rubrics and the pattern of dramatic movement indicate the use of this sepulchre in the Easter play at Magdeburg. All textual references are to "ymaginarium Sepulcrum"—an uncommon qualification—the opening of the *Depositio* noting "parabunt eciam ymaginarium Sepulcrum Domini ante altare Sancti Laurencii." A cross would be buried in it, wrapped with a cloth on top and a cloth beneath, and with a pair of stones. The church possessed one or more relics of St. Lawrence, but we have no information as to the location of that altar. The stage directions have the two disciples explicitly enter the tomb to receive the gravecloths.

Just before the close of Easter Matins a candlelight procession moves out of the east choir (rood-screen begun in 1445) and takes up a position proximate to the baptismal font, probably in the second bay of the nave. In fact, members of the procession seem to form a rectangle around it. Those with Easter candles and banners stand on either side of the font, perhaps on the north and south sides. The canons are directed to line up on the west side facing east, the choir boys lin-

ing up on the east side facing west. Thus clergy and choir boys face each other.[12] Close by stands the archbishop. Two canons with thuribles, as the Marys, go to the sepulchre; we are not told explicitly whether they begin their walk from the font area. The chorus sings "Maria Magdalena." Two angels sit at the sepulchre, to the right and left. After the "Quem quaeritis" exchange, the women turn back, stand between the baptismal font and the chorus, possibly at the center of the rectangle, and sing "Ad monumentum venimus." There is a distance of twenty-five meters between the sepulchre and the font.

Peter and John run to the tomb, John arrives first, and then they enter to receive the two gravecloths. Meanwhile the chorus sings "Currebant duo." The rubric thereupon only notes that the pair of disciples sings "Cernitis, o socii," their demonstration to the assembly of the empty grave after they have taken up the linen, "accipient duo linthea." Perhaps they then return to the clerical group. It would seem that the Marys' report is directed to the chorus while that of the disciples is the public announcement and is therefore made from the place of the sepulchre.

The archbishop, near the chorus, begins "Surrexit Dominus," which is followed by the *Te Deum*, the bells ring out, and the procession returns to the choir as the subcustos removes the cloth coverings from the relics at the altar, presumably the high altar (deponet velamen de reliquiis in altari).

This general pattern of movement can be considered as quite common when the sepulchre stands in the vicinity of the nave. The chorus descends into the body of the church and takes up a position at some remove from the tomb, while the Marys and Peter and John make their way between that group as surrogate disciples, and the sepulchre. The performance concludes with a return procession and is often decorated with lighted candles and banners. Here as elsewhere through a dramatic act the high altar is transformed from a death memorial to a place of life.

Dramatic Performance and Permanent
Replicas of the Holy Sepulchre

Imitations of the Holy Sepulchre in Jerusalem were erected in numerous European churches during and after the era of the Crusades, and most of them were used for the ceremonies of Easter. After the fall of Jerusalem in 1099, the Pope founded the Order of the Holy Cross, in 1113, and the following year the Augustinians established the cult of the Holy Sepulchre.

Figure 16. Cathedral of Aquileia. Easter Sepulchre at the western end of the north aisle.

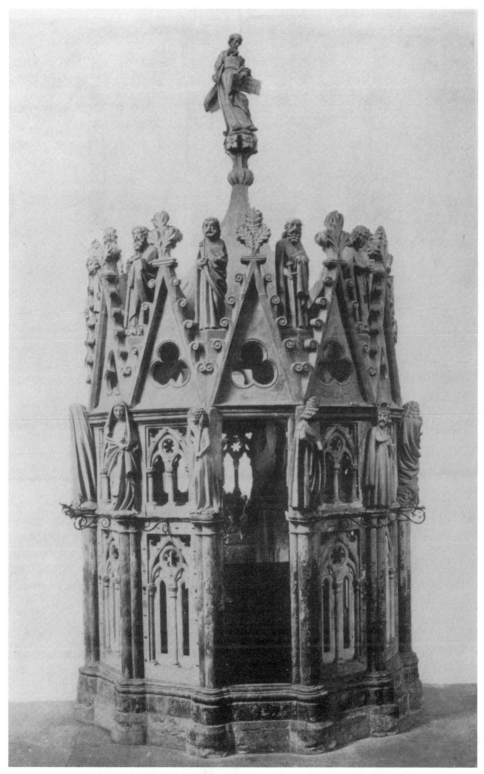

Figure 17. Constance, St. Mary's Cathedral. Easter Sepulchre, in St. Mauritius Rotunda.

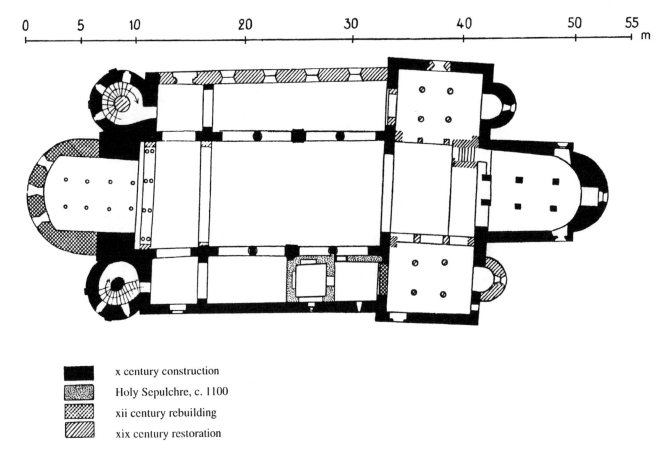

x century construction

Holy Sepulchre, c. 1100

xii century rebuilding

xix century restoration

Figure 18. Church of Gernrode. Floor level, showing entrance to the Holy Sepulchre.

Sepulchres and chapels dedicated to the Holy Sepulchre began to appear all over Europe. By no means, however, does the presence of an Easter sepulchre mean the presence of a full-fledged Easter drama. To be sure many were used for ceremonials, and many without notice in the rubrics, but only a rare few served as sites for the drama, and nowhere do the rubrics actually describe the monument. Those occasional rubrics that provide any information at all mention such matters as the presence of one or more angels, the acts of entering and exiting, and the use of the cross, host, and gravecloths. Indeed the presence of such a replica in a church that staged the *Visitatio Sepulchri* does not necessarily mean that the replica became part of the dramatic performance. However, those unusual plays that did incorporate a stone replica are significant for the concept of mansions on the medieval stage.

Today four Easter sepulchres still survive at churches that also possess a related dramatic text, a text with some internal evidence of focus on the existing permanent sepulchre. Magdeburg is one of the four. The others are at Aquileia, Constance, and Gernrode.

The one at Aquileia dates from the middle of the eleventh century.[13] There a cylindrical, stone structure, about 3.8 meters in diameter and 2 meters in height, surmounted by an open grille and a conical roof, with a small door at the west, stands in the north aisle toward the western end of the church. It contains a niche, an altar, and a ceremonial sarcophagus. Its early date of the mid-eleventh century—coeval with the construction of the cathedral itself—is particularly important to a chronological consideration of theatrical mansions.

The earliest text from Aquileia (in the vicinity of Trieste), from ca. 1100, indicates a movement of the chorus out of the choir into the body of the church for the *Visitatio Sepulchri*, the Marys turning "ad Populum et ad chorum," Peter and John showing the linen to everyone (aliis), and "Populus" singing "Kyrieleison" after "Te Deum laudamus." From the beginning these Aquileian texts are concerned explicitly with communication with the laity, shutting them out of the church during the *Elevatio Crucis* and then opening the doors of the church to them for Easter

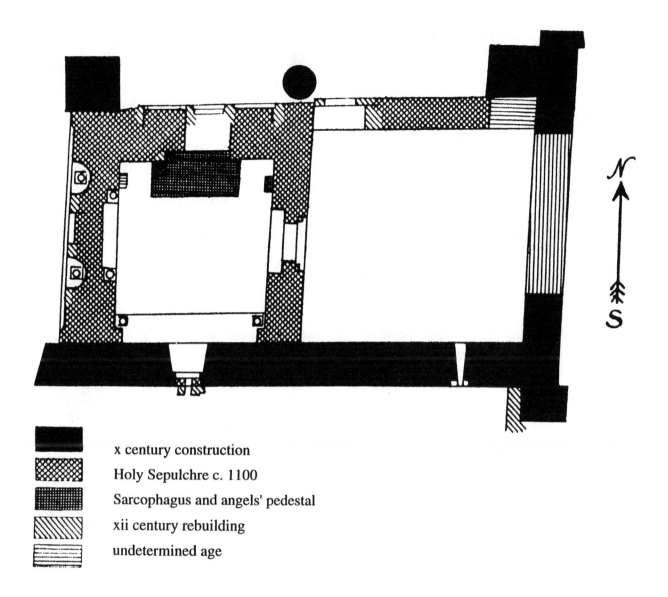

x century construction

Holy Sepulchre c. 1100

Sarcophagus and angels' pedestal

xii century rebuilding

undetermined age

Figure 19. Church of Gernrode. Plan of the Holy Sepulchre, showing entrance into antechamber, entrance into grave chamber, and "window" opening in north wall behind the sarcophagus.

Matins. A thirteenth-century text from Aquileia or its region says specifically that Peter and John enter the sepulchre and then carry the linen "ad medium Monasterium" (referring to the nave or body of the church) to display it. Their movement pattern may have been quite interesting: out the westward-facing door of the Monument, at the west end of the church in the north aisle, then around into the nave, and eastward all along the nave through the congregation to the waiting chorus. A different thirteenth-century text adds that after the chorus takes up a position "in corpore ecclesie," the two women emerge from the sacristy. Fifteenth-century documentation says that the door of the sepulchre was closed and sealed during the *Depositio:* "Locata autem Cruce in Sepulchro clauso ostio et sub sigillo firmato: Dominus Pontifex advolvat lapidem ad ostium Monumenti." Since at least ca. 1100 the two Marys had approached the sepulchre with the antiphon "Quis reuoluet nobis ab hostio lapidem?".

A permanent Easter sepulchre from this same early date (ca. 1080) also survives at Gernrode (East Harz Mountain area), together with a dramatic text certainly associated with that sepulchre. The church was dedicated in 961. In the south aisle, in the two east-ernmost bays, stands the sepulchre, this one an at-tempt to reproduce the configurations of the Holy Sepulchre in Jerusalem. It consists of an antechamber or forecourt, called the St. Aegidius Chapel, which opens westward into the grave chamber itself. Origi-nally the antechamber was entered on the east side from the transept; in the twelfth century that entrance was closed up and a small door on the north side opened directly onto the nave. On the outside the two rooms are rectangular in shape, slightly over 2 meters in height. The antechamber is open above, whereas the grave chamber once had a rotunda roof, now de-stroyed. Inside, the antechamber gives the impression of a small forecourt about 5 meters square with an al-tar, dedicated to St. Aegidius. To the west of it stands the grave room itself, about 2.5 meters square. There in the north wall is a niche and low platform for a sar-cophagus (1.6 meters long, 60 centimeters wide). Originally a window-like aperture in the north wall at about sarcophagus height opened into the church. It would emit candlelight from the grave into the nave, or from the nave one could see moving shadows and light and hear voices within the grave room. From outside in the nave one could peer in. This window was eventually closed up with stone work, but one does not know when. As in the case of the other repli-cas discussed here—at Aquileia, Magdeburg, and Constance—in early times an onlooker from outside the sepulchre could make out something of whatever sights and sounds and odors were within. Perceived in this atmosphere, events taking place inside were rather hidden and thus mysterious. Because one can-not date the closure of this "window" at Gernrode (nor does one know why), one cannot be certain that this special effect marked the "Quem quaeritis" scene as late as the present text, around 1500. However, it is clear that the Gernrode text reflects dramatic practice which is very old, perhaps even antedating the con-struction of the sepulchre around 1080, and that the extant text fits the extant structure.

As noted the text dates to ca. 1500, its rubrics strangely enough in German, and happily enough very precise.[14] Also of special interest, it documents one of twenty-three instances in the staging of this drama where the roles of the Marys were played by women. Gernrode was a Damenstift, a community of canon-esses. There the *Visitatio Sepulchri* developed out of the *Elevatio Crucis* either before or during Easter Matins, and was celebrated not partly in secret as in Aquileia but all together in a colorful enactment. The worshippers present were probably not townsfolk but members of the canonesses' households and commu-nity.

Early in the Easter night the canonesses are awak-ened with traditional Good Friday rattles, and the canons, who live outside the grounds, gather in the east choir (dedicated to the patron, St. Cyriacus). The canonesses will have passed from their quarters south of the church directly into their own choir gallery, somewhat raised in the south transept. Two flanks of steps, at the front edge of the raised east choir, on the right and on the left, lead directly down into the cross-ing. The men move down the choir steps, through the crossing, turn and stoop through the little door into the St. Aegidius Chapel and from thence into the grave room, and remove the cross buried there in the sepulchre the previous Friday. The women descend and wait at the Altar of St. John, near the sepulchre. The men remove the cross to the All Souls Altar (sele-messen-altar), according to the rubrics, probably at the confessio entrance between the two flanks of east choir steps.[15] Apparently it required two men to carry the cross; the 1.6 meter by 60 centimeter sarcophagus platform might indicate its size. This movement of some ten or a dozen meters is symbolic of the Har-rowing of Hell. The three Marys follow in procession, wearing nuns' habits with special wimples decorated with red crosses. Then come the other women. All canonesses carry lighted candles. The Marys stand to the left of the cross and altar, the others to the right. When the cross is set in place, the three Marys make their Easter offerings and then proceed some twenty-five or thirty meters along the length of the nave, tak-ing up a position at the westwork beneath the belfry, the bells hanging in a housing between the two great west towers. Meanwhile the other women make their traditional Easter offering at the cross. Whether other people are also to make such an offering, one does not know. Thereupon the three Marys begin their journey toward the sepulchre. They move eastward to stand and sing at the All Saints Altar, probably in mid-nave, halfway between the crossing and the westwork. When the canonesses' chorus begins "Maria Mag-dalena," the three continue eastward back through the church to the sepulchre, and they enter it. Inside and invisible to the rest of the church, save through the window if still extant at the sarcophagus, they ex-change the "Quem quaeritis" lines with two angels. They emerge and move over to the grave of highly revered Abbess Hathui (the first of Gernrode), lo-cated just in front of the Altar of the Holy Cross.

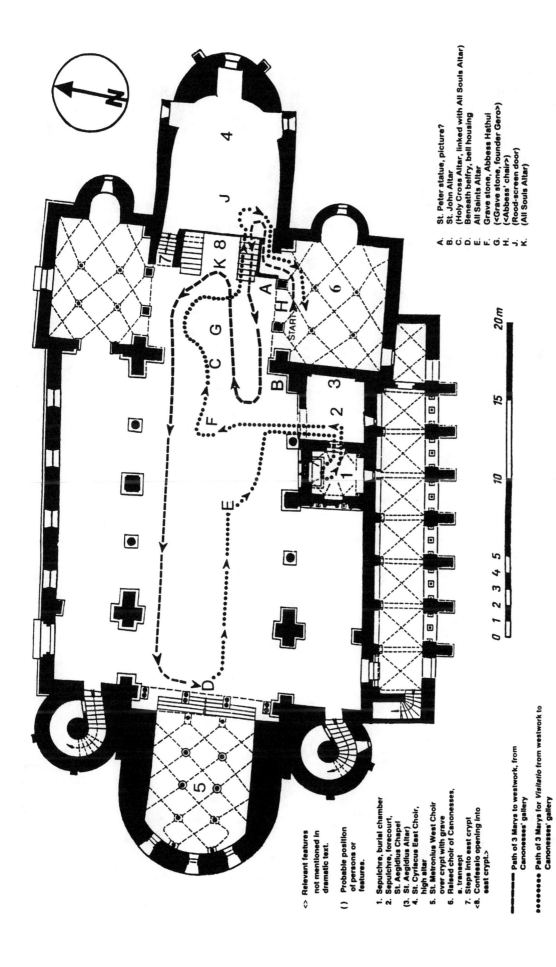

<> Relevant features
   not mentioned in
   dramatic text.

() Probable position
   of persons or
   features.

1. Sepulchre, burial chamber
2. Sepulchre, forecourt,
(3. St. Aegidius Chapel)
4. St. Cyriacus East Choir,
   high altar
5. St. Metronius West Choir
   over crypt with grave
6. Raised choir of Canonesses,
7. transept
<8. Confessio opening into
   east crypt>

A. St. Peter statue, picture?
B. St. John Altar
C. (Holy Cross Altar, linked with All Souls Altar)
D. Beneath belfry, bell housing
E. All Saints Altar
F. Grave stone, Abbess Hathui
G. (<Grave stone, founder Gero>)
H. (<Abbess' chair>)
J. (Rood-screen door)
K. (All Souls Altar)

▬▬▬▬ Path of 3 Marys to westwork, from
      Canonesses' gallery

▬ ▬ ▬ Path of 3 Marys for *Visitatio* from westwork to
      Canonesses' gallery

•••••••• Path of 3 Marys for *Visitatio* from westwork to
        Canonesses' gallery

0 1 2 3 4 5   10   15   20m

Figure 20. Church of Gernrode. *Visitatio Sepulchri*, ca. 1500.

Figure 21. Church of Gernrode, Holy Sepulchre, ca. 1080. Note the gestures. *"Noli me tangere."*

Figure 22. Church of Gernrode, Holy Sepulchre, ca. 1080. Mary Magdalen. Note the gesture.

A great cross hung just above the altar, where the nave meets the crossing, from a beam spanning the arch of the crossing. From early on these enactments of the Resurrection discovery would often incorporate in their movement patterns a grave or graves of persons important to the life of the particular community. There, at Hathui's grave the celebrant (of the Easter Mass to come) meets them and sings to them as Christ, "Maria, quid ploras?"; his speech ascription calls him "Der Homessen Here," the High Mass priest, not Christ. The three respond as the one addressed, Mary Magdalen, and singing they move to the Abbess. Their next lines, the joyful announcement of "Surrexit dominus de sepulchro," they sing directly to her, each woman taking a line beginning with "the one in the middle" (Magdalen). The abbess was probably standing with her canonesses. There in response the cantrix commences the recital about Peter and John, "Currebant duo," and a deacon and subdeacon come out from the sepulchre to sing "Cernitis, o socii." Earlier they had probably been the singers of the angels' lines. It seems likely that they are standing in front of the sepulchre, facing the women some ten or a dozen meters away at the All Souls Altar. In response, priests and canonesses sing together; the High Mass priest reads the Collect; and then when the cantrix begins the final "Te decet laus" (not the *Te Deum*), the women take up the hymn and climb the (south?) steps to the east choir, pausing there at the rood-screen door to finish their music. Thereupon they turn south-west and ascend a few more steps into their south-transept gallery, where the Abbess collects their candles. For a full study of the performers' movement patterns at Gernrode, see Appendix B at the end of this chapter. The text itself and its direct linking of the *Elevatio* with the *Visitatio Sepulchri* indicate very early usage, as do the text and *Elevatio-Visitatio* performance at Constance. As at Aquileia, one is struck by the way the mise-en-scène embraces the whole church, as well as by the variety of sound and the deployment of lights.

The Sepulchre Outside the Church

At the Cathedral of Constance stands the fourth extant replica of the Holy Sepulchre that one can associate with a *Visitatio Sepulchri* text. It is a first cousin to the one at Magdeburg, reflecting many parallels and ties between the Magdeburg of Otto I and the Constance of Bishop Konrad. The sepulchre at Magdeburg dates to 1240; at Constance to 1280. Both

are Gothic in style and polygonal in shape; sixteen-sided at Magdeburg, and twelve-sided at Constance. The Constance sepulchre stands slightly smaller, 2.74 meters in diameter, with pierced walls 2.49 meters high, a conical roof, and a narrow door opening eastward. The tenth-century cathedral at Magdeburg is dedicated to St. Mauritius; the tenth-century chapel containing the Constance sepulchre is also dedicated to St. Mauritius. In fact, the present sepulchre at Constance may have replaced an original tenth-century sepulchre erected by Bishop Konrad after his Holy Land pilgrimage; or the round chapel in which it stands, some eleven meters in diameter, may have been Konrad's original replica of the Holy Sepulchre. The present fifteenth- and sixteenth-century cathedral replaced an eleventh-century cathedral.

But the related sepulchres differ in one key respect: whereas the one at Magdeburg stood conspicuously in the nave of the cathedral, the one at Constance has been hidden away from the very beginning. It is not in the cathedral at all, but in a Chapel of St. Mauritius, at the edge of the cathedral cemetery. In order to reach it one must exit from the north transept of the cathedral and continue north some thirty or thirty-five meters. The chapel itself is a small rotunda.

Although each cathedral has a sepulchre and a dramatic text from the same era, their texts reflect the contrast in staging space. The two embody very different dynamics of drama.

At Constance one brief, fifteenth-century text records an *Elevatio* observance just preceding Easter Matins. There a procession moves to the sepulchre. Boys (Scolares) sing "Quem queris mulier," the only appearance of this antiphon in these celebrations. They seem to address a single, festively vested priest (Sacerdos ornatus), not three Marys. Upon returning, the procession sings "Dum transisset" and pauses at the entrance to the (east) choir. Then the canons continue on into the choir carrying the Host (cum Corpore Domini) while the chorus led by the cantor remains at the entrance to sing first an antiphon and then the *Te Deum*. Thereupon the chorus enters the choir area and Matins commences, eventually to conclude with a second singing of the *Te Deum*.

Another text from Constance, one that may or may not be a play, dates to 1502.[16] Here too a pre-Matins procession goes "ad sanctum Sepulchrum." Uniquely each of three angels sings separately "Quem queritis," "Non est hic," and "Ite nunciate." The Marys (Cantent Marie) sing only the "Iesum Nazarenum" line; they have no journeying antiphon. Whether sung while

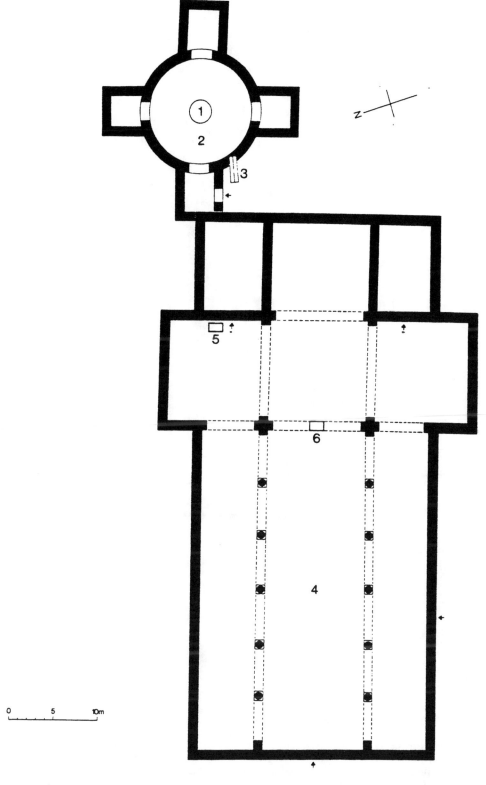

Figure 23. Constance, St. Mary's Cathedral and St. Mauritius Rotunda. Erdmann's conjectural ground plan ca. 1000 with later documented altars. (1.) Holy Sepulchre, (2.) St. Mauritius Rotunda, (3.) Grave of Konrad, (4.) St. Mary's Cathedral (Nave), (5.) Altar of the Holy Cross, (6.) Parish Altar.

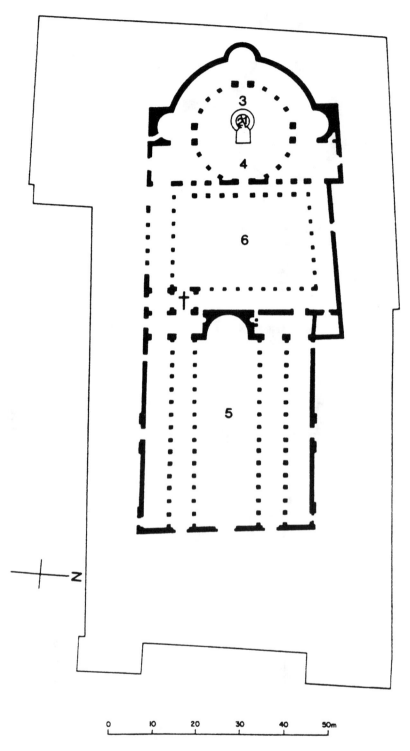

Figure 24. Jerusalem, Plan of Golgotha. From Coüasnon's Plan. (1.) Sepul-
chrum Domini, (2.) Spelunca, (3.) Tegurium, (4.) *Anastasis*-Rotunda, (5.)
Basilica of Constantine, (6.) Golgotha courtyard. Note similarities of the
Cathedral and Rotunda at Constance.

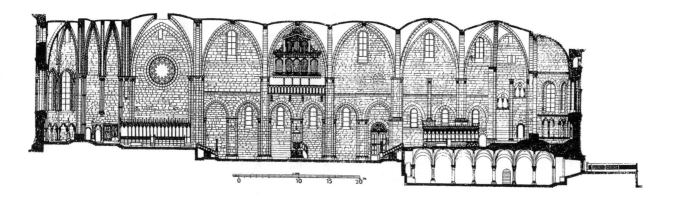

West

East

Figure 25. Cathedral of Bamberg, interior. (In the xvi century the now central tomb of Heinrich II and Kunigunde was somewhat to the east, and both choirs were closed off with screens.)

processing or after entering the St. Mauritius Chapel one cannot say. The piece feels a great deal like the tenth-century pre-Mass processionals from northern Italy with their antiphonal voices. The chorus chants "Et recordate sunt verborum eius," presumably on the return, and when back in the (east) choir they commence "Surrexit Dominus," then "Te Deum laudamus." The Constance texts document very ancient practice. The more elegant solution, recorded at Winchester for example and adopted almost everywhere, was to leave the *Elevatio* before Matins but to insert the *Visitatio Sepulchri* just prior to the close of Matins so that the little play imbued the normal end-of-Matins *Te Deum* with new meaning for worshippers celebrating the Resurrection.

In sum, at Constance the "Quem quaeritis" lines in connection with the sequestered replica of the Holy Sepulchre remain part of an in-house rite, encouraged or enforced by the staging space, whereas at Magdeburg with the publicly located replica, the "Quem quaeritis" lines lead off a presentation for *clerus et populus*. With a sepulchre removed from chancel and nave such as the one at Constance, the dramatic ceremony enhances the *Feierlichkeit,* the solemnity, of the Resurrection announcement: a festive procession returns and brings the news, perhaps also gravecloths. But in this instance a drama which develops out of the lines at the sepulchre hardly comes into being. By contrast, when the performers are physically out in the midst of a congregation, as at Magdeburg, they tend to turn overtly toward the clergy and the worshippers. Their purposes tend toward demonstrating and teach-

ing, and there the impulse for drama is generated. Such is also the case at Aquileia and Gernrode, where the Easter sepulchre stands in the body of the church. Let us hasten to add that when naming a didactic element at the inception or execution of this drama, by no means is there an implication that the dynamic of the performance is limited in its symbolic, ritualistic, and aesthetic power; no more than the didactic element in the works of Sophocles or Shakespeare limits the thrust of those works in performance.[17]

At sepulchres outside the major church there is ceremony with minimal "Quem quaeritis" lines and little or no elaboration of the drama. The procession at Constance compasses in fact a semisecret event. At Augsburg the *Visitatio Sepulchri* is a public processional event with one moment of turning dramatically to the audience—but not at the scene at the sepulchre. At Laon with its theology students and Templars' Chapel the processional grows into a victory march. Quite the reverse is the case at Magdeburg, Gernrode, and Aquileia, where the purpose of the Easter procession is to bring the performers out among the worshippers.

With the use of the Holy Sepulchre replica inside the church and the direct contact with the townspeople, the performers turn to those around them and do something quite different from the liturgy—musically and visually different. They make a presentation. A presentation is a gift, an act of gift-giving, whereas a ritual is an act enclosed within itself. To the congregations at Magdeburg, Gernrode, and Aquileia the performers give a play, and then their return march into the east choir becomes part of their play's finale.

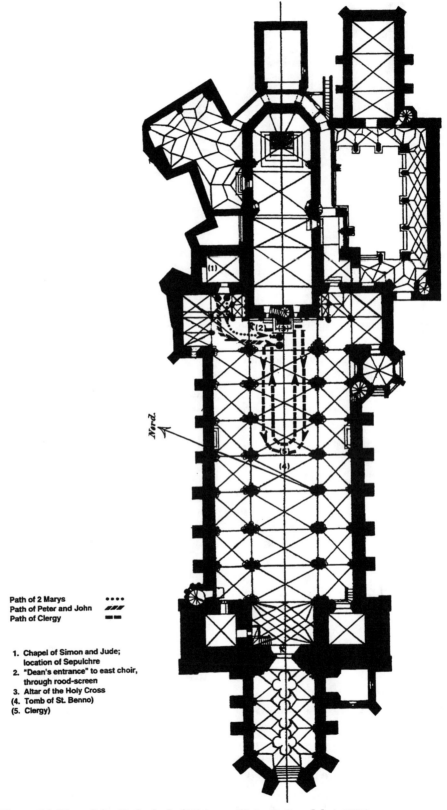

Path of 2 Marys ••••
Path of Peter and John ▰▰▰
Path of Clergy ▬ ▬

1. Chapel of Simon and Jude;
   location of Sepulchre
2. "Dean's entrance" to east choir,
   through rood-screen
3. Altar of the Holy Cross
(4. Tomb of St. Benno)
(5. Clergy)

Figure 26. Plan of the Cathedral of Meissen. *Visitatio Sepulchri*, 1520.

Cathedral of Meissen—the Sepulchre in a Chapel

A blocking pattern rather similar to that at Magdeburg is indicated by a text, dated 1520, from the Cathedral of Meissen, save that here the sepulchre is in the Chapel of Simon and Jude.[18] The cathedral is a Gothic hall church mainly built in the thirteenth and fourteenth centuries. This dark chapel, dedicated about 1300, is located adjacent to the east choir, at the extreme of the north aisle and opens onto that aisle. The rubrics of the *Depositio* tell us that the sepulchre was prepared in the chapel and that during the ceremony the Host and a bier supporting a crucifix (*Imago Resurrectionis*) were placed upon the altar there. The text of the *Visitatio* does not say specifically that characters go into the chapel, but the angels disclose the sepulchre to the woman (Angeli Sepulchrum aperientes), perhaps by merely stepping aside from the doorway.

The play commences with a candlelight procession out of the east choir and into the nave, the senior clergy (canons, domini) passing through the chorus standing on either side (per choros alternatim stantes). The two rood-screen doors used by the chorus in previous Easter ceremonies would suggest their filing out via both doors to form a kind of corridor for the canons. They take up a central position before the tomb of Bishop Benno. The first Bishop of Meissen (1066–1106), he was declared a saint in 1525. Apparently some members of the cathedral community remain in the choir. The antiphon "Maria Magdalena" is sung, whereupon two Marys dressed in red stand before the sepulchre and carry on the "Quem quaeritis" exchange with the angels, who then reveal the tomb. The women look in, come back before the Altar of the Holy Cross, just in front of the rood-screen, and sing "Ad monumentum venimus," facing east.

The chorus sings "Currebant duo" as Peter, limping, and John, both in red vestments like the chorus, run to the sepulchre, receive the sudary, and return before the Altar of the Holy Cross to sing "Cernitis, o socii," facing westward. We are not told the starting point of either the women or the disciples. The facts that at least a portion of the chorus remains in the east choir and that the Marys address "Ad monumentum venimus" in the direction of the east choir might indicate the subsequent exit of the disciples from that position.

Two priests then appear at the north (the "Dean's") entrance to the choir, begin "Surrexit Dominus," and display the *Imago Resurrectionis* which had been placed on the high altar during the *Elevatio*. This may have

been a kind of effigy of Christ which would be detached from a cross.[19] After twice leading off "Surrexit Dominus," each time picked up by the chorus, the two priests then intone the vernacular "Christ ist erstanden," clearly creating a three-step progression to the climactic moment when the congregation participates. The performance ends with the *Te Deum*. The Marys had faced east, bringing their news to the Jerusalem community, while Peter and John had faced west, bringing their news to the contemporary community.[20]

Usage in Two Double-Choired Churches: Bamberg and Besançon

Cathedral of Bamberg—the Sepulchre in the Subsidiary Choir

The high altar of the thirteenth-century Cathedral of Bamberg is in the raised, west choir (dedicated to St. Peter), while the altar which served for the sixteenth-century *Visitatio Sepulchri* was located in the raised, east choir (dedicated to St. George), at the opposite extreme of the church. Texts dating to as early as the thirteenth century document the elaborate processionals into these two choirs and between them, characterizing the Paschal ceremonies.[21]

Easter Matins is held in the main (west) choir. Then a procession with candles moves out into the church and stops near an alms receptacle at the very center of the nave, placing lights at the Altar of St. Kunigunde, somewhat to the east. The boys' chorus remains in the west choir, singing "Ad tumulum venere gementes."

Then three priests as Marys, dressed in white and carrying thuribles, go to the sepulchre at the Altar of St. George in the east choir, where two angels are seated. "Quem quaeritis" follows, and when the angels announce "Surrexit Dominus," the women leave the sepulchre, make their way to the Altar of St. Stephen, located between the two flights of steps that lead on either side from the nave up into the east choir, and face the chorus. A first cantor from the chorus asks "Dic nobis, Maria," and each in turn responds with a verse. "Christ ist erstanden" is begun, and the whole procession returns to the west choir for the final *Te Deum*.

It is important to distinguish here those moments which by means of the staging are made most public. The whole cathedral glows and reverberates with the light and sound of the ritual, while the actual visit to the sepulchre is carried on almost in private at the far apse of the church. Both choirs were closed off with

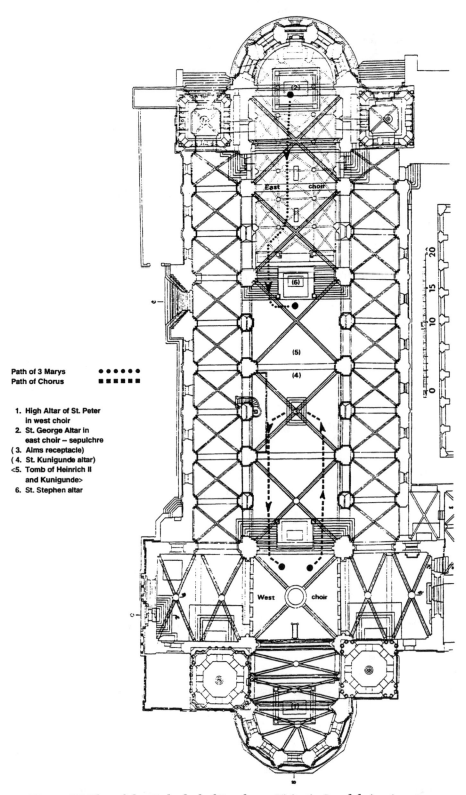

Figure 27. Plan of the Cathedral of Bamberg. *Visitatio Sepulchri,* **xvi century.**

screens above the steps leading up from the nave. A dramatic parallel can be drawn to the performance at Trier rather than to that at Essen, for in the former instance, as at Bamberg, the women are heard in the distance and then questioned when they return from their journey, by those who have descended into the nave. Again two essential stations are established— the sepulchre and the waiting community.

One is especially aware of the pastoral nature of these Easter celebrations at Bamberg. The *populus* participated not only in the little drama but also, and this is rare indeed, in the *Depositio* and *Elevatio*. Not only do they sing, but they are part of the *Depositio* procession, while the *Elevatio* procession cuts a figure eight through their midst in moving between the west and east choir. One is also especially aware of the hieratic nature of *Visitato Sepulchri* here because with one exception all nine of the Bamberg Cathedral texts, ranging from the thirteenth to the sixteenth century, have speech ascriptions referring not to the characters (Angel, *Angelus,* or the Marys, *Marie*) but to the ecclesiastical performers—such as *Sacerdotes* (priests) and *Dyaconi* (deacons)—or the texts simply mark the alternating lines as *Versus* and *Responsio* and the like.

Church of St. John the Evangelist at Besançon— the Sepulchre and the Manger at the High Altar

The two-apsed Church of St. John at Besançon was built largely in the twelfth and thirteenth centuries, with the high altar at the western end and the main choir extending to the fifth bay of the nave, only closed off by a rood-loft (possibly with a rood-screen) in the mid-sixteenth century. The text of the *Visitatio Sepulchri* dates from the fourteenth century; the sepulchre was located at the high altar, approached immediately by a set of steps.[22]

Matins is celebrated with the chorus dressed in black. Then three Marys, wearing white dalmatics with their amices over their heads and carrying gold or silver vessels, advance from the Chapel of St. Oyan, at the western extreme of the south aisle, to the Altar of the Holy Cross. A kind of performance director leads the way, a cantor with cope and staff. They are accompanied by a small procession with candles. They sing "Quis revolvet," eventually turning toward the main altar. The Altar of the Holy Cross was usually located in mid-nave, just before the choir entrance; here the rubric adds that at this point they are "in medio ecclesie et ad introitum chori." It seems, then, that they come eastward along the south aisle, turn into the

nave at about the sixth bay (if not farther to the east) and begin to move westward, stopping at the Altar of the Holy Cross before the choir entrance. Two winged angels at the high altar—on the left and right sides— ask "Quem quaeritis." Singing "Non est hic" they uncover the veiled altar, and the women sing "Alleluia, surrexit Dominus," proceeding through the choir to kneel and offer their vessels. As they then stand on the steps at the altar, the cantor who was in their procession approaches and questions the first Mary: "Dic nobis, Maria." Each responds in turn, the second bearing the sudary. The cantor looks back to the chorus as he sings "Credendum est magis," and the chorus follows with "Scimus Christum." The *Te Deum* is begun, the women return to the chapel, and the chorus members divest themselves of their black copes, probably emerging in white.

At Besançon the view of the high altar and sepulchre was unobstructed by a rood-screen, and nave and choir were on the same level up to the raised altar. Rather surprising here is the distance between the women and the angels during the moments of "Quem quaeritis," a scene conceived and executed in a more formal mode than many of those previously examined in this chapter. The symbolic offerings by the women convey a strong sense of ritual, while the cantor's query and the three-fold response to it do not contain that dramatic necessity which we have noted in productions where the sepulchre stands in a less overt position.

If as some have suggested this play has roots in a pre-tenth-century ceremony for converts returning from baptism on the night of Easter, then of all of our reconstructions in this chapter I believe that we are closest here to that part of the ancient Easter Vigil. Echoes of that early mise-en-scène may be found in the facts that the small procession begins in a chapel that was associated with baptism even prior to the construction of the present cathedral; that when the women face about toward the main altar, they take up a position between the congregation and the chorus; and that their white dalmatics contrast strikingly with the black of the chorus. The angels must call out "Quem quaeritis" to them from a distance of more than twenty meters.

One senses the same feeling for expansive use of space and visual as well as aural effect in a Christmas text from Besançon, an *Officium Stellae* probably dating from the latter part of the sixteenth century. The performance employed the whole extent of the nave. Here an elaborate procession, including three crowned kings with their respective servants carrying gold vessels, leaves the sacristy and makes its way to the Altar of the Virgin in the eastern apse, the site of some other Christmas ceremonies. Possibly the Magi advance eastward along the south aisle, as did the Marys, but I do not know where the sacristy was located in this period. (The present sacristy, off the western end of the north aisle, was built in the eighteenth century.) In any case, they proceed the length of the church, singing "Nouae geniturae/cedit ius naturae . . . nato Christo." Turning then in the direction of the chorus, they advance to the choir entrance, having stopped twice to say verses along the way. They thereupon ascend the *pulpitum,* the pulpit or the rood-loft constructed between 1550–58, in order to read the Gospel. As they read, the cantors presumably over in the west choir also chant or read a verse alternately with them. At the conclusion of the reading the first king points to the star and each exclaims "Ecce stella!" They descend and walk through the choir entrance up to the main altar, where they place their offerings, the star apparently moving before them (tandemque Stella duce progressi).

The position of the main altar in the west makes for geographic verisimilitude when the Magi approach along the nave from the east, and the long journeys from one end of the church to the other display the regal pomp of the performers. But the tenor of the performance is predominantly ritualistic, the high altar, as far as we know, only defined as the manger by the presentation of gifts.

Productions at the Cathedral of Rouen and in the Fleury Playbook

Cathedral of Rouen

Five manuscripts associated with the cathedral preserve nineteen copies of five different plays—the *Visitatio Sepulchri, Peregrinus, Officium Pastorum, Officium Stellae,* and *Ordo Prophetarum*—attesting to at least three hundred years of dramatic performances, from the thirteenth, fourteenth, and fifteenth centuries. In 1200 a fire nearly completely destroyed the old church; the present Gothic, cruciform cathedral was built in the first half of the thirteenth century.[23]

VISITATIO SEPULCHRI

The *Visitatio Sepulchri,* with the appearance of Christ to Mary Magdalen and two other women, was performed in the east choir, where a sepulchre that could

be entered was positioned near the main altar. The following description derives from the fourteenth-century text, with some variants from that of the thirteenth century.[24]

At the end of Matins three clergy, their amices over their heads "ad similitudinem Mulierum" and carrying vessels, come through the east choir toward the sepulchre with the lines "Quis reuoluet." The thirteenth-century text says that they move from the choir entrance. An angel before the tomb asks "Quem quaeritis," and at his reply to the women, "Non est hic," points to the grave and departs very quickly (citissime discedat). The earlier text does not add "very quickly."

Two angels sitting in the tomb inquire, "Mulier, quid ploras?," the women having entered. The woman in the middle (called Mary Magdalen in the thirteenth-century text) responds; the three kiss "the place" and emerge. A priest impersonating Christ, carrying a cross, appears at the left (probably south) corner of the altar and addresses Magdalen; "Mulier, quid ploras?" He shows her the cross, speaks her name, and she falls at his feet: "Rabboni." Christ makes a sign with his hand (in the thirteenth-century text he draws back), sings "Noli me tangere," and apparently goes behind the altar to reappear at the right corner of the altar before all three Marys. It is interesting to note here greater congruity in the fourteenth-century play, for in the earlier text all three Marys address Christ and then prostrate themselves when they recognize him.

Christ assures the women, commands them to report to the disciples that they shall see him in Galilee, and vanishes (se abscondat). The earlier text says only that he goes away (discedente). The women bow toward the altar and turn toward the chorus to sing "Alleluia, resurrexit Dominus," whereupon the archbishop or priest with a thurible commences the *Te Deum* before the altar.

What exactly the spatial relationship was between the altar and the sepulchre cannot be determined, but apparently they stood close to each other. However, the symbolic point is that Christ does not emerge from the tomb for the second scene of the drama but, having risen, he is now associated with the altar. In addition, we note the heightened visual effect of his disappearance behind the altar and his final vanishing.

Unlike most of the German productions which we have examined in this chapter, this performance was apparently meant chiefly for the clerical community.

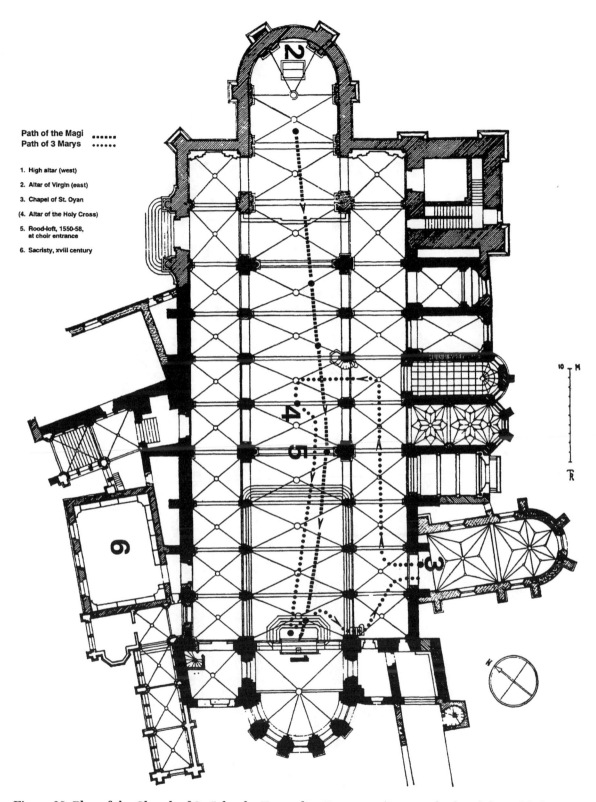

Figure 28. Plan of the Church of St. John the Evangelist, Besançon. (Steps in the fourth bay added in xviii century; eastern end, a reconstruction of the original form.) *Visitatio Sepulchri*, **xiv century.** *Officium Stellae*, **xvi (?) century.**

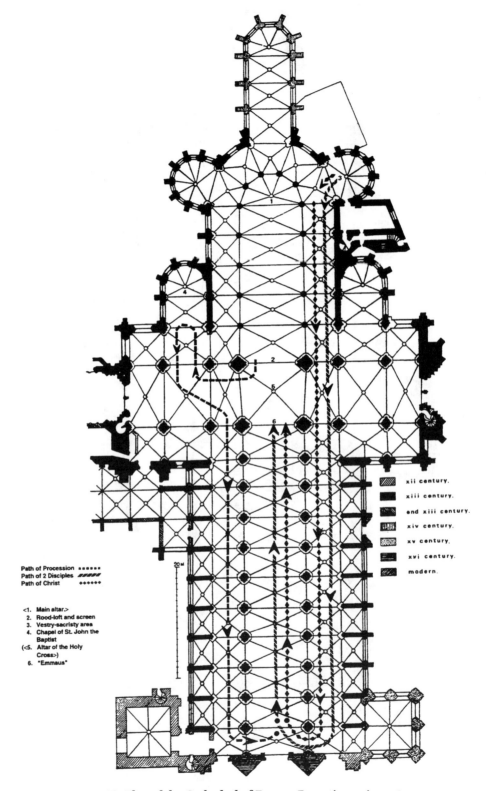

Path of Procession ● ● ● ● ● ●
Path of 2 Disciples ▬ ▬ ▬ ▬ ▬
Path of Christ ◆ ◆ ◆ ◆ ◆ ◆

<1. Main altar.>
2. Rood-loft and screen
3. Vestry-sacristy area
4. Chapel of St. John the Baptist
<5. Altar of the Holy Cross>
6. "Emmaus"

xii century.
xiii century.
end xiii century.
xiv century.
xv century.
xvi century.
modern.

Figure 29. Plan of the Cathedral of Rouen. *Peregrinus,* **xiv century.**

Since the thirteenth century a rood-screen with a central door 2.13 meters high, and two side doors closed off the east choir, thus blocking the view of the main altar from the nave. Curiously enough, however, the thirteenth-century *Adoratio Crucis,* prior to the burial ceremony *(Depositio)*, mentions the populace specifically: "Quando Crux adorata fuerit a clero et populo, eleuet eam sacerdos alte. . . . Quo uiso, clerus et populus genuflectant. . . ." The cross was then washed with water and wine, ". . . de quo commemorationem sacram clerus bibat et populus." It was then carried by the clergy to the sepulchre in the east choir, put in "pedibus uersis ad orientem," covered with a cloth, censed by the archbishop or priest, and the door closed (claudat ostium Sepulchri). These rubrics suggest an observance in the crossing, in contact with the populace outside of the east choir. Then in order to bury the cross the clergy took it from the Altar of the Holy Cross (in the crossing) into the east choir, to the sepulchre.

Could this thirteenth-century manuscript hearken back to an earlier, pre-rood-screen time when the *populus* had a view of the east choir, did partake of the communion wine, and the drama was more ceremonial? For instance, in the thirteenth-century text we find the more ritualistic prostration of all three Marys toward the Risen Christ, an act changed to the one Mary, Mary Magdalen, in the fourteenth-century text: a slight shift from ritual to drama.

Through these texts there runs an overt awareness of worshipper-audience. By that token it seems that at Rouen certain of the music-dramas were conceived of as secret mysteries, performed only for the clerical community, whereas others were acted out both for the clergy and the townspeople. As we have seen, the *Visitatio Sepulchri* was sung wholly within the confines of the east choir, by the thirteenth century effectively shut off from the general populace. Surprisingly, as we shall see, the *Officium Pastorum* was also staged totally inside the east choir. It too occurred in relation to Matins, on Christmas Day right after the *Te Deum* instead of just before it like the *Visitatio*. Also like the *Visitatio,* the little shepherd play derives from a dialogue trope, "Quem quaeritis in praesepe?" (Whom do you seek in the manger?), modelled on the earlier Easter trope "Quem quaeritis in sepulchro?" (Whom do you seek in the Sepulchre?). Furthermore, the *Officium Pastorum* may well have early roots in the liturgy at Rouen because a Christmas play where angels sing to shepherds is described for the first time by Jean, Bishop of Avranches (1060–67), who later became Archbishop of

Rouen. The earliest surviving text of the shepherd play comes a bit later, from the twelfth century.[25]

Quite by contrast at Rouen, the *Peregrinus* at Vespers on Easter Monday, the *Ordo Prophetarum* with its twenty-eight speaking personages prior to Mass on January 1, and the *Officium Stellae* with public gift-giving prior to Mass on Epiphany could not have been more spectacularly conceived for a lay public: with Cathedral-long processions, singing from atop the rood-loft, and a built-up city of Emmaus and a fiery furnace located, say the rubrics, right "in the middle of the nave of the church" (in medio navis ecclesie).

PEREGRINUS

At Rouen the *Peregrinus* play (The Wayfarer) was presented during Vespers of Easter Monday, after the procession to the baptismal font. The following description derives from the fourteenth-century text, with some variants from that of the thirteenth century.[26]

The choral group leaves the east choir, perhaps by the side door at the north of the rood-screen, and moves to the baptismal area before the Altar of St. John the Baptist. This was located in a chapel off the east side of the north transept. Then during the singing of a psalm the procession makes its way down the north aisle and takes up a position before the central door at the western end of the nave.

Singing "Jhesu, nostra redempcio," two disciples come out of the vestry, off the south-east extreme of the ambulatory, advance slowly down the south aisle all the way to the south door in the western façade, turn into the nave, and stand at the head of the procession there. They are bearded and wear the garb of pilgrims, with staffs, purses, special hats. At the conclusion of the fourth stanza of this hymn (there are six stanzas), a priest as Christ—barefoot, wearing an alb and amice, and carrying a cross on his right shoulder—comes up to them from the south aisle, presumably likewise having departed from the vestry.

A change in the mise-en-scène from the thirteenth century has heightened the theatrical effect, for in the earlier performance the two disciples entered the church from the south door in the western façade and approached the procession while Christ entered through the north door there. The fourteenth-century staging allowed the two journeys to occur along the entire length of the cathedral.

Christ suddenly stands between the two. They fail to recognize him. A moment of dramatic irony follows as Christ asks them about their discussion. They look at him in surprise, this man who does not know what has happened in Jerusalem, and then they tell him of Christ's death. He had approached them with downcast face. Now he looks at them intently. He reproaches them for their lack of faith and makes as if to go on, but they hasten to him and invite him to remain with them, pointing with their staffs at the *castellum* which is Emmaus. Singing, they lead him "usque ad tabernaculum, in medio navis Ecclesie, in similitudinem castelli Emaux preparatum." They ascend and sit at a table prepared there, Christ in the middle. As he breaks bread in their midst, they recognize him, and he suddenly vanishes.

A structure represented both the village of Emmaus and a room or house somewhere in the town. Nowhere in the drama of the medieval church do we have better documentation as to such a construction, one that also characterized the staging of religious plays out of doors. A raised platform, possibly decorated with painted hangings, with at least a table and three seats, it was erected in the nave, perhaps toward the western side of the crossing.[27] The Altar of the Holy Cross seems to have stood in the crossing. One might even surmise that the scaffolding had a trap-door in the floor for the sudden disappearance of Christ.

The two disciples rise, astonished, face each other and sing mournfully (in the thirteenth-century text they look to the procession) before turning about toward the *pulpitum* to address Mary Magdalen: "Dic nobis, Maria." This questioning does not occur in the *Visitatio Sepulchri*. Magdalen, dressed in a dalmatic and amice with her head bound "in modum Mulieris," responds "Sepulchrum Christi," showing and spreading out a gravecloth on one side and a second on the other side, then casting them down (proiciat) before the great central door of the rood-screen. She is standing in the pulpit or up on the rood-loft, where she can be seen clearly by all those west of the scaffolding. This would mean that her exchange with the two disciples is carried out between two raised positions, a striking theatrical effect.

Mary Magdalen concludes with "Surrexit Christus," the chorus takes up the music, the actors depart, and the procession returns into the east choir.

We possess thirteen *Peregrinus* texts from eight localities; four of them from Rouen. Of the nine other *Peregrinus* texts the one from Beauvais (twelfth century) seems to place Emmaus in the choir; one of two reflecting Norman-French usage in Sicily (Syracuse, twelfth century) says that the scene occurs "ad altare" while the other (Palermo) places the action outside

the choir; performances at Padua (thirteenth century) and in the Fleury Playbook (late twelfth century) put the repast in the nave. Subsequent dramatized appearances of Christ to other disciples in Jerusalem took place in the choir in the Fleury Playbook and in Palermo. The only scenic description comparable to that at Rouen is found in the Fleury Playbook rubrics. Usually, though, a table or altar as table is noted or implied.[28]

Whereas the *Visitatio* production on Easter morning has characters moving to and away from the site of the sepulchre, the progress of the *Peregrinus* demands an extensive playing space for its depiction of travellers on a journey. The tomb of Christ had the aura of an essentially secret place, where a passive scene occurred, a discovery of a past event, while the house at Emmaus was the locale of an open, theatrically direct show of dramatic irony, wonder, and recognition unfolding *coram populo,* and as such the latter play with its scaffolding exhibits practices of dramaturgy becoming independent from liturgy rather than the more static scenes never far removed from ecclesiastical ritual. From the latter, the ceremony of Easter Sunday, comes lyric poetry; while from the former, the story of the wayfarers, comes narrative action. And whereas the *Visitatio Sepulchri* at Rouen was restricted to the vicinity of the high altar, the performance of the *Peregrinus* spread through the whole body of the church, creating in addition a climactic, public witness to the Resurrection by transferring the interrogation of Mary Magdalen and the display of the gravecloths to this concluding position. Such a change has its foundation in the dynamics of performance rather than in the texts of liturgy.

OFFICIUM PASTORUM

A similar comparison is evident between the separate Christmas plays of the shepherds and of the Magi at Rouen, the former with the manger at the high altar and the latter with the manger at the Altar of the Holy Cross in the nave.

The *Officium Pastorum* was performed at Rouen just after the concluding *Te Deum* of Matins, and it led into the first Mass of Christmas Day. The following description derives from the fourteenth-century text, with some variants from that of the thirteenth century.[29]

At the back of the main altar was placed the manger, with artificial figures of the Virgin (Ymago Sancte Marie) and the Child concealed by a curtain which a pair of midwives pulled aside during the performance—an arrangement for the display of reliquaries often found on altars of this period.

As five shepherds, in tunics with amices (and staffs, according to the thirteenth-century text), enter the central portal of the choir, a boy as an angel announces the Nativity from a high place: "Nolite timere." A number of angels (seven in the thirteenth-century text) up under the vaulting continue with "Gloria in excelsis Deo," and the shepherds begin to make their way toward the manger, singing "Pax in terris." Two midwives, dressed in dalmatics, ask "Quem queritis in presepe," and at the response of the shepherds they draw the curtain and point first to the Christ Child, "Adest hic paruulus," and then to the Virgin, "Ecce uirgo." The shepherds bow before the Child as they sing "Salue, uirgo singularis," then turn and go back to the chorus with "Alleluia," whereupon Mass begins and they rule the choir. The thirteenth-century text has them address "Salue, uirgo singularis" directly to the Mother and then worship the Child just before their return.

The pattern of movement, as the concept of the play, is of the simplest sort, perhaps originally an imitation of the earlier Easter drama beginning with the idea of the altar as manger and modeled on the "Quem quaeritis" lines. In any case, the basic ingredient of the static scene is the same with the expected discovery made a revelatory experience for all onlookers through the sudden opening of the curtain before the figures of Mother and Child.

The earliest indication of mise-en-scène for the *Officium Pastorum* appears in an eleventh-century text from Novalesa, where two deacons behind the altar address two cantors as shepherds standing in the choir, doubtless in front of the altar. The only other *Officium Pastorum* with notes as to the position of the manger is found in a thirteenth-century text from Padua, where it was set up in the choir area before the altar and contained a covered image of Virgin and Child (cum Beata Uirgine Maria et Filio, nitido pallio cooperta), disclosed by the midwives at the approach of two shepherds.[30]

From the beginning the *Officium Pastorum* was closely attached to the Mass and never became the inventive, independent kind of work that we find in the freer Magi plays, some of which include the shepherds.

OFFICIUM STELLAE

A prelude to the Mass of Epiphany as of the thirteenth century, the *Officium Stellae* at Rouen portrays the coming of the Magi to Bethlehem without introducing the character of Herod and episodes associated with him. Its conception differs markedly from that of the shepherd play. Here the manger was established in the nave—not in the east choir—on the Altar of the Holy Cross, probably in the crossing, with a figure or figures of the Virgin and the Child concealed behind a curtain that was drawn at the appropriate moment by two midwives. As in the *Officium Pastorum,* a rubric refers to the "Ymago Sancte Marie" and a subsequent direction has lines addressed to the Child. Above the altar hung a *corona*, a cluster of lights, as the star.

The following description derives from the fourteenth-century manuscript with some variants from the whole text and the fragmentary text of the thirteenth century; for convenience the former is cited as "the thirteenth-century text" and the latter as "the thirteenth-century fragment."[31]

The three Magi come from different directions, from the east, north, and south, and meet before the main altar, each with a servant bearing his particular gift. The thirteenth-century text notes the first king's appearance from behind the altar but does not have the respective servants carrying the offerings, while the attendants do perform this function in the thirteenth-century fragment. (Could the thirteenth-century text reflect practice in the pre-rood-screen era—as possibly with the thirteenth-century *Visitatio* from Rouen and the early shepherd play? Then with the erection of the rood-screen and the greater separation of clergy from laity, could the *Visitatio* and *Officium Pastorum* have been consciously confined to the east choir at Rouen?) The king from the east points to the star with his staff, "Stella fulgore," each king responds with a line, they kiss, and after the cantor begins the responsory "Magi ueniunt," the procession moves out of the choir, also singing "Interrogabat Magos" if necessary (si necesse fuerit), and takes up a position in the nave, probably west of the Altar of the Holy Cross. Because the rood-screen (thirteenth century) blocks the worshippers' view of the high altar, the emerging Magi must now become visible to the populace. The Magi (at the entrance to the nave in the thirteenth-century text) point to the lighted *corona* suspended before the cross and go to the altar: "Ecce stella." Whether there are in fact two stars, the *corona* here and one at the high altar, where Mass and a second offering are to take place, is a moot point; the kings could have seen the *corona* from the main altar if the cluster were raised high enough, and there is no indication that a star moves.[32]

Two clerics at either end of the altar open the curtain to reveal the images, "Ecce puer," and the kings prostrate themselves in adoration of the Child. The first takes gold from his servant and presents it, the other two following with frankincense and myrrh. Thereupon the clergy and the populace bring their gifts.

The Magi pray and fall asleep, and a boy as an angel appears before the altar warning them to return home by another way. The cantor begins the responsory "Tria sunt" at the entrance to the choir, and the performance concludes as the procession presumably reenters the choir via the middle door for Mass, at which the Magi rule the choir.

The two fifteenth-century texts record a dramatic change in this final scene: here the angel stands "in pulpito," apparently up on the rood-loft, to deliver the warning, and the Magi then make a detour, withdrawing via the north aisle near the baptismal area (in the north transept; see the plan) and entering the choir through the north door. The rood-screen had a central door and a smaller entrance on either side of it. The procession then enters the choir, "as is customary on Sunday," probably through the large portal, the cantor commencing the responsory.

The fourteenth- and fifteenth-century texts reveal a double offering, whereby gifts were not only presented during the course of the performance at the Altar of the Holy Cross but also during the subsequent Mass at the high altar by the Magi and others who so wished, presumably of the clerical community. The thirteenth-century text does not mention the participation by the laity, while the thirteenth-century fragment removes this act from the center of the drama and places it during the singing of the final responsory.

The pattern of this performance is very like that of the *Officium Pastorum*, with the manger and the revelatory experience there quite similarly executed, but the major differences being in the implications of the more extensive opening journey with its east-to-west orientation, the additional final scene, made more theatrical and literal by the action in the later texts, and, of course, the fact of public exhibition in the nave with the overt participation of the congregation.

We shall compare the staging of other Magi plays when we come to the productions of the Christmas season in the Fleury Playbook.

ORDO PROPHETARUM

Two Rouen texts, from the fourteenth and fifteenth century, record the most extensive extant version of the *Ordo Prophetarum* with its twenty-eight major speaking personages, acted just prior to Mass on the feast of the Circumcision (January 1). Of particular interest are the rather detailed descriptions of costumes, which will be dealt with in the ensuing chapter, and an imitation furnace erected in the nave and set on fire toward the conclusion of the presentation.[33]

The pre-Mass performance opens with a procession of the performers from the cloister into the middle of the church, by what route we are not told. One by one each prophet is announced by summoners, he apparently steps forward to deliver his prophecy in the nave, and is then escorted by the summoners to a position beyond the furnace (ultra fornacem), while the chorus sings "Quod Iudea," the summoners then returning to call on the next speaker. At the end of the speeches all prophets and ministers stand "in pulpito"—probably on the rood-loft—to sing "Ortum predestinacio," whereupon the cantor at the choir entrance begins a responsory, the chorus doubtless moving into the east choir for Mass, where the prophets and ministers rule the choir.

Within the processional-type performance are two dramatic scenes: one with Balaam spurring on his donkey as the beast refuses to budge before an angel, to whose presence Balaam is momentarily blind, and with the crying out of the player inside the animal costume; the other, the climactic display, with Nebuchadnezzar's futile attempt to coerce homage from Shadrach, Meshach, and Abednego, who are then thrown into a fiery furnace.

The furnace, constructed of oakum and cloth, was erected "in medio nauis ecclesie"—the same phrase applied to the *castellum* of Emmaus—perhaps west of the crossing (and of the Altar of the Holy Cross). King Nebuchadnezzar, the last but one of the twenty-eight chief figures, points to an idol and commands two of his soldiers to have the three youths bow before it. When they spurn the image, the soldiers bring them before the king, and he orders them thrown into the fiery furnace. The command is carried out and the structure lighted. Nebuchadnezzar hears the unharmed boys singing "Benedictus es, Domine Deus," asks his soldiers about it, and is told "Deum laudant," and then at the query of the summoners he concludes the episode with a statement of the event. Just how the actors escaped from the spectacular effect we are not told.

The formal line of recitals is hardly dramatic, but the work is not far removed from that kind of outdoor performance whereby a processional group advanced from station to station, stopping at the given points to act out a progressive series of scenes.[34]

*The Fleury Playbook and the Church
of St.-Benoît-sur-Loire*

A twelfth-century manuscript from the library of the Abbey of St.-Benoît-sur-Loire, at Fleury, contains the most extraordinary collection of dramas which we possess from the medieval church. This anthology of ten works, all copied at Fleury in the same hand in the third quarter of the twelfth century, has come to be known as the Fleury Playbook. However, it may not have originated in Fleury. The neums, for one thing, are not characteristic of those from Fleury. In addition, we possess no earlier evidence of dramatic activity there, and no rubric names any unique feature of the church—a specific tomb, altar, or chapel. Some scholars have suggested that student circles of either Orléans or Paris generated the compendium. Whatever the originating community, the plays evince a certain homogeneity in their emphasis on theatrical display, love of rhymed verse, and integration into a liturgical Office (at least eight of the ten have such liturgical links). Nevertheless, the copying of the manuscript at Fleury, in the twelfth century, and housing it in that library might well indicate production in that church, and as a whole the Playbook reveals important concepts for the staging of the music-drama.[35]

As to the rubrical evidence revealing location of performance, the plays fall into two categories: the *Visitatio Sepulchri, Peregrinus, Officium Stellae,* and *Ordo Rachelis* contain direct references to choir and nave; the plays of St. Nicholas, St. Paul, and Lazarus do not. However, each of the latter texts concludes with a choral work normally attached to a worship service. Unfortunately no singular feature of the building or its furnishings is named in the plays, unless hinted at by the references to Galilee in the *Ordo Rachelis* and *Resuscitatio Lazari,* but what we can reconstruct of the mise-en-scène fits admirably the church of St.-Benoît-sur-Loire. As to the inventive spirit evidenced by the manuscript, this was an abbey long renowned as a brilliant center of the arts in the Middle Ages. Bishop Ethelwold, for one, acknowledged his debt to the monks of Fleury in the *Regularis Concordia.*

The major building of the church as it now stands occurred in the eleventh and twelfth centuries: reconstruction work on its famous west tower and porch began in 1067, the east choir and transept were finished in 1108, and the nave was dedicated in 1218. Originally the main altar, consecrated to the Virgin, stood in the middle of the east choir. Toward the east-ern end of the choir, beyond the main altar, rose a wall about two meters high, with narrow openings into the crypt. On the raised floor level which extended eastward from the top of this wall (the roof of the crypt) stood an altar to St. Benoît, with the remains of the saint in the crypt directly beneath. The floor of the choir westward from the foot of this wall was approximately level with that of the nave, and as far as I can determine, no rood-screen closed off the east choir. Rubrical references to a direct relationship between characters in the choir and the congregation support this point.

In the early part of the sixteenth century the choir stalls were moved into the sixth and seventh bays of the nave, a rood-screen was built between the fifth piers of the nave (1518), and the floor of the east choir was raised by sets of two, five, and two steps up to the top of the crypt wall, thus covering it (1531–35). Therefore, after these major interior changes the staging of the plays as indicated by the late-twelfth-century rubrics would seem no longer to obtain in all particulars, and the *terminus ad quem* for the productions at Fleury might well be this period.

VISITATIO SEPULCHRI

The sepulchre for this production, a structure which could contain at least four persons, was located in the east choir, perhaps close to the choir entrance. There is no indication as to the use of the pierced crypt wall.

Three monks as the Marys, "vested in imitation of the three Marys" approach "haltingly and as though sorrowful," alternately singing quite a long lament. Perhaps they move the whole length of the church. Entering the choir, they go as if seeking to the monument, where a very ornate angel sits, dressed in a gilded alb, wearing a miter, and holding a palm in his left hand and a candelabrum in his right. After the "Quem quaeritis" dialogue, the women turn "ad populum" and sing "Ad monumentum Domini venimus." I believe that here in order to address the populace they move westward from the sepulchre to the choir entrance at the transept. Mary Magdalen thereupon leaves the other two, goes back to the sepulchre, looks in, mourning, and then hastens to Peter and John, an older and a younger man, who apparently stand up at their places in the choir (pr[e]stare debent ere[cti]). Sadly she tells them of the empty tomb and the grave-cloths within. They run to the sepulchre; John arrives first but waits and enters after Peter; they emerge bewildered.

After they depart, Mary Magdalen returns, lamenting, and two angels seated within ask "Mulier, quid ploras?" and comfort her. Meanwhile Christ comes dressed as a gardener, stands at the head of the sepulchre, and asks the same question. The recognition scene occurs, Magdalen falling at his feet, and Christ withdraws a little, sings "Noli me tangere," and goes away.

Mary Magdalen turns "ad populum" with "Congratulamini michi," and the two angels show themselves at the entrance to the sepulchre, inviting the women to view the place and exhorting them to tell the disciples. The Marys depart from the sepulchre, apparently having obtained the gravecloths. They go over to the populace (ad plebem) and announce "Surrexit Dominus," spreading out the linen before the populace (ad plebem). The two expressions "ad populum" and "ad plebem" seem to refer to the congregation. After then placing the linen on the altar, they return, alternately singing verses of praise.

As they start to leave the choir, the actor playing Christ appears to them. Now he is in a brilliant costume as Resurrectus, wearing a white dalmatic with a white chasuble, a precious cloth or a phylactery on his head, and carrying a cross with a banner in his right hand and a gilded (Gospel?) book or cloth in his left hand. He commands the women to tell the disciples that he will come to them in Galilee. The drama ends with choral rejoicing and the final *Te Deum*.

The whole production moves about the spacious east choir, save possibly for the initial approach of the women through the church into the choir entrance. Moreover, in the rubrics one finds four explicit references to the congregation, indicating, I believe, lines delivered by performers within the east choir but having walked over toward the transept. There the front ranks of the congregation would have stood with their unobstructed view of the east choir. The pattern of movement is no longer simply the one or two journeys between the grave and a waiting assembly. Instead, the adroitly prolonged penetration of the tomb's mystery involves the staging of a progressive series of confrontations between individual characters within a well-defined acting space directly in front of the gathered spectators, the entire playing area conceived and used as a polyscenic stage of juxtaposition. Peter and John apparently are seated with the monastic community, in rows along the north and south flanks of the choir, on either side of the altar and sepulchre. These two actors are visible even during the opening scene, where they have no part. Likewise Mary Magdalen's

two companions stand aside but no doubt remain in view during both the race to the tomb and the appearance of Christ as gardener, later reentering the action at the invitation of the angels. A characteristic of medieval staging is the presence of actors in the vicinity of the playing space who do not participate in a given scene, a complement to the principle of polyscenic setting. But here we find a mixture or hybrid form in that Christ must leave the stage, as it were, for his sumptuous costume change and subsequent reappearance.

This *Visitatio* combines visibility when the Marys come through the nave, and blocked visibility at moments of secrecy, all dwelling in a kind of crucial ambivalence as to how much the congregation is supposed to see. All the ambiguities as to what extent the congregation is and is not "audience" coruscate through the performance—all the ambivalences as to whether, in our terms, the church cares about "sight lines." These Fleury plays are skillfully staged—a characteristic of the whole Playbook—where the sense of who is the audience is manifestly complex.

Built textually on the foundation of the Rouen play, as de Boor has pointed out, it is the Fleury staging that draws the congregation into repeated witness to the Resurrection. Four times characters turn explicitly to the populace during the course of performance, and finally in a spectacular climax they present the audience with the Risen Christ.

PEREGRINUS

The *Peregrinus* play took place during Vespers on Tuesday of Easter week. Because the two disciples advance into the choir after the repast, it seems that Emmaus was established in mid-nave, the journey of the wayfarers beginning at the western end.

Dressed in tunics and copes with their cowls concealed to resemble cloaks, and with hats and staffs, the two disciples proceed "a competenti loco," singing "[J]esu, nostra redempcio." They look like Compostela pilgrims. Christ, in a tunic, a real cloak (hacla), and a hat but barefoot and with a wallet and palm branch, follows stealthily behind them and then begins to question them. As he finally feigns a departure, they invite him to stay with them, and they sit at a table prepared with an uncut loaf, three wafers, and a cup of wine. Water is brought for the washing of hands. Christ then reenacts Communion, with the breaking of bread and offering of wine, and as they eat the wafers he secretly goes away, unnoticed by them. Discovering his absence, the two sadly rise and walk, lamenting, toward the choir. As they enter the choir, the chorus sings "Surrexit Dominus et apparuit Petro," and a second scene commences, an appearance of Christ to ten disciples in Jerusalem.

Christ comes to them garbed in a white sleeveless tunic, red cope, white embroidered miter, and carrying a gold cross. Whether there are more than two disciples singled out or whether members of the chorus add to the group, we are not told. Christ addresses them three times with "Pax uobis" and shows the wounds in his hands and feet; the disciples approach and touch the stigmata; and, raising his hand over them with a blessing, Christ goes out by an entrance probably in the south flank of the choir (per hostium ex aduerso chori) since the sacristy lay in that direction.

A slow movement and song by the disciples marks a transition to the final scene, when Thomas joins them, likewise dressed as a pilgrim with a tunic, cloak, hat, and staff. Upon Thomas' declaration of disbelief Christ appears for the third time, now wearing a crown formed of his amice and philacteries and carrying a gold cross with a banner in his right hand and the Gospels in his left. Again he repeats the three-fold "Pax uobis," answered by the chorus. When Thomas has touched the wounds, he prostrates himself before Christ.

Thereupon the composer-author builds up to the climax dramatically and musically by having Dominus sing four songs found nowhere else in the canon of this drama. In them Christ charges the disciples to go forth and preach the Gospel. The play closes with a festive procession as the disciples lead him through the choir singing "Salue festa dies," explicitly so that the congregation may see him. This is the high point.

The blocking of the opening scene seems to begin like that at Rouen with the journey along the nave from the west. Two more episodes are then played out in the east choir, the pair of wayfarers making the transition by their walk into that area. Here, as in the *Visitatio Sepulchri*, emphasis is placed on spectacular costume change, costumes in the two plays with similarly if not identically ornate features. In fact one is struck by the attention paid both to costume and to the details of the repast at Emmaus, with kinds of realistic touches in direct contrast to the formal conception and execution of the work as a whole. The immediacy of the Communion scene in the nave, the removal to the east choir, and the final turn directly to the worshippers underscore the strong consciousness

of relationship between actors and spectators, and the definition of playing areas in the church—in the nave and choir—connected by the moves of individual characters. One senses, for instance, the marked contrast between Emmaus in full view and the action in the choir. We shall have occasion to note again the location of Jerusalem in the vicinity of the main altar, in the east.

In addition to hosting multitudes of pilgrims arriving to draw spiritual sustenance from the relics of St. Benedict, Fleury served as a major stopping place on the pilgrimage route to Santiago de Compostela in northwest Spain—the third greatest pilgrimage site in medieval Christendom after Jeruselum and Rome. Many were housed and fed in Fleury's western tower, with its second-story interior apertures looking directly out to the nave. To dress Cleophas and Luke as Compostela pilgrims and to have them commence their journey from beneath this western tower would have fused fittingly dramatic episode with contemporary event. That same fusion of act and ambience may also have marked the Christmas journeys of the shepherds and the Magi as they made their way westward along the nave to the manger, at the place beneath this tower where as wayfarers Mary and Joseph had sought refuge.

OFFICIUM STELLAE

Let us continue our supposition that from the twelfth century the plays of the Fleury Playbook were staged in the church of St.-Benoît-sur-Loire. The position of the Christmas manger there has been the subject of a good deal of speculation. The relevant rubric says: "and let them [the shepherds] thus proceed to the manger, which will have been readied at the doors of the church" (et sic procedant [shepherds] usque ad Presepe, quod ad ianuas monasterii paratum erit). Shortly thereafter the shepherds invite the members of the congregation standing nearby to worship the Christ Child (inuitent populum circumstantem adorandum Infantem); meanwhile the Magi gather before the main altar; eventually after their interview with Herod, they will meet the shepherds returning from the manger.

The phrase "ad ianuas monasterii" might be construed as referring to one of two locations at Fleury: to an entrance on the south side, the monastery lying south of the church, or to the entrance at the west end of the nave. Both external evidence and theatrical logic indicate the latter as the correct position. To erect the manger in the south transept or aisle would be to obscure it. The term *monasterium* appears frequently in other texts referring not to the monastery buildings but to the body of the church as distinct from the choir, and more specifically to the nave.[36] The likelihood of the meaning here is increased by position, usage, and symbolic association. The main public entrance to the church for dignitaries and townspeople was on the north side, opposite the fourth bay, while the doors at the western end led from the porch of the western tower directly into the nave. At ground level this westwork stood on a dozen unenclosed pillars, an open assembly point for processions that could enter the nave of the abbey, in the playwright's phrase, "ad ianuas monasterii." Moreover, as we have noted with the *Peregrinus* play, the westwork was strongly associated with pilgrimage, pilgrims en route to Santiago de Compostela and pilgrims coming in acts of devotion toward the remains of St. Benedict, founder of European monasticism. The sacred remains had been transferred from Monte Cassino to Fleury in the seventh or eighth century. Pilgrims were fed by the monastery in this ground-level area and were lodged in the second story, from which they could witness services. To locate Bethlehem and the manger at those doors where wanderers were given food and shelter would seem particularly appropriate.

The performance commences with Herod and his court in position, probably to one side of the nave not far from the crossing. An angel in a high place, perhaps somewhere over the crossing, announces the Nativity to a group of shepherds, and a chorus of angels joins in the "Gloria in excelsis Deo." The shepherds, at first frightened, rise and proceed to the manger, singing "Transeamus usque Bethleem." There the midwives ask "Quem queritis." The shepherds fall down in worship, and then invite the congregation nearby to do the same.

Meanwhile the Magi come forward, each from a different direction, and meet with a kiss before the main altar, calling attention to the star. The star moves, either running on a string or carried in front of them, and they follow it to the choir entrance, where they inquire of those standing there—as citizens of Jerusalem—where the king of the Jews has been born. This is a clear indication of a sense of geography and, I believe, the second time in the play where the congregation is drawn into the action.

Herod sees the Magi and twice sends a soldier as messenger to them. Then he sends his interpreters. Once again the messenger is dispatched, and at last he leads the Magi to the king. After asking further questions and examining the gifts of gold, frankincense, and myrrh, Herod commands young courtiers (symmistae) seated with him to fetch scribes. The latter, bearded, are brought with their prophetic writings, having been "in diuersorio"—perhaps in the area of the sacristy. They search the pages for a while and finally show Herod the prophecy of Christ's birth. The king becomes furious, hurls the book to the ground, and his son, hearing the commotion, comes to pacify his father by speaking contemptuously of the supposed usurper. Whereupon Herod asks the Magi to find the Child and return to him so that he too may go and worship. It seems evident from the context that the audience would understand these lines as Herod's act of deception.

The Magi leave, pointing to and following the star, which precedes them. Herod has not seen it. When he does, he and his son brandish their swords—no doubt foreboding *The Slaughter of the Innocents*, a separate play in the Fleury Playbook. Just how literally the star was kept out of his sight until this moment is impossible to guess: it could have been suspended at a considerable height, and perhaps a canopy stretched above the royal throne; there could have been two stars, as some have suggested for the performance at Rouen.

The Magi meet the returning shepherds, who tell them what they have seen and then go away, perhaps on into the choir. Following the star, the Magi come to the manger, are shown the Child by the midwives, offer their gifts, and sleep there. An angel appears above, possibly from one of the openings in the western tower, and warns them to return by another way. An altar to St. Michael had stood in that upper story since earliest times. Singing "O admirabile commercium," the Magi follow the instructions so that Herod does not see them, probably moving along one of the side aisles, and enter the choir, whereupon the cantor begins the *Te Deum*.

In this play, which combines the *Officium Pastorum* with the *Officium Stellae,* there are three major stations: the meeting place of the Magi at the main altar, the court of Herod, and the manger. Herod is probably on a throne since his young companions are noted as being seated; he is surrounded by quite an entourage, all of whom may have been on some kind of raised platform. Whether the manger was in some way covered with a curtain we are not told; the two midwives show the Christ Child; above it was a place for an angel.

Of particular significance is the use of the whole

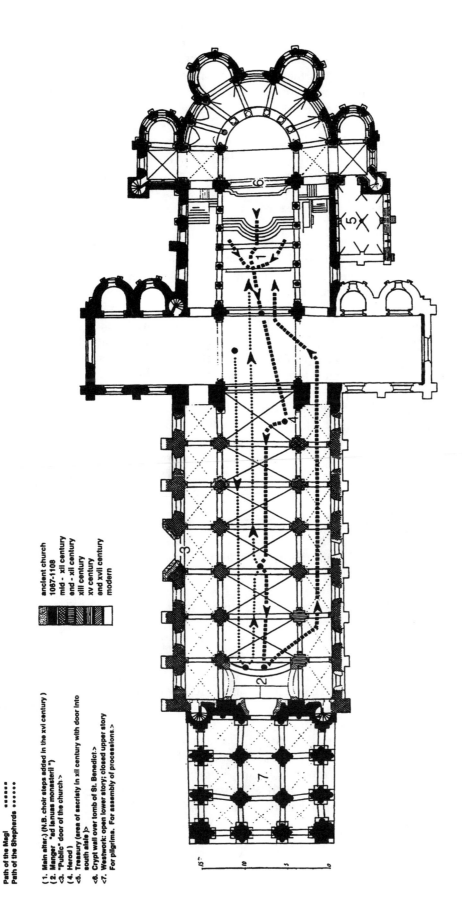

Path of the Magi ▪▪▪▪▪▪
Path of the Shepherds ●●●●●

1. Main altar.) (N.B. choir steps added in the xvi century)
(2. Manger "ad Ianuas monasterii ")
<3. "Public" door of the church>
(4. Herod)
<5. Treasury (area of sacristy in xii century with door into south aisle)>

<6. Crypt wall over tomb of St. Benedict.>
<7. Westwork: open lower story; closed upper story
For pilgrims. For assembly of processions.>

ancient church
1067-1108
mid - xii century
end - xii century
xiii century
xv century
end xvii century
modern

Figure 30. Plan of the church of St.-Benoît-sur-Loire. (Steps in the east choir added in the xvi century.) *Officium Stellae*, xii century.

length of the church with stations at either end, a station in the middle, and the congregation between, so that in fact the action proceeds amongst the onlookers, who at one extreme are directed to the manger and who at the other extreme are addressed as citizens of Jerusalem. The pattern of journeys to and from specific localities is most clearly laid out, each move dramatically motivated. Furthermore, this pattern of journeys is matched by a sequence of overlapping scenes, where in one example the shepherds pay homage at the manger while in the east choir some distance away the Magi begin their approach toward each other. Rubrics are quite explicit about this simultaneity of action. The opening rubric, "Ordo ad representandum Herodem," points to the work's two modes: the more ritualistic and traditional advances to the manger, and the more inventively dramatic episode in and near Herod's court. The mise-en-scène of the former is essentially processional in nature, while the center of the play, probably set in something like a "mansion," is defined in terms of intense questioning and rather realistic touches—hurrying messengers, diligent scribes searching their pages, a raging monarch menacing with his sword. The Herod play is acted out within the ceremonial framework of the drama.[37]

ORDO RACHELIS (THE SLAUGHTER OF THE INNOCENTS)

The one version of this play which permits a tentative reconstruction of the performance is that in the Fleury Playbook, acted at the end of Matins, perhaps on Innocents' Day (28 December). A procession of boys advances, singing, along the nave of the church (per monasterium) and is suddenly preceded by a lamb carrying a cross "hither and thither" (huc et illuc). The rubrics reveal no more information as to this symbol of sacrifice. Meanwhile Herod's armor-bearer offers the king his scepter, and an angel above the manger warns Joseph to flee with Mary and Child into Egypt. Joseph follows the instructions, traveling so that he is not seen by Herod. Hearing from the armor-bearer that the Magi have returned home via another route, Herod in his anger attempts suicide, is pacified, and then orders the massacre of the children.

As the killers come forward, the lamb is secretly removed, the mothers pray in vain for mercy, and the prostrate children cry out to an angel who appears above. Rachel comes with the "Consolatrices" and sings a series of four laments over the bodies of the

children during which the "Consolatrices" accompany her and support her in moments of fainting, finally leading her away.

An angel from above summons the innocents, who rise and enter the choir. Then follows a dumb show in which Archelaus replaces his father, Herod, on the throne. An angel now calls Joseph back to Israel, and the Holy Family returns, "withdrawing into Galilee," whereupon the cantor begins the Te Deum.

There are two obvious clues as to areas of the church: the opening procession of the innocents "per monasterium," and their entrance into the choir. It seems that the term monasterium refers here as in the Officium Stellae to the nave of the church. Since the massacre and Rachel's extensive lament over the fallen children, the high point of the drama, apparently occur in the crossing before the choir entrance, the innocents probably proceed through the western entrance and eastward along the nave.[38] If the murder takes place in the crossing, Herod's court could stand as in the Officium Stellae, that is, to one side of the eastern part of the nave.

These rubrics as to the nave and choir leave the position of the manger and the locations of "Egypt" and "Galilee" to be accounted for. Again the most likely place for the former seems to be as in the Magi play, at the western doors, where an angel appears "super Presepe" to warn Joseph just as he appears "desuper" to warn the sleeping Magi. The Holy Family then departs into Egypt, "non uidente Herode"—exactly the wording of the rubric describing the return of the Magi. If Herod is seated on the south side of the nave with his back to the south aisle, then, as we have suggested for the Magi, the Holy Family might move eastward along this aisle, perhaps stopping in the south transept as "Egypt."

An angel appears in a high place four different times during the course of the performance: to warn Joseph at the manger, to admonish the prostrate children, to call the children after Rachel departs, and finally to summon Joseph back to Israel. Considering the structure of the church, the logical place for the latter three would be above the area of the crossing, although neither necessarily by the same angel nor from exactly the same position.

Finally we come to the problem of Galilee and a possible reference to a singular feature of the church. Just before the cantor begins the Te Deum, a rubric has Joseph return, withdrawing into Galilee with Mary and the Child, and singing "Gaude, gaude, gaude, Maria uirgo": "Tunc Ioseph reuertatur cum Maria

Figure 31. Church of St.-Benoît-sur-Loire, east choir with pierced crypt wall, xii to xvi centuries. Main altar stood in mid-choir, west of crypt wall.

et Puero, secedens in parte[s] Galilee." The latter phraseology is a paraphrase of the Vulgate (Matthew 2:22): "secessit in partes Galilaeae." The emendation of "parte[s]" is Young's. I would suggest that the Holy Family leaves the south transept, passes behind Archelaus, now on his father's throne but feared by Joseph according to the Scriptural account, and moves out along the nave and on through the western doors into the porch of the western tower that was known elsewhere by the name of "Galilee." The term "Galilee" was applied in this way in the eleventh century at Cluny, for example, which monastery had particularly strong ties with St.-Benoît-sur-Loire.[39] That the author of the play paraphrased the Vulgate in his stage direction weakens the case for this being an overt reference to the western porch of the church, although by the same token a previous descriptive rubric has the angel warn Joseph "fugere in Egiptum" (Vulgate: "Fuge in Aegyptum") while the next rubric merely notes "Ioseph abiens," not paraphrasing the Vulgate (et secessit in Aegyptum). The fact that Joseph, Mary, and the Child come back would seem to indicate their being seen and heard in the vicinity of where they had been before, particularly since their return follows immediately the dumb show in which Archelaus becomes king; and the fact that only the innocents explicitly enter the choir would seem to preclude this as the destination of the Holy Family.

No other drama of the medieval church portrays this journey out of Egypt, but in the play of Lazarus in the Fleury Playbook a special place representing Galilee is prepared for Christ and the disciples, possibly at the western extreme of the nave.

RESUSCITATIO LAZARI

The Raising of Lazarus requires the representation of a house (domus) used first by Simon and then by Mary, Martha, and Lazarus; two geographical places (locus) Galilee and Jerusalem; and Lazarus' tomb. It is the only play that comes within the scope of this study which employs the term *platea* in the rubrics, here apparently referring to a neutral playing area. But nowhere in the text is there an indication of position in relation to choir or nave, although the closing *Te Deum* by the chorus suggests a performance during Matins.

At the outset Simon "resideat in domu sua" as Jesus comes "in plateam" with disciples. The house, probably a decorated platform, contained a table, for Simon comes to Jesus and leads him into a meal,

"posita mensa." Mary Magdalen as a prostitute appears (in habitu per plateam meretricio) and falls at Jesus' feet.

At the conclusion of this scene Jesus departs with his disciples toward Galilee, where a locale is prepared for him (abeat quasi in Galileam; et sit ex aduerso preparatus quidam locus ubi resideat), while a group of Jews goes to another *locus* representing Jerusalem. Nowhere in the plays of the medieval church do we find the word *locus* indisputably employed as a technical term to mean scaffolding. Mary remains in the *domus* at Bethany, now the home of Mary, Martha, and their brother, Lazarus: "Domus uero ipsius Simonis, ipso remoto, efficiatur quasi Betthania."

Mary sends messengers to Jesus, asking him to aid her infirm brother, the Jews come to comfort the sisters, and Lazarus dies. As Jesus approaches, Martha runs to meet him, Mary comes out of the house (a domo egrediente), Jesus crosses to the tomb (transiens ante monumentum), and at his prayer Lazarus sits up. The play closes with the choral *Te Deum*.

The best that we can do in a consideration of the staging space is to suggest parallels with other performances at the monastery, first eliminating the choir as too restricted a place for the whole production. If the Easter sepulchre served as Lazarus's tomb, then it would have been in a forward area of the choir: Christ mentions the stone that blocked the entrance and calls Lazarus to come out; rubrics in this play and in the *Visitatio* refer to it with the frequently used term *monumentum;* and this would have created a fitting *tableau* as the chorus behind sings the final *Te Deum*. The *domus* was certainly close by, perhaps in the crossing coincidental with the position of Emmaus in the *Peregrinus*. That area referred to as *platea* would then have been just in front of it. Jerusalem, the starting place of the comforters but not the setting for a scene, might have been in the choir, the same location as in the *Peregrinus*. However, Galilee was at some remove; if placed at the western doors, this would give appropriate scope not only to the journey of the messengers but especially to Jesus' meetings first with Martha and then with Mary as he approached Bethany and the climactic scene of the miracle.

If this conjectural arrangement of stations is correct, then the general pattern of movement in the Lazarus play would seem to approximate that of the Magi, innocents, and wayfarers in the placement of major journeys along the nave of the church with a structure not far from the choir entrance. All of these characters are in the choir at the conclusion of the respective plays.

CONVERSIO SANCTI PAULI

Four *sedes* (literally "seats") are called for in the opening stage direction of *The Conversion of Saint Paul*, two in Jerusalem and two in Damascus:

> For representing the conversion of the blessed apostle Paul, let there be prepared in a suitable place, as if it were Jerusalem, a seat [sedes], and upon it the High Priest. Let there be prepared also another seat [sedes] and upon it a young man in the likeness of Saul; and let him have with him armed attendants. On the other side, somewhat removed from these seats [sedes], let there be, as it were in Damascus, two seats [sedes] prepared; in one of which let there be seated a man called Judas, and in the other, the High Priest of the Synagogue of Damascus. And between these two seats [sedes] let there be a bed [lectus] prepared, in which let a man lie impersonating Ananias.[40]

Paul in Jerusalem, dispatches his soldiers to capture Christians, and at the report that all save two have fled to Damascus, he obtains letters from the High Priest authorizing him to follow them. "Dominus" appears to him on the road to Damascus, he is struck blind and led to the house of Judas, and the Lord then sends Ananias to counsel him. Paul's preaching angers the Chief of the Synagogue in Damascus, whereupon he is forced to flee, and he and his followers are lowered from a wall in a basket. He returns to Jerusalem, where he is received by Barnabas and other apostles, who begin the *Te Deum*.

These *sedes* seem in fact to be raised scaffolds, each with a seat for the respective major figure and probably with sufficient space for an accompanying group, such as the soldiers of Paul and of the Chief of the Synagogue in Damascus. Between the pair as Jerusalem and the pair as Damascus there is an open area, where Paul is struck blind and falls to the ground, and through which area he eventually returns to Jerusalem. The *sedes* of Judas is also referred to as *domus*, the term used in the Lazarus play, and perhaps the spectacular escape of Paul involved part of the construction of Judas' house: "Saulus cum Discipulis suis in sporta ab aliquo alto loco, quasi a muro, ad terram demittatur." In addition to the wall, another set piece often to stand on the Elizabethan public stage is a bed, located here between the two *sedes* in Damascus; Ananias lies on it before going to the house of Judas.

As to the positions of the *sedes* within the church, the text gives us virtually no hints; neither choir nor nave is mentioned. We have already noted the east choir as the location of Jerusalem in the *Peregrinus* and probably in the Lazarus play; and since the apostles begin the *Te Deum* in this production, the two *sedes* of Jerusalem may have been in the vicinity of the choir. Considering the spread of the *Officium Stellae*, for example, it is hardly conceivable that the four *sedes* were all arranged either in the choir or in the crossing. One could envision the two of Damascus as standing toward the western end of the nave (Ex alia uero parte, aliquantulum longe ab his sedibus [of Jerusalem]); the major journeys taking place along the nave; Paul's sermon addressed to the onlookers in the nave just as the shepherds had turned to them; the high place from which Paul is lowered that used in the appearance of the angel to the Magi; and the usual choral conclusion occurring back up at the choir entrance.

FILIUS GETRONIS

Aside from a reference in the opening rubric of the *Iconia Sancti Nicolai* to the image as being in a house (domus), the directions in three of the St. Nicholas plays from the Fleury Playbook tell us virtually nothing about arrangements for staging. But the requirements given for the fourth, *The Son of Getron*, are extensive. These were all apparently performed in connection with the celebrations of St. Nicholas' Day (6 December), a festival of some importance wherever there was a school.

Marmorinus, a heathen king, sends out his soldiers to conquer nations, and they overrun the church of St. Nicholas in the city of Excoranda, abducting the boy Adeodatus from the church and bringing him to Marmorinus. After a year the boy's grieving parents, Getron and Euphrosina, observe the feast of St. Nicholas in the church and return home to offer a meal to the clergy and the poor. Meanwhile Marmorinus calls for a banquet, commands Adeodatus to serve his wine, and, overhearing the boy's sighs, orders that the boy shall remain. Thereupon St. Nicholas appears and magically conveys Adeodatus, goblet still in hand, to the gates of Excoranda. Hearing the good news from a citizen, Euphrosina runs out to meet her son.

The opening stage direction describes the juxtaposition of Marmorinus' court and the city of Excoranda:

... let there be prepared in a suitable place King Marmorinus sitting upon a high seat [in alta sede] with his armed attendants, as though in his own kingdom. And in another place let there be prepared Excoranda, the city of Getron, and in it Getron, with his comforters, his wife Euphrosina, and their son Adeodatus; and let there be in the eastern part of the city of Excoranda [ab orientali parte ciuitatis Excorande] the church of Saint Nicholas, in which the boy is to be seized.

On one side was probably a platform with a throne for the king, space for his soldiers and servants, and possibly a table. Opposite this stood the representation of Excoranda, perhaps a platform or low wall surrounded by cloths painted to suggest a city. St. Nicholas deposits the boy before the city gates (ante fores), not, I believe, right at the entrance to his home. On the platform or in this area must have been some indication of a house, for at one point Euphrosina leaves the church and enters her house (in domum suam), where she prepares a table furnished with bread and wine for the clergy and paupers. The rubric "Tunc resurgant," referring to the parents, and this staged meal would also imply seats.

Whether the church of St. Nicholas was shown by a kind of frame doorway, the rubrics do not reveal. At the outset Getron and his wife go to the church "cum multitudine Clericorum," suggesting a rather large area, probably with an altar, while the phrase "ab orientali parte ciuitatis Excorande" might indicate a position at the choir entrance, with Marmorinus' court then at one side and Excoranda at the other in the crossing. In the first scene the frightened people flee from the church "ad ciuitatem suam." Clearly the directions "ad ecclesiam Sancti Nicolai eant, in quam cum introierint" and "exeat ab ecclesia, et eat in domum suam" refer to different, distinct entranceways.

There was a good deal of action in the central playing area with the passage of the king's soldiers, the movement to and from the representation of the church, and finally the Saint's deliverance of the boy from Marmorinus' court across to his rightful home, perhaps accomplished with a mechanical device.

The arrangement of the staging resembles most closely that of the St. Paul play, with its juxtaposition of Jerusalem and Damascus and probable use of raised platforms. But the crucial miracle in the St. Paul play takes place during what seems to be a prolonged journey from one city to another, while a triangular arrangement of what are apparently three distinct locales would satisfy all the theatrical requirements of the *Filius Getronis*: the church of the Saint

at the apex, perhaps at the choir entrance, with the other two structures at either side of the crossing.

Summary of Information on the Staging of the Plays in the Fleury Playbook

The plays in Orleans MS 201 were all copied at Fleury in the second half of the twelfth century, and copied in the same hand. They reflect traditions of staging not conceived by a single author but rather belonging to or adopted by a particular abbey in this era. There is no positive proof, no external evidence, as to performance of the dramas in the church of St.-Benoît-sur-Loire, nor is there any reason to deny them to Fleury save for the possibility that the neums are not characteristic of the monastery. On the other hand, all references in the rubrics to physical aspects of the church suit this structure quite well and, most important, the texts afford us a unique opportunity to examine a group of productions associated with a single monastic community at a particular time. It is possible that the plays were set down in this manuscript with some view toward performances in different churches, and for that reason references to such items as local altars were omitted. The phrase "in competenti loco" (in a suitable place) referring to the location of actors and set pieces, appears in the *Peregrinus* and in the Lazarus, St. Paul, and Getron plays. Nonetheless, in general those play texts which cite named features of a known church are rare indeed.

Each of the plays in this collection with more traditional dramatic subject matter contains at least one note as to the area of the choir. In the *Visitatio Sepulchri*, women enter the choir and go to the sepulchre; at the conclusion they place the linen on the altar. After the miracle at Emmaus, the two wayfarers come into the choir; Christ leaves the disciples in Jerusalem "per hostium ex aduerso chori" before reappearing to Thomas; and at the conclusion the group leads Christ "per chorum" so that he may be seen by the congregation. The *Officium Stellae* has the Magi meet before the altar and then advance to the choir entrance; the performance ends as they come "in choro." And the children in the *Ordo Rachelis* rise and enter the choir.

There seem to be two explicit references to the nave: the manger in the Magi play is placed "ad ianuas monasterii," and the Innocents begin the *Ordo Rachelis* "gaudentes per monasterium." We have cited examples for the use of the term *monasterium* in referring to the body of the church beyond the choir, and specifically to the nave. This designation appears theatrically logical for the staging of the two plays here; and it is significant that nowhere in the manuscript do we find another designation for the nave, such as *navis* or *in medio ecclesiae*. Furthermore, the westwork at Fleury as place for providing pilgrims with food and shelter as well as starting point for processions would appear to strengthen the argument for locating the Christmas manger at its doors.

Finally, it is possible that the withdrawal of the Holy Family "in parte[s] Galilee" at the conclusion of the *Ordo Rachelis* was associated by the writer with the porch of the western tower and that when Jesus goes "quasi in Galileam" during the Lazarus play, this locale would have been placed at the western extreme of the nave. The references might hint at that particular feature of many major Romanesque churches called "the Galilee church."

The direct evidence for performance of the other plays (including the St. Nicholas dramas) within the church rests on the fact that each production concludes with the choral singing of a piece normally attached to the liturgy: the plays of St. Paul and Lazarus with the *Te Deum* of Matins; the *Filius Getronis* with "Copiose caritatis," found accompanying the *Benedictus* of Lauds and the *Magnificat* of Second Vespers.

Two general organizations of staging space mark the productions: the action revolving around two or more locales in a given area before the congregation, such as the sepulchre and altar of the *Visitatio Sepulchri* in the choir; and the action extending along the nave, among the spectators and between stations in the extreme west and the choir, such as those in the *Peregrinus* and *Officium Stellae*. In the latter instances a major scene occurs in the crossing or in mid-nave—the meal at Emmaus, the inquiry of Herod, the slaughter and Rachel's lament—and travellers or processions advance west-to-east and vice versa.

Reconstruction of stage arrangements for the Lazarus, St. Paul, and Getron plays is more problematic. *Lazarus* has one *domus*, two geographical places, and a tomb; *St. Paul* has four *sedes* and a bed; *Getron* has a *sedes*, a *domus* in a city, and a church. I have suggested the crossing as a major focal point of each play: the arrangement of *Filius Getronis* is similar to that of the *Visitatio Sepulchri* in that the set pieces and the action appear grouped in a space before the onlookers; the arrangement of the St. Paul and Lazarus plays extended out along the nave with some scenes played away from the stations. In the *Conversio Sancti Pauli* we have noted a distinct sense of distance between the

two *sedes* representing Jerusalem and the two *sedes* (plus a bed) representing Damascus; Paul is struck blind on the journey to Damascus and returns to the Holy City for the final moments of the production. A similar sense of distance is evident in the *Resuscitatio Lazari* between Jesus' place of sojourn in Galilee and the house at Bethany, from which first Martha and then Mary run to meet Jesus as he approaches. In addition, the rather large groups involved in these two dramatizations of New Testament stories seem to preclude crowding all of the mise-en-scène into either the choir or the crossing, but just how much space would have been employed for their respective journeys is impossible to conjecture. I have suggested their progress to and from the western extreme of the nave because of the precedent of the *Officium Stellae* and the theatrical effect thus created. Such a placement, then, draws the presentation in among the spectators.

We shall devote separate sections of this study to set pieces, special effects, and costume, but at this point let us summarize our data on the major scenic units called for in the Fleury Playbook. The chief set piece of the *Visitatio* is the sepulchre, here a structure large enough to allow a pair of angels to sit within and Peter and John to enter it. Apparently built especially for this occasion—there is no evidence of a permanent sepulchre at Fleury—it had an entrance from which the two angels emerge "ita ut appareant foris," probably indicating an enclosure the interior of which was not visible save from the doorway and which resembled in general form those found at Aquileia, Constance, and Magdeburg.

All of the other structures erected for the productions were quite open, affording full view of the proceedings at them. At Emmaus the wayfarers sat at a table prepared with a loaf, three wafers, a cup of wine; and there was water for washing. In order for the scene to be visible to a standing congregation, there must have been at least a raised platform, perhaps like that at Rouen.

What sort of arrangement formed the *praesepe*, the Christmas manger of the *Officium Stellae*, we are not told; certainly it was a major scenic element. The two midwives are present and the rubrics refer explicitly to the Child, but we do not hear of a curtain. In the *Ordo Rachelis* the non-speaking part of Mary was probably played by an actor.

There can be little doubt that Herod in the Magi play was on a throne—his companions are noted as being seated—and the area of the court seems to have been defined by some physical means. It was full of people, including his son, at least one soldier, advisers, scribes, and the Magi. These all may have been on a platform with a throne in the center, and we have suggested a canopy which would obscure Herod's view of the star until it had moved on down the nave toward the manger.

The plays with less traditionally dramatized subject matter tell us more about major scenic units; only here do the terms *sedes* and *domus* appear. The opening stage direction of the St. Paul play calls for four *sedes* and we subsequently learn that each has a seat for at least the major character associated with that station, surrounded by various groups of people. It seems likely, in fact, that each was a raised scaffolding of some sort, appropriately decorated. The *sedes* of Judas is twice referred to as *domus* and it had a clearly defined entrance (Annanias domum Iude introeat) and also a place for Paul to sit. Such an elevated position would be particularly suitable for Paul's preaching, and it seems that he is lowered in a basket from some part of this structure meant to represent the wall (ab aliquo alto loco, quasi a muro). I envision here a construction not unlike that representation of Emmaus at Rouen: a wooden platform about five or six feet in height surrounded with cloths painted to represent walls, possibly with a railing, and supplied with at least a few pieces of furniture. The bed of Ananias stood between this *sedes* and that of the chief of the Damascan synagogue; here too may have been a raised platform.

For the double-purpose *domus* of the Lazarus play, used for Christ's meal with Simon and as the house of Mary, Martha, and Lazarus at Bethany, I would also conjecture such a scaffolding. The fact that the word *sedes* is not applied to it, whereas we are told of Judas' *sedes* and later *domus* in the St. Paul play, indicates the frequently encountered ambiguity of the term *sedes*. The mansion was equipped at least with a table for the repast and probably with a bed for Lazarus; it too had a clearly defined place of entrance. A more uncertain term is the word *locus*, applied here both to Galilee and to Jerusalem. Nowhere in the drama of the medieval church does it appear in an unequivocally technical sense to define a structure but seems to be used, as here, to imply simply a position or locality. Galilee and Jerusalem are selected stations in the church, but we have no hint as to any attendant scenic elements.[41] The *monumentum* of *Lazarus* may have been the Easter sepulchre: Christ refers to the stone that closed the entrance and commands Lazarus to come out of it. In front of the *domus* was the *platea*—not, I believe, a structure, but rather an open area meant as the street before the house.

Three stations are called for in the *Filius Getronis*: the high *sedes* of King Marmorinus, opposite it the *domus* of Adeodatus and his parents in the city of Excoranda, and the church of St. Nicholas to the east of the city. The royal throne, surrounded by courtiers and soldiers and from which the monarch orders a banquet, may have been on a raised scaffolding much like that for Herod's court; it may have had a table, and, as in the *Peregrinus* play, there was water for washing. The *domus* was furnished with a large table, with bread and wine, and probably a number of seats; at least one entrance opened toward the representation of the church. Like the *domus* of Judas in the St. Paul play, I believe that the dwelling of Adeodatus and his parents was a raised platform. It is difficult to imagine whether there was a visual distinction made between a house and a city. Judas' house was one of two structures which, together with Ananias' bed, composed the city of Damascus. The direction from the Lazarus play, "Domus uero ipsius Simonis . . . efficiatur quasi Betthania," would seem to indicate town and domicile presented as one structure, unless the *platea* before Simon's house were ringed about with something like a low wall. Such a suggestion might solve the problem of Excoranda with the house and possibly the church within its boundaries: "Paretur et in alio loco Excoranda, Getronis ciuitas. . . . Sitque ab orientali parte ciuitatis Excorande ecclesia Sancti Nicholai. . . ." St. Nicholas conveys Adeodatus before the gates of the city (ante fores), where a citizen addresses him and to which place his mother runs to meet him. The church, east of the *domus* and closely associated with if not made part of the city, has a distinct entranceway and must have encompassed a number of characters. The family enters "cum multitudine Clericorum." I have suggested the possible construction of a frame doorway at the choir entrance; perhaps there was an altar or possibly the main altar was used.

If the *Filius Getronis* was performed during the vigil on 5 December, with the other three St. Nicholas plays presented at Matins, just prior to Mass, and at Vespers on 6 December, St. Nicholas' Day, the same basic scenic arrangements probably would have been employed for all productions, and this procedure might account for the almost total absence of descriptive rubrics in the latter three texts.[42] Each play requires three locales, the most important of which representing a domicile. The *Tres Clerici* wander in a foreign land and are given shelter in an inn, where they sleep; here there seem to be two rooms and at least a table. St. Nicholas comes to the inn at the end of the play. The opening rubric of the *Iconia Sancti Nicolai* mentions the house (*domus*) of the Jew, who leaves his possessions in an unlocked chest before a statue of the saint. Three robbers steal the goods and withdraw to a retreat, but St. Nicholas comes to them with a severe warning and they return the plunder, whereupon the Jew leads those nearby, apparently the chorus, in rejoicing. The *Tres Filiae* propose to their father that they alleviate his impecunious state by means of prostitution, whereupon gold is miraculously thrown in through the window and a suitor comes for the first daughter and the dowry. The miracle is repeated for each daughter. After the third time the father runs out and discovers that St. Nicholas has been the mysterious benefactor. In each performance the *domus* of the Getron play could have served as the center of the action, St. Nicholas coming from the area of the church or choir (the conclusion of the *Iconia* indicates the proximity of the *domus* to the chorus), and the clerks, robbers, and suitors coming from the somewhat more removed position of Marmorinus' court.

In these performances I would suggest, then, combinations of platforms, raised seats at ground level or on scaffolding, and playing areas or stopping places at times defined by other scenic elements. The very presence of various locales all visible during a given play—the opposition of court and manger, or the contrast of two cities—makes for the central meaning of the production. Simultaneity of action even occurs, where in a cinematic manner the end of one scene may overlap the beginning of the next. This usage will characterize the outdoor polyscenic stage of juxtaposition and eventually Shakespeare's public theatre.

Special Stage Arrangements at Tegernsee (twelfth century), Avignon (ca. 1372), and Bozen (1514)

The Play of Antichrist, from Tegernsee (twelfth century)

This remarkable 417-line play from the Benedictine monastery at Tegernsee dates from sometime between the 1160s and 1180s.[43] The Roman Emperor demands tribute from the kings of the earth: the kings of Greece and of Jerusalem yield without struggle, the ruler of the Franks submits after a battle, and the king of Babylonia is subdued in his attempted assault on Jerusalem. The Emperor, accompanied by Ecclesia, thereupon enters the Temple and lays his royal in-

signia before the altar, proclaiming Christ the true ruler, and returns to his former domain no doubt as king of the Teutons. Antichrist appears and overcomes the king of Jerusalem, assuming his crown and presumably having his throne removed to the Temple, from whence he drives out Ecclesia and, with threats and bribes, subdues the kings of the Greeks and the Franks. The king of the Teutons defeats Antichrist's army but becomes a believer when he witnesses Antichrist raising a soldier from the dead. The German with Antichrist's army conquers the king of Babylonia and *Gentilitas*, the personification of heathendom; and Synagoga finally gives in. During Antichrist's declaration of his omnipotence before a gathering of the kings, thunder crashes, he collapses, and his followers flee. But Ecclesia calls them all to the Christian faith, and the play closes with a hymn of praise.

The opening stage direction reads as follows:

> First let the Temple of the Lord and seven regal seats [*sedes regales*] be arranged in this manner: the Temple of the Lord to the east; near this let the seat [*sedes*] of the king of Jerusalem and the seat [*sedes*] of Synagoga be placed. To the west the seat [*sedes*] of the Roman Emperor; near this let the seat [*sedes*] of the German king and the seat [*sedes*] of the French king be placed. To the south the seat [*sedes*] of the Greek king. To the south the seat [*sedes*] of the king of Babylonia and of *Gentilitas*.

There is no external evidence as to the production, nor does the text mention specific features of a church. Some critics have suggested performance out of doors because of the work's scope and lack of liturgical connection. However, we know that the church of the monastery was a very large Romanesque basilica with a total length of sixty-nine meters. This fact together with the orientation of the playing area—the temple (and altar) positioned in the east—and the use of a chorus, the only musical notation in the text being for a passage based on a responsory, lead me to believe that it was in fact acted within the church.

Eight structures enclose a neutral playing area on three sides. The Temple seems to be the most complex; it has an entrance, contains an altar, and eventually a throne for Antichrist is placed within it, probably that of the deposed king of Jerusalem. It is possible that an area at the choir entrance served for the Temple, as we have suggested for the church of St. Nicholas in the *Getron* play of the Fleury Playbook. The other *sedes* are in the east, that for the king of Jerusalem, very close to the Temple, and that for

Synagoga. Opposite these in the west, and I suspect at the western doors of the church, stand three *sedes:* for the Roman Emperor (together with Ecclesia), for the king of the Teutons (the position taken by the Emperor after his conquest of nations), and for the king of the Franks. Along the south side are two *sedes:* one shared by the king of Babylonia and *Gentilitas,* and one for the Greek king. These geographic locations are obvious: Jerusalem in the east, as we have noted in the Fleury Playbook, for example; the connection between the church of Rome and the Teutonic Emperor (possibly Frederick Barbarossa) in the west; and Babylonia and Greece, the southern lands. The flow of movement and various battles occur in the encompassed rectangular space.

This leaves the north side of the church for the onlookers at this huge spectacle—a unique arrangement with the audience separated from the playing area and spread along the flank of the rectangle, facing south.

Here I believe that the term *sedes* indicates raised scaffolding—a platform for each major group with a throne on it. The rubrics refer to a *tronus* for each ruler save the king of Babylonia, but there can be little doubt that he too had such a royal seat because *Gentilitas,* who occupies the same *sedes,* is noted as having a *tronus.* Whether the Temple was also formed with a platform is unclear; at one point the Teutonic king ascends to Antichrist there. The use of the verb *ascendere* throughout the text seems to indicate not merely a movement from one locale to another but

Figure 32. Church of the Friars Minor, Avignon (during the French Revolution).

specifically in every instance a mounting of a throne or platform—to occupy a throne, to render homage, to request aid, to complete a conquest.

If, as we have suggested, the Antichrist play was acted in a church, with the Temple in or near the east choir, then we have here a singular example of an audience placed over at one side of the nave and the most extensive recorded indoor employment of the polyscenic stage of juxtaposition, save perhaps for the rather anomalous situation at Bozen in the sixteenth century, where a Passion play was produced indoors. The mise-en-scène at Tegernsee predicts one kind of late medieval and Renaissance stage arrangement whereby the audience was located along the front side of a wide and rather shallow stage.

The Presentation of the Blessed Virgin,
by Philippe de Mézières (Avignon, ca. 1372)

The richest details as to the performance of any drama within the medieval church survive in a manuscript which belonged to Philippe de Mézières (1326 or 1327–1405), who introduced the ceremony of *The Presentation of the Blessed Virgin* in the West, first officially celebrated on 21 November 1372, in the Church of the Friars Minor at Avignon during the era of the Popes there. The dramatic observance, based on an apocryphal account of Mary's parents, Joachim and Anne, dedicating their child at the Temple, included the celebration of Mass.[44]

So full is the information in Mézières' descriptive text, that we can reconstruct the performance with considerable accuracy, but we cannot be certain that the author had the Avignon church specifically in mind when he set down his instructions.

Here we find our only dimensions for platforms erected within the church. In this case there were two, each usually referred to with the term *solarium*. The first wooden construction had to be especially well built: "Let the strongest boards be used in the construction of the platform, and let it be well put together so that the weight of the people standing on it will not be enough to make it cave in" (Fiat igitur edificium seu solarium de lignis fortissimis et bene ligatis ne propter pressuram populi astantis aliquomodo cadere valeat). Located in mid-nave (in medio ecclesie), slightly closer to the choir entrance than to the western portal, it was six feet high, ten feet wide from north to south, and eight feet wide from east to west. The ancient French foot here was 32.48 centimeters; the present English foot, 30.48 centimeters. But still the podium was crowded, and Mézières knew it. As many as a dozen persons would take their places on it at one time. Steps, three feet wide and entered via a wooden gate, led up to the scaffolding on the east and west sides, and a railing, two feet high, surrounded the platform.

A bench (scampnum) was placed toward the north side, extending east-west, on which Mary was to sit between her parents; the central seat was raised a little for Mary. She was played by a three- or four-year-old girl. Opposite the bench were two seats or stools (sedes or scabella) for Synagoga and Ecclesia, respectively. Carpeting or tapestry covered the floor of the platform and the seats. At the northeast corner was to stand Gabriel, with Raphael at the northwest corner, and two musicians (pulsatores) at the remaining corners. Other members of the opening procession were to pass up the western steps, between Synagoga and Ecclesia and the bench with Mary and her parents, and down the eastern steps toward the choir area.

The actors were prepared in the chapter house, whence an elaborate procession moved through the monastery area before the church, and entered the western doors; then the above-mentioned characters took their respective places on this first platform. Each of nine angels ascended before Mary, sang a hymn, and proceeded toward the choir entrance. Rather comic scenes of the expulsion of Synagoga and Michael's ejection of Lucifer resulted in the hurried and forced disappearance of these two figures via the western doors. Those on the platform rose and moved up the nave, grouping themselves in front of the high altar for the presentation of Mary to the bishop (in 1385 dressed as a Jewish high priest). Then all but five of the characters left the church, Mass was said, and the observance closed with a formal recessional.

Mary heard Mass from the second platform (in loco eminenti . . . solarium), located toward the north side of the chancel, between the high altar and the choir stalls. This scaffold was six feet square, seven or eight feet high, carpeted, and surrounded by a one-foot railing. Mary sat on a silk cushion or knelt on a smaller silk cushion in the center, facing south. In front of her was a prayer stool (scabellum) with a little book of the hours. At the beginning of Mass she let a dove fly off which she had held since the opening processional. Behind her stood Gabriel and Raphael; near her sat two young girls, who, together with Mary, had deposited their candles in candelabra on the podium.

When Mézières introduced and described *The Presentation of the Blessed Virgin,* he modelled the mise-en-scène on already long familiar and traditional staging practice. I believe that we can accept the dimensions of the first platform as rather typical for

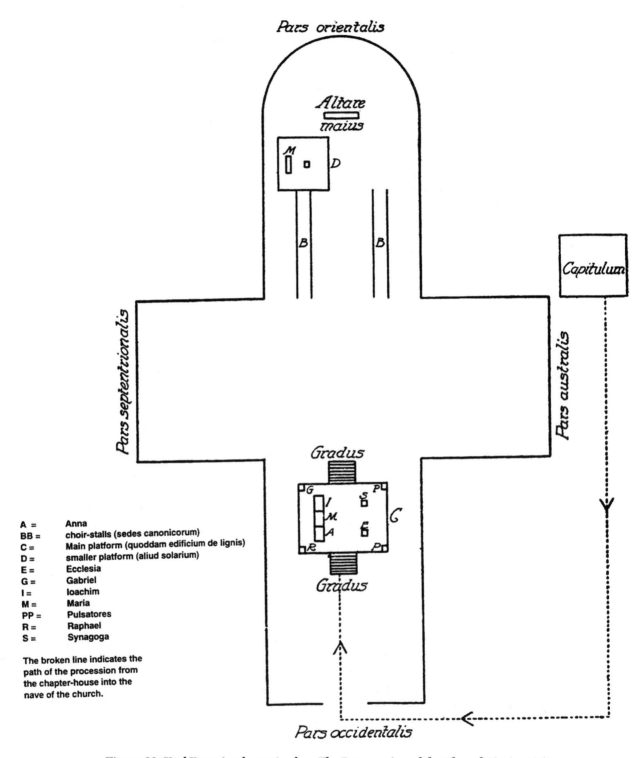

Pars orientalis

Altare maius

M *D*

B *B*

Capitulum

Pars septentrionalis

Pars australis

Gradus

G | *S* P
I
M | G
A | E
R | P

Gradus

A =   Anna
BB =   choir-stalls (sedes canonicorum)
C =   Main platform (quoddam edificium de lignis)
D =   smaller platform (aliud solarium)
E =   Ecclesia
G =   Gabriel
I =   Ioachim
M =   Maria
PP =   Pulsatores
R =   Raphael
S =   Synagoga

The broken line indicates the
path of the procession from
the chapter-house into the
nave of the church.

Pars occidentalis

Figure 33. Karl Young's schematic plan: *The Presentation of the Blessed Virgin*, 1372.

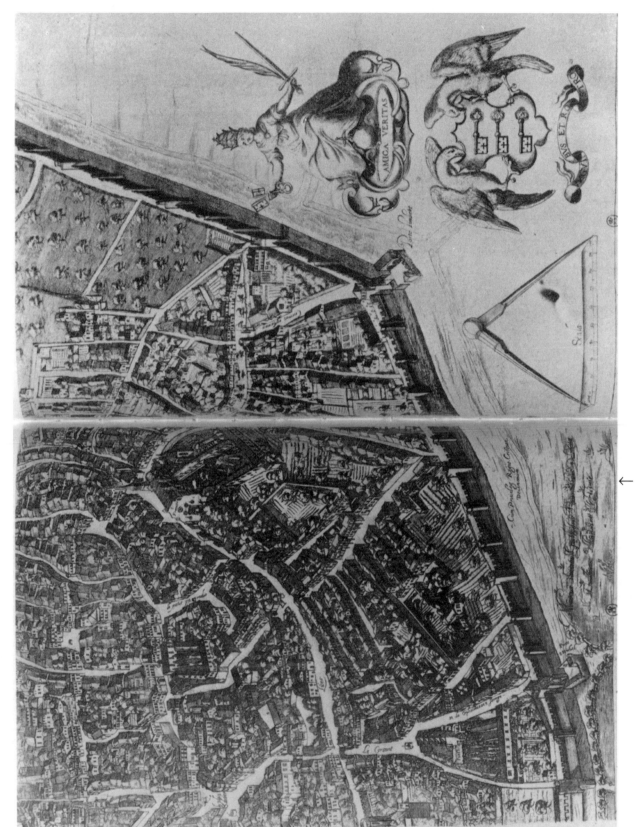

Figure 34. Avignon (detail) 1618, with church and monastery of the Friars Minor. Reprinted by permission of Les Éditions de Minuit.

such a structure in the nave, a height of about five or six feet generally shown in late medieval depictions of raised stages in city marketplaces, where they are also surrounded by standing spectators. In this text the author repeatedly emphasizes his awareness of the audience, of the problems of sightlines and of the pushing throng: the first platform is built so that it can be seen quite clearly from all parts of the church (vt ab omnibus partibus ecclesie lucidius videri possit) and its steps are to be closed off with gates so that no one can go up except in the proper way for the performance (ita quod nemo ascendere valeat nisi cum ordine ad representationem faciendam). The view of the act of presentation at the high altar is not to be hindered by other participants: "vt videlicet misterium Presentationis Marie ab omnibus videri possit sine impedimento." He also recognizes the rather jammed situation on the first platform, where the railing should serve as a protective device for the actors: "et ne illi qui super solario erunt a solario leuiter cadere possint." The second platform seems unusually high at seven or eight feet, clearly to enhance sightlines where it might have been partially obscured by choir stalls and celebrants before the main altar.

Equally in accord with what we know of contemporary staging practice are the blocking pattern and employment of the scaffolds. A procession draws toward the first locale, scenes are acted out on it, a processional journey proceeds to the main altar for another scene there, and finally a *tableau vivant* is established in the chancel. Symbolically the high altar represents the most sacred place, the goal toward which the performance is directed—here the Temple—while other events occur in the nave until the focus shifts toward the east.

Mézières' description is particularly suited to what we know of the Church of the Friars Minor in Avignon, built during the first quarter of the fourteenth century and demolished after the Revolution. A type found especially in Provence, it was a huge, austere structure, with a single nave flanked by lateral chapels between the buttresses. Judging from Berthault's engraving, the nave must have been about forty feet in width, where the view of a platform ten feet wide would not have been obstructed by columns. Because of Mézières' concern for the visibility of the action at the high altar and of the platform nearby, it seems certain that the rood-screen shown in the eighteenth-century engraving did not exist in 1372.

A map of Avignon from 1618 (see Figure) reveals features of the monastery, adjacent to the south side of the church, that coincide with the outlined progress of the opening procession. The chapter house, where the author suggests the actors be prepared, may have been the detached chapel at the southeast corner of the church. From here, the procession advances through the monastery and through the portal that leads to the area before the western entrance of the church: "Ibit autem processio per claustrum usque ad portam que ducit ad plateam que est ante valuas magnas ecclesie occidentales." A courtyard with an *allée* of trees is shown here on the map, with a cemetery just to the south. Mézières anticipates a crush of spectators in the cloister garden. The procession then circles about, turns, and moves through the western doors and to the first platform.

Of course most monasteries had a similar layout. When Philippe de Mézières wrote this description, he was probably thinking of the 1372 production, but at the same time, he intended his instructions for general adoption and usage.

The Passion Play, in Bozen, 1514

In 1514 Vigil Raber (d. 1552), a painter by profession, served as the director of a seven-day performance in the parish-church of Bozen, in Tyrol.[45] Other religious plays had been acted in Bozen, and some of these texts were no doubt incorporated in the undertaking of 1514 together with texts from the city of Hall, but this was the only time that such an extensive drama was seen there. Tyrol was rich in dramatic activity, particularly during the fifteenth and sixteenth centuries, mutual borrowing of local versions among towns was quite common, and references in several texts as well as in financial accounts indicate practices of both indoor and outdoor production. The plays are in the vernacular, the rubrics in Latin.

Of particular significance is a rough sketch of the stage made by Raber for the *Vorspiel*, the opening play on Palm Sunday which text Raber copied and adapted from a drama performed out of doors in 1511 in the town of Hall. The plan shows an approximately square stage with seven locales positioned on the periphery—Caiaphas, Annas, Simon the Leper, *Infernum*, *Angeli*, Synagoga, Mount of Olives—and the Temple, the largest mansion, in the center. The *Porta magna* seems to show the western entrance of the church, and *Ingress* the path of the opening processional through this portal to the staging area. Only one extant text can be associated directly with the 1514 production and with the sketch, Raber's copy of the Palm Sunday play containing the plan on the first page

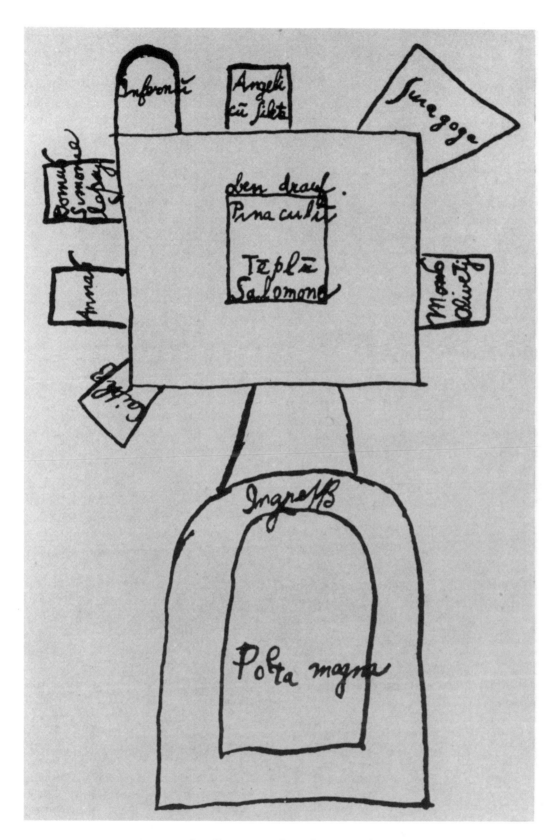

Figure 35. Vigil Raber's stage plan—the *Vorspiel*, Bozen, 1514.

of the manuscript. Certainly the same basic stage was employed on Thursday, Friday, Saturday, and Sunday of Holy Week and on the following Monday, the dramatization of the Ascension occurring somewhat later and not requiring such construction, but the stage was changed from day to day. For example, the *Vorspiel* barely incorporates the Mount of Olives while there is no place noted for the Crucifixion. The *Vorspiel*, which exhibited episodes in the life of Christ leading up to the Last Supper, demanded the largest number of scenic units, judging from other Tyrolean texts of the remaining six plays.

Reinhold Nordsieck and Wolfgang Michael have attempted reconstructions of the stage in the church of Bozen. Nordsieck believes that the plan shows a raised stage about eight meters square, located toward the eastern end of the nave, surmounted by the Temple, and surrounded by seven mansions. He suggests that the lines for each mansion represent its ground plan. Michael, on the other hand, feels that these lines indicate an entranceway for each locale, in some instances formed simply by a wooden frame, those for Caiaphas and Synagoga, like the *Porta magna*, drawn in perspective as viewed from above. Michael reconstructs a wooden stage taking up the entire eastern half of the church before the choir, about 24 meters square and about 1.3 meters high (thus covering the altars in the nave). *Infernum* was the already present, rounded doorway north of the choir entrance with heaven (*Angeli*) at the choir entrance. The sacristy is assumed as the place of the sepulchre on Easter Sunday.

Samples of accounts published by Wackernell tell us of large amounts of material and labor that went into the preparations. One master carpenter, for example, was paid for thirty-four days of work. A testimony to the fact that the production did occur in the church comes from a recorded payment to carpenters for changes made on the stage for each day's performance: "Den zimerleiten, alls sy am palmtag, am weihen pfintztag, am karfreitag, am Osterabent, am Ostertag dye pün in der khirch zu den Spillen zu geholffen haben. . . ."[46]

Over one hundred actors took their given places on the stage for the opening day, each remaining there until his particular scene occurred. But what the locales looked like, we cannot be certain. The *Templum Salomonis* is also marked on the plan "oben drauf Pinaculum," presumably the elevated position from which Satan challenges Christ to throw himself and possibly the high place to which they go (ad altum locum) in order to survey the kingdoms of the earth. Michael suggests a frame formed by a pair of central piers in the church and bridged above by a narrow walkway. At one point Christ "ambulat in portico Salomonis," apparently indicating a forward area of the Temple. Specific entrances and exits are made to the Temple, and one scene has tables and baskets there containing fowl.

The sketch identifies the house of Simon as *Domus*. There are at least eight or nine characters in it during the meal served by Christ, as well as a table and seats. The place of Caiaphas is also termed *domus* in one stage direction. We have cited the probable use for hell of a structural door beside the choir entrance, to which Satan enters in order to change his costume before tempting Christ. In fact heaven and hell are usually placed at opposite extremes on the medieval stage. The Mount of Olives was probably a three-dimensional construction. In the *Vorspiel* Christ sends Peter and John to it in order to fetch the donkey on which he is to make his triumphal entry into Jerusalem.

> Geet hin, petre und Johannes, drat
> In das Castel, das vor euch stat;
> Da wert ir vinden angebunten schir
> Ein eslin unnd ein jungs. . . .

Of course it was used more fully later on. As to the other locales, the rubrics hold no clues. Stage directions mention half a dozen places which do not appear on Raber's plan: a desert, a pond, Bethany, the Jordan River, Jericho; at one point Jesus leaves the Temple area "et vadit ad locum specialem." Only Bethany need have been represented by a structural scenic unit, and perhaps it was the *domus* of Simon the Leper.

Because of the sightlines along the north side of the church for Caiaphas, Annas, and the *domus* of Simon, I suspect that in fact frame doorways were employed for all locales save *Infernum* (an already existing entrance), the Mount of Olives (a full mansion), and perhaps the *Angeli* (at the enclosed choir entrance). The employment of neutral stage areas makes it quite evident that scenes begun at specific places spilled out of bounded locations. Although figures at the repast in Simon's house are mentioned as being seated, nowhere in the rubrics do we find notes as to seats, thrones, or the like. One item in the 1514 accounts raises a question as to whether the locales were curtained off:

> mer umb 200 klaine nageler, die debich damit aufzuslagen. . . . *In diese Teppiche waren wahrscheinlich Figuren mit Seide eingestickt; denn es begegnet auch der Posten* ausgeben dem maister Silvester, maler, von zwayen pildern zu entwerffen (*für den*) Seydennatter. . . .[47]

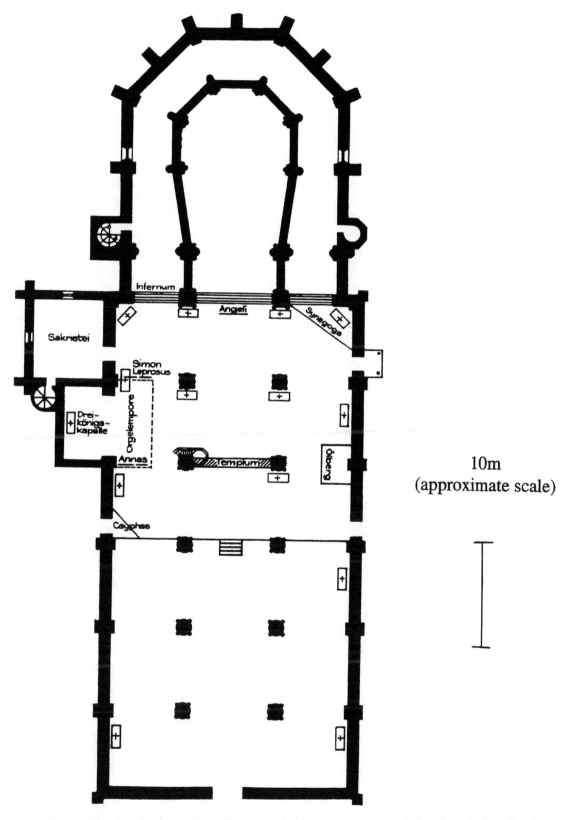

Infernum

Angeli

Synagoge

Sakristei

Simon
Leprosus

Drei-
könings-
kapelle

Orgelempore

Annas

Templum

Ölberg

Cayphas

10m
(approximate scale)

Figure 36. Parish Church of Bozen. Wolfgang Michael's reconstruction of church and of Vigil Raber's stage plan, 1514.

Within the context of the present study, the situation at Bozen is anomalous. It represents in fact the placement in the church of essentially outdoor drama—a kind of performance which flourished in city squares during this last era of the medieval Passion play—granted that traditions of indoor staging on a smaller scale also existed in Tyrol at this time. Never again was such an undertaking seen in Bozen. Here we witness the now clear division between spectator area and playing place, with the stage at one end of a rectangular hall, as it were, the audience at one side of that stage. The acting space is the polyscenic stage of juxtaposition, enclosed within itself. In that scenic units surround not simply an open neutral performance area as at Tegernsee but rather a large, dominant structure, the concept of this indoor theatre hints at the more central focus of Renaissance mise-en-scène.

The Use of Church Space: Summary

Taken as a whole, perhaps the most intriguing evidence throughout this study of staging space manifests its huge variety, variations that for compelling local reasons or ideologies veer back and forth over time. For instance, a great sense of mystery coruscates through many texts, making the moment of discovery secret. Performances of early "Quem quaeritis" ceremonials could have no congregation present at all, only the monastic community unto itself. Other texts with their rubrics demand spectacularly public display. Between these two extremes we have discovered an entire spectrum of relationships among celebrants and between celebrants and worshippers-audiences. At the risk of seeming developmental, overly diachronic instead of synchronic, let us survey patterns of action, geographical designations in the rubrics, and textual references to particular areas in the church.

Centers of Action and the Playing Area

We can distinguish four general patterns of the mise-en-scène in the church, determined by the location of major set pieces and by points at which distinct moments of action occur. The first of these concentrates the drama at one place or center, best exemplified by the simple *Visitatio Sepulchri* with movement to and from the tomb. If the sepulchre stands outside the chancel area, then we usually find opening and closing processions of clergy and chorus to its vicinity, while the Marys emerge from the choir or from this assembled group. When the sepulchre is the main altar or near it, then the

play takes place in the choir area, already the chief focal point of the church building. Some of the Christmas plays also restrict performance to one area, the east choir. This kind of arrangement, however, could only satisfy demands for several sets when the picture-frame stage of the Renaissance became dynamic, that is, where sets were changed. But in the medieval church the solution for multiple settings of stage action was precisely that for multiple settings of liturgical observance: they were all visible all the time.

The second arrangement incorporates essentially two centers of action: in the *Visitatio*, the sepulchre and, at a remove, the display area for the linen, the meeting point of the Marys and the disciples, or site of the questioning of Mary Magdalen; in the *Pastores*, the location of the angels' appearance and the manger; in the *Magi*, their first gathering place and the manger; in the *Peregrinus*, the road to Emmaus and the *castellum;* in Mézières' *Presentation*, the scaffold in the nave and that at the high altar. Here we have a number of instances in which the movement flows between the nave and the chancel area or occurs almost wholly in the nave and at the choir entrance.

With the inclusion of a third locale, the action often extends east and west along the length of the nave. In the *Officium Stellae* of the Fleury Playbook the kings meet at the high altar, proceed through the choir entrance to Herod, and make their way to the manger, probably at the western doors. The pattern is just reversed in the *Peregrinus* at Rouen where the wayfarers walk from the west to Emmaus in mid-nave and where finally Christ appears to disciples in Jerusalem, probably in the choir area. It is this kind of movement among an aligned series of centers, with the audience on either side, that we find enlarged in the sixteenth-century stage plans for outdoor performances of Passion plays at Lucerne and Villingen. I have suggested such staging for the St. Paul play in the Fleury Playbook, with Damascus and Jerusalem at either extreme of the nave, the blinding episode somewhere in between.

The fourth category of stage arrangement has to do with those plays which call for several centers established so that within themselves they form a distinct staging area viewed by an audience at one side— similar to our first category but with more stations. The *Visitatio Sepulchri* in the choir in the Fleury Playbook is a good example, as is the *Vorspiel* at Bozen. Here the scenic units either fill the staging space so that the action passes among them or, as at Tegernsee, the scenic units are placed on the periphery of an open area and thus define it as playing area. In all instances it has seemed logical to conjecture a grouping of locales in the vicinity of the choir entrance, save for the production at Tegernsee and the complex versions of the *Visitatio Sepulchri* that occurred in the choir.

The Daniel play of Beauvais (twelfth century) takes place in one geographical location, as does the Isaac play of Vorau (twelfth century): the former in Babylon, with the throne of the king, the den of lions, the house of Daniel, and a place for Habakkuk; the latter in Canaan, with platforms (tabernacula) for Isaac, Jacob, and Esau.[48] It would seem logical to envision a semi-circular arrangement of these locales, possibly at the choir entrance or in the crossing of the church, thus forming an open area in their midst for movement from one station to another. The play of Joseph from Laon (thirteenth century) has two separate geographic areas: Canaan with a place for Jacob and a cistern, and Egypt with places for Pharaoh, and a prison; the groups could have been established opposite each other in the crossing.[49] In the St. Nicholas plays from the Fleury Playbook three localities seem necessary: I have suggested a triangular formation for the *Filius Getronis*, the church of St. Nicholas at the choir entrance flanked by the *sedes* of King Marmorinus toward the north side of the crossing and the city of Excoranda with the house of Getron toward the south.

If the series of aligned locales predicts the outdoor Lucerne plan (1583), the grouping of the Tegernsee platforms is a forerunner of the outdoor Valenciennes stage (1547) and an arrangement akin to that of the Anglo-Norman *Jeu d'Adam* (twelfth century), acted just in front of a church with the exterior façade as its background.[50] Each places the audience before a wide, open playing area flanked along the back and perhaps at either end by scenic units. And each has the main action occur between two extreme poles: the Temple in the east and the *sedes* of the Roman Emperor in the west at Tegernsee; terrestrial paradise and hell in the *Jeu d'Adam;* heaven and hell at Valenciennes.

The acting area thus encompassed is often called the *platea* in documents relevant to outdoor medieval productions, but the term is employed to refer to playing space in only one drama inside the church. At the beginning of the Lazarus play from the Fleury Playbook, Simon takes his place in his house and then Jesus comes "in plateam." At the invitation of Simon, Jesus enters the house and then "ueniat Maria in habitu per plateam meretricio" and falls at Jesus' feet. In fact, even here the word conveys the sense of a street (before Simon's house) rather than naming a neutral acting space.[51]

Geographical Places Designated in Rubrics

The shape of the church with its usually east-west orientation, normal liturgical practice, and the layers of symbolic meaning attached to its various parts determined the location of staging. But if rubrics reveal a consciousness as to the geographic position of Jerusalem, for example, where would a scene set in that city have been played? Conflicting demands of other dramatized episodes, overlapping and changing symbolism, special customs and shrines in individual churches, and varying degrees of topographical awareness or emphasis make it obvious that we cannot expect to find consistent practice. The following discussion takes into account only plays where rubrics name a geographic locality. "Jerusalem," for example, never appears in stage directions for the *Visitatio Sepulchri.*

In general the Holy City seems to have been conceived of as being near the chancel: at the choir entrance the Magi of Fleury and Freising speak to the citizens of Jerusalem. In the *Peregrinus* plays from the Fleury Playbook and from Sicily, Christ probably appears to his disciples assembled in this vicinity. The king of Jerusalem is at the east of the Tegernsee *Antichrist* stage. Apparently the east choir served for the Holy City in the Lazarus and St. Paul plays in the Fleury Playbook.

The Temple, meaning the Temple of Jerusalem, is located at the main altar for the Padua *Purification* and Mézières' *Presentation*. It is on the east side of the Tegernsee *Antichrist* (as are Synagoga and the king of Jerusalem). Perhaps then the church of St. Nicholas from the *Filius Getronis* from Fleury and the high priest from the Fleury *St. Paul* are placed in or close to the east choir. Synagoga stands at the southeast corner of the stage at Bozen with the temple in the center.

That the Magi came from the East is reflected in Christmas plays from Bilsen, Fleury, and Rouen, where they meet at the main altar before proceeding westward. Galilee figures in the Fleury plays of *Lazarus* and the Innocents: it was probably at the west end of the nave where a porch, a chapel, or the narthex in this period was sometimes called "Galilee." Emmaus is usually in the nave, sometimes at an altar. Bethlehem, like the sepulchre, could be in the choir, nave, or even at the western doors. Egypt is called for in the Beauvais *Daniel*, in plays of the Innocents from Fleury and Freising, and in the Christmas play from Benediktbeuern, but no hints as to directions are found in them.

In general the sense of geography is akin to the

sense of history as reflected in these plays in that they reveal only selective attention to such matters when the dramatized story particularly underscores the ancient or foreign. Of much greater significance are priorities of sanctity. Jerusalem is near or in the east choir when Christ appears to his disciples there; Herod's court is always away from the chancel.

The Parts of the Church

We have noted the frequent location of the sepulchre in the east choir, especially in France, and the occasional placement of the manger in the east choir. In addition, the Magi meet at this position (Bilsen, Fleury, Rouen), while *Annunciation* scenes (Padua, Saint-Omer, Tournai), the *Purification* (Padua), and the *Presentation* (Mézières) are centered there. A major concept of medieval ecclesiastical architecture, both Romanesque and Gothic, is that of the church as shrine, as reliquary, with the chancel as the shrine par excellence; and therefore it is wholly in keeping that the reliquary of Christ in the drama be located at or near the high altar, that gravecloths be displayed from this position, that the choir area serve as the Temple within the church, and that the worship of the Virgin and Child occur there.

The placement of the sepulchre outside the choir as well illustrates both theatrical exigencies and possible local associative symbolism, for in general the crossing and the nave are the most frequently used staging areas. Here most journeys take place; here are located Herod's court, Emmaus, the murder of the Innocents, the moment of Ascension; here was usually set up the Altar of the Holy Cross, a focal point for Easter celebration. When we find reference to the *pulpitum*, it may have been either a raised pulpit, often where the Gospel was read, or a rood-loft before the choir: an angel appears on it in the Rouen *Magi*, the Magi read from it at Besançon, prophets stand here in the Rouen *Ordo Prophetarum*, Mary Magdalen addresses the *peregrini* from this position at Rouen, the *Annunciation* of Parma occurs here, and the gravecloths are exhibited here at Hildesheim.

The western doors form the usual grand entrance to the church, often the commencement of a processional approach toward the high altar. We have discussed the possibility suggested by the placement of the sepulchre here at Essen that the Romanesque westwork was particularly associated with the cult of the Savior, this being the traditional direction of the Second Coming. The tomb of Christ may also have

been located here in Soissons (twelfth-thirteenth centuries), in Prague (fourteenth century), and in Venice (1523), but our documentation is ambiguous. More obvious is the theatrical employment of this area for the *Presentation*, the commencement of the wayfarers at Fleury and Rouen, the spice seller of the Tours *Ludus*, the rulers of Rome, France, and Germany at Tegernsee, and the manger of the Fleury Playbook, all performances which extended through the church. At Rouen the *peregrini* (fourteenth, fifteenth centuries) used the aisles as well, as did probably the Magi at Fleury and Rouen; the *Visitatio* at Aquileia centered around a permanent sepulchre at the western end of the north aisle; in the Gernrode church, the Marys processed from the eastern to the western choir and then eventually returned eastward the length of the nave to the replica of the Holy Sepulchre; angels and apostles moved to and from the western sepulchre at Essen along the north and south galleries of that Romanesque church.

It is a gripping moment when one can observe the dramatic imagination at work in these ecclesiastical spaces. For example, a thirteenth-century text from Rheinau has the chorus wait at the Altar of the Holy Cross while the Marys go to the grave chapel out in the western porch; by 1600 the whole community processes out to the grave chapel. In earlier *Visitatio* texts from Braunschweig, Mary Magdalen remains in the vicinity of the sepulchre; in a later text she wanders through half the church, a solitary figure searching for the Risen Christ. And at Bozen on Palm Sunday more than one hundred players entered the *Porta magna* and proceeded to the stage.

Separate chapels contained or formed the sepulchre in churches at Barking, Gernrode, Mainz, Meissen, Rheinau, St. Gall, and Soissons. Augsburg, Constance, and Laon made use of chapels outside the church structure, such as Templars' chapels. The crypt served as the center of the *Visitatio* at Sion, Trier, Verdun, and Würzburg. Augsburg and Gernrode (and possibly Eichstätt) could employ replicas of the Holy Sepulchre in their mise-en-scène. Entrances for the *Visitatio* were made from the sacristy or vestry at Angers, Besançon, Cividale, Châlons-sur-Marne, Cracow, Moosburg, and Zwickau, and for the *Peregrinus* at Padua and Rouen.

From high places, usually over the nave, came the voices of angels to shepherds at Rouen and to Magi at Fleury and Nevers, instrumental music, and special effects of descent and ascent during the celebrations of the Annunciation (Parma, Tournai), Ascension (Bamberg, Berlin, Moosburg), Assumption (Halle), and Pentecost (Halle, St. Paul's in London).

Both the Easter drama and the Christmas drama were born in churches where there was no major barrier between choir and congregation, in an era when the members of the monastic community were not cut off from the remainder of the sanctuary and when all shared the elements of the Sacrament. As we noted in Chapter 1, Bishop Ethelwold's express purpose in his mise-en-scène at the high altar was "for the strengthening of the faith of unlearned common persons and neophytes."

In the thirteenth century a general trend toward greater separation of laity and clergy brought with it the construction of the rood-screen, partially to be sure as a means of protecting the monks from the cold during their long observances, causing a more pronounced distinction between scenes presented for the congregation and those more exclusively for the ecclesiastical body. In German-language areas especially this seems to have been a factor in the enactment of the Easter drama outside the main choir with processionals through the church. At Rouen we have a clear record of dramatic elements in Christmas celebrations divided between choir and nave, while at Fleury with its late-twelfth-century plays, as far as we know a rood-screen was first erected in the sixteenth century.

Set Pieces and Special Effects

Perhaps one could say that the greater the distance from liturgy, the more varied the exercise of theatrical imagination. The theatrically complex examples of medieval church staging are to be found in those liturgical dramas which are less embedded in the liturgy. Their rubrics reveal enormous variety in the mise-en-scène, particularly in the implications of stage directions calling for set pieces and special effects.

By contrast, however, from its inception the *Visitatio Sepulchri* remained intimate to liturgical observance—in its music, its words, its staging—in its overall character. It was the first liturgical drama, with its origins in Easter celebration. Its centerpiece was a replica of the Holy Sepulchre, and, although the Easter Tomb may be called the first set piece, it always served as a locus of solemn sacred observance, partaking of the tone of the Canonical Hours and the Mass. When the sepulchre was part of a drama, for example, special theatrical effects occurred there quite rarely, except perhaps for the appearance of the Risen Christ in a radiantly ornate costume.

But non-liturgical invention often marked the plays less fused with the liturgy, and these are the dramas that I shall survey in the present section of the book. Heretofore we have only had occasion to allude to the following play texts, rubrics, and other records of performance which add particularly to our information on scenery and properties.

Isaac, Joseph, and Daniel: tabernacula, thrones and pits

Preserved at Vorau in Austria is a unique twelfth-century fragment of an *Ordo de Ysaac et Rebecca et Filiis eorum Recitandus*, which opens with the following rubric:

> Tria tabernacula disparatim disponenda *sunt* cum lectis et aliis ornatibus prout facultas erit, vnum Ysaac, secundum Iacob et Rebecce, tercium Esau. Coquine Esau et Iacob, vbi delicate dapes cum pane et uino promte sint. Capreolus, si esse p*otest*. Duo hedi. Tece manuum pilose. Pellis, que tegat collum, pilosa. Pillea Iudaica Ysaac et filiis, et coloribus uari-

ata; cetera simplicia aptentur. Vestes prout decentiores prouideantur. Arcus cum pharetris.[52]

(Three *tabernacula* are separately arranged with beds and other available decor, one for Isaac, a second for Jacob and Rebecca, a third for Esau. Kitchens for Esau and Jacob, where delectable food with bread and wine should be prepared. A roe-buck, if possible. Two kids. Hairy coverings for the hands [and] a hairy skin which should cover the neck [of Jacob]. Jewish caps of various colors for Isaac and his sons; otherwise they should be simply outfitted. Suitable clothes should be provided. A bow and arrows.)

A choir interjects allegorical passages and narrative into the main dramatic action, which begins as the aged Isaac goes to his bed. He calls for his elder son, Esau, messengers "intrantes ad Esau" summon the son, the father requests food, and Esau goes off to the hunt, represented by a dumb show. Encouraged by his mother, Jacob covers his hands and neck with hairy pelts and dresses in clothes left at the house of Esau (et uestibus optimis domi Esau relictis) in order to deceive his father. Jacob takes up a tray with bread and wine and "intrans ad Ysaac" represents himself as Esau in order to obtain the father's blessing. At this point the play breaks off. The text reveals neither a liturgical connection nor an indication as to place of performance, but there is no reason to suspect that it was not intended to be staged within a church.

The three *tabernacula* were probably platforms, each with a bed and two with kitchen equipment. This term is used to describe Emmaus in the thirteenth-century Rouen *Peregrinus*, for the curtained sepulchre at Angers (1655, entered by the two Marys), and *tabernacles* for the curtained pavilions in the dramatization of the Annunciation at Saint-Omer in the sixteenth century.[53] Two appearances of the verb *intrare* and a reference to the *domus* of Esau would strengthen the argument, implying distinctive structures. The dumb show of the hunt must have occurred somewhere in the neutral playing area, away from the *tabernaculum* of Esau, for at the beginning he goes out (abeat) with bow and arrows. A bed is called for in Hilarius' play of *Lazarus* and in the Fleury play of the *Conversion of St. Paul,* but only at Vorau do we seem to have an indication of placement on some kind of scaffolding.[54]

The representation of a lions' den appears in two twelfth-century plays of Daniel, one by Hilarius and another from Beauvais. And a thirteenth-century play of Joseph, from Laon, uses the same word, *lacus,* to indicate the pit into which Joseph was placed before being sold into Egypt by his brothers.[55]

The play by Hilarius, performed either at Matins or Vespers, must have exhibited considerable splendor and spectacle, but the stage directions only mention two major set pieces: a throne (tronus) for the king and the pit. In that Daniel is made to sit to the right of the monarch, there was probably a second seat of some sort, but despite the indications of an elaborate court (the king enters "cum ponpa sua") and a royal feast in which vessels are used from the Temple of Jerusalem, we know nothing of a raised scaffolding.

As in the biblical account, a written warning to the king mysteriously appears on the wall during the banquet. Here the rubric reads "Postea ap[p]arebit quedam dextera super capud Regis scribens: Mane, Techel, Phares." Hilarius mentions neither the wall nor the means for creating the effect. On the advice of the queen, Daniel is brought to interpret the writing and is subsequently seated beside King Balthasar (Belshazzar) while the sacred vessels are removed.

A dumb show battle ensues in which Darius kills Balthasar, takes his crown, and places himself upon the throne. Jealous courtiers bring about Daniel's fall into disfavor, and he is brought to the den of lions, either a constructed locale, perhaps simply an enclosed area, or a side chapel or crypt: "Daniel intrans lacum sic orabit. . . ." Here an angel with a sword appears and closes the mouths of the lions, perhaps appropriately costumed men or older boys with masks. Another angel brings Habakkuk with food for Daniel, Darius visits the den, and eventually the evil courtiers are substituted for Daniel (Inuidi mittentur in lacum) and are devoured by the lions. Daniel sits again beside the king's throne and utters his prophecy concerning the coming of Christ.

In addition to the two specific locales, the battle must have occurred in a central playing area, the soldiers probably brought the vessels from the sacristy or vestry, and a place of some sort was needed for Habakkuk. No areas of the church are mentioned, but in that Darius is made to begin the final *Te Deum* (or *Magnificat* if the production occurs at Vespers) we might envision the king's court set up in the vicinity of the choir, perhaps at its entrance.

Four locales are designated in the *Daniel* play from Beauvais. The king's throne may have been raised, for Balthasar "ascendat . . . in solium," and later Darius comes to the lions' den "descendens de solio suo." When in favor, Daniel sits near the king, while the mysterious writing appears in front of the monarch "in pariete," possibly a set piece resembling a wall. These two seats and the wall might well have been placed on a platform representing the palace if the rubric "relicto palatio," referring to the removal of the sacred vessels, is anything more than a literary embellishment.

A second possible structure or especially furnished area represented Daniel's house, to which he withdraws from his seat beside the king after the conspiracy of the detractors: "Daniel . . . ibit in domum suam." He is seen praying there (perhaps an altar is part of the set). Eventually he is thrown into the lions' den (proicient Danielem in lacum), where he is saved by the sword-wielding angel and fed by Habakkuk before being restored. The evil courtiers are then thrown "in lacum," where they are consumed. A fourth locale seems to be indicated, one for Habakkuk because the second angel leads him back "in locum suum." The concluding *Te Deum* is begun by "cantores," but no specific places within the church are noted.

An even greater display of pomp is implied for this performance, with onstage instrumentalists (Cythariste) who accompany Darius. A pair of soldiers expel and kill Balthasar before the new king sits "in maiestate sua," and the production swarms with princes and satraps, including an opening chorus.

The thirteenth-century fragment of a Joseph play from Laon seems to demand at least six distinct places of action. A hint as to the liturgical connection may have been contained in the now lost conclusion to the work, and although the text does not assure us that it was intended for indoor production, its implied mise-en-scène is quite similar to the Daniel plays. Three areas represent the land of Canaan and three represent Egypt. Jacob sends his son Joseph to his other sons in the fields. The rubric "Iacob pauefactus surgit" probably indicates a seat for the old man, perhaps with other seats where later "sedent Filij eius circa eum." The second area would have represented the fields, where the brothers plot against Joseph, not far from a cistern in which they put him while sending his coat stained with a kid's blood to Jacob as evidence of Joseph's death. Joseph is drawn out of the cistern and sold to Midianite merchants, who eventually bring him to the household of Potiphar in Egypt. The cistern (cisterna) is also referred to as *lacus* and *puteus.*

In Egypt there is Potiphar's locale, where Joseph receives council (Consiliarij surgunt) and where, in pantomime, Potiphar's wife vainly attempts to seduce Joseph. She thereupon falsely accuses him to her husband and as a result Joseph is put in prison (carcer, lacus). Having correctly interpreted the dreams of two fellow prisoners, Joseph is brought before Pharaoh, for whom there must have been a royal seat (Ioseph . . . genu inclinans Regi sessum uadit).

Because of famine in Canaan, Jacob sends his sons to Egypt for food, but keeps the youngest, Benjamin, at home. Joseph, unrecognized by the brothers, furnishes them with sacks of grain, secretly places silver in the bags, then calls them back, reveals the money, accuses them of theft, retains one brother as a hostage, and sends them home with the order that they bring Benjamin. The fragment concludes with the sons attempting to persuade Jacob to allow Benjamin to accompany them.

A playing area with Canaan on one side and Egypt on the other would seem logical here, but we have no written evidence as to platforms and only hints as to seats for Pharaoh, Jacob and his sons, or for Potiphar's counsellors. The cistern and the prison may well have been simply enclosed areas. However, the sense of distance between the fields of Canaan and the home of Jacob, between Canaan and Egypt implies a rather extensive place of performance.

Annunciation, Ascension, and Pentecost: curtained pavilions and flying devices

Pavilions

A number of liturgical celebrations employed especially constructed theatrical effects and devices, often during moments when Matins or the Mass gave way to brief drama. Several records of the angelic Annunciation to Mary reveal significant staging, one a description of the so-called Golden Mass (Aurea Missa) by Pierre Cotrel at Tournai in the sixteenth century.[56] Two curtained structures (stallagia), probably platforms, were erected by carpenters in the choir, one for Mary, on the bishop's side, and the other opposite it for the angel. That of the Virgin, also referred to as her oratorium, contained a cushion on which she was revealed kneeling at the beginning of Mass, with a book of the hours in her hands. At the singing of the Gloria, the curtain before the angel opened, the Virgin bowed to him and a dove with lighted candles, symbolizing the Holy Spirit, was let down by means of a cord from the roof to a position in front of Mary's platform:

> Et dum cantabit Angelus Spiritus Sanctus superveniet in te, etc., tunc Angelus vertet faciem suam versus columbam illam ostendendo, et subito descendet ex loco in altis carolis ordinato, cum candelis in circuitu ipsius ardentibus, ante stallagium sive oratorium Virginis, ubi remanebit, usque post ultimum Agnus Dei.

At the end of Mass, Mary and the angel, accompanied by candlebearers, return to the vestry.

This is our only certain reference in a dramatic text to a curtained structure of this type designed to reveal at a given moment a character standing within, aside from the revelations of the sepulchre and manger. The latter seems always to have contained an image to be revealed when midwives drew aside the curtain, while in the former angelic figures show an empty tomb with gravecloths. On the other hand, the descending dove was not an uncommon feature of the Annunciation observance and of a symbolic representation of Pentecost.

At Saint-Omer the Golden Mass was established in 1535 by the will of a cantor, Robert Fabri. The will is in French.[57] The Virgin was at the right of the altar, the angel at the left of the altar, on two platforms referred to as passés and as eschaffaulx. The following properties derive from an inventory, dated 1557, of the church, where they were stored in a wooden box:

> Huict pendans de cortines et deux voies de toille blanche servans aux deux tabernacles, armoiez des armes dudit S' Fabri.

> Deux cielz de mesme, semez de chacun ung soleil millieu, et de plusieurs estolles de taffetas.

> Huict coupettes de bois doré pour mettre aux pilliers des deux tabernacles.

From these items we might surmise that each platform was surrounded on four sides by curtains, supported by poles with gilded caps at each corner, and covered with cloth sewn with a sun and stars to represent the heavens. Somewhere on each was hung a white cloth with the arms of Fabri depicted on it. The inventory also lists a wooden dove covered with white damask, but as we have no text from Saint-Omer, we do not know precisely how it was used.

Flying devices

At the celebration of the Annunciation in Padua in the fourteenth century, a dove was let down and received by Mary under her cloak, probably in the choir area, while in the fifteenth century at Parma it appears that the angel was lowered by means of ropes: "a fenestris voltarum dictae ecclesiae, versus sanctam Agatham, per funes Angelum transmittendo, usque per directum pulpiti super quo evangelium cantatur, in quo fit reverenter et decenter repraesentatio Virginis Mariae." The Assumption of the Virgin was celebrated at Halle in the sixteenth century with an elaborate procession at the conclusion of which an image of the Virgin, on a bench before the choir, was drawn up through an opening in the roof by means of cords.[58]

A similar effort enhanced the celebration of Pentecost at Halle when, during the singing of a hymn, the figure of a dove as the Holy Spirit amidst a circle of lights was slowly lowered over the high altar from a hole in the roof. "Magister fabrice et scriniarius Columbam significantem Spiritum Sanctum de hiatu testudinis cum arcu et circulo suo pleno cereis suspendent, et tempore suo sensim demittent." The ropes and the dove were removed during the ensuing sermon. A live pigeon and a descending censer were described by an eyewitness, William Lambarde, at St. Paul's Cathedral in London, in the sixteenth century:

> The like Toye I my selfe (beinge then a Chyld) once saw in *Poules* Churche at *London,* at a Feast of *Witsontyde,* wheare the comynge downe of the *Holy Gost* was set forthe by a white Pigion, that was let to fly out of a Hole, that yet is to be sene in the mydst of the Roofe of the great Ile, and by a longe Censer, which descendinge out of the same Place almost to the verie Grounde, was swinged up and downe at suche a Lengthe, that it reached with thone Swepe almost to the West Gate of the Churche, and with the other to the Quyre Staires of the same, breathinge out over the whole Churche and Companie a most pleasant Perfume of suche swete Things as burned thearin.[59]

Apertures in the roofs of several European churches remain as witnesses to such ceremonies.

A most elaborate flying effect is attested to by a fourteenth-century manuscript from Moosburg, which describes a genuinely dramatic text of the Ascension within a church.[60] In the middle of the nave stood a structure referred to with the words *tentorium* and *domuncula,* probably implying an enclosure of cloths like a tent. The term *tentorium* was also used to describe the place of the tomb for the *Visitatio Sepulchri* at Essen. Within the *tentorium* representing Mount Sinai in the Moosburg ceremony was an effigy of Christ, suspended from the roof by a rope, and a person to speak Christ's role was also present. Three rings were hung from the upper area. The effigy was to be drawn up through a ring of silk cloths, while the two other rings could be raised and lowered: the first

of flowers with the likeness of a dove and the second encircling the likeness of an angel.

Fifteen persons proceed from the sacristy toward the western side of the *tentorium*: two angels, Mary, and twelve apostles. The image is drawn up so that it is visible above the *tentorium*; the dove and then the figure of the angel are lowered over it. Following a dialogue between Christ and Phillip, the image is raised to a halfway point, Mary lifts her hands and sings "Jhesu, nostra redempcio," the apostles surround the enclosure, and the image is finally pulled up out of sight.

Appended to this text is a very interesting note which forbids the apparently not uncommon practice of casting down the image of the devil together with lighted sulphur and squibs or colored water, and other acts of irreverence. The note goes on to recommend a final shower of wafers, roses, lilies, and sundry flowers, to be gathered by poorly dressed children of the *schola,* who are to clap their hands and sing. Another reference to this custom occurs at the end of the sixteenth-century *ordo* for the Assumption at Halle: "Obmittentur autem hic effusiones aquarum et alie leuitates sub Assumptione."

But it was not omitted from the sixteenth-century Ascension ceremony at Bamberg, where a table or altar (mensa) was set up outside the choir and an image of Christ placed on it.[61] After two boys stationed at the roof opening where the image was to be received sang the incipit of "Viri Galilaei" and were answered by the chorus, the effigy was drawn up slowly by means of cords, and particles of the Host together with some drops of water were let fall through the aperture.

In a sixteenth-century text from Berlin the celebration of the Ascension is reported to have been concluded to the roll of drums for thunder (timpanum est percuciendum in representacionem tonitrui) as Host particles were thrown from the roof.[62] Here four images were employed. The effigy of Christ was placed on a bench in mid-nave, together with an image of the Virgin and reliquaries. Eventually two figures of angels were lowered from the aperture above, the clergy carefully fastened the effigy of Christ with ropes (duo dicti prelati prudenter et diligenter alligabunt Imaginem cum funibus), and it was then raised up out of sight with one angel at its head and the other at its feet. To prevent possible damage to the effigy, members of the clergy held a gold cloth directly beneath the place of ascent.

Accounts from the years 1481 and 1494–96 refer to performances of an Ascension play in the church at Bozen, where a stage was especially erected (ain pün

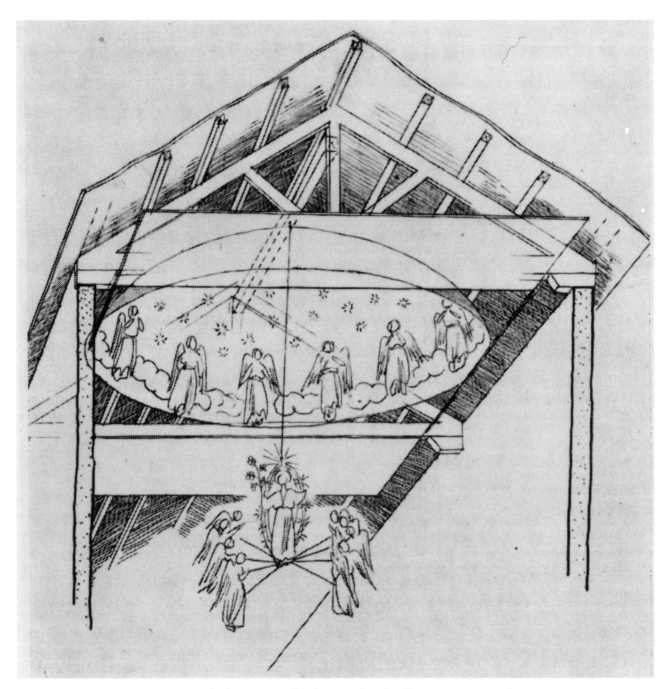

Figure 37. Reconstruction of Filippo Brunelleschi's paradise for the *Annunciation*, Florence, XV century.

auff der kirchen).[63] By means of a pulley mechanism Christ and two angels were conveyed upward in three large baskets (3 spreuslkörb, sessel, dar inn der salvator und die engel sein auff gefarn), while a devil seems to have been lowered in a harness (umb geriem dem Tewfel, dar inn er herab gefarn ist).

This contrivance is somewhat reminiscent of the basket specified in the Fleury Playbook to lower St. Paul from a high wall (Saulus cum Discipulis suis in sporta ab aliquo alto loco, quasi a muro, ad terram de-

mittatur), here possibly from the side of one of the platforms in the production.[64]

The most complicated technical apparatus made possible spectacles given in Florentine churches during the fifteenth century. While visiting in that city in 1439, the Russian Bishop Abraham of Suzdal saw two such productions and recorded eyewitness accounts of them. In the church of S. Annunziata the visit of the angel Gabriel to the Virgin was enacted by means of a device so that the assembled congregation watched the

Figure 38. The *Annunciation* (Florence, ca. 1500), showing a *mandorla* (almond-shaped glory machine).

heavenly being flap his wings and fly overhead between the throne of God and the position of Mary. A raised scaffolding 10.5 feet square was erected up above the entrance to the church. On a throne there sat God the Father, surrounded by seven moving rings of lights and angels who produced the music of the spheres on cymbals, flutes, citterns, and drums. A rood-loft, 21 feet high, spanned the middle of the church, 175 feet from the entrance, and on one side of this gallery Mary was seated near a bed. Both scaffolding and rood-loft had curtains which were pulled aside as the action began. The performance commenced with a half-hour debate among four prophets on the rood-loft, then God the Father sent Gabriel to the Virgin, the Annunciation was acted out, and, as the angel returned, fire descending from the throne to the rood-loft increased as it moved and ignited the candles of the whole church. Wheels running along a pair of strong ropes, attached to the scaffolding and to the rood-loft near Mary, supported the angel, who was let down and pulled back up by means of a third, fine rope operated by technicians who were hidden above. The fire effect was created by means of three other ropes which extended from celestial paradise to the center of the rood-loft.[65]

The Bishop witnessed an even more ornate production in the Carmelite Church of the Ascension (S. Maria del Carmine). To the left of the rood-loft was a stone replica of Jerusalem with towers and bastions; opposite it stood the Mount of Olives, 10.5 feet high. Celestial paradise was formed by a 28 foot square platform at a height of 56 feet, with a hole in the center 14 feet in diameter. A cloth with the sun, moon, and stars painted on it covered the aperture until the moment of the Ascension, at which time the cloth was removed to reveal God the Father miraculously suspended and surrounded by angels with musical instruments and many lights. The performance began as Christ, accompanied by four angels, entered into Jerusalem and then emerged leading out Mary the Virgin, Mary Magdalen, and the apostles, all of whom moved across to the foot of the Mount of Olives. Christ then took up a position on the Mount and by means of cords and pulleys was raised upward as a large cloud with two angels and revolving rings descended from the heavens. The cloud enveloped him, lights shone out from its interior, the angels knelt, music played, and the whole was drawn up through the opening to God the Father.[66]

To the architect Filippo Brunelleschi (1377–1446) must go the credit for having created the mechanical apparatus for these productions, both within and outside of churches, and, as A. M. Nagler has pointed out,

"Due to his efforts, the Florentines learned to look upon their religious theater as a work of art."[67] Giorgio Vasari tells us about a paradise machine that Brunelleschi devised for an enactment of the Annunciation in the church of S. Felice in Piazza. To the rafters of the roof was attached an immense inverted half-globe with lights and clouds and twelve youths as angels stationed around its circumference. This paradise could be closed and opened by means of two horizontal five-braccia (i.e., about ten-foot) sliding doors. A copper, almond-shaped glory machine (mandorla) containing the angel who was to appear to Mary descended from the center of the heavens. It was operated by means of a windlass and counterweights, filled with lights and surrounded by eight angels. Accompanied by music, the *mandorla* was lowered to a stage. The angel stepped out and moved across to the Virgin, then returned to the device and was drawn back up into the celestial area, where God the Father was also positioned.

Later the Florentine carpenter Francesco d'Angelo, called Il Cecca (1447–88), modelled his apparatus for the Ascension in the Carmelite Church on that invented by Brunelleschi. A similar half-globe represented paradise into which Christ was received. Above it ten moving circles of copper lanterns represented the ten heavens. Two cables with pulleys ran down and were attached to the rood-loft, by means of which a great cloud full of angels descended and, along with Christ, reascended. Christ left his apostles standing on a mountain constructed of wood, apparently on the rood-loft.[68]

Other Special Effects: light, sound, appearances and disappearances, effigies

Light and Sound

A catalogue of textual references to lighting in play texts and rubrics would only hint at the festive glow of Christmas processionals, the secret shadows within the openings of the Holy Sepulchre, the solemn brilliance of Easter morn piercing the darkness of Good Friday, the highlighting of sacred shrines and heathen courts, the single flickering taper illuminating the face and costume of many an actor. The significance of these moments in the drama emanates from human sensibility toward seasonal daylight and extends the metaphysics and the aesthetics of light that pervaded the consciousness of medieval church stonemasons. Ultimately the flying buttresses of the Gothic style were invented to support great new walls of light. The reds and blues of stained glass windows were conceived to match the interior walls of sculpted and painted surfaces—and in some instances to create a special haze of light. The God-light aesthetic so evident in the drama of Easter and Christmas derived from the fifth century, from Augustine and Dionysius the Pseudo-Areopagite. It developed in particular in France as early as the eighth century and reached a climax with the cathedral builders of the thirteenth century.

The arrays of candles and lanterns that adorned the cloud- and paradise-constructions in fifteenth-century Florence and the Annunciation fire witnessed by the Bishop of Suzdal in that city constitute the most technically ambitious effects created specifically for the liturgical drama. Two singular phenomena demand our particular attention here: the star which led the Magi to Bethlehem and the flaming sword or semblance of lightning in the hand of an angel.

The Christmas star in its simplest form appeared in the Swiss Cathedral of Sion (Sitten) in the thirteenth century. There a procession of the three Magi (tres magos) from nave to high altar was preceded by a boy carrying a candelabrum with three candles. At Limoges in the eleventh or twelfth century, the three kings come to the choir entrance, see the star "hanging from a cord" in mid-choir, and move to the high altar, the star preceding them. In the twelfth-century Fleury Playbook, the star appears to have traveled from the main altar all the way to the manger, probably at the western doors, but whether suspended and moved along a wire the rubrics do not reveal: the Magi see it at their eastern meeting place, follow it to the choir entrance, and, after the episode with Herod, continue behind it to the manger; Herod only notices it after their departure from his court. In the thirteenth and fourteenth centuries at Rouen, the Magi viewed the star from their initial position in the choir and then advanced toward it, a cluster of lights (corona) hanging over the manger at the Altar of the Holy Cross: the "corona . . . pendens in modum Stelle" seems to have been stationary. Certainly a star was necessary for this play, but other texts give us no hints as to its nature, whether suspended, sliding on a wire, or possibly in some instances a candelabrum carried before the kings. We find a moving star used in the twelfth or thirteenth century in the *Visitatio* at the Cathedral of Soissons, where a cord was stretched from the high altar to the door of the sepulchre chapel somewhere outside the choir and possibly in the west. Here was suspended an iron ring with seven candles, which then preceded the procession returning with the Host from the sepulchre to the high altar.[69]

In the thirteenth-century *Ludus Paschalis* from Benediktbeuern, an angel strikes one of the guards at the tomb with a flaming sword (ferens ensem flammeum), and all four soldiers fall to the ground as if dead. In the Tours *Ludus* of the same century, he causes lightning (iniiciat eis fulgura). As will be observed in our study of costume, it was not uncommon for an angel to appear, as in the Fleury Playbook, with a taper or even with a candelabrum, which could have been shaped as a sword with candles fixed to it. At Coutances in the fifteenth century, a pair of angels carry rods with ten burning candles in them (virgas decorticatas, in quibus sint decem candele ardentes), at the sight of which the soldiers at the grave fall to the ground, and in Philippe de Mézières' *Presentation of the Blessed Virgin* at Avignon in the fourteenth century, Michael holds erect a flaming or flashing sword in his right hand (gladio fulgenti). It is interesting to note that in fifteenth- and sixteenth-century manuscripts of the *Visitatio* from Klosterneuburg an angel carries a sword fitted with numerous lights, but the scene with the soldiers is omitted, while in the thirteenth-century *Ludus Paschalis* from the same monastery an angel strikes the soldiers with an unsheathed sword. This may well be a small illustration of the point that after the great inventive and experimental periods of the twelfth and thirteenth centuries came a decorative era, an epoch reflected in the late Gothic style in architecture and art and resulting in productions where decor became ornament for its own sake.[70]

Thunder accompanied the angel's blow at Benediktbeuern (et medio fiant tonitrva magna), crashed over the head of the vanquished Antichrist in the twelfth century at Tegernsee (Statim fit sonitus super caput Antichristi), and in the sixteenth century rumbled at the shower of wafers concluding the *Ascension* at Berlin (timpanum est percuciendum in representacionem tonitrui). The rolling doors of Brunelleschi's paradise made this sound, and the Bishop of Suzdal heard thunder in the Florentine churches of the Annunciation and of the Carmelites. A Spanish play possibly dated in the fourteenth century, in the vernacular from Vich but with rubrics in Latin, calls for an earthquake "and other tumult" to strike down in terror the sleeping guards at the tomb (Tunc fiet terre motus cum alio tumulto qui dum fiet angeli venient ad monumentum quorum omnium timore vigiles cadent in terra facie versu pro nimio timore quasi dormientes).[71]

Appearances, Disappearances, and Effigies

When the scene of Christ's disappearance from the table at Emmaus came to be enacted in the church, was there some provision made for a particular device by means of which he vanished, or did the actor simply step behind a column or merely walk away quickly? The wording of the Gospel account in Luke— "et ipse evanuit ex oculis eorum" (24:31)—is often paraphrased or quoted in stage directions, but the verb "to disappear" is not usually elaborated upon. Further, in some instances, as in the Benediktbeuern play, Christ reappears to other disciples. However, texts from three different churches may hint at a special effect. At Saintes in the fourteenth century the *peregrini* and Christ sat down, Christ broke bread, "Et postea euanescit ab occulis eorum, intrans opertum locum." He immediately emerged from this secret or covered place, but no other details as to any set piece are given. The *tabernaculum* representing Emmaus in the middle of the nave at Rouen, to which the three actors ascended, has already been discussed. Christ sat at the table between the two disciples and "in fractione panis agnitus ab illis subito recedens ab occulis eorum euanescat." A trap-door would have been possible on this raised scaffolding, the phenomenon did happen suddenly, but the verb *recedere,* commonly used for a character's exit, may just as well indicate a departure. He did not reappear, as he does in the Fleury Playbook, where he secretly leaves an elaborately prepared table—"ipse latenter discedat, quasi illis nescientibus"—to return after a costume change to the disciples assembled in the choir.[72]

Some rubrics enlarge upon the Biblical account of the scene between Christ and Magdalen near the sepulchre to the extent of suggesting his magical appearance and disappearance. At Rouen the sepulchre seems to have been in the choir area, perhaps somewhat apart from the main altar. Here, in the fourteenth- and fifteenth-century texts, Christ appears (obuians) at the left corner of the altar—not at the tomb—then reveals himself (appareat) to all the women at the right corner of the altar, and finally vanishes (se abscondat). The thirteenth-century Rouen text notes the two-fold appearance (appareat), after which he goes away (discedente). It seems that the effect was achieved by the actor's suddenly stepping out from behind the main altar, the intention of the moment more clearly expressed in the later versions. This sequence at Rouen resembles that at Barking in the fourteenth century where, however, the sepulchre was outside the choir. Christ appeared (appareat) at the left side of the altar, presumably in the choir, withdrew (disparuerit), and met the three women at the right side of the altar. At Rheinau in the thirteenth century, Christ may have been concealed within the enterable

sepulchre until this scene, during which he revealed himself to Magdalen (ei se manifestans) and then vanished (euanescit). At the conclusion of the scene in Coutances near an enterable sepulchre, Christ disappeared (dispereat). The tomb at Coutances and at Rheinau was located outside the choir area, as was that at Chiemsee in the thirteenth century, to the side of which Christ suddenly advanced (ex inprouiso Dominica Persona adueniens). There is, then, no explicit documentation as to Christ's place of concealment in this scene, but the intent of a surprising appearance from behind the altar or from within the sepulchre is implied by some of the rubrics cited above.[73]

In addition to those effigies employed in flying devices, an image of the Virgin, probably together with the Christ Child, almost always served as the focal point of adoration in the Christmas plays. The cult of the Virgin, the creation of a shrine to which gifts were brought, the lack of lines for her in the Biblical account—all of these were factors contributing to the almost universal employment of carved or sculptured figures, probably already part of the treasures of most churches. At Rouen the three kings approached "ad Ymaginem Sancte Marie" on the Altar of the Holy Cross, where two clerics drew aside curtains revealing the Christ Child. The *Officium Pastorum* of Rouen placed the manger behind the main altar—"Ymago Sancte Marie sit in eo posita"—and midwives opened a curtain to show the Child. The earliest reference comes from Nevers in the eleventh century, where midwives displayed an image to the three kings; the lines mention the Child. At Milan in 1336 an outdoor procession moved into the Church of St. Eustorgio to find a manger scene with a cow, a donkey, and "Christus parvulus in brachiis Virginis Matris," possibly an image. An effigy of the child Jesus was used in the *Purification* from Augsburg in the fifteenth century, an idol was needed for the *Ordo Prophetarum* at Rouen in the fourteenth or fifteenth century, and the image of St. Nicholas in the two plays on this subject—by Hilarius and in the Fleury Playbook. A figure of Christ, undoubtedly a crucifix, stands at the center of the fourteenth-century Cividale *Planctus Mariae.* In a few instances the cross was displayed at the conclusion of the *Visitatio Sepulchri,* usually devoid of an effigy of Christ. In the early sixteenth century at the Easter celebrations of Granada, a special structure served for the sepulchre, which was draped with rich hangings and contained two statues of angels holding a cloth imprinted with Christ's wounds (Estan dentro puestos dos angeles de los dorados que estan puestos en el altar mayor que tengan un paño de lienço en que esten pintadas o scñaladas algunas çicatriçes).[74]

A number of miraculous effects are called for in rubrics without further elucidation as to their execution, two of these from Benediktbeuern, where a group of idols falls down as the Holy Family enters Egypt *(Ludus de Rege Aegypti),* and Herod, after the murder of the Innocents, is eaten by worms (corrodatur a uermibus), carried from his throne, and received by devils with much rejoicing. How the murder of the Innocents was staged at Benediktbeuern, Freising (in the eleventh or twelfth century), and Laon (in the thirteenth century) we do not know; a lamb was borne by the boys in the latter *Ordo Rachelis.* In the Fleury Playbook a procession of singing boys enters the nave and is joined by a lamb bearing a cross, symbolic of the sacrifice of the lamb of God, which is secretly removed during the slaughter (subtrahatur agnus clam); the fallen cry out; Rachel and her companions weep over the bodies; and finally at the command of an angel the boys rise and enter the choir.[75]

The mysterious appearance of writing on the wall at Belshazzar's feast is called for in the two plays of Daniel; Hilarius notes merely "Postea ap[p]arebit quedam dextera super capud Regis scribens," while in the Beauvais text a wall is specifically mentioned: "Interim apparebit dextra in conspectu Regis scribens in pariete." In the *Ordo Prophetarum* at Rouen in the fourteenth- and fifteenth-century texts, the fiery furnace at the court of Nebuchadnezzar was constructed of oakum and cloth, but the rubrics of this play do not reveal how its three inhabitants were saved from the flames.[76]

It is in these kinds of special effects—flying machines, staged horrors, vanishings, the use of fire—that we witness most clearly the oneness of the natural and the supernatural, the characteristic admixture of the realistic and the symbolic within the fundamental conceptualization of these dramatic actions in the immediate present, where the so-called miraculous is an integral part of the human experience. The Resurrection of Christ is at one and the same time as immediate and eternal as the recurrence of the seasons.

But in the fourteenth century one begins to sense a growing attention to the trappings of the scene within the church. In fifteenth-century Florence the role of the artist-machinist dominated that of the clerical poet, and even a cursory examination of the outdoor productions of religious drama, which became prominent in this period, reveals the tendency toward more elaborate, detailed staging and an ever-increasing emphasis on pageantry for its own sake, both in costumes and scenic effects. This tendency culminated in the fantastic theatrical displays of the sixteenth century and coincided with the cessation of this kind of performance and the

church's control over it, as the move in thirteenth-century Europe toward nationalism, inadequately answered by the church's establishment of an immense ecclesiastical bureaucracy, finally came to a head in the sixteenth century: with the Reformation, the Counter-Reformation, the sack of Rome (1527), Henry VIII's break with the Pope (1531), the abdication of Charles V in Germany (1556), the purge by the Council of Trent (1570) of tropes, sequences, music-drama, and much else from the liturgy, and the dominance of the crown over the nobility in France under Henry IV (1589). As vehicles of religious expression the outdoor vernacular Passion plays of Bourges, Valenciennes, York, Coventry, Frankfurt, and Lucerne became anachronistic in the course of the sixteenth century for a number of reasons. But whereas the new dramatists of the sixteenth century nourished a new poetry and celebrated those values of human individuality and a sense of history that mark the Renaissance, yet on the Renaissance stage they dressed their mise-en-scène in much medieval garb.

Summary: Major Scenic Elements

The idea of the theatrical "mansion" seems to have evolved from the notion of providing a small replica of an edifice and from the practical necessity of having a raised acting space with some items of furniture. The original prototype for the miniature edifice came into being during the Crusades with imitations of the Holy Sepulchre in Jerusalem, the earliest extant examples of which are at Aquileia and Gernrode, both built in the eleventh century. They were erected for Easter ceremonials, probably including genuine dramatic performances at Aquileia and certainly including the *Visitatio Sepulchri* at Gernrode. The example now at Constance (1280) replaced such a replica from the tenth century— or the little tenth-century chapel where the replica stands was itself the original "replica"—and I have examined what is probably a theatrical employment of the sepulchre at Magdeburg (1240). The twelfth- or thirteenth-century drama at Soissons took place at a sepulchre which had a window and an altar within: angels stood "ad fenestram . . . Sepulchri."[77] Large, temporary enclosures for the tomb are indicated by the fourteenth-century *tentorium* at Essen and the *habitaculum* at Mont-St.-Michel, while a Bamberg *Agenda* (1587) describes a sort of room formed by curtains, and the sepulchre at Angers (1655) is noted "quasi tabernaculum extemporaneum."[78] The early sixteenth-century Easter celebrations at Granada called for a special structure draped with hangings and containing two stat-

ues of angels.[79] On occasion an external chapel such as
that at Augsburg and Laon became a locale for the play.
But the Easter tomb differs essentially from all other
major scenic elements in that it serves not so much as a
place within which an action occurs as the repository of
circumstantial evidence for the central event which has
already taken place—the Resurrection—and therefore
the mystery of its interior is revealed to the spectators
not at first hand but through witnesses.

For the most part the Christmas manger served a
theatrical function akin to that of the sepulchre in that
it always remained a kind of shrine—the main altar,
this or another altar with the figure(s) of Mary and/or
the Child, or a crèche in some other area—to which
gifts were brought and near which the angel appeared
to the Magi. No dramatic text mentions a distinctly enclosed locale to be entered by shepherds or kings, although in the *Ordo Rachelis* from Freising, Fleury,
and Laon, and in the Benediktbeuern Christmas play
there are indications of live actors portraying members of the Holy Family. However, of greater significance for the scenic means is the concept of a tableau
hidden from view by curtains which midwives suddenly draw aside at the crucial dramatic movement to
reveal the manger or an image both to the visitors and
to the congregation. In the earliest period of the *Officium Stellae*—in the eleventh-century play from Nevers—*Custodes* show an image to the Magi, and in the
twelfth-century Montpellier text midwives open the
manger and hint at a special form of altar at which an
object of particular religious veneration such as a reliquary often stood within a curtained-off space. Florentine spectacles of the fifteenth century enlarged
the *tableaux vivants* discovered in this manner, as did
French Annunciation scenes in the following century.

The second and more important element, the decorated platform, was needed for sightlines and to define performance area—an adjunct to the church interior originally designed for presentations before a
body of spectators. From the earliest times the scaffold had been a major chattel of traveling troupes, the
raised podium or dais had always been employed to
exhibit people and elements in church ritual, and once
the drama began to unfold elsewhere than at steps of
the east choir, the necessity and desirability of small
stages in the church became quite evident.

The fullest description of a mansion comes from the
early *Jeu d'Adam,* a twelfth-century Anglo-Norman
text meant for performance not within the sanctuary
but in the area immediately outside in front of the
church façade. Terrestrial paradise was a raised scaffold, surrounded with beautifully decorated cloths:

Constituatur paradisus loco eminenciori; circumpo-
nantur cortine et panni serici, ea altitudine, ut per-
sone, que in paradiso fuerint, possint videri sursum ad
humeris [humeros]; servantur [serantur] odoriferi
flores et frondes; sint in eo diverse arbores et fructus
in eis dependentes, ut amenissemus locus videratur
[videatur].

(Let Paradise be set up in a somewhat lofty place; let
there be put about it curtains and silken hangings, at
such an height that those persons who shall be in Paradise can be seen from the shoulders upward; let there
be planted there sweet-smelling flowers and foliage;
let divers trees be therein, and fruits hanging upon
them, so that it may seem a most delectable place.)[80]

Some scenic units within the church probably resembled this one, and, although nowhere except in the
Florentine spectacles is there such full documentation, nevertheless as the material from the rubrics is
surveyed, it is useful to have a clear example in mind.

From Freising come the earliest references to set
pieces other than to the sepulchre—a throne (solium)
for the eleventh-century *Officium Stellae* and a bed
(stratus) for the eleventh- or twelfth-century *Ordo
Rachelis*. The seat or throne is in fact the most important and most frequently mentioned property in the
mise-en-scène through the ages.

It is with the great theatrical experiments of the
twelfth century that we first find records of construc-
tions similar to the *Jeu d'Adam.* At Tegernsee thrones
were probably placed on seven platforms (sedes), and
the Temple area was indicated with at least an altar and
a throne if not formed by a frame doorway at the east
choir or by scaffolding. Although normally meaning
"seat," the term *sedes* may imply also a trestle, as it
seems to here. Even more furnishings make up the dé-
cor of the three rooms (tabernacula) for the Vorau
Isaac, including beds and kitchen equipment, which
appear to have been set up on separate raised platforms; whenever rubrics mention a *domus,* as in this
case, an open, defined, and visible interior space is
nearly always required. In addition to naming the
palace and a *domus,* the Beauvais *Daniel* and the
Daniel by Hilarius call for a lions' den or pit (lacus), but
there are no further hints concerning its construction.

The Fleury Playbook *Peregrinus* with its rich staging details dates to the twelfth century, while the first
record of the *Peregrinus* at Rouen occurs in the thirteenth century. But it is this latter text which attests to
a scaffolding (tabernaculum) in mid-nave, decorated
to look like the village of Emmaus—possibly with
hangings similar to those in the *Jeu d'Adam*—and furnished with a table and seats; it was raised since the

travelers are said to ascend up into it, and for Christ's vanishing it may well have been trapped. The four *sedes* called for in the opening rubric of the Fleury *St. Paul* are probably separate platforms, each equipped at least with a seat for the respective major personage; one of them, also termed *domus,* could have had a simulated wall from which Paul was lowered. Like the *Antichrist,* the *Son of Getron* requires the representation of a particular place of worship—in this instance the church of St. Nicholas, possibly a separate platform or an extension of the same area occupied by the *domus* of Getron, or an especially decorated part of the east choir perhaps with a frame doorway.

Three of our most significant pieces of evidence derive from fourteenth-century records. For the *Ordo Prophetarum* at Rouen a furnace was built of cloth and oakum in mid-nave and was set on fire during the course of the performance—an enclosed hut-like structure large enough to contain several actors. A hollow representation of Mt. Sinai, made of cloth and wood and containing an actor and an effigy of Christ, was erected in the nave for the *Ascension* at Moosburg. And Philippe de Mézières' meticulous description of the *Presentation of the Blessed Virgin Mary in the Temple* records our earliest dimensions for platforms (solarium), built in the nave and near the high altar: the first, ten-by-eight feet and six feet high; the second, six feet square and seven or eight feet high; both with railings, seats, and carpeting.

Fantastic machinery invented by Brunelleschi marked the spectacles in fifteenth-century Florence. Bishop Abraham of Suzdal reported having seen, in 1439, a flying device carry an angel between the throne of God and Mary for the *Annunciation,* God the Father with numerous angels situated on a platform ten-and-a-half feet square up over the entrance of the church and surrounded by seven rings of light, and Mary on a seat beside a bed positioned 175 feet away and up on the rood-loft. Both stages were closed off by curtains. A cloth painted with the sun, moon, and stars was removed from the opening of heaven into which Christ was drawn by means of a cloud machine at the performance of the *Ascension* that same year. Bishop Abraham described celestial paradise as a platform twenty-eight feet square with a fourteen-foot opening, suspended above the Mount of Olives at a height of fifty-six feet. At one side of the rood-loft stood a stone representation of Jerusalem into which Christ first disappeared in order to lead more than a dozen persons concealed there out across to the base of the Mount of Olives, ten-and-a-half feet high and situated at the opposite end of the gallery. The structure of Jerusalem is related to the permanent

Easter sepulchre in that it was enterable and closed all about, while it was perhaps akin to some representations of Emmaus in that it showed aspects of a medieval stronghold or city. As for the Mount of Olives—a hollow construction of wood and cloth at Moosburg—the Bishop says that it was hung about with red materials and reached by means of steps. Inside celestial paradise, God the Father was revealed miraculously suspended in mid-air and encircled by angels and lights as the cloud descended by means of seven cords.

Brunelleschi built an inverted half-sphere up in the rafters of S. Felice to represent the heavens, which he could close off by means of a pair of sliding horizontal doors. A *mandorla* surrounded by angels swung down from the brilliantly illuminated paradise to a platform on which Mary was seated, and Gabriel stepped out and moved across the stage for the act of the Annunciation. To this device Il Cecca later added a second level of concentric rings, the ten heavens, above the suspended platform that was to receive Christ upon his Ascension.

From the sixteenth century there are two clear indications of the use of pavilions, both for the *Annunciation.* At Tournai a pair of *stallagia* was set up, opposite each other in the east choir. Each was surrounded and closed off by curtains and silk cloths, and each was opened at the appropriate dramatic moment (et ante *Confiteor* immediate cortine circumquaque oratorium Virginis solum aperientur), first revealing the Virgin at her prayers and then the angel. Of particular interest here is the probability that the pavilions opened at least on three sides.[81] At Saint-Omer two *eschaffaulx* or *tabernacles* were erected for the same scene, one on either side of the high altar. An inventory dated 1557 from the church indicates that they were small platforms with posts at each corner to which curtains and silk hangings were fastened on all sides; the top of each was covered with cloth embroidered with a sun and stars.[82]

Finally, Vigil Raber's rather puzzling sketch for the *Vorspiel* of the seven-day Passion at Bozen in 1514 reflects outdoor practices of mise-en-scène.[83] Here it seems that a large single stage extended across half of the church's interior, just west of the main choir—the only such documented structure. On it four wooden frame doorways, perhaps curtained, appear to have indicated specific localities. In addition, an already present structural door served for *Infernum,* and the entrance to the east choir as the area of celestial paradise. In the center of the stage an upper gallery may have spanned two of the church's columns, which, with a curtain that could be drawn between them, formed the Temple. Similar techniques may have been employed earlier at Tegernsee and Fleury.

And the Mount of Olives was probably a pavilion with movable hangings on at least two sides.

Raised platforms, seats, tables, and beds comprise standard equipment for indicating a city, a house, or a room from the eleventh and twelfth centuries onward, and, as of the twelfth century, rubrics calling for walls, pits or dens, even a prison indicate sizeable decorated scenic elements. One is constantly reminded both of the sepulchre at Aquileia and of the Garden of Eden in the *Jeu d'Adam*. Although the closed manger dates from this earliest period, it is not until the fifteenth century that we have specific evidence as to other large *tableaux vivants* revealed by means of movable curtains—a device essentially Renaissance in spirit that would lead to the monoscenic, picture-frame stage as opposed to the open polyscenic stage characteristic of the Middle Ages.

The period of dramatic performances from the tenth through the thirteenth century belongs primarily to the church as far as extant source materials disclose, although there is no denying *homo ludens* and a constant but sparsely recorded stream of folk play, mime, dance, and other forms of presentational entertainment. The principles of the placement or layout of the mise-en-scène within the church derive from and with ecclesiastical ritual just as the changing shape of the church's architectural interior affected and is affected by its usage. It is not so much in the patterns of movement and employment of church space that one feels the influence of other dramatic productions, but rather in the scenic means as of the fourteenth century at a time when religious performance in marketplaces, city streets, and similar spaces began to mark the dominant dramatic genres. In the subsequent periods the influence was no doubt mutual, fundamental concepts of staging having been established within the church and then elements of the greater outdoor spectacles and more elaborate theatrical techniques adapted to the sanctuary. To this activity we must add the rise of humanism: the publishing of Vitruvius' *De Architectura* in 1486, and the acting of Roman drama in schools and academies. From Vitruvius scholars learned about a curtained scene and tried to imitate it when producing Terence. Although the texts of the church drama do not vary considerably with regard to subject matter in the latter centuries, one senses in those conservative productions something of the spirit of the Renaissance. The Florentine machinery seems oddly out of place in the church, yet it predicts the Renaissance stage, while by 1514 Raber's pageant with its frames and baskets smacks of a rather old-fashioned show that has

lost something of its inner didactic and mnemonic fire to the pedestrian mind of the realist.

APPENDIX A

Sion: On the Border between Ceremony and Drama

Texts linked with two churches in Sion (Sitten, Switzerland) document the use of the hidden sepulchre. A fourteenth-fifteenth-century text of a *Depositio* from the Cathedral of Sion (Romanesque, eleventh century to ca. 1450, then Gothic reconstruction) locates the burial place of Host and cross at the Altar of St. James in the ancient Romanesque crypt, directly beneath the east choir and high altar. We shall call it "the cathedral *Depositio*." A different text, dated to the same period, of a *Depositio* from the Valeria Church of Sion locates the burial of Host and cross at the Altar of St. Catherine in the Chapel of St. Catherine, probably the apsidal chapel of the Romanesque church (ca. 1100–ca. 1300) on the north side of the main apse and east choir. Neither manuscript preserves a *Visitatio Sepulchri*.

However, an earlier, thirteenth-century manuscript from Sion does contain a *Visitatio Sepulchri*, together with a *Depositio* and *Elevatio* (L746). For the sepulchre, did it use the St. James Altar in the crypt of the cathedral, or the St. Catherine Chapel in the Valeria Church? The manuscript, an *Ordinarium*, belongs to one of the two churches, and quite possibly to both. But its rubrics are not specific as to the place of the sepulchre. On Good Friday the Host and cross are to be taken from the high altar "ad locum deputatum" for the burial, and early on Sunday morning, the clergy go "ad locum Sepelitionis" for the *Elevatio*. In this context the word *sepelio* appears only in texts from Sion, and, in reference to the crypt in the *Visitatio*, only in a text from Trier (Young, 1:142).

Although one cannot be certain of the locus of the grave dialogue in this thirteenth-century manuscript, we know that as of 1474 it was enacted in the Chapel of St. Barbara, in the cathedral. A fifteenth-century hand has emended this *Visitatio* text to fit new conditions in the cathedral. The eleventh-century Romanesque church was rebuilt as a Gothic church in the mid-fifteenth century. Over the words "ad locum deputatum" is written "sacellem Divae Barbarae." In 1471–74, Bishop Walter Supersaxo built the apsidal Chapel of St. Barbara, abutting on the south wall of the apsidal east choir. He was buried in it, just in front of its altar. Thus, according to the text, as of 1474 the three Marys would gather behind the main altar of the cathedral and proceed in single file, the oldest first, out of the east choir, circle around south and then back eastward to enter the Chapel of St. Barbara. After the brief, three-line exchange with the angel, they would return with the gravecloth to hold it up before the chorus. There they probably stopped in front of the east choir and faced west. Choir stalls stood on the south and north sides of the fore-choir area. The observance did not end as usual with the *Te Deum*, but reached its climax and conclusion immediately thereafter as the celebrant intoned "Resurrexit Dominus, alleluia."

If this *Visitatio* text already reflected Easter observance in the cathedral before the fifteenth-century hand altered it, then it seems highly likely that during services prior to 1474 the Marys had descended from the high altar into the crypt for the exchange with the angel at the Altar of St. James. The cathedral *Depositio* puts the Host and cross there. The fifteenth-century alteration in mise-en-scène made the discovery moment slightly more public—but just slightly, for the Chapel of St. Barbara stood off to one side so that even bystanders in that area could only vaguely perceive an occurrence within it.

In addition, it is quite possible that this thirteenth-century *Visitatio* text reflects Easter celebration in the Valeria Church of Sion. In earlier times the ancient church had served as cathedral, and continuing as the collegiate church for canons living up on the hill of Valeria, it shared much liturgical practice with the cathedral in the town below. Thus for the cathedral, the fifteenth-century hand may have altered a text borrowed from the Valeria Church or, in some sense, shared between the two churches.

At Valeria also the dialogue with the angel would have been hidden away from the canons, as well as any other worshippers, for Valeria has an unusual configuration. A solid rood-screen in mid-church with walls and choir stalls extending eastward toward the high altar created an isolated, walled-in choir for the canons. The rood-screen, dating to the thirteenth century, can still be seen today. If this thirteenth-century *Visitatio* was performed in the Valeria Church together with the *Depositio* from Valeria, the three Marys would have gathered behind the high altar, moved out in front of it, and then turned and disappeared from view of the canons into the Chapel of St. Catherine, probably the north apsidal chapel. In conclusion, after the three-line exchange there, they would have returned to a position in front of the high altar to hold up the gravecloth before the canons in their enclosed area. Any worshippers beyond them out in the nave of the church could have caught only the most fleeting glimpses of the gravecloth through the narrow rood-screen door, while hearing the sounds and seeing the flickering lights and shadows of the obscured observance.

These Sion texts also reveal close relationships between ceremony and drama. The dialogue between the women and the angel constitutes the observance of a mystery, not the didactic enactment of an event. One is reminded of the Easter Matins ceremony at Constance, where the replica of the Sepulchre stands outside of the cathedral. At Sion only one angel is stationed at the sepulchre: a boy "who can sing very well." Secreted away either in the Chapel of St. Catherine at Valeria, or in the crypt and later the Chapel of St. Barbara in the cathedral, he must be heard. Whereas the women are to sing softly (submissa voce), his voice must penetrate (alta voce) from the recess of the sepulchre. As noted above, the Marys "all together" display the gravecloth to the chorus, not to a populace: to the canons enclosed in their east choir at Valeria, or to those in the flanking rows of choir stalls just in front of the east choir in the cathedral. And this *Visitatio* is the only one to reach its climax not with the *Te Deum* but immediately thereafter with the concluding "Resurrexit Dominus, alleluia."

Not only the dialogue that was sung in the chapels but the very selection of the altars and chapels where it was sung lent significance to the observance. Most obviously the cathedral crypt Altar of St. James infused the moment with the aura of the saint highly venerated in pilgrimages to Santiago de Compostela, together with Rome and Jerusalem one of the three greatest pilgrimage centers in medieval Europe. The change in the mise-en-scène to the newly built Chapel of St. Barbara changed the moment to imbue it with the sanctity of her presence, while up in the Valeria Church, extant documentation of the Easter use of the St. Catherine Chapel dates exactly to the era of veneration for St. Catherine, the patron. Thus the ceremony derived assurance of Resurrection from altars sacred to those who were certainly in heavenly bliss. By the same token, the Easter enactment not only derived power but also created power akin to that of a Mass for the dead. A move or a procession gave special liturgical assurance of life after death to the altars and tombs at which the participants stopped to pray or chant: to those in the crypt, and to St. Catherine and St. Barbara. Founding church patrons and high-ranking ecclesiastical officials, ecclesiastical and secular, wished to be buried as close to the high altar as possible—or to have an altar of their own. At Sion, Bishop Walter Supersaxo had his burial place located in the St. Barbara Chapel for precisely these two reasons. The Marys in the *Visitatio Sepulchri* at Gernrode stopped at the grave of founding Abbess Hathui; at Rheinau, at the grave of founder St. Fintan; at Trier, at the tomb of Archbishop Theodoric; at Meissen, at the tomb of the recently beatified Meissner bishop St. Benno. They honored and derived honor from the sacred place; they gave assurance of Resurrection to the person revered and received assurance of Resurrection from him or her, as it were.

The same thirteenth-century manuscript with its *Visitatio Sepulchri* also contains the simplest form of a dramatic Christmas celebration, the *Officium Stellae*. It unfolds even closer to the liturgy. During the Mass of Epiphany, three Magi ("tres magos," as in the Bible, not "Kings") read the Gospel, perhaps from up on the rood-screen if at Valeria. Then they proceed in single file—like the Marys except that the youngest goes first—with their gold, frankincense, and myrrh. A boy with a three-branched candelabrum precedes them. According to the rubrics they move out into the nave, then back up toward the high altar, go into the east choir at the entrance in front of the Altar of St. Michael, and finally give their gifts to the celebrant who is waiting for them at the high altar. Mass continues. An Altar of St. Michael existed at this period in both Sion churches; southwest of the high altar in the cathedral, its location uncertain at Valeria.

As noted above, the extant text could derive from either—or from both churches. Thus if they commenced their procession in the east choir, then they would have moved westward out into the nave, turning either into the north or south aisle (the south aisle in the cathedral) and proceeding eastward toward the St. Michael Altar and then to the high altar. No Christmas manger serves as a center of action, no gifts are given to a Christ Child, and in fact, not even a line of dialogue is sung. This is a ceremony, a procession added in the midst of Mass, not a drama. But it contains presentational elements that marked Christmas plays in other churches, such as the designation of roles, the move out into the nave, the procession led by a star, and the handing over of the three gifts. It remained ceremony when embedded in the Mass, for there one did not add words and music. It became drama when embedded in Matins, for there one exercised greater freedom with the liturgy. As noted in the opening chapter, the same principle holds true for the *Visitatio Sepulchri*: the "Quem quaeritis" lines as trope when in a procession preceding Easter Mass; the "Quem quaeritis" lines as dramatic dialogue when in a play concluding Easter Matins.

Whereas the *Depositio-Elevatio-Visitatio* series at Sion constituted an in-house ceremony for the clerical community, the Easter liturgy in the same thirteenth-century manuscript also provided a public ceremony for the lay community. That took place a week earlier, on Palm Sunday. Textual rubrics describe a major ecclesiastical procession with townspeople. They left the great, south door of the cathedral and wound their way singing to the Church of St. Peter at the foot of the Valeria hill. There palm branches were blessed. The procession then exited from the church, circled south to make a detour "by the path through the Lord Bishop's meadow" (today the "Planta") outside the immediate town area, and arrived at the Church of St. Theodul, just south of the cathedral. There a sermon was delivered in front of the church. Meanwhile the boys' choir left the procession and went over and ascended the westwork tower of the cathedral. They represented the children of Jerusalem (pueri Haebreorum). As the procession approached the west tower and entrance of the cathedral, the boys' choir began the hymn "Gloria laus." The rubric carefully notes that the timing had to be right: the procession was to move slowly enough so that "Gloria laus" up in the tower finished just as the procession reached the cathedral's west door directly below. Thereupon, with more chant, the procession reentered the cathedral.

In this awareness of private versus public ceremony, two hundred years later the fifteenth-century alterer of the manuscript added a public ceremony to the *Elevatio*. He wrote in the margin. His mention of the Chapel of St. Barbara in his addition assures locus in the cathedral, not at Valeria, while the public nature of the event belongs to the cathedral of the townsfolk, not the Valeria Church of the canons. Just prior to Easter Matins, instead of going "ad locum Sepelitionis" for the *Elevatio* and removing the Host directly to the main altar, the leader of a procession—the

bishop if present—takes the Host (and cross presumably) from the St. Barbara Chapel, intones "Christ ist erstanden" (vulgari voce), leads the way out of the cathedral (probably by the great south door) and around to the west tower entrance, and knocks on the closed door with the cross. This is a Harrowing of Hell, the celebrant singing "Atollite" and the chorus responding "Quis est." The procession then moves forward through the cathedral to the high altar, with special blessings of the people. Easter Matins commences. This is public ceremony. By contrast, the subsequent *Visitatio* in this fifteenth-century version is almost private. As described above, the three-line exchange between the angel and the Marys at the Chapel of St. Barbara transpired out of sight of all but a few. For the worshippers nevertheless, the preceding *Elevatio* with its public procession had established the chapel as locus of the Holy Sepulchre.

With these observances at Sion one has singular documentation of borders between dramatic ceremony and drama. Where private Easter liturgy removes the Host and cross from the main altar to the Chapel of St. Catherine at Valeria and to the Altar of St. James in the cathedral crypt, a change in mise-en-scène in the cathedral later employs the more visible Chapel of St. Barbara as sepulchre. And where in the cathedral the Easter Sunday liturgy of the thirteenth century remained hieratic, the Palm Sunday procession from church to church in town created an extended, dramatic event for the populace. In an innovation, the cathedral—not Valeria—altered the *Elevatio* in the fifteenth century to make it too a dramatic, public event. Thus it seems that it is with the overt inclusion of the larger lay community that drama emerges from liturgical practice at Sion.

Textual Materials Relevant to the *Visitatio Sepulchri* at Sion—Summary

The Visitatio Sepulchri *at Sion—Summary of Textual Evidence for Performance in the Cathedral and in the Valeria Church*

MS 47, Kapitelsarchiv, Sitten, thirteenth century, no altars named

Dep.	*El.*
Altered, xv cent. hand, Cath., Sep. in Chapel of St. Barbara	Altered, xv cent. hand, Cath., Sep. in Chapel of St. Barbara

MS 17, Kapitelsbibl. [sic], Sitten, fourteenth-fifteenth century

Dep.	*El.*
Cath., Sep. at St. James Altar (in crypt)	Cath., Sep. at St. James Altar (in crypt)

MS 46, Kapitelsarchiv, Sitten, thirteenth century

Dep.

Valeria Church, Sep. at
St. Catherine Altar
(in Chapel of St. Catherine)

In the thirteenth century, the *Visitatio Sepulchri* in MS 47
was performed either in the Valeria Church or in the Cathedral of Sion, or in both. If performed in the Valeria Church,
the sepulchre could have been in the St. Catherine Chapel,
or elsewhere. If performed in the Cathedral, the sepulchre
could have been in the crypt, or elsewhere. As of 1474, the
Visitatio in MS 47 was certainly performed in the Cathedral
with the sepulchre in the Chapel of St. Barbara.

List of Sion Texts

1. *VS,* xiii, with *Dep.* and *El.* MS 47, Bl. 16a–b, 18b–19a,
19a–b. Sitten, Kapitelsarchiv. No altars named. Altered by
fifteenth-century hand, with *Dep.* and *El.* at Chapel of St.
Barbara (in the Cathedral); and knocking on tower door of
the Cathedral in *El.*

Published by:
Lipphardt, L746, "Ordinarium der Kathedrale von Sitten,
vor 1300"; Carlen, *VS* only, "Ordinarium Cathedralis Ec-
clesiae Sedunensis pro Choro Valeriano."
N.B. Holderegger, 56 n. 1: "sehr häufig auch ist die
Datierung 'in choro Valeria,'" referring to ways in which the
Valeria Church is cited in contemporary documents.
N.B. *Vallesia*, 89, dates MS 1250–70.

L746a ("Sermones et Liber ordinarius, der Kathedrale von
Sitten"), L746b ("Ordinarium der Kathedrale von Sitten"):
copies of L746 from fifteenth century and 1365, respectively.

2. *Dep.*, xiv–xv. MS 17, Bl. 289b–90a, Sitten, Kapitelsarchiv.

Published by:
L746c, "Missale der Kathedrale." Text different from #1
Dep. above.

3. *Dep.* and *El.*, xiv–xv. MS 17, Bl. 292r, Sitten, Kapitelsarchiv.

Published by: *Vallesia*, 118, "Missale Sedun." Text different
from *Dep.* #1 and #2 above. With Sepulchre at "the Altar of
St. James beneath the high altar" (in the Cathedral crypt).

4. *Dep.*, 1455. MS 21, Bl. 240, Sitten, Kapitelsarchiv.

Published by: *Vallesia*, 129, "Missale Sedun." Text virtually
a copy of *Dep.* #3 above. With Sepulchre at "the Altar of St.
James beneath the high altar" (in the Cathedral crypt).

5. *Dep.*, xiii. MS 46, Sitten, Kapitelsarchiv.

Published by: L747, "Prozessionale der Wallfahrtskirche
Valeria bei Sitten." Text different from #1–4. With Sepul-
chre at the Altar of St. Catherine (in the Chapel of St.
Catherine, Valeria Church).

6. Palm Sunday Procession, xiii. MS 47 above.

Published by: Carlen.

7. *Officium Stellae*, xiii. MS 47 above.

Published by: Carlen.

Features Named in the Rubrics of
Sion Texts—Documentation

Altar of St. Catherine—Valeria Church

The Chapel of St. Catherine (with altar) was probably the
north apsidal chapel in the thirteenth century; it certainly
was by the sixteenth century. The Valeria Church has three
side-by-side apses at its east end, opening westward: the
larger, central apse at the rear of the east choir; and two
smaller apses, to the north and south of it respectively, each
separated from it by a wall.

—See Holderegger's ground plan, fig. 6.
—Written documentation regarding the Chapel of St.
Catherine (with altar) as of the thirteenth century: ibid., 31.
—Cult of St. Catherine, by this time patron of Valeria
Church, as of the thirteenth century: ibid., 31.
—Position unsure of Chapel of St. Catherine in north apsi-
dal chapel in the thirteenth century; position certain
there by the sixteenth century: ibid., 90*ff.*
—No reference found to St. Catherine Altar in Cathedral
in medieval period.

Altar of St. James—Cathedral of Sion

—Written documentation regarding the St. James Altar in
the Cathedral as of the thirteenth century; written documentation of its position in the crypt "beneath the main
altar," fourteenth century: *Vallesia*, 88, 118. Note access
to crypt under east choir—on south side: *Vallesia*, 98
(same side as St. Michael Altar).
—No reference found to St. James Altar in Valeria in medieval period.

Chapel of St. Barbara—Cathedral

—Written and architectural documentation regarding the
St. Barbara Chapel in the Cathedral, built 1471–74 by
Bishop Walter Supersaxo: *Vallesia*, 94*ff.* See diagrams,
90, fig. 3.
—Chapel exists today.

Altar of St. Michael—Valeria Church and Cathedral

VALERIA

—Written documentation regarding the St. Michael Altar at Valeria as of the thirteenth century: Holderegger, 37.
—Holderegger and Carlen suppose that the St. Michael Altar is in the south apsidal chapel, Valeria.
—Written evidence from the seventeenth century seems to indicate a position in the nave: Holderegger, 197.

CATHEDRAL

—Written documentation regarding the St. Michael Altar in the Cathedral as of the thirteenth century: *Vallesia*, 118.
—Probable position in east choir, southwest of high altar, at crypt entrance: ibid. 118, 144. Note proximity to the certain location of St. Martin Altar, to rear of high altar.

Reconstructions—Drama and Ceremony at Sion

Text #1, *VS.*

Carlen assigns the *VS* only to the Valeria Church. He places the Sepulchre at the altar west of the rood-screen, on the south side, "so dass das Volk den dramatischen Szenen folgen kann" (354). He does not mention the Chapel of St. Catherine. Therefore, he has the Marys move from behind the main altar out through the central door of the rood-screen, and after the grave dialogue he has them reenter the choir through that door to display the gravecloth in the east choir. See his diagram, 353, and photo of the Valeria Church interior, opposite 364, as well as a photo of a page from MS 47, facing 350, with fifteenth-century alterations.

Text #1, *VS.*

Michael also assigns the *VS* only to the Valeria Church. But he envisions all the worshippers in the east choir area and therefore "das Sepulchrum auch im Chorraum befand, [so] konnten von dort die Zuschauer leicht die ganze Handlung übersehen" (14). He too does not mention the Chapel of St. Catherine and assumes that the enactment was for "das Volk" and wholly visible to them.

Text #1, *VS.*

Lipphardt, 8:649: His posthumously published notes to this text seem to confuse the two churches.

Text #3, *Dep.* and *El.*

Vallesia (88, 89; text, 118) quotes and paraphrases the rubrics, noting that "the Altar of St. James beneath the high altar" (so cited in the *Dep.* rubric) stood in the crypt.

Text #6, Palm Sunday Procession

Carlen (357*ff.*) reconstructs the procession, adding details for which I cannot find a source.

Elsewhere in Switzerland—not at Sion as far as I know—and in southern Germany and Austria, the Palm Sunday procession included a life-sized carved figure of Jesus riding on a donkey. It stood on wheels and was pulled along in the procession, often decked out with flowers. See, for example, Möbius; a photo in Young, facing 1:94; an eighteenth-century example stands in the City Museum of Überlingen, south Germany.

Text #7, *Officium Stellae.*

Carlen (362*ff.*, with diagram, 363) assigns the dramatic procession only to the Valeria Church. He has the three "magos" read the Gospel from the rood-loft, descend and process out into the nave through the central rood-screen door (as did the Marys in his reconstruction of the *Visitatio*), turn south, then east, moving eastward along the south aisle toward the apsidal chapel that abutted on the south wall of the choir. Following Holderegger, he believes the St. Michael Altar stood there. In front of the St. Michael Altar the Magi turn north to reenter the choir and present their gifts to the celebrant at the high altar.

Text #7, *Officium Stellae.*

Michael (18, with diagram, 14) also assigns the dramatic procession only to the Valeria Church and follows Carlen in all other details. His references are to a "Gemeinde" in the east choir area with their backs to the rood-screen. The canons were the major people there. Moreover, their stalls stood against the north and south walls, respectively, of the choir area, but not against the west wall, the rood-screen. Where Carlen with Holderegger assumes the position of the St. Michael Altar in the apse on the south side of the choir, for Wolfgang Michael that position becomes fact.

Sion—Bibliography

Antonini, Dubuis and Lugon, "Les fouilles récentes dans la cathédrale de Sion." *Vallesia* 44 (1989):61–78.

Carlen, "Das Ordinarium Sedunense." Carlen was the first to publish the dramatic texts from Sion and to suggest reconstructions of their performances, including a prototype of the *Officium Stellae* and the Palm Sunday procession. Excepting the latter, he assumed that all were performed in the Valeria Church.

Dubuis and Lugon, "La Cathédrale Notre-Dame de Sion." *Vallesia* 44 (1989): 79–114.

Holderegger, "Die Kirche von Valeria bei Sitten," 31: 51*ff.*, 109*ff.*, 207*ff.*, 260*ff.*, 32: 26*ff.*, 90*ff.*, 191*ff.* Major work on the Church of Valeria, both written and architectural documentation.

Lipphardt, *Lateinische Osterfeiern und Osterspiele;* published eleven Easter-season texts from Valeria, L746–752.

Lugon, "Documents relatifs à la cathédrale de Sion." *Vallesia* 44 (1989): 115–210.

Michael, *Frühformen der deutschen Bühne.* He discusses (13–18) Carlen's reconstructions, with some alterations. Reproduces Carlen's photo and ground plan for the *Officium Stellae.*

I wish to thank two people in particular for their generous assistance at Sion: Domherr Dr. Paul Werlen, Archivar des Domkapitels; and M. Maurice Wenger, Directeur, Festival de l'orgue ancien, Valère.

APPENDIX B

Movement Patterns of the Performers in the *Visitatio Sepulchri* at Gernrode

Gernrode, text ca. 1500 (MS copied 1502): Lipphardt, 786–86a. See also Lipphardt, "Die Visitatio Sepulchri."

For the Gernrode church and sepulchre, see Voigtländer, *Die Stiftskirche zu Gernrode.* See also Erdmann, et al., "Neue Untersuchungen." In addition, see Schulze, *Das Stift Gernrode;* also Schwarzweber, *Das heilige Grab,* 7–8.

For Lipphardt's sense that the extant text of the *Visitatio Sepulchri* from Gernrode (ca. 1500) may be a shortened version of a text older than the construction of the Sepulchre itself there, see Voigtländer, *Die Stiftskirche zu Gernrode,* 90 n. 12.

In this regard, the figure of Mary Magdalen often plays a special role in these Easter plays when acted in nunneries and by communities with canonesses. The Gernrode text does not include the scene between Jesus as gardener and Mary Magdalen, though it singles her out from the three women with the "Dic nobis, Maria" line; however, she does appear with Jesus in the recognition scene in the carving on the north wall of the Sepulchre, and also, on the west wall, standing alone.

Special Notes on the Location of Features of the Gernrode Church Related to the Staging of the *Visitatio Sepulchri* There

The features are numbered as given on the plan. Items 1 through 8 are major parts of the church relevant to the mise-en-scène of the *Visitatio Sepulchri* text. Items A through K are features relevant to the stage directions.

1. Holy Sepulchre, grave room.
2. Holy Sepulchre, forecourt.
3. Holy Sepulchre, St. Aegidius (St. Giles) Altar. Probably against inner east wall of the forecourt, St. Aegidius Chapel.

    1, 2, and 3. The replica of the Holy Sepulchre ca. 1080, with burial chamber (1) and (2) forecourt called the St. Aegidius Chapel. The forecourt-chapel had an altar, probably against its inner east wall (3). Thus when the *Depositio Crucis* says the canonesses enter the St. Aegidius Chapel and "bliben vor dem altar püssen [zwischen] dem heyligen Grabe stan," they would have been in the center of the forecourt-chapel, its altar (3) east of them and the burial chamber (1) west of them. A small door leads from the forecourt into the burial chamber. Originally the burial chamber had a dome, like that in Jerusalem. The dimensions are nearly those of the burial chamber and forecourt in Jerusalem at that time. Against the north wall of the burial chamber stood a sarcophagus (for the burial of the cross at Easter). In the north wall was an opening, a kind of window; one could stand in the nave and peer through the window into the burial chamber and into its sarcophagus. The north-wall door into the forecourt was cut in the twelfth century. Originally one entered from the south transept. In the twelfth century that entrance was blocked up during the construction of the canonesses' gallery and at that time the north-wall forecourt door was cut. It has been suggested that the statue of a bishop in the burial chamber is a depiction of the Risen Christ; textual rubrics do not indicate that a bishop sang Christ's line in the play (the "Homessen Here" did, the High Mass priest). Figures carved on the exterior walls of the Sepulchre, dating to the period of its construction, show Mary Magdalen alone, then the "Noli me tangere" scene with the Risen Christ above, as well as remains of a Peter and John scene in the race to the tomb. The extant play, of course, has neither of the latter scenes, but the gestures of Mary Magdalen and Christ in the sculpture are strikingly appropriate for their lines in the text, gestures of apprehension and of blessing.

4. The raised St. Cyriacus east (main) choir and Altar, with crypt below. The canons had their seats in the raised east choir. The ca. 1500 text refers to a choir door, probably a central door in a rood-screen at the top of the east choir steps. Originally two sets of steps led down into the crossing, on the north and south sides, not the present single flank. Between them was a confessio opening (8), a small opening in the east crypt wall probably giving access to the relic of St. Cyriacus enshrined in the crypt (Erdmann, "Neue Untersuchungen," 247*ff.* Horn and Born, 1:144–99). An altar—perhaps the All Souls Altar—might have stood between the steps. One finds this arrangement in other Romanesque churches as well, in the Cathedral of Braunschweig, for example, and nearby Quedlinburg.

5. The St. Metronius west choir, with crypt. High above it was the bell housing of the westwork.

6. The canonesses' raised gallery in the south transept. This gallery was erected around 1130, with a door in its south wall leading directly to the canonesses' quarters, on the south side of the church. When in their gallery the canonesses wishing to reach the crossing and nave of the church would have filed down several

narrow steps at the northeast corner of their gallery into the east choir; then turning west they would have filed down the south flank of east-choir-to-crossing steps. With its construction, the canonesses' gallery blocked the original, open east entrance to the antechamber of the replica of the Holy Sepulchre. That east entrance was sealed up and, as noted above, a small door was cut into the north wall of the antechamber—the present door and the one used by performers of the ca. 1500 *Visitatio Sepulchri* text.

7. Steps down into the east crypt.
8. Confessio opening into east crypt, perhaps also the location of the All Souls Altar.

Note. After several Reformation-inspired attacks on images, all altars were finally removed from the church in 1616, making it difficult now to reconstruct exact positions of many of them.

A. The St. Peter statue or picture was located at the foot of these steps. Rubrics refer to it frequently in these ways: "sso gheen dy Frouwichnn zcu sunte Peter abe" and "wedder vff eren kor zcu Sunte Peter vff."
B. The St. John Altar was near the (north) entrance to the forecourt of the Sepulchre. An earlier document refers to it as "s. Johannis an dem hiligen grabe."
C. The procession symbolizing the Harrowing of Hell goes "vor den sele-messen-altar," before the All Souls Altar. Voigtländer, as well as earlier scholars, have been able to find only one other reference to this altar: "ad altare, quod dicitur altare animarum, ibidem in monasterio" (1357, Voigtländer, *Die Stiftskirche zu Gernrode,* 140). The document is a record of a contribution to the altar, not of its establishment. I suspect that the All Souls Altar stood between the two flanks of steps leading up into the east choir, at the confessio opening.

I wish to thank in particular Dr. Ross of the Landeshauptarchiv Sachsen-Anhalt, Aussenstelle Oranienbaum, for a painstaking search which also turned up only the one reference (1357), cited above (correspondence 25 May 1992).

The Altar of the Holy Cross served as the center for burials and for the daily Masses for the dead. There are many references to it from as early as 1014. It stood somewhere in the crossing, perhaps under the cross-bearing beam which spanned the arch of the crossing from its original construction. The founding patron of the abbey, Gero, was probably buried in the crossing, perhaps between the Altar of the Holy Cross and the confessio (Erdmann, "Neue Untersuchungen," 258–60). The highly revered first Abbess, Hathui, was buried just in front of the Altar of the Holy Cross, with other Abbesses buried nearby in the east end of the nave. In 1394 the Holy Cross Altar received a thorn from the Crown of Thorns.

The cross first buried in the Holy Sepulchre replica and then later brought out during the *Visitatio Sepulchri* was carried to the All Souls Altar. According to the rubrics the canons "take it up" or "pick it up" to carry it—"dass crücze haben vffgenomen," a second manuscript copy says "vff gehoben"—and then "Wan nu dass crucze gesatzt iss," the women make their offerings at the cross. The phrase "When the cross is set" seems to indicate a rather large cross with a base or socket. If on Good Friday it was actually fit into the sarcophagus, then the size of the extant sarcophagus platform might be indicative of its size: 1.6 meters by 60 centimeters. Earlier, on Palm Sunday, the men had carried the cross from the Sepulchre to the Holy Cross Altar (vor dess heyligen crüecess altar), and then specifically two men, the High Mass priest and the deacon, had carried it to a position in front of the east choir, "vor sunte ciriaci chor" (Voigtländer, *Die Stiftskirche zu Gernrode,* 141), where perhaps the All Souls Altar stood. In addition, a designated place for offerings, according to a 1489 reference, was "ante Crucem" (ibid., 149), before the cross. Thus the canonesses could have made their Easter offerings at the All Souls Altar, positioned just in front of the east choir.

Note. Apparently Lipphardt, 8:731, confused either the two major saints of the church or the east and west crypts when he noted that the All Souls Altar "befand sich vor dem Lettner im Osten der Kirche in nächster Nähe des Metronius-Grabes." I suspect a similar east-west confusion occurs in his note on the choir entrances in the double-choired Cathedral of Bamberg; Lipphardt, 7:143 notes 17, 31.

D. Beneath the bell housing, the belfry. After making their special Easter offerings the Marys go "vnder dy glocken." From the beginning the westwork above this position contained the bells of the church. In the twelfth century the original rectangular tower flanked by two round towers was replaced by the present, rounded westwork. From other references in the manuscript, it is clear that the expression "dy glocken" served for purposes of orienting or locating. For instance, at one point on Palm Sunday the women move to the St. Aegidius Chapel and stand "mit dem rücken zcu den glocken."
E. The All Saints Altar. When the Marys then move from the westwork area to a position "vor aller heyligen altar, dar bliben dy drye personen"—they are probably in mid-nave. An earlier document locates the All Saints Altar there, "in medio monasterii." A contemporary copy of the ca. 1500 *Visitatio* manuscript instructs: "dar bliben dy drye personen stande," adding the word *stande* for extra clarity because this particular altar had seats or benches. Its location satisfies the symbolism of the staging and also fits with the other pieces of the mosaic in the reconstruction.
F. The grave of Abbess Hathui (Hadwig, Hedwig), the first

Abbess, was just west of the Altar of the Holy Cross: "in medio aecclesiae coram sanctae crucis altari" (Voigtländer, *Die Stiftskirche zu Gernrode*, 136, document from 1014). The carved grave stone, and that of Gero, were flush with the pavement. The Marys emerge from the Sepulchre and go to this position, where the chief celebrant is waiting for them, to ask "Maria, quid ploras?".

G. Grave stone of founder Gero (flush with pavement). The exact location is not known. A position in the crossing is highly likely. Erdmann, "Neue Untersuchungen" (260), suggests between the Altar of the Holy Cross and the confessio.

H. Possible location of the chair of the Abbess. Her chair (Stuhl) is documented (Voigtländer, *Die Stiftskirche zu Gernrode*, 116 n. 9). But where it stood, I do not know, perhaps at the front of the canonesses' gallery. The Abbess probably descended with her canonesses and stood with them at the All Souls Altar. During the performance the Marys leave the grave of Hathui and "go with the antiphon [singing] before the Abbess" (gheen myt der An[tiffen] vor dy eptischen). They then sing their "Surrexit dominus" to her. At the end the canonesses climb the east-choir steps and stand at the rood-screen door, all the while singing the final hymn. Whereupon they go on up into their gallery. And "then the Abbess takes their candles" (Danne sso nympt dy Eptisthynne ore lichte wedder). Clearly at that point she is with them in their gallery.

Other *Visitatio* texts such as that at Magdeburg have the bishop or archbishop standing with or near the chorus when the chorus has moved out into the nave of the church for the *Visitatio* and then return to the east choir with the chorus.

When the deacon and subdeacon emerge from the Sepulchre at Gernrode and sing "Cernitis, o socii"—they had apparently also sung the angels' "Quem quaeritis" lines—they probably stand in front of the Sepulchre and sing toward the entire company of canonesses in the crossing, including the three Marys. For the finale the women sing together with the men, and then the women as a group proceed expressly to the choir door (Chor-thoer), probably to the top of the east choir steps, to sing a final hymn, "Te decet laus." And from there they return to their choir (vff oren chorn), where the Abbess collects their candles.

J. Rood-screen door (Chor-thoer), documented as of ca. 1500.

K. All Souls Altar, probable location.

Note. A number of factors indicate reasons for the uniqueness of this *Visitatio Sepulchri*. As Lipphardt has pointed out, its text reflects a very ancient form. Moreover, it was fit specifically to the construction of the Holy Sepulchre replica. Voigtländer reports Lipphardt's agreeing with him that the present text derives from a Gernrode play that antedates the construction of the sepulchre and that it was abbreviated over the ensuing years (Voigtländer, *Die Stiftskirche zu Gernrode*, 90 n. 12).

Of particular interest is the relation between concepts of ritual and drama as manifested by this text. For example, the *Visitatio* emerges directly out of the ceremony of the *Elevatio Crucis*. Thereupon the role of the three women as the three Marys is spelled out: "Drye frouwichenn, dy Margen" (three women, the Marys). They also wear special veils or wimples, with a red cross on each of the four sides. Yet in further speech ascriptions they are called "Dy Dry Personen" (the three persons). Inside the Sepulchre "Dy Engel" (the angels) sing the "Quem quaeritis" exchange, but when they emerge to sing "Cernitis, o socii" (normally sung by Peter and John), the singers are "Der Dyaken vnde Subdyaken" (the deacon and subdeacon). The priest who delivers Christ's only line, "Maria, quid ploras?", is called "Der Homessen Here" (the High Mass celebrant). And although he addresses Maria in the singular, all three women respond. When then proclaiming the Resurrection, each in turn delivers her line "zcu der eptischen," to the Abbess, the most powerful ruling person in their lives. One senses here a very hieratic, hierarchical, in-house celebration. Moreover, it is unlikely that townsfolk were present. But each of these canonesses—there were about eight at this period, almost all members of the nobility—had her own servants and an entourage, among whom there were even members of the lower nobility. These people may well have been in the abbey church on Easter Sunday.

It is not clear where the enactment fit in the liturgy. The rubrics and text of the piece seem very self-contained, a whole work. The stage directions begin with the waking of the canonesses on Easter night (in der heyligen osternacht), using the rattles of Good Friday, and then the gathering of the canons in the east choir (they lived outside the immediate abbey grounds); and the performance ends with the ancient Benedictine hymn "Te decet laus." This is the only *Visitatio* text that concludes with this hymn, instead of the usual *Te Deum* of Matins. Lipphardt reports that it was sung in the monastic Cursus at Sunday Matins instead of the *Te Deum* ("Die Visitatio Sepulchri," 5). Was the play at Gernrode meant for performance at the end of Easter Matins? Or as a substitute for Matins? Did Easter Mass follow directly? One cannot be sure. From its founding the abbey came directly under both royal (960) and papal protection (961). Eventually in the fourteenth century it was named an *ecclesia exempta*. Thus in its practices it did not follow Benedictine rule, as did most of the churches where one finds the *Visitatio Sepulchri* and other plays.

There are important architectural and liturgical links and parallels with the St. Georg church for canonesses in Prague (L387) and the Cathedral of Essen (L564).

I wish to express my gratitude to Stiftskirche Gernrode Pfarrer and Frau Christian Günther for their help with my work in Gernrode.

APPENDIX C

Set Pieces: Terminology

In the following list of terms, unless otherwise noted the references in parenthesis are to Karl Young, *The Drama of the Medieval Church*, Walther Lipphardt, *Lateinische Osterfeiern und Osterspiele* (Lipphardt's text number preceded by an L), and J. E. Wackernell, *Altdeutsche Passionsspiele aus Tirol* (Wackernell).

arbor   tree. Benediktbeuern Passion (13th century) (1:519).

archa   ark, box. Essen *Visitatio* (14th century) (1:333).

ascabellum   foot-stool. Palma di Mallorca (14th century) (L58, "uel aliud stagnum").

cadafale   catafalque. Gerona, Cathedral *Ludus Paschalis* (16th century) (L821).

carcer   prison. *Officium Stellae*, Bilsen (12th century) (2:77); *Joseph*, Laon (13th century) (2:271).

castellum   castle, stronghold, village; from the Vulgate referring to Emmaus. *Peregrinus*: Benediktbeuern (13th century) (1:463); Padua (13th century) (1:482); Rouen (13th–15th century) (1:462, 693= *tabernaculum*).

crux   cross for crucifixion scenes. Benediktbeuern Passion (13th century) (1:516, 530); Sulmona Passion (14th century) (1:705); Tyrol Passion (15th–16th century) (Wackernell, 126 ff).

discus   altar top, table. Padua *Peregrinus* (13th century) (1:482).

dolium   cask. Tyrol Passion (15th–16th century) (Wackernell, 258).

domuncula   tent-like construction. Moosburg *Ascension* (14th century) (1:484 = *tentorium*).

domus   house, room. Beauvais *Daniel* (12th century) (2:298); Vorau *Isaac* (12th century) (2:263 = *tabernaculum*); Fleury Playbook (12th century): *Lazarus, St. Paul, Iconia, Getron* (2:199–224, 220–21= sedes?, 344, 355); Tyrol Passion, (15th–16th century) (Wackernell, 83 = *sedes?*, 87 = *pretorium*); Bozen *Vorspiel*, 1514 (Wackernell, 446–47, 449, 465).

foris   door, gate. Fleury Playbook, *Getron* (12th century) (2:356). N.B.: Christ breaks down gates of hell in the Klosterneuburg *Ludus Paschalis* (13th century) (1:428: *porta*) and kicks in the door of hell in Tyrol Passion, Tyrol (15th–16th century) (Wackernell, 209 = *janua*).

fornax   furnace. Rouen *Ordo Prophetarum* (14th–15th century) (2:154, 164–65).

habitaculum   abode, dwelling; enterable sepulchre (?). Mont-St.-Michel *Visitatio* (14th century) (1:575).

hospitium   lodging. Beauvais *Peregrinus* (12th century) (1:468); Rouen *Peregrinus* (13th–15th century) (1:461, 693 = *castellum, tabernaculum*).

infernum   Hell. Klosterneuburg *Ludus Paschalis* (13th century) (1:425. "Ihesus ueniens ad portas Inferni").

lacus   den, pit. Hilarius, *Daniel*, and Beauvais *Daniel* (both 12th century) (2:276 ff, 300–301); Laon *Joseph* (13th century) (2:268–69 = *cisterna, puteus*).

lapis   stone at sepulchre entrance or opening. *Depositio*: Admont (ca. 1500) (L485a); Aquileia (1494)(L495); Basel (1488) (L197). St. Lambrecht *Depositio, Visitatio* (ca. 1200) (L728).

lectulus   bed, couch. Hilarius, *Lazarus* (12th century) (2:212).

lectus   bed, couch. Vorau *Isaac* (12th century) (2:259); Benediktbeuern Christmas play (13th century) (2:180); *St. Paul*, Fleury Playbook (12th century) (2:219).

limbus   underworld picture. *Elevatio*: Brixen-Innsbruck, Hofkirche (1628) (L542c, *patrum et infantorum*).

litus maris   sea-shore. Benediktbeuern Passion (13th century) (1:518).

locus   place. N.B.: often used as a general designation of locality or position—e.g., Beauvais *Daniel* (12th century) (2:300). Apparently only as a technical term for a set piece in Tyrol Passion (15th–16th century) (e.g., Wackernell, 181), and possibly Benediktbeuern Passion (13th century) (1:514, 518). Occasionally used referring to an actor's role—e.g., Soissons *Visitatio* (12th–13th century) (1:305); Benediktbeuern Christmas play (13th century) (2:180); also position of actors before and after participation in performance.

mensa   altar top, table. *Peregrinus*: Beauvais (12th century) (1:468); Sicily (12th century) (1:478); Fleury Playbook (12th century) (1:472); Rouen (13th–15th century) (1:462, 693). Benediktbeuern Passion (13th century) (1:514). Fleury Playbook (12th century): *Lazarus, Tres Clerici, Getron* (2:200, 331, 355). *Ascension*: Bamberg (1587) (1:694); Berlin (16th century) (1:696). Tyrol Passion (15th–16th century) (Wackernell, 24); Bozen *Vorspiel* (1514) (Wackernell, 446–47, 457).

murus   wall. *St. Paul*, Fleury Playbook (12th century) (2:222).

palatium   palace. Beauvais *Daniel* (12th century) (2:295).

paries   wall. Beauvais *Daniel* (12th century) (2:292).

platea   courtyard, street. N.B.: only possible example of use as a technical term for neutral playing area: *Lazarus*, Fleury Playbook (12th century) (2:199).

scabellum   bench, stool. Philippe de Mézières, *Presentation of the Blessed Virgin Mary* (1372) (2:232, 235); Bamberg *Ascension* (1587) (1:694).

scam(p)num bench, stool. Mézières, *Presentation* (1372) (2:231); Berlin *Ascension* (16th century) (1:696); Halle *Assumption* (1532) (2:256).

sedes seat, platform (?). Tegernsee *Antichrist* (12th century) (2:371); Bilsen *Officium Stellae* (12th century) (2:79); Benediktbeuern Christmas play (13th century) (2:172, 189). Fleury Playbook (12th century): *Getron* (2:351); *Peregrinus* (1:472); *St. Paul* (2:219, 220–21 = *domus?*). Mézières, *Presentation* (1372) (2:231). Tyrol Passion (15th–16th century) (Wackernell, 24, 68, 81–82).

solarium balcony, platform, terrace. Mézières, *Presentation* (1372) (2:231, 232 = *edificium de lignis*).

solium seat, throne. Freising *Officium Stellae* (11th century) (2:93: in first line, not in rubrics); Beauvais *Daniel* (12th century) (2:291, 296, 300).

stallagium pavilion, stall. Tournai *Annunciation* (16th century) (2:480–82 = *oratorium*).

statio place, residence, station. Tyrol Passion (15th–16th century) (Wackernell, 81); Bozen *Vorspiel* (1514) (Wackernell, 452–53). N.B.: usually the stopping position of a procession—e.g., Besançon *Officium Stellae* (2:433).

stratus bed, couch. Freising *Ordo Rachelis* (11th–12th century) (2:118).

tabernaculum lodging. Vorau *Isaac* (12th century) (2:259, 263 = *domus*); Rouen *Peregrinus* (13th–15th century) (1:461, 693 = *castellum, hospitium*).

tabernaculum, MG Sarch, Tabernackl sepulchre. Brixen, Dom *Depositio* (1553) (L542a); Augsburg *Elevatio* (1612) (L527).

templum church, temple. Tegernsee *Antichrist* (12th century) (2:371); Padua *Purification* (14th century) (2:253); Bozen *Vorspiel* (1514). N.B.: St. Nicholas church, *Getron*, Fleury Playbook (12th century) (2:351 = *ecclesia*).

tentorium canopy, tent. Essen *Visitatio* (14th century) (1:333); Moosburg *Ascension* (14th century) (1:484 = *domuncula*).

t(h)ronus throne. Tegernsee *Antichrist* (12th century) (2:372); Hilarius, *Daniel* (12th century) (2:276, 281, 286); Montpellier *Officium Stellae* (12th century) (2:69).

turris citadel, tower. Tyrol Passion (15th–16th century) (Wackernell, 214, 247).

viculnea fig tree. Bozen *Vorspiel* (1514) (Wackernell, 463).

Chapter 4

The Costumes

The rubrics of the liturgical drama and dramatic ceremonies contain far more information about the costumes of the characters than about any other aspect of staging. The apparel can be classified in three types. Almost all sacred and royal figures wore ecclesiastical vestments. However, a few characters were dressed in the clothing of contemporary daily life: for instance, Christ as gardener in the *Hortulanus* scene in the *Visitatio Sepulchri* and the wayfarers Cleophas and Luke as medieval pilgrims in the *Peregrinus*. There is a third category of rare, exotic figures such as the speaking donkey in the Balaam scene in the *Ordo Prophetarum* and Diabolus in the *Ludus Paschalis* from Klosterneuburg. But the sacristy contained most of the costumes.[1]

By far the strongest visual element in the mise-en-scène was the costuming with rich vestments from the sacristy that lent the wearer a long-traditional aura of ancient sanctity. If the production took place in a cathedral, we can be sure of a display of silks, satins, brocades, and the precious embroidery that constituted one of the finest crafts of the medieval world.

A good deal is known about ecclesiastical vestments and medieval dress in general from paintings, miniatures, sculpture, and stained glass. Although nowhere can we be certain that we have before us a pictorial reproduction of a theatrical scene set in a church, nevertheless the subject matter of the visual arts often coincides with that of the stage, deriving from the same great well of human understanding and interpretation of Biblical material. Such manuscript illuminations do provide important details (e.g., the presence of thuribles in the common visualization of the *Visitatio* scene at this time), and they also serve to identify the mnemonic and devotional function of both plays and pictures. The garments worn by the characters served to join the present with the past, and to make those in attendance at the play experience the sacred time in history when the Incarnation was a present reality—a time when the eternal and the temporal intersected. To the worshipper-playgoer, the past meant an indefinite yesterday. In these dramatic and nondramatic portrayals one rarely distinguished between the local and the foreign. And the medieval burgher lived in a world where spirits mingled with men. Thus the garb of the plays as a concept of scenes was at one and the same time contemporary and timeless, representing the earthly and the eternal, and was hallowed by the special vesture of religious observance.

Bishop Ethelwold instructed that the angel seated at the altar-sepulchre be dressed in an alb (a white tunic), holding a palm branch, while the three Marys wear copes (festive cloaks) and carry thuribles. From the inception of this drama the purpose of the costume was to endow the actor with appropriate qualities, to make the character immediately identifiable to the spectators, and to contribute to the magnificence of the whole spectacle as part of the festive ceremonies.[2]

Visitatio Sepulchri: The Variety and Kinds of Vestments

The costumes worn by participants in the *Visitatio Sepulchri* included at least some of the vestments used in the celebration of the Mass since the performers were members of the clergy in most cases and often also assisted in the Mass, stepping out for a few moments for this *Quem quaeritis* scene.[3] Liturgical vestments of the Church of Rome evolved not from Jewish ritual but rather independently from various items of fine clothing worn by citizens of the Greco-Roman world during the period of the Empire. Thus in the first such services the apparel of the celebrant did not differ essentially from that of the laity, consisting of the *tunica alba,* from which developed the liturgical alb and surplice, the *tunica dalmatica,* which

123

became the liturgical dalmatic and tunicle, and the *paenula,* the ancestor of the chasuble. The *tunica* was a simple, sack-like undergarment with a hole in it for the head, with (tunica manicata, manulaeta) or without sleeves (colobium). Later it was lengthened from the knees to the ankles, and after the fourth century it was made of linen instead of white wool. By the sixth century civil fashions had changed but the church retained this garb. The *dalmatica* formed the outer garment—a long, sleeved tunic. And the large, hanging cloak similar to the Spanish poncho, once the dress of slaves and soldiers, had been adapted as the daily dress of senators with the sumptuary law of 382 A.D.

There are two chief periods in the development of liturgical vestments of the Holy Roman Church: the period up to the ninth century, and from the ninth century through the thirteenth century.[4] It was not, however, until the advent of the Reformation that the dress of the clergy, in and out of official ecclesiastical functions, was finally completely unified, but by the end of the thirteenth century most of the additions to the ninth-century vestments had been made.[5] And after the ninth-century rich embroidery and jeweller's work enhanced the garments, previously distinguished only by the quality of their materials. In the eleventh century the chasuble, which had been worn by all ministers at the Eucharist as well as in processions, became the chief vestment, reserved only for the celebrant. The processional cope and the surplice were also introduced (twelfth century). Since most extant texts of the liturgical drama were set down after the vestments had been established in use, we can be fairly certain about the appearance of the garments mentioned in the stage directions.

A well-documented series of variant costumings for angels—more than twenty in all—incorporates as a whole nearly all of the garments important for the liturgy found in the sacristy. The alb is the basic article of clothing with which we are concerned. This garment was a simple sleeved tunic, made of linen or even wool prior to the expansion of the silk trade along the famous "Silk Road" from Asia and subsequently the development of silk manufacture in the Mediterranean region—manufacture which expanded even to Paris and London in the later Middle Ages. The alb remained without ornamentation until the twelfth century, at which time trade with the East increased considerably and Sicily began to produce silk. However, as Braun points out, in the medieval period the word *alba* was not infrequently applied to vestments ranging from a camise to the liturgical tunic of a deacon, and later it did not always retain its white color. Often our sources mention simply an *alba* as being the

costume of the angel(s) at the sepulchre without any further qualification. In the rubrics of the Senlis text the angels are specifically wearing "albis non paratis." Judging from the body of extant source material, we can assume that the *alba* was white unless otherwise specified, as at Mainz (1547), where the angels have "rubeis albis."[6]

The second most frequently mentioned vestment is the dalmatic—a liturgical outer garment in the form of a tunic with long, wide sleeves, decorated in the early Middle Ages with parallel stripes running from the neck to the border and a pair of such stripes about each sleeve. It was usually made of white silk after the fabric had become available, with the stripes in red, although the stripes were later left off. When worn with the chasuble, it was often the color of the chasuble. The dalmatic is often mentioned alone as the garb of the angels and occasionally along with the alb. Rarely do we find the color specified; for example, it seems that "albis et tunicis candidis" refers to the dalmatic-like tunicle.[7]

The stole, a long (2.5 meters), narrow strip of material, usually silk (also of wool or linen), designated rank. It was worn about the neck with the ends hanging down the length of the front of the dalmatic in the case of bishops and popes. It was also worn over the shoulder, especially by deacons, from the left shoulder across the chest. By the thirteenth century deacons seem to have begun crossing the stole across the breast, and this practice, at first optional, became standard for the priests. It is sometimes part of angelic apparel, worn with the alb or with the alb and dalmatic. More frequently, however, we find "coopertus stola candida" as the only reference to the dress of an angel sitting at the sepulchre—as indeed in Mark's account in the Vulgate the angel is so described (Mark 16:5)—or in other cases "ad caput coopertus stola candida," in which instances the color is specifically given. In Mark it is a "beautiful garment."[8]

We also find references to angels appareled in surplices, *superpellicium,* originally white and worn over fur garments, as the term implies. In the medieval period it reached to the ankles or calves (now to the hips) and had rather extended sleeves, as had early forms of the alb. In the *Visitatio* at Essen two canons "erunt induti dalmaticis albis super superpeliciis suis," and at Augsburg (1449) "induti dalmaticis super superliciis suis" probably means the same thing. Jacques Eveillon, in describing the Angers *Visitatio,* says that the angels were dressed in "superpellicio & cappa candida."[9]

No doubt the surplice was worn underneath the white cope or pluvial (cappa, pluviale), a liturgical

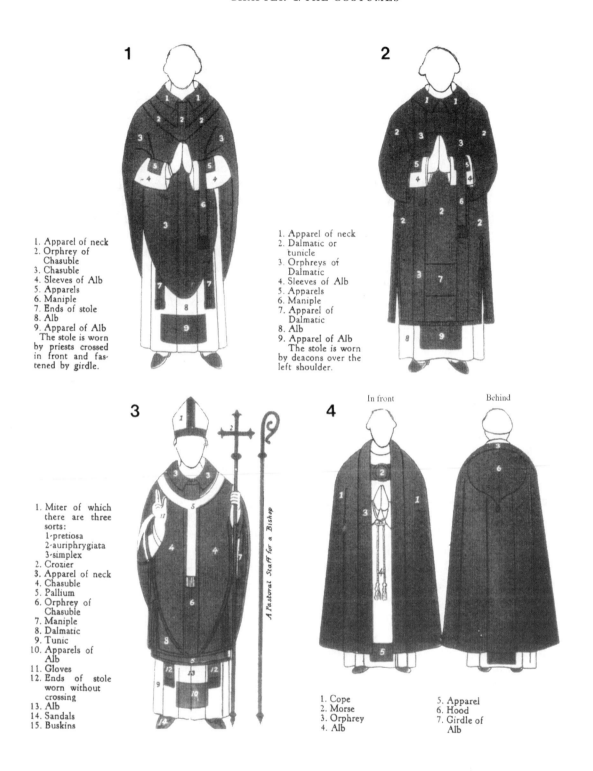

Figure 39. Ecclesiastical Vestments. (1.) Priest Vested for Mass, (2.) Deacon Vested, (3.) Archbishop Vested for Mass, (4.) Priest in Cope.

cloak, usually of silk with rich ornamentation, that reaches to the feet and is closed with a clasp or morse on the chest of the wearer. The cope was the processional garment of priests. Apparently by the twelfth or thirteenth century the hood on the cope was vanish-

ing, and it was just beginning to develop into the shield or decorated flap of the early Renaissance. The fourteenth-century angel of the Mont-St.-Michel *Visitatio* wore simply a "capa alba" and was crowned, while two other angels in the sepulchre were dressed in "capis rubeis." The angels in the Metz *Visitatio* dated 1240 are "cappis et albis induti." But, as we shall note, the cope seems to have been reserved chiefly for the Marys and for the Risen Christ.[10]

In some cases the headdress of the angels is specified, e.g., "stolam habens in capite," though it is clear that this aspect of costuming is much more important in the presentation of the Marys. But several references indicate angels wearing head-covering rather like the Marys'. At Zwiefalten and Rheinau the angels have "dalmaticis, uelatis similiter capitibus," and the Marys have their heads and shoulders wrapped, as have the angels in a Stuttgart manuscript and in an unidentified German monastery. The amice is mentioned neither for the angels nor for the Marys in these four instances. Once we find as angels "pueri induti albis et operti capita." More frequently the amice is specifically noted as the covering for angels' heads, although they are usually without such. "Amictus super capita" or "alba et amictu" and "albis . . . amictus super capita" exemplify the simplest references, but, as we shall note, the amice is called for when the dress of the angels becomes more complicated. In the medieval Western Church this was a rectangular piece of cloth, usually of linen, that could be worn over the head and shoulders as a type of hood (e.g., "amictu capita operti"). Sometimes the amice was decorated with embroidery, but was usually it was simply white and folded down about the neck to form a sort of large collar.[11]

The finest angels in the *Visitatio Sepulchri* are equipped with wings—first mentioned in thirteenth-century texts—and sometimes draped with a stole, but the rubrics do not indicate the actual composition of the wings, usually stating only that they were to be fastened to the shoulders. A stage direction from the Cathedral of Padua reads, "duo scolares ad modum Angelorum, cum alis et liliis" (two scholars in the manner of angels, with wings and lilies), but more often if such elaborate equipment as wings is noted, very ornate dress for the angels is also called for. At Besançon two boys are dressed in "admictis albis paratis, et super humeros alas habentes et stolas rubeas super humeros circumdantes alas in modum quo ponunt diaconi" (in ornate albs and amices, and having wings on their shoulders and red stoles over their shoulders and draped over the wings in the manner that deacons wear them [stoles]). Another version from Besançon has the two boys in "admictis albis paratis, et super humeros alas habentes et capas plicatas rubeas super humeros circumdantes alas in modum quo ponunt diaconi stolas" (in ornate albs and amices, and having

wings on their shoulders and red copes folded over their shoulders and draped over the wings in the manner that deacons wear their stoles). In an unidentified French monastery boys at the right and left of the altar are wearing albs with "rubicundis amictis capitibus et uultibus coopertis" (with red amices covering their heads and faces); and at Soissons two deacons are appareled in "albis simplicibus, capitibus amictis coopertis, niueis dalmaticis superindutj" (in unembroidered albs, their heads covered by amices, dressed in snowy-white dalmatics). The two Besançon texts are especially interesting for their differing descriptions; in both cases boys are dressed in white amices with wings, but whereas the first pair wear red stoles on their shoulders over the wings in the manner of the deacons, the second two wear red copes folded on their shoulders and "surrounding" the wings in the manner in which deacons wear stoles. Braun notes that deacons wore stoles draped from the left shoulder and fastened on the right side, but he does not deal with the possible ambiguity of *stola* as a synonym for either *orarium* or simply meaning "cloak" or "garment." Du Cange recognizes the problem.[12] Nonetheless we can perhaps infer that the red copes in the second instance were folded together, especially if made of silk, and draped from the shoulders of the angels in order that the wings might be visible.[13]

In the latter instances both pairs have their heads covered with amices, as have the Besançon angels, and in the French monastery we find an unusual reference to a red or ruddy amice. The *Visitatio* from Narbonne presents two winged boys wearing albs and amices, specifically clad "cum stolis violatis et sindone rubea in facies eorum." There can be no doubt about the stoles in this instance; and the "sindone rubea" could be either liturgical winding sheets or perhaps more likely simply linen or muslin cloth draped over the head, veiling the face. This is the only mention I have found of such an item.[14]

Perhaps the most resplendent angel, if one may judge from the rubrics, appears at the sepulchre in the Fleury Playbook. He wears an "alba deaurata, mitra tectus caput etsi deinfulatus, palmam in sinistra, ramum candelarum plenum tenens in manu dextera" (a gilded alb, head covered with a miter although without a chasuble, holding a palm in the left hand, a candelabrum full of candles in the right hand). His miter incorporates an aspect of the appearance of a bishop or abbot. The specifying of the properties to be held with each hand in the Fleury play is unusual but not unique. But the mitered angel is singular. Since the text is dated in the twelfth century, it seems reasonable that the angel had a miter of the type that was a dented cap with the peaks at each side; however, by the later part of the century the miter could instead have peaks at the front and back.[15] The term *deinfulatus*, the reading of the first syllable of which Young says is "uncertain," could also in this context refer to bandlike pendants (infula) hanging from the back of the miter. They were introduced about this period. But *infulatus* normally meant "wearing a chasuble" or, metaphorically, "vested in priestly office": "mitra . . . etsi deinfulatus," thus, he is wearing a miter "but without a chasuble," or "not vested in priestly (or episcopal) office."[16]

The chasuble is the vestment of the Mass, *par excellence.* In its early form it was a long, conical cloak, closed on all sides save for an opening for the head of the wearer, but heavy embroidery and brocades made this form impractical, and as of the thirteenth century the "Gothic chasuble" began to become popular, the areas at the arms cut away and the panels in front and back even more highly ornamented.

Most of the angels in the *Visitatio Sepulchri* are not specifically mentioned as having anything in their hands. Palm branches, however, are not infrequent; they also carry tapers or candles or a sword.[17]

As we have noted, the major color of these costumes was white—a traditional angelic color associated with purity (see Matthew 28:3: "et vestimentum eius candidum sicut nix"; also Revelation 6:11 and 7:9)—often supplemented with red stoles or even copes. From about 1200 the official colors of the church in the West had been firmly established, first set down in a treatise by Innocent III, *De sacro altaris mysterio* (cap. 10). The four liturgical colors for the clergy and for the altar mark seasons and prominent feasts and festivals: white, red, green, and violet and black. The major times at which white is used include: festivals of Christ (except the Passion), of the Virgin, the Angels and Confessors, and it is worn during ordinary days, between Easter and Whitsuntide, and in sacramental processions. Red is the dominant color at festivals commemorating the suffering of Christ—the Passion, the Blood, the Elevation of the Cross—and is worn on festivals of the apostles and martyrs. Green dominates on Sundays and weekdays between Epiphany and Septuagesima, the pre-Lent season, and between Trinity and Advent, except at festivals. Violet is worn at Advent, at Lent between Septuagesima and Maundy Thursday, on vigils or fast days, on Candlemas Day, and on days of intercession and in votive Masses. Black, considered along with violet, especially belongs to Masses for the dead, adult funerals, and is worn on Good Friday. The *Visitatio Sepulchri* would then be performed in white, but red would be used as a reminder of Christ's suffering and as the most logical decorative effect. These uses of liturgical color seem to hold true in general, but we also find evidence of local variations.[18]

The approaching Marys are usually dressed in white, but visually they must be sharply distinguished from the angels. Frequently the rubrics simply specify "in [ad] modum Mulierum," or "uestibus muliebribus," or "tenentes figuram Mulierum," or "in similitudinem trium Mariarum." The cope is the costume most frequently mentioned, designated specifically as being white and as "bonis cappis" without regularity, leading us to assume that this was the standard color. However, the cope is seldom mentioned together with the amice, and in one case the Marys are "in superpelliceis et in capis sericis, capitibus uelatis," perhaps indicating that they are to pull up their amices, the scarf-like collars that in this way could serve the function of making them appear more like women. A text from Sion specifies that they are to wear their amices on top of the head: "habet . . . amictum super caput." Thus someone who was to play the role of one of the Marys would first lay the amice on his head, then slip on an alb, and then a cope, finally pulling down the amice and wrapping it around his neck like a collar. However, if the rubric specifies a raised amice, he would have simply left it up over his head somewhat like a hood.[19]

Among the more than eighty *Visitatio* texts edited by Karl Young and Walter Lipphardt which mention the costuming of the Marys, there are several instances where color is introduced in the costume, one of which occurs in a very complete description of the women's garb—the Eveillon text of Angers, in which "duo corbicularii, alba et dalmatica candida ornati, capite amictu circumtecto, sed amictui superinducta mitella purpurea, Mulieres."[20] Not only have they albs, white dalmatics, and amices, but the latter are trimmed with a purple band. At Fleury the two respondents to "Quem queritis" wear "lion copes," albeit they sing the Easter Mass Introit trope and not the *Visitatio.* In the fourteenth-century play of the monastery of Fécamp a red cope is used to distinguish one of the Marys, who also carries a thurible while the others have "uasa in modum pissidarum": "tres fratres in specie Mulierum, quorum unus in capa rubea portet thuribulum inter duos alios, et ceteri duo ex utroque latere eius in dalmaticis candidis." The Mary with the red cope is also distinct because the outside two wear white dalmatics. While the text does not tell us that the central Mary is the Magdalen, the identification seems evident. In the thirteenth-century play at Trier we find "tres domini . . . cum candelis suis et assumptis cappis purpureis"; a fourteenth-century text from the same place shows that the custom persisted. A fifteenth-century text from Urgel states that someone should hand the Marys a "capam rubeam." Rarely do Marys wear chasubles: in a sixteenth-century service book from Meissen the women are dressed in "casulis rubeis"; in a piece from Moosburg they wear "rubeis casulis." Considered against the number of times that we have a note on the costume of the women, these examples of red costuming form only a small percent of the evidence.[21]

The combinations of albs, dalmatics, and amices are almost as numerous as the descriptions of the costumes, the head being covered in nearly all of the instances which do not mention the cope. In almost all texts they carry thuribles and sometimes specifically "thuribula cum incensu." Occasionally we also read of gold or silver vases, or simply vases, or pyxes, or candles or tapers, and less frequently of casks. In the *Visitatio* of Metz each held a thurible in one hand and a palm branch in the other. At Wolfenbüttel we find the only other instance in the *Visitatio* where one of the Marys is singled out by costume or hand property. Here the three visit the tomb dressed in white copes: "prima et secunda cum thuribulo, tercia cum pixide aurea."[22]

Our last examples in this portion of the study involve first a fascinating and singular performance in the nunnery of Barking, near London (1363–76), in which three nuns impersonated the Marys, and a cleric the angel. The abbess, Katherine of Sutton, costumed them herself. The nuns put off their black habits, dressed in "nitidissimis superpellicijs," with "niueis velis," and carried silver vessels.[23] A more curious addition is in the account by the French traveler de Moléon (1651–1731) of the *Visitatio* ceremony at Angers, in which two Marys, each wearing an amice with an embroidered skullcap and gloves, take up ostrich eggs wrapped in silk before they enter the sepulchre. This touch recalls the iconography of the ostrich egg, which hatches in the sand by only the heat of the sun and was thus regarded as symbolic of Christ's Resurrection. An ostrich egg was suspended in certain churches from Good Friday to Easter Sunday.[24]

In the Type II *Visitatio*, which adds the race of Peter and John to the tomb in the *Visitatio*, Peter is sometimes depicted as being the older and slower, even limping. The most detailed description of the apostles' costumes occurs in the fourteenth-century text from the Church of St. John the Evangelist in Dublin. After the Marys have left the sepulchre, two

persons enter "nude pedes, sub personis Apostolorum Iohannis et Petri, indute albis sine paruris cum tunicis, quarum Iohannes amictus tunica alba, palmam in manu gestans, Petrus uero rubea tunica indutus, claues in manu ferens." They are barefoot and are clad in unembroidered albs and tunicles; John is in white, he wears an amice and carries a palm, while Peter is dressed in red and carries the keys, which are his standard symbol.

In a sixteenth-century breviary from Meissen they are both wearing red dalmatics, and Peter is distinguished only by his limp (Petro claudicante). At Moosburg we find Peter and John played by canons wearing a "dalmatica et subtili induti." The "subtile" seems to be the tunicle or "tunica," a garment similar to the dalmatic in form and frequently colored and decorated. It was sometimes worn under the dalmatic, and it served as an outer vestment for deacons and subdeacons. Here the garments seem to distinguish the two disciples, Peter the higher ranking in a dalmatic, and John in a tunicle. Apparently the Dublin costumes also involved this garment, put on over the alb.

In a late fourteenth-century version from Prague two brothers are dressed in copes and are carrying candles. The only mention of the apparel of the two apostles in the Type III *Visitatio* occurs in a play from the monastery of Rheinau, where they are also recorded as wearing copes.[25]

The appearance of Christ to Mary began simply— without an attempt to portray the Risen Lord as a gardener. At Rouen he wore an alb with a stole and carried a cross. He appeared in a St. Gall version at the right corner of the altar dressed in a red chasuble, "rubea casula indutus, ad dextrum cornu altaris habens vexillum in manu"—that is, with the cross staff and banner that had come often to accompany the Risen Christ in iconography. It is this fifteenth-century play that distinguishes Mary Magdalen with a pyx instead of a thurible. At Brixen the Christ figure was dressed all in red: in an alb with red trim and a sash, an amice, a stole, and a cope (ain mantl).

But as soon as Christ appeared "in similitudinem Hortolani," we discover the first costume change in the *Visitatio*. This occurs at Fleury. He does indeed enter "like a gardener." However, the change of costume does not effect a recognition scene, for upon his second line Mary Magdalen recognizes him: "Raboni!" and one line later, "Sic descedat Hortolanus." He leaves. Mary Magdalen then tells the congregation of her meeting with Christ, the angels bid the Marys go and inform the other disciples, and the Marys exhibit the gravecloths. "Interea his [is] qui ante fuit Hortolanus in similitudinem Domini ueniat, dalmaticus [dalmaticatus] candida dalmatica, candida infula infulatus, filacteria preciosa in capite, crucem cum labaro in dextra, textum auro paratum in sinistra habens." He is wearing a white dalmatic and a chasuble of the same color; in his right hand is a cross with a banner (labarum), and in his left hand a (Gospel?) book or cloth decorated with gold.[26] But the "filacteria preciosa" seems to be rare. It could be a cloth or a phylactery. In biblical usage phylacteries were small cases with sacred texts written on them; they were attached to forehead or arm, as a reminder to keep the Law. The phylactery in the play may be different, perhaps an amulet containing relics. At Easter time special attention was devoted to relics. They were often covered on Good Friday and uncovered on Easter morning. In any case, if Christ does have a "costly phylactery," it probably hangs from a head-band or headdress.

Although not so specified in the Fleury play, when Christ is robed in an ornate fashion, he usually has bare feet. For example, in a play from Chiemsee he is dressed in a "dalmatica, casulamque complicatam super humeros habeat, coronamque capiti superimpositam, nudis pedibus incedat." A cross staff with banner is not called for, but wearing a dalmatic he has a soft (or, folded) chasuble over his shoulders and he is crowned.

Also without sumptuous array he is sometimes noted as appearing barefoot. In the fourteenth-century *Visitatio* at Mont-St.-Michel, Christ enters bearing a cross and silently moves across the choir and returns to the vestry just prior to the Marys' entrance. It is a small dumb show, a prelude to the play. *Deus* is wearing an alb "as if dyed in blood" (de alba tincta sicut in sanguine). He is barefoot, with a diadem and a beard. Later in this Type III *Visitatio*, when *Deus* comes to Mary Magdalen, the rubrics indicate no alteration in his appearance.

Another German *Visitatio*, this one from Nottuln (ca. 1500), describes Christ as "stantem discalciatum et pilleatum, fossorium in manu habentem." The spade in his hand clearly suggests the basis for Mary Magdalen's first impression. The two characters' interaction is highly articulated in this play: in addition to the usual action of his calling her back after she has turned away (eam . . . iam revertentem . . . Et conversa Maria recognoscit eum et dicit: "Tibi gloria in secula!"), the play also presents—uniquely, I believe—no fewer than four points at which Jesus retreats from Mary Magdalen (ille secedet paulisper; Rusumque Jhesus recedet; illo fugiente retrorsum, sequatur [Maria] eum; Iterum Ille recedat) suggesting the insistent and repeated urgency of her attempts to touch him.

Finally, in examples of the *Visitatio* at Coutances and Vich the texts call for soldiers at the tomb. The rubrics of the fifteenth-century Coutances play refer to "quatuor clerici armati." Christ appears "in habitu Ortolani" and addresses Mary Magdalen, who does not recognize him. "Tunc ille recedat et satis cito redeat, indutus capa serica vel pallio serico, tenens crucem" (Then he goes away and comes back very quickly, dressed in a silk cope or silk pallium, and holding a cross), at which he says "Maria!" and she replies "Raboni!" In contrast to the Fleury play, the change of costume has effected the recognition in the scene. Perhaps a choice of garment is indicated so that he may be distinguished from the angels, also clad in silk copes.[27]

Ludus Paschalis

In the large-scale *Ludus Paschalis* from Klosterneuburg, thirteenth century, Christ appears to Mary "in specie Ortulani," addresses her twice, and then: "Ihesus in specie Christi: *Maria!*" at which she recognizes him. The same scene is repeated again in the text (ll. 176–82), but we have no indication as to the costume nor does Christ seem to change his apparel anywhere out of sight.[28]

Apparently Christ has three costumes in the thirteenth-century *Ludus Paschalis* from the Tours manuscript, although no garments are mentioned for anyone else; and Christ's appearance in the garden to Mary Magdalen is lost. He approaches his disciples wearing a dalmatic and carrying a cross, and then he comes again to the disciples for the scene with Thomas "indutus sacerdotalibus uestimentis candidis," which probably indicates a chasuble.

In the Klosterneuburg *Ludus Paschalis* an angel is equipped with an "euaginato gladio," and in the *Carmina Burana* of Benediktbeuern we find one of the rare instances in which the two angels are differentiated: "unus ferens ensem flammeum et uestem rubeam, alter uero uestem albam et crucem in manv" (one in a red garment and carrying a flaming sword, the other, however, in a white garment with a cross in his hand). The first angel stabs one of the guards, thunder follows, and the soldiers fall down as if dead.[29]

Peregrinus

Realistic touches and a sense of disguise are found in some of the *Peregrinus* plays. In the twelfth-century text from Sicily the two "clerici" as wayfarers wear copes, while the thirteenth-century *Peregrinus* from Rouen has two clerics dressed in "tunicis et desuper capis" and carrying staffs and wallets (baculos et peras) "in simili-tudinem Peregrinorum."[30] This wallet seems to be the first real addition to costume obtainable from some source other than the sacristy. Christ in the Rouen play, on the other hand, wears an alb with an amice, has bare feet, and carries a cross in his hands—but he does not appear to Mary Magdalen although she is used to exhibit the gravecloths, wearing a dalmatic and amice "et uinc-tus in modum mulieris caput circumligatus."

At Maastricht ca. 1200, Salvator comes along the Emmaus road wearing a coarse or hairy cloak and car-rying a staff (habens cocem hispidum et baculum in manu). The performer has just changed from his dea-con's vestments with amice worn during his preceding appearance to Mary Magdalen. A thirteenth-century *Peregrinus* play in the Cathedral of Padua has the dis-ciples wearing short cloaks and the long woolen cloaks characteristic of pilgrims, and carrying staffs "ad modum Peregrinorum." Christ likewise has the long pilgrim's cloak and staff, and, in addition, a wine flask "ad modum Peregrini." Lipphardt feels that in the thirteenth century the congregation would have rec-ognized them immediately as Compostela pilgrims. A fourteenth-century text from Rouen attests to some interesting additions: besides the copes, staffs, and wallets, the *peregrini* now "habeant capellos super capita, et sint barbati." Christ, barefoot, wears an alb and an amice, but he bears a cross "super dextrum humerum."

However, the two *peregrini* do not recognize the risen Christ according to the Gospel, and therefore in order to make this event more convincing and to in-crease the dramatic irony of their talk about the events of the previous week, he also must be dressed as a trav-eler or pilgrim. This is the case in the most elaborate rubrics from the twelfth-century Fleury Playbook. First come two men "uestiti tunicis solummodo et cappis, capuciis absconsis ad modum clamidis, pilleos in capitibus habentes et baculos." They wear simple tunics and copes, with felt or fur hats, and they are car-rying staffs; apparently the hoods are hidden in the form of the chlamys, a cape associated with the peas-antry. Christ has a similar costume: "pera[m] cum longa palma gestans, bene ad modum Peregrini para-tus, pilleum in capite habens, hacla uestitus et tunica, nudus pedes." In addition he carries a wallet and a palm branch, and has a similar hat; over his tunic he probably wears a chlamys, which would better match his bare feet. According to Dante in *La vita nuova*, one could discern three types of pilgrims: *palmieri*, the Jerusalem pilgrims; *romei*, the Rome pilgrims; and *peregrini*, ones who had journeyed to Santiago de Compostela.[31] The pilgrims bearing the palm branch enjoyed particular distinction, for they had made their pilgrimage to Jerusalem.

After the meal has been shared and Jesus has disap-peared, he appears a second time—to the apostles—and he has a different costume: "colobio candido uesti-tus, cappa rubea superindutus, ob signum Passionis crucem auream in manu gestans, infulatus candida in-fula cum aurifrisia." Now he is wearing a sleeveless, white tunic under a red cope, and a white miter (a *mi-tra auriphygiata*, of brocaded or embroidered silk in gold and studded with tiny pearls), and he is carrying a gold cross—the sign of his Passion and Resurrection. To the disciples Christ shows his hands and feet "minio rubicatos." This is one of the very rare specific require-ments for makeup, in this case to simulate wounds, though no doubt Mary Magdalen uses such coloring when she appears in the *Raising of Lazarus* in the same manuscript, and face painting seems to have been needed for one of the kings in the *Officium Stellae* since he was traditionally an African.[32]

Christ's third appearance will come after the en-trance of Thomas, "uestitus tunica et clamide serico, baculum in manu habens et pilleum aptum in capite." He too is a traveler, dressed in a tunic and chlamys, carrying a staff and wearing a hat. Dominus still has his white "colobium" and red cope, but now "coronam gestans in capite ex amicto et philacteriis compositam, crucem auream cum uexillo in dextra, textum Evvan-gelii habens in sinistra." The crown seems to be made of an amice decorated with phylacteries; in his right hand he carries a cross of gold with a banner and a Gospel-book in his left hand.[33]

The Passion Play

Prior to 1936 it was believed that the only Latin Church plays directly presenting the Passion were produced after the mid-thirteenth century, and that the earliest were from German regions. In 1936, how-ever, Dom Mauro Inguanez published the somewhat fragmentary text of a mid-twelfth-century Latin Pas-sion play (beginning with Judas' bargain and ending with Mary's *planctus*) from Monte Cassino, the home of the founder of Benedictine Monasticism. This early Passion play is remarkable in the detail and realism that its rubrics and dialogues present, for they reveal a very living Christ. At least one other extant Passion play, the fourteenth-century smaller fragment from Sulmona, is clearly dependent on it.[34]

The few examples of the Passion plays all indicate

points at which costume forms an important part of the spectacle. In the Monte Cassino play, Christ is stripped and given a scarlet robe, a reed, and the crown of thorns, then re-dressed in his own garments and then stripped again before being crucified, during which first the soldiers divide his clothes and then one of the priests "standing some distance off" tears his own clothes and the priests inveigh against Christ. The rubrics read: "Milites dividant vestimenta Christi et [dicant]: [V]estes sorte. . . . His dictis sacerdotes . . . [text missing] stans a longe . . . [text missing] et scindat vestimenta sua."[35] In the fourteenth-century Sulmona fragment the casting of lots by the soldiers for Christ's garment is also present, described here as "Et mittentes sortes super uestes primus Milex dicit: *Vestem sorte*" (l. 133). The Sulmona fragment adds that the soldiers dress Jesus in a "ueste alba" before presenting him to Pilate; in the Monte Cassino play he is simply described as "ligatus."

We have noted the costume changes of Christ in his scene with Mary Magdalen in the garden, with especial reference to the recognition effect of his altered appearance. The thirteenth-century Benediktbeuern Passion plays present us with the seed of what was to become one of the big production numbers of the mysteries: the conversion of Mary Magdalen and her consequent putting off of mundane dress, which was to become as rich and outlandish as the directors could dream up. Similarly, the rubrics in the *Raising of Lazarus* in the Fleury Playbook describe her as costumed like a streetwalker: "Maria in habitu per plateam meretricio." In the Benediktbeuern play, Magdalen has been enjoying worldly companions and purchasing cosmetics for herself to enhance her erotic lure. She falls asleep. An angel visits her. And then the rubric reads: "Tunc deponat uestimenta secularia et induat nigrum pallium, et Amator recedat, et Diabolus." She buys ointment and goes to Christ. She has put off her secular garments and has dressed in a black cloak, which frightens off her lover—and even the devil.[36]

The tradition of Jesus' changing to white apparel before being taken from Herod to Pilate is also here in evidence. At line 216 we read: "Tunc Iesus induitur ueste alba, et reducunt Ihesum ad Pilatum" (Then Jesus is dressed in a white garment, and they lead Jesus back to Pilate). What he was originally wearing we do not know. And then, following the Biblical narrative: "Tunc ducitur Ihesus ad flagellandum. Postea Ihesus induatur ueste purpurea et spinea corona" (Then Jesus is led to be whipped. Afterwards, Jesus is dressed in a purple garment and a crown of thorns).

A number of Tyrolean productions of the Passion in the fifteenth and sixteenth centuries belong more to the tradition and practice of outdoor performances, but some of these plays, acted in the vernacular with casts of local townspeople, occurred within the church: texts from Bozen (now Bolzano), 1495 and 1496, refer to the sacristy; Vigil Raber's plan is for the church in Bozen, 1514; financial accounts from Sterzing, 1541 and 1543, cite the church there.[37]

Texts from Bozen note Christ's white garment given him as "ain Narr" by Herod and refer to the purple robe in which he is mocked.[38] When he meets the wayfarers on the road to Emmaus, he is dressed "in vesti mendicy."[39] Most intriguing is the scene with the appearance of Hortulanus to Mary Magdalen. Here the whole concept of mistaken identity has been discarded. After the Harrowing of Hell, Christ takes Joseph to paradise, and "ipse recedit ad sacristiam manens in ornamentis." Then, with Mary Magdalen at the sepulchre near the entrance to the sacristy, out steps a second actor—Raber himself in 1514—who in fact impersonates a gardener, shovel in hand. Mary questions him, he moves back, and Christ emerges for the recognition scene, no doubt still carrying the banner and wearing the diadem given him by one of the angels at the moment of the Resurrection.[40] Financial records from Bozen, 1495, note brown cloth for what is probably Christ's normal garment, cloth for the robe of purple, a pair of gloves, and thongs for the accomplishment of the Crucifixion. A wig was prepared for him in the Ascension play of 1494.

The devils' clothing needed much attention, attested to by numerous expenditures for renewal and repair. In 1514 there are records of masks and the use of a cow's tail; the 1495 accounts list woolen and black garments, gloves, staffs, and possibly forks; in 1496 eight new faces were painted onto the costumes; and in Sterzing, Raber was paid for preparing masks that covered the whole head of the actor.

Angels had wings, one at least gilded, and white shoes. One who was present at the sepulchre used a fiery sword (Cum gladeo igneo).[41] Fleshlings were apparently employed for the souls in hell; in Sterzing these figures also wore masks. Pilate and Herod needed special hats, Caiaphas and Annas "15 innfel," and the caps of the Jews were full of buttons and other odd ornaments (schusl). Judas wore yellow and also probably black, the characteristic colors of much medieval Jewish clothing; a coin sack and a rope, for his suicide, were prepared. Peter carried keys. The Virgin wore a wig and a crown at the Ascension; she had a mask in Sterzing, 1469: "air larffn fur unser liebe fraw."[42] One of Raber's innovations was that of casting women in female roles, but in 1514 the Virgin was still played by a boy. Nowhere else to my knowledge do we hear of her wearing a mask, however.

Raber even saw to it that there was a kind of "dress parade" prior to the undertaking of 1514 so that he could check the costumes, but Wackernell records no use of vestments. Since many of the bills were paid by church provosts (in 1541 "die spil undt teufls claider" were locked up in the Sterzing church) and since no mention is made of alternative clothing for those characters who traditionally wore albs, dalmatics, or copes, we can assume that numerous major costumes came from the sacristy; others were probably supplied from the private wardrobes of the actors.

Annunciation and Ascension

Information on the Florentine productions of the *Annunciation* and *Ascension* reveals most about the angels. The celestial being whom the Bishop of Suzdal saw appear to the Virgin (1439) was dressed in white and gold, held a branch in his hand, and had movable wings which he set in motion as he flew. Those who accompanied Christ's rise to heaven wore golden wings. In paradise they were crowned and carried musical instruments: citterns, flutes, and chime bells. In the former production God the Father was dressed in priestly vestments, wore a crown, and bore a Gospel-book.

The prophets in the *Annunciation* resembled those in pictures, according to the Bishop, with ample beards, ruffled hair, gold haloes, and long, wide, white surplices with girdles; each had a red band (a stole?) running from the right shoulder to the left side. Each carried prophetic writings. The apostles at the Mount of Olives in the *Ascension* were barefoot, also modelled on artistic representations, each individualized, for example, with or without a beard.[43]

Officium Pastorum and Officium Stellae

When we turn our attention to the Christmas season and Epiphany, we are concerned with some other characters or groups of characters: the *Officium Pastorum* yields scanty information as to the shepherds, but the *Officium Stellae* reveals a good deal about the presentation of royalty. In a thirteenth-century *ordo* from the Cathedral of Padua there are no realistic touches in the clothes of the shepherds. They are dressed in copes (cum duobos pluuialibus), as are also the two canons playing the roles of midwives. The Virgin is wrapped in a "nitido pallio." A twelfth-century

text from Montpellier has boys "in uno loco ecclesie baculis se sustentantes in similtudine Pastorum consistant"; and another boy played an angel in an amice and alb. Rouen texts from the fourteenth and fifteenth centuries call for shepherds wearing tunics and amices, as well as midwives played by priests dressed in dalmatics. A thirteenth-century manuscript from Rouen notes only that the *pastores* carry staffs.[44]

Some French and Spanish texts of the *Officium Pastorum* convey more detail, color, and movement. A fourteenth-century text from Pleinpied, an Augustinian monastery near Bourges, describes two shepherds as having capes (capas), belted on the outside, and with their heads hooded. They hold shepherds' staves and sing in turn (unus a dextris et alius a sinistris uultibus in sese inuicem conuersis). After Lauds they advance through the church "playing in the manner of shepherds" (tunc pueri eant per ecclesiam ludentes ad modum pastorum). The shepherds also are described in a sixteenth-century text from Narbonne as wearing capes. A lively Toledo presentation performed at Lauds on Christmas Eve is recorded in Canon (later Archbishop) Felipe Fernández Vallejo's *Disertación V. sobre la música* (1785). In this ceremony, choir boys clothed as shepherds (vestidos de Pastores) advance from the sacristy straight up to the main altar. There, while Mass is being celebrated, the shepherds occupy themselves in dancing and whirling (estan arriba en lo plano mientra se dice esta Misa danzando, y bailando). After Mass certain chanters take two of the shepherd-boys by the hands (asen de las manos) and engage them in a vernacular song based on the traditional antiphon for Lauds. Vallejo notes that the dancing has been forbidden in his own day "por evitar excesos, por considerarla abuso." Another text from Toledo, drawn up by Vallejo's contemporary, the historian Father Enrique Flórez (the text was begun in 1773), describes the same ceremony and adds that the shepherds wore a kind of white hood (capillos de paño blanco), perhaps like that described in the fourteenth-century text from Pleinpied.[45]

An investigation of the *Officium Stellae* proves even more profitable, since from about the sixth century the term Μάγος (Magus) has been interpreted as meaning "king." Because gold, frankincense, and myrrh are mentioned in the Gospel of Matthew as being the gifts they carried, their traditional number has been three. It was the period of the Crusades together with the writings of Bede and St. Bonaventura which brought about another tradition—that one was a Moor—these Magi having become representatives of the far corners of the earth. Here an opportunity for pomp and rich show presented itself, and grew to colossal proportions when towns such as Bourges began producing their outdoor Passion plays.[46]

In a service-book of St. Stephen's at Besançon we find the three kings dressed "amictis, albis, paratis, stolis, et tunicis colore differentibus. Apponuntur etiam humeris cappae, dantur capelli cum coronis, et vnicuique famuli, qui deferant phialas." They wear ornate albs with amices, stoles, and tunicles of different colors. Copes are laid over their shoulders, they are given hoods with crowns, and the servant of each carries a vessel.

Another later description of the Besançon celebration (by Francis Guenard, 1629) shows in what directions it developed:

trois petits garcons à la mode de pages de Perses auec habillements a ce propres, l'un desquelz on doibt noircir par le visage et les mains, qui represente le Roy more, et tous trois tiennent en main vne coupe . . . [les Roys] auec aulbes, Tunicques, et pluuiales toutes de diuerses couleurs auec les ceintures et Chapeaux coronnez a ce propres ayant chascun la palme en main et chascun vn liburet où est noté et escript ce qui doibuent fere et chanter.

(three young boys in the manner of Persian pages with suitable garments, one of whom, because he resembles the king of the Moors, should have his face and hands blackened; and all three, each carries a chalice in his hands . . . [the kings] with albs, tunicles, and pluvials, all of different colors, with the appropriate belts and crowned hats, each carries a palm in his hand and each a script where it is noted and written what they must do and sing.)

The three little boys who were pages to the kings wore Persian costumes; one was to have his face and hands blackened. The kings, in turn, were to dress in albs, tunicles, and copes of different colors with belts and proper crowns. Each carried a palm in one hand and a script in the other. The pages followed. At the end of the performance they retired to the vestry "pour mettre bas leurs habillementz."

At Limoges the Magi wore silk vestments, each having a gold crown on his head "et cyphum deauratum, seu aliud jocale pretiosum in manibus suis." A Rouen text distinguishes quite obviously between the kings and their trains, the former in "cappis et coronis ornati" and "cum suis famulis tunicis et amictis indutis."

When Herod enters into these plays, he immediately begins to dominate the action and even the liturgy. At Padua, Herod and his chaplain come out in a fury. He carries a wooden spear, which he hurls at the chorus; and they "sunt induti uilissimis strictis et infulis." They seem to be wearing the cheapest tunicles and chasubles. In the Fleury Playbook version of the drama, only Herod's messengers, "in habitu iuuenili," and scribes, "in diuersorio parati sunt barbati," are described, not Herod.[47]

Ordo Prophetarum

Because each of the large number of speakers in the Ordo Prophetarum had little action and only a brief appearance, it was of utmost importance that on sight he be immediately distinguishable from the other prophets. Biblical record and church custom suggested the necessary attributes of person, habit, and hand properties. Texts from two churches preserve full information: the thirteenth-century version of the Ordo Prophetarum from the Cathedral of Laon contains a list of the prophets at the beginning of the play; a fourteenth- or fifteenth-century manuscript from the Cathedral of Rouen—the so-called Festum Asinorum—has appropriate indications of costume accompanying each individual as he begins his lines.[48]

The order of speaking is as follows:

Laon:	Rouen:
	Moyses
	Amos
Ysaias	Ysaias
	Aaron
Iheremias	Iheremias
Daniel	Daniel
Moyses	Abacuc
	Balaam
	Samuel
Dauid	Dauid
Abacuc	Osee
	Iohel
	Abdias
	Ionas
	Micheas
	Naum
	Sophonias
	Aggeus
	Zacharias
	Ezechiel
	Malachias
	Zacharias
Elisabeth	Elyzabeth
Iohannes Baptista	Sanctus Iohannes Baptista
	Symeon
Virgilius	Virgilius
Nabugodonosor	Nabugodonosor
Sibilla	Sibilla
Symeon	
Balaam	

The Rouen version includes fifteen more speakers, but the order of the appearances remains essentially the same. In each of the ensuing comparisons the Laon figure is given first.

Isaiah. *Laon:* "barbatus, dalmatica indutus, stola rubea per medium uerticis ante et retro dependens." *Rouen:* "barbatus, alba indutus, per mediam frontem rubea stola discrinitus." The Laon version has the prophet with a beard and wearing a dalmatic with a red stole across his head, hanging down in the front and back. At Rouen he is without long hair and wears a red stole across his forehead.

Jeremiah. *Laon:* "similiter, absque stola." *Rouen:* "sacerdotali habitu ornatus et barbatus tenens rotulum." The Laon play does not mention the scroll.

Daniel. *Laon:* "adolescens, ueste splendida indutus." *Rouen:* "indutus uiridi tunica, iuuenilem uultum habens, tenens spicam." "Youth" is defined at Rouen in terms of a green tunicle, which color has not appeared before, and he is holding an ear or spike of grain. It is interesting to note that fourteenth- and fifteenth-century texts of the *Visitatio* from Rouen mention the angel before the sepulchre "et tenens spicam in manu."[49]

Moses. *Laon:* "cum dalmatica, barbatus, tabulas legis ferens." *Rouen:* "tenens tabulas legis apertas, indutus alba et cappa, et cornuta facie, barbatus, tenens uirgam in manu." At Rouen he is also bearded, carries the Tables of the Law, and instead of a dalmatic he wears an alb and a cope. He carries a rod, and the rubric uses the same expression as the Vulgate (Exodus 34:29–30): "cornuta facie," which has been traditionally accepted as "having horns," as well as a radiant countenance. The Hebrew words seem to be ambiguous, and modern scholarship has accepted this as meaning "beams." However, here he has some sort of horns.[50]

David. *Laon:* "regio habitu." *Rouen:* "ornatus regalibus ornamentis." This implies at least a crown and probably a cope.

Habakkuk. *Laon:* "barbatus, curuus, gibosus." *Rouen:* "senex claudus, dalmatica indutus, habens in peram radices, et longas palmas habens unde gentes per/cuciat [sic], comedens." He is bearded, bent, and hunchbacked at Laon; the Rouen text only says that he is old and lame, dressed in a dalmatic, but equipped with a bag of roots and long palm branches that he uses to hit people, and he is eating.

Elizabeth. *Laon:* "femineo habitu, pregnans." *Rouen:* "In persona alba, quasi pregnans." The Rouen text glosses feminine attire with "alb," and in both instances she is visibly pregnant—carrying the child who was to be John the Baptist. I assume that this was effected simply with a pillow.

John the Baptist. *Laon:* "pilosa ueste et longis capillis, barbatus, palmam tenens." *Rouen:* "nudus pedes, tenens textum." The Laon text has him wearing a hairshirt and with long hair and a beard, holding a palm leaf. The Rouen text specifies only that he is barefoot and carries a book.

Virgil. *Laon:* "cum cornu et calamo, edera coronatus, scriptorium tenens." *Rouen:* "in iuuenili habitu bene ornatus." In both texts he is addressed as "Maro." Here we find the introduction of a figure from outside either of the Testaments. On account of his authorship of the Fourth Eclogue, the Roman poet Virgil was regarded as a prophet who foretold the coming of Christ. The Laon text has him crowned with ivy and carrying an ink horn and a reed-pen—and writing board or material. Rouen depicts him only as being dressed as a young man.

Nabuchadnezzar. *Laon:* "regio habitu, superbo incessu." *Rouen:* "quasi rex paratus." Garbed as a king in both cases, as is David, his walk is haughty at Laon.

Sibyl. *Laon:* "ueste feminea, decapillata, edera coronata, insanienti simillima." *Rouen:* "coronata et muliebri habitu ornata." In both instances she is dressed as a woman, but it is perhaps significant that she is specifically without hair in the Laon text. At Rouen she is crowned, but in Laon the crown is expressly of ivy—and she has an insane expression. Perhaps makeup was used. Spanish texts present special evidence for Sibyl costumes, for from locations across medieval Spain comes a drama or semidrama specifically devoted to her prophetic declarations. The eighteenth-century canon Felipe Fernández Vallejo, who claims that the drama is "una ceremonia antiquissima, y venerable, que en lo substancial no ha padecido alteración," describes the Sibyl as dressed "á la Oriental," representing either the Sibyl Herophila or Eritrea. Vallejo's study includes a drawing which shows a woman in a richly embroidered dress, wearing a peaked coronet, necklace, pendant, and perhaps earrings; in her hands she holds a scroll with the words and music of her prophecy.[51] This was the final prophet in the Rouen *Ordo.*

Simeon. *Laon:* "barbatus, capa serica in/dutus [sic], palmam tenens." *Rouen:* "senex." At Laon he wore a silk cope.

Balaam. *Laon:* "super asinam, curuus, barbatus, palmam tenens, calcaribus urgens." "Hic ueniat Angelus cum gladio." *Rouen:* "ornatus sedens super Asinam, habens calcaria retineat lora et calcaribus percuciat Asinam. Et quidam iuuenis habens alas, tenens gladium, obstet Asine." Apparently a crooked or bent figure, as was also the case with Habakkuk, incited humor, and this little scene with the ass is saved until the end of the Laon *Ordo.* As to be expected, the scene is enlarged in the *Festum Asinorum,* and once Habakkuk has been introduced, Balaam follows immediately. In both cases he uses his spurs, and at Rouen he has a whip as well. The angel is also equipped with wings. We have no specific information as to the ass, but one line in the *Festum* is interesting: "Quidam sub Asina dicat," and in Laon, "Puer sub Asina respondet." Whether the speaker was tied "underneath" a live donkey or whether this is a costume we cannot judge.

Of the figures mentioned only in the Rouen *Festum Asinorum,* Aaron is especially noteworthy: "ornatus pontificalibus indumentis et mitra, barbatus, tenens florem." Pontifically robed, which would include at least a chasuble, he is also specifically mentioned as wearing a miter and as carrying the rod that has bloomed. The Jewish high priest appeared in the outdoor productions consistently as a bishop.

Otherwise at Rouen, Amos carries an ear or spike of grain; and Jonas is bald.

In general there seems to have been a prophetic look, a hint of the ancient, with a particular prophet made distinguishable by his particular props, makeup, and items of apparel. This standard garb to which pieces were added is attested to in a manuscript from the Cathedral of Padua. There at the Feast of the Purification we read of four priests "in modum Prophetarum" at the Temple at the circumcision of Christ. The four priests appear in a New Testament event, but they must have the feel of Old Testament prophets.

Singular New Testament Characterizations Through Costume

However, in contrast to this prophetic type, the same Purification play assigns distinctive personality to Joseph, the husband of Mary, by means of a prop. Joseph "asociate calato portanti super humerum"—he carries a basket on his shoulders. In the basket he may be transporting doves, as occasionally depicted in the visual arts, but the rubrics do not give us any further information.

Another important mention of Joseph's appearance

is found among the *Carmina Burana* of Benediktbeuern. There he is "in habitu honesto et prolixa barba." He is dressed in a dignified manner, but his beard might also indicate the early stages of what later could become a somewhat comic figure.

Of other plays based on New Testament material, besides the Nativity and Resurrection, *The Raising of Lazarus* in the playbook of Fleury contains a description of Mary Magdalen's costume before (or rather at the time of) her conversion: "Maria in habitu per plateam meretricio." She is a prostitute.[52] No doubt a costume change of some sort marked her subsequent appearance with Lazarus and Martha. As we have seen, a costume change can signal an alteration in both the external and the internal condition of the character. That is manifestly the case with Mary Magdalen in the *Carmina Burana,* where she sheds her mundane clothing and dresses in black.

Old Testament Plays

Of the dramatic pieces based on Old Testament material, three are of interest here: *Isaac and Rebecca, Joseph and His Brothers,* and the dramatization of the story of Daniel. The rubrics in these cases provide a special perspective on the liturgical drama because they present a very different setting from the later vernacular drama and demonstrate that we have here two entirely distinct genres.

In the twelfth-century fragment from Vorau we find a description of items necessary for the kitchen in the Isaac story and of properties for the deception of the old father: "Tece manuum pilose. Pellis, que tegat collum, pilosa." In addition, the clothing is specified: "Pillea Iudaica Ysaac et filiis, et coloribus uariata; . . . Vestes prout decentiores prouideantur. Arcus cum pharetris." There must be hair to cover the hands of Jacob, hairy skins to cover his neck; also Jewish caps (or hats) for Isaac and his sons, in various colors. Appropriate clothes are to be provided, and a bow, quiver, and eventually arrows. As for these caps, it is difficult to be more specific about their appearance, but the deception of Isaac, who is rather blind, is carried off with much shrewdness (following 1. 120): "Interim, dum mater protegit manus et collum Iacob pellibus pilosis [et ues]tibus optimis domi Esau relictis aromatizantibus uestit eum" (In the meanwhile, his mother covers the hands and neck of Jacob with hairy skins, and she puts on him Esau's best clothes, that were in the house, and his fragrances that were there). The bow and arrows are for Esau the hunter.

Joseph's coat becomes important in the thirteenth-century play from Laon concerning him and his brothers. Interestingly enough, Jacob gives Joseph only a staff when sending him out to his brothers, who promptly put him in a pit (cisternam), planning to dip his garment in blood. Joseph is sold to merchants and we read: "Hismaelite Ioseph splendida ueste indutum ducunt." As he is led into Egypt he is still dressed in a fine garment. No mention is made of the tunic until the brothers see a traveler: "Dant illi tunicam Ioseph." They give it to him. The man brings the garment to Jacob, the father, who recognizes it (Tunicam agnoscens), and believes that a wild beast has killed Joseph. In Egypt the captive Joseph, now risen in rank, rejects the illicit approaches of Potiphar's wife: "Ioseph non concedit consilio, quo uolente discedere, illa clamidem rapit. Ioseph dimisit et fugit." She then goes to her husband "clamidem secum ferens," and complains that Joseph has attacked her—holding out the chlamys, or cloak. And consequently, "Ioseph in carcerem uadit," Joseph ends up in prison. Obviously the rubrics contain some dramatic flaws as to the apparel of the young man, depicting him as departing quite well dressed. However, since he probably does not disappear from view, no costume change is possible—at least we infer this from the rubrics—so that at the beginning he must have the cloak which Potiphar's wife grasps.

The play of *Daniel* by Hilarius contains little information about costumes. Baltasar enters "cum ponpa sua" wearing a crown, and Daniel is clad "pulcherrimis indumentis." We have no indication as to how the lions were brought on stage or how they "devoured" Daniel's accusers. Perhaps they were played by persons wearing skins and masks of some sort, if they were made to appear at all. The Beauvais text of *Daniel* adds nothing on the subject. The king has Daniel garbed in "ornamentis regalibus" and, as in the work by Hilarius, the angel who closes the mouths of the lions carries a sword. But the accusers are properly consumed by the beasts. Young prints a description of a costume from an inventory of the treasury of Beauvais (1464) which Desjardins infers may have been used in the play of Daniel: "*Item* ung tissu noir de soye à usage de homme ferré tout autour d'argent lequel avoir [sic] au bout une petite chaenne laquelle estoit d'argent" (Item, a black silk cloth for a man, with a silver border all around it and a little silver chain at the top).[53] However, no internal evidence supports the assertion.

Festum Praesentationis Beatae Mariae Virginis

The final celebration within the church which we shall discuss here is a costume show: Mézières' *Presentation of the Blessed Virgin Mary in the Temple* (1372). In the text of the *repraesentatio figurata* we have a description of the apparel of twenty-two people, given for the most part with meticulous attention to detail.[54]

Mary, three or four years old,

shall have a pure white tunic of sendal, without any unnecessary decoration, with a narrow hem [plicatura] encircling the lower edge of the tunic. The tunic should be loose [lata] everywhere except in the sleeves, which should be tight [adiacentes], and she should not wear a belt around the tunic. Next she should put on a cloak, also very white, of sendal or of silk muslin, open in front the whole length of her body, with a little cord of gold embroidery [cordula de frizello aureo] for fastening the cloak over the breast in the manner of a bridal mantle. Around the collar of the tunic and all along the opening of the cloak should be sewn a narrow gold embroidered border [paruus frizellus aureus], and around the lower edge of the cloak there should also be a hem, visible on the outside of the cloak. Mary's head should be bare, and her hair should fall back over her shoulders. She should also wear on the top of her head a circlet of gold decorated with silver, about the width of a finger, along with a diadem of moderate width, decorated with silver gilt, carefully fastened around the back of her head. Such will be the ornamentation for Mary's head. She should not wear rings or a girdle or anything else unless of white and gold, demonstrating the purity and virginity of Mary and the brightness of her charity.

Two young girls accompany her. One "will be dressed in green silk or sendal, figuring Mary's humility, and the other in a blue or azure color [celestine], symbolizing Mary's faith and hope. . . . These two young girls will not wear a cloak as Mary does, but they should wear the loose tunics with a hem around the lower edge described above. They also should not have any ornamentation on their tunics. On their bare heads they should wear circlets of silver, as described above, but not the diadems at the back. And their hair should hang down behind as was specified above concerning Mary."

As for Joachim, Mary's father, he will be dressed in a priest's alb [induetur alba sacerdotis], tied at the top like a priest's, with a stole around his neck extending across his chest in the form of a cross, as does a priest's. Over this he should wear an old-style *pluvialis* without an opening [non fracto, i.e., a pluvial that does not open in the front]. On his head he should wear a delicate and rather long, and, if such can be found, rather elaborate, piece of cloth [aliqualiter laboratum], with which he should wrap his head and neck [i.e., probably a type of hood that one laid across the shoulders when not pulled up]. The two ends of the hood-cloth, about the length of two palms or a little more [seven or eight inches], should be thrown over his shoulders, right and left, over the *pluvialis.* In front he should wear a long, thick white beard hanging down over his chest, and he should carry in his hand, outside the *pluvialis,* a medium-sized glass cup filled with red wine [vnum vas mediocre vitreum plenum vino rubeo].

Anna, the mother, "should be dressed in white linen, covering both her body and her head, in the manner of an honest matron of antiquity, and she should carry in her hand a round loaf of bread [in manu vnum pannum], as white as possible and rather large."

The two angels, Gabriel and Raphael, should be dressed in albs with amices [cum amictibus albis], a cincture at the top, with stoles around the neck and crossed in front of the chest. On their heads, they should wear birettas fastened around the head above the ear [barretas adiacentes in capite super aures]. Around the head and on the top these should have the form of not very wide triangles or quadrangles, and should have two flaps [fanis] behind like a bishop's miter. These birettas should be made out of white sendal or silk cloth, or out of papyrus or parchment, and should have little embroidered borders with a design sewn around them, and pictures of flowers scattered over them [cum quodam frizello in circulo barreti de pictura aliqua et floribus seminatis picture super barretam]. As well, whoever might like to could place behind the birettas little fringes of varicolored silk. The two angels should also have on two wings each, and they should each carry in the right hand a red staff.

The nine angels should be dressed like Gabriel and Raphael, except that the three who represent the highest orders of angels, the cherubim and so forth, will wear birettas colored red, as described above, while the three of the second rank should have birettas of a blue or azure color, and the three of the third rank of angels, white birettas. All nine orders should carry lilies on delicate green-colored staves [super quandam virgam subtilem viridis coloris], with the lilies of the first orders, gold, those of the second

orders colored azure [celestine], and of the third, silver.

Ecclesia will be played by some attractive young man of about twenty without a beard, and will be dressed in a deacon's habit, entirely of gold, with the hair of a most beautiful woman hanging down over the shoulders.[55] On her head she will wear some sort of golden crown set with lilies and precious stones. Attached with a small cord in front of her chest will be a silver and gold chalice without any paten, which chalice signifies the New Testament. In the left hand she will carry a long cross, as wide as her body; and the top of this cross should be a red staff highly polished for its whole width [et capitis cuius crucis virga rubea erit latitudine pollicis magni], while the whole cross should be gilded and without any ornamentation. In the right hand she will carry a round ball, entirely gilded, signifying the universal dominion of the Church.

Synagoga will be dressed in the style of an old woman of antiquity with a worn-out tunic reaching to the ankles made of some kind of plain-colored cloth [cum tunica talari inueterata alicuius panni simplicis coloris], and a torn, black mantle. Her head, in the style of an old woman, should be covered with a veil of a dark color, and she should wear a black veil in front of her face and eyes, though she should be able to see through it. And in her left hand she should carry a reddish banner whose black staff appears to be broken [cuius hasta nigra fracta apparebit], with the banner draped over her shoulder. On this red banner there should be written in letters of gold, "S.P.Q.R.," which are the arms of the Romans. And in her right hand she should carry two stone tablets inclined towards the earth, on which tablets should be engraved letters looking like Hebrew letters, signifying the law of Moses and the Old Testament.

The two youths who will play the sweet [soft, indoor] instruments will be dressed like the angels, except that they will not wear stoles or wings, but definitely will wear birettas of a green color.

The Archangel Michael will be armed with splendid armor from his feet to his head, and above his helmet or basinet or visor he will wear some sort of gilded crown as the sign of victorious soldiers and as a sign of Christ triumphant. Also, in his right hand Michael will hold a naked sword, shining and held up towards heaven; and in his left hand he will hold an iron chain, on which Lucifer, tied at the neck will follow behind Michael.

Lucifer will be decked out with those ornaments which themselves befit what is most shameful and abominable [turpissimo et abhominabili], with horrible horns, teeth, and face. And in his right hand Lucifer will hold some kind of trundling hook or barbed hook of iron carried over the shoulder; and with his left hand he will hold the chain, as if trying to rebel against Michael.

In the production of 1385 at Avignon the priest who received Mary was dressed in Jewish garb: "induto habitu summorum pontificum Iudeorum."[56]

Mézières even describes the arrangements for a dressing room—a chamber "large enough to be used as a dressing room or place of preparation for the cast of the representation." He suggests that it might be the chapter house of the brothers, "closed off temporarily by curtains [borrowed] from some house near the church suitable for the purpose." In the procession the two young girls carry candles, the colors of which match their tunics. So too Mary carries a white candle in her right hand, and in her left hand "a pure white dove at her left breast."

Sources of Garments

The above survey of vestments and other costumes will raise questions about the sources of these spectacular garments, which not only provided brilliant effects for the liturgical drama and to related ceremonies but were also regularly worn in the worship services of the Church from day to day and week to week. The sources of these vestments are often shrouded in a certain amount of mystery. We know that the fifteenth-century cope that is extant at Vadstena joined the workmanship of Flemish embroiderers with that of local artists at the Brigittine house, and a supply of vestments at Vadstena includes chasubles and other vestments that came from as far away as Italy. Elsewhere, the most valued vestments seem to have been those embroidered in England and termed *opus anglicanum*, regarded as the finest in Europe. An inventory of 1295 from the Vatican treasury, for example, lists 113 embroideries designated as *opus anglicanum*.[57]

While nuns were often famous for their needlework and also for their appreciation of embroidered vestments—for example, the Syon Cope now in the Victoria and Albert Museum was one of those acquired by Syon Abbey, the Brigittine house established by Henry V—much work was clearly done in secular workshops.[58] Property records in London indicate that at one time there were a half dozen or so workshops where "borderers" supplied Church, Crown, and nobility. Marc Fitch has suggested that the number of secular workers in London in the late thirteenth century, men and women, "might be estimated as between 70 and 80."[59]

In France it was not until 1471 that the embroiderers of Paris formed a guild, but as early as 1292–1303 the Provost of Paris approved an extensive set of regulations for them, the earliest regulation of any embroiderers in Europe. Included is a list of approximately two hundred masters and mistresses. Regulations were strict and included prohibitions against working at night, and no one was permitted to use gold costing less than eight sols per rod. Sewing was to be done with silk. Silk thread and fabric, for example, were produced by "silk women," who are on record as receiving raw materials from Italy in the fourteenth century.[60]

The designs used by the embroiderers seem usually to have been based on cartoons produced by other artists, whose drawings served as guides to the elaborate iconography demanded by the patrons of their art. Fortunately, an artist's manual survives which gives detailed instructions to those who supplied embroiderers with such designs. This is Cennino Cennini's *Il libro dell'arte*, which lays out procedures such as spanning "cloth or fine silk on stretchers." The first step is to draw on the taut cloth with charcoal, then to "take a sponge, . . . [and] rub the cloth with it, on the reverse, where it has not been drawn on; and go on working the sponge until the cloth is damp as far as the figure extends." Now the artist will take a small brush with which to ink in the design; the object is "to shade with it in the darkest places, coming back and softening gradually." Cennini judged this method to be highly satisfactory: "You will find that there will not be any cloth so coarse but that, by this method, you will get your shadows so soft that it will seem to you miraculous."[61]

The intricacy of the designs and the colors of the vestments must indeed have made the liturgical dramas and other ceremonies seem miraculous to those who witnessed them in the cathedrals, churches, and monasteries of medieval Europe. It is also worth remarking that in many cases the participants in the liturgical drama would have had the same scenes embroidered on their vestments as they were presenting in their plays.

Summary

Costume created much of the spectacle. It also served as an important means of character identification, becoming increasingly realistic within certain conventions. And it began to function not only as a decorative element but as a genuine part of the dramatic action.

From the outset the appearance of the characters in the earliest performances at the high altar did not vary in kind from that of the other clergy participating in the worship service: all wore vestments. Robing in the garb of the church endowed the wearer with a peculiar aura of sanctity. It associated him with the other-worldly miracle of the Mass, placed him in the course of long-evolved tradition, gave him a visual aspect of the ancient, and identified him within priestly hierarchy. These silks and linens—gilded, dyed, richly embroidered—made for a brilliant hieratic pageant. The snow-white alb or dalmatic of celestial beings became so traditional that rubrics often call merely for a figure apparelled "as an angel." The copes of the Marys suggest ornate processional, while the chasuble of the Risen Christ imbues him with the high mystery and holiness of the fulfilled Resurrection, reenacted daily at the Eucharist by a wearer of a chasuble. It was impossible to achieve a solely decorative effect by putting on a vestment.

With a dramatic action came immediately the need to single out the participating personages through physical attributes, a means of instant characterization already at hand in the sacristy. To the selected vestments were added individualistic touches: the Marys raised their amices so as more nearly to resemble women, one of them dressed in red instead of white, the angel bore a taper or palm branch and later had wings, Peter and John ran barefoot to the tomb, the Magi wore crowns—all otherwise in vestments.

Certain aspects of costuming became more realistic, many deriving from contemporary, secular habit, as an increasing sense of verisimilitude infused the performances. The *peregrini* were to drape the cope in a particular manner as a chlamys; they were given wallets, staffs and the typical hats of pilgrims, and at Rouen the later texts call for beards. Most striking are the characteristics of the prophets in the *Ordo Prophetarum* of the fourteenth and fifteenth centuries. The basic apparel is from the vestry, but Elizabeth simulates pregnancy, Daniel carries an ear of grain, Virgil has writing materials, and Habakkuk with a bag of roots is old, bent, and bearded. Many subsidiary characters, such as soldiers and merchants, about whose appearance we are rarely informed, seem to have had no vestments. Such early, less traditional works as the Vorau *Isaac* and the Tegernsee *Antichrist* (both twelfth century) are peopled for the most part with those in contemporary, medieval clothing; Isaac and his sons, for example, wear variously colored Jewish caps.

Often imaginative features were designed for personifications, demons, and animals. The allegorical figures of Synagoga and Ecclesia first appear on the stage in the *Antichrist*, but it is Mézières who describes them (1372): Ecclesia in a gold costume of a deacon (probably an alb or dalmatic), crowned, and carrying a cross and an orb; Synagoga as an old woman in a shabby tunic and black mantle, a veil over her face, with a broken banner and tablets representing the Law of Moses and the Old Testament. From the very beginnings, however, as the vestments brought with them a multiplicity of symbolic overtones, so also did the thuribles of the Marys, for example—hallowed vessels of church ritual and at the same time specific properties in the dramatized story. It was just as natural to give Peter his traditional keys, Jeremiah a scroll, and Resurrectus a gilded Gospel-book as it was to have Peter limp, Jeremiah wear a beard, and Resurrectus display his wounds.

Devils ran about the area outside in front of the church in the twelfth-century *Jeu d'Adam*, a devil appears to Pilate's wife to implant a dream in the twelfth-century Monte Cassino Passion, and they drag Herod off to hell at Benediktbeuern (thirteenth century), but their roles in the sanctuary were rare. One such creature is called for by Mézières, with horns and fangs and what is perhaps the earliest record of a mask used inside the church. However, Tyrolean documents of the fifteenth and sixteenth centuries are full of masks, especially for devils, and we even hear of a facial covering for the Virgin Mary (probably acted by a boy or young man, 1469). Both Daniel plays of the twelfth century require some representation of lions; these may well have been appropriately costumed actors, as no doubt was the case with Balaam's speaking donkey.

In general there are three kinds of theatrical costumes within the church—the sacred, the secular, and those special creations for abstract figures, devils, and animals—which categories also remain valid for the outdoor productions. The sacred are distinguished by vestments and the secular by local habit of the Middle Ages, but it is, of course, as impossible to draw these lines firmly as it is to separate the symbolic from the so-called historical. The Magi wore vestments; some of the prophets did not. This constellation of characters and their apparel vividly illustrates that same immediacy of the human and the divine found in the pictorial arts of the Middle Ages, where men and angels commune in the continuing present.

Two of the earliest examples of costume change demonstrate a dynamic function of costume in a dramatic action: disguise for nefarious purpose. The character of Antichrist enters the scene with a breastplate concealed beneath his outer cloak, which he then casts aside as he reveals his intent to conquer the king of Jerusalem. Subjugated monarchs offer him their crowns, and he returns the crowns—acts of submission and domination. In the Vorau *Isaac,* Jacob impersonates his brother in order to obtain their father's blessing by clothing himself in Esau's garments and covering his hands and neck with hairy pelts. Related to this use of disguise is the staging of Christ's temptations in Raber's *Vorspiel* at Bozen, 1514, where "Sathanas" first disappears into hell in order in some way to alter his appearance (mutat habitum); he then addresses Christ as "Lieber prueder," indicating perhaps a more human garment such as that of a traveler.[62]

In the thirteenth century Christ is sometimes actually given the apparel of Hortulanus in his appearance at the tomb to Mary Magdalen, the latter mistaking him at first for a gardener. This tendency toward verisimilitude in turn led to a costume change, and at Klosterneuburg and Coutances the new visual impression of Resurrectus accompanied and effected the recognition.

The same sense of disguise is inherent, for example, in the *Peregrinus* of the Fleury Playbook, where Christ is dressed like the two pilgrims, thus making more believable their failure to recognize him. But here costume change is also employed to heighten by degrees the radiant magnificence of the Risen Lord during the progress of the play: at first he is a wayfarer; then later with other disciples in Jerusalem he wears a white miter and a red cope over a white tunic; and before Thomas, at the conclusion, he is crowned. Also in the *Ludus Paschalis* from the Tours manuscript he seems to appear as a gardener, then in a dalmatic, and finally in a chasuble, but at Bozen and Sterzing the notion of mistaken identify was removed, for a second actor emerged from the sacristy, playing not even Christ disguised but in fact a gardener.

Finally, the change of apparel can indicate a modification of a character's exterior or interior condition.

Most interesting is the example of Mary Magdalen in the *Carmina Burana* of Benediktbeuern, where she puts off her worldly clothing and dresses in black. In the Fleury Playbook she comes at first as a prostitute in the Lazarus play and then probably makes alterations in her appearance for the subsequent scenes.

Almost all of the major innovations and experiments with the physical appearance of characters in the church had occurred by the end of the thirteenth century. Again one is struck by the frequency with which the first documentation of a particular theatrical phenomenon does not derive from the *Visitatio Sepulchri.* Once the *Visitatio* had come into being, it remained close to its ceremonial roots whereas other, later liturgical dramas diverged more from liturgy and employed more theatrical costuming and acting. We also sense from the source materials as of the late twelfth century a growing tendency toward emphasis on decoration for its own sake, as in the Fleury Playbook, where the most elaborate angel sits at the sepulchre and where the magnificence of Resurrectus is displayed through increasingly ornate costumes. Brunelleschi and his imitators created shows in fifteenth-century Florence that left little to the imagination as to the appearance of paradise, filled with hosts of white and gold angels; the celestial being who came to Mary not only had wings, but he flapped them as he flew. Mézières' *Presentation* is one great costume display. And the entourages of the Magi swell in pomp, as at Besançon, while even the *Visitatio* is decked out in more color and light. The later influence, to a degree the competition of performances in the city square made itself felt within the church, particularly in the fifteenth and sixteenth centuries, and fostered greater ornament in the sanctuary.

These traditions and varieties of theatrical costume established within the church obtained as well in the outdoor religious drama, and, in fact, the sacristy remained a major source of supply for clothing the actors.

Chapter 5

Acting

Introduction: Performers of Ceremonies

When in the tenth century members of the clergy began to act out the *Visitatio Sepulchri,* they employed the vocal and physical means long practiced in the celebration of ecclesiastical rites. In fact, the emergence of drama occurred in a period of extreme emphasis on the interpretation of the Mass as a symbolic enactment of episodes in the Gospels, associating the celebrant with Christ. In the ninth century Amalarius of Metz, one of the leaders and chief spokesmen in this movement, prefaced his *De ecclesiasticis officiis* with the following statement:

> Sacraments should have likeness to the things for which they are sacraments. Therefore the priest should be like Christ, just as the bread, wine, and water are similar to the body of Christ. Thus the sacrifice of the priest on the altar is in a way like the sacrifice of Christ on the cross.[1]

Writing about the year 1100, Honorius of Autun (Augsburg?) in his *Gemma animae* went even further, under the probable influence of Aristotle, declaring the Mass a dramatic form and the celebrant an impersonator of Christ in the use of voice and gesture:

> It is known that those who recited tragedies in theatres presented the actions of opponents by gestures before the people. In the same way our tragic author [i.e., the celebrant] represents by his gestures in the theatre of the Church before the Christian people the struggle of Christ and teaches to them the victory of His redemption. Thus when the celebrant [presbyter] says the *Orate* [*fratres*] he expresses Christ placed for us in agony, when he commanded His apostles to pray. By the silence of the *Secreta* he expresses Christ as a lamb without voice being led to the sacrifice. By the extension of his hands he represents the extension of Christ on the Cross. By the chant of

the Preface he expresses the cry of Christ hanging from the Cross. . . . By the *Pax* and its communication [i.e., the "Kiss of Peace"] he represents the peace given after the Resurrection and the sharing of joy.[2]

Throughout the Middle Ages, in the writings of Sicardus of Cremona (d. 1215), Pope Innocent III (d. 1216), Albertus Magnus (1206–80), and Durandus of Mende (ca. 1237–96), runs this view of the Mass, albeit not without considerable dissent from a number of quarters.

Such discussion dealt with a whole catalogue of ritualistic gesture and attitude which formed the heritage of dramatic presentation in the church: bowing, kissing, kneeling; extending the arms, folding the hands, striking the breast; raising the Communion chalice, swinging the censer. These actions were enshrouded in layers of symbolic meaning and ancient tradition hallowed by religious usage. Furthermore, the celebrant's most important instrument was his voice, vigorously trained from his earliest days as a choir boy under the tutelage of the *Magister Cantus* or the *Magister Scholae,* and there can be little doubt that the excellence of a priest's conduct of ceremony was judged on the quality, strength, and accuracy of his voice. Writing as early as the seventh century, Isidore of Seville says that the three primary qualities of the voice in Divine Service are *alta* (intense), *clara* (clear), and *suavis* (sweet). Rubrics in the plays reiterate these characteristics, in particular the demand for *voce alta.*

In regard to what we know of early tropes, additions to the liturgy, Notker Balbulus (ca. 840–912) of St. Gall tells us that he had encountered much difficulty in remembering the extended melodies sung to the final *a* in the *Alleluia,* until he discovered words, *versus ad sequentias,* written under them in a choir book brought from Jumièges. These words seen by Notker were tropes. This use of the early tropes may have been as a mnemonic device, which function would have contributed to their propagation and development.

In addition to a long-established emphasis on voice and an anthology of traditional, symbolic gesture, the clerical actor of the tenth century was heir to a number of commemorations which contained or consisted of prolonged mimetic acts reflecting Biblical events. At the center of the Mass is the Eucharist, from the earliest days of Christianity an enactment of the Last Supper, itself a memorial meal at the time of the Passover. As of the seventh or eighth century, the Adoration of the Cross had been introduced in the West from Jerusalem as well as Palm Sunday observances that approach the borders of genuine drama. Performance of the *Mandatum*, an imitation of Christ's washing the feet of his disciples, and the burial of the cross and Host were germinal within the Church by the sixth century.

Two points should be noted here about the style of the liturgical drama and the attitude of its participants. First, the clerical actors in the *Visitatio Sepulchri* of the tenth century were participating in one more reenactment, a basic ingredient of the ecclesiastical ceremonial in which they and their forefathers had grown up and been educated. But, although costume, voice, and gesture did not vary essentially, none the less the new extended action together with greater consciousness of impersonation required touches of verisimilitude special to the particular drama. And second, the clerical performers of the church productions throughout the Middle Ages continued to be trained and to function in the complex, formal rituals of worship.

The role-words in the rubrics of the drama hint, however faintly, at a distinction between the imitation of an action (the play) and the act itself (the liturgy). They partake of the attitude expressed in the rubrics by words such as Bishop Ethelwold's *quasi*, as if, and *figuro*, literally to figure or represent. They signal an awareness of make-believe, that fundamental element common to all drama: *exprimo* (express, represent), *facio* (make, depict), *figura* (figure, role), *fingo* (depict, feign), *forma* (image, role), *ludus* (play), *persona* (person, role), *personagium* (person, role), *prefiguro* (figure, play), *representatio* (representation), *represento* (represent), *significatio* (representation, drama), *in similitudine mulierum* (in the likeness of women), *in similitudinem peregrinorum* (in the likeness of pilgrims), *simulo* (act, impersonate), *species* (appearance, role), *teneo* (hold [a role]), *typum* (type, role), *vicis* (like, in the role of).

We shall find that medieval acting in the church varies from place to place and from age to age, as far as the texts reveal, but I believe that we can begin to characterize the style generally as solemn in tone, presentational in manner, unsubtle in the portrayal of emotion, and full of symbolic gesture and vocal effects taken directly from the liturgy. The major means of characterization was costume, the vestments themselves indicative of the formal mode of character portrayal. The conduct of those plays closely connected to the regular observances resembled most the liturgy as recited, while touches of verisimilitude increase quite considerably in, for example, some of the early Old Testament plays. Sparks of originality and individuality are usually found in the acting of less sacred or heathen characters.

Once in a great while the rubrics afford us a glimpse of an ecclesiastical actor's face and head: *annuo* (nod to), *demitto* (*vultu demisso*, with the face turned downward), *se inclino* (*inclinatis capitibus*, with bowed heads), *reclino* (lean, bow), *Capite in dextram manum reclinato* (Her head leaning on her right hand), *submitto* (*vultibus submissis*, with faces turned to the ground), *verto* (turn, *vultibus versis ad clerum*, with faces turned to the clergy; *versis vultibus ad orientem*, with faces turned to the east; *versis contra conventum*, turned toward the [monastic] community). But delicate facial nuances and the physical display of secondary emotions are rare and more difficult for the singer than for the speaker of a role; the mode of the operatic tends toward the presentational and away from so-called realistic detail. Moreover, it would be a serious mistake to limit our conception of the clerical actor to hints given by textual rubrics, to suggest, for example, that he stands rooted to the spot if stage directions do not assign him any stage business. Bishop Ethelwold and Philippe de Mézières introduced dramatic performance for widespread adoption and therefore included rather full descriptive material concerning the acting. But nearly all other manuscripts represent local custom, where the manner of acting like the manner of vocal training was a matter of largely unrecorded tradition.

As with the liturgy itself, so first in importance for exact preservation was the text and second, the music, the former a product of centuries of scrupulous formulation and the latter a development transmitted as much by oral as by written means. Who performed the particular functions was of vital concern, and so we know rather a good deal about personnel and their apparel. Most of the physical properties which served the scenic means were already at hand; the rubrics generally contain less about set pieces unless some special item had to be arranged or until the scenery and machinery became dominant elements. But the method of executing a particular movement was a matter of unwritten tradition, inherited and learned from other ceremonies and performances. Thus our glimpses of the clerical actor are sparse and our general picture a mosaic of often little-related pieces. Bishop Abraham of Suzdal is our first witness with an eye on the actors. A fourteenth-century *Planctus* from Cividale seems to note every move and gesture of the players.

Most phenomenal is the twelfth-century *Jeu d'Adam,* which can be regarded with Ethelwold's *Regularis Concordia* and Mézières' *Presentation* as a kind of prompt-book. The subtleties of acting revealed in its stage directions are found nowhere else in the early Middle Ages. What tradition of performance lies behind the scene of the temptation of Eve, for example, is unknown, yet it must reflect some of the acting necessary to the spate of highly original plays from this period, such as those by Hilarius, which contain hardly a hint as to the playing and yet demand great mimetic skill.

Of all facets of dramatic art, the most elusive one is the art of acting. Its very essence is the transitory, its very substance the fact of change. It is the least possible for the historian to capture. Ironically, perhaps, it is also the most significant aspect of theatre, for the actor in a given instant on the stage is the life of the art. Yet nowhere is our vocabulary more limited than in terminology necessary to describe exactly what an actor does or to delineate the manner and mode of expression. It is, then, only through an attempt to examine examples and to place evidence in a milieu and context that we can hope to envision a few theatrical moments on the stage of the church and to lend substance to designations of style.

The Actors

Women Play Women

Rare indeed are women in the roles of the Marys. Each of these unusual performances took place in a nunnery or in a church, usually a cathedral, with a nunnery-like chapter of canonesses attached to it. In this study of acting we shall examine the women's performances in particular detail because they often magnify issues of acting common to all liturgical plays. For instance, with a woman instead of a man playing the role of Mary Magdalen, verisimilar gesture and vocal coloring in some texts contrasts with formal ritualistic movement and chant-delivery in others. In certain manuscripts the rubrics and lines and music make her gesture of reaching out to touch the Risen Lord seem deeply emotional; whereas in other manuscripts her repeated acts of prostration bestow the staid cast of a rite on the moment. This tension between the two tendencies in the figure of Mary Magdalen runs through the whole canon of medieval church drama: the personal and the priestly, the human and the hieratic. Its presence is felt everywhere, sometimes more tangibly, sometimes less, but it becomes vividly apparent with dramatic performances by nuns and canonesses.

As we have noted, all roles in the liturgical drama were sung by male clergy, including the Marys, as well as the roles of angels (with a few boys as angels), the Risen Christ, and the disciples Peter and John when their scene was included in the *Visitatio.* With one striking exception: performance in the nunnery. In every extant text of the *Visitatio* from a nunnery or from a chapter of cathedral canonesses, and we possess twenty-three, the roles of the women were taken by women. No other liturgical dramas were performed in nunneries. The roles of the three Marys provided the first, the oldest, and the longest performance practice for women in the drama of the western world.[3]

One could argue that these twenty-three music-dramas performed by women comprise a precious, isolated phenomenon, born in the twelfth century and dying out around 1600. Certainly one does not trace direct theatrical lines from these nuns to the professional actresses on the stages of sixteenth-century Spain and Italy. Nor does the liturgical drama bear direct import upon the flourishing of Renaissance drama. Yet with their cult of Mary Magdalen, and their practices over seven centuries in music, language, and movement, the dramas feed and were fed by the wellsprings of medieval culture. They answer a need for dramatic expression by women and for the education of women. A number of the women's dramas seem to reveal new work by a single hand, some one individual who has meticulously crafted the coalescing of traditional antiphons with new composition. That person may have been the Abbess.

What, if anything, distinguished the twenty-three performance traditions with women from the usual, all-male performances? What happened when women instead of men played the Marys at the Easter sepulchre? And when a woman took the part of Mary Magdalen? Are there any traces left, however faint? Did the sound of female voices, the appearance of female body language, the very presence of women make any impression on the remaining texts, our only sources, with their words and music and their stage directions? Who composed them? Or compiled them?

The Abbess

Chief among the women of a convent stood the Abbess. She was the head of the house: usually a woman of some social rank (as were most nuns) and with some education, and frequently authoritarian in her rule. It was she who would take in hand any cloistral performance. Rarely in the Middle Ages could a woman exert independence and exercise leadership, but as an Abbess a women might reach beyond the confines of quotidian routine toward power and invention. When we come upon an unusual rendering of the *Visitatio Sepulchri* from a convent, it is quite likely that an Abbess was the one who made it for her nuns to perform, annealing existing music and texts with fresh compositions, perhaps even her own.

Two of the twenty-three surviving women's manuscripts actually name an Abbess. At Barking, it was Katherine of Sutton (Abbess, 1363–76) who, according to the manuscript, promoted the *Visitatio* with its singular Harrowing of Hell ceremony. She encouraged this dramatization in order to counteract what she perceived as "stultified devotion" and local "indifference" toward Easter celebration. At Origny, one manuscript of the *Visitatio* records the name of Isabelle d'Acy (Abbess 1286–1324) as the Abbess who had had the older text copied; she was probably responsible also for its stage directions in French; whether she augmented the text and music in any way, we do not know. These pioneers belong to the ranks of other powerful, often autocratic Abbesses who emerged in the Middle Ages such as Hildegard von Bingen (1089–1179) with her original musical compositions, her writings on natural science, and her wide-ranging correspondence. Some Abbesses were known for their homilies. The daughters of the Lüneburg nobility and the House of Braunschweig were educated at the convent of Medingen, where Abbesses enjoyed a considerable reputation as preachers and where, in the *Visitatio*, women played the Mary-roles.

One piece of evidence comes from the Ruhr area in Germany, from Essen. It is very probable that a woman, perhaps the Abbess, created the fourteenth-century *Visitatio* for the Collegiate Church of Canons and Canonesses at Essen. Also, from the St. George Nunnery in Prague comes a unique thirteenth-century *Visitatio* which, as Susan Rankin, the leading authority on this music, points out, reveals "its own newly composed melodies." There, as elsewhere, the figure of Mary Magdalen began to emerge. Rankin goes on with her musical analysis: new composition in the Mary Magdalen scene with the Risen Christ made it possible to realize modal and stylistic unity with the surrounding texts and melodies. In fact, because its set of texts and melodies was transmitted *en bloc*, the Mary Magdalen scene may have been composed "by one person at one time."[4]

Manuscripts from nunneries reflect a sense of the Abbess and her women. In fact, from beginning to end the Abbess presided. Nuns in a convent normally observed the hours unto themselves, including Matins. However, Easter Matins was a special event, and it seems that even in a convent members of the male clergy participated in it with the nuns. When Easter Matins included the little drama and the time came for its performance, the male celebrant might lead off a procession; and when the play was finished he or his cantor usually intoned the music that concluded Matins, the *Te Deum*.

But when the drama was sung by nuns or canonesses one felt everywhere the presence of the Abbess. It was she who processed from the nuns' or canonesses' choir loft with the women's chorus (the *conventus*) out into the nave of the church for the *Visitatio*. At Prague she led off a great procession into mid-church as prelude to the performance; at Troyes, with a light, a book, and the Marys, she marched at the climax of a huge procession of male clergy. At Poitiers she took up a central position in the east choir as the drama commenced, with the angel, two servant-nuns, and her sacristan distributing lights to the participants. It was she who at Nottuln signalled her *Cantrix* to conclude the *Visitatio* with the singing of the *Te Deum*.

From beginning to end the Abbess presided. At Gandersheim only the Abbess entered the sepulchre during the *Depositio* (the Good-Friday burial ceremony of the cross)—in the presence of novices as well as townspeople. During the *Depositio* at Essen she led her convent out into the nuns' cemetery, where she then stood on one dish of a giant scale, symbolizing Christ's sacrifice as righting the balance over against the weight of human sin. During the *Visitatio* at the convent of Gernrode the three Marys emerged from the sepulchre (a stone replica of the Holy Sepulchre in Jerusalem) to move through the church to the Abbess, singing of their discovery, "Surrexit dominus," directly to her. They also paused in mid-church to sing an antiphon at the tomb of Hathui, the much-revered founding Abbess. This gesture linked Hathui with Christ's Resurrection, bestowing a special blessing upon Hathui. At the same time, the gesture drew from Hathui's tomb an assurance to the Gernrode nuns of their own eventual resurrection. At the end of Matins as the nuns of Gernrode ascended again back into their choir loft, the manuscript says that the Abbess collected from them the candles she had distributed at the outset of the *Visitatio*.

The Marys or, if included in the play, Peter and John (always played by male clergy) finished every version of the *Visitatio* by taking the sacred gravecloth from the sepulchre and holding it up for all to see, tangible evidence to the Resurrection. In the early performance at the St. George Convent of Prague (from the twelfth century), Peter and John concluded the drama with that public gesture. But the convent at Prague added a unique touch. There the Abbess initiated a little ceremony by going over and kissing the gravecloth—followed by the nuns (sorores) and then the townspeople standing nearby (populus circumstans).[5]

The Rite of Purification: The Abbess and the Three Marys

At Origny the nuns who were to play the Mary-roles first went through a rite of purification. This little ritual is documented for four convents: Barking (manuscript copied from 1363–76); Origny (a manuscript copied 1286, and a 1315–17 manuscript); Troyes (thirteenth century manuscript); and the Abbey of St. Edith's at Wilton (1250–1320 manuscript). Such a ritual of cleansing does not occur in a single one of the approximately 680 churches where men played the roles of the Marys, in either secular or monastic churches.

The manuscript rubrics from the French convent of Origny read as follows:

. . . they [the three to play the roles of the Marys] should confess and go to my Lady during the canticles of Matins, and each one should give [donate] some possession [propriété] on her own and place

[there] whatever they have of their own will, and they should say *Confiteor*, and my Lady should say *Misereatur* and *Indulgentiam*. Afterward, the Marys should go and get dressed [in their white shifts and in their cloaks (mantles) and in white kerchiefs without (a) veil] and come before the Altar of Magdalen, and they should be at prayer until the time set for going to the sepulchre.

Since the ninth century this *Confiteor* or Confession, a formulaic prayer, was said by the celebrant during two of the canonical hours, Prime and Compline. With the *Confiteor* he was acknowledging his sinfulness and begging the mediation of those who assisted him in the service. They immediately give him this mediation, saying the *Misereatur*, and, in turn, saying the *Confiteor*. The priest-celebrant responded with the *Misereatur* and went on to give them Absolution, saying the *Indulgentiam*. By the early eleventh century this observance had also been inserted into the Mass. In each instance it was performed at the high altar. It is a liturgical Confession, a formal act using established formulaic wording just like the rest of the liturgy.

A second type of Confession marked monastic as well as secular life of the Middle Ages: sacramental Confession. A monk said Confession weekly to a spiritual director selected from the monastic community. In like manner it was often the case in the monastery that the celebrant-priest, before going out to say Mass, said a private Confession to his spiritual father. And at the farther range, each Christian believer was required to make Confession at least once a year, normally preparatory to Easter. In every instance, the basic formula for this private, or sacramental Confession was the same as for the public, liturgical Confession. The confessing individual said the *Confiteor*, and the spiritual father responded with the *Misereatur* and granted him Absolution with the *Indulgentiam*. This sacramental Confession was part of personal purification, whereas liturgical Confession was part of public ceremony.

In the convent at Origny, the rite between the Abbess and the Mary-role players partakes of both liturgical Confession and sacramental Confession. In the spirit of liturgical Confession, the Marys make Confession to the Abbess just as those assisting in the canonical hours and at Mass make Confession to the priest-celebrant. Thereupon the Marys receive Absolution from the Abbess just as those assisting in the hours and at Mass receive Absolution from the priest-celebrant. In that sense, the Abbess is taking on special powers reserved for the male priesthood. And just as in the liturgical Confession, so the Mary-role play-ers will kneel at prayer at an altar at Origny, here sig-nificantly the Altar of Mary Magdalen.

In addition, this rite just before the *Visitatio Sepul-chri* is also like the second kind of Confession, sacra-mental Confession. In that sense, removed from the ongoing service of Matins the Marys say the private *Confiteor* to the Abbess as their spiritual director, just as each of them in her life as a nun used the formula *Confiteor* in her weekly Confession to her spiritual director. This individual cleansing is reinforced at Origny with the giving of a personal gift, each pre-sented by the nun expressly of her own free will.

Moreover, in this private, sacramental sense, the Confession of the Mary-role players parallels the pri-vate, sacramental Confession of the priest-celebrant in a monastery before he goes out into the main church to say Mass. Upon receiving personal Absolu-tion from the Abbess, each of the nuns will dress in white, pray at the Altar of Mary Magdalen, and then go out into the main church to carry a sacred reli-quary—a blessed cloth between her hands and the reliquary—to the Easter sepulchre. In that moment they are the *celebrants*.

This rite embodies some remarkable phenomena. Here the Abbess takes unto herself sacred powers re-served for the male clergy. Moreover, these women undergo a rite of purification before they can perform the roles of the Marys. It is both public-liturgical and private-sacramental. It is a rite that not a single member of the male clergy underwent before playing in a liturgical drama—a rite that links to numerous religious acts where women must be cleansed in some special way before participating in a sacred observance.[6]

The order of events in this Confessional act signals symbolic steps in preparing the nuns to perform their roles. At Origny they first confessed at the Magdalen altar, then dressed in white (dens leur blans chainses et leurs mantiaus et en blans cueurechies sans voil [French-Picardy dialect]); then they prayed at the Magdalen altar; finally they rose and each received a reliquary on a blessed cloth; and then they went out into the church and moved to the sepulchre.

At St. Edith's at Wilton the order is the same: first they are cleansed, then they change clothing. The three *cantrices* get up from the choir, wash their hands, take off their veils (absconso velamine), and put white veils on their heads "in similitudine mulierum." Then they take up phylacteries, candlesticks, and thuribles, and go out searching for the sepulchre. There is this literal

washing, but no *Confiteor*. Wilton and Origny had strong ties.

In the English nunnery of Barking the order is re-versed. The Abbess herself dressed the Marys, and *af-ter* that—rather than *before*—she heard their Confes-sion. First came a Harrowing of Hell ceremony. Then the Abbess and the three nuns chosen to play the Marys entered into the Chapel of St. Mary Magdalen. There the nuns exchanged their black vestments for white surplices, and the Abbess put a snow-white veil on each of them. Then each, holding a silver vessel, said Confession (the *Confiteor*) to the Abbess and she gave them Absolution. Thereupon Mary Magdalen commenced the *Visitatio*.

As at Barking, so in the Notre Dame Convent of Troyes there was first the costume change, then the Confession. At Troyes the Marys dressed in white (toutes blanches et creuechie blanc sor lor testes)—together with two children as the angels; then the Marys came before the high altar, knelt down, and said Confession (the *Confiteor*); then each received a can-dle, a cloth, and a vessel; whereupon a great procession led them out into the church and to the western ex-treme of the nave for the *Visitatio*.

The positioning of the Confessional rite in the ob-servance also imbued it with special power. At Origny, to say Confession prepared the nuns to wear white (and to handle sacred relics). Whereas at Barking and at Troyes, to wear white prepared the nuns to say Con-fession. But at Troyes, they said their Confession not to their Abbess but to the celebrant-priest. It was he who, in turn, said the *Misereatur* and gave them Absolution—and then presented each with a candle, cloth, and vessel. There at Troyes the Marys per-formed a much more public act of Confession than at Origny and Barking, and in kneeling at the high altar they were undertaking the same age-old Confession as did a celebrant-priest before he said Mass.

Nowhere is such a practice of purification recorded when the *Visitatio Sepulchri* was performed by the male clergy. The little Confessional rite is an act of inner purification. It retains the sense that women must be cleansed, a folk-practice reaching back into the mists of prehistory as it reaches forward into our own day.

Furthermore, in presiding over the solemnity of Confession the Abbess at Origny and at Barking ap-propriated to herself a religious power normally re-served solely for men, for priests. Thus not only does this ceremonial appear to carry age-old practice of cleansing women, but it also reveals a singular, sacred act by the Abbess.

Fresh Composition and Human Feeling at Origny and at Barking

Origny St. Benoît

Examinations of the three texts from the French nunnery of Origny and then, comparatively, of the ceremony and play from the English nunnery of Barking reveal patterns of new creation, work possibly even composed in these women's religious institutions by the women themselves.

Let us first examine the exchange between Mary Magdalen and Jesus in the dramatic *Visitatio* from Origny in order to perceive exactly what distinguishes this moment from its counterparts in versions performed by men and from its counterparts in other versions where the Marys were played by women.

According to texts L303 (copied 1286) and L303a (1315–17), toward the end of Easter Matins the three nuns who are to play the three Marys are prepared before the Altar of the Blessed Mary Magdalen, offstage as it were. As we have noted, each says Confession and is given Absolution by the Abbess. Thereupon they dress in white—albs, copes, and headdresses without veils—and pray at the Magdalen Altar until it is time to go to the sepulchre for the drama. A ceremonial occurs at the sepulchre, an exchange that one can just barely call a drama.

But a third text (with music) from Origny (1315–17, L825) contains a remarkably ample dramatic composition. From here we follow L825. A priest with a censer then leads a procession. Each of the Marys has a lighted candle; Mary Magdalen also carries a (spice) box. Then comes the chorus, each of the women with a lighted candle. The antiphon here, "Quis reuoluet ergo nobis ab hostio lapidem" (Who will roll the stone away from the entrance for us), is a new composition.[7]

They meet the merchant (li Marchans), this and all other roles—except the Marys—played by male clergy. Mary Magdalen pauses, alone in pain, while the other two Marys bargain for spices. Nowhere else do we find such a moment, with Magdalen grieving while the other two deal with a spice-seller. There follow ten stanzas of dialogue sung in French that are unique to this drama; they are original, not translations of Latin. The merchant is young and caring, eager to honor "tres grant Signeur."

The two Marys return to Magdalen, and the three continue their journey. Two angels await them—one at the head of the sepulchre, one at the foot. The angels open the sepulchre "un peu" and point with their fingers, singing "Non iacet hic." Then the angels open up the sepulchre completely, the three Marys approach it and kiss it, and the angels close it. This is the only such gestural sequence that I know. The Marys' kissing the sepulchre also occurs at Barking convent and at the Cathedral of Rouen, while only here do we find this partial opening, full opening, and then closing.[8] The Marys' ensuing lament, "Heu, infelices"—they are left unsatisfied by the sight of the empty grave—is unique. It extends and underscores their grief. The two Marys leave and Mary Magdalen remains by herself. Continuing the newly composed lament, "Infelix ego misera," she carries forth her exchange with the angels, and then Jesus appears, singing the familiar text "Mulier, quid ploras? Quem queris?" but to a new melody. Magdalen bows to him (thinking him the gardener), asking "Domine, si tu sustulisti eum" (Sir, if you have taken him [the body]). Immediately the recognition takes place. Mary Magdalen sings "Raboni!" at Jesus' feet and then "throws herself" on the ground as Jesus sings "Noli me tangere."

This act of prostration occurs in two other Mary Magdalen scenes when played by a woman, at Barking and at Wilton, but in eight or nine such scenes where men play Mary Magdalen. Could this body language suggest a different concept of character, perhaps a more abject, self-abnegating Magdalen when performed by male clergy?

The text through here belongs to a French tradition, but the melodies are unique. Mary Magdalen thereupon gets up and remains alone in front of the sepulchre while Jesus goes over to the other two Marys. Barking convent and the Cathedral of Rouen provide the only other texts in which the Risen Christ appears first to Mary Magdalen and then proceeds to the other two Marys. They also throw themselves at his feet—again, an act singular to Origny, Barking, and Rouen. The two Marys then rise before him as he sings to them, "Ite, nuntiate fratribus meis."[9]

In the Origny manuscript Jesus exits and the three sing "Eya nobis internas mentes," a unique adaptation of "Heu nobis internas mentes." The composer has taken a stanza that belongs to the opening lament of the three Marys (just prior to "Iam percusso"), moved it to this scene ending position, and turned it into a triumphal song. Rarely does one discover such sophisticated little alterations of the original material toward the creation of a new version of the *Visitatio*.

The Marys sing of their discovery, as usual, and the

chorus of nuns responds "Deo gratias." Thereupon two apostles (Peter and John) come to the Marys. A unique gestural sequence follows: "taking Magdalen a little aside by the sleeve" (prendent le manche le Magdelainne vn peu de lons), the apostles ask the standard question about what she has seen, "Dic nobis, Maria . . . ?" (Tell us, Mary . . . ?). They then let go of her sleeve (laissent le manche le Magdelainne), and she points with her finger to the sepulchre (demoustre au doit le Sepuchre [sic]), singing forcefully (en haut) "Sepulcrum Cristi." When the two Marys come over, Magdalen again points with her finger to the sepulchre. Finally she lays her hand on her breast (met se main a sen pis), singing "Spes nostra" (Our hope) instead of the usual "Spes mea" (My hope). She thereupon turns to point with her finger in another direction (trestourne sen doit dautre part), to sing "Precedet uos in Galileam." Other characters in a few other texts do point sometimes, but not Mary Magdalen. This pointing or gesturing in a direction seems to be a French tradition. I find four similar examples, but none—except at Barking—matched in this way to this particular exchange where she stands unaccompanied by the other women and, while singing, points with her finger.[10]

As the two disciples go to the sepulchre, the normal antiphon at this point, "Currebant duo simul," has been turned into an exchange between disciples and chorus. This is the only such instance in the *Visitatio* drama. The disciples emerge with the sudary, the three Marys kneel and kiss it, and the disciples then carry it away from the sepulchre. This act may have to do with one of the many relics at the cloister.[11] In the convents at Barking, Prague, and Wilton we find similar gestural patterns. At Barking, at "Dic nobis, Maria," Mary Magdalen points with her finger to the angel at the sepulchre and then offers the sudary to be kissed by the clergy. At Prague, Peter and John hold the sudary while the Abbess, the nuns, and then the people standing nearby kiss it. At Wilton the Marys first venerate a sacred book (textum), and then the nuns and the populace may kiss it. The Origny manuscript breaks off at this point.

No men's religious order had the *Visitatio* so publicly led by an Abbot or Bishop as the Convent of Origny was led by its Abbess; and none had the role-players say Confession. No other men's or women's religious order had Mary Magdalen sing this amount of freshly composed music, engage with the other Marys in kissing the sudary, point with her finger to the sepulchre and to Galilee, or be pulled aside by the sleeve.

Barking

In the fourteenth century, Abbesses from both Origny and Barking seem to have augmented thirteenth-century *Visitatio* texts from their respective abbeys. The Barking text is also *sui generis*, a whole composition unified in its conception, where likewise the composer-author has woven together threads from both the Anglo-Norman and the French practice, intertwined with new, unique composition. Would that the music from Barking had survived, as it has from Origny.

Here too, at Barking, one feels the controlling presence of the Abbess. The *Elevatio* of the surviving text actually names Abbess Katherine of Sutton (Abbess of Barking, 1363–76). She promoted and may have elaborated the much older Easter ceremony and drama, because, according to the rubrics, she was concerned about "rooting out indifference" in the gathering of the people (populorum concursus), "and in order to stimulate the most ardent celebration." Here too a general populace was present.

A unique *Elevatio* served as antecedent to the *Visitatio*, both performed just before the end of Matins. A procession led by the Abbess, with the entire convent together with some priests and clerks, each priest and clerk with a palm and an unlighted candle, entered the Chapel of St. Mary Magdalen, apparently within the main church. Then they closed the chapel door. A Harrowing of Hell ceremony followed, where from outside a priest beat on the door three times—Christ knocking on the gates of hell—whereupon "the gates should fly open," and the priest led the group out "like the patriarchs," through the middle of the choir, and over to the sepulchre. What the sepulchre looked like, we do not know. The priest entered the sepulchre, removed the Host, and took it to the high altar. The procession moved on to the Holy Trinity Altar, "in the manner in which Christ proceeded to Galilee after the Resurrection, with His disciples following."

This is the only such Harrowing of Hell sequence in a women's institution, and, together with the *Ludus Paschalis* from Klosterneuburg, the only one performed within Matins (not before) and located within a church chapel. Otherwise, wherever the rare Harrowing of Hell is presented, a procession winds around the outside of the church prior to Easter Matins, and the knocking, with singing from within, occurs at an exterior door.

At Barking thereupon three sisters (Tres Sorores) selected by the Abbess, together with the Abbess herself, return to the Chapel of St. Mary Magdalen. They, like the entire convent, were dressed in black. The Abbess then dresses the Marys in the purest white surplices with white veils on their heads. Thus prepared, and each holding a silver vessel, they make Confession (they say the *Confiteor*) to the Abbess and she gives them Absolution (et ab ea absolute). They then sing three passages unique to Barking. As previously noted, the convents of Barking, Origny, Troyes, and Wilton contain the only documentation of such a costume change done at this point and in this manner, and at Barking, Origny, and Troyes the only saying of Confession by the role-players (at Troyes, not to the Abbess but to a priest).[12]

After the exchange with one of the two angels, played by a clerk (clericus), the women enter and kiss the sepulchre, a gesture also found only at Origny and Rouen Cathedral. Magdalen picks up the sudary. During the subsequent exchange the angels say or sing (we have no music from Barking) "Quid queritis viventem cum mortuis?" (Why do you seek the living among the dead?), a direct quote from Luke 24:5.[13] It is followed by a unique rubric, "Then they still doubting the Resurrection of the Lord shall say mourning to each other: 'Heu dolor . . .'" (Tunc ille de Resurrexione Domini adhuc dubitantes plangendo dicant ad inuicem: "Heu, dolor . . ."). Only at Barking does a stage direction convey this doubt as to the Resurrection. Mary Magdalen sighs, *suspirando*, singing "Te suspiro . . ."; only in the text from Coutances Cathedral do we hear again this particular expression of vocal mourning.

Jesus appears, at the left side of the altar—whether now the high altar, we do not know—and eventually Mary Magdalen prostrates herself at his feet singing "Raboni!" Jesus, singing "Noli me tangere," draws back and then goes away. Thereupon follows a moment unique to this drama—

Maria gaudium suum consociabus communicet uoce letabunda hos concinendo versus:
   Gratulari et letari. . . .

[Mary joyfully imparts to her companions, singing in a glad voice this verse:
   Give thanks and rejoice. . . .]

As at Origny, Jesus reappears—to the right of the altar—now to the three Marys together. And they, prostrate on the ground, hold and kiss his feet. This prostration also occurs at Origny, but not the holding and kissing.[14] Again, something original follows here

from the composer-author. Not only is the ensuing piece, "Ihesus ille Nazarenus," newly composed and unique to Barking, but, the prostration finished, each of the three women is instructed to sing a different stanza each to a different melody.

The next piece is also unique to Barking: "Alleluia, surrexit Dominus." In singing it the three Marys stand on the step in front of the altar and turn toward the populace. The nuns' chorus responds in repeating the "Alleluia."

Another newly composed piece introduces a turn in the scene as priests and clerks in the role of disciples come forward to sing "O gens dira."

The "Dic nobis, Maria" is very similar to that from the convents of Origny and Troyes. As in Origny, Mary Magdalen points with her finger to the sepulchre— "where the angel was sitting," the Barking text adds.

But quite different from the Magdalen at Origny, at Barking she holds the sudarium and offers it to the clergy and clerks (sacerdotes et clerici) to be kissed. Only at Origny, otherwise, do participants kiss the sudary—there the Marys—and at Prague, where the Abbess, convent (sorores), and populace kiss the gravecloth (held by Peter and John). It is a liturgical kiss that parallels the kissing of the sepulchre by the women at Origny.

Men and women sing together the *Credendum est* and the *Scimus Christum*, whereupon Magdalen begins *Christus resurgens* and both the clergy and the women's chorus pick it up. We also find men and women explicitly singing together at Origny.

During the singing of the *Te Deum*, the priests who had been the disciples (now in their usual vestments) reenter from "the chapel," probably the Magdalen Chapel, and with candles they cross through the choir to the sepulchre, pray, return, and pause—here a unique, mimed reminder of the race to the tomb by Peter and John. The Abbess then gives them the signal to exit. And Lauds commences.

Special Features of Men's Texts

It is also in the *Visitatio* texts that the scene between the Marys and the spice-seller first emerges—at Vich in Spain (eleventh-twelfth-century manuscript). The spice-seller's second oldest appearance occurs in a women's text, from the St. George Nunnery in Prague. The Marys purchase their funeral ointments from him. And thereafter he appears in men's texts: for example, a single spice-seller at Klosterneuburg, and together with a younger merchant at Egmond (Spe-cionarius, mercator juvenis). At Benediktbeuern *Apothecarius* even has a wife (Uxor Apothecarii). In the Tours manuscript the cast includes a *Mercator* and a *mercator juvenis*, but is the manuscript linked to nuns or canonesses?

Many of the twenty-one extant men's plays with an emphasis on the character of Mary Magdalen also manifest other inventive variations; but *all* of the twenty-three womens' plays contain fresh material (fifteen that add something special to the Magdalen role among the Marys; and eight that do not).[15]

Women Identify with the Marys

In addition to the role of the Abbess and the purification rite, what is particular about these drama texts from women's orders with women singing the Mary-roles? One is struck, first of all, by the emerging presence of Mary Magdalen in them. Her role can be augmented with features ranging from a hand gesture to a whole scene such as her recognition of the Risen Christ. She is thus singled out in liturgical plays from a total of thirty-six different monastic and secular churches, counting both men's and women's institutions. Her role is em-phasized in sixty-five percent of the texts originating from women's orders (15 out of 23), and in only three percent of the texts deriving from men's orders and from secular churches (21 out of about 680). Some of the dra-matic texts actually make use of a Mary Magdalen chapel (plays from the nunneries of Barking and Marienberg; a Mary Magdalen altar at Origny). These chapels and altars are a sign of the cult of Mary Mag-dalen that arose in the twelfth and thirteenth cen-turies.[16] Nuns and canonesses—as women, they could identify with the Marys and especially with Mary Mag-dalen. According to the Biblical narratives it was to the women that the news of the Resurrection was first given. It was to Mary Magdalen that the Risen Christ first ap-peared—she a "fallen woman," a sinner given special blessing, one with a unique relationship to Jesus. Nuns, from the beginning of female monasticism, could see themselves reflected in these Biblical women. Then as now they were "the brides of Christ," in their devotions and liturgies. To make the next move from singing an-tiphons and other ecclesiastical music in the Divine Of-fice to singing antiphons and other verses in the *Visita-tio Sepulchri* demanded but a small step.

The liturgical drama emerged from ceremony with the creation of mimetic action and character. Mary Magdalen was central to that process because she was featured in the first truly dramatic Easter scene where

at the Sepulchre she weeps over Jesus' death, Jesus appears to her, she mistakes him for the gardener, and then in the most famous recognition scene in western literature he sings only her name, "Maria" in the litur-gical drama, and she, recognizing him, sings "Rab-boni" (teacher), falling at his feet, as he backs away, singing, "Do not touch me."

This little scene gave impetus to new poetic and musical creation. Whereas the earliest texts of the *Vis-itatio* itself date to the tenth century, the earliest texts with Mary Magdalen as a character date to the twelfth century. In these plays and in almost every one of the subsequent Easter plays with Mary Magdalen as a character, something unusual occurs, whether played by a man or a woman: fresh musical composition, a new ceremonial moment, a unique gestural pattern. At the women's convent of Wienhausen perhaps the most radical alteration of the moment took place. There, according to a fourteenth-century text, the "Maria" and "Raboni" exchange was sung not once but three times. After singing each "Raboni," Magdalen spoke in German a two- or four-line rhymed verse, and the music of each "Maria/Raboni" was altered from the original in order to stagger the rising emo-tional impact.[17]

The following manuscripts of the *Visitatio* from convents are unique in another respect: those from Gernrode, Origny, Regensberg, and Troyes contain descriptive rubrics that are not in Latin, as is the case with all other extant manuscripts of liturgical drama. From Gernrode and Regensburg, rubrics are in Ger-man; from Origny and Troyes, rubrics are in French. Why the vernacular in manuscripts from 4 out of 700 localities? Perhaps they acknowledge the rarity of women trained in Latin. It is only from women's or-ders that liturgical drama texts exhibit this vernacular phenomenon. The Origny play, moreover, includes some newly composed passages to be sung in French.

A different kind of rubric also suggests fresh com-position rather than a copy of a *Visitatio* text and mu-sic borrowed from another church. Four of the dra-mas with women as the Marys call for the use of special prompt-scripts during performance—and at Origny, a prompter. There in the fourteenth-century Origny manuscript, when the Marys come to the door of the sepulchre, "the cantor [masculine] should be with them, who should teach them what they should say." At Poitiers the *capiceria* (sacristan) gave various participants—including the Abbess—each "a taper or candle to illuminate what they say [sing]." At Regens-burg-Obermünster each of the three Marys took a "Zetl" with her, presumably a slip of paper with the role written out. At Essen the angels seated in the tent used as the Sepulchre "have a book which contains the songs they are to sing if they do not know them by heart, and candles in order to see." This direction also suggests a special lighting effect because the candles provided the only illumination within the sepulchre. At Troyes the Marys were guided by a nun processing along beside them with a torch "to light them and bringing the book into which they look." There too a special lighting effect was achieved. At the proper dramatic moment two candelabra-bearers entered the sepulchre with the Marys and the door was then shut. Whether or not the rest of the congregants could see flickering firelight through openings in the sepulchre walls, we do not know. But after a ceremony at the altar inside the sepulchre, the Marys emerged with the gravecloth to move to the convent-choir and sing the good news to them: "Surrexit Dominus de sepulcro."

If any one characteristic of these innovative details makes the performances by women as Mary Magdalen and the other Marys distinctive, it seems to exist in the expression of human feeling. Something from inside the characters is revealed a little more frequently and a little more insistently than in the men's texts. To single out one graphic example let us recall the previously discussed emotional moment where, after Mary Magdalen has met the Risen Christ in the *Visitatio* at the nunnery of Origny, the apostles come and ask what she has seen, singing the traditional "Dic nobis, Maria" (Tell us, Mary). At Origny the stage direction reads: "And the two apostles [Peter and John] come before the Marys, and, taking Magdalen a little aside by the sleeve, they say [sing], 'Dic nobis, Maria.'"

Nowhere else in the entire canon of the liturgical drama does that tiny gesture occur. It is a moment of intimacy, an expression of urgency, perhaps a tug to one side for secrecy, possibly driven by fear—or excitement. It is a fleeting glimpse of intense human feeling.

Three Types of *Visitatio* Performances by Women

The twenty-three texts where women played women fall into three groups. Examples of the first kind of drama come from Origny and Barking, and from Wilton. As already discussed, each comprises several scenes with extended sung dialogue.

A second type of women's *Visitatio* comprises a briefer drama than the first and seems to play out within Matins somewhat less altered by appended ceremony. Yet each of this second group is also marked by some unique feature: for instance, the

Abbess alone entering the sepulchre in the *Depositio* at Gandersheim; or a pair of alternative melodies provided for the "Surrexit Dominus" in a manuscript from Andernach.

Most examples of the women's *Visitatio* belong to a third type. Here the drama is also a simple little play, but it is embedded within the framework of an elaborate processional celebration: at Essen, Gernrode, Nottuln, Poitiers, Prague, Regensburg, Troyes, and the two earlier texts from Origny. Each of this third kind of women's text exhibits unique features. For instance, as just noted, a light and a book for prompting were carried in the processionals at Essen, Poitiers, Regensburg, and Troyes. At Gernrode the three Marys wore special nuns' habits, including a white wimple or veil with a red cross on each of its four sides. Likewise at Regensburg each of the Marys donned a special nun's habit, there with wide sleeves (weit Ermel). At Nottuln, Christ appeared barefoot, carrying a spade and wearing a wool cap; after Mary twice genuflected and then prostrated herself, Christ bent down and raised her up. Extensive processions occurred at Poitiers (into the westwork, with a singular scene between Mary Magdalen and an angel), at Troyes (where the Marys said Confession and dressed in white), and at Prague, with its character of the spice-seller and its major juxtapositions and fusions of men's and women's voices.

Voices

In addition to the striking visual impact often specified in these women's texts, the sound of their music was different. One did on occasion hear a coalescing of men's and boys' voices in the drama, as in the liturgy, in monastic and non-monastic churches. Once in a while the roles of the angels were sung by boys; more frequently, the schola of boys joined with the clergy to form the chorus. But in the nunneries one always heard the conjoining and alternating of male and female pitch, timbre, and resonance. There the male roles—Jesus, the angel(s), and, in some dramas, the disciples Peter and John—were always taken by men. Thus one heard a singular mixture of male and female voices in the exchanges between the Marys and the angel(s), between Mary Magdalen and Jesus, and, when the scene was included, between the women and the disciples. In the latter scene an almost operatic effect must have been achieved at Wilton. After her visit to the sepulchre, Mary Magdalen is questioned by five monks, "Dic nobis, Maria." She displays the gravecloth, sings "Angelicos testes" (Angelic witnesses), and then sings "Credendum est magis" (The single, truthful Mary) together with the five monks.

In a convent the nuns alone, without a priest, could and did celebrate the canonical hours that divided each of their days. At Mass and other special services they always formed the house choir. Thus at their Matins on Easter morning (the first service of the day) they became the chorus for the drama. Often the manuscript rubrics direct the women to leave their own reserved choir area and move into the nave of the church in order to sing the *Visitatio*. An ordained priest always celebrated the Mass with its sacrament of the Eucharist—in all churches, including convents. Interestingly enough, in each of the women's *Visitatio Sepulchri* texts from the twenty-three different localities, not only did male clergy sing the male roles (including the angels) but one or more members of the male clergy also participated in the Matins service.[18]

Even more striking must have been those performances where male and female choruses sang the chant together, for instance, in a convent directly linked to a monastery such as at Gernrode, Münster, and Marienberg bei Helmstadt, or in a cathedral with a chapter of canonesses as well as canons, as at Essen. There at Essen three canonesses sang the roles of the Marys. During the performance the chorus of canonesses, descending from their own choir loft, joined the chorus of canons and the boys' schola on the main floor of the cathedral in front of the east choir. When the time came, the women sang the antiphon "Maria Magdalena" while up above the Marys passed along the second-story, south gallery toward the sepulchre in the westwork. At a later point in the drama the men sang "Currebant duo simul" (Two ran together) while Peter and John in like fashion passed along the second-story, north gallery to the sepulchre. The sepulchre, a coffer (*archa*) within a tent, stood in the second gallery of the westwork (a major architectural structure at the western extreme of the nave). The three Marys (played by canonesses) bent over and peered into the tent and said, "'Ubi est Jhesus?' vel similia verba" ('Where is Jesus?' or similar words). But they did not go in. Only the men, Peter and John (played by canons), were allowed to enter; not the women. Toward the end, when one of the disciples sang out the announcement of the Resurrection from the third story of the westwork, the canonesses' chorus down below responded with "Deo gratias." At the drama's finish, it was their *Cantrix* (choir leader) who led off the concluding music of the service, the singing of the *Te Deum*, whereupon everyone joined in—women, men, boys, and the townspeople of Essen and vicinity.

Women Play Women

Did the presence of women in the liturgical drama effect any substantive difference? Taken together the innovations in medieval texts with women as role-players begin to point toward a more general pattern in societal change. From this point of view, perhaps the *Visitatio* in the convent can be looked upon as a kind of paradigm. The convent as a community of women had existed for an extensive period of time. Then along came a pioneer, a literate individual and an explorer in many different areas. In the liturgical drama the innovator was most likely a woman, an Abbess. She functioned not *de novo* but as someone who galvanized what had been in existence for centuries: in this instance, bringing together the nuns and the already widespread and thriving *Visitatio*. As head of the convent she worked with the establishment, with the men of the Church of Rome. Much of the Abbess' leadership consisted in collaboration: in this example, men and women performing the *Visitatio* together. As a result of the sudden coalescence in the long-established community of women, many often surprising innovations burst from a single, central invention.

When one thinks of women and the drama of the Middle Ages, perhaps one thinks first of Hrotswitha from Gandersheim (ca. 935–after 973), with her six Latin one-act plays composed as Christian imitations of Terence. But these little dialogues with their sometimes elaborate, discursive stage directions must be considered as moral disquisitions, to be read aloud—there was no silent reading in this era—along with other didactic and devotional literature such as sacred history and saints' lives. Hrotswitha herself was not a nun but a noblewoman living voluntarily within a women's religious order, writing her histories and other poetic works in the brilliant cultural matrix of Gandersheim convent together with its monastic counterpart, Hildesheim. So far as we know, she had nothing to do with the liturgical drama, nor with any other plays that might have been acted.

For dramatic performance in the cloister one must look not to a Hrotswitha but to the person of the Abbess and to the *Visitatio Sepulchri*.

Convents for women had flourished under the aegis of the Church of Rome almost from its inception. When the women of the convent began to play the Marys, other distinctive phenomena also sprang up. Mary Magdalen emerged as a character, unusual acting instructions appeared, details of emotional expression evolved, new phrases and whole pieces of music were composed, original poetry was written, costumes were changed from black to white at the miraculous moment, and in some convents the female role-players first underwent a purification rite.

The longer *Visitatio* from Origny best exhibits this pattern of innovation. It manifests an important inception principle, a combining of elements from two major traditions of the *Visitatio*: one belonging to the Anglo-Norman area, the other French. The composer of this particular drama fused elements from the two traditions together with her (or his?) own original compositions, textual and musical, fashioning finally not a collage but a complete and new artistic entity. Each detail has been shaped or carefully reshaped to fit an artistic unit. Taken as a whole, the plethora of minute elements that we can single out as musically and dramatically unique—from rearranged stanzas to fresh dialogue to singular gesture and body language—all yield a movement toward greater emotive expressiveness on the part of the characters, in particular on the part of Mary Magdalen.

Most likely the composer was an Abbess. It is she who may even have freshly compiled, composed, and written a distinctive version of the *Visitatio* for her convent. Indeed she seems to have taken the *Visitatio* into her own hands just at the time when, toward 1200, medieval Europe was on the verge of a momentous period in the history of music and the development of the liturgical drama. With the *Visitatio* the Abbess made manifest the female religious experience: in the act of cleansing, in emotional expression, and in identification with the figure of Mary Magdalen.

Texts of the *Visitatio Sepulchri*—from the Lipphardt edition: marked with "L" followed by Lipphardt text number and manuscript date

Note that the respective play itself often dates to a period earlier than the extant manuscript. Walther Lipphardt, *Lateinische Osterfeiern und Osterspiele,* 9 vols. (Berlin: Walter de Gruyter, 1975–90).

Visitatio Texts from Churches and Women's Convents with Women as the Marys

Andernach, St. Thomas, L355a (14th century)
Asbeck, L182–184 (1518, 16th c., 1524)
Barking, L770 (1363–76, 15th c. copy, text from 13th c. or earlier)
Brescia, St. Julia, L8 (1438)
Essen, Cathedral, L564 (14th c.)
Gandersheim, L785 (1438, 16th c. copy)
Gernrode, L786 (ca. 1500)
Gerresheim, L213 (15th c.), L214 and L574 (1685–1692)

Havelberg, L787 (15th c.)
Lichtenthal bei Baden-Baden, L832 (13th c.)
Marienberg bei Helmstedt, L791 (13th c.)
Medingen bei Lüneburg, L792 (c. 1320)
Münster, Liebfrauen, L793 (ca. 1600)
Nottuln, L794 (ca. 1420), L795 (pre–1493)
Origny St. Benoît, L303 (pre–1214, copied 1286), L303a, L304, and L825 (1315–17, text and music from ca. 1220 or earlier)
Poitiers, Holy Cross Nunnery, L151–153 (13th–14th c.)
Prague, St. George Nunnery, L798–806 (12th–14th c.), L387 (15th c.)
Regensburg-Obermünster, L796 (1567–87)
Salzburg Nonnberg, L718 (15th c.)
Troyes, Notre Dame, L170 (13th c.)
Wienhausen, (Lipphardt "Die Visitato Sepulchri") (14th c.)
Wilton, St. Edith's, (Rankin "New English Source") (1250–1320, copied in the 18th c.)
Wöltingerrode, L766 (13th c.)

Visitatio Texts from Churches and Monasteries with Men as the Marys—the Magdalen Role Emphasized

Besançon, L94 (13th c.)
Braunschweig, Cathedral, L780 (14th c.) [canonesses as Marys?]
Chiemsee, L782 (13th c.)
Cividale, Cathedral, L781 (14th c.)
Coutances, Cathedral, L771 (c. 1400) [canonesses as Marys?]
Dublin, L772 (14th c.)
Egmond, L827 (15th c.) [Rijnsberg Nunnery performance?]
Einsiedeln, L783 (12th–13th c.)
Engelberg, L784 (14th c.)
Fleury Playbook, L779 (12th c.)
Hersfeld, L788 (15th c.)
Joachimsthal (former Czechoslovakia), L789 (1520–23)
Klagenfurt, L790 (13th c.)
Klosterneuburg, L829 (13th c.)
Maastricht, L826 (ca. 1200) [canonesses as Marys?]
Mont-St.-Michel, L773–74 (14th c.)
Narbonne, L116 (n.d.)
Padua, Cathedral, L427 (13th c.), L428 (14th–15th c.)
Rheinau, L316 (ca. 1600), L797 (13th c.)
Rouen, Cathedral, L775–78 (12th–14th c.) [Rouen, *Peregrinus,* L812 (13th c.)]
Vich, L823 (11th–12th c.)

Visitatio Text with Unknown Ecclesiastical Origins—the Magdalen Role Emphasized

Tours, L824 (13th c.)

The Actors

The actors from the ranks of the clergy, choir boys, and in these few instances, nuns, are identified in numerous manuscripts of Easter and Christmas plays, whereas the following important dramas reveal virtually nothing as to their casts: the Tegernsee *Antichrist,* Laon *Joseph,* plays by Hilarius, the two Passion plays from Benediktbeuern, the four examples of the so-called *Ludus Paschalis,* and the St. Nicholas dramas and *Lazarus* and *St. Paul* in the Fleury Playbook. It is probable that these too were performed by clerical actors because of their liturgical choruses, apparent production in churches, association with monastic communities, and their kinship to works that do mention the clergy as performers—although there has been some speculation about traveling players at Benediktbeuern, for example.[19] All we know about the casting of the Beauvais *Daniel* comes from a line in the opening piece: it was "devised by the youth of Beauvais Cathedral." Mézières' requirement of a three- or four-year-old girl as Mary is the first documented instance of a secular participant, aside from choir boys, and it is not until the era of productions in Bozen, in the sixteenth century, that there is proof of numerous townspeople as actors within the church.

From the beginning it was the lower-ranking members of the ecclesiastical community who took the roles—canons, priests, deacons, brothers, *clerici* (clerks or priests), *pueri*—and one often perceives a recognition of hierarchy in the assignment of more important roles to more important participants. In general the angels at the tomb were played by deacons, ordained ministers below the rank of priest, who may have appeared younger than the priests who played the Marys, while the bishop or abbot often presided over the presentation, commencing the *Te Deum.*[20]

Shepherds, Magi, and midwives seem to have been impersonated by canons, priests, or *clerici,* the status of the *obstetrices* usually beneath that of the visitors, while from the era of the earliest Christmas dramas, the eleventh century, boys appeared as angels.[21] Boys also played the shepherds in the Montpellier text and the midwives in a German production and at Clermont-Ferrand. Whereas the Christmas celebrations were especially filled with the voices of boys, who, as angels, could easily perch up in the lantern tower, gallery, or triforium, it was more in keeping with the solemn spirit of the occasion if the heavenly beings at the Easter sepulchre were played by an adult. By the

thirteenth century, however, it was not uncommon for boys to take the parts of angels in the *Visitatio,* although by no means does this constitute a general or consistent practice.

Boys' choirs and schools had long been an integral part of monastic and collegiate life, and their choruses resounded in every large church. Provision is frequently made in the Easter dramas for their placement in processionals, the early play of *Isaac* from Vorau has a chorus of *pueri,* and the hosts of angels in Brunelleschi's paradise machines are a natural, theatrical extension of these groups.[22] Apparently toward the latter part of the Middle Ages productions of drama where children figure in a major way became fashionable in some quarters. The trend is reflected in a note appended to the fifteenth-century "Modus antiquus visitandi sepulchrum" from Cleves: "This manner of priests' [per presbyteros] visiting the sepulchre has fallen out of use, but it is performed by boys [scholares] according to the book called the *Agenda.*"[23]

Besides a general tendency to have younger individuals impersonate angels, typecasting on occasion solved the problem of John's winning the race to the tomb—for which there is no Biblical explanation. Texts from the twelfth and fourteenth centuries instruct that at the Austrian monastery of St. Lambrecht an older man should take the part of Peter, a younger man that of John. The same arrangement is called for in a thirteenth-century version from Rheinau. At Zurich canons represent the angel and the women, but "two old and honorable canons" play the disciples, of whom Peter is visibly the older. John must also be his junior at Essen, the otherwise very formal production in which canonesses portray the Marys. A sixteenth-century text from Augsburg merely notes that whereas priests (sacerdotes) enact the Marys, two "seniores sacerdotes" play the apostles, but they are not distinguished in the manner of the race. The most intriguing pair appear at Meissen and at Moosburg. In both performances Peter must have a limp, the realistic medieval mind making visible the cause of his losing the race to the tomb (Petro claudicante; precurratque Johannes, Petro sequenti et claudicanti).[24]

Tutors proximate to the performance were necessary for small children. Anna and Joachim, and later guardian angels, look after the little girl in Mézières' *Presentation:* "Throughout the Mass Mary will conduct herself with maturity and devotion, Gabriel and Raphael giving her instructions."[25]

Actors' Sides

Unique among the documents relevant to the medieval theatre are two extant examples of actors' sides: the fourteenth-century Sulmona fragment with the role of the fourth soldier in a Passion play, and the so-called Shrewsbury fragments, a fifteenth-century English manuscript containing for a single actor the part of the third shepherd in an *Officium Pastorum*, the third Mary in a simple *Visitatio Sepulchri*, and one of the two wayfarers in a *Peregrinus* play. Unfortunately there is no other information as to conditions under which these two players performed. The Sulmona text consists of the soldier's lines, usually delivered together with his companions, a few rubrical indications of his stage business, and the opening words, rather than the tag lines, of the immediately preceding speaker. The actor delivers five speeches alone, three together with the third soldier, and the remainder he recites with the group (Omnes). The role commences as soldiers three and four fight with one and two, go before Pilate, participate in the arrest of Christ—falling to the ground at the sound of an earthquake—bind Christ to a column before the magistrates, lead him to Pilate and then to Herod, dress him in white, bring him again to Pilate—calling for the crucifixion—bow mockingly in front of Christ, put a cross to his shoulders, quarrel over the division of his garment, "crucifigant eum inter duos latrones," mock those at the foot of the cross, eventually go and march around the sepulchre upon Pilate's orders to guard it. Discovering the sepulchre empty, they fear for their lives, run to Pilate, and the last we hear of soldier number four he and the third soldier believe that Christ has in fact risen from the dead and they sing "Alleluya." His role seems to be at an end here.

The Shrewsbury sides represent a transition to vernacular usage, for some of the speeches are in Latin, others in English. Actor's business is not given here—save in quotations from the Gospel of Luke as to the fear of the shepherds and the fact of their going to Bethlehem, and a note as to the Marys' approaching the sepulchre—but the cues are more effectively recorded in that they consist of the final words instead of the first two or three delivered by a previous speaker. Of course, tag lines set down in this manner hardly indicate attempts at depth in the portrayal of character relationships. The only extant actor's part from the Elizabethan public stage, that of Edward Alleyn in the title role of Robert Greene's *Orlando Furioso,* has the same kind of cue-line notation.[26]

Actors' Voices

Admonitions as to the quality of the actor's voice reflect what had always been self-understood and of greatest importance. From Aldersbach a fourteenth-to-fifteenth-century text requires specifically that the angel in the *Visitatio* be played by a "cleric who should have a sonorous voice" (sonoram uocem). The same instruction appears in texts from Strassburg, Aschaffenburg, and Melk. A fifteenth-century manuscript from St. Florian, one dated 1500 from Vienna, and six from Passau all employ the same descriptive adjective: the angel is to be sung by someone "having a suitable voice" (aptam vocem). The actor here is usually a deacon; a *clericus* as the angel at Passau must be selected "qui habet sonorem vocem." And at Tournai the two youths chosen by the *magister cantus* to play the *Annunciation* are to be those "having sweet and full [or intense] voices" (voces dulces et altas).[27]

Rarest of all are specific notes as to desirable characteristics of the role-players. At Marienberg bei Helmstedt each of the two actors to play Peter and John should be someone "who is suitable for them" (qui eis expedit). The only physical characteristic of a character-in-action that I know of is Peter's limp at Meissen and Moosburg, already mentioned. And at Sion the boy chosen to sing the angel must be one "who knows how to sing well" (qui bene sciat cantare).[28]

This specification for the angel selection at Sion points to the single most powerful and expressive element in the liturgy: the human voice. The performers of the liturgical drama had been trained since childhood as singers. They had committed huge swatches of the liturgy to memory, hour after hour singing the Mass and the Divine Office. They trained from early on toward the mastery of tone, pitch, rhythm, intensity, sonority—the infinite shadings of the chant, the varieties of sound in the multitude of architectural spaces, the myriad moods of worship from mourning to thanksgiving to celebration.

With the insertion of the drama into the liturgy appears an astonishing vocabulary related to the voice. Because the plays demanded something new from the singers, the textual rubrics team with instructions as to vocal quality, for instance, a passage to be sung "sweetly" or "intensely" or "tearfully." The regular singing of the chant passed on from one generation to the next through repetition and the instruction of the Magister Scholae, transmitted orally for the most part, memorized for the most part, but then with the introduction of the new material—such innovation in the liturgy was unusual, to say the least—the Magister and his singers required new "how to" phrases in the rubrics in addition to the words and music. Thus the rubrics of the liturgical drama in general fill with words to coach singers, words that, taken together, provide a treasury of vocal properties.

The following vocabulary contains a compendium of words in rubrics specific to vocal characteristic and line delivery. In the ensuing discussions we shall mine it for information on the technical use of the voice, the creation of mood, and the expression of emotion, mindful of nuances that distinguish ritual observance from mimetic episode.

Voice Vocabulary

Quality of Voice, Word or Line Delivery

Young references are noted first (with no identifier for volume 1), then Lipphardt (L), and Donovan (D). A Roman numeral refers to the date, the century, of the respective manuscript. Plays other than the *Visitatio Sepulchri* and *Ludus Paschalis* are denoted by the following abbreviations:

2 = Young, vol. 2	OR = *Ordo Rachelis*
3F = *Tres Filiae*	OS = *Officium Stellae*
Ann = *Annunciation*	Pass = Benediktbeuern Passion
Ant = *Antichrist*	Paul = *St. Paul*
Dan = *Daniel*	Per = *Peregrinus*
Get = *Getron*	Pres = Mézières' *Presentation*
Isa = *Isaac*	Pur = *Purification*
Jos = *Joseph*	Shep= Shepherds' Play
Laz = *Lazarus*	Xmas = Benediktbeuern Christmas Play

Voice:

ad diapason   at the octave.
   xiii: L71

alacer   animated, brisk, lively, sharp.
   xvi: 324

MG. allein   alone.
   xvii: L793

alternae modulationes   antiphonal tones.
   xv: 383

alterno   sing antiphonally.
   xii: Per 473

altisonus   high-sounding.
   xvi: 614

altissimus   highest.
   xiii: L826 (voice)

altus   elevated, high, loud, intense.
   xi: 628
   xii: 248, 262, 364, Per 472, Per 480, OS 2:35, Paul 2:221, Dan 2:286, L408, L775
   xiii: 305, 320, 442, 446, 447, Pass 516, L71, L86, L269, L492

   xiv: 268, 349, 350, 364, 371, 376, 589, 591, 594, Pres 2:233, 235, 237–40, Ann 2:249, Pur 2:254, L108, L153, L275, L306, L307, L350, L352, L494, L746, D Shep 125
   xv: 252, 317, 409, 580, 591, 593, 602, 631, 661, L233, L361, L362a, L453, L454, L464, L604a, L699
   xvi: 261, 342, L354, L715a
   xvii: 603, L214, L624

apertus   clear, free, plain, open.
   xiii: Pass 532
   xv: 630 (voice)
   xvi: 341, 643

aptus   fitting, suitable.
   xv: 354, 355, 646, 655, L633–34, L647–49, L762
   xvi: 652, L654

auctorabilis   authoritative, commanding.
   xiii: 399

blandus   smooth.
   xv: L453, L454

brevissimus   shortest.
   xviii: L444 (tone: a simpler version of chant)

cachinnus   loud laughter.
   xiii: Xmas 2:176
   xiv: Pres 2:233

cano   sing.
   xv: 627 (*simul* "likewise")
   xvi: L536n

clamare   to complain, cry out, proclaim, shout, wail.
   xii: 354, 365, Jos 2:270, Dan 2:292, 300
   xiii: 442, 660, Pass: 515, 516, 530, 532
   xiv: 334, 364, 365
   xvi: 341

clarus   bright, clear, distinct, loud.
   xii: 242, 364
   xiii: 656
   xiv: 364, L108
   xv: 580, L449
   xvii: 603, L573

clementer   gently, softly.
   x: 578

conqueri   to complain bitterly of.
   xiii: Pass 530

consolatio   comforting, consolation.
   x: 254
   xi: 587

despective   contemptuously.
   xii: OS 2:87

discretus   discreet, prudent.
   xiii: Xmas 2:172

dulcis   sweet, friendly.
   xiii: 660

dulcisonus   dulcet, sweet sounding.
    x: 581
    xi: 249

dulciter   pleasantly, sweetly.
    xii: Isa 2:259

elatus   elated, elevated.
    xvii: 251

excelsus   elevated, high, lofty.
    xii: 267
    xiii: L492
    xiv: 244, L494
    xv: 410, L106, L464, D Shep 34

exclamare   to call out, cry out, exclaim.
    xii: Dan 2:297, 300, 301

exultans   joyful.
    xii: 241

flebilis   mournful, tearful.
    xv: 382

flere   to cry, lament, weep.
    xiii: Pass 523, 524, 529, 530
    xiv: Pres 2:238
    xv: 409

fractus   broken.
    xvii: L214

fremere   to moan, murmur, wail.
    xii: Laz 2:207

furor   frenzy, passion.
    xiii: OS 2:99

gaudere   to rejoice.
    xii: OS 2:88, OR 2:110, Dan 2:300
    xiii: 400
    xiv: 349, 350

gravis   bass, deep-toned, grave, low.
    xii: Per 471, Get 2:356
    xiii: 394
    xiv: 334
    xvi: L435

gravitas   dignity, gravity.
    xvi: Ann 2:481

grossus   grandiloquent, important, strong.
    xiv: Pres 2:237

hilaris   joyful.
    xv: L795

humilis   abject, humble, low, submissive.
    xii: 241
    xiii: 304, 385, L269
    xiv: 244, 264, 329, Ann 2:249, D 90
    xv: 640, L106, L736
    xvi: 639, L600a, L795
    xviii: L444

increpare   to exclaim loudly, rebuke, passionately lament.
    xii: Per 471

insusurrare   to whisper.
    xii: Ant 2:378

iubeo   order, command.
    xii: 297

iubilo   shout with joy.
    xi (xv copy): 299

iucundus   joyous.
    xiv: L780
    xv: 409

lacrimabilis   melancholy, mournful, tearful, weepy.
    xii: Dan 2:300
    xv: 408

lacrimare   to weep.
    xii: Laz 2:207

lamentabilis   lamenting, weepy.
    xii: Get 2:353

lamentabiliter   lamentably.
    xv: L795

lamentari   to lament, weep.
    xiii: Pass 524
    xiv: 347

lenis   gentle, mild, quiet.
    xiii: 399

letabundus   joyful.
    xv: 383

lete   gladly, joyfully.
    xv: 593

maestus   sad.
    xii: L93 [in Vol. 6] (*vox* "voice")

maternus   motherly, maternal.
    xvi: 672 (*vox* "voice")

media voce   medium, moderate (voice).
    xv: L464

mediocer   medium, moderate.
    x: 581
    xi: 249
    xii: 267, 597, L315
    xiii: 312, 597
    xiv: 260
    xv: 252, L213, L485

moderatus   moderate.
    xii: 394
    xv: 409

modicus   moderate, modest.
    xii: Per 471

modulatio   modulation, rhythmical measure.
    x: 254
    xi: 587

morose   soberly, solemnly.
    xvi: Ann 2:481

murmurare   to grumble, murmur, mutter.
    xiii: 428, Xmas 2:176
    xiv: Pres 2:238

nuntio   announce.
  xiii: 400
paulatim   gradually, slowly.
  xiii: Pass 528
plangere   to bewail, cry, lament.
  xii: 3F 2:318
  xv: 383
planus   clear, distinct, plain, flat.
  xiii: 294
  xiv: Ann 2:249
plorare   to lament, weep.
  xii: OR 2:119
  xiii: 443, Pass: 524, 525, 530
  xiv: Pres 2:238
  xv: 409
precelsus   exalted, lofty, very high.
  xii: 597
  xiii: 597
  xv: 596
pronuntio   pronounce, proclaim.
  xii: 311
prorumpo   break forth into song.
  xii: 311
  xv: 630
  xvi: 342, L260
publica   public, audible.
  xiii: 572 (voice)
quasi   as if.
  xiii: L102
quero   ask.
  xv: 362
querulus   plainitive, complaining.
  xvi: 324
remissus   gentle soft, held back, restrained.
  xii: 363
  xiii: 314, L728
  xiv: 363
respondeo   answer.
  xiv: 381
  xv: 667, L625, L795
  xvi: L785
reticeo   return to silence.
  xv: L795
silentium   silence.
  xii: 310
  xiii: L728
  xiv: L494
  xvi: L344
simplex   plain, simple, sincere.
  xiii: OS 2:436
sobrius   moderate, sober.
  xiii: Xmas 2:177

sollemniter   solemnly.
  xv: 593
  xvi: 601
sonorus   loud, sonorous.
  xii: 365
  xiv: L615a
  xv: 648, 649
  xvi: L344, L503
suaviter   sweetly.
  xii: Laz 2:200
  xiv: OS 2:44
  xv: OS 2:437
subiungo   order, command.
  xii: Dan 2:284
submissior   lower, quite low.
  xiv: L536a
summissus   gentle, humble, soft, submissive.
  xii: 263, 597, 632, L315
  xiii: 313, 597, OS 2:436
  xiv: 268, L230, L447, L536a, L536d, L536y, L746
  xv: 382, 591, 592, 593, 594, 596, 668, L213, L233,
       L234, L307, L308, L352, L449, L485, L536q,
       L536r, L536x, L795
  xvi: L370, L576g
  xvii: 251
suppressus   subdued.
  xii: 266
  xiii: 399
suspirare   to sigh.
  xii: Isa 2:260, Get 2:356
  xv: 383, 409
susurrare   to murmur, whisper.
  xii: Laz 2:207
taceo   to be silent.
  xiii: Per 463
tacitus   quiet.
  xiv: 649, L632, L635, L761, L762
  xv: 649, L719
tonaliter   with tone, with singing.
  xiii: L728
ululare   to howl, shriek.
  xiv: Pres 2:233, 238
vicis   turn, exchange.
  xii: Per 479 (*tribus vicibus* "by threes")
  xvi: 672 (*tribus vicibus* "by threes")

The Qualities and Use of the Voice

One can commence with a working distinction between words from the rubrics connected with the
sound of the voice (high, loud, sonorous) and those
which prescribe the attitude of the singer (joyful, sor-

rowful). At the same time, one recognizes that both have their roots in the meaning of the text or in the intention of the composer-playwright.

The dramatic attitudes or moods for which the vocality is most frequently described are those of joy—repeatedly a glad proclamation—and sorrow; the sound of the voice for joy most often called for being *alta*, that for sorrow being *lugubris*. Of all words in this context *alta* provides the most ambiguities. Although often one does not know whether *alta* refers to pitch, volume, or intensity, in the instances cited below, the translation of "intense" usually seems appropriate. As to "pitch," when we have the music, we can determine whether a given part is higher (altus) than the preceding or following part. If "volume" refers to the loudness of a voice, then "intensity" refers to that particular characteristic of the voice where the sound—whether loud or soft—carries or pierces through a given distance or space.[29]

In addition, it is difficult to distinguish between lines intended to be delivered in an intensely emotional manner, *voce alta*, as opposed to those sung or spoken in a more intense voice in keeping with the music of the ceremony, for *altus* can and does refer to choral singing as well as to passages by individual characters. Toward the conclusion of the fourteenth-century *Visitatio* from Essen, one of the disciples ascends to the organ-loft and proclaims "Christus Dominus surrexit" three times: "primo in gravibus, secundo altius, et tertio bene alte, et conventus respondebit ei toties in simili tono." Here it is a matter of pitch. A thirteenth-century text from Haarlem concludes with a triple elevation of the cross, whereby the pitch of "Christus Dominus resurrexit" is repeatedly raised, "alte," "altius," and "altissime."[30]

This descriptive adjective is usually applied to lines that conclude a play in a joyous, celebrative manner, such as those accompanying the display of linen in the *Visitatio*. The fourteenth-century play from Dublin has the women emerge from the tomb singing "Alleluya," "*alta uoce* as if rejoicing and wondering" (quasi gaudentes et admirantes), and the final chorus is sung "*alta uoce* as if rejoicing and exulting" (quasi guadentes et exultantes).

By the eleventh or twelfth century, texts of the *Visitatio* reveal an explicit sense of vocal contrast between the sorrowful mission of the Marys at the outset and the concluding triumph, a moving dramatic crescendo that begins in subdued tones. An eleventh- or twelfth-century play from Melk has the women reply humbly (humili uoce) to the angels' opening question; the angels joyfully (uoce exultanti) announce "Non est hic"; and the Marys sing the final antiphon in a loud, clear voice (uoce

clara). Such a transition is implicit in Bishop Ethelwold's description, where the angel sings "Quem quaeritis" in a medium voice (mediocri uoce) and the final *Te Deum* is begun by the prior "sharing in their [the Marys'] gladness" (congaudens). Elsewhere the Marys start out with humble, tearful, mournful, gentle, low or subdued sounds (voce humili, lacrimabili, lugubri, remissa, summissa, suppressa); the angels commence sweetly, moderately, or in humble or gentle tones (mediocriter, voce humili or summissa); subsequent lines of the play may be delivered solemnly, in a medium or joyful voice, somewhat higher or louder (sollempniter, mediocri voce, iocunda, or voce altiori quam prius); and the witness to the Resurrection, usually with the showing of the gravecloths, is celebrated in an intense, high, exalted, or sonorous voice (voce alta, excelsa, precelsa, sonora). Some of these words, such as *humilis* and *lacrimabilis*, clearly refer to the attitude of the singer; others to the sound, such as *sonorus* and *mediocriter*; whereas words such as *remissus* and *suppressus* could refer to either.[31]

In fact this gradual swelling from lower or softer tones—and from a muted mode toward rich, festive sounds and an exultant mood—characterizes most of the performances in the church. The overall pattern of the productions can be called comic because they begin in perplexity or seeming misfortune and conclude happily. The *Peregrinus* of Fleury opens with the two wayfarers singing in a medium voice (modica uoce), Christ rebukes them in a low or grave voice ("graui uoce," his usual voice when the Gospel was intoned), and in a version for Sicily all the disciples sing "alta uoce" the concluding "Surrexit Dominus" after Christ's appearance to them. In the *Officium Stellae* from Rouen, the Magi point to the star "simplici uoce," and the first line of the midwives is spoken in a gentle or soft manner (submissa uoce) before the three kings rule the choir in the subsequent Mass. Conversely, the *Ordo Rachelis* at Fleury opens on an exultant note as the innocents go "gaudentes per monasterium," then sinks to despair as Rachel weeps over the bodies of the children, but is saved from final tragedy when the innocents rise and enter the choir while Joseph returns singing, "Gaude, gaude, gaude." One also perceives the overall auditory design of the *Annunciation* at Padua, where the angel commences "alta uoce" his address to the Virgin, while Mary answers in a simple or clear manner (plana uoce), finally turning toward the congregation at the conclusion and delivering the *Magnificat* "alta uoce."

Strong contrast of vocal effect distinctly marks certain individual scenes such as the opening exchange of the Benediktbeuern Christmas play, between Archisynagogus, the chief representative of anti-Christian forces, and Augustine, his major adversary. Archisynagogus sets forth with a display of anger and then derisive laughter (cum nimio cachinno), while Augustine answers him with dignity and restraint (Voce sobria et discreta). To the shrieking and howling Lucifer (cachinnantem et aliquando vlulantem) in the *Presentation,* Mézières opposes the full voices of Michael and other angels (alta voce), and close to the grandiloquent speeches (grossa voce) of Mary's parents he contrasts the crying, lamenting, and murmuring (flendo, plorando, murmurando) of the expelled Synagoga.

The most intense and frequently portrayed sudden reversal of emotions occurs in Mary Magdalen's recognition of Christ. At Chiemsee she bends down and looks into the sepulchre three times as she mourns; Christ suddenly advances and gently questions her (leni uoce) and she responds in a subdued or suppressed voice (suppressa uoce), making as if to depart; when she recognizes him, she throws herself at his feet, attempting to embrace him; she then listens reverently as he addresses her in an authoritative manner (auctorabili uoce); and Mary Magdalen runs jubilantly to the disciples (quasi gaudens).[32]

The raised voice (alta) is also employed elsewhere for the high note of conclusion, the full tone of public proclamation, and the excitement of discovery. This is the quality of the angel's first announcement in Hilarius' play of *Daniel,* and Symeon receives the Christ Child at the finale of the Paduan *Purification* with this voice. Paul preaches at Damascus and Thomas in the *Ludus Paschalis* from the Tours manuscript declares his belief "alta uoce." This is the qualification cited most by Mézières for important moments in the *Presentation*: in the procession to the church the angel must sing loudly, accompanied by instruments, "to rouse the populace to devotion"; the angels, Ecclesia, and Michael address Mary "alta voce"; Anna and Joachim speak thus in presenting their child at the high altar; and the bishop receives her with a full voice. A twelfth-century *Officium Stellae* from Limoges has the Magi proceed "cum gravitate," but when the first king spies the star, he sings "altiori voce."[33]

Aside from the use of the raised voice, the rubrics disclose little as to subtleties and variations of rejoicing. Certainly the more important key to the vocal portrayal of emotions lies with the mode of the particular musical passages. A general tone of exuberance is noted at Fleury for the shepherds returning from the manger "gaudentes," while more specifically personal expressions of joy in individual dramatic moments are sometimes indicated through the character's delivering his speech as a loud exclamation (clamare). In the Beauvais *Daniel,* King Darius "gaudens exclamabit" as he discovers Daniel safe from the lions. At Rouen, Mary Magdalen "clamando" recognizes Christ, "Raboni"; later *Visitatio* texts from that cathedral have her speak the word "alta voce." At Wilton convent the three Marys announce the Resurrection with "Alleluya resurrexit" singing "iussionis voce"—they had begun the performance "lamentantes"—and the whole community celebrates, "Omnes congaudent."[34]

The sound of exclamation conveys a range of moods and emotions. As a proclamation (exclamare) it is the manner in which the Curia of the Beauvais *Daniel* hails the new king, and the angel closes the same play; the "Surrexit" of the *Visitatio* is announced at St. Lambrecht "sonora uoce conclamantes," and at Essen "Sic clamabit." Or "clamare" can be an outcry, such as that of Judas when he betrays Christ and of the Jews as they demand the crucifixion in the Benediktbeuern Passion. It is the sign of the kind of shock experienced by King Belshazzar in the Beauvais *Daniel* as he witnesses the handwriting on the wall (stupefactus clamabit). In distress, Potiphar's wife shouts out her false indictment of Joseph before her husband's house, and Daniel's accusers vent their confessions in this manner. The sense of suffering is extreme in Christ's cry "Ely, Ely" (alta uoce clamet) from the cross in the Benediktbeuern Passion.[35]

Sorrow and lamentation form the other major mood which the ecclesiastical actor had to convey with his voice, whereby he was often instructed to use a plaintive tone in the delivery of his lines or to shed tears during certain speeches: mourning over the dead, bewailing one's own suffering or misfortune, or repenting. Some rather late texts have the Marys approach the sepulchre lamenting or weeping instead of the more usual subdued tone: *lamentari, plangere, voce lacrimabili.* These expressions of anguish usually occur in moments of bereavement for the dead. King Darius comes to the den of lions mourning over the awaited destruction of Daniel (Beauvais), and he speaks "lacrimabiliter." Rachel (at Freising) weeps over the slaughtered innocents (plorare). Christ is moved to tears in the Fleury play of *Lazarus* (fremens et lacrimans in se), as are Lazarus' sisters in the Benediktbeuern Passion (flere), and in the latter play Mary the mother of Christ stands at the foot of the cross and "cries out to the weeping women, lamenting bitterly" (clamat ad Mulieres flentes et conquerendo valde). Euphrosina bewails (lamentabili uoce) the loss of her son in *Getron* (Fleury). And the father of the *Tres Filiae* cries (plangere) over the threatened misfortune of his daughters before St. Nicholas performs his miracles (Fleury). The voice of lamentation also accompanies acts of repentance: in the Benediktbeuern Passion, Mary Magdalen is converted, dresses in black, and with ointment comes "flendo" and "lamentando" to Christ; in the same play Judas is weeping (flendo) as he returns the pieces of silver to the high priests.[36]

Besides the extremes of joy and sorrow, some characters portray such muted feelings as restrained grief or gentle consolation through the use of the middle registers, the low voice, or a sweet tone. But again the terminology of the rubrics does not permit more than vague distinctions between pitch and volume, conveying rather a general sense of the vocal quality and attitude in the dramatic moment. We have already alluded to the fact that the Marys frequently begin their journey to the tomb in a humble, soft, low, or medium voice, the angels questioning them in a similar manner. The earliest description, from Winchester, stresses sweetness in the angel's delivery (mediocri uoce/dulcisone cantare), and in the Fleury Playbook the heavenly beings sing in deep tones (moderata et admodum graui uoce). At Coutances the Marys sing in a modest or restrained manner (vereconde). At Zwiefalten and at Barking, there is a more explicit suggestion of sadness in the voices of the women, "multum suppressa uoce" and "flebili uoce et submissa." Barking was a nunnery, a rare abbey where as we have noted one could hear the difference between male and female voices in this drama.[37]

So was the Abbey of Origny St. Benoît. There the translation of the *Visitatio* rubrics by the early fourteenth-century Abbess Isabelle d'Acy suggests an increasing loudness in the dialogue on the part of both questioner and answerer. In French there is a distinction between "bas instruments" (e.g., strings) and "hauts instruments" (e.g., shawms and trumpets). This distinction informs Isabelle d'Acy's stage directions for the Origny play. The Marys, sung here by women, are first to sing softly (bien bas) and high (à fausset, in falsetto): "Quis revolvet." The priest as angel is also to sing softly (bien bas): "Quem queritis." Then the Marys sing a little louder (un peu plus haut): "Jhesum Nazarenum." And then the priest sings with a loud voice (à haute vois): "Non est hic." Presumably there

is not much difference in pitch, except the difference between the male and female voices.[38]

Parallel with the *Visitatio* is the scene in the Rouen *Officium Stellae* where the midwives at the manger speak in a gentle or soft voice (submissa uoce) or respond sweetly (suauiter). When Christ appears as Hortulanus to Mary Magdalen, he first addresses her in a gentle or soft tone (leni uoce, submisse cantat) (Chiemsee, Havelberg), and when the Marys deliver their rather militant outburst against the Jews, "Dicant nunc Iudei," just prior to the final display of the linen, they sing "mediocri uoce" or "summissa uoce" (Zwiefalten, Prüfening, Rheinau, Hirsau).[39]

Every now and then a descriptive word or phrase suggests an actor's attempt at a kind of verisimilitude in his voice that is quite out of the ordinary. As early as the twelfth century, the actor playing Isaac at Vorau imitated an old man by sighing (suspiria ut senes). Other examples of the sigh accompany speeches of mourning: the captive son of Getron is overheard by the king as "suspiret grauiter" (Fleury); at Barking and at Coutances, Mary Magdalen sighs during her lamentation near the sepulchre. Only twice are there documented moments in which characters whisper: in the *Antichrist* play the figure of Hypocrisy whispers of the advent of Antichrist to a group of Hypocrites, but he has no recorded audible lines; while one of the few passages unaccompanied by music in the Fleury drama of *Lazarus* is the message whispered by Martha to her sister, Mary, that Christ, approaching Bethany, has called for her. Murmuring seems to be an expression both of grief and anger: in the *Ludus Paschalis* from Klosterneuburg the apostles "sine cessatione murmurant ymnum istum plangentes Dominum" before hearing of what the Marys have witnessed, while in the Christmas play from Benediktbeuern, Archisynagogus appears in a tumultuous fury "cum magno murmure."[40]

One is struck by the sheer amount of movement, the activity, the comings and goings indicated by the rubrics. And one is struck by the qualities of movement and gesture that are called for. What is done is done fittingly or decorously (aptate), or with certainty (modo certificate).[41] Elsewhere the actors are to go or step quickly (cito, celeri gressu), or quite quickly (citius).[42] The Marys go wandering, tentative (erraneos), or step by step (pedetemptim); or they wander through the choir (vagando per chorum).[43] They often walk slowly (lente).[44] Peter and John go at a run (cursorie), or hurriedly (festinanter); as do Cleophas and Luke in the *Peregrinus*.[45]

Characters hesitate (dubito), or act immediately (immediate), or do something often (sepe), or move unexpectedly or unforeseen (ex inproviso).[46] They wait for another (exspecto), or expect someone (prestolor).[47] They do something humbly (humiliter), or in a modest or restrained way (vereconde), or greet each other gently or tenderly (clementer eos salutantes).[48]

Perhaps among the most affecting components in the music and pageantry are the occasional moments of silence. After singing the *Maria Magdalena et alia Maria* at Nottuln, the nuns' chorus returns to silence (reticeo), and the play proper begins. Similarly two twelfth-century versions of the *Visitatio*, from Augsburg and St. Lambrecht, which start with a major procession out of the choir, call for stillness before the women then make their way toward the sepulchre. Three texts—from Prüfening, Rheinau, and Hirsau have the Marys, returning from the scene at the sepulchre, enter the choir silently and then burst out "precelsa uoce" with the *Surrexit*. These are rests scored for the modulation of each work as a whole, but there is only a single example of a character's silence as indicative of his own inner tension. Following Scriptural accounts, the composer of the Benediktbeuern Passion has Pilate interrogate Christ, saying "Your own people and the chief priests have handed you over to me." Christ delivers his next reply slowly (paulatim); "My Kingdom is not of this world." "What are you, then?" asks Pilate, and Christ speaks no more (Iesus vero taceat).[49]

The Anglo-Norman *Jeu d'Adam* and the *Planctus Mariae* of Cividale: Prompt-scripts for the Actors

One of the most remarkable dramas of the twelfth century is the *Jeu d'Adam*.[50] It is written in Norman French with such extensive Latin rubrics that we can call it a prompt-book. It was apparently designed for production immediately in front of a church. If indeed this structural façade serves as the background, then the central entrance of the church would be celestial paradise. At one side of the open playing area would stand a scaffolding decorated to represent terrestrial paradise and at the opposite side a full-sized hell, probably a hell mouth. The drama has three scenes: the fall of Adam and Eve, Cain's murder of Abel, and an *Ordo Prophetarum*.

A chorus (probably a church choir) is present, per-

haps proximate to the central door because their plainchant singing—two Latin lessons and seven responsories, all traditional—is always associated with the presence of God the Father. Thus musical passages shape out the spoken scenes. In performance one experiences a powerful and subtle partnership in alternating sound, the human voice singing and speaking, juxtaposing contemporary telling of the myth (in the people's language) with age-old ritual chant (in Latin). Has liturgical music been appropriated to frame mimetic action, or have dramatic scenes been interspersed within blocks of music?

Although apparently not intended to be played within the sanctuary, the stage directions of the *Adam* furnish an amazing source of information as to the standards possible for medieval acting and as to the kinds of demands that could be made upon the actor. Who performed the play, we do not know, but in that God the Father, called "Figura" and dressed in a dalmatic, has a major role, that a chorus is used, that an exterior of a church seems to provide the setting, and that the work closes with a not uncommon Christmas observance, we might well assume that clergy were involved. Because of the drastic and in one instance complex nature of demonic performance, for example, it may be that some members of the cast were professional mimes. In any case, the author shows keen concern for the proper use of voice and gesture and adherence to the text; he instructs Figura, Adam, Eve, Cain, and Abel at almost every juncture while giving the devils quite a free hand in their improvised exploits in which they are to use "fitting" gestures.

After opening directions as to set construction and costuming, there follows the kind of admonition which Hamlet would deliver to the players at Elsinore four centuries later:

> And let Adam himself be well instructed when he shall make his answers, lest in answering he be either too swift or too slow. Let not only Adam, but all the persons, be so instructed that they shall speak composedly and shall use such gestures as become the matter whereof they are speaking; and in uttering the verses, let them neither add a syllable nor take away any, but let them pronounce all clearly; and let those things that are to be said be said in their due order.

To begin with, a great deal of attention is paid to the tone of voice and to the use of facial expression: Adam stands before Figura "with composed countenance" (vultu composito), and Eve "with countenance a little more subdued" (parum demissiori). Perhaps the most subtle piece of acting in the work is carried out by the Devil as he tempts first Adam and then Eve. He tells Adam that he is a fool for not tasting the forbidden fruit, but Adam refuses, so the Devil runs about a bit with the other demons before returning. Now he puts on a "cheerful" face, "and rejoicing" he continues, but still to no avail. This time he departs "sadly and with downcast countenance" to have a mimed conference with his fellows. Then he spies Eve, reassumes his "cheerful countenance and [with] much blandishment" approaches her to deliver a considerable line of flattery. However, eventually it takes a serpent "cunningly put together"—possibly the Devil now in a disguise—to bring about her downfall. At the end of this section, with "great dancing and jubilation," the devils drag the unhappy couple off to hell. What we witness here is something unique in the drama of the church: a character masks his real emotion, and the quality of joy which the devil originally feigns is the opposite of his usual fiendish exuberance in victory.

Pious pleasure is the emotion played by Adam and Eve as they first enter terrestrial paradise, "walking about, innocently delighting themselves." Displeasure, anger, sorrow, scorn, fear, and wonder are all to be portrayed explicitly with the face and voice. In addition, Abel addresses his brother "in a fond and friendly fashion," while Cain replies "as if mocking him," and "more mildly than is his wont." The only technical terms used to describe the voice are those applied to the prophets, who should speak loudly and distinctly (aperte et distincte), Abraham commencing "alta voce."

Physical attitude and gesture must also give expression to a whole range of feeling, indeed hardly another actor on the medieval stage of the church is called upon to sustain such a series of emotional transitions as those required of Adam and Eve. Their opening moods are of composure and delight. Then after eating the fruit, they rise in shame from their hiding place to confront Figura, "yet not fully upright, but . . . bending forward a little," their altered costumes also indicating a change in spiritual condition. Driven from the garden, "sad and confounded in appearance, they shall bow themselves to the ground, even unto their feet." In misery they beat their breasts, and as their wretchedness grows, they prostrate themselves, striking their breasts and thighs. Here we find a rising scale of physical expressions for degrees of sorrow. As Adam then laments, he looks back with terrible regret at paradise, lifting up "both hands toward it; and devoutly bowing his head."

Thereupon his mood changes to anger, and he raises his hand against Eve, "moving his head with great indignation."

The raising of the right hand also constitutes a threat, a gesture employed by Cain. And "manifesting wonder and fear," the prophet Habakkuk extends both hands toward the church. Even the sense of fatigue is to be conveyed, by Adam and Eve and then by Cain and Abel as they sit down after agricultural labors.

In addition to numerous instances of pointing to objects, places, and people, there are two examples of mimed speech. When the Devil first fails in his attempt on Adam, he goes to hell and "Shall hold converse there with the other demons." And when the serpent ascends the trunk of the forbidden tree, "Eve shall approach her ear, as if hearkening unto its counsel." In neither case are lines given.

If anywhere there is an indication of the traveling mimes' influence on the early religious drama, it is to be found in two episodes of the *Jeu d'Adam* acted out wholly in pantomime on the neutral playing area. The first shows Adam and Eve cast out of the garden:

> Then shall Adam have a spade, and Eve a mattock, and they shall begin to till the ground, and they shall sow wheat therein. After they shall have finished their sowing, they shall go and sit for a season in a certain place, as if wearied with their toil, and with tearful eyes shall they look back ofttimes at Paradise, beating their breasts. Meanwhile shall the Devil come and plant thorns and thistles in their tillage, and then he shall depart. When Adam and Eve shall come to their tillage, and when they shall have beheld the thorns and thistles that have sprung up, stricken with grievous sorrow, they shall cast themselves down upon the ground; and remaining there, they shall beat their breasts and their thighs, manifesting their grief by their gestures. . . .

The second scene depicts the offerings of Cain and Abel:

> Then shall they go unto two great stones, which shall have been made ready for this purpose. The one stone shall be set at such a distance from the other that, when the Figure appeareth, Abel's stone shall be on his right hand, but the stone of Cain on his left. Abel shall offer up a lamb, and incense, whence he shall cause smoke to arise. Cain shall offer a handful of corn. Then the Figure shall appear, and he shall bless Abel's offering, but the offering of Cain shall he regard with scorn. Wherefore, after the oblation, Cain shall set his face against Abel; and when their sacrifices are ended, they shall go again unto their own places.

Each moment constitutes in itself a miniature play, requiring considerable skill on the part of the performers, the first especially revealing some of the means of expression necessary to a mimetic artist playing without words a scene of labor, fatigue, and progressive grief. Additionally, it would take little to locate these same tragic elements in a comic action.

As to characterization, there is one note of particular interest in the otherwise formal sequence of prophets. Abraham, Balaam, and Habakkuk are old; Solomon is dressed like David, but appears younger; while Daniel is played by an actor "in years a youth, but in his demeanor like unto an old man." That is, Daniel is to act against type.

In contrast to the *Adam,* this free work of inventive genius, is the ceremonial *Planctus Mariae* in a fourteenth-century manuscript with music from the Cathedral of Cividale del Friuli. Probably performed during the Adoration of the Cross on Good Friday, the *Planctus* consists of lamentations by five speakers—the Virgin, Mary Magdalen, two other Marys, and the disciple John—standing beneath what seems to be a figured crucifixion scene with Christ and the two thieves. Of extraordinary value in the 127-line piece are seventy-nine stage directions noting gesture, added to the text above each respective line. Otherwise there is no movement in this static, musical composition.

By far the gestures which occur the most often are a character's beating his or her breast in lamentation (some eighteen times), and pointing to the image of Christ (some sixteen times), and specifically to his side, the crown of thorns, the cross, the thieves. Striking the hands together is called for twice as an expression of misery, the relaxed or dropped hand a sign of despair. Once Magdalen wipes away her tears, and twice actors mourn with their hands to their eyes. Consolation is displayed by means of an embrace— the arms sometimes placed around the neck of the second actor—an act of affection by the Virgin for John.

Only once does someone prostrate him- or herself—Magdalen at the feet of Christ—while bowing with the inclined head and genuflection are signs of veneration. Outstretched arms and open hands accompany entreaty and other forms of address to Christ, to other characters, and to the congregation.

A rather late document, this *Planctus* serves as a kind of anthology of gesture which we find sporadically indicated throughout the corpus of church drama, and it tells us a great deal about the possible expressiveness of the hands especially in the frequent portrayals of grief.

The Use of the Body

Characterization

When a stage direction such as that from Rouen Cathedral says that actors playing the Marys move toward the tomb "dressed in dalamatics, and having amices on their heads in the manner of women, carrying vases in their hands," it reveals the major means of characterization—the costume and hand property. Nowhere is the necessity for the instant attachment of individual features to the *dramatis personae* more clearly discernible than in the *Ordo Prophetarum,* accompanied at Laon and Rouen by extensive notes distinguishing aspects of their physical appearance. This manner of characterization, ritual-oriented in that most actors wear some form of ecclesiastical vestment, reflects quintessentially the ceremonial quality of movement and gesture in these musical pieces.

Yet as early as the twelfth century we begin to find a few prominent, singular additions to the usual dress and deportment, as some of the stage directions in the *Jeu d'Adam* would lead one to suspect. In the Vorau *Isaac* there is a portrait of great age: the father goes to his bed and delivers his opening lines "having raised his hands and repeatedly coughing and sighing like an old man." We have already cited the type-casting of an older and a younger man as Peter and John; in the race to the tomb at Moosburg and at Meissen, Peter is also made to limp. In the *Ordo Prophetarum* from Rouen, Habakkuk is lame; at Laon, Nebuchadnezzar has a haughty walk, the Sibyl feigns madness, and Balaam furiously drives the donkey with his spurs. The Sibyl in the Benediktbeuern Christmas play also simulates insanity "cum gestu mobili," while Archisynagogus is instructed explicitly to imitate Jewish behavior (imitando gestus Iudei in omnibus).[51]

A scene with what Karl Young calls, "The boldest effort toward realistic impersonation . . . encountered thus far," occurs at the interview between the Magi and Herod in the twelfth-century Montpellier text of the *Officium Stellae.* Here two of the kings do not speak Herod's language. The first hails him in Latin and is made to sit at Herod's right, but the second suddenly begins in gibberish, "Ase ai ase elo . . . ." He is given a place by the first. Then the third spouts more nonsense, "O some tholica . . . ." Obviously perplexed, Herod puts him by the others and starts to question them as to their identity and mission, and they continue as they had spoken earlier—in Latin. As Albert Weiner observes, "This is no matter of realistic impersonation; it is an instant, sudden flash of originality."[52] Although a matter of language rather than gesture, the stroke epitomizes the sporadic evidence of fitful attempts at verisimilitude in acting which punctuate the performances.

As will be seen from the following discussion, it is usually the evil or non-Christian characters—Herod, Archisynagogus, soldiers—who have moments where they reach toward more elaborate variety in acting, the imitation of less ceremonial behavior, for, as Grace Frank has pointed out, "Herod's was the first role capable of giving us a real person and not a type."[53] The other character with these seeds of genuine personality is Mary Magdalen, depicted in a range of highly emotional episodes beginning with her life as a prostitute.

Means of Conveying Emotions

The most frequently expressed mood on the part of a character is that of awe or veneration; then come the primary emotions of joy, sorrow, fear, and anger. Secondary feelings such as jealousy or fatigue occur seldom, and the rubrics reveal no especial instructions as to acting them. The unique stage direction from the Cividale Visitatio, "Yhesus admirans" (Jesus wondering), provides an exception—perhaps the call for delicate facial expression as Jesus sings "Mulier, quid ploras?" to Mary Magdalen (Woman, why do you weep?).[54] Moreover, we should not make the mistake of ascribing our modes or habits of behavior to the performers in these plays. Whereas it appears that the embodiment of emotion is often exaggerated, characters too often falling to the ground voluntarily or involuntarily, we must take into consideration the facts that the playing space of a large church demands broad gestures—the ordinary lifting of a finger must become the turning of the whole head; that the tenor of the performance is operatic and gesture should harmonize with the voice of singing and declamation rather than match a conversational tone; that commonly accepted, everyday expressions of grief or pleasure can and do vary quite considerably from area to area and from period to period; that with rare exceptions these texts are not prompt-books and usually record only major matters of acting; that a fundamental characteristic of many of these plays is the often uneven interspersing of relatively realistically conceived moments within the more formal unfolding of the

work; and that behind and beside the attitudes of the players lies a whole catalogue of gesture inherent in and appropriate to regular ecclesiastical observances. Just as the voice of the actor was trained first to read, chant, and sing the Office, so the body of the actor was schooled first to move through and gesticulate in liturgical ritual.

Acts showing awe, homage, humility, respect, or reverence almost always involve bowing the head, kneeling, or prostration, the latter as the most extreme physical position frequently reserved for moments of particular emotional pitch such as Mary Magdalen's recognition of Christ. The earliest example of this latter action, which, to be sure, also involves joy and shock, occurs in a twelfth-thirteenth-century Visitatio from Einsiedeln, where at Christ's pronouncement of her name Mary falls down (procidens) and remains prostrate (adorans in terra) for possibly a twenty-line exchange. At Rouen there is an evident sense of contrast between Mary at Christ's feet and then the three women as they merely bow (inclinent) to the chorus at the conclusion. At Wilton Nunnery one feels the influence of the Cult of the Holy Sepulchre where the Marys approach the sepulchre and prostrate themselves one by one, "worship the place where Dominus lay," and deposit phylacteries in the sepulchre. Later, in the same performance, Mary Magdalen prostrates herself, again, at the sepulchre, rises and genuflects, and prostrates herself once more at the recognition scene with the Risen Christ. Both the feeling of Mary's excitement and her desire to touch Christ are made explicit in the thirteenth-century Visitatio from Rheinau: "Hec cantando currens procidit ad pedes eius et nititur eum tangere." Christ raises his hand to stop her, and during the course of the subsequent exchange she twice more throws herself at his feet (procidendo ad pedes eius). As of the fourteenth century this action seems to become more exaggerated in some places: at Barking, Magdalen prostrates herself before him, and then when he reappears at the other side of the altar, all three fall down and grasp and kiss his feet. At Münster, Magdalen genuflects twice, then falls, and he bends over and with a benediction raises her up.

A clear sign of repentance is Magdalen's prostration before Christ both in the Benediktbeuern Passion and in the Lazarus of Fleury. At Beauvais, Tours, Benediktbeuern, and Fleury, Thomas falls at Christ's feet after being shown his wounds; and the father of the Tres Filiae at Fleury performs this act before St. Nicholas.

More commonly the shepherds and the Magi bow their heads or kneel at the Christmas manger. The

Montpellier text is exceptional in that it indicates a comparison between the kings' genuflecting to Herod but prostrating themselves on the ground at the manger. The inclined head or bended knee is the sign generally of homage to a superior personage: the Marys genuflect before the angel (Sens), the messenger kneels to Herod (Fleury), soldiers do obeisance to mock Christ (Sulmona), merchants having sold Joseph, bow to Pharaoh (Laon), in Florence Bishop Suzdal saw the apostles and angels kneel and bow to Christ at the *Ascension,* and in his *Presentatio,* Mézières has Joachim and Anna ascend the stage "capite modicum inclinato quasi reuerendo Mariam."[55]

Besides the standard shows of reverence, there are several other varieties of attitude. Regal forms of allegiance usually include bowing and genuflecting but when, in the Beauvais *Daniel,* Belshazzar ascends his throne, his cheering satraps applaud him. Pious forms include the ceremonial kissing of a sacred object or place, such as the altar of the sepulchre in the *Visitatio* from Toul. Bishop Suzdal paints a vivid picture of the Virgin in the Florentine *Annunciation*: she rises suddenly at the approach of the angel, answers him in a shy voice, and finally she looks heavenward meekly and folds her hands in her lap.[56]

The pleasure in the mundane exhibited by Mary Magdalen prior to her conversion and the fiendish delight of satanic beings in their triumphs are kinds of joy usually seen on the outdoor stages. Inside the church joy is almost always the spirit of the celebrative finale, conveyed by loud singing, or the instant of excited relief in the face of anticipated misfortune. Besides the exultant voice, running seems to be its major physical expression. In the earliest era of the *Visitatio,* at Verdun, the Marys hasten to announce the Resurrection. Peter and John, having heard the good news, race to the sepulchre. At Rheinau, Magdalen must be some little distance from the Risen Christ, for upon recognizing him—not before—she rushes over to him. At Chiemsee, after this scene, she runs rejoicing to tell the two disciples: "procedat in occursum Discipulorum quasi gaudens nunciatura eis Resurrectionem Domini."

In throwing themselves at Christ's feet after the Resurrection, Mary Magdalen and Thomas are expressing a profusion of emotions, among them great joy. When at the end of the play of *Getron* a citizen discovers the long-lost son miraculously standing before the city gates, he hastens off to bring the happy message, and the boy's mother runs to kiss and embrace her returned child.[57]

The slow, searching step described by Ethelwold for the Marys as they approach the sepulchre is clearly enunciated as an expression of sorrow in the Fleury text, where the women move "pedetemtim et quasi tristes." At Wilton the opening rubric gives a graphic picture of a whole little scene. The women carry phylacteries in their hands, and candlesticks and thuribles. They approach "looking around and lamenting" (querentes et lamentates). Eventually they will go to the sepulchre one by one (singillatim), where each will then prostrate herself. Some later texts, such as that from Indersdorf, have them circle about the tomb, mourning. The opening mood of the *Peregrinus* is expressed in the same manner, as at Rouen, where the wayfarers begin to walk "lento pede."[58]

With the first examples of prostration as a show of veneration in the thirteenth century also appear the most detailed descriptions of grief, on the parts of Mary Magdalen at the sepulchre and Rachel over the murdered innocents. In the *Ludus Paschalis* from the Tours manuscript, Mary commences from the left side of the church, clapping her hands and crying (plausis manibus, plorando). When the angel sings "Non est hic," she raises her hands toward heaven, mourns, and then faints, for both of the other two women must support her. Most detailed is the description of Magdalen's acting in a text from Coutances (ca. 1400). Here, alone, she looks repeatedly into the sepulchre, begins to cry (fingat se flere), and withdraws a little, whereupon the angels return. She sits down nearby and laments, then rises and stands again weeping at the sepulchre. As she once more bends down peering into the tomb, the angels inquire, "Mulier, quid ploras?" and she sighs out her answer (quasi suspirans). When she recognizes Christ, she throws herself at his feet, and he draws back singing, "Noli me tangere." Mary returns to the other women and, coming into the choir, they sing the *Victimae paschali* "voce iocunda."

The early *Ordo Rachelis* from Freising has a comforter wipe Rachel's eyes as she weeps over the slaughtered children, while her portrayal in the twelfth-century play from Fleury resembles one of the more drastic displays by Magdalen. Here an extended series of four laments forms the heart of the work: Rachel, with two comforters, sheds tears over the bodies of the innocents and faints; they take her up; she faints again; the two finally lead her off. Sorrow is also a major factor in Martha's and then Mary's throwing themselves at Christ's feet in the Fleury drama of *Lazarus.*

The bending of the body accompanies the mourning of the apostles at the Florentine *Ascension,* perhaps members of the group attempting mutually to console each other, and Mézières sketches a portrait of despair in a stage direction for the *Presentation*: "Synagoga will rise to her feet in her place, with her face bowed to the left side, turn in all directions as if sad, and as if weeping will sing." She is then driven from the stage, weeping and wailing and throwing aside her banner and the tablets of the Mosaic law.[59]

Fear or anxiety usually causes characters to collapse or to withdraw a little. At Klosterneuberg the soldiers placed to guard the sepulchre fall to the ground when the angel with the brilliant sword approaches, and at the sight of him, the Marys are terrified and pull back. In the Sulmona fragment the soldiers fall down during the earthquake which occurs while they are arresting Christ, and at Coutances they are to remain "quasi mortui" until the singing of the *Te Deum*.

In the Fleury *Officium Stellae* the shepherds are terrified at the sight of the angels, and perhaps they too fall down, for when reassured, they get up and move toward the manger. In the Laon *Joseph*, fear causes old Jacob to rise at the sight of Joseph's bloodstained coat, before then collapsing in grief. But Lucifer in Mézières' *Presentation* embodies a parody of fright as "trembling, he will allow himself to fall on his face" before the Virgin.

Concern that Mary will touch him causes the Risen Christ often to raise his hand in prohibiting her or even to pull away a few steps from her. The *Visitatio* from Nottuln directs that Jesus retreat, and therefore that Mary Magdalen advance, no fewer than four times: "ille secedet paulisper"; "Rursumque Jhesus recedet"; "illo fugiente retrorsum, sequatur [Maria] eum"; "Iterum Ille recedat."

When an angel suddenly appears before Balaam riding on a donkey in the Benediktbeuern Christmas play, the ass sees the angel and backs up out of sheer terror.[60]

Shock and confusion are often coupled with fear in these dramas. When in Hilarius' *Daniel* play the king sees the mysterious handwriting on the wall, "conturbatus" he sends for interpreters, and at Beauvais he cries out "stupefactus." When the German king refuses Antichrist's bribes, the latter's Hypocrites turn away "confusi," and Mary "stupefacta" replies to the angel in the Benediktbeuern Christmas play. These moments were probably depicted more by means of facial expression and vocal intonation, while the act of standing up shows the two disciples' sudden bewilderment at the disappearance of Christ in *Peregrinus* plays: at Beauvais they rise, the direction from Rouen reads explicitly "quasi stupefacti surgentes cantent," and at Fleury, after a pause, "quasi tristes surgant."

Whereas, like the soldiers at the sepulchre, Paul on the road to Damascus falls to the ground "quasi semimortuus" when he hears the voice of God.[61]

Displays of anger belong almost exclusively to Herod's province, to his discovery of prophecies concerning the Christ Child, his reaction to the detour taken by the Magi, and his threat of murdering the innocents. Despite what seems to be his excessive behavior "cum magna indignatione" (Benediktbeuern), it is generally thought that only on the outdoor stage did he emerge as a comic figure. Anger, of course, was a major sin. It is difficult to judge whether a medieval church audience would have found him comic or seriously threatening. As early as the eleventh-century *Officium Stellae* from Freising, we find him hurling prophetic writings to the ground and brandishing his sword. These are the hallmarks of his performance: in the Montpellier text, where his officers enter with drawn swords, and at Fleury, where his son joins him in the latter gesture. At Bilsen he throws down swords before clapping the Magi into prison. In the *Ordo Rachelis* of Fleury the depiction moves toward that of madness, for at the news of the detour made by the Magi, Herod "quasi corruptus" attempts to kill himself with his sword. Almost a parody of fury is displayed by the villainous Archisynagogus in the Benediktbeuern Christmas play: he pushes his companion, moves his head and whole body back and forth, waves his staff, and stamps his foot; this is accompanied by a considerable tumult and much murmuring from his followers, and violent laughter on his part. In the Fleury play of *St. Paul*, the titular character stands up "quasi iratus," and in the *Presentation*, Mary kicks the cowering Lucifer.[62]

Special acts of affection are much rarer than those of grief or anger, and usually consist of formal greetings such as the kiss exchanged by the Magi as they meet or are coupled with an expression of sympathy or consolation, such as the support which comforters give Rachel in moments of fainting. In the Laon *Joseph*, the old father embraces his youngest son when it appears that the latter will have to depart for Egypt. Standing beneath the cross in the Benediktbeuern Passion, the mourning mother of Christ holds John in her arms and then the latter, in turn, takes her by the shoulders and leads her away. Most moving is the gesture made by Elizabeth as she comes to visit Mary in the fourteenth-century *Annunciation* at Padua: she kneels before Mary and blesses her in a humble voice (humili uoce), touching her body with both hands.[63]

Attitudes and Acts Adapted from Ritual

Five major acts are taken over into drama directly from the conduct of liturgical ceremony: greeting, blessing, offering or dedicating, rendering homage, and praying. It is often impossible to draw distinct lines between these practices either in terms of content or form, but the emphasis of this discussion rests on documented physical attitudes of the actors employed in religious rite and in the drama, suggesting that in the adoption of a given attitude the actor was using a familiar language of gesture which carried with it well-known symbolic overtones and long-established associative patterns.[64]

The kiss, as the *Pax* or "Kiss of Peace," often occurs as part of the conclusion of the *Visitatio*. It is the standard kind of salutation used as of the eleventh century by the Magi as they first meet and view the star, in the Fleury Playbook made into a little ritual: "Et osculentur sese; sic medius ad sinistrum, sic sinister ad dextrum" (And let them kiss each other; in like manner the one in the middle to him at the left, and the one at the left to him at the right). Texts from Compiègne and Montpellier have Herod receive them with a kiss as well. After the Resurrection in the *Ludus Paschalis* in the Tours manuscript, a group of disciples kiss Christ when he appears to them saying, "Pax uobis." The more terrifying on the stage in the Benediktbeuern Passion is Judas' betrayal of Christ with this gesture, a complete inversion of its meaning.

Both the sense of greeting and of blessing are contained in the appearance of Gabriel to the Virgin in the *Annunciation*. The sixteenth-century version from Tournai gives very explicit instructions as to how the angel is to make a three-fold salutation while singing "Ave, gratia plena, Dominus tecum": at "Ave" he bows both head and body, then straightens up in a dignified manner; at "gratia plena" he bends his knees about half way (mediocriter) and rises; at "Dominus tecum" he genuflects with his knees touching the ground, standing up again when he has finished.

In the *Peregrinus* of Fleury, Christ appears to a gathering of disciples and blesses them, "Accipite Spiritum Sanctum," by raising his hand over them. Both of Mary's parents kiss her during the *Presentation*—a sign of benediction—prior to their then leading her to the bishop at the high altar. To begin the meal at Emmaus in *Peregrinus* plays, Christ is often made not only to bless the food but to echo the progress of the Last Supper: at Fleury he raises first the bread in his right hand and then the wine cup; in the Beauvais manuscript Christ's spoken line has two directions inserted in it—

He took bread, and when he had blessed (he shall make +) and broken it (he shall break it), he gave it to them.

[The "+" seems to indicate "the sign of the cross."]

A similar act commences the process of offering or consecration on the part of Mary's parents in the *Presentation*, where first Anna raises high a loaf in her left hand and then Joachim a cup of wine, eventually placing the two items on the high altar after the bishop has taken Mary in his arms. In the *Antichrist* play the Roman Emperor enters the temple, having completed his conquests, and places his crown, scepter, and insignia before the altar there. These are acts of dedication.

When Antichrist then begins his reign, he establishes a miniature rite of homage, consecration, and investiture for each ruler who gives him his allegiance: the respective king kneels and offers his crown; Antichrist kisses him, inscribes the first letter of his name on the forehead of the king and his followers, and replaces the proffered crown. Ecclesiastical and royal ceremony coincide here.

With gifts one can render homage. The holding up of the object and the subsequent laying of it on the altar mark the presentation of gifts to the Christ Child in Christmas plays: in an especially ceremonial performance at Besançon (1629), each of the Magi, standing up on the rood-loft, raises his particular gift with the appropriate music.

Such offertory moments are almost always accompanied by such gestures of homage and reverence as have been examined in this chapter as expressions of emotion: bowing, kneeling, prostration, and kissing not only of persons but also of sacred objects, including the altar.

Attitudes of prayer have differed quite considerably over the ages and from locality to locality, and a few of these variations are documented in the drama of the church. In the *Lazarus* plays, by Hilarius and from the Fleury Playbook, Christ looks toward heaven as he makes his supplication, and ascending the Mt. of Olives in the Benediktbeuern Passion, he kneels, gazes upward, and weeps. Getron's wife (Fleury) enters the church of St. Nicholas to pray for the return of her son, raising her hands in her plea.

Prayer often combines with a gesture of abasement. Before the high altar at the *Presentation*, the parents of Mary kneel for a brief prayer with their heads apparently touching the ground (capitibus in terram inclinatis), while until the conclusion of the *Annunciation* from Tournai, Mary stays in the genuflectory position as if at her orisons. An interesting transition from homage or prayer to sleep occurs in some texts of the *Officium Stellae:* in the Fleury Playbook the Magi make their offerings and then sleep before the manger so that the angel can warn them as in a dream to return via a different route. Two thirteenth-century texts from Rouen have the Magi fall down in worship and then explicitly pray and dream, while fourteenth- and fifteenth-century texts from Rouen call for offerings made by the clergy and laity during the time that the kings remain silently praying or sleeping.[65]

A Summary Catalogue of Movement and Gesture

The term "liturgical" conjures up images of solemn tone and movement. One might think the liturgical drama as staid as the liturgy. But not always so. The church when used as dramatic staging area burgeons with the activity of daily life as well as ritualistic life. The actors handle props and deal with set pieces: *accipio* (take, accept), *aperio* (open), *appono* (put in place), and the like.[66] Speech ascriptions call for dynamics of daily exchange: for example, *pronuntio* (pronounce, proclaim), *quaero* (ask), *recipio* (receive).[67]

The vocabulary of gesture manifests an intentional partnership with the singing: such as, *demonstro* (*digitto*, to point out . . . with a finger), *erigo* (to stand straight after bowing), *exsero* (to thrust out, stretch forth—*exertis manibus*, with hands stretched forth), *indico* (to point to), *ostendo* (cum manu, to show . . . with the hand), *palpo* (to press, touch), *sustento* (*brachium*, to stretch out . . . the arms), *tango* (to touch). The verbs of the rubrics reveal ecclesiastical spaces filling with the lively doings of the characters: *advolvo* (to roll [the stone] into place), *baiulo* (to carry a load, to bear), *commestio* (to eat [a meal]), and the like.[68]

From the earliest era of the *Visitatio*, the act of running signified joy on the part of the women who had been at the tomb (Verdun); a sense of relief and anticipation cause Peter and John's race, as is also the case with Getron's wife (Fleury) when she rushes out to meet her lost son. Haste marks the movements of the bereaved Martha and Mary as they go out to meet Christ *(Lazarus),* of Judas as he comes to the high priests in order to betray Christ (Benediktbeuern Passion), and of messengers going between the Magi and Herod—all moments of dramatic tension.

In addition to underscoring the solemnity of a procession, slow walking often conveys a mood of sadness or bewilderment on the part of the actor. The *Regularis Concordia* instructs the women to approach the Easter sepulchre "stepping delicately as those who seek something," and "like lost folk"; the *Visitatio* from Fleury has them move "slowly as if sad." This is also the way in which the wayfarers are to begin the journey in the *Peregrinus* at Rouen, "lento pede." In the Tournai *Annunciation,* Mary must preserve dignity and modesty as she rises and gradually turns.

Rapid standing up can accompany a sudden change of emotion. In the *St. Paul* of the Fleury Playbook, the titular character rises from his seat in anger at news of escaped Christians; Jacob gets up fearfully as Joseph's blood-stained tunic is brought in (Laon); at Christ's disappearance from the table at Emmaus the *peregrini* rise, shocked and bewildered (Beauvais, Rouen); and in the Tegernsee *Antichrist,* the king of Babylonia stands up to assert himself against the Christian world.

In the actor's use of the body one might well single out the limp of Peter, the bent backs of aged prophets, and the fainting of Rachel as tendencies toward more human portrayal—tendencies documented as of the thirteenth century.

Commonly recorded attitudes of the body are bowing, kneeling, and prostration. Bowing is used as a sign of respect and humility by the Marys as they address the angel at the tomb, and by figures such as angels showing reverence for Christ; it is indicated as an expression of grief by Rachel and by the apostles; and it is part of making verisimilar the Marys' inspection of the empty sepulchre. Kneeling constitutes a stronger yet formal and restrained act of veneration or a physical position for prayer. While willed prostration expresses extremes of self-abasement and obeisance, an unwilled collapse expresses extremes of grief or fear.

In addition to bowing, there are some indications as to positions of the head and in fact a few hints as to ways in which facial expression was employed. While the Teutonic king observes Antichrist's three healing miracles, the stage direction says that the king's faith wavers, then that his doubt grows, and finally that he capitulates; in that he has no lines until the end, one would certainly expect appropriate facial reactions by the German king. At the moment in which Christ dies on the cross in the Benediktbeuern Passion, he inclines his head. This is also a means of portraying despair at the *Presentation* in the figure of Synagoga, "facie inclinata ad partem sinistram, quasi tristis," while Mary ascends the platform with a joyous face (hylari facie). The lowered head and eyes also show humility, specifically for Mary during the *Annunciation* at Tournai, "submissis oculis, erit semper intenta ad orationem," and indicated in Rouen texts for the three women as they approach the tomb "uultibus submissis." Christ is described in Rouen texts of the *Peregrinus* as coming up to the wayfarers "uultu demisso"; they, in turn, look at him "quasi admirantes." The head and eyes are raised in prayer by Christ in the *Lazarus* plays, and in awe or wonder by Mary in the Florentine *Annunciation* and in the Moosburg *Ascension*. Bishop Suzdal tells us that at the *Ascension* in Florence, Christ looks across from the Mt. of Olives back to Jerusalem in a moment of farewell.

The most frequently documented gesture with the hand or arm is that of indicating or pointing—the angels to the sepulchre, the Magi to the star, the midwives to the manger—and in the display of the gravecloths or making of offerings. These gestures can be said generally to consist of two sorts: those of a rather realistic nature and those which belong to ritual. In the *Ludus Paschalis* from Benediktbeuern, the apothecary shows the Marys the way to the sepulchre, while as a conclusion to the *Ludus Paschalis* from the Tours manuscript, Magdalen answers the question of the disciples by pointing with each line first to the sepulchre, then to the angel, to the sudarium, and to the cross. In the text from Origny St. Benoît, Peter and John come to the women and catch hold of the sleeve of Magdalen as they inquire as to what she has seen; she in turn points toward the sepulchre, at "spes nostra" she places her hand on her breast, and finally while telling them that Christ will appear to them in Galilee, she points in the opposite direction. When at Rheinau, Magdalen recognizes Christ before the tomb, she falls at his feet and attempts to touch him, but he extends his hand and prevents her—a gesture he also uses in Rouen texts. Embracing sometimes accompanies sorrow and consolation, as in the Benediktbeuern Passion, where the mother of Christ takes John in her arms and then he holds her by the shoulders. In the Florentine *Annunciation*, Mary folds her hands in her lap as a sign of humility. Part of Magdalen's mourning at Tours, prior to her fainting, includes the clapping of her hands and her raising of her hands toward heaven.

This latter gesture tends toward what seems to be a not uncommon attitude of prayer and supplication, closely associated with ceremonial practices. Getron's wife adopts the same stance in pleading for the return of her son (Fleury), while in Mézières' *Presentation*, Anna and Joachim hold up their arms in moments of proclamation and praise. Mary the mother of Christ also raises her hands to sing "Jhesu, nostra redempcio"

at the Moosburg *Ascension*. Part of the symbolic meaning of the arms raised in supplication has to do with the desire of the supplicant to receive that for which he asks. In the *Annunciation* from Padua, the Virgin stands with arms outstretched toward the descending dove, which she then places under her garment.

The speaker of a benediction often raises one hand in the direction of the recipient. Quite specific details are given the angel in the Paduan *Annunciation*: at "Ave, Maria" he is to kneel and lift his right hand with two fingers raised; the open right hand is then extended by the standing angel as he allays Mary's fears. It is this text which also calls for Elizabeth to kneel before Mary and touch her body with both hands as she pronounces a blessing.

In a moment of royal ceremonial enacted during the Beauvais play of *Daniel*, the king, Belshazzar, enters and ascends his throne, and the courtiers surrounding him applaud and cry out "Rex, in eternum uiue!" We hear the same cry from them 210 lines later and perhaps witness the same form of greeting—this time, however, for Belshazzar's murderer and successor.[69]

Especially Mimed Moments

The kind of representation possible through mime is suggested by the following passage from the revels of Innocents' Day celebrated during the thirteenth century in the Cathedral of Padua. Here boys take over the service, led by the Boy Bishop, and after the reading of the epistle, at a special Mass, a brief dumb show takes place illustrating the Flight into Egypt:

There are some soldiers who . . . go about the church searching for the infant with his mother, that is, Christ with the Blessed Virgin Mary. And there is one dressed as a woman who sits on a donkey with her son at her breast; someone who impersonates Joseph leads the donkey fleeing through the church, representing the escape of the Virgin with the child into Egypt as the angel of the Lord had instructed Joseph in a dream.

All of this was in pantomime and apparently took place throughout the extent of the church interior. The actors as soldiers had to portray both by facial expression and manner of gesture the sense of the threatening hunt, Mary and Joseph the mood of fear in hurried movement.

When, in the tenth century, Bishop Ethelwold says that the Marys are to go toward the Easter sepulchre as if searching, he is directing a mimed attitude. In the twelfth century we find a variety of such indications together with major innovations in the literature of drama, as well as in the amount of dumb show. With time the dumb show seems to increase. A twelfth-century *Visitatio* from St. Lambrecht has the women incline their heads in order to peer into the tomb—the same play which cast an older and a younger man, respectively, in the roles of Peter and John. A thirteenth-century text from Chiemsee describes the Marys coming back from the tomb "as wishing to announce [the Resurrection] to the apostles," and later Magdalen turns from Hortulanus, not knowing him and "wishing to go away." Christ almost always makes the same gesture after meeting the *peregrini*, feigning a departure from them. At Rouen they hasten after him and hold him back "as if inviting him to the lodging," pointing with their staffs toward Emmaus. In the Fleury Playbook, Christ secretly comes up to them and follows along behind them before they see him.

A good deal of action is involved in Herod's interview with the Magi. Most vivid is the scene with his scribes in the Fleury Playbook, where they turn through their writings at some length (diu reuoluant librum), finally come upon the relevant prophetic passage, and pointing to it hand the book over to the incredulous Herod, who eventually hurls it to the ground. Hearing the uproar, his son goes through an attempt to pacify the king. Both in the *Presentation* and in the *Annunciation* from Tournai, the Virgin looks at a book of the hours, and in the former she is instructed to turn the pages "as if saying her hours."

Examples of these smaller bits of stage business are comparatively rare, but the fact that they abound in Mézières' *Presentation* reflects its conscious creation as a prompt-book and suggests a multiplicity of such detail simply unrecorded for similar productions. In his essay on medieval acting, Albert Weiner is bothered by what he envisions as possibly long transitional pauses during a production, but this sometimes justified conclusion should be tempered with an awareness of the music and with the realization that the few glimpses we are given of mimed moments probably stand for many more considered by the writer or scribe as unnecessary to a grasp of the text. Even when a hand property is listed, its use is usually implied or self-understood. Mézières however, not only has Mary carry a little dove, which she will let fly at the end of Mass, but while she is seated, she is to kiss it, pet it, and press it to her breast from time to time. The lines of the early *Antichrist* play cease during the numerous battles that are waged in the open playing space, but on occasion actors are specifically instructed to deliver an interchange as they move from one place to another. In the Christmas play from Benediktbeuern and in the *Ordo Rachelis* from Laon, the Magi discuss the star as they walk.

Two rather late texts of the *Visitatio* suggest improvisation for the guards at the sepulchre: that in Sainte-Chapelle, Paris, is optional, whereby at the conclusion the soldiers may get up and carry out whatever business seems best to them—"Surgant Milites, si ibidem fuerint, et faciant quod eis bonum viderint faciendum"; at Coutances the four men speak among themselves (dicant personagia sua)—no lines are given—until they fall as if dead before the angel.

The Sulmona Passion opens with four soldiers fighting among themselves; later, as in the Monte Cassino Passion, they draw lots for Christ's garment. A considerable amount of mimed action is required for the Benediktbeuern Passion: the fishing of Peter and Andrew, the purchase of ointment, the torture, crucifixion, and burial of Christ, the suicide of Judas. In the Laon *Joseph*, merchants produce their scales and weigh their silver. At Florence (fifteenth century) the angel making the *Annunciation* to Mary waves his arms simulating flight as he is conveyed through the air by means of a pulley.[70]

Eating, sleeping, washing, and dressing occur with some frequency in the plays, particularly the repast. In the *Peregrinus* of Fleury a table holds an uncut loaf, three wafers, and a cup of wine; there is first a washing of hands, and then after the ritual blessing Christ goes away explicitly while the two disciples are eating. Meals are also served in the Fleury plays of *Lazarus* and of *Getron*, and in the Passion play of Benediktbeuern. Food is prepared in the Vorau *Isaac*. In the *Getron* play the king washes his hands before commencing a banquet, and Pilate performs the act as a symbolic gesture in the Passion plays.

While the Magi sleep before the manger, an angel warns them as in a dream. The same motif occurs in the Benediktbeuern Passion as an angel appears to the sleeping Mary Magdalen, resulting in her repentance. Her spiritual change is shown on stage as she puts off her worldly clothing and dresses in black. Antichrist's throwing off of his outer garment reveals him as a war-like figure. And in the Benediktbeuern Passion, Christ is mocked first in a white tunic and then in a purple robe. The most elaborate example of on-stage dressing occurs in a fourteenth-century *Marien-klage* from Innsbruck, where a king clothes himself while he delivers a series of speeches.[71]

Extended Mime or Dumb Show

There are a dozen or more points during the course of the Tegernsee *Antichrist* when major action such as the preparation and conduct of battles or the execution of regal ritual and pageantry is carried out in dumb show. Prior to Antichrist's entrance, a group of Hypocrites come in, "bowing silently and in apparent humility to all sides and currying the favour of the laity. Finally they all gather before Ecclesia and the *sedes* of the king of Jerusalem, who receives them honorably and places himself wholly under their counsel." Another moment which seems to demand mimed speech occurs as "the Hypocrites lead Antichrist into the temple of the Lord, placing his throne there. Ecclesia, however, who had remained there is attacked with many insults and blows and returns to the *sedes* of the Pope."

In fact, the chief subject of lengthy dumb show is usually violence. In the Fleury play of *Getron*, an army advances against the church of St. Nicholas and over-runs it, causing the worshippers to flee to their city. Both twelfth-century *Daniel* plays show Darius' men attacking and killing King Belshazzar and Darius assuming the throne; later an angel appears with a sword and closes the mouths of the lions. Murder is committed not only in the *Antichrist* play but forms a central part of the *Ordo Rachelis,* with the mothers crying out for their children (Fleury, Benedikt-beuern). And at the conclusion of the Fleury drama, a stage direction says that Herod is replaced by his son, Archelaus, who is then exalted, while the Benediktbeuern Christmas play ends with a most curious spectacle as "Herod is gnawed by worms, and carried dead from his throne, he is received by devils with much rejoicing. Herod's crown is placed on Archelaus, his son."

The play of *Isaac* calls for an extensively mimed hunt, for which a bow, arrows, and a roebuck had been prepared, and the almost simultaneous beginning of the next sequence:

> Then Esau shall depart as if to hunt with bow and quiver, surrounded by his companions. When he blows a horn, they shall run about from different di-

rections. He shall attack and kill some animal with arrows, and then he shall do whatever he sees fit; but they shall have the above-mentioned food at hand, which he shall bring in silver vessels to Isaac with bread and wine after Jacob leaves the father. And, after Esau, Rebecca goes out from her place, where she shall have overheard Isaac's words with his son about the hunt, and she shall sing, telling Jacob . . . .

Also the attempted seduction of Joseph by Potiphar's wife in the thirteenth-century play from Laon is en-acted in pantomime:

> Meanwhile Potiphar's wife, attentive to Joseph, calls him secretly. Joseph does not yield to her design, and as he tries to go away, she seizes his cloak. Joseph leaves it and flees. She keeps it so as to incriminate the innocent man. Carrying the cloak with her, she comes before her husband and cries out . . . .

These cited scenes derive mostly from source material which in the twelfth and thirteenth centuries had been woven rather recently into the fabric of liturgy. The material had not been adapted for fre-quent usage as antiphons and responsories, nor had the subject matter become a traditional part of the canon of ecclesiastical drama. Therefore, as compared to many of those playwrights who embellished the *Vis-itatio,* for example, the creators of these scenes were experimenting with essentially new theatrical mater-ial. It is significant that in the twelfth century—the era of Hilarius, the *Jeu d'Adam,* the Tegernsee *Antichrist,* and the Vorau *Isaac*—these dramatists could expect actors to execute such sophisticated mimetic imita-tions, behind which lie the documented dramatic tra-ditions of the Church in the tenth and eleventh cen-turies and, perhaps more importantly, those largely undocumented practices of folk performance and of the medieval mime.[72]

Verisimilitude versus Ritual: The Style

The evidence of the acting, as that of the other aspects of production, indicates generally four periods of de-velopment. In the tenth and eleventh centuries, the era of origins, one finds gesture, movement, and the use of the voice taken simply and directly from the conduct of ecclesiastical ceremony, while there is a sudden burst of experimental theatrical activity in the twelfth century, employing more natural physical and vocal effects especially in performances less intimately integrated within the worship service. The late twelfth and thirteenth century can be called the apogee of that development, the full expansion and extension of the Christmas play and *Ludus Paschalis*, for example, marked by greater concern to record matters necessary to the mise-en-scène and demands made upon the actor. As of the fourteenth century what occurs within the church is largely a matter of elaboration. More attention was paid both to spectacle and to increased detail and verisimilitude in the acting, tendencies influenced by the rise of those outdoor productions of religious drama and of morality plays which culminated in the massive shows of the sixteenth century. The uses of scenery and practices in costuming match the same chronology, tending toward elaboration of spectacle as of the fourteenth century.

In conclusion, the nature of the clerical acting was fundamentally presentational. The following factors provide clues to the style of performance: the works were largely sung, with what was probably interspersed declamation or intoned speech; characterization was chiefly created through costumes and most of these were vestments; with only rare exceptions women's roles were played by men or boys; and much of the gesture was derived from ritual. Touches of realism were added from the beginning and apparently increased as time went on: sighing, whispering, calling out; some typecasting; physical attitudes and facial expressions noted in the portrayal of emotions.

To be sure, we are discussing general trends, for just as there is a wide variance in the texts as to information on acting, and just as there were major divergences in the interpretation and execution of the Mass, so the manner of dramatic performance, even of the same play, must have varied quite considerably from place to place and from period to period. While great theatrical traditions flourished in the twelfth-century performance venue(s) of the Fleury Playbook and in the thirteenth century at Benediktbeuern and Rouen, other monastic groups and collegiate chapters performed only the *Visitatio* through the sixteenth century and in its simplest form. In fact, virtually an offertory rite at Rouen, the *Officium Stellae* at Fleury in the same era was a complex drama of Herod. And whereas thirteenth- and fourteenth-century plays of the *Visitatio* from Chiemsee and Coutances, respectively, create lengthy scenes with elaborate acting instructions for Mary Magdalen in her recognition of Christ, elsewhere the moment is carried out quickly and formally.

Proximity of a scene's subject matter to that of church ritual affected the manner in which it was acted: no more startling contrast can be found than that between the highly imaginative, subtle workings of the Devil in the twelfth-century *Jeu d'Adam*, the rigid repetition of prophecies at the end of that play, and the formal, meticulously recorded gestures of Mary in the fourteenth-century *Planctus* from Cividale. In the period of the tenth through the thirteenth century the major portion of extant Easter and Christmas plays belonged very much in the main stream of liturgical performances, conceived and executed by the clergy largely in traditions of ritualistic conduct; while in the twelfth and thirteenth centuries appears a group of plays based on other Biblical material— *Daniel, Isaac, Joseph, Lazarus, St. Paul*—and on hagiographic and eschatological writings—*Antichrist*, the St. Nicholas dramas—the texts of which expressly require new and considerable mimetic skill from the actors. It would seem that these latter works were inspired by and derive more directly from the presence of the ubiquitous medieval mimes in and near monastic communities. But the sacred progress of the worship service had little place for theatrical experiment on a grand scale, nor did Rome feel that this was the business of ordained priests. When in the thirteenth century movements toward nationalism across the map of Europe were answered by the Church with elaborate institutional machinery, the open Church of the twelfth century closed into smaller pockets and undertook purges, which have always punctuated its history. The new modes of drama, never having fit comfortably into official religious observances, eventually found their more suitable locales beyond the Church's doors, albeit not beyond its all-pervasive control, while as of the thirteenth century the innovations in acting and attention to acting learned at least in part from the mimes came to be reflected in the productions of those plays more in keeping with the liturgy. Furthermore, in the retained and sometimes elaborated dramas of Easter and Christmas it became increasingly necessary to set down those matters of gesture for the clerical actor which were not inherent in his performance of the regular service.

In the playing of roles within the church there can hardly be a question of sustained illusion, only the kind of sporadic originality illustrated by the Magi in the twelfth-century Montpellier text who speak to Herod in a "foreign" tongue and then revert to Latin. The murdered Innocents in the Fleury Playbook, after the symbolic lamb has been removed, eventually rise and proceed into the choir, and the "dead" soldiers lying at the sepulchre of the fifteenth-century Coutances *Visitatio* get up again when the final *Te Deum* is begun.

Just as the *dynamis,* the underlying power, of this drama is a deep sense of religious belief, so the performance of a role was a very genuine act of worship on the part of the performer, and the playing style of the actor matched the ceremonial nature of the drama, both born and nurtured in the execution of some of the richest ritual devised by the human mind. This is the foundation of the acting style and at the same time the cause of a fundamental conflict for the player which we find reflected in what we have termed "touches of verisimilitude." First, there is the drive in every actor to resemble that figure whom he impersonates, yet the embodiment of particularly sacred figures in this context had to stop short, for one could only present Christ. Second, the more tangible or believable the representation, the greater the fulfillment of the drama's basically didactic purpose, in part the principle which led medieval painters and sculptors to depict Christ in every detail as a tortured man on the cross. Herein lies the paradox of the artist in the Gothic cathedral: his desire on the one hand to create a thing of beauty to the glory of God and on the other hand to make vivid the suffering, violence, and evil of his own world—the cool, partially cerebral act of worship versus the drive to represent and to teach through the most palpable means possible.

Chapter 6
The Music

The *Gesamtkunstwerk*

Every dramatic text belonging to the medieval church must be regarded as a kind of libretto, a composition or compilation of poetry and music, with as much variety in language and scene as in music. In the same breath we must add that it would be a great mistake to consider these works as miniature operas, a tendency in many modern productions of them. Most might be regarded as collages assembled from different parts of the liturgy, while on rare occasions one discovers moments of fresh composition. For example, the service of the shepherds at Rouen (*Officium Pastorum*, thirteenth-fourteenth century) includes two songs that contrast in their musical styles with the other, traditional pieces that comprise the work. Such moments glow, however faintly, with the embers of something new, something different from ritual. It is drama.

These two plainchant songs may have been composed especially for this drama, both words and music: "Pax in terris" and "Salve, virgo singularis." They are metrical whereas the other texts are not, and they combine balanced phrases with a rare kind of melodic repetition. This sort of melodic repetition occurs in plainchant at this date only in some hymns and some other metrical chants such as the *conductus*, from about 1200. With thoughts of performance in mind, one is struck here by the way in which each of the new songs as a whole creates a particularly theatrical moment in the drama. The first, "Pax in terris," sung by the shepherds as they approach the manger, announces the news of peace on earth. Furthermore, the pattern of musical repetition within the piece draws attention to the key line of its text. Its melodic form runs *a, a, b, a*, where *a* repeats the same musical phrase while *b*, the most important

line of text, is set to a new and richly ornamented melody line: "The Man-God mediator descends to his own."

The other new song creates the climax of the drama, where the shepherds reverence the Christ Child: "Salve, virgo singularis." They have come to a statue of the Virgin and Child, revealed from behind a curtain during the "Quem queritis in presepe" [sic] dialogue. Again, the pattern of the musical repetition emphasizes the thrust of the words. The melodic form runs *a, b, b / a, b, b*. The first *a* line begins, "Hail, matchless Virgin," the recognition and greeting; the second *a* line tells how "peace on earth" is achieved: "Mary, by your prayers cleanse us from the dregs of sin." That is to say, the new words and music deliver the substantive message of the play matched to its theatrical highpoints. Example 4 is John Stevens' transcription and translation.[1]

> Fear not: for, behold, I bring you tidings of great joy, which shall be to all people. For unto you is born this day in the city of David the saviour of the world. And this shall be a sign unto you: ye shall find the babe wrapped in swaddling clothes, lying in a manger.

> Glory be to God on high and on earth peace to men of good will.

> Peace is announced on earth, glory on high; earth and heaven are joined through the agency of grace. The Man-God mediator descends to his own, so that guilty man may ascend to the joys which are sanctioned. *Refr.* Eya, eya, let us go and see this Word which has been born; let us go, that we may know what has been proclaimed.

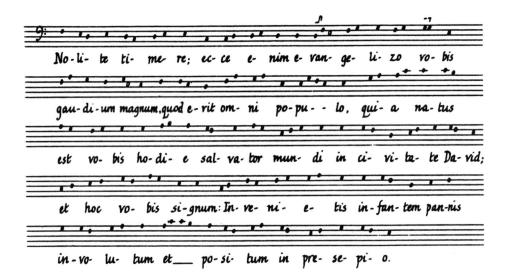

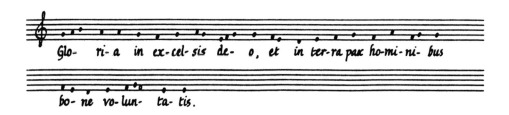

Example 4. Music from the Christmas play of the shepherds (*Officium Pastorum*) from Rouen Cathedral (xiii–xiv century).

Trans-e- a mus us-que Beth-le- em et ri- de- a- mus hoc ver-bum

quod fa- ctum est, quod fe- cit do- mi- nus et os- ten- dit no- bis.

Midwives Quem que- ri- tis in pre-se- pe,____ pas- to- res, di- ci-

te ____

Shepherds Sal- va- to- rem Chri-stum do- mi- num, in- fan- tem

pan- nis in- vo- lu- tum, se- cun- dum ser- mo- nem

an- ge- li- cum.

Midwives Ad-est hic___ par- ru- lus cum Ma-ri- a ma- tre___

su- a, de quo du- dum va-ti- ci- nan- do Y- sa- y- as

di- xe- rat pro-phe-ta:

Midwives Ec- ce vir- go con- ci- pi- et et pa- - ri- et___

fi- li- um; et e- - un- tes di- ci- te qui- a___

na- tus est.

Example 4 (continued).

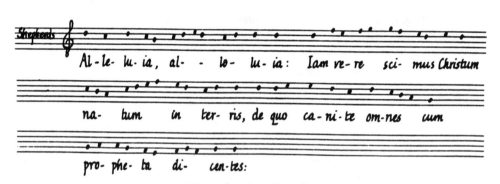

Example 4 (*continued*).

Let us go to Bethlehem and see this Word which has been created, the Lord's doing which he shows to us.

Whom are you seeking in the crib, shepherds? Tell / The Saviour who is Christ the Lord, a babe wrapped in swaddling clothes, according to, the words of the angels. / The little one is here with Mary his mother; it is he of whom formerly Isaiah the prophet had prophesied, saying: / Behold, a virgin shall conceive and bear a son. As you journey, declare that he is born.

Hail, matchless Virgin; remaining a virgin you give birth to God, conceived in the heart of the Father before all time. Now let us worship him created from the flesh of his mother. Mary, by your prayers cleanse us from the dregs of sin. So dispose the course of our

dwelling [in this world] that your Son may grant us to enjoy the vision of himself [in the hereafter].

Alleluia, alleluia, now we know truly that Christ is born on earth: of him sing you all, saying with the prophet.

"Quem quaeritis in praesepe" imitates the Easter line "Quem quaeritis in sepulchro," even holding a strain of the earlier death music in the music of new life. Unlike the puzzles still surrounding the origins of the Easter trope, whether it began in the Introit of Easter Mass or in Easter Matins, we know that "Quem quaeritis in praesepe" first appeared in the late tenth century as a trope of the Introit of the third Christmas Mass, which opens with "Puer natus est nobis" (A son is born unto us). Thereafter in imitation of locating

"Quem quaeritis in sepulchro" at the end of Easter Matins, "Quem quaeritis in praesepe" was also put at the end of Christmas Matins. It was in the Matins position that it became part of a drama, as did "Quem quaeritis in sepulchro." Instead of an angel or two at the sepulchre singing "Whom do you seek?" to the approaching Marys, a pair of midwives at the Christmas manger sang the question to the approaching shepherds. Midwives also sang the line in the Christmas plays where the Magi (three kings) come to the manger.[2]

Throughout this study of staging we are searching through original records of liturgical observance to discover rare bits of evidence of the drama: the glimmerings that we might call *play* instead of *rite, ludus* instead of *ordo* or *officium, Spiel* instead of *Feier, jeu* instead of *rituel.* Where are the moments when the special quality of the music carries an emotional or narrative passage?

Plainchant was the vehicle for the delivery of the musical parts of the Mass and the Canonical Office. Responsories and antiphons were intoned by the single voice of a cantor and sung by the choir, the stanzas of hymns by the two halves of the choir alternating. In the sixth century Gregory the Great had codified the liturgy with the "Roman" form of the chant. What we know now is a Frankish version of that chant which was developed as of about 750 in the Carolingian empire, was appropriated by Rome in the eleventh and twelfth centuries, and became the foundation of all western Church music. In the tenth and eleventh centuries the notation was written at first over the words of texts, not on staff lines with key signatures but in so-called neumes meant only to remind the singer of what he had already committed to memory. No stronger traditions passed from generation to generation than those of the chant which emanated from Rome. As of the twelfth and thirteenth centuries the always single-line notation (without rhythmic values) came to be recorded more and more on staff lines (often four) with marked pitch, and scholarship over the last hundred years has generally succeeded in interpreting the neumes by collation of sources, demonstrating the endurance of liturgical melodies through the medieval period.

It was in the twelfth and thirteenth centuries that the inventive genius of these clerical composers burned brightest, a few even known by name but most anonymous. Certainly *the* great creative period for the major repertory lies back in the mists of time, but later on in the two hundred years between ca. 1100 and 1300 new composers contributed new songs to the existing liturgical repertory of tropes, sequences, and rhymed offices. Rather suddenly in the thirteenth century large repertories of song, both religious and secular, were collected in manuscript anthologies. Thereafter ecclesiastical music and texts from the fourteenth, fifteenth, and sixteenth centuries preserve with rare exceptions recopyings and rearrangements of familiar material.

"One of the most striking aspects of sacred Latin chant after 1000," writes Richard Crocker, "is the increase in lyricism." Nowhere does the new clarity of phrase and song-like quality of the music stand out more distinctly than in the liturgical drama. For instance, new cults of St. Nicholas and of Mary Magdalen in the twelfth century engendered new verse and musical composition within the liturgy. "During the period 1000–1150," Crocker writes, "the primary determinant form seems to have been the texts and the new shapes they took." New rhyming, accentual songs marked newly composed Offices (extended ceremonies). Liturgical dramas often resembled these Offices in gathering and shaping a variety of musical items, but as dramas they did so in order to tell a story.[3]

In the vanguard stands the tenth-century *Visitatio Sepulchri* of Winchester. It consisted of freshly composed music, such as that for the *Quem quaeritis* lines, and made use of already traditional antiphons. Placed at the turning point from Matins to Lauds and the Easter Mass, it barely emerges from this continuous flow of music. When performed, it passes quickly in a few minutes forming a fulcrum for two massive ecclesiastical rituals. In most locations throughout its seven-hundred-year history, clergy seemed to have performed it in a liturgical style undifferentiated from other liturgical observances. Yet in Bishop Ethelwold's mind its original purpose differed from that of ritual. He wished to teach "uninstructed people and especially neophytes." Ritual does not teach. Drama can.

The musical core of the work throughout its history always remained that of the questioning and answering at the Easter sepulchre, to which other pieces were added sometimes together with original melodies. Except for a few late texts that call for organ accompaniment to the closing hymn, all was sung *a capella.* As William Smoldon wrote, "There is a great variety in the voice-groupings: long and elaborate solos; singing together in twos and threes; single voices and groups answering each other; solos with refrain choruses; and finally the triumphant choral conclusion" of the *Te Deum laudamus.*[4]

A production of the medieval church drama may be termed fairly a *Gesamtkunstwerk,* an amalgamation of the arts into a genuinely composite art form. Into that great continuing work of art, the liturgy, was introduced this new art with its additional characteristic of narrative. In certain rare examples of the music-drama we discover moments where the aura or mood of a given moment is underscored by the quality of the unaccompanied monody, where the kinetic power of the music at times unleashes an emotion more emphatically than the words of the dialogue, where an onstage figure is even occasionally characterized by his particular tune, and where there is ample opportunity for melodic reminders of other passages in the performance or in the liturgy. But the beginnings are small.

Like the texts, the scenery, the patterns of movement, and the costumes—the music can summon an ancient mood and at the same time a contemporary mood. The music partakes of ritual's timelessness. For in that some of the Easter and Christmas dramas contained both plainsong taken over from regular observances and tunes especially composed for the work, the total appeal in performances to the mind and senses of the medieval spectator would certainly have aroused a feeling of sanctity created by the known melodies and a dynamic response to the uniqueness of the work as a whole, formed in no small part by fresh and at times very theatrical sounds.

Words and Music

One must exercise extreme caution when imagining and performing these dramatic works lest one bring modern attitudes to the relation between their words and their music. An audience today expects music connected with words to create an atmosphere or mood, especially in a drama, and to convey dramatic character through the underscoring of emotions. As a rule plainchant does neither, save to sustain the solemnity of liturgical observance. Most liturgical music-drama also functions in this way. But there are exceptions, and in those exceptions one perceives the steps by which drama begins to break away from ritual.

The very selection of long-familiar antiphons and the order in which one sings them creates a sequence of moods. They shape an overall rhythm of performance. For example, the *Te Deum* at the end of the *Visitatio Sepulchri* at Winchester finishes not only Matins but also the little drama. In addition, with Mary Magdalen's first appearance, in the eleventh century, we perceive dramatic music specific to the moment. When the Risen Christ sings Mary Magdalen's name (Maria), and she responds with "Rab-

boni" (teacher), each word is marked by a sudden burst of many tones called "melisma." All at once the music theatricalizes the moment. In fact, the music throughout this whole exchange, says Susan Rankin, shows "no connection with available chant models."[5] The melodies were composed specifically for the play. This kind of invention appears in about ten percent of the surviving *Visitatio* texts, and in almost all other liturgical dramas, where tones relate directly to storytelling elements such as emotion and character, as distinct from the qualities of words and music in the Mass and the Canonical Hours.

Quite often it is the music more than any other single factor which colors a significant word and conveys the emotion of a given moment. Florid, melismatic passages stand out from usually syllabic passages, which match a note to a syllable, and can emphasize laments, express joy, or create a more reflective mood such as Christ's compassionate questioning of Mary Magdalen in the fourteenth-century *Visitatio* from Cividale.[6]

The music in the Cividale manuscript is original and of especial beauty. Mary commences her *planctus* in a solemn manner, rather syllabic in form. All at once Jesus delivers a very emotional line—"Mulier, quid ploras?" (Woman, why weepest thou?)—with an efflorescence of notes. The emotional quality of this melisma is even underscored by the stage direction, "Yhesus admirans" (Jesus, wondering). But in her reply to the supposed gardener, Mary continues in her measured mood, for the most part still matching each syllable to a single note. In the musical contrast one feels perhaps a sense of urgency. Then from Jesus comes another outburst, singing her name in a rich, rising melisma, exactly the same setting as the beginning of his question to her. And running to Jesus, Magdalen sings out the suddenly and appropriately high-pitched word of recognition, "Raboni!" Here Mary's leap to high notes carries her emotional leap. Jesus had begun "Mulier, quid ploras?" right on the concluding note of Mary's opening *planctus,* picking up where she had left off and leading her dramatically. Now the abrupt jump in pitch between singers, together with the melismata, conveys excitement.

Fleury, "The Slaughter of the Innocents" (*Ordo Rachelis*), and "The Image of St. Nicholas" (*Iconia Sancti Nicolai*)

Together with the Beauvais *Daniel* perhaps the most impressive of all music-dramas is that of "The Slaugh-

(Maria:) Dolor crescit, tremunt praecordia
(My grief grows and my heart trembles)

de magistri pii absentia,
(because of the absence of my Lord,)

qui salvavit me plenam vitiis,
(who saved me when I was full of wickedness,)

pulsis a me septem demoniis.
(and drove out of me seven devils.)

Yhesus admirans respondit ei dicendo:
(Jesus, wondering, answers her, saying:)
Mulier, quid ploras?
(Woman, why weepest thou?)

Maria respondit ei dicens:
(Mary answers him, saying:)
Quia tulerunt Dominum meum, et
(Because they have taken away my Lord)

nescio ubi posuerunt eum. Domine, si tu sustulisti eum, dicite
(and I know not where they have laid him. Sir, if thou hast borne him)

michi ubi posuisti eum, et ego eum tollam.
(hence, tell me where thou hast laid him, and I will take him away.)

Ihesus dicit statim:
(Jesus at once replies:)
Maria!
(Mary!)

Maria currendo ad Yhesum dicit:
(Mary runs to Jesus and says:)
Raboni!
(Master!)

Tunc Jesus dicit:
(Then Jesus says:)
O Maria, noli me tangere, --- (etc.)
(O Mary, touch me not, ---)

Example 5. Mary Magdalen recognizes the Risen Christ in the *Visitatio Sepulchri* from Cividale Cathedral (xiv century).

ter of the Innocents." If one were to imagine a scale with dramatic ceremony at one end and a miniature liturgical opera at the other end, then ninety percent of the *Visitatio Sepulchri* versions would stand at the one extreme and the *Ordo Rachelis* at the far extreme. It comes from the late twelfth-century Fleury Playbook. Here is John Stevens' summary of it.

It opens with the Innocents (the choristers of the choir) processing through the church singing "O quam gloriosum est regnum" (liturgical antiphon). Then "a Lamb, suddenly appearing, bearing a cross, shall go before them . . . and they following shall sing 'Emitte agnum, Domine'" (liturgical antiphon). This process continues during the Angel's warning to Joseph, Herod's attempted suicide and his command for the slaying of the children. As the slayers approach, the Innocents salute the Lamb once more, "Salve, Agnus

Dei." The distraught mothers are allowed a prayer of five words for mercy. Immediately an angel appears and exhorts the murdered children to rise and cry out. Dead on the ground, they sing a sentence from the Matins responsory of the Limoges manuscript . . . , "Quare non defendis sanguinem nostrum, Deus noster?" They continue to lie prostrate during Rachel's long lament but rise to their feet when the Angel sings the antiphon "Sinite parvulos" (Christ's words "Suffer the little children . . ."). They then process to the choir, praising Christ in the words of the sequence "Festa Christi." Archelaus succeeds Herod as king (in dumbshow); the angel summons the Holy Family back to Galilee; Joseph sings "Gaude, gaude" (liturgical antiphon), and the play ends with the *Te Deum*.[7]

A close examination of the choice and placement of familiar antiphons and of the word-tone relationships in the new compositions reveals a singularly sensitive and talented composer, both when working within the liturgical traditions of the late twelfth century and when pioneering with nuances of performance.

A Twelfth-Century Lament of a Jew: The Texts of Words and Notes

When composer-playwrights added new songs in the making of a liturgical drama, they tended to bind the words with the music more specifically than in the traditional chant. For example, where a downward sweep of notes often served in the inherited chant as a marking, or a demonstrative device, in the drama it could well serve an emotive purpose, as an affective device. Where the former could create perhaps a general mood, the latter could create a vivid moment.

To illustrate the point one could hardly find a more dynamic piece than the twelfth-century monologue of the Jew in *The Image of St. Nicholas,* from the Fleury Playbook. It was sung just before the Introit to the Mass on 6 December, St. Nicholas' Day. In it a Jew (Judaeus) returns home to find his treasure chest empty. His icon of St. Nicholas had not prevented a robbery. First he bewails his loss, and then he grows angry—all in hexameters, quite unusual for the chant. The two modern transcriptions printed in Example 6 indicate rhythmic patterns that are probably stricter than in the original performance, where much freer rhythms would have conveyed more accurately the emotional ups and downs of the Jew's distress. A closer relationship between the meanings of the lines and corresponding patterns of music one can hardly find in the chant, dramatic and nondramatic. For one thing, rhymes among syllables often reflect in matching musical repetitions.

The piece opens with what William Smoldon called, "the first yell to be set to Gregorian music," a descent into poverty embodied in a rapid descent of seven notes: "Vah!" *Judaeus* goes on, "perii!" (All is lost!). Next, in his second line he asks why his parents brought him into the world. Then in his third line he almost repeats the opening seven-note descent but with a more familiar Latin wail: "Heu!" "Why was I born," he continues, finishing the third line with the same pattern of notes as at the end of the first line. Each of his questions rises in tone at the end, like speech. The three melodic phrases end on *a*; their end syllables also rhyme—*pi, sti, ri.* This kind of note-word-sound linkage characterizes the entire piece,

just as each whole line or pair of lines links its patterns of notes with the sounds and meanings of the words. Furthermore, through the course of the solo, *Judaeus* expresses his upwrought state with despairing and then angry words carried in music that also tacks back and forth through changes of tempo, ascents, descents, repeats, contrasts, echoes, and bursts.

The initial three lines form a unit, both musically and verbally. Then from it the opening outburst goes on to punctuate the whole monologue, taking on various shades of meaning that climax in this motif at the finale when *Judaeus* threatens St. Nicholas with flagellation followed by incineration if the Saint does not see to it that the treasure is returned—and that very night.

To return to the beginning of the monologue—lines 4 and 5, and 6 and 7, are paired. Each pair shapes a unit of music and language, a mood of questioning and lamenting. With line 8, "Pollens argento" (Loaded with money), the mood of the Jew swings as do his notes, marching upward. In lines 9 and 10, again a musical and verbal pair, he feels low with a six-note descent on "miser" (miserable) and again on "Nam latet" (Nothing remains), both lines also ending with an identical musical configuration.

Thereupon he comes to a new mood—and the turning point of the twenty-one-line solo—in four lines each rather independent from the others. The four-line fulcrum of the monologue begins at line 11: "Quod levius" (How light-hearted I was) . . . "Sed, ni decipior" (But, not to fool myself) . . . "Sic ego" (So much for me) . . . and "Quidni noxa?" (Why shouldn't I feel hurt?). Lines 11 and 12—"Quod levius" and "Sed, ni decipior"—start with the same music, respectively, and then the music of each line goes its own way, as does the thought expressed in the words.

Lines 15 and 16 pick up again the practice of pairing lines both in sense and in identical beginning and ending note patterns. But now *Judaeus* changes the direction of his address. And his mood. *Judaeus* talks directly to the icon, blaming St. Nicholas for his loss. Line 17, "Nec solus flebo" (Nor do I merely cry) opens and closes with a downward sweep of five notes. He is returning to his opening yell, but starting on a higher note. Thereupon, with lines 18 and 19—"Tu meritis" (You deserve . . . to be thrashed with whips) and "Sed fessus cedam" (But tired I am)—he raises himself to punish the image, then sinks with the thought of "whips" in a five-note fall; raises himself again, but again sinks with five downward notes as he gives St. Nicholas "the space of a night" to restore the stolen property. The ends of 17, 18, and 19 are also melodi-

Planctus Iudei (Ms. Orléans 201, S. 191-193)

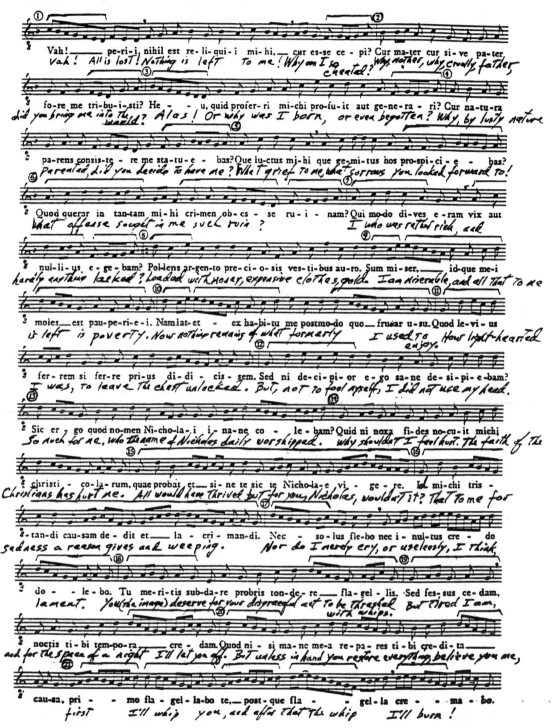

Example 6. Monologue of *Judaeus*, finding his treasure chest empty, in the *Iconia Sancti Nicolai* (*The Image of St. Nicholas*) from the Fleury Playbook (xii century)—first of two transcriptions.

Example 6 (continued). Iconia Sancti Nicolai—second of two transcriptions.

Example 6 (*continued*).

cally related—the melody of 18 is very similar to that of 19—so that by means of this thrice-repeated pattern he shapes a musical springboard for his final outburst.

The monologue concludes as *Judaeus* delivers two single-standing lines. Line 20, "Quod nisi" (But unless ... you restore everything), opens and closes with a five-note downward sweep. The first sweep starts on *d*, the second again up to *d*. He is climbing to his line 21 finale. The seven-note and six-note sweeps that opened his initial outcries of "Vah!" and "Heu!" had begun on *c* and *b* respectively. Now he finishes the piece by swearing that if St. Nicholas does not restore his treasure, and it must happen tonight, he will whip him and then burn him. There he reaches to the top of his performance: "fla-" ("fla-gella," the whip) initiates a seven-note descent with *e* at the top; "cre-" ("cre-mabo!", I'll burn!), a final six-note descent from *e* (not *e*-flat).

One of the most memorable solos in the corpus of the church drama, the furious lament stands out because it is so unchant-like. In fact, it is so different even from other solos found in the drama, that it has been suggested that the composer was reproducing a Jewish hymn. From the wandering scholar Hilarius, probably a student of Abelard in the twelfth century, we possess a Daniel play, a Lazarus play, and a *Ludus super Iconia Sancti Nicolai*. Hilarius follows the orig-

inal story as told in the Vita of St. Nicholas insofar as it was a heathen who had put an ill-gotten icon of the Saint in charge of his gold and silver. He is referred to as *barbarus*, an African in the Vita, and named Barbarus in Hilarius' play. The Fleury Playbook playwright turned him into a Jew. What conditions could have inspired such a striking alteration, from *barbarus* to *Judaeus*? In general Jews seem to have been tolerated and treated humanely in that part of the world at that time because they were money lenders and collectors of interest, a practice expressly forbidden to Christians by their Church. Increased building as well as Crusade activity in the twelfth century intensified the demand for financing, and to this end Jews were necessary to the social structure.

Partially as a consequence of this role in the community, much discussion as to belief took place between Jews and Christians. That trend may well be reflected in the finale of the Fleury play where, when the Saint does effect the return of the Jew's treasure, *Judaeus* "sings intensely" (dicat alta voce) four times the joyful refrain "Gaudeamus!", converted not by Christians but through his own new-found conviction.

Historical events gave the theme a poignant importance. In 1171, a pogrom was carried out in nearby Blois, where thirty-four Jews were arrested and burned. Their rabbi, who was able to escape, wrote to a colleague in Orléans about their singing in the fire: "When the flames licked up, the Jews raised their voices together such that the Christians said, 'We have never heard such a beautiful song before this day.' And it actually became known that this song that the Christians had heard in those terrible moments was the [Jewish] hymn *Alenu.*" Perhaps that incident also inspired the Fleury playwright to add "I'll burn!" as the climax of the Jew's lament.

Echoes of that lament would be heard four centuries later by audiences in the English theatre—in Christopher Marlowe's play *The Jew of Malta* (ca. 1590). Then instead of *Judaeus* his name was Barabas. Then, instead of Robbers, it was the Knights and Officers of Malta who seized Barabas' possessions.

Barabas.
My gold, my gold, and all my wealth is gone!
You partial heavens, have I deserved this plague?
What, will you thus oppose me, luckless stars,
To make me desperate in my poverty?
And knowing me impatient in distress,
Think me so mad as I will hang myself,
That I may vanish o'er the earth in air,
And leave no memory that e'er I was?
No, I will live: nor loathe I this my life;
And since you leave me in the ocean thus
To sink or swim, and put me to my shifts,
I'll rouse my senses, and awake myself.

(I.ii.258–69)

When Barabas is dispossessed, he can turn in mid-speech from lamentation to action. In that regard he is like the *Judaeus* of Fleury. But when Shakespeare's Shylock is dispossessed, like the *Judaeus* of the Fleury Playbook he can move an audience. One such moment comes toward the end of the trial scene in *The Merchant of Venice* (ca. 1600).

Shylock.
You take my house when you do take the prop
That doth sustain my house; you take my life
When you do take the means whereby I live.

(IV.i.374–76)[8]

Other Music Dramas

The extant versions of the *Peregrinus,* the *Officium Pastorum,* the *Officium Stellae,* and the *Ordo Rachelis* all combine the free rhythms of prose settings with lyrical poetic stanzas and blend original music with traditional antiphons and hymns. The *Peregrinus* con-

sists mostly of a number of antiphons, recitative-like musical passages. Whereas the *Officium Pastorum,* inspired by the text of the Easter trope but with an entirely original setting, remains musically close to the liturgy. In the *Officium Stellae* one finds a sudden burst of free composition and new music with spare employment of familiar ecclesiastical pieces. And the *planctus* of Rachel from the Fleury Playbook constitutes one of the melodic high points not only in this genre of theatre but in all medieval art-music, the more remarkable because it differs so radically from the by then three-hundred-year-old nondramatic tradition of Rachel's lament.

Such variety did not underlie the heritage of other church dramas, each perhaps a product of a single act of composition, for when, as of the twelfth century, a new style of Latin poetry employed regular meter and rhyme, this stanzaic form became reflected in the incantatory strophic settings of new plays as opposed to the theatrically more lively settings of prose. From the Fleury Playbook, all verses of the *Three Clerks* are sung to a single tune, with the exception of St. Nicholas' prayer; the opening laments of the *Three Daughters* have one tune, whereupon the father then commences a new tune which is repeated more than thirty times; and each stanza of the *Lazarus* reiterates the same melody, save the opening prose section. The *Conversion of St. Paul* goes to the opposite extreme, with a different tune for nearly every new verse while exhibiting clearly patterned verse form. A strongly unified artistic whole is the *Planctus Mariae* from Cividale, essentially a poem with great melodic variety and beauty, whereas the *Ordo Prophetarum* remains musically repetitive and incantatory.

But of especial musical interest are the *Son of Getron* and the *Image of St. Nicholas* from the Fleury Playbook, the eleventh- or twelfth-century *Sponsus (Wise and Foolish Virgins)* from Limoges (was it in fact produced in a church?), and the twelfth-century *Daniel* from Beauvais, for these works tend toward the use of leitmotiv, a melody assigned to a particular character or group of characters, with some singularly effective moments created by the human voice in performance. Each figure or onstage group has its given tune in *Getron;* with a few exceptions such is also the case in the *Image,* set strophically but with nearly a dozen melodies; and the *Sponsus* employs four melodies of non-Gregorian character—for the prologue, Gabriel, the *prudentes,* and both the merchants and the *fatuae.* Perhaps the most remarkable musical composition is the play of *Daniel* from Beauvais, consisting of almost fifty melodies, each usually assigned

Primus:

Stel - la ful - go - re ni - mi - o ru - ti - lat

Secundus veniens a meridie:

Que re - gem re - gum na - tum mon - strat

Tertius ab australi parte:

Quem ven - tu - rum o - lim pro - phe - ti - a si - gna - ve - rat

Example 7. The three kings see the star in the Christmas play of the Magi (*Officium Stellae*) from Ste. Corneille de Compiègne (xi century).

[Rex]

Re - gem quem que - ri - tis

na - tum es - se quo si - gno di - di - cis - tis?

Magi:

Il - lum na - tum es - se di - di - ci - mus

in o - ri - en - te stel - la mon - stran - te.

Rex:

Si il - lum reg - na - re cre - di - tis di - ci - te mic - hi.

Magi:

Hunc reg - na - re fa - ten - tes cum mis - ti - cis mu - ne - ri - bus

de ter - ra lon - gin - qua a - do - ra - re ve - ni - mus

tri - num de - um ve - ne - ran - tes tri - bus in mu - ne - ri - bus.

Primus: **Secundus:** **Tertius:**

Au - re re - gem Tu - re sa - cer - do - tem Mir - ra mor - ta - lem

Example 8. Herod interviews the three kings in the Christmas play of the Magi (*Officium Stellae*) from Ste. Corneille de Compiègne (xi century).

to a new speaker, and some of which may have a dance-rhythm quality found nowhere else in the drama of the medieval church save at Benediktbeuern.[9]

Dramatic Character Through Music

The earliest, complete manuscript of the Magi play reveals establishment of character through music. It comes from the Abbey of Ste. Corneille de Compiègne (eleventh century). From the opening lines each king is singled out musically. At the same time, the three phrases as a group create a musical unity embodying the single purpose of the three Magi.

Not only does the music shape individual character, but as the drama unfolds it underscores the heightening tension between the Magi and Herod.

Herod asks each of his questions in the plagal G-mode. The Magi answer each in the authentic D-mode. The very shift back and forth in modes expresses conflict. Furthermore, where Herod opens each interrogative with the jump of a fourth, the Magi counter each with the jump of a fifth, a little higher. In this way the music underscores their diametrically opposed purposes: Herod wants to find the Christ Child in order to kill him, the Magi in order to worship him. Another version of the Magi play, from the early twelfth century, goes so far as to have two of the three Magi speak to Herod in total gibberish—an invented foreign tongue.[10]

In an even more sophisticated way, the students at Beauvais Cathedral used music to create character and character relationships in their *Play of Daniel* (mid-twelfth century). No other liturgical drama displays such a wealth of musical and poetic invention, pushing the bounds of the chant well into the territory of secular lyrics. The student-composers of the *Daniel* associated certain characters with particular modal idioms, and with their music they created dramatic juxtapositions, as Rankin notes,

> by altering the mode of successive texts sung by different characters, and [by] contrasting simple with elaborate melodic styles, as well as wide and small ranges. For example, the three songs with the widest range in the play (a tenth) are associated with particularly impressive or dramatic moments: "Iubilemus regi nostro," sung in praise of Belshazzar near the beginning of the play, "Ecce rex," which accompanies the entrance, and "Heu, heu," Daniel's plea for pardon after Darius' order that he should be thrown to the lions.[11]

Unfortunately, the difficult neumes of the *Ludus Paschalis,* the larger Passion play, and the Christmas play from Benediktbeuern cannot be transcribed into plainsong notation. However, we do know that the latter was set strophically, and Thomas Binkley has traced the musical incipits to related service books and then produced the resulting work.[12] No music is given for the shorter Passion in *Carmina Burana.* Scanty neumes accompany the fragment of the Vorau *Esau,* but we have no music for *Antichrist,* Mézières' *Presentation,* the Laon *Joseph,* or for the plays by Hilarius. The more the pity. Yet there can be little doubt that the respective roles were sung.

Herein lies the most obvious and frequently overlooked distinction between productions in the sanctuary and in the city square. Whereas the former were conceived and acted as music-dramas, the latter were spoken in the vernacular no longer supplied with musical settings and at a remove from the church service. Clerics rigorously trained in music sang the liturgical drama, whereas civic laity spoke the mystery, miracle, and Passion plays. Music did not play such a large part in the open-air performances, where angelic choirs, the raucous sounds of demons, the singing school in the Temple, the blowing of fanfares and accompaniment by stringed instruments all served the action in an incidental fashion.

Modes and Dramatic Music

Medieval music was based on a system of eight modes, codified in the ninth century and well established by the time of the inception of church drama. A mode is a way of patterning tones. It comprises a diatonic scale with the compass of one octave. Not only were modes assigned quasi-classical names (as of the ninth century), but theorists as early as Guido d'Arezzo (ca. 995–1050) imitated the Greeks in attributing ethos or a singular aesthetic quality to each mode: Dorian (grave), Hypodorian (sad), Phrygian (mystical), Hypophrygian (harmonious), Lydian (joyful), Hypolydian (devout), Mixolydian (angelic), and Hypomixolydian (perfect).

For the study of modes in the music-drama a key question is this: in an antiphon selected for a moment in the drama (or in a newly composed piece of music for the drama), was the music with its particular mode supposed to elicit a particular feeling in the singers and listeners during that moment? At the birth of medieval drama, Gregorian melodies were said to convey a range of moods, and these musical moods underscored the theatrical presentations as they did the liturgy. Clearly the employment of traditional plainchant in the drama transferred associations of liturgical usage to the drama. But can one take one more step in relationships between sound and mood? Were there really "mode-affects," or were these theorists' games? We have no definite answer. The attribution of ethos varies among theorists. It often seems a rather personal matter. And yet there reigns a prevailing sense throughout this period that the tonal pattern of the melodies matched, or should match, the meaning of the words.[13]

For example, the *Quem quaeritis* lines were set to a second-mode melody, with what theorists generally spoke of as a sad feeling, whereas, as one would expect, the majority of music in such a play as the *Ludus Paschalis* from the Tours manuscript is in Dorian and Hypodorian modes. While half of the numbers in the Beauvais *Daniel* are written in the favorite Dorian and Hypodorian modes, including the dignified passages of the two kings, the pathos of Daniel's prayer and thanks and Darius' mourning are expressed in the Phrygian or the Hypophrygian modes. In the Fleury *Officium Stellae* the angelic chorus sings "Gloria in excelsis Deo" in the Hypomixolydian mode; the Magi spy the star, "Ecce stella," in the Lydian mode; and most of the exchanges at Herod's court are in the Dorian mode.[14]

One of the most striking theatrical contributions of music to performance consists in an elementary kind of leitmotiv technique hinted at in the Magi play of Campiègne and deployed though not rigidly so throughout the Beauvais *Daniel*. It is characteristic of the *Son of Getron* in the Fleury Playbook, where a distinctive melody is assigned each to King Marmorinus, to Getron, Euphrosina, Adeodatus (the son), the king's attendants, and to the citizens of the city. When Adeodatus, captive at Marmorinus' court, sighs his longing for home, in one verse he sings his mother's music, and her consolers also take up her melody. A similar occurrence of this phenomenon is found in the *Sponsus* of Limoges, where the prologue, the angel Gabriel, the wise, and the foolish virgins are each furnished a singular tune. When the merchants refuse oil to the foolish virgins, they sing their melody; and when Christ concludes the play, he does so apparently first with the melody of the prologue and then with that of Gabriel.[15]

Subtle shadings in mood are nowhere better exemplified than in a parallel scene from the *Ludus Paschalis* of Tours, where nine changes of mode underscore the lines. It is in this latter play especially that the music sets the women's feelings about the grave against the attitudes of the guards, deepening the sadness of the women and later of Thomas.[16]

A lyrical passage such as the lamentation of Mary Magdalen from Cividale or in the *Visitatio* from the Fleury Playbook is often reserved by a playwright for an intensely emotional moment, where perhaps foregoing recitative or melismatic chant-music contrasts sharply with the then highly charged lyric. The buildup in the *Peregrinus* of Beauvais toward the tense confrontation between doubting Thomas and the Risen Christ reaches a crescendo in vigorous lyrical passages. After much song in prose at Herod's court in the *Officium Stellae* from Fleury, Archelaus races on with a song in rhythmic verses, "All hail . . . ," and attempts to raise the spirits of the company. He succeeds, for Herod immediately takes up the melody, and Archelaus, with some slight musical variations, concludes by threatening the life of the Christ Child. In fact, it has been observed that in numerous church dramas "free rhythm of a prose setting followed by the measured melody of a lyrical poetic stanza suggests an anticipation by many centuries of the dramatic device of *recitative* followed by *arioso*, one that emerged in the early baroque era."[17]

One of the most remarkable achievements with some of the most fervent music in all church drama forms the climax of the earlier discussed *Ordo Rachelis* from Fleury: the threefold lament of Rachel. Here the plea of the mothers begins in an original Mixolydian phrase, and then Rachel's opening solo, haunted by that plea, presents in Hypomixolydian mode a development of a theme which is subsequently varied by her consolers. Melismatic passages mark Rachel's second solo, while the theme remains insistent. Then the consolers alternate with Rachel in delivering an impassioned recitative set to a new melody. Rachel is singing in her Hypomixolydian mode, the consolers in the rare Phrygian mode. Finally, singing a familiar antiphon from Good Friday, in a Hypophrygian mode Rachel collapses over the bodies of the slain children and the *Consolatrices* lead her away as they intone an antiphon from Innocents' Day. Throughout the scene one experiences a flow from one mode to a related mode as one experiences the flow of Rachel's joining and mourning with her companions. Moreover, the rest of the play, taken as a whole, shapes a musical and textual framework around this *planctus*. The frame comprises a mosaic of separate liturgical chants from at least half a dozen different Offices, a dramatic ceremony into which has been placed this singular mourning song in dialogue form. Indeed one might view the *Ordo Rachelis* of the Fleury Playbook, a lamentation acted out within a more ritualistic presentation, as a paradigm of the medieval music-drama acted out within the liturgy of church ritual.[18]

In analyzing the ways in which the creators of the drama fashioned a parquetry of traditional chants, adding new music here and there, one runs the risk of possible assumption that the idioms of plainchant, for example the recurrent formulae of a particular mode, are specific and individual in their liturgical connotations and "moods." Given the *huge* corpus of the chant, such association does not generally occur.

However, some remarkable exceptions survive, demonstrating that even in repetitive stanzaic works certain passages could be set off by the foil of a new melody, while where there already existed such a treasury of liturgical music, composers could thread their strands of melody with an almost limitless number of familiar jewels that would reflect on the present action—fleeting reminders of moods in other services or of earlier moments in the given play. In that each stanza of the *Three Clerks* from Fleury is set to the same tune save for St. Nicholas' supplication, that prayer is thus singled out by its very sound from the remainder of the play. In the Beauvais *Daniel*, the bewilderment of Belshazzar's wise men is admirably illustrated by the redundant quality of their melody. Although the central lines of the *Officium Pastorum*, "Quem quaeritis in praesepe," are modelled on the Easter lines, the musical setting presents an original composition; but in the shepherds' play from Rouen the midwives at the manger suddenly use the Easter tune for these opening four words, creating a subtle echo before resuming the usual setting. This same effect is found in the *Officium Stellae* of the Fleury Playbook for the first two words. Something quite rare happens musically in those moments at Fleury and Rouen. Even more interesting and demonstrative of the dramatic overtones which the sound of performance could supply is the passage in the latter play where the shepherds sing to the Magi a portion of what the angel had first told them, and while so doing they also quote excerpts from the angel's music.

Soloists, Choruses, and Instruments

Several contemporary titles of plays indicate dominance or emergence of a single, major figure: the designation *Ordo Rachelis* first occurs in an eleventh-to-twelfth-century manuscript from Freising; the twelfth-century Norman-French Epiphany play for Sicily has the superscript "Versus ad Herodem faciendum," and that from Fleury "Ordo ad representandum Herodem"; and a Dutch Easter play from ca. 1200 was called *Visitatio Marie Magdalene* when a new version of it was created in the fifteenth century.[19] Certainly Rachel might well be considered a soloist, while more prominent and increasingly difficult parts were being written for the singer of the role of Mary Magdalen, her long performance in the *Ludus Paschalis* from the Tours manuscript containing several solos found nowhere else in the music or drama of the church.

The part of the Virgin Mary in the *Planctus* of Cividale and the role of Daniel at Beauvais both illustrate focus on a central figure. But more characteristic is the corporate sound, the monophonic enrichment of an action through juxtaposition of single voices and vocal combinations and the relationship of the individual singers to choral groups.

The chorus in the music-drama performed two different dramatic functions. First, the choir of men's and boys' voices served as it did during the Mass: singing hymns, sequences, and antiphons, completing the *Visitatio Sepulchri* with "Surrexit Dominus de sepulchro" and the *Te Deum*, occasionally narrating an action with one of these traditional pieces such as "Currebant duo," sometimes sung as the race to the tomb was mimed. But when the choir receives the report of the Marys and of Peter and John, the gathering becomes for the moment surrogate disciples if not the apostles in Jerusalem. Thus they begin to take on dramatic identity within the play. A special part is assigned to the chorus in the Vorau *Isaac*, where boys sing allegorical material between episodes.

The second function of the choral body has to do with its acting a role, assuming character and distinctively theatrical costume. Nearly every kind of ecclesiastical drama contains an example: the angels in Christmas plays, disciples in the *Peregrinus* and *Conversion of St. Paul*, Jews and "Assessores" in the Benediktbeuern *Ludus Paschalis*, satraps and attendants in the Beauvais *Daniel* (who punctuate the play with ringing choruses and repetitions of "Rex, vive in aeternum"). It is in the *Sponsus* of Limoges that groups—the wise and foolish virgins—actually sing the roles of the protagonists.

It was the *a capella* voice which carried these melodies, made possible by the vocalizing technique of the ardently trained, skilled clerical singer, who had no need for instrumental accompaniment. Church councils of the twelfth and thirteenth centuries actually included showy singers in their reiterated interdicts on the playing of all instruments in the liturgy save the organ, which appeared more frequently in churches during this period and was heard on festive occasions and at special moments. The drama, usually performed within the liturgy, remained musically in keeping with the service. Only about a dozen plays, with two exceptions all of the fifteenth century or later, call for organ participation—usually with final choruses.[20] Also a handful of references mention the ringing of bells at the conclusion of the *Visitatio Sepulchri*: either those in the church tower or chime-bells, hung in a row and struck, used to teach the chant and sometimes played together with the organ.[21]

One important production may present an exception to this ban on instruments, the Beauvais *Daniel*, and Mézières' *Presentation of the Blessed Virgin* certainly does. When the Queen enters the scene of *Daniel* in the Cathedral of Beauvais, her escorts chant, "Let strings [cordis] and voices / Resound in sonorous music," and the courtiers of Darius' entourage sing, "Let the drums resound [resonent et tympana], the harpists pluck their strings [Cythariste tangant cordas], / And the pipes of the musicians sound / To his honor." The lines paraphrase the biblical account. But the rubric for the latter, the one rubrical hint of instrumentation in the text, only mentions string players and courtiers: "Cythariste et Principes sui psallentes hec." They precede Darius and sing the ensuing conductus. The *citharae* of the stage direction like the lines may well belong to verbal poetry, and, like all other liturgical drama, the *Daniel* may well have been sung entirely *a capella*.[22]

Unfortunately no music accompanies Mézières' directions for *The Presentation of the Blessed Virgin*, but two instrumentalists, perhaps with harps, lutes, or psalteries (pulsabunt instrumenta dulcia), have places on the platform in the nave and are instructed to play during certain processionals and to accompany angels' singing an unspecified vernacular piece.[23] With all of the outdoor mystery-play activity of this period in France, it might perhaps seem surprising that no more than those quiet instruments penetrated the new observance, yet I believe that the restriction is indicative of the strength of church custom.

Here too practices in open-air staging of religious drama differed radically, employing all known instruments for incidental music, and such usage no doubt influenced the depictions of celestial paradise, full of angels with bells, citherns, cymbals, drums, and flutes, created by Brunelleschi and others within and outside of Florentine churches.[24] Moreover, the *Ars nova* of the Renaissance wrought major changes in the conduct of ecclesiastical ritual, and ties between clergy and private chapels, for example, resulted in the common sound of instrumental music in processionals. Doubtless the calls for pipes and trumpets, together with the organ, in mid-sixteenth-century texts for cel-

ebrations of Pentecost and the Assumption at Halle reflect this new, nonmedieval spirit.[25] But the composers of the liturgical *dramma per musica*, which with its incomparable store of medieval melody waxed and waned in the church over a period of seven hundred years, adopted and invented almost wholly vocal music, wherein many a clerical performer must have been the match for many a minstrel or trouvère.

Dramatic Qualities of the Music

The composer of the *Visitatio Sepulchri* for Cividale employs melisma for emotional impact. So does the composer-compiler of the *Ordo Rachelis* from Fleury. Immediately we must take warning that by no means does a melismatic passage in the music-drama always signal a charged theatrical moment. Certain composers do provide melisma on a word that conveys intense feeling. This practice has precedence in the nondramatic singing of a sometimes prolonged and florid "Alleluia." Also, as discussed with the Cividale text, a sudden change of pitch from one character to another can be intended to convey an emotional exchange. Pronounced, percussive beats such as those that appear in the Beauvais *Daniel* can mark the movement of a procession. Now and then in what we have singled out as very theatrical plays, we hear intense lyrical passages, such as those sung by Rachel and by Mary Magdalen, this quality of music analogous to lyrical poetry. The insertion of the non-liturgical *planctus* into the music-drama reveals this rare tendency toward musical lyricism. When in an unusual instance such as the *Officium Stellae* in the Fleury Playbook, we hear the Easter music sung at the Christmas line "Quem quaeritis in praesepe?" (Whom do you seek in the manger?), we recognize the use of a musical theme quoted or reiterated for dramatic purposes. Such is also the case with the hints of leitmotiv already discussed, though for the most part thematic material is repeated in these plays with no dramatic intent. The *Ludus Paschalis* from the Tours manuscript repeats one cadence fifteen times, another ten or eleven, and a third more than fifteen, apparently without any conscious theatrical shading. On the other hand, from the very inception of this drama, whole pieces were transplanted to it specifically as musical as well as textual reminders. That is, both of Ethelwold's well-known Easter antiphons—"Alleluia, surrexit dominus de sepulchro" and "Venite et videte locum"—intensified in his drama the evocation there of traditional Easter liturgy. Finally, a shift in mode, such as the shift from the predominant D mode to the

F mode for the scene between the spice-seller and the Marys in the *Ludus Paschalis* of Tours *may* have to do with an overtly dramatic intention on the part of the composer-dramatist. Musically the scene contains a single melody repeated ten times. In the *Visitatio Sepulchri* from Fleury, the predominant mode is D. But right at the center of the play a major shift to the E mode occurs, beginning as the angels ask Mary Magdalen, "Mulier, quid ploras?". When the women lay the gravecloth on the altar, there are six phrases moving between F and G—the Marys celebrating the Resurrection—then two well-known antiphons on E, and the finale, "Resurrexit hodie dominus," back on the original, dominating D. Here too we must exercise the greatest caution, for only in the rarest of instances do we know what mood a mode was intended to evoke; the intent, if it existed at all, probably varied from place to place; and many a shift in mode in the drama, like many a thematic repetition, seems to have occurred with no theatrical design. The very dramatic *Tres Filiae* from the Fleury Playbook, a St. Nicholas play, uses the same melody almost entirely throughout, and the near-comic merchant scene in the *Ludus Paschalis* from Origny repeats one tune sixteen times. Perhaps this practice, and the Origny melody itself, reflects the manner of singing narrative poems: *chansons de geste* and saints' lives.

In any case, the dominant characteristics of this music in the liturgy remain primarily staid, solemn, reverent, and ceremonial when carried over into the drama. Only once in a great while do we find a musical quality, like the melismata in the *Visitatio Sepulchri* of Cividale, that seems to have been chosen or shaped precisely to convey personal emotion of a character or to carry forward a theatrical action.[26]

Dramatic Functions of the Music

Bishop Ethelwold revealed a firm instinct for dramatic structure when he placed his *Visitatio Sepulchri* just prior to the regular singing of "Te Deum laudamus" (We Praise Thee, O God) by whole assembly at end of Matins. This music creates the triumphant finale of the play, just as with the same keen sense for shaping the theatrical experience he created a quiet opening when the angel slips surreptitiously over to the high altar and, after the third responsory ("Dum transisset sabbatum"), leads into the play with the gentle, rising notes of "Quem quaeritis." One could devote an entire study of the music-drama to the dramaturgical choices of opening and closing

music conveying the action and creating impact, choices tutored by long liturgical practice.

We discover links between music and dramatic structure in the shift to a new mode for the spice-sellers in the *Ludus Paschalis* from Tours, the processions of the *Daniel*, the placement of the Christmas angels' hymns, the musical buildup in the three-scene version of the *Visitatio Sepulchri* from the walk of the Marys to the race to the tomb to the joyous singing of Mary Magdalen. In the unfolding of one of these dramas, the composer-compiler selected a familiar piece of music for one of four reasons. An antiphon such as "Currebant duo" (Two ran to the Tomb) sung by the chorus can be used to narrate what the actors are doing, here the approach to the sepulchre by Peter and John. We find this type of structural element commonly employed in the Japanese Noh drama and in ancient Greek tragedy and comedy. The composer-compiler through his choice of music can also provide the actors with dialogue (for example, "Quem quaeritis"), or he can conjure up mood or atmosphere at a given moment (for example, with a *planctus*), or he can introduce or underscore dramatic themes at appropriate junctures ("Resurrexit dominus"). In the blueprint of a play each of the musical pieces is located strategically for overall dramatic effect. The *Peregrinus* plays illustrate the point. Though vivid in episode and dramatic action, they contain little original composition because, as Rankin observes, "for no other play was so much textual material already set as Gregorian chant."[27] Its authors compiled and joined together already existing liturgical pieces.

While making a dramatic effect because of its characteristics and its placement, a piece of music can also express a character's feeling, as in the powerful impact of Rachel's lament over the bodies of the Innocents. However, during Herod's fury, another emotional high point in the Fleury Playbook, the music conveys no especial "anger" whatsoever. As Herod rages and his son tries to pacify him, both sing the same, staid tune. Specific emotional expression through music links rarely to a dramatically charged moment. When words and music do conjoin in this manner, a spark of a *ludus* contrasts with the generally cool temper of an *ordo* or *officium*.

To take a second example, the exchange between Rachel and her *Consolatrices* in the *Ordo Rachelis* of Fleury occurs in six segments before they lead her off: first Rachel, then the *Consolatrices*, then Rachel and so on. But the music of this dialogue is all of one piece. It does not vary in major ways between characters: the

Example 9. The lament of Rachel, with her *Consolatrices*, in the *Ordo Rachelis (Slaughter of the Innocents)* from the Fleury Playbook (xii century)—first of two transcriptions.

sounds and rhythms and patterns of Rachel lamenting intermingle with those of the *Consolatrices* consoling. Each refers to the other, as it were. Only two elements link word and sound to express feeling of the moment: the settings of the words "Heu" (Alas) and "O." The two-note settings of the two-syllable "Heu" begin six of the seven lines in Rachel's first lament. It is insistent, its two syllables sounding G four times, then rising to sound D

twice. After the first consolation passage, Rachel picks up with "Heu" three times, each in a descending pair of notes, then continues to drop to "Quomodo gaudebo" (How shall I rejoice?). This is her second lament. Her third lament returns to D, repeating "Heu" three times on that note. In the first lament, the repeated "Heu" fits in the rhythmical pattern of the lines. In the second and third laments it does not. A listener hears the disjointed

Example 9 (continued).

Example 9 (continued).

quality of her cry. The second moment where one hears the sensibilities of "play" emerging from the mind-set of "dramatic ceremony" occurs with the repeated melismas of the name "Rachel" sung by the *Consolatrices* and later in "O dolor, O patrum" (O grief! O [joys] of fathers and mothers . . . turned now to mourning) sung by Rachel. These moments carry particular anguish as compared with the overall tone of the lament. "The music of medieval drama," writes John Stevens, "when not wholly subject to laws of liturgical ceremony, is a sort of extended song, a lyrical narrative shared by different voices." Example 9 is his transcription.

Then Rachel should be brought in, and two consolers, and standing over the children she weeps, sometimes falling, she says:

Alas! tender youths, what mangled limbs we see!
Alas! sweet children, murdered by madness alone!
Alas! whom neither piety nor young age restrained!
Alas! wretched mothers, who are forced to see this!
Alas! what now shall we do? Why do we not submit to these deeds? because joys cannot lighten our sorrows,
Alas! we are mindful of the sweet pledges of love who are no more.

Lament of Rachel from the Fleury Play Slaughter of the Innocents

Then Rachel is brought in, and two consolers, and standing over the children she weeps, sometimes falling, saying:

He-u! te-ne-ri par-tus la-ce-ros quos cer-ni-mus ar-tus!

He-u! dul-ces na-ti, so-la ra-bi-e ju-gu-la-ti!

He-u! quem nec pi-e-tas nec ve-stra co-er-cu-it e-tas!

He-u! ma-tres mi-se-re quae co-gi-mur i-sta vi-de-re!

He-u! quid nunc a-gi-mus cur non hec fa-cta su-bi-mus!

He-u! qui-a me-mo-res no-stro-que le-va-re do-lo-res!

Gau-di-a non pos-sunt, nam dul-ci-a pi-gno-ra de-sunt!

The Consolers support her as she falls, saying:

No-li, vir-go Ra-chel, no-li dul-cis-si-ma ma-ter,

Pro ne-ce par-vo-rum fle-tus re-ti-ne-re do-lo-rum. Si-que tri-sta-ris

ex-ul-ta-que la-cri-ma-ris. Nam-que tu-i na-ti vi-vunt su-per a-stra be-a-ti.

Facsimile in N. Greenberg, ed., *The Play of Herod* (New York, 1965), pp. 94–96.

Again Rachel laments:

He-u! He-u! He-u! Quo-mo-do gau-de-bo; dum mor-tu-a mem-bra vi-de-bo;

Dum sic com-mo-ta fu-e-re per vi-sce-ra to-ta? Me fa-ci-ent ve-re pu-e-ri

si-ne fi-ne do-lo-re O do-lor! O pa-trum!

mu-ta-ta-que gau-di-a ma-trum Ad lu-gu-bres luc-tus!

La-cri-ma-rum fun-di-te fle-tus, Ju-de-e flo-rem pa-tri-e la-cri-man-do do-lo-rem!

Again the Consolers:

Quid tu, vir-go, ma-ter Ra-chel, plo-rans for-mo-sa, cu-ius vul-tus Ja-cob

de-le-ctat? Ce-u so-ro-ris a-gni-cu-le lip-pi-tu-do e-um ju-vat!

Ter-ge, ma-ter, flen-tes o-cu-los. Quam te de-cent ge-na-rum ri-vu-li!

Then Rachel:

He-u, he-u, he-u! Quid me in-cu-sa-stis fle-tus in-cas-sum fu-di-sse.

Cum sim or-ba-ta na-to, pau-per-ta-tem me-am cu-ra-ret;

Qui non hos-ti-bus ce-de-ret an-gus-tos ter-mi-nos,

quos mi-chi Ja-cob ad-qui-si-vit, Qui-que sto-li-dis fra-tri-bus.

quos mul-tos, proh do-lor, ex-tu-lit es-set pro-fu-tu-rus?

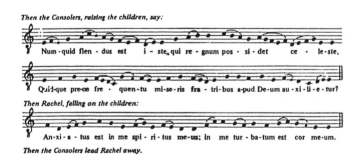

Then the Consolers, raising the children, say:

Num-quid flen-dus est i-ste, qui re-gnum pos-si-det ce-le-ste,

Quid-que pre-ce fre-quen-tu mi-se-ris fra-tri-bus a-pud De-um au-xi-li-e-tur?

Then Rachel, falling on the children:

An-xi-a-tus est in me spi-ri-tus me-us; in me tur-ba-tum est cor me-um.

Then the Consolers lead Rachel away.

Example 9 *(continued): Ordo Rachelis*—second of two transcriptions.

The consolers support her as she falls, saying:

Do not, pure Rachel, do not sweetest mother, hold back the tears of your grief for the murder of the little ones. But if you are sad about these things, rejoice at what you weep for; assuredly your children live blessed above the stars.

Again Rachel laments:

Alas, alas, alas! How shall I rejoice while I see these dead bodies; when my whole body is so troubled? Truly, the children will make me grieve forever. O sorrow! O joy of fathers and mothers changed to sorrowful mourning! Shed floods of tears, mourning the flower of Judea, the sorrow of the country.

Again the consolers:

Why do you weep, pure Rachel, lovely mother, in whose features Jacob delights? As if a bleary-eyed old wife of a sister could be pleasing to him.

Dry, mother, your flowing eyes. How do these rivers of your cheeks become you?

Then Rachel:

Alas, alas, alas! Why do you reproach me for having shed tears in vain; When I am deprived of my son, who alone would care for my poverty; who would not yield to the enemies the hallowed bounds that Jacob acquired for me? To his dull brothers—how many, O sorrow, have I brought forth—he would have been useful.

Then the consolers, raising the children, say:

Why must you weep for him who possesses a celestial kingdom? By frequent prayer to God, will he not help the wretched brothers?

Then Rachel, falling on the children:

My spirit is anxious within me; my heart is troubled within me.

The consolers lead Rachel away.[28]

In addition, music often serves the practicalities of production. Philippe de Mézières, in the specifications for his *Presentation of the Blessed Virgin,* provides an anthology of such sound. A pair of *pulsatores*—two players each with a "sweet stringed instrument"—produce music for an entry, for several ensuing processions, music to cover a long exit, sound that will underscore the weight of a dramatic moment, and even some playing by the *pulsatores* to cover the "uproarious laughter" anticipated from the crowd at the scene where Synagoga is

expelled from the church. The drama of the medieval church also provides the first costume change when at the *Visitatio Sepulchri* of the Fleury Playbook a cleric initially dressed as a gardener appears to Mary Magdalen, disappears, and later returns garbed as "Resurrectus" in the white vestments of a bishop. Mary Magdalen sings her long *planctus* during his absence, thus providing sufficient time for the "gardener" to put on the vestments.[29]

But rarely does the music impart strong human feeling, while familiar chants are put one after the other in order to tell the story. The Padua *Annunciation* (fourteenth century), discussed in Chapter 3, illustrates the point. It comprises a mixture of well-known chants and closes with the *Magnificat* where Mary sings the first three verses and then for subsequent verses the organ and the choir alternate. Though the subject matter invites expression of individual experience, nowhere is that quality found in the music. Rather the music conjures up an atmosphere of liturgical solemnity and communal celebration, and, through the pacing of its various parts, builds structurally to a climax.

We can contrast the *Annunciation* with the *Ordo Rachelis* just discussed. At the center of the *Ordo Rachelis* stands the deeply emotional, threefold lament of Rachel over the bodies of the slain Innocents. Her non-liturgical *planctus* echoes secular ceremony and courtly song. Melisma is used emotionally and so are strong melodic jumps. Also musical "rhyme" accentuates the human feeling of the moment. On the other hand, in contrast to Rachel's lament the rest of the play derives from at least ten different liturgical chants in half a dozen services, or it was composed in imitation of those chants. This layering of the familiar with the unfamiliar creates an overall unification of tone, and the resulting musical associations create an emotional impact. For instance, Rachel makes the transition between her *planctus* and the conclusion with a well-known psalm-antiphon "Anxiatus est in me spiritus meus," as she collapses over the bodies of the children. It is the antiphon of Lauds of Good Friday. With her music she embodies the grief of an individual woman, the sorrow of the psalmist, and the suffering of Christ. The function of the music is to create individual expression, and, at the same time to move in a meditative sphere.

The Congregation

A picture of a silent, docile, stationary body of worshippers reverently intent upon witnessing these productions may well be generally accurate, but it is somewhat dispelled by a few of Mézières' notes on the *Presentation.* Here a phalanx of young spear carriers must march on either side of the procession from the chapter house up to the church doors so that the performers "may have a clear path and not be harmed by the pressing of the people." Further, accompanied by the two instrumentalists, angels while marching sing a vernacular piece specifically "in order to arouse the people to devotion." Inside the church—men *and* women are in the crowd—gates are needed to close off the two sets of steps up to the platform in the nave in order to prevent the jostling throng from encroaching on this acting area, and the spear carriers must clear a path from the western doors to the first platform and then cordon off a space before the high altar where the actors are to proceed from the mid-church scaffolding. Mézières even reveals one moment of audience reaction to the production, for the instrumentalists must play a little while laughter subsides at the expulsion of Synagoga.[30] For the *Peregrinus* at Padua (thirteenth century), the cantor or *magister scolarium* made a way for the wayfarers from the sacristy through the press of people to the place of Emmaus in the church. Members of the congregation later scrambled for wafers dropped from over head at the conclusion of the performance.[31]

But one would surmise a usually more quiet atmosphere, such as witnessed by Bishop Suzdal in Florence, where he twice comments on the stillness of the congregations which had filled the respective churches, all people looking up toward the scenes of the Annunciation and of the Ascension on the roodloft. From his note that the final fire effect in the former production damaged none of the spectators' garments, one could imagine that the moving flames probably did cause some momentary consternation.[32]

When performers in a play address the spectators, their underlying attitude differs from their attitude in the observance of Matins or the Mass. Here we can perceive the threshold between religious ritual and drama. Whether Bishop Ethelwold intended his *Visitatio Sepulchri* only for an assembled monastic community alone or also for townsfolk at Easter service one does not know. In any case, when the third respond of Easter Matins is sung and he begins to coach his actors, they are performing for an audience. At that moment worshippers become audience; celebrants become actors. His language in his rubrics reveals this attitude: the Marys move "as if," "these things are done in imitation of," and they are to hold up the linen "as though the Lord was no longer wrapped in it." Then when the play is finished, for the finale of the service he has the entire assembly engage in a worshipping act by singing together the traditional *Te Deum*. Actors become cele-

brants again; specators become worshippers again. Whether the singers of the *Te Deum* were monks and the monastic community worshipping by themselves, or monks singing in front of townsfolk, or monks singing together with townsfolk, we cannot tell. But clearly, during the play Bishop Ethelwold establishes a performer-onlooker relationship in an act of make-believe, and during the closing *Te Deum* he establishes a return to the celebrant-worshipper relationship.

However, when other monastic communities absorbed the *Visitatio Sepulchri* into their observance of Matins and when those monks in their stalls enclosed it in the east choir as another in-house rite, I suspect that their underlying attitude was often closer to ritual than Ethelwold's.

Who were the spectators? With his Easter drama, Ethelwold is attentive to "uninstructed people and especially neophytes." These certainly comprised lay brothers, school- or choirboys, others connected with the monastery, and especially those training for monkhood or priesthood. In view of the fact that Winchester both observed monastic rule and served as a secular cathedral, it is quite conceivable that his own intended audience also included people from outside the monastery. That may well also have been the situation at Dunstan's Canterbury. But it was certainly not the case everywhere among the Benedictines in England. The monastic-laity relationship varied from monastery to monastery among those for whom Ethelwold and his colleagues composed the *Regularis Concordia*. When textual rubrics in later centuries instruct that German-speaking congregations are to join in at the end of the play by singing the vernacular hymn "Christ ist erstanden," one can be more certain of the presence of laity. Morever, in general the texts seem to indicate that the wider the audience or the more public the audience, the more dynamic are the characteristics of the drama.

Public Enactment and Hidden Rite

More definitely than the compilers of the *Regularis Concordia* in Anglo-Saxon England, the playwright-composers of the Fleury Playbook stepped decisively across the threshold from ritual to drama.[33] The Playbook refers to *populus* and to *plebs*. Whether these words designate a monastic community or the presence of a lay congregation one cannot tell except from the context. But it seems that at Fleury (or wherever else the Playbook might have originated) a lay congregation is meant.[34] There in the *Visitatio Sepulchri* the Marys turn "to the people" (ad populum) with the news of the Resurrection, Mary Magdalen sings the *Congratulamini michi* "to the people" (ad populum) after the *Hortu-lanus* scene—i.e., the episode with Christ as gardener—and the Marys depart from the sepulchre singing "Surrexit Dominus" (The Lord has risen) *ad plebem;* finally, when they lay out the gravecloth on the high altar, they sing *ad plebem* the words "Cernite, vos socii, sunt corporis ista beati / Linthea . . ." (Behold, you companions, here is the shroud of the blessed body . . .). At this moment the congregation becomes directly involved. In fact, it is even given a role as part of the original Jerusalem community that first received the news of the Resurrection from the women; it becomes contemporary with the events that are being depicted.[35]

The congregation becomes a similarly symbolic community in the *Peregrinus* of Fleury. Toward the conclusion, the Risen Christ bids the gathered disciples to go out and preach the Gospel. They are in the east choir, in Jerusalem. The stage direction then has the disciples lead Christ *per chorum ut videatur a populo*—"through the choir in order that he may be seen by the people." It is the present congregation that is to be taught. In the *Officium Stellae* at Fleury the worshippers are drawn directly into the dramatic proceedings at two junctures. In fact, they are even given roles to play. First the shepherds make their way to the Christ Child and then invite those standing nearby to worship at the manger (populum circumstantem). Then after the Magi have met at the high altar and have seen the star, they move to the crossing and address the spectators there as citizens of Jerusalem (Dicite nobis, O Ierosolimitani).[36] During Mass which follows the *Officium Pastorum* at Rouen, staged at the high altar in the east choir, the shepherds receive offerings possibly from clergy and laity (Offerant omnes qui uoluerint). But the play itself could have been witnessed only by the clergy in the east choir or ambulatory, shut off from the remainder of the cathedral by a rood-screen. The crib had been erected behind the main altar, with an *imago* of the Virgin Mary. A similar offertory occurs at Rouen during the *Officium Stellae*, where the manger is set up at the Altar of the Holy Cross before the east choir: a thirteenth-century text has the priests and the congregation present gifts after the Magi have completed their journey and departed (et fiat oblatio a clero et populo), however, fourteenth- and fifteenth-century texts place this act while the Magi are sleeping, prior to their being warned by an angel to return by another route. Here a general custom of the Christmas season has been incorporated directly into the mise-en-scène.[37]

Furthermore, frequent participation by the worshippers occurs in moments of congregational singing which often accompany the conclusion of the *Visita-*

tio Sepulchri. Some six dozen texts from German areas beginning in the twelfth century include familiar hymns in the vernacular (notably "Christ ist erstanden"), the congregation vocally joining together with the *dramatis personae* and church choir in the celebration of the Resurrection. A thirteenth-century text from the women's convent of Wöltingerrode calls for not one but three hymns in German to conclude the *Visitatio*. The rubric reads: *populo acclamante.*

The numerous rubrics in these plays directing actors and officiating clergy to turn to the congregation—in order to display or present some object or person, and to address, exhort, and bless the hearers—reveal an immediacy of contact between celebrant and worshipper. One can interpret this shifting character of the "audience" as a recognition and a realization of the community of worshippers. Precisely this shift effects Bishop Ethelwold's expressed intent to propagate drama "for the strengthening of the faith."

Yet of all the liturgical dramas, the *Visitatio Sepulchri* could also have a different function. In some primarily monastic churches the exchange between the Marys and the angel(s) actually occurred out of sight of the worshipping community, as a private episode. The Marys would then return with the gravecloth, and the community, seeing them, would celebrate the discovery of the Resurrection by singing the traditional *Te Deum*. For instance, at Constance the dialogue at the Tomb involved at a stone replica of the Holy Sepulchre that was located in a chapel altogether separate from the cathedral. The Marys left the Constance cathedral in procession, sang the dialogue with the angels either while processing toward the chapel or in the chapel, and then returned into the church to sing "Surrexit Dominus" and conclude with the *Te Deum*. Thereupon Easter-morning Matins commenced, eventually to finish with a second singing of the *Te Deum*. The text makes no mention of a gravecloth. A different text from Constance also records a pre-Matins observance, an *Elevatio* with a unique antiphon, "Quem queris mulier" (Whom do you seek, woman?), sung at the sepulchre in the chapel. Then a procession returned from the sepulchre (from the chapel) to the church with the Host (cum Corpore Domini) and moved to the choir entrance. The canons with the Host entered the choir, whereupon the cantor with the chorus (Cantores) commenced an antiphon, presumably the "Surrexit Dominus," repeating it three times. Finally they sang the *Te Deum*, the procession (Omnes) entered the choir area, and then Easter Matins began, the opening proclaimed with an intense voice—"sequitur festive alta voce: 'Domine labia mea'." Both texts from the Cathedral of Constance seem to reflect early practices at the birth of the liturgical drama.[38]

Since before the turn of the millennium Constance had already had numerous ties with Magdeburg. And at Magdeburg there is also a stone replica of the Holy Sepulchre (1240) related in many ways to the one at Constance (1280). However, there is one major difference. At Magdeburg it is located not outside the cathedral but in the nave of the church, so that there the *Visitatio Sepulchri* was performed right in the midst of the standing populace. The time of performance also varied: at Magdeburg, just at the end of Matins (the "normal" time); at Constance, just prior to Matins. At Magdeburg a story was told; at Constance, a mystical moment was created. At Magdeburg one feels the drama; at Constance one feels the ceremony. Different dramatic purposes required different architectural spaces.

To cite another pair of contrasting examples, at Braunschweig, Mary Magdalen actually went searching for Salvator through the crowd of worshippers standing in the nave of the cathedral; whereas at Sion (Sitten, in Switzerland) prior to 1474, the choir members in their stalls and the lay worshippers could only have heard faint music from the Marys and the angel in the crypt beneath the high altar—a rubric for the angel specifies "quidam Puer, qui sciat cantare" (a boy who can sing very well).

In these examples at Sion and at Constance a hidden rite was celebrated. At Constance the procession to the tomb actually exited from the cathedral (or formed outside of it) and moved some thirty or thirty-five meters eastward to enter the ancient (tenth century) Chapel of St. Mauritius with its stone replica of the Holy Sepulchre. The exchange between the angels and the women could have been neither seen nor heard by the worshippers inside the cathedral. Similarly, in the Cathedral of Sion the Marys departed from the raised east choir and descended into the crypt underneath the east choir to sing their lines with the angel at the subterranean Altar of St. James and to receive the gravecloth. Worshippers did not witness the scene at the sepulchre, and only those near the entrance to the crypt could possibly have caught even muffled sounds of the *Quem quaeritis* chant from down there.

Behind the two types of staging—the hidden and the open exchange at the sepulchre—lie almost opposing concepts of the relationship between performer and audience or congregation. The concealment of the event at Sion bestowed a miraculous nature upon the gravecloth in the hands of the women as they emerged from the crypt. That act was akin to the secret miracle of the Eucharist as the act was dramatized at Constance. Furthermore, when the exchange at the tomb was hidden away, as at Sion and Constance, the work tended to remain a brief, dramatic ceremony almost indistinguishable in form from its liturgical contexts; but where the *Visitatio Sepulchri* served as a public, didactic, and mnemonic instrument as at Magdeburg and Braunschweig, its lines, music, and its dramatic characteristics tended to increase.

There are, in fact, two plays surviving from Sion where one can recover the mise-en-scène: the *Visitatio Sepulchri* for Easter and an *Officium Stellae* for Christmas. Both appear to record very ancient forms. However, in the strictest sense the second one, the *Officium Stellae,* is really not a drama. It is not a play acted out but rather a procession with special props and costumes. Like the early (many Italian) pre-Mass processions augmenting the Introit at Easter with added tropes, both the Easter and the Christmas observance at Sion augmented the *Feierlichkeit* (the celebrative solemnity) of the particular observance. The populace caught sounds, smells, and glimpses of the *Feierlichkeit,* just as it caught sounds, smells, and glimpses of the sacred moments of the Mass. On the other hand, for the townspeople in thirteenth-century Sion the Holy Week festivity at the cathedral was not on Easter Sunday but on the preceding Palm Sunday, when a great public procession wound its way from the cathedral to various neighboring churches and eventually back to the cathedral.

Neither the partially secreted *Visitatio Sepulchri* nor the *Officium Stellae* at Sion was intended to teach. It seems that in certain churches the liturgical drama had a teaching function; in others it did not. That is, in some instances its mnemonic function was more pronounced (i.e., bringing back to mind what was already known), and in other instances its devotional function was more pronounced. Like the tropes added to the Introit of the Easter Mass to make the entering procession more *feierlich,* so some forms of the *Visitatio Sepulchri* and the *Officium Stellae* were included in order to create a more festive event than the liturgy would otherwise allow. Such was the case at Sion. Where the events at the sepulchre itself are hidden away, as is the situation at Sion and at the Cathedral of Constance and at other Easter sepulchres located in removed chapels, the waiting on the part of clergy and congregation creates anticipation toward the reentry of the Marys into the chancel and the glorious announcement of the Resurrection. That is the augmented *Feierlichkeit,* but not a drama enacted in front of an audience. The mountain isolation of Sion may have resulted in our having texts that although dating to the thirteenth century contain practices and attitudes reflecting a more ancient *Feierlichkeit.* This isolation may also have been the reason for the continued use of these texts in Sion into the seventeenth century.

By contrast, the early liturgical drama in some areas was certainly intended to serve a teaching or mnemonic function within a monastic community. And in a third situation, this drama often served to instruct a general populace. Such was the case at Winchester circa 973, teaching apparently both townsfolk and members of the monastic community; and such was the case in churches with texts calling for the singing of a final hymn in the vernacular, often "Christ ist erstanden."

In other words, the evidence suggests that in some monastic communities the overt teaching and mnemonic functions of this drama in its simple form occurred to the monastery's leadership no more or less than the teaching and mnemonic functions of a given hymn or procession, whereas elsewhere, as at Winchester, such purposes became primary elements from the outset, either for the monastic community or for the townspeople, or for both. It is in the latter instances that the drama separated increasingly from the liturgy, became more distinct as a genre, and took on more narrative and characterological features. As to the question of origins, it seems that in the tenth century somewhere between the Easter Mass Introit tropes of Italy and southern France, and Easter Matins tropes of German areas—and the Council of Winchester—the idea was born of using this special *Feierlichkeit* in order to bring back to memory and to teach.[39] As time went on, monastic communities whose observances were strictly intramural tended toward the enhancement of their Easter *Feierlichkeit* if they used *Quem quaeritis* at all, whereas monastic communities and especially cathedral chapters whose observances included extramural congregations, such as townspeople and pilgrims and students, tended toward demonstrating and teaching if they used *Quem quaeritis.* It was there that the antiphonally exchanged *Quem quaeritis* lines came to be acted out and expanded—and extended to various sites in the church—as were the lines of Christmas plays and other music-dramas in the eleventh and twelfth centuries.

The Tourist and the Native in the Theatre

As noted in Chapter 1 and in the preceding discussion, Ethelwold was certainly addressing his play to the monastic community; probably also to a lay community. In any case, most surviving texts of church dramas belong to in-house ritual and not to public celebration, but as at Winchester a vibrant sense of interaction between performer and community runs through their rubrics. There are at least 559 direct references in as many texts to monastics or laity (e.g., if *populus* means laity) or both as recipients of a dramatic event. For example, 45 texts of the *Visitatio Sepulchri* note explicitly to whom the Marys or Peter and John display the gravecloth(s), while 204 specifically call for a sung response to the discovery of the Resurrection, including 73 instances of the vernacular "Christ ist erstanden." References include *ad chorum, ad populum, coram omnibus hominibus, coram omnibus, coram hominibus, coram omni populo,* and *ad clerum populumque.* More than 53 mention the chorus or choir (ad chorum) as "audience"; about 54 suggest a partially lay congregation (ad populum); and 15 give both. Yet *ad populum* could refer to the monastic community. Winchester, Beauvais, Magdeburg, and Rouen are the most likely centers for the rare meeting of the two audiences because their cathedrals were both monastic and secular. The source church of the Fleury Playbook probably belongs to this list. With the widespread construction of rood-screens, beginning in the thirteenth century, a dramatic performance in the east choir such as the *Officium Pastorum* at Rouen would be exclusively for monks, young trainees, and possibly other clergy. By contrast, the *Officium Stellae* at Rouen was performed at the Altar of the Holy Cross, in the nave, where it concluded with gift-giving by the congregation.[40]

Certain monastic communities such as Rouen and Benediktbeuern—and probably the source community for the Fleury Playbook—seem to be centers of dramatic activity in part because of their size, variety of membership, and attraction for pilgrims. Ritualistic observance in small, rather closed monasteries appears to have remained more formally ritualistic and less dramatic. At cathedrals one sometimes encounters Easter ceremony more suited to the resident monastic community or chapter as well as drama for a lay audience. It is a more general public presence, it appears, that might press the monastic leadership toward producing what we would call a genuine play. That new element among the worshippers might have consisted of members of the wider monastic community itself, as perhaps in the case of Bishop Ethelwold, or laity from the nearby region. Furthermore, at Beauvais Cathedral it was clearly a student populace that gave impetus to the creation of the drama, as perhaps was the impetus for the Fleury Playbook.

Most of the time a dramatic performance can make its fullest possible impact when the actors and the audience members share the same language. The composers of the church drama used languages in performance that were very well known to their audiences—musical, verbal, and visual languages—and in this familiarity resides a major source of their power. Layfolk could certainly not understand enough Latin to follow a new text, nor could many members of many a monastic community for that matter, but they would know the story, and that story could be conveyed through the familiar languages of gesture, movement, sound, color, smell, touch, and even taste. For his *Visitatio Sepulchri*, Bishop Ethelwold employed not new customs but native customs. From earliest childhood members of the monastery had a daily church-going habit, members of the local laity at least a weekly church-going habit, and pilgrims' avowed purposes were to spend extended hours at worship. The church space provided a very familiar ambiance, where celebrants and congregants had long been reading the languages of pictures and spaces. When a member of a monastic community or a medieval burgher went inside the church, he or she brought to the rituals of Divine Office a whole lifetime of associations: great familiarity with the vocal language of Gregorian chant, with the body language of ritual gesture, with configurations of movements, with the meanings of ecclesiastical vestments, with the sights and sounds and smells of ritual process as well as familiarity with the metaphorical vocabulary of stories from Christian myth woven into the repeated patterns of this repeated event. Out of all of those forms of communication—native languages—from a sequence of sung sounds to a hand gesture, producers such as Bishop Ethelwold fashioned the drama of the medieval church and located it in a native setting.

Vocal Language

If we judge the medieval church performer's craft from the rubrics of dramatic texts, then we must conclude that the singers placed chief emphasis on the voice. They were able to express and to elicit primary emotions of joy and sorrow and multiple nuances of feeling because of a lifetime of training and practice in Gregorian chant. Moreover, from early childhood their audiences, mostly monastics, were conditioned to "read" their vocal language. With Gregorian chant the performers and their congregations shared a familiar "language."

Body Language

Just as the voice of the ecclesiastical performer was trained to read, to chant, and above all to sing the Mass and the Office, so from boyhood his body was schooled to move through liturgical ritual: to raise his hand in blessing, to open or fold his hands in prayer, to bow his head, to kiss, to genuflect, to prostrate himself. By the same token, his audience shared with him this rich, formal language of gesture and movement in ritual observance. A survey of the rubrics in these dramatic texts reveals that the most frequently expressed mood through body language is that of awe or veneration. Then, according to the rubrics, gesture expressed the primary emotions of joy, sorrow, fear, and anger. Secondary feelings such as jealousy and fatigue occur seldom in these plays, and the rubrics contain no special instructions as to acting them. When in this drama we have rubrical evidence of emotional expression and when the corresponding music survives, once in a great while we can even discover changes in the music corresponding to the emotional passages.[41]

The creators of the church drama had the advantage of myth—familiarity with the language of plot intimately linked to the language of music. At the conclusion of Bishop Ethelwold's *Visitatio Sepulchri*, the angel shows the three Marys the empty sepulchre. They take the gravecloth, hold it up for the assembly, and sing "Surrexit Dominus de sepulchro" (The Lord is risen from the sepulchre). That is their invitation to the audience—to celebrate. The audience accepts the invitation and once again becomes congregation, singing the *Te Deum*. With its standard closing hymn, the ritual of Matins has the language of response to the invitation already built into it.

In this moment the performers and the audience-turned-worshippers invest the old hymn with new meaning, and they do it because of the play. Bishop Ethelwold finishes the event by having all of the church bells ring out. It is through the language of myth that the Easter play joins the past and the present. It is commemorative, so that audience members, whether monks or local peasants, pass immediately beyond the level of puzzlement or wonder at newness toward filling the bare moments with their own associations. They can experience not a new story but a new meaning.

Clearly the levels of response to the music-drama

spread over a wide range. If laity were present, they were in a sense tourists compared to the natives of the monastery, for the most part less reponsive to the nuances of performance than the producing monks, who were familiar with each use of sound and gesture. Furthermore, as Bishop Ethelwold makes clear, such a range of diversity existed within the respective monastery itself.

Conclusion

Let us, for a few moments, indulge in a small fantasy, imagining a well-dressed medieval burgher approaching the monastery of St.-Benoît-sur-Loire in the dim, early morning of 6 January, about the year 1170, in order to participate in worship services of Epiphany. As he enters the north door, he gazes up at what he considers one of the glories of the church—the sculpted tympan of Christ flanked by the evangelists and angels—crosses himself, and then slips in among the standing crowd. When his eyes have adjusted to the brilliance of a hundred candles, he edges toward the center of the nave so as to obtain a better view of the proceedings. Everywhere there are monks and others who live in the monastery, together with some village folk who like himself have come for this special occasion.

Matins is underway: the air hangs heavy with incense and the great stone vaulting echoes with the familiar mixture of men's and boys' voices alternating with the chant of a single priest. In the east choir rows of white-robed chorus members stand before their carved stalls, on either side of the glowing central altar. Before it move stately, richly arrayed celebrants. At the rear and towering over the monastic figures, the tomb of the patron saint stands above a stone wall, through pierced openings of which one catches a glimpse now and again of the flickering lights in the crypt.

While the third responsory is being sung, officials from the monastery direct members of the congregation to make a path along the nave and to clear the crossing immediately before the east choir. At the same time a solemn figure dressed in a purple, brocaded cope, wearing a gold crown, and carrying a scepter, emerges from the ambulatory to the spectator's right of the east choir and makes his way toward a large wooden platform, about six-feet high, erected between the first two piers at the south side of the nave. A woven carpet covers the floor and ornate hangings decorate the sides. In the center stands a carved

chair with a baldachin and several stools nearby, the whole stage backed by a wide tapestry. Like other members of the congregation, our spectator recognizes the priest as king Herod, having witnessed a play about the *Murder of the Innocents* on 28 December and having heard local talk of preparations in the monastery for an even more splendid Epiphany celebration. Behind Herod march half a dozen members of his court, some in vestments and one in armour. They file up the steps of the platform, some occupy stools, others light several candelabra there, and Herod sits motionless on his throne. Meanwhile, as the responsory comes to an end, three boys, carrying staffs and resembling local peasants in their dress, move toward the center of the crossing and sit on the floor.

There is silence. Suddenly from up in the lantern tower comes a high voice singing "Be not affrighted! For behold, I bring you good tidings. . . ." The congregation looks upward to see the singer, a boy clad in a radiant white and gold alb, surrounded by half a dozen of his fellows similarly apparelled, one of whom our spectator recognizes as his son.

Everyone knows these words, but the melody sounds unfamiliar. The shepherds cringe; one of them automatically shields his face with his arm; another one kneels. And then the whole angelic chorus bursts forth with "Glory to God in the highest." As the angels retreat into the tower, the shepherds rise, face each other, and to an old Christmas setting they resolve, "Let us now go unto Bethlehem," moving slowly through the crowd down the main aisle toward the western extreme of the church while they sing.

There, before the doors leading out to the porch and beneath an overhanging balcony, the worshippers see two young clerics in copes, their heads covered with their amices, standing in front of a small platform with velvet curtains hung across it on brass rods. When the shepherds arrive, the midwives question them with words from a Christmas Mass, "Whom do you seek, O shepherds?", but the opening of the tune is that which the congregation has heard the angel at the Easter sepulchre use many times when addressing the three Marys. It is a momentary reminder that at this birth comes the conquest of death, presented both with visual and aural parallels between the visit to the manger and the visit to the tomb. At the shepherds' reply, the midwives draw aside the curtains and reveal a *tableau vivant* surrounded by several dozen candles: a doll in a straw-filled crib, with clerics as Mary and Joseph stationed behind, Mary in a rich blue and white vestment with her head covered. The shepherds prostrate themselves, sing "All hail, King of the ages," rise, and beckon the nearby members of the congregation to approach as they continue with an antiphon, "Come hither, come hither." A number of men and women press forward, others genuflect and make the sign of the cross, and the shepherds kneel to one side of the platform, becoming part of the *tableau*.

All eyes are turned toward this scene as a deeper voice rings out from beyond the high altar, "With an exceeding brightness this star doth blaze," and the congregation wheels about to see three lavishly arrayed priests emerge from different areas of the east choir and converge before the main altar. Each is dressed in a different colored cope, wears a gold crown, and carries a large gold vase or jewelled casket. The second and third chant a succeeding line of the music, each greets the other with a kiss, and then excitedly they point to the then newly lighted cluster of candles suspended on a wire over their heads, exclaiming, "See, the star." This wire, almost invisible because of its great height, stretches all the way along the nave and disappears into an upper-level opening at the famous west tower. Hidden there is a man who can then draw the burning star westward, ultimately to a position directly above the manger.

The cluster now moves and the Magi follow it to the crossing, where they address the bystanders with an especially composed piece: "Make known unto us, O ye citizens of Jerusalem, where now is he, expected of the people?". Clearly the Magi have journeyed from the East and have now arrived in the Holy City.

Herod stirs. He has seen them. Quickly he gestures to his armed messenger and sends him from the court over to the Magi. The messenger's recitative—a series of questions as to their race, their home, their purposes—is answered by the kings in a soaring, lyrical passage ("We are Chaldaeans"), a kind of poetic pause before the recitative continues as the emissary rushes back, greets Herod formally on bended knee, and reports the search for a new king. Herod is visibly upset: he waves the man aside, and instructs several courtiers to find out about this rumor. They depart, exchange words with the newcomers, return to Herod, and finally Herod directs the messenger to summon the strangers. All of this has a sense of perplexity and increasing urgency about it, reinforced by the frantic movements back and forth through the crossing and Herod's uneasy gestures.

Herod himself sets forth the interrogation as the kings ascend his platform and finally open their caskets, displaying gold, frankincense, and myrrh. At the sight of these gifts meant for another king, Herod turns to his young courtiers and commands them to summon his wise men. Loudly singing "You, learned in the law," a pair of courtiers hasten from the platform, disappear around the corner into the transept, and immediately reemerge with two actors in dalmatics, wearing long beards and carrying heavy books. The old men struggle along, unable to keep the pace of the courtiers, and no sooner do they come into Herod's line of vision, than the king springs to his feet: "Hear us, you scribes. . . ." A tense pause ensues. Herod sits in nervous agitation as the old men deliberately and methodically turn pages and peer at the writings. Finally one points out a passage to the other, the second nods approval, and together they sing, "We see, O Sire, in the lines that the Prophets have written . . . ," handing the book to Herod. He pours incredulously over the page as the chorus in the east choir suddenly fills the church with an antiphon—"Thou, Bethlehem, art not least among the princes of Judah."

Herod rises and hurls the book to the floor. His son, Archelaus, comes running from out of the south transept, dashes up onto the stage singing "All hail, father," and tries desperately in a vigorous lyric to pacify the enraged monarch. He is somewhat successful because the father answers using Archelaus' music, but to further allay Herod's spoken fears, Archelaus speaks deprecatingly of Christ: he will take up arms against this boy. The king pulls himself together and turns with feigned grace to the Magi, asking them to search out the child and return so that he too "may come to offer homage."

The Magi bow, circle about, descend the steps into the nave, and see and point to the light cluster now beginning to progress again toward the west: "Lo! the star." While looking after the departing men, Herod and Archelaus suddenly spy the star, which because of its height has been out of their direct line of vision; they draw their swords, brandishing them menacingly. Vivid in our spectator's memory is the enactment of the *Murder of the Innocents* with the moving scene of Rachel's lamentation that he saw performed here a little over a week ago. From that very spot Herod had ordered and overseen the awful slaughter in the crossing, while Mary and Joseph had escaped with the Christ Child from the manger in the west up the south aisle. In fact, snatches of Herod's music in his last speech recall his conference with the armed messenger just prior to that killing.

With a familiar, celebrative Christmas antiphon the shepherds now rise and start to make their way back along the nave, where they meet the approaching

Magi, who question them: "Whom have you seen?". The shepherds' reply rings out with some of the melodic phrases sung to them by the first angel. Our spectator could reach over and touch these monastic actors, so close are they now to him. Then as the shepherds continue up the aisle and into the choir, the star glides along and the Magi proceed in the direction toward which the shepherds had pointed, singing an ancient liturgical sequence but set to new and magnificent music.

Seeing them, the midwives turn to each other questioningly, "Who are these . . . ?". At the reply, the women draw the curtains, and the Magi greet the Christ Child first with the shepherds' melody of salutation and, then prostrating themselves, each makes his offering by placing his gold receptacle on the platform before the crib, and each remains in a posture of sleep on the ground. The curtains are closed.

From an aperture up in the west wall, the angel who opened the performance comes out with a candle onto the balcony over the manger and warns the sleeping Magi to return homeward by another way. The three kings rise, sing their resolve to follow the angel's instructions, and, chanting a familiar Christmas antiphon, make their way through the crowd and then eastward along the south aisle. Our spectator catches glimpses of them as they progress solemnly beyond the piers, pass behind Herod's court, and finally emerge into the crossing; they go into the east choir and, facing back to the congregation, sing "Let us rejoice, O brothers." Whereupon the cantor intones the concluding part of Matins, the joyous *Te Deum,* and the church resounds with voices of the choir and congregation as the remaining actors file out toward the vestry.

As Lauds begins our spectator reflects upon the striking similarities between figures in some of the newly finished frescoes near him and the people he has just seen as angels, kings, and the Virgin. He knows one of the painters in the monastery, a man recently come from Rouen, and he cannot help wondering whether his friend has had a hand in this special service or whether perhaps he had modelled some of the fresco figures after a similar celebration he had witnessed elsewhere. The costumes were certainly similar, and a few of the postures. . . . Also that manger scene looked very like a relief carved on the high altar, with the crib and Mary and Joseph behind. As to Herod's court, local fairs were full of people selling goods and playing scenes on such platforms with chairs, tables, and colorful cloth backings, but it proved a suitable and useful device in the church, where participants in observances were often lost from view if one found no place near the front. Above all else there was the music, full of tunes often repeated at Christmas time yet richly interwoven with many especially invented melodies. The monastery must have acquired a new choir master. Our spectator would have to ask his son.

Notes

Introduction

1. Editions of liturgical drama texts: Lange, *Die lateinischen Osterfeiern*. Lipphardt, *Lateinische Osterfeiern und Osterspiele*. Lipphardt references of the form "L" followed by a number, without a volume, refer to text number, not page. Young, *The Drama of the Medieval Church*. Henceforth, this work will be referred to as "Young" and will be followed by volume and page numbers. Two books about the staging of liturgical dramas that derive from the respective authors' theatrical experiences: Collins, *Production*. Davidson and Davidson, *Performing Medieval Music Drama*. The term "drama" in this study refers to a play, whereas "theatre" refers to performance—dance, circus—as well as to the drama when staged.

2. The term *dynamis* comes from the opening of *The Poetics*, where Aristotle sets about to examine the *dynamis* of a *synolon*—the secret power of a poetic whole or entity. Musicologists: Crocker and Hiley, *New Oxford History of Music*. Dolan, *Le Drame liturgique*. Rankin, *Medieval Liturgical Drama*. Stevens, *Words and Music in the Middle Ages*. Vellekoop, "De klank van licht en donker." Also Vellekoop, "'Orality versus Literacy'—and Music." Textual study, liturgical dramas: de Boor, *Die Textgeschichte der lateinischen Osterfeiern*.

3. More recent discussions have stressed the element of recreation which seems implied in twelfth-century uses of the word *ludus* (a play) and even *comoedia* instead of *ordo* or *officium*, and consideration of particular pieces has sought support in liturgical and non-liturgical contexts of the manuscripts to determine a degree of dramatic self-consciousness in the minds of the redactors. Such speculation is an important refinement of our understanding.

   On the significance of the change from *ordo* to *ludus* see Woolf, *English Mystery Plays*, 25–40, and Wickham, "Romanesque Style in Medieval Drama." C. Clifford Flanigan has studied the non-liturgical manuscript context of the Fleury Playbook in relation to changing audience expectations, which Flanigan considers primary in the development from ritual to drama: "Fleury Playbook." Flanigan cautions against assuming that such contemporary understandings can be proven or easily known.

4. Milchsack, "Die Oster- und Passionsspiele."

5. Young, 1:xiv–xv.

6. Young, 1:xiii, xiv. New work such as that by Garnier provides a visual gloss where we can begin to compare directives for gesture in the rubrics of the drama texts with gestures depicted in pictorial sources.

Chapter 1: Winchester and the *Visitatio Sepulchri* in the Tenth Century

1. Writing about the year 1005, the monk Aelfric attributed the whole *Regularis Concordia* to Bishop Ethelwold. See Symons, "Sources," 289.

2. Translation from Symons, *Regularis Concordia*. The two surviving manuscripts of the *Regularis Concordia* from this period are located in the British Library: Cotton MS Faustina B 3 (late tenth or eleventh century); and Cotton MS Tiberius A 3 (ca. 1050–1100), with Anglo-Saxon glosses.

3. Brooks, "Sepulchre of Christ in Art and Liturgy," 13.

4. From Rankin, "Liturgical Drama," 313, ex. 90.

5. Ibid., 314, ex. 91.

6. For Novalesa, see Young, 1:215; Lipphardt, L29. For Melk, see Young, 1:241; Lipphardt, L264.

7. Rankin, "Liturgical Drama," 318, ex. 92.

   The two extant manuscripts of the *Regularis Concordia* contain text and stage directions but no music. The Winchester Tropers—a tenth-century manuscript and an eleventh-century manuscript—preserve text (with almost no stage directions) and music. An incipit—the first word(s)—for "Cito euntes" appears in the Winchester Tropers but not in the *Regularis Concordia*. The "Cito euntes" incipit was probably omitted from the *Regularis Concordia* because it is sung immediately after the "Venite et videte" and by the same Angel.

   Recently, however, it has been suggested that there may be two traditions behind the two *Quem quaeritis* versions at Winchester. A close scrutiny of the relationships among the four Winchester manuscripts has led Nils Holgar Petersen to posit an earlier tradition of a performance of a *Quem quaeritis* ceremony linked to the grave monument of St. Swithin. See Petersen, "Operaens liturgiske forankring." See also Drumbl, *Fremde Texte*, 53.

   Strictly speaking, we can only cite two *Visitatio* plays in the tenth century: the Winchester Troper-*Regularis Concordia* text and the text from Verdun. For a detailed analysis of the relationship between the Winchester Troper and the *Regularis Concordia* see Petersen, "*Quem quaeritis* in Winchester as Authentic Roman Liturgy." See also Planchart, *Repertory of Tropes at Winchester*, 1:237–38.

8. Symons, *Regularis*, 44. At St. Lambrecht, Austria, in the Easter procession march *Indocti*, presumably young trainees in the monastery (ca. 1200), L728.

   Beginning with the advent of James Frazer's *Golden Bough* a group of scholars has wanted to see the origins of medieval religious drama in folklore. That there were ex-

tra-liturgical embellishments and that popular forms of entertainment did affect the outdoor performance of later religious plays, there can be little doubt, and there can be no
question of a certain common ground shared by all ritualistic, ceremonial practice, but beyond the citation of general parallels these scholars do not submit any proof of significant influence of popular-secular festivities on the early
sacred drama of the medieval church. As to the origins of
the ecclesiastical play, medieval *homo ludens* found a central place for his creative urge within liturgical celebrations.
See Hunningher, *Origin of the Theater,* and Toschi, *Le
origini del teatro italiano.*

9. Symons, *Regularis,* 3.

10. Hardison, *Christian Rite,* 196 n. 34. Symons, *Regularis,*
    45, 49, 58. More recently Clyde W. Brockett has said that
    drama seems not to have been cultivated at Fleury during
    the tenth century but evidently it was cultivated at Ghent.
    See Brockett, "Role of the Office Antiphon," 15–16 and
    notes 23, 24.

11. When he was Abbot of Abingdon, Ethelwold brought
    monks from Corbie in order to give his own community
    special musical instruction. Symons, *Regularis,* xxi. See
    also Planchart, *Repertory of Tropes at Winchester.*

12. Hardison, *Christian Rite,* 194–95, shows the close parallel
    between Ethelwold's note on imitation in his *Visitatio* and
    Amalarius's interpretation of the use of thuribles (*propter
    mulierum imitationem*) only for the Gospel procession of
    the Easter Vigil Mass. For the references from Amalarius
    see Symons, *Regularis,* xlix, 5.

13. Hardison, *Christian Rite,* 78–79.

14. However, I cannot accept the assurance with which
    Hardin Craig writes: "The ecclesiastical persons responsi-
    ble for this combination of elements [impersonation, ac-
    tion, and dialogue] were at first and for a long time entirely
    ignorant of the nature of what they had done. . . ." See
    Craig, *English Religious Drama of the Middle Ages,* 19. He
    bases this statement on his acceptance of the theory that
    this drama derived from tropes of the Mass.

15. Symons, *Regularis,* 42–45.

16. Symons, *Regularis,* 17; *Elevatio* in *Regularis,* 49. Two schol-
    ars in the field of medieval ecclesiastical architecture have
    suggested recently that the authors of the *Regularis Concor-
    dia* had in mind a chapel in the westwork for the perfor-
    mance of the *Visitatio Sepulchri.* See Heitz, *Recherches;*
    Klukas, "Liturgy and Architecture."

17. The one reference in the *Regularis Concordia* to other altars
    speaks of washing "the altars"; see Symons, *Regularis,* 39.

18. The Anglo-Saxon gloss is published by Logeman, "De con-
    suetudine monachorum"; see also his description of the
    sepulchre, 421. E. K. Chambers agrees, ". . . I think that
    the sepulchre was made on the altar, not in the hollow of
    it, and," he adds, "covered from sight until wanted by a veil
    let down all round it from a circular support above." See
    The Mediaeval Stage, 2:17 n. 1.

19. Symons, *Regularis,* 13, 16, 36, 39, 56, 61. On 43, 44, for ex-
    ample, we find reference to "the brethren of the right hand
    side of the choir" and to "the brethren of the left hand side
    of the choir."

20. Hardison, *Christian Rite,* 77.

21. Symons, *Regularis,* 44, 49.

22. Symons, *Regularis,* liv, lvi. We might also add that Aelphege,
    the successor to Ethelwold as Bishop of Winchester, went to
    serve as Archbishop of Canterbury from 1005 to 1012.

For Dunstan's mentorship of Oswald, see the *Vita Os-
waldi,* in Raine, *Historians of the Church of York,* 1:420–21.
A tangible sign of intellectual, spiritual, and artistic interaction between the two men may appear in an unusual manuscript thought to be in Dunstan's own hand, which is the direct exemplar of another copy from Oswald's Worcester. See
Bishop, *Aethici Istrici Cosmographia Vergilio Salisburgensi
Rectius Adscripta,* viii–xvii. Close interaction among all three
reformers may appear in the architectural similarities between additions made at Deerhurst Priory, probably while
under Oswald's care, and those made at Dunstan's Canterbury and Ethelwold's Winchester, as well as other tenth-century churches. The evidence is discussed by Klukas, "Liturgy
and Architecture," esp. 90–91 with references. Klukas notes
that the three altars and the chapels elevated above the choir
which he and others have posited in these churches would
be well suited to the possibly different kinds of chapel space
mentioned in the strictly liturgical devotions of the *Regularis
Concordia.* Even if this is accepted, however, it does not
prove that the *Depositio* and *Visitatio* were included in the
liturgy from the *Regularis Concordia* used in these lesser
churches, and it does not support Klukas' assumption that
the drama of tenth-century England was performed at the
altars of the west end of the church as in fourteenth-century
Essen (see Klukas, "Liturgy and Architecture," 92–93). On
the latter question see below, Chapter 1, discussion of the
westwork, and Chapter 3, discussions of Essen, Braunschweig, and other uses of the western area of the church in
the staging of the drama.

23. Hope, "Plan and Arrangement of the First Cathedral
    Church of Canterbury."

24. Ibid., 138. The contemporary description comes from
    Eadmer the precentor, who recalled his early years in the
    church, during the mid-eleventh century.

25. A summary of the written evidence is given by Quirk,
    "Winchester Cathedral." An important interim report on
    the dig, together with the plan reproduced here, comes
    from Biddle, *Excavations.* The most recent report on the
    dig comes from Biddle, "Felix Urbs Winthonia."

26. Biddle, *Excavations,* 74. Klukas, "Liturgy and Architec-
    ture," 91, names the dedications of the altars in the Old
    Minster, Winchester. His source of information is unclear.

27. Biddle, *Excavations,* 74–77; Quirk, "Winchester Cathedral,"
    56–59. See also the discussion by Petersen, "Quem quaeri-
    tis." With reference to Biddle, Petersen notes that in 974 re-
    mains of St. Swithin were placed in a shrine at the high altar.
    In the present study we shall discover many links of this kind
    between a local saint or sacred personage and the perfor-
    mance of the *Visitatio Sepulchri.*

The reason for building these often large western structures, rather common in Europe from the ninth through the
first half of the eleventh century, has long puzzled students of
medieval ecclesiastical architecture. Some of the answers to
the westwork problem include suggestions that it was intended for additional choirs, for additional tombs and altars,
or that it served as a place set apart for the use of royalty. Recently Carol Heitz has proposed that the westwork was dedicated to the cult of the Savior, a movement in the so-called
Carolingian Renaissance, and that here was performed the
Depositio-Elevatio-Visitatio sequence—not in the east at the
high altar. Evidence as to altars, tombs, and choirs as well as
associations with angels and the notion of the Second Coming as occurring in the West, could certainly be construed to

fit the thesis. Heitz shows plainly a number of examples of Easter ritual in the westwork, and it is very much to his credit that in his *Architecture et liturgie* he has examined fundamental questions about the use for which ecclesiastical structures were intended and to which they were put.

More recently Arnold W. Klukas has suggested that the *Visitatio Sepulchri* of the *Regularis Concordia* was intended specifically to be performed in a raised western chapel. He cites as evidence the existence of such a chapel at Deerhurst, probably reformed with new construction of this chapel by Oswald, "the most important extant example for liturgical and architectural forms before the Conquest."

Heitz and Klukas can cite only one indisputable example of a *Visitatio Sepulchri* performed in the west end of a church: the *Visitatio* at Essen, recorded in a fourteenth-century manuscript. Yet at Winchester too Carol Heitz (p. 181) would envision the *Depositio-Elevatio-Visitatio* sequence as taking place in this western structure: "On peut affirmer toutefois que le sépulcre improvisé ne se trouvait pas obligatoirement dans l'autel majeur. Nulle part il n'est fait allusion au choeur principal de l'église et l'on peut imaginer la veillée nocturne tout aussi bien ailleurs que dans l'abside orientale."

That the Easter sepulchre was often set up elsewhere than at the high altar we shall demonstrate in Chapter 3, but in almost every such instance where the texts are precise we find the sepulchre located at least in the vicinity of the east choir, in the nave or sometimes in a crypt or in a nearby chapel. Nevertheless, the coincidence of the cult of the Savior, the writings of Amalarius and others, and the birth of church drama, indicate something of the new quality and tenor in the conduct and emphasis of Christian worship, and, indeed, in medieval religious thought. Concomitantly, whereas clusters of *Visitatio* texts from various churches and monasteries are almost identical, no two are alike as far as performance is concerned.

For additional examples of the west as site of the Easter sepulchre for dramatic performance see Chapter 3 of the present study. For instance, at Aquileia a permanent sepulchre was constructed at the western end of the north aisle (eleventh-century structure); at Soissons (twelfth-thirteenth-century text) it may have been in a western chapel; at Bamberg (sixteenth-century text) the high altar was in the western apse of a bicephalic church, the sepulchre in the eastern choir; at Braunschweig (fourteenth-century text) the Marys met the Risen Christ in the western end of the church; and at Rheinau (1600) the *Visitatio* was enacted at the Chapel of St. Fintan out in the western porch.

28. See Warner and Wilson, *Benedictional of Saint Aethelwold,* for a facsimile edition of the manuscript, with a reproduction of this illumination in color (fol. 51v). A Benedictional contains a collection of pontifical blessings, spoken only by a bishop.

29. Ibid., xxiv. An analogy might be found in Quirk's conclusion that the exterior tomb of St. Swithin at Winchester consisted of a four-sided, walled structure, probably with a gabled roof, and furnished with holes or a doorway through which pilgrims could touch the burial slab. The chamber behind the main altar to which at least part of St. Swithin's relics were translated in ca. 971 might provide a second analogy. See Quirk, "Winchester Cathedral," 40, 42. When translated indoors, one reliquary of St. Swithin was on an altar, inside a guarded enclosure with an opening.

30. See, for example, Heitz, *Recherches,* plates 44, 45—interpreted as evidence for the *Visitatio Sepulchri* in the westwork.

31. See the facsimile of the entire manuscript in Morcquereau and Gajard, *Paléographie musicale.*

For the Hartker text, see Young, "Origin of the Easter Play," 52–53. See also Lipphardt, L80.

32. See Young, 1:134–35, for a discussion of Jewish burial custom.

Chapter 2: Plays of the Medieval Church— The Texts

1. There are two major collections of texts. One was edited and published by Karl Young, *The Drama of the Medieval Church.* More recently Walther Lipphardt edited and published about a thousand texts of the *Visitatio Sepulchri*—three times as many as published by Young—reediting most of those that appear in Young and often adding to them the corresponding *Depositio, Elevatio,* and *Adoratio* ("Adoration of the Cross" ceremony). See his *Lateinische Osterfeiern und Osterspiele.* In addition, the chief work on the Spanish texts is that of Donovan, *Liturgical Drama.*

For a useful census of extant liturgical drama texts see also Stevens and Sage, "Medieval Drama."

The sessions of the Council of Trent fell into three periods. 1–10: 1545–47, under Paul III; 11–16: 1551–52, under Julius III; 17–25: 1562–63, under Pius IV.

2. Rankin, "Liturgical Drama," 2:333.

3. Rankin, *Medieval Liturgical Drama,* 1:61.

4. Ibid., 1:297, 16.

5. Ibid., 1:293.

Chapter 3: Staging Space and Patterns of Movement—with Set Pieces and Special Effects

1. Brooks, *Sepulchre,* 53. See Brooks, chapter 7, for a discussion of types of Easter sepulchres. See also Sheingorn, *Easter Sepulchre in England.*

2. Young, 1:214–15. Lipphardt, L19, L14.

Monte Cassino (1058-1087):

Finita tercia [Terce] uadat Unus Sacerdos ante altare, alba ueste indutus, et uersus ad chorum dicat alta uoce:
Quem queritis [. . .]
Et Duo Alii Clerici stantes in medio chori respondeant:
Jesum Nazarenum [. . .]

Monte Cassino (ca. 1100):

Qua [procession] finita vadat Sacerdos post altare et uersus ad chorum dicat alta uoce:
Quem queritis [. . .]
Et Duo Alii Clerici stantes in medio chori respondeant:
Jesum Nazarenum [. . .]

3. St. Gall, *Visitatio,* L328. Regensburg, *Visitatio,* L686.

4. Text of *Visitatio Sepulchri* from Trier (called Treves by Young): Young, 1:280-1; Lipphardt, L349. Texts, tenth–eleventh century to 1767: L347-357c. The east crypt dedicated to St.Helena was accessible again as of 1196, after the building work on the east area of the cathedral was finished. In the eleventh-century westwork there was also a crypt but as of the earliest *Visitatio Sepulchri* with indications of staging, from 1305–7, the eastern crypt was employed.

Depositio and *Elevatio* from Trier: Young, 1: 142–43.

For information on the Cathedral of Trier, see Irsch, *Der Dom zu Trier.* Particular evidence for assigning the play to this church is the reference in the rubrics to the tomb of Archbishop Theodoric von Wied (1212–42). See also Ronig, *Der Trier Dom;* Kurzeja, *Der älteste Liber Ordinarius der Trierer Domkirche,* 3:689–714.

5. Acquisition of spices in thirteenth- and fourteenth-century plays from Toul and Prague: Young, 1:265–66, 402–7; L168, L168a, L801–5.

A text from Braunschweig, dated to the second half of the fourteenth century, has the three Marys come together from different directions, and as they meet they sing the first verse from the French spice-seller scene ("Omnipotens pater altissime"), but there is no hint of a spice-seller: L780. This text also has an alternative ending where Mary Magdalen gives an extraordinary performance—moving away from the sepulchre at the westwork and through the church to the pillar opposite the great exterior door, then to the Altar of St. Bartholomew in mid-nave, on to the south tower area, and finally back to the westwork, where she meets Salvator.

For assistance with my work on documentation relating to the Cathedral of Braunschweig, I wish to thank Dr. Luitgard Camerer from the Stadtbibliothek and Herrn Nickel from the Stadtarchiv Braunschweig.

6. For the descent into the crypt on Good Friday, to carry out the Burial of the Cross, the procession had explicitly removed the cross from the St. Agnes Altar (people's altar) and had used the north steps there down into the crypt. One senses here a strong feeling for spatial and related symbolic balance.

7. The only other uses of the crypt known to me in this connection come from Sion, Verdun, and Würzburg. The one from Verdun is of especial interest because of its very early date, the tenth century. Having gone "in subterraneis specubus," two brothers return to the chorus, about whose location we are not informed. Because the "Quem quaeritis" dialogue itself takes place out of sight and, for the most part, out of earshot of the worshippers, illustrative spectacle such as that at Trier characterizes the return of the Marys. At Verdun they bring thuribles with them, which they had not had upon their descent, and they bring an empty cross. The Würzburg play, dated by Young to the fourteenth century but by Lipphardt to the thirteenth century, has first a little procession by two angels with candlebearers from the choir into the crypt, and then the three Marys descend via a different route from the choir into the crypt. There the "Quem quaeritis" exchange occurs. Before the Marys reappear three choir boys move to the high altar and lead off the singing of "Ad tumulum." Thereupon the women emerge to sing an antiphon at the Altar of St. Martin and then climb the steps to the tomb of a bishop (the founder, Bishop Heinrich?) to display the gravecloth expressly before the "canons and people." At Sion in 1474 the earlier locus of the sepulchre in dramatic performance was brought up from the subterranean east crypt to the St. Barbara Chapel, directly south of the east choir. At Laon the "Quem quaeritis" exchange took place below in the lower story of a two-story chapel, with the celebrant and chorus and others waiting above; a procession had exited from the church to the external chapel, so that when the Marys ascended to announce the Resurrection, a major festive procession developed in the chapel and then back into the cathedral. For a full discussion of liturgical drama at Sion, see Appendix A at the end of this chapter.

In his reconstruction of the *Visitatio Sepulchri* in the Cathedral of Braunschweig (L780, second half of the fourteenth century), Wolfgang Michael assumes that sepulchre was at one of the two crypt entrances which opened onto the nave from either side of the east choir steps. Thus the scene with the women at the grave and the subsequent appearance of Christ to Mary Magdalen would have occurred in plain view, simply indicating the crypt as burial place. See Michael, *Frühformen,* 17. However, the text does not mention the crypt or its entrances. Nor do two earlier Braunschweig texts (L534, L535, twelfth and fourteenth centuries).

It is my conclusion that the sepulchre was not at a crypt entrance in the east but at the west end of the nave, at the westwork. The later fourteenth-century text says that the Marys begin their journey at the foot of the east choir steps and move to the St. Bartholomew Altar. It stood in mid-nave. From there they go to the sepulchre. Peter and John go to the sepulchre, presumably from the east choir, and then take up a position at the St. Bartholomew Altar to display the gravecloth.

Texts of the play from Verdun: Young, 1:578; L360–62a. Texts of the play from Würzburg: Young, 1:257–58; L371–77. Also of interest is that three fifteenth-century copies of the Verdun play may have been musical copies for the performers (see Lipphardt, 7:284). A fuller discussion of Laon is in the present chapter at "The Sepulchre Outside the Church."

8. Text of *Visitatio Sepulchri* from Essen: Young, 1:333–35; L564.

Depositio and *Elevatio* from Essen are abstracted in: Arens, ed., *Der Liber Ordinarius der Essener Stiftskirche.* The full texts are printed in Lipphardt, L564.

For information on the Collegiate Church, Essen, see Zimmermann, *Das Münster zu Essen;* Borger, "Die Architektur und ihre Geschichte."

For a reconstruction of the movement patterns during the *Visitatio Sepulchri,* with a cutaway drawing of the church, see Klukas, "Liturgy and Architecture."

There are many links and parallels between the nunneries of Essen and Gernrode (L786). In the area of architecture, for example, Gernrode also has a gallery running along the north and one along the south side of the nave, eastward from the westwork to the transept. But unlike the high galleries at Essen, there is no evidence that these were used in performance. There are also important parallels with the nunnery at Prague (L387).

9. Text of *Visitatio Sepulchri* from Braunschweig, L780.

Recently Norbert Koch has demonstrated that the St. Bartholomew Altar, where the three Marys come together before continuing on to the sepulchre, stood in the middle of the nave. According to the textual rubrics, the three Marys departed separately from the east choir, joined at the St. Bartholomew Altar, and proceeded on their journey together to the sepulchre. The sepulchre was, in all likelihood, not as Wolfgang Michael proposed in the east near a crypt entrance but at the west end of the church, at the westwork. It was there that the women met the angel, and, after the other women returned to the St. Bartholomew Altar, Mary Magdalen met Salvator. In the alternative staging of Mary Magdalen's scene with Salvator, as given by the rubrics, the other women return to mid-nave to the St. Bartholomew Altar while she begins to sing her *planctus.* But then, instead of singing at the sepulchre, she goes among the bystanders searching for Jesus: first to the pillar opposite the great church

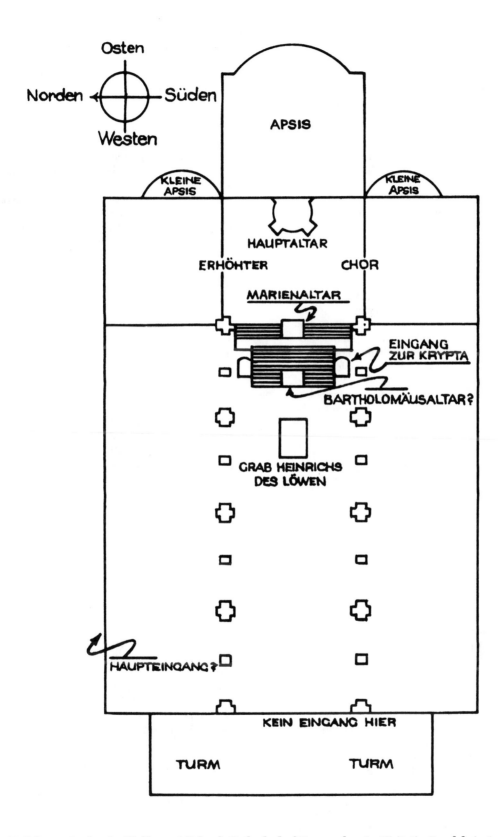

Figure 40. Schematic plan by Wolfgang Michael, Cathedral of Braunschweig. *Visitatio Sepulchri,* **xiv century. Mary Magdalen's search for Salvator throughout the church.**

door to the town, then eastward to the St. Bartholomew Altar in the middle of the church, then back westward to the pillar opposite the great tower (part of the westwork), and finally, going "a little farther" she meets Salvator. This alternative staging reveals a step toward the creation of a dramatic figure as individual, a remarkable use of space and movement without altering any lines or music, to create a powerful performer-congregation relationship. See Koch, "Der Innenraum des Braunschweiger Domes." Because the location of the St. Bartholomew Altar is critical for this reconstruction, I wish to express my particular gratitude to Herr Nikel in the Stadtarchiv von Braunschweig for a photocopy of the printed edition of the manuscript on which Koch based his conclusion (Koch, 497 n. 9): *Origines Guelfici (1222),* 3, "in medio Ecclesie beati Blasii Bruneswic altare in honore beati Bartolomei Apostoli fieri iussimus." The MS in the Niedersächsischen Staatsarchiv Wolfenbüttel is: StA Wolfenbüttel VII B HS 133, Vol. 1.

Text of *Visitatio Sepulchri* from St. Joachimsthal (Zwickau, Jugoslavia, 1520–23), L789: Mary Magdalen "facit circuitum per Ecclesiam."

At Rheinau, L797, in a thirteenth-century text, the chorus processed out of the east choir at the beginning of the play to stand in the nave at the Altar of the Holy Cross. The sepulchre was in the west choir (in minori choro). After the Marys brought their news from the sepulchre to the chorus, Mary Magdalen returned to the sepulchre area searching (redit Maria Magdalena ad Sepulchrum querendo). A later text from Rheinau (1600) documents a procession that moved the entire length of the church, east to west, to perform the *Visitatio Sepulchri* at the Chapel (sacellum) of St. Fintan out in the western porch.

One also finds this embrace of the east-west axial space in the mise-en-scène at Aquileia, Laon, and Gernrode. The permanent Easter sepulchre at Aquileia, erected in the middle of the eleventh century, is located in the north aisle toward the western end of that ancient church; at Laon (twelfth- and seventeenth-century texts) the *Visitatio Sepulchri* developed into a major procession through the western doors of the cathedral to and from a separate, exterior chapel; and from an eastern area in the church at Gernrode the three Marys took up a position in the west apse before returning eastward through the church to a permanent sepulchre near the south transept. When we are well informed as to the location of the sepulchre outside the main (normally east) choir, we usually find it in the vicinity of the crossing or near the middle of the church.

For texts from Aquileia, see Young, 1:320–21, and Lipphardt, L487–99. For texts from Laon, see Young, 1:302–4, 620, and Lipphardt, L109–12.

Parallel with the situation at Laon, at Metz in 1180 the Templars also built a round chapel in imitation of the Holy Sepulchre of Jerusalem. Lipphardt believes that the thirteenth-fourteenth-century dramatic texts recording French-Norman influences at St. Arnould of Metz reflect the earlier influences by these Crusaders. However, the surviving *Visitatio Sepulchri* text from St. Arnould with staging rubrics (1240) locates the performance in the church, expressly using the tomb of St. Arnould, the high altar, as the sepulchre. See L269.

It is largely on the basis of the play at Essen that Heitz, *Recherches,* 189*ff.,* puts forward a theory as to the performance generally of the *Visitatio* in the western part of the church during the early period. However, this text is late

(fourteenth century), and tenth- and eleventh-century rubrics do not corroborate the thesis. Arnold W. Klukas also supports the theory on the architectural evidence of tenth-century Deerhurst, very probably reformed by Oswald. See Klukas, "Liturgy and Architecture."

10. Texts of *Visitatio Sepulchri, Depositio* and *Elevatio* from Magdeburg: Young, 1:630, 152–53; L608–11. Lipphardt (7:520) believes that the *velamen* may have been part of the relic of Veronica's cloth (Schweisstuch) for which the church in Halle was named (Ad velum aureum). Fifteenth- and sixteenth-century Bamberg texts related to Magdeburg, among others, use the term *velamen* to refer to the cloth covering for the ciborium or monstrance, in which the Host was kept, e.g., L195, L195a (deposito velamine). Whether singular or plural, relic or relics, the Latin does not reveal. Most plausible, however, is reference here to the well-documented practice at Magdeburg of uncovering a whole array of relics at the high altar on special occasions such as Easter. See Kroos, "Quellen zur liturgischen Benutzung des Domes und zu seiner Ausstattung."

The burial of the two stones with the cross is very unusual. An undisclosed number of stones were buried with the cross at Gnesen, in Poland (fourteenth to sixteenth century): L576–576i.

For information on the Cathedral of Magdeburg, see Walther Greischel, *Der Magdeburger Dom;* Clemens, Mellin, Rosenthal, *Der Dom zu Magdeburg;* author unknown, *Eigentliche Beschreibung,* describes the sepulchre as a model of Otto's original church, and also mentions the Pantheon and the burial Chapel of St. Mauritius as its models. Note the round shape of the Chapel of St. Mauritius in Constance (see the Constance ground plan in the present study). For discussion of "Otto I Chapel," see Dalman, *Das Grab Christi in Deutschland,* 34–35. For reference to the St. Lawrence relic(s), see Dresserus, *Sächsisch Chronicon,* 271–73.

A second apparently somewhat earlier copy of the Magdeburg Ordinarium, now lost, referred to the "ymaginarium sepulchrum Domini ad altare s. Laurentii," rather than "ante altare Sancti Laurencii." In her study of published excerpts from this copy as well as of the manuscript quoted by Lipphardt and Young, Renate Kroos ("Quellen zur liturgischen Benutzung des Domes und zu seiner Ausstattung") has recently concluded that the sepulchre used in the Easter play was especially constructed in front of the St. Laurentius Altar, whereas the permanent sixteen-sided structure in the nave is what the Ordinarium called the "Capellam sancte marie rotundam." She too has been unsuccessful in her attempt to locate the St. Laurentius Altar. The second copy of the Ordinarium disappeared during World War II. Kroos cites excerpts from it published by G. Sello, "Dom Altertümer," *Geschichtsblätter* 26 (1891) [her citation], among others. The quotation above of the relevant passage comes from Wentz and Schwineköper, *Das Erzbistum Magdeburg,* 28.

I wish to express my gratitude to Domprediger Giselher Quast at Magdeburg for his generous assistance in this research.

11. Dresserus, *Sächsisch Chronicon,* 133; *Eigentliche Beschreibung,* fol. B3r.

12. Lipphardt, L608: "Et tunc Processio cum candelis ardentibus exhibit in Monasterium, quam precedent primo cerei Pascales, deinde cruces cum vexillis. Hii stabunt circa baptismum

hinc et inde. Conventus vero stabit hoc modo, quo Pueri versus occidentem et Domini versus orientem, et Chori stabunt versi contra se invicem." (Also in Young, 1:630.)

13. For the photograph and fifteenth-century text from Aquileia, see Young, 1:320–21. For texts ca. 1100–1688, see L487–99. For a summary of Easter rituals derived in part from thirteenth-century texts, see Vale, "Storia della Basilica doppo il secolo IX," 55–58. For a description and drawings of the Aquileia sepulchre, see Lanckoronski, *Der Dom von Aquileia*, 8–10, 124–26.

14. Why the rubrics in the Gernrode text are in German is not entirely clear. Could it be because this was a Damenstift, not a nunnery, and thus with lower expectations as to ability in Latin? The canonesses had nothing like the stringent vows of nuns. Many came from noble families. Only the Abbess had to refrain from marriage. At the end of the manuscript, the copyer has put his name and the date 1502 with a note: "Item Dyss büchelin hoerth frouwichen barberen von der wessenburg." [Lipphardt, "Die Visitatio Sepulchri (III. Stufe)," 6.] Was her German stronger than her Latin? Is this Barbara von Weissenberg (nobility from Oberlausitz)]? See Schulze, *Das Stift Gernrode*, 53.

From the Damenstift Obermünster, near Regensburg, comes another *Visitatio* text in German, from 1567–87, L796. Here too the Marys were played by women, as at Troyes, Gandersheim, and Münster. See the discussion of "Women Play Women" in Chapter 5 of the present study.

15. Lipphardt says that the All Souls Altar was in front of the rood-screen in the eastern part of the church, but he adds, "near the grave of St. Metronius" (Lipphardt, 8:731). All other information that I can find indicates that the grave of St. Metronius was in the west crypt, beneath the west apse, which was constructed in the twelfth century and dedicated to that saint. The All Souls Altar may indeed have been at the confessio opening into the east crypt, just in front of the rood-screen.

16. Lipphardt does call this text a play, a *Visitatio Sepulchri*. He finds no other example in the corpus of the liturgical drama where these particular antiphons are linked (Lipphardt, 7:185).

Lipphardt, 7:187, thinks that the 1502 *Visitatio* at Constance developed out of a procession that preceded Matins, not that concluded Matins. Jezler agrees. The rubric reads: "Ad matutinum ante compulsationem fit Processio ad sanctum Sepulchrum . . ." L241. This would mean that the "Surrexit Dominus de sepulcro" and the *Te Deum* were sung before Matins and repeated at the close of Matins. I find these pieces preceding Easter Matins only at Fulda, Rheinau, and St. Gall, recording very old practice. The positioning of the ceremony or drama with "Quem quaeritis" was in flux. Lipphardt also notes that nowhere else does one find this particular relationship of three antiphons in performance: "Venite et videte," "Et recordate," and "Surrexit Dominus."

As noted, the earlier *Elevatio* text from Constance (fifteenth century, L239) also puts the procession to the sepulchre as a prelude to Matins, with an antiphon (presumably the "Surrexit Dominus") when the Host is carried into the east choir, and then the *Te Deum,* followed by the beginning of Matins with "Domine labia mea." There the opening stage direction for the procession reads: "In die sancto Pasce ad Matutinas secundo pulsu angularis Domini ibunt ad sacrum Sepulcrum. . . ." The striking of a rectangular, probably hand-held bell (secundo pulsu angularis) sum-

moned participants to form the procession before Matins. It was not the kind of bell ringing that often signaled the beginning of Matins (see above "ante compulsationem," referring to the before-the-start-of-Matins bell). For the rectangular bell see Horn and Born, 1:131. For a thorough discussion of architecture and text, see Jezler, "Gab es in Konstanz ein ottonisches Osterspiel?".

Constance, photograph and sixteenth-century text: Young, 1:301–2. Fifteenth- and sixteenth-century texts: L239-246. Description and photograph: Dalman *Das Grab Christi*, 30ff., Tafel III, IV.

17. Two other extramural replicas of the Holy Sepulchre can probably be linked with the *Visitatio Sepulchri*. The Holy Sepulchre Chapel in Augsburg was torn down in 1611, and it was not replaced. It had been dedicated very early, in 1128. Located in the Weinmarkt square, it was a product of the Augsburg citizens' active participation in the First Crusade. It was a rotunda and one could enter it. We do not possess more information. The dramatic texts as of the twelfth century refer to it when they refer to "tumulum." The earliest, the twelfth-century *Visitatio Sepulchri* text, has a procession move to the "Sepulchrum imaginarium," presumably this chapel outside the cathedral in the Weinmarkt. The Magdeburg text also uses this unusual term, "Sepulchrum imaginarium." Two angels sit inside, at the head and foot of a sepulchre. The women enter it, take up the grave linen, exit, and "post intervallum"—presumably the interval while they return to the cathedral—they stand in the nave (in medio), display the linen "in publicum" and sing the "Cernitis, o socii" (usually sung by Peter and John). Peter and John run to the sepulchre (ad Monumentum), and the Marys begin "Surrexit Dominus." Presumably Peter and John then return, although the rubrics are silent on this point. The chorus erupts in joy (prorumpens in gaudium, alta voca) with the *Te Deum* and the *Populus* concludes with "Christ ist erstanden" as the empty cross is raised up over the choir entrance. Whether the *Populus* had also processed out of the church to the "Sepulchrum imaginarium" and then reentered the church we do not know. Also of particular interest here are the earliest references to the performers as being "in the role of": "ex Personis Mulierum," "ex Persona Angelorum," "ex Persona Discipulorum Petri et Johannes." "Sepulchrum imaginarium" is also a descriptive expression used by Johannes Belethus (ca. 1165), Sicardus von Cremona (ca. 1215), and Wilhelm Durandus (1286–91). See L120–22.

Beginning in 1487, Augsburg texts introduce a Harrowing of Hell sequence with the first indoor devil. For the procession before Easter Matins the bells ring in order to inform the laity, instead of shutting them out. First the Host and cross are brought in to a cathedral altar, in a small procession. At this point the archbishop, presumably with Host and cross, leads a procession out along the monastery wall or churchyard (per ambitum vel cimiterium). This procession includes the townspeople. "Tollite portas" (Open up ye gates) is sung, finishing with "Et introibit rex glorie" (And the king of glory shall come in), as he knocks with his bishop's staff on the closed church door. Inside the church a young student (Levita Iunior vel Alius) "in Figura Diaboli grossa voce" sings out, "Quis est iste rex glorie?" (Who is the king of glory?). [As of 1612 a processional cross would be used to knock on the door, and the singer inside the church would no longer be identfied as "Diabolus," only as "Cantor."] This sequence is repeated three times, whereupon the door opens and the procession moves around into the "new choir," the newly built east choir dedicated in 1431. They then go to the Altar of the Holy Cross at the crossing, where they put the Host. Country and town folk also proceed to that altar (Rurales tamen et Oppidani simpliciter), singing "Kyrieleyson. Christie . . . ." The butchers' guildsmen are carrying the cross. They place it in front of the altar. The Host is then put in a monstrance and displayed to the people.

Thereupon Matins commences, eventually to conclude with the *Visitatio Sepulchri*. It is not clear whether the external Holy Sepulchre at the Weinmarkt is being used. A procession moves "ad locum sepulchri," where the chorus takes up a position. When the two Marys sing their lines, they do not leave the chorus. Two students (levite) in the sepulchre represent the angels. After their exchange with the Marys, two senior priests approach the sepulchre, take up the gravecloth, turn toward the chorus, hold it up, and sing "Cernitis o socii . . . ." Presumably the procession returns to the church, for at the singing of the *Victimae paschali* the crucifix is put back in its proper place. All finish by singing "Christ ist erstanden."

It may seem surprising at first glance that at Augsburg heightened moments of drama do not occur in relation to the extramural replica of the Easter Sepulchre. At Augsburg the Marys do not even move over to the sepulchre for the exchange with the angels; they are explicitly held within the chorus. The tendency toward drama emerges not in the brief ceremonial at the sepulchre outside the church but rather when the ecclesiastical performers reenter the church and then address the congregation. One senses the same principle at work here as discovered in the contrast between the uses of the sepulchres at Constance and Magdeburg: the former a procession out into the cemetery and a ceremony, the latter a procession into the nave and a drama.

In the tenth century Augsburg already had a Holy Sepulchre outside the cathedral, in the now no longer extant Church of St. Ambrose. Lipphardt publishes some thirty Augsburg texts, including the *Depositio* and *Elevatio* as well as the *Visitatio Sepulchri*, ranging from the twelfth century to 1764. Augsburg: L505–529, L779a (in Vol. 6). Schwarzweber, *Das heilige Grab*, 4. Texts from 1580 and 1612 repeat the mise-en-scène in the 1487 Augsburg text. The Bamberg *Agenda* (1587) was initiated from Augsburg for churches in the Bamberg diocese. Taking its cue from earlier Augsburg texts, the 1587 Bamberg *Agenda* contains the high point of Harrowing of Hell scenes with a devil explicitly hammering on the church door with a piece of iron or a hammer or a chain. See L530–531.

Outside the Cathedral at Laon one can still visit the twelfth-century Templars' Chapel, a rather large two-story structure with an altar above and the sepulchre below. Two twelfth-century texts and two texts by Antoine Bellotte dating to 1652 reveal an elaborate pre-Matins procession to the sepulchre characterized by unusual texts and the participation of students from the Laon theological faculty. The 1652 texts surely refer to this chapel, while the twelfth-century texts may be referring to it. In 1652 the festive procession goes to the chapel, pauses for a brief four-line exchange between an angel figure hidden from view (stans in abscondito) and two deacons (as Marys), the celebrant descends and reascends, and the procession winds around the chapel (Proceditur autem circumcirca ecclesiam a praedicte loco Sepulchri) and through the western door into the nave of the cathedral and to the crucifix, then on into the east choir. In the twelfth-century text the celebrant emerges from the

sepulchre with the Host. Here and in the 1652 texts a pallium or portable baldachin covers him in procession.

At Laon the processional elements dominate completely, where the return to the cathedral develops into a triumphal parade, the high point of the event. There the *Victimae paschali* is to be sung by the chorus "in jubilum erumpentes." Nowhere does one find the performers turning to the worshippers, save in the priest's ritual display of the Host. For Laon texts, see Young, 1:302–3; L109–12.

A fifteenth-century *Visitatio* text from the Cathedral of Regensburg documents the use of an exterior chapel as the Holy Sepulchre. The St. Johannes Chapel, it stood on the north side of the cathedral. At the expansion of the cathedral in 1380 it had been moved from the ancient east choir area to that location and rebuilt; it was rebuilt again in 1766. At least as early as the eleventh century it had served as the baptistry. Like other texts linked with an exterior chapel, so here the "Quem quaeritis" exchange is very brief, while the major event consists in a colorful procession out of the cathedral and then back into it for a climactic public display of the gravecloths from the steps of the altar to the Virgin. The *populus* responds with "Christ ist erstanden," and there is a great ringing of all the bells (Et fit compulsacio cum omnibus campanis clare sonantibus). See L684.

Texts ranging from the fourteenth century to 1798 record usage at Eichstätt (L550–62). One finds an interesting situation there because at Eichstätt in the mid-twelfth century a rotunda-shaped Holy Sepulchre Chapel was erected at the edge of town, containing within it a stone replica four-fifths the size of the Holy Sepulchre in Jerusalem. However, as far as I can tell the extant dramatic texts refer not to this replica but to preparation and dramatic use of a sepulchre in the nave of the Eichstätt Cathedral.

The stone replica is a ten-minute walk from the cathedral. It is a structure now free-standing inside a baroque church. It comprises two rooms: a small rectangular chamber with an altar and, entered through a low door at the west side, a narrow rectangular grave chamber with an 80-centimeter-high stone sarcophagus or stone bench on which a nearly life-size image could be laid out. In the south wall is a niche that one can close up for the Host.

Originally the replica stood in a chapel. The chapel was torn down in 1611 and replaced with the present baroque church, and the replica of the sepulchre was positioned in a side arm or chapel of the church. Marks on the stones of the replica suggest that it was disassembled and reassembled at some point, perhaps at the rebuilding of the old chapel into the baroque church in 1611. From its original construction in the mid-twelfth century the replica had been housed in a chapel that was part of a monastic complex, Scottish or Irish at the time of its construction, an entity entirely separate from the cathedral in town.

At the close of Easter Matins in the Cathedral of Eichstätt the 1326 text (the earliest) has a group, probably chorus and performers, go "itur ad monasterium" for the *Visitatio Sepulchri*. Once again, I take "monasterium" here to refer to the nave. This procession seems to move from the east choir into the nave of the cathedral. A later, fifteenth-century text of the *Visitatio* says specifically "fit Processio in ecclesia kathedrali ad monasterium," and at the conclusion of the play, all singers return to the (east) choir, "In reditu canitur ad chorum," singing the *Te Deum*. After the procession into the nave, according to the 1326 text, two "precentores cum Cantore" as the Marys go to stand "ante Sepulchrum." There the "precentores" exchange "Quem quaeritis" lines with "Duo Scolares in Sepulchro." These angels later emerge to show the grave linen, and the "precentores" turn back (or return) to the nave (reuertuntur ad monasterium) singing "Ad monumentum venimus." The three singers report "Ad monumentum," the chorus asks "Dic nobis, Maria?" and finally all sing the *Te Deum.* As just noted, the fifteenth-century text is specific about the return of the chorus into the (east) choir. Other fifteenth-century texts from Eichstätt also record this pattern: that the chorus moved into the nave to sing "Dum transisset sabbatum, Maria Iacobi et Salome" as the women departed, and reentered the (east) choir while singing the *Te Deum.* But Walther Lipphardt to the contrary thinks the performers left the cathedral and made the ten-minute walk to the monastic chapel to act out the *Visitatio Sepulchri* at the stone replica: "'revertuntur ad monasterium,' woraus deutlich hervorgeht, dass das Sepulchrum ausserhalb des Münsters lag" (Lipphardt, 7:464); but no texts reveal any exit from the cathedral by performers, chorus, or congregation.

Eichstätt: L550–562. Schwarzweber, *Das heilige Grab,* 4–5. I wish to thank Diözesanarchivar Brun Appel in Eichstätt for an examination of available documentation, and for his view, as opposed to Lipphardt's, based on that documentation that the Eichstätt *Visitatio* text has nothing to do with the replica of the Holy Sepulchre (correspondence with author, 27 January 1992). Brun Appel's findings corroborate my own.

See also: Young, 2:509 n. 7; Dalman, 56*ff.* (Eichstätt), 96*ff.* (Augsburg).

18. For the text of the *Visitatio Sepulchri* from Meissen, see Young, 1:330–31. For the *Depositio, Elevatio,* and *Visitatio Sepulchri* from Meissen, see L612–14.

Regarding the *Depositio* and *Elevatio* from Meissen, see Young, *Dramatic Associations of the Easter Sepulchre,* 107–9.

For information on the Cathedral of Meissen, see Ebert, *Der Dom zu Meissen;* Schwechten, *Der Dom zu Meissen.*

For information on the tomb of St. Benno, see Gersdorf, *Urkundenbuch des Hochstifts Meissen,* 3:365. Ursinus, *Geschichte der Domkirche,* 113, 116, 188; Schoettgen and Kreysig, "Calendarium ecclesiae cathedralis Misnensis," 3:120.

For information on entrances to the east choir, see Ursinus, *Geschichte der Domkirche,* 166, 275; and 127, 277.

19. The *Imago Resurrectionis* is also referred to in the *Depositio* and *Elevatio* as *corpus, crux,* and *imago.* For a discussion of the subject see Young, 1:139.

20. Numerous churches had special chapels dedicated to the Holy Sepulchre, but as already noted we lack evidence for their use in staging the liturgical drama. On the other hand, documentation does show that Chapels of St. Andrew, St. Fintan, St. Barbara, and St. Sebastian served respectively in productions of the *Visitatio Sepulchri* at Strassburg (1364), Rheinau (1600), Sion (Sitten, 1474), and St. Gall (1582, 1583).

At Strassburg the chapel itself formed the sepulchre. Earlier documents (1150) refer to it as the Holy Sepulchre Chapel. It stands at the north side of the east choir. The St. Fintan Chapel (*sacellum,* the container of the founder-saint's relics) was in the western porch of the church at Rheinau; in the drama it became the Holy Sepulchre. In the case of Gernrode, the founder-saint's tomb was also in the western end, but here the Marys only paused at the tomb on their way eastward in the church toward a stone replica of the Holy Sepulchre.

Like the movement patterns at Gernrode, the Cathedral of Meissen, the Cathedral of Trier (and the Abbey of St. Simeon at Trier), as well as at the Cathedral of Bamberg, the dramatic performance at Rheinau linked its Resurrection message directly with the grave of the church's founder. At Meissen, Bamberg, and at St. Simeon in Trier the chorus took up a position at the founder's tomb, waiting for the news of the Resurrection. While at Trier Cathedral and Gernrode the Marys paused at the founder's tomb, at Gernrode on their way to the sepulchre and at Trier returning from the sepulchre, announcing the Resurrection to the chorus from that position.

At St. Arnould of Metz, the sepulchre was behind the high altar, the St. Arnould Altar, where two angels sat; while the Marys ascended the steps in front of it from the choir. For texts of the Rheinau *Depositio, Elevatio,* and *Visitatio,* see L315–16, L797. For the text from St. Arnould, Metz, see L269.

At the Abbey of St. Simeon, Trier, the procession prior to the *Visitatio Sepulchri* (fifteenth century) took up a position before the tomb of St. Simeon. See L356.

Brooks, *Sepulchre,* 65.

For texts of the Strassburg *Depositio, Elevatio,* and *Visitatio Sepulchri,* see L341–45. Strassburg was the center of an ancient, widespread Holy Sepulchre cult. The St. Andrew Chapel, on the north side of the east choir, is the oldest part of the present cathedral. At the *Elevatio* of 1364 the host was brought out of the chapel and displayed to the people (Populo coram) before being taken to the Altar of St. Laurence and again held up to the populace. Later, when in the *Visitatio* the Marys return from the sepulchre, they enter the choir, climb to the top step of the high altar, face westward toward the chorus, and expand what must have been a fairly large sudary betwen them.

For the texts of the St. Gall *Depositio, Elevatio,* and *Visitatio Sepulchri,* see Young, 1:621–22; L327–32. Apparently St. Gall had a Holy Sepulchre Chapel, outside to the north of the church. It was taken down early in the sixteenth century. Whether it was used for dramatic production we do not know.

A fuller discussion of Sion (Sitten, in Switzerland) is in Appendix A, which follows the present chapter. Regarding mise-en-scène, the two plays from Sion appear to be very ancient forms. The Christmas *Officium Stellae* at Sion is really not a drama. It is not a play acted out but rather a procession with special props and costumes. Like the early (mainly Italian) Easter pre-Mass processions augmenting the Introit with added tropes, both the Easter and the Christmas observances at Sion augment the *Feierlichkeit* of the particular observance. The populace catches sounds, smells, and glimpses of the solemnity just as it catches sounds, smells, and glimpses of the sacred moments of the Mass. On the other hand, the Easter festivity at the Cathedral of Sion that was distinctly for the townspeople in the thirteenth century was not on Easter Sunday but on the preceding Palm Sunday, in a great public procession that wound from the cathedral to various neighboring churches, and eventually back to the cathedral.

For a discussion of the didactic role of the *Visitatio Sepulchri* and the *Officium Stellae* at Sion, see "Public Enactment and Hidden Rite" in Chapter 6.

21. For the text of the *Visitatio Sepulchri* from Bamberg, see Young, 1:617–18.

For the *Depositio* and *Elevatio* from Bamberg, see Brooks, *Sepulchre,* 92–93.

For the *Depositio, Elevatio,* and *Visitatio Sepulchri* texts from Bamberg, see L187–95a, L530–31.

For information on the Cathedral of Bamberg, see Mayer, *Bamberg als Kunststadt;* von Reitzenstein, "Die Baugeschichte des Bamberger Domes."

The tomb of Heinrich II and Kunigunde now stands at the center of the nave; the Altar of St. Kunigunde no longer exists. Since 1937 one flight of steps leading up into the east choir spans the entire width of the nave. We can only guess as to which set of steps the Marys used in the east and the choir used in the west. The *Visitatio* text notes the boys' chorus as remaining in the west choir before the Altar of St. Michael. This altar is usually found at the western end of medieval churches, for example in the westwork, but I have not been able to locate it at Bamberg. An earlier, thirteenth-century text from Bamberg has the boys up in the ambo (in pulpito).

A service-book, an *Agenda Bambergensia* (Ingolstadt, 1587) describes a curtained place of the sepulchre: "Ubi notandum est, quod in templo designari atque tapete, vel antependio claudi debet locus quidam ad repraesentandum Christi Sepulchrum conveniens, in quo inter caetera stratum iaceat linteum . . . ," see L530. However, this *Agenda* was intended for general usage, not specifically for the Bamberg Cathedral. See also Young, 1:323.

22. For the text of the *Visitatio Sepulchri* from Besançon, see Young, 1:290–91; L93–95.

A very similar *Visitatio Sepulchri* text (thirteenth century) comes from the no longer extant Church of St. Etienne (St. Stephen) in Besançon. There too a kind of performance director, in a red cope and with a staff, leads the Marys rather a long way, from the bell tower to mid-choir. At the conclusion the Marys return by their former route and the play ends with a costume show. As at the Church of St. John, the winged angels at St. Etienne wear white with red cloth draped over one shoulder (at St. Etienne a folded red cope, at St. John a red stole). Choral leaders and the performance director are in red at St. Etienne; the women, in white. Now during the singing of the *Te Deum* the choral leaders change from red to white copes and the chorus from black to white, thus creating a visual transformation to match their spiritual transformation effected by the Marys and the angels.

For the text and summary of the *Officium Stellae* from Besançon, see Young, 2:37–40, 433; reprinted from Crombach, *Primitae Gentium,* 732–34. Young notes, "The dates of the manuscripts upon which Crombach draws cannot be determined." Crombach's text is a composite, the opening and closing rubrics from the Church of St. Stephen at Besançon (destroyed in 1676). His summary of the Magi play from the Church of St. John is "ex veteri consuetudine." If the textual reference to the ascent of the Magi "supra ad pulpitum" concerns the rood-loft, then Crombach's manuscript is later than 1550–58, the date of the rood-loft. For a very full description in French (1629) of the *Officium Stellae* from the Church of St. Stephen, Besançon, see Young, 2:433–34.

For information on the church of St. John the Evangelist, Besançon, see Fohlen, *Histoire de Besançon;* Tournier, "La Cathédrale de Besançon"; Tournier, *Les Églises comtoises.*

See also comments by A. M. Nagler, where he locates these reconstructions within the documentation of *The Medieval Religious Stage.* Nagler responds in particular to the article by D. H. Ogden, "The Use of Architectural Space in Medieval Music-Drama."

23. Summary of play texts from Rouen published by Lipphardt (text number given) and Young (volume, page number given):

Play	MS date	MS	Lip	Young
Visitatio Sepulchri	13th c.	904	775	1:660
				(*Depositio,* 1:135)
	14th c.	384	776	1:370
	15th c.	1213	777	1:661
	15th c.	382	778	1:661
Peregrinus	13th c.	222	812	1:461
	14th c.[a]	384	813	1:693
	15th c.	1213	815	1:693
	15th c.	382	814	1:693
Officium Pastorum	13th c.	904		2:16
	14th c.	384[b]		2:14
	15th c.	1213		2:428
	15th c.	382		2:428
Officium Stellae	13th c.	222		2:438
				(fragment)
	13th c.	904		2:435
	14th c.	384		2:43
	15th c.	1213		2:437
	15th c.	382		2:437
Ordo Prophetarum	14th c.	384		2:154
	15th c.	382		2:154

[a]Play reconstructed in the figure of the Cathedral of Rouen in the main text.
[b]Listed by Young as: Rouen, Bibl. de la Ville, MS 384 (*olim* Y. 110), Ordin. ad usum cathedralis Rothomagensis saec. 14. Lipphardt, *Visitatio Sepulchri,* L775–79; *Peregrinus,* L812–14.

List of manuscripts:
Rouen, Bibl. de la Ville, MS 222 (*olim* A. 551), Process. Rothomagense saec. 13th c..
Paris, Bibl. Nat., MS lat. 904, Grad. Rothomagense saec. 13th c.
Rouen, Bibl. de la Ville, MS 384 (*olim* Y. 110), Ordin. Rothomagense saec. 14th c.
Paris, Bibl. Nat., MS 1213, Ordin. Rothomagense saec. 15th c.
Rouen, Bibl. de la Ville, MS 382 (*olim* Y. 108), Ordin. Rothomagense saec. 15th c.

For information on the Cathedral of Rouen, see Aubert, "La Cathédrale [de Rouen]"; Carment-Lanfry, *La Cathédrale de Rouen;* Loisel, *La Cathédrale de Rouen;* Loth, *La Cathédrale de Rouen.*

24. The two fifteenth-century *Visitatio* texts from Rouen are quite similar to the fourteenth-century text in details of mise-en-scène.

25. Delamare, *Le De officiis ecclesiasticis de Jean d'Avranches.*

26. The two fifteenth-century *Peregrinus* texts from Rouen are quite similar to the fourteenth-century text in details of mise-en-scène.

For the text for the *ordo* of Easter Vespers (fourteenth century), see Young, 1:692.

27. For a reference (1570) to a scaffold erected for another occasion in the Cathedral of Rouen, see Le Verdier, *Mystère de l'incarnation,* 1:xi. Le Verdier (1:xlvii) also cites deliberations (1452) of the cathedral chapter concerning a *Peregrinus* play.

28. For *Peregrinus* texts with indications as to staging, see Young: Beauvais (twelfth century), 1:467; Sicily (Syracuse, twelfth century) 1:459; (Palermo, twelfth century) 1:477; Benediktbeuern (thirteenth century), 1:463; Padua (thirteenth century, a description of a performance), 1:482; Fleury Playbook (St.-Benoît-sur-Loire, twelfth century), 1:471; Saintes (fourteenth century), 1:453.

See also Lipphardt: L808 (Beauvais), L811 (Palermo),

L812–15 (Rouen), L816 (Saintes), L817 (Fleury Playbook), L818–19 (Syracuse), L820 (Seckau [Benediktbeuern]). Two *Peregrinus* texts from Durham (twelfth century) have no stage directions (L809–10).

29. The two fifteenth-century texts of the *Officium Pastorum* are quite similar to the fourteenth-century text in details of mise-en-scène, save that "Ecce uirgo" is omitted in the two and no rubric in MS 1213 says specifically that the shepherds worship the Christ Child. The emphasis on the Virgin in the thirteenth-century text seems to diminish slightly in the later versions.

30. For texts of the *Officium Pastorum* from Novalesa (eleventh century) and Padua (thirteenth century), see Young, 2:8–9.

31. The two fifteenth-century texts of the *Officium Stellae* from Rouen are quite similar to the fourteenth-century text in details of mise-en-scène save in the following particulars: (1) Neither says specifically that the *corona* is lighted; (2) both place the angel "in pulpito" instead of before the Altar of the Holy Cross; (3) both note that the Magi return through the north aisle, before the baptismal area, and enter the choir via the north door; (4) both say that the procession enters the choir as on Sunday, MS 1213 omitting the position of the cantor at the choir entrance; (5) both add that the final verse at the withdrawal of the procession, "Salutis nostre auctorem," is sung if necessary.

The thirteenth-century fragment (MS 222) begins with the offering at the manger by the first king.

32. Young (2:48), among others, thinks there were two stars. This suggestion is supported by the fact of the double offerings, but no other text of the *Officium Stellae* known to me proves such an arrangement.

33. No other separate text of the *Ordo Prophetarum* contains information as to staging save the notes on costume from Laon (thirteenth century; see Young, 2:145). The presentation of prophecies which opens the Christmas play at Benediktbeuern will be dealt with after the consideration of the Magi play in the Fleury Playbook.

34. I have as yet found no document giving the exact location of the Altar of the Holy Cross during the periods relevant here. It was the site of the manger for the *Officium Stellae*, the only play text where it is mentioned, and I believe that its position affects the conjectural location of both the Emmaus scaffolding (*Peregrinus*) and Nebuchadnezzar's furnace (*Ordo Prophetarum*), both "in medio nauis ecclesie."

Normally the Altar of the Holy Cross was erected before the choir entrance, which at Rouen was spanned by a roodscreen (as of the thirteenth century) with three doors. Just to the south of the central portal, before the screen, stood the Altar of the Virgin (or "autel du Voeu"); to the north, the Altar of St. Cecilia. A central position of the Altar of the Holy Cross somewhere before the rood-screen fits all rubrical hints and theatrical exigencies.

In the eastern most bay of the nave the depiction of a lamb carrying a cross decorated the keystone of the vault; it can be dated around 1220 because it is inscribed with the name of the architect: "Durandus me fecit." One historian noted its position of honor proximate to the Altar of the Holy Cross "au centre de l'église." For the preceding reconstructions I have suggested a location of the altar in the center of the crossing (approximately eleven meters square), directly beneath the lantern tower, with the structures of Emmaus and the furnace somewhat west of it. See Deville, *Revue des architectes de la cathédrale de Rouen*, 13. See also Loth, "La Cathédrale de Rouen," 29; Aubert, "La Cathédrale [de Rouen]" 30. The inscription: "Durandus me fecit."

35. The dramas which make up what is generally referred to as the Fleury Playbook appear in the following order in Orléans, Bibl. de la Ville, MS 201 (*olim* 178), Miscellanea Floriacensia saec. 13th [12th c.]:

Play	Text in Young
(1) *Tres Filiae* (St. Nicholas play)	2:316
(2) *Tres Clerici* (St. Nicholas play)	2:330
(3) *Iconia Sancti Nicholai* (St. Nicholas play)	2:343
(4) *Filius Getronis* (St. Nicholas play)	2:351
(5) *Officium Stellae*	2:84
(6) *Ordo Rachelis*	2:110
(7) *Visitatio Sepulchri*	1:393
(8) *Peregrinus*	1:471
(9) *Conversio Sancti Pauli*	2:219
(10) *Resuscitatio Lazari*	2:199

For the *Visitatio Sepulchri*, see Lipphardt, L779; *Peregrinus*, L817.

For information on the church of St.-Benoît-sur-Loire, see Chenesseau, *L'Abbaye de Fleury*; Aubert, "Saint-Benoît-sur-Loire"; Banchereau, *L'Église de Saint-Benoît-sur-Loire*; Rocher, *Histoire de l'abbaye royale de Saint-Benoît-sur-Loire*.

Largely on the basis of the music, the fact that the MS is bound with a sequence dedicated to St. Lomer, and the lack of external evidence particularly as to a cult of St. Nicholas at Fleury, Solange Corbin has suggested the Abbey of St. Lomer at Blois as the original site of the productions. See Corbin, "Le Manuscrit 201 d'Orléans." In *The Medieval French Drama*, 44 n. 1, Grace Frank refutes the arguments. The musical evidence is founded on comparison with a single manuscript; the fourteenth-century sequence to St. Lomer has no connection with the play texts; the library of Fleury "reveals a sympathy for S. Nicholas" logical in a medieval school. Corbin would deny Fleury's dramatic activity as indicated by the *Regularis Concordia*, though there can be no question of Fleury's influence on Ethelwold's work.

As to the staging, one is struck by remarkable coincidences with the *Visitatio Sepulchri* in the tenth-century *Regularis Concordia*. At Fleury the women approach "pedetemtim et quasi tristes." Bishop Ethelwold used that word (step-bystep) (L394). "Pedetemtim" also occurs at Aquileia (Moggio?, thirteenth century, L490), Sainte-Chapelle, Paris (fifteenth century, L149), and in Hirsau reform churches: Hirsau (fifteenth century, L223), Prüfening (twelfth century, L311a), Rheinau (twelfth and twelfth-thirteenth century, L315, L315a), and Admont (fifteenth century, L485). As at Fleury, so too in the *Regularis Concordia* the angel carries a palm; also at Mont-St.-Michel (fourteenth-century, L773, L774), and Rouen (thirteenth century, L775, the palm exchanged for a rod, "spica," in later Rouen texts and at Wilton. See Rankin, "New English Source," 10). The play in the *Regularis Concordia* and the Fleury play are the only texts where the women place the graveclooth on the high altar at the conclusion. The unusual line 68 in the Fleury play, "surrexit a morte," sounds very like the "surrexit a mortuis" in the *Regularis Concordia*. Arras (St. Vedastus, eleventh century, L91), Beauvais (thirteenth century, L92, L808), Châlons-sur-Marne (fourteenth century, L99–102), Metz (Gorze, twelfth century, L266–70, L270a in Vol. 6), and Münster (fourteenth century, L274–99) also use it. Finally, also as Lipphardt points out, the "Surrexit Dominus de sepulchro" in the Fleury Playbook comes from the English or Lotharingian tradition.

Solange Corbin's reading of the music in the Fleury Playbook has been brought into question. See Monterosso, *Sacre
rappresentazioni,* xiii–xiv. On the basis of the notation, Monterosso would assign the manuscript to the last decades of the
thirteenth century. Nevertheless, Lipphardt (8:703–5) came
down on the side of Corbin.

For recent musical studies see Stevens, *Words and Music in the Middle Ages;* Rankin, *Medieval Liturgical Drama.*

The doubts raised by Solange Corbin over the Fleury
provenance of the plays are summarized and answered by
Collins, "Home of the Fleury *Playbook.*" See also Bevington,
"Staging of Twelfth-Century Liturgical Drama," 115 n. 1.

I wish to thank Marco Mostert of the University of Amsterdam, for sharing with me his intimate knowledge of the library of Fleury during a discussion on 27 May 1992 at Wassenaar. He is certain that the extant Fleury Playbook manuscript
was copied at Fleury and in the twelfth century. Whether play
texts in it derived from elsewhere, that is another question.

36. For the term *monasterium* as referring to the body of the
church or nave, see Young: 1:163, 247, 283, 315, 330, 333,
337, 342, 352, 355, 361, 363, 484, 586, 612, 630, 640, 642,
646, 649, 652, 668. In order to perform the play at St. Em-
meram, Regensburg, a procession first moves out of the east
choir "ad Monasterium ante altare Sancte Crucis" (Young,
1:295; L323); another text from Regensburg has a group
come from outdoors in the cloister area "usque sub ianuam
Monasterii" and then enter the church (Young, 1:504;
L684). In the *Ordo Rachelis* at St.-Benoît-sur-Loire the
children advance "per monasterium" and then go on into
the choir at the conclusion of the play (Young, 2:110).

We have noted the ancient use of the westwork at Fleury
both to feed and shelter pilgrims and penitents and as a
gathering place for processions. These two functions would
support the argument for placing the Bethlehem manger
at its doors. Furthermore, in the fourteenth century the upper story was converted from a shelter for pilgrims to a
chapel for the community, a continuation of active ties with
the non-monastic world.

The door from the church directly into the cloister is located in the seventh bay of the south aisle, right at the
south-west corner of the south transept. It still has remains
of a curious stone cupboard, apparently for non-liturgical
books. It is at this door that a number of scholars would locate the Christmas manger, taking the word *monasterium*
to refer to the monastery complex.

For a recent reconstruction of the *Officium Stellae* with a
diagram see Michael, *Frühformen* (especially 20); Michael
places the manger at the western doors, but he has the high
altar at the tomb of St. Benoît. Steps were added to the east
choir only in the sixteenth century.

The term *infula* in these plays is quite rare. A twelfth-
century text from Soissons has a subdeacon use his infula
to cover the container with the Host when on Good Friday
he secretly conveys it to the altar in the sepulchre (L167).

37. In addition to the Magi plays from the Fleury Playbook, the
Church of St. John at Besançon, and the Cathedral of Rouen,
texts from nine other churches give us some hints as to mise-
en-scène, but only for the thirteenth-century performance in
the Swiss Cathedral of Sion can we document the pattern of
movement with some confidence. There the Magi laid their
gifts on the main altar. First they read the Gospel, probably
from the rood-loft, and then, led by a boy with a three-candle
candelabrum, they moved along an aisle to the south of the

choir and finally over to the main altar. At Limoges (twelfth
century?) and in the Church of St. Stephen at Besançon
(1629), the high altar served as the repository, in the latter instance the three kings having first advanced to seven stations
within the church and having read the Gospel from the rood-
loft. An outdoor procession in Milan (1336) progressed
through the city and into the Church of St. Eustorgio, where
the Magi offered their gifts at a Nativity scene set up beside
the main altar (Ubi in latere altaris majoris erat Praesepium
cum bove, et asino, et in Praesepio erat Christus parvulus in
brachiis Virginis Matris).

Whenever Herod appears, he seems to be placed in the
nave, at a distance from the sacred area of the altar. At Nevers (eleventh century) the Magi meet at the high altar, go to
Herod, and then on to the manger; the same pattern obtains
in the Montpellier text (twelfth century), where Herod is on
a throne and the three newcomers sit for a time beside him.
Herod ascends a throne at Freising (eleventh century) and
presumably at Bilsen (twelfth century), where he eventually
has the Magi thrown into prison.

To summarize, then, when neither Herod nor the shepherds appear in the *Officium Stellae,* the blocking pattern
is generally that of the *Officium Pastorum* and the simple
Visitatio: a move by the Magi to and then away from the
manger or repository of their offerings, often the main altar. With Herod on the scene, they make two detours: first
to the court in the nave and then back from the manger via
a different route. Here the manger seems to be outside the
main choir, though only in the Fleury Playbook do rubrics
appear to indicate its position in the extreme west. The
second detour occurs in the fifteenth century at Rouen
without the presence of Herod.

When the shepherds participate in the same performance with the Magi, they are considerably overshadowed
by the regal pomp of the climactic visit to the Christ Child.
In the Fleury Playbook, at Freising, and at Bilsen the shepherds begin the play; perhaps their quest commences in
mid-nave; then as the three kings make their way toward
the manger, the meeting with the shepherds is quite brief.

For a reconstruction of the performance in the St. Valeria
Church in Sion (Sitten, Switzerland, thirteenth century) with a
diagram and photograph of the church, see Michael, *Frühformen,* 14–16, 18. For a full discussion of dramatic performances
at Sion, see Appendix A at the end of the present chapter.

For Magi plays with clues as to mise-en-scène, see Young:
Freising (eleventh century), 2:93; Nevers (eleventh century), 2:50; Bilsen (twelfth century), 2:75; Limoges (twelfth
century?), 2:34; Montpellier(?) (twelfth century), 2:68;
Benediktbeuern (thirteenth century), 2:172; Milan (1336),
2:451; St. Stephen at Besançon (1629), 2:434.

The 575-line Christmas play of Benediktbeuern belonging
to the *Carmina Burana,* opens with an *Ordo Prophetarum* and a debate with "Archisynagogus"; then follow
the Annunciation, birth of Christ, journey of the Magi and interview with Herod, adoration by the shepherds, presentation
of gifts by the Magi, and slaughter of the Innocents. At the
conclusion a rubric says that Herod is gnawed by worms, carried "de sede," and received by devils; his son takes the crown;
Mary, riding on a donkey, and Joseph depart for Egypt.

The first stage direction contains the only clue to the location of set pieces: "Primo ponatur sedes Augustino in
fronte ecclesie, et Augustinus habeat a dextera parte Ysa-
iam et Danielem et alios Prophetes, a sinistra autem

Archisynagogum et suos Iudeos." Some scholars have felt that seats or platforms for actors were positioned outside the church; Young, on the other hand, suggested that "in fronte ecclesiae" could well refer to the western end of the nave. I see no reason for positing an outdoor performance here. Moreover, it seems likely that the prophets were at the eastern end of the nave, near the choir, as at Rouen; the *Antichrist* of Tegernsee has the temple, the king of Jerusalem, and Synagoga in the east. At the conclusion of the *Ordo Prophetarum* from Benediktbeuern, the prophets may either withdraw or sit in their proper places (uel sedeant in locis suis propter honorem ludi).

Certainly the play was performed with movement among several specific stations, either raised platforms or thrones for Augustine and Herod. The manger contained a bed for Mary (Maria uadat in lectum suum), Joseph was present, and for the first time we can be certain that the Virgin was not represented by an image.

The star is first viewed by the Sybil, who is no doubt with the other prophets. It then appears at the birth of the Christ Child and is immediately seen by the Magi, coming from different parts of the earth. They advance toward Herod's area (usque in terram Herodis); the last we hear of the star is at this position; the Magi then meet the shepherds and continue on to the manger.

Perhaps the most logical suggestion would be that of an arrangement not unlike that in the Fleury Playbook, with the *sedes* and locations of action extending from the prophets in or near the choir to the manger at the western extreme of the nave. Herod and the slaughter of the children would then have been placed in mid-nave.

For the Benediktbeuern Christmas play, see Young, 2:196. E. K. Chambers, for example, suggests outdoor performance: *Mediaeval Stage*, 2:79.

Of the six plays in *Carmina Burana*, four begin with a direction as to the actors moving to an assigned place (locus), while the comprehensive Christmas drama notes the *sedes*, and the action of the *Peregrinus* commences immediately with the conversation of the wayfarers. Only the *Ludus Paschalis* from this collection can be associated with the liturgy, coming at the end of Matins. For a summary of the Benediktbeuern play texts see Young, 1:686–87; for the Christmas play text, see Young, 2:172–90.

For the Tegernsee *Antichrist*, see Young, 2:371, and the discussion of it in this chapter.

38. From the Christmas productions at Rouen we have already noted the danger of assuming the same position of the manger, for example, in two plays performed on different days.

39. On "Galilee," see Migne, ed., *Patrologiae Cursus Completus: Patrologia Latina*, vol. 150, 1249ff. The source of the term is unknown. Heitz, 206–9, attempts to associate it with the Easter liturgy, more specifically with the Easter drama.

Walter Horn and Ernest Born in their work *Plan of St. Gall*, 3, 153, connect the term with church architecture:

galilea: Narthex, porch, or chapel at the entrance of a church, from the province of Galilee, a name applied, in medieval architectural language, to outer annexes of the church, probably an allusion to Galilee as an outlying portion of the Holy Land, or to the phrase "Galilee of the Gentiles"—Matthew 4:15.

40. Translations from Adams, *Chief Pre-Shakespearean Dramas*, 51 (St. Paul play), 63 (Getron play).

In reference to this opening stage direction, Adams notes: "It is not easy to understand exactly what is meant here by *sedes*. The 'seats' may have been on platforms, or may have been merely set in cleared spaces."

Bevington ("Staging of Twelfth-Century Liturgical Drama," 111) counts "five seats or *sedes* in all." It seems that to the four *sedes* mentioned in the stage direction he adds the bed as the fifth *sedes*.

41. In other texts the word *locus* is also used in referring to an actor's role. For example, in the Christmas play of Benediktbeuern, Elizabeth leaves because her part is at an end: "Deinde recedat Elysabeth, quia amplius non habebit locum hec persona" (Young, 2:180).

42. See, for example, Creizenach, *Geschichte des neueren Dramas*, 199.

By no means do I wish to suggest one author for the St. Nicholas plays; their quality varies quite considerably.

43. For the text of *The Play of Antichrist*, see Young, 2:371–87.

For notes on the Romanesque basilica at Tegernsee, see Dehio, *Handbuch der deutschen Kunstdenkmäler*, 529–30.

44. From a manuscript belonging to Mézières, the following items are published in Young, vol. 2:

(1) *Officium Presentacionis Beate Marie Virginis in Templo*, 2:227–42: a description and text of a performance; probable association with a production of 21 November 1372, in the church of the Friars Minor (Franciscans), Avignon.

(2) A note concerning a dramatic performance in the church of the Augustinians at Avignon, 1385, 2:478–79.

(3) A letter written by Mézières after 21 November 1372, about the reception of the celebration in Italy and France, 2:473–78.

For information on the Church of the Friars Minor, Avignon, see Girard, *Évocation du vieil Avignon*, 311–12, and 1618 map between 294–95; Labande, "Guide archéologique du congrès d'Avignon," 31–32; Castrucci, *Istoria della città d'Avignone*, 57.

On measurement, see "Sistema francese antico," 23:118: one piede equals 32.48 centimeters. One English foot equals 30.48 centimeters.

For an English translation, see Mézières, *Presentation Play*; see also Meredith and Tailby, *Staging of Religious Drama*, 207–25.

45. For the text of the *Vorspiel* from Bozen, see Wackernell, *Altdeutsche Passionsspiele*, 433–72.

For information on performances in Bozen, see Wackernell, xl–l, ccxxxv–ccxlv.

For reconstructions of Vigil Raber's plan and information on the parish-church at Bozen, see Michael, *Frühformen*, 37–44; Michael, "Staging of the Bozen Passion Play"; Nordsieck, "Der Bühnenplan des Vigil Raber."

Much of the source material relevant to medieval theatrical activity in Tyrol has gone astray during the last decades, and Wackernell's book is our major source of information. He published texts from eight related manuscripts.

Financial records from Bozen and Sterzing attest to both indoor and outdoor performances of various religious plays in the fifteenth and sixteenth centuries, but Wackernell's excerpts do not reveal where the stage was erected for the Passion play in Bozen, 1495, or in Sterzing, 1496 and 1503. Wackernell is certain that the latter took place inside the church because the provost paid the bills and because of references to the sacristy in the play texts; in 1541 and 1543 accounts give the name of the church in

Text	Place of Performance	Date of Performance	Notes (Th, Fri, Sun=Holy Week days on which the Last Supper, Crucifixion, Resurrection were acted.)
1. "Bozener" Passion	Bozen	1495	3-day performance (Th, Fri, Sun).
2. "Amerikaner" Passion	Bozen	1495	Text of same Passion as "Bozener."
3. "Vorspiel"	Bozen	1514	Palm Sunday of 7-day performance. Raber's copy of play acted in Hall, 1511, with his 1514 stage plan.
4. "Sterzinger" Passion	Sterzing	1496, 1503	3-day performance (Th, Fri, Sun). Text for Sun. lost.
5. "Pfarrkircher" Passion	Sterzing	(copied 1486)	4-day performance(Th, Fri, Sun, and *Peregrinus* on Mon, after Easter).
6. "Haller" Passion	Hall	1511 (copied 1514)	4-day performance (Palm Sun, Th, Fri, Sun). Palm Sun "Vorspiel" lost. Raber's copy made late in 1514 for intended performance in Trento. Raber's "Vorspiel" (3) in Bozen he copied and adapted from now lost "Vorspiel" of Hall, 1511.
7. "Brixener" Passion	Brixen?	?	3-day performance (Th, Fri, Sun).
8. "Mischhandschrift"	—	(copied 1530–50)	"Vorspiel," Last Supper. Probably not for performance.

Sterzing. See Wackernell, "Pfarrkirche zu unserer lieben Frau im Moos," xcv, xcix.

The only internal evidence of production within the church at Bozen and at Sterzing comes from two stage directions. The first has to do with the removal of Christ's body to the sacristy after the Crucifixion (Wackernell, 173):

Et tunc quasy violenter recipiunt corpus Jhesu, differunt ad sacristiam et canunt: "Ecce, quam moritur justus!"

With minor variations this rubric appears in the "Bozener," "Amerikaner," "Sterzinger," and "Pfarrkircher" plays. The "Sterzinger" adds a procession: "Vadunt pussillam viatu"; Joseph has some lines; "Et sic vadunt et canunt ultra."

Then after the Harrowing of Hell, Christ frees Joseph of Arimathaea from prison and then withdraws into the sacristy but retains the same costume (Wackernell, 215): "et ipse recedit ad sacristiam manens in ornamentis." This rubric appears in the "Bozener," "Amerikaner," and "Pfarrkircher" versions; the "Sterzinger" text for Easter Sunday is lost.

References in the stage directions of these four texts contain few clues as to actual stage construction. After the Last Supper, Christ goes with his disciples "ad monttem Oliveti," where eventually an angel appears to him, perhaps having been concealed in a structure like that shown on Raber's plan (Wackernell, 47). The phrase "ad locum" is used rather frequently, but rarely with additional descriptive information.

For the Last Supper the disciples sit at a prepared table. Caiaphas, at one point, rises "a sede." Herod goes "ad sedem suum" on the second day (the "Sterzinger" text says "ascendit"), addressed by his servant: "Herr, sitzt her in dissen sall." Pilate also goes "ad sedem," and his servant begins, "Herr, nu tret her in den sal" (Wackernell, 81, 82).

Pilate's is the locale most clearly indicated by the rubrics as a mansion. In the "Sterzinger" and "Pfarrkircher" plays, Pharisees and others bring Christ "ad Pilatum stantes ante domum"; the "Bozener" direction reads, "ad Pilatum stans ante dominum"; the "Amerikaner," "ad Pilatum stantem ante Jesum." The first rubric is correct, for the Jews go "in kain haydnisch haws," and so Pilate must come out to them. He appears, then "Pilatus introducit Jhesum in pretorium," and after an interview "Pilatus exit ad judeos" (Wackernell, 83, 87, 89).

As to the grave, we have already noted the deposit of Christ's body in the sacristy. On Easter morning an angel "circuit sepulchrum"; then one stands at the head, another at the foot. "Tunc resurget dominus et stans circa sepulchrum . . ."

("Brixener" and "Amerikaner": "stans percutienti") before the Harrowing of Hell. Later Peter says to John (Wackernell, 239):

Nw schleuff in das grab und puckh dich,
Wan dw pist vil junger dan ich.

Michael suggests that at Bozen the doorway to the sacristy would have been reduced from 2.9 meters to 1.6 meters by a stage 1.3 meters in height, thus forcing the disciples to bend down when entering the small opening.

When Christ goes to *Infernum*, he kicks the door, "Salvator trudit januam inferni cum pede et aperit," setting off much shrieking among the devils inside (Wackernell, 209). At Bozen this was probably the structural door north of the choir entrance.

He then makes his way "ad turrim," where the Jews have incarcerated Joseph of Arimathaea, and leads Joseph "ad paradisum." Later the Jews return and wonder at the miracle: "Nu ist der turen worden lär!" (Wackernell, 214, 247).

And for the devils' scene in the "Pfarrkircher" version, Lucifer "ascendit super dolium" before hell in order to preside over the array of *diaboli* and damned souls from the cask or raised seat (Wackernell, 257).

Financial accounts from Hall record performances there either in the city square or park (in der Stat gartten); fourteen days before Easter, 1511, work began "an der pün im garten zu dem Spil des passions" (Wackernell, ccxxxii). The stage directions in the "Haller" Passion mention the table where Christ sits with his disciples. At the beginning of the Friday performance he is brought "a domo" and eventually led "ante domum Pilati" (Wackernell, 297, 320–21).

As far as the texts reveal, then, save for the use of the sacristy, the mise-en-scène of these plays was very similar, whether acted indoors or not.

46. Wackernell, *Altdeutsche Passionsspiele*, ccxl.

47. Ibid., ccxli. Wackernell's comments are in italics.

48. For texts of the Beauvais *Daniel* and Vorau *Isaac*, see Young, 2:290–301, 259–64. These plays are further discussed under "Set Pieces and Special Effects" in this chapter.

For a manuscript facsimile, transcription, and discussions of staging, cultural contexts, and music of the Beauvais *Daniel*, see Ogden, *Play of Daniel*.

49. For the text of the Laon *Joseph*, see Young, 2:267–74.

50. For a reproduction of the Lucerne and Valenciennes outdoor Passion play plans, see Nicoll, *Development of the Theatre*, 68–69, 71. For the Villingen Passion plan, see

Michael, *Frühformen,* 49. See also Nagler, *Medieval Religious Stage.*

For the text of *Adam,* see Aebischer, *Le Mystère d'Adam.*

51. The *Jeu d'Adam* has devils run about "per plateam" and "per plateas"—the staging area. See Aebischer, *Le Mystère d'Adam,* 35, 42.

For a helpful summary of the use of stage space in the Latin Easter drama see Roeder, "Raumregie."

52. Some of the evidence which I examine here has been surveyed by Haastrup, "Medieval Props." Her approach emphasizes the physical evidence for stage properties used in various plays, including the *Visitatio Sepulchri* and related Good Friday Easter dramas and ceremonies that are not under consideration in this section. See also Davidson, "Ceremonies and Liturgical Plays."

For the text of the Vorau *Isaac,* see Young, 2:259–64.

53. For Rouen, see Young, 1:461, 691–93; L812–14. For Angers, see Young, 1:251; L89: "Paratur altare maius vice Monumenti Christi, velis supra et ab anteriori parte obtentis, quasi tabernaculum extemporaneum." For Saint-Omer, see Young, 2:482–83; see also the discussion of "Pavilions" in this chapter.

54. For the Fleury *St. Paul,* and Hilarius, *Lazarus,* see Young, 2:212, 219.

55. For texts of Hilarius' *Daniel,* Beauvais *Daniel,* Laon *Joseph,* see Young, 2:276–86, 290–301, 267–74.

For a more complete examination of the rubrics of the Beauvais *Ludus Danielis,* see also Ogden, "Staging of *The Play of Daniel.*"

56. For the text of Cotrel's *Aurea Missa,* see Young, 2:480–82.

57. For the *Missa Aurea* at Saint-Omer, see Young, 2:482–83. In 1543 a carpenter was instructed to make "deux petis passés," called "eschaffaulx."

58. For references from Padua, Parma, and Halle, see Young, 2:248, 479–80, 256.

For a survey of the staging of Assumption plays, see Massip, "Staging of the Assumption in Europe." For further information about the play which has survived into modern times at Elche (Elx), in Catalonia, see Massip, "Cloud."

59. For references from Halle and London, see Young, 1:490.

William Lambarde, *Dictionarium Angliae Topographicum et Historicum* (London, 1730), 459–60, quoted by Young, 1:490. For identification of the large thurible used in this ceremony, see Davidson, "Heaven's Fragrance."

For further uses of a dove, real or artificial, at celebrations of Pentecost, see Donovan, *Liturgical Drama,* 143–44 (at Valencia) and 157–60 (at Perpingnan, France). Donovan notes that the custom was traditional at Toledo, Valencia, Huesca, Badajoz, Burgo de Osma, Seville, and elsewhere (144 n. 21).

For extant apertures in European church roofs see Haastrup, "Medieval Props," 154, 159–61, fig. 20.

60. For the text from Moosburg, see Young, 1:484–88; Brooks, "Eine liturgisch-dramatische Himmelfahrtsfeier," 91–96; Haastrup, "Medieval Props," 151–52. On Ascension images, see also Larson, "Ascension Images in Art and Theatre," and on Ascension ceremonies, see Davidson, "Saints and Angels," 3–7.

For the text from Essen, see Young, 1:334.

For the text from Halle, see Young, 2:256.

61. For the text from Bamberg, see Young, 1:694.

62. For the text from Berlin, see Young, 1:696.

63. Wackernell, *Altdeutsche Passionsspiele,* xlvii–xlix.

64. Young, 2:222.

65. Wesselofsky, "Italienische Mysterien," 427–31. The description of the machinery is as follows (430): "Sein Niedersteigen geschieht folgendermassen: er [the angel] hat hinter sich zwei Räderchen befestigt, die von unten, wegen der grossen Entfernung, unsichtbar sind, und in welche die zwei Stricke passen, während am dritten, feinsten Stricke Leute, die oben aufgestellt und ebenfalls unsichtbar sind, den Engel herablassen und wieder nach oben ziehen." (The descent is effected in this way: behind him [the angel] there are two small wheels secured, invisible from below because of the distance, into which the two ropes fit, while some people who cannot be seen stand up above and by means of the third very thin rope lower and lift up the angel.) The fire effect (431): "das Feuer kommt vom oberen Gerüste in immer grösserer Fülle und mit furchtbarem Gedonner, die Lichter in der Kirche anzündend, aber ohne die Kleider der Zuschauer zu versengen oder irgend Uebles zuzufügen." (The fire poured forth and spread with increasing intensity and noise from the high scaffold, lighting the lamps in the church but without burning the clothes of the spectators or causing any harm.) The English translation of the full text is from Meredith and Tailby, *Staging of Religious Drama,* 243–45.

66. Wesselofsky, "Italienische Mysterien," 436–39; Meredith and Tailby, *Staging of Religious Drama,* 245–47.

67. Nagler, *Sources of Theatrical History,* 41.

The production in S. Felice is described by Vasari, *Le vite,* 1:627–31.

For a consideration of these four Florentine productions, together with conjectural diagrams and information on the churches, see Molinari, *Spettacoli fiorentini del quattrocento,* 35–54.

For a reconstructed model of Brunelleschi's man-powered crane, see Maas, "Castello IV," 1–7.

68. Vasari, *Le vite,* 1:821–22.

69. For useful observations on light in the church and bibliography on the subject, see Koch, "Der Innenraum des Braunschweiger Domes," 4:487, 498 n. 17. See also Sachs, Badstübner, Neumann, *Christliche Ikonographie in Stichworten,* 240ff.

An aesthetic of light also pervaded the consciousness of Church musicians. "Higher tones more than lower tones were associated with light" in medieval Gregorian chant, writes Kees Vellekoop in his study of "De klank van licht en donker."

For the descriptions by Abraham, Bishop of Suzdal, see Wesselofsky, "Italienische Mysterien"; English translation may be found in Meredith and Tailby, *Staging of Religious Drama,* 243–47.

The "star" was carried by a boy at (Sion) Sitten: "et quidam puer debet eos precedere qui portet cereum. in cuius summitate sunt tres candele ardentes" [sic]. See Carlen, "Das Ordinarium Sedunense," 362–63. For references to stars in Magi plays from Limoges, Fleury, and Rouen, see Young, 2:35, 84, 44, 437. Young (2:42) thinks that the star at Besançon (seventeenth century) was drawn on a string, his evidence coming from a contemporary description in French included in Francis Guenard's *Liber Caeremoniarum et Officiorum divinorum quae fiunt in ecclesia Sancti Stephani Bisuntini* (1629): "laquelle Estoille doibt estre arrestée au droit du pulpite qu'est au choeur." See Young, 2:434.

The relevant passages from Soissons read as follows (see Young, 1:625, 305; L167): "Ecclesia [nave?] preterea, cereis accensis, a capite usque ad pedes per circuitum uestiatur. Altare sacrosanctum amplificato numero cereorum lumine circumdetur. Numerus uero cereorum circa altare et ante sit lxxxxᵃ, et unus funiculus insuper a capite usque ad pedes pretendatur; in quo circulus quidam ferreus habens vii cereos super ostium Sepulchri in altum dependeat. Circulus autem iste qui et stella a nobis nuncupatur...." "Presbyteri nempe predicti [two Marys at sepulchre], acceptis thuribus [thuribulis], conducant illud semper incensantes, unus a dexteris et alius a sinistris, stella predicta semper duce [back toward high altar]."

This text from Soissons and a thirteenth-century text from the nunnery of the Holy Cross at Poitiers (Young, 1:571; L151) refer to dramatic use of windows in the respective sepulchres. Flickering lights and music barely audible through the open work in the replicas of the Sepulchre at Aquileia, Constance, Gernrode (original ca. 1080 openings were sealed up by 1500), and Magdeburg must have increased the mystery—and perhaps the sanctity—of the moments chanted within them.

70. For references to fire-wielding angels, see Young, 1:435, L830 (Seckau, Benediktbeuern); Young, 1:439, L824 (Tours); Young, 1:394, L779 (Fleury); Young, 1:408, L771 (Coutances); Young, 2:233 (Mézières, Avignon), Meredith and Tailby, *Staging of Religious Drama*, 207–25; Young, 1:423, 639–40, L829, L601, L598–99 (Klosterneuburg). A flaming sword is specified in a further early sixteenth-century text from Klosterneuburg (L600a).

About the effect in the Tours manuscript, Gustave Cohen remarks: "Sans doute la poudre lycopode de nos artificiers...." *Anthologie du drame liturgique*, 39 n. 1.

71. See references to thunder in Young, 1:435, L830 (Seckau, Benediktbeuern); Young, 2:387 (Tegernsee); Young, 1:697 (Berlin); Vasari, 1:630 (Brunelleschi); Wesselofsky, "Italienische Mysterien," 431, 438 (Bishop of Suzdal) trans. in Meredith and Tailby, *Staging of Religious Drama*, 245.

The play from Vich was first printed by J. Gudiol in *Vida Cristiana* 1 (1914): 238–40; it was ignored until Donovan, *Liturgical Drama*, (87–91) reprinted it in 1958.

72. For references to Christ at Emmaus, see Young, 1:464, L820 (Seckau, Benediktbeuern); Young, 1:454, L816 (Saintes); Young, 1:462, L812 (Rouen), Young, 1:472, L817 (Fleury). The two remaining *Peregrinus* play texts are quite similar to Rouen—Palermo (twelfth or thirteenth century), "et fra[n]gat panem, eisque det, ac post ab oculi[s] eorum evanescat," Young, 1:478, L811; and Syracuse (twelfth century), "et frangat panem eisque det, ac postea ab oculis eorum evanescat," Young, 1:460, L819.

73. For references to Christ before Magdalen, see Young, 1:371, 660, 661, L776, 775, 777, 778 (Rouen); Young, 1:383, L770 (Barking); Young, 1:387–88, L797 (Rheinau); Young, 1:409, L771 (Coutances); Young, 1:399, L782 (Chiemsee, previously called "Nürnberger Osterspiel").

74. For references to effigies, see Young, 2:14, 17, 44, 164, 437 (Rouen); 2:51 (Nevers); 2:451 (Milan); 2:251 (Augsburg); 2:337–41 (Hilarius); 2:344–48 (Fleury); 1:506–12 (Cividale). Donovan (*Liturgical Drama*) prints the play from Granada (61–62).

75. See Young: *Ludus de Rege Aegypti*, and the Christmas play of Benediktbeuern, 2:465, 189; *Ordo Rachelis* (Freising, Laon, Fleury); 2:119, 105–6, 110–13.

76. For references to Daniel plays, see Young, 2:278 (Hilarius); 2:292 (Beauvais); 2:154 (Rouen *Ordo Prophetarum*).

77. Ogden, "*Visitatio Sepulchri*," 95–102; Young, 1:304; L166, L167.

78. Young, 1:333, 575, 323, 251; L564, L773–74, L530, L89.

79. Donovan, *Liturgical Drama*, 61–62.
80. Stone, *Adam*, 159. Aebischer, *Le Mystère d'Adam*, 27.
81. Ogden, "Set Pieces and Special Effects," 88 n. 24–48; Young, 2:481.
82. Young, 2:483.
83. Vigil Raber's sketch was first reproduced by Nordsieck, "Der Bühnenplan des Vigil Raber."

Chapter 4: The Costumes

1. For these plays, see Young, 1:522, 2:150, 159. For another *Ordo Prophetarum* containing the Balaam episode, see Brockett, "Previously Unknown *Ordo Prophetarum*," 117, 121–24. Some of the documentation in the present chapter was discussed in a different form in Davidson, *Material Culture and Medieval Drama*.

2. The standard work on ecclesiastical vestments is: Braun, *Die liturgische Gewandung*. Perhaps the finest study of the portrayal in art of the characters relevant to this study is: Réau, *Iconographie de l'art chrétien*.

Mayer-Thurman, *Raiment for the Lord's Service*, contains useful photographs with descriptions of medieval vestments. During the period of the liturgical drama, in addition to a certain amount of local amateur work, vestments in England were made chiefly by paid, professional needlework guilds, composed of men and women and run by men. Their work, called *Opus Anglicanum*, was famous and much sought after all over Europe. See Mayer-Thurman, 46. See also Flüeler, *Das sakrale Gewand*; Victoria and Albert Museum, *Opus Anglicanum*; "AVISTA Sessions 1996."

3. Young, 2:403: *pueri, fratres,* or *clerici.* Examples in the text at Young, 1:244, 249, 264, 310, 370, 381. Apparently dignitaries as a rule did not act. For Marys played by women see Chapter 5.

4. The dress of the Eastern Church had been fairly well unified by the ninth century.

5. Pontifical gloves (eleventh century); miter (tenth century); liturgical shoes and stockings restricted to bishops and cardinals; occasionally the *rationale*.

6. For the *Alba* of the angel(s) without further qualification, see Young, 1:249, 279, 370, 580, 581, 592; Mainz text, 1:614; Senlis text, 1:245. For *paratus* meaning ornate or decorated (e.g., with embroidery), see Braun, *Gewandung*, 79, 80 n. 3, 292.

The fourteenth-century *Visitatio* of Fécamp (Young, 1:264) mentions "unus frater in albis in specie Angeli"; from St. Gall (Young, 1:621) there are four "scholastici" "induti angelico habitu"; and at Klosterneuburg (Young, 1:639) the deacon is dressed in "solemni alba veste" and carries a sword.

Braun, *Gewandung*, 59–61. For commerce in silk and a map showing the "Silk Road," see Singer, "Epilogue," 2:761–64, fig. 684. See also Geijer, *History of Textile Art*, 226–39.

7. For the dalmatic alone as the garb of the angels, see Young 1:247, 253, 281, 577, 595; L190a, L207, L256, L315 (with heads covered), L447, L449, L485, L522, L612, and occasionally along with the alb, L350. For the color of the dalmatic, see Young, 1:333, 385. It seems that "albis et tunicis candidis" (1:603) refers to the tunicles over albs. *Tunica* is translated "tunic" unless the context suggests the dalmatic-like "tunicle."

The dalmatic appears alone in an example of the *Visitatio* from the Brigittine abbey at Vadstena in Sweden—a location of considerable interest because of the extant vestments used prior to the Reformation there. When the dalmatic alone is specified, it is common to find the role of the angel(s) played by the deacon(s); such is the case at Vadstena.

    See Davidson, *Holy Week and Easter Ceremonies;* Estham, "Medeltida Textilier."

8. For the stole as part of angelic apparel, worn with the alb, see Young, 1:248; L662, L664, L673, L677, L678, L678a, L679, L680, L681, L793, L795, or with the alb and dalmatic, Young, 1:263. For the "coopertus stola candida" as the only reference to the dress of an angel sitting at the sepulchre, see Young, 1:321, 326, 352; L545, L633, L639, L694, L695, L696, L698, L706, L756, L765; in Mark's account in the Vulgate the angel is so described (Mark 16:5). See in addition "ad caput coopertus stola candida," Young, 1:648, 652; L615a, L647, L654, L719, L738, L762, where the color is specifically given.

    Young, 1:362: Two angels are "cooperti quasi stola candida"; this and the expression "clericus alba stola indutus" (Young, 1:382) make one wonder if perhaps *stola* is sometimes used in the classical sense of the word—that is, a dress, a gown. Here a beautiful garment is called for, "alba stola" probably a "tunica alba."

    In addition, we have found mostly deacons and canons mentioned as taking these roles, implying that they simply wore the stole over their normal dress.

9. Texts from Essen (Young, 1:333), Augsburg (Young, 1:645), Angers (Young, 1:251). Eveillon, *De Processionibus Ecclesiasticis Liber,* 177.

10. Text from Mont-St.-Michel (Young, 1:373). Text from Metz (L269).

11. Texts from Zwiefalten (Young, 1:267), Rheinau (L315), Stuttgart (Young, 1:596), and unidentified German monastery (Young, 1:313). Texts from Le Mans (Young, 1:288), Jerusalem (Young, 1:262, 591; L408), Rouen (Young, 1:661), and Nottuln (L:795: "amictu capita operti"). Angels in Prague "stolam habens in capite" (L662–81, not L674).

12. *Glossarium Mediae,* 7:603.

    Texts from Padua (Young, 1:294), Besançon (Young, 1:290, 614), an unidentified French monastery (Young, 1:293), Soissons (Young, 1:304).

13. For a thirteenth-century example see Braun, *Gewandung,* 586–7; 166–67 for *planeta plicata*; 79–80, 292 for *paratus* meaning ornate or decorated. Jungmann, 1:411 for *planeta plicata*, a deacon's or subdeacon's soft chasuble that could be rolled up or tucked up in front; e.g., Young, 1:399 (*Visitatio,* Chiemsee).

14. Text from Narbonne (Young, 1:285).

15. See Mayer-Thurman, *Raiment for the Lord's Service,* 33.

16. Text from the Fleury Playbook. See Young, 1:394, 1:394 n. 1; Latham, *Revised Medieval Latin Word-List,* 249. See also Braun, *Gewandung,* 153, 426–29.

    Today *infula* refers to "One of two lappets that hang from the back of a bishop's miter." See *Webster's New International Dictionary,* s.v. *infula.*

    For the ambiguity of meaning see also Du Cange, *Glossarium Mediae,* 4:358–59.

    For photographs of miters and a study of their types, see Mayer-Thurman, *Raiment for the Lord's Service,* 33.

    Uses of the words *infula* and *infulatus* in the Fleury Playbook rubrics: *Peregrinus* (the Risen Christ, Young, 1:472), *Visitatio Sepulchri* (the angel, Young, 1:394; the Risen Christ, Young, 1:396).

    If *mitra . . . etsi deinfulatus* means "a miter . . . but without a chasuble" or "a miter . . . but not vested as a bishop,"

it may serve two functions. It would emphasize the fact that the angel does not wear full episcopal regalia but only the miter, a great rarity in itself for an angel. And it would set up the visual contrast between beginning and ending characters of the drama, the angel juxtaposed to the even more glorious Risen Christ, who will indeed wear a chasuble, a white one, and, on his head, not a miter but a precious phylacterium. Visually the angel presages the Christ. For angels with headgear "reminiscent of a bishop's miter," see Gabriel and Raphael in Mézières' *Presentation* (Young, 2:229).

    The *Peregrinus* in the Fleury Playbook exhibits a parallel to this theatrical effect. There Jesus appears to the disciples in a white colobium (a sleeveless tunic), over it a red cope, and wearing a miter aurifrigiata (with embroideries). He carries a gold cross. He exits, soon to return to Thomas and to finish the play, having exchanged the miter for a crown formed by an amice and phylacteries. He carries a gold cross with a banner and now, in his left hand, a Gospel-book. See Young, 1:472–74.

17. For palm branches in the hands of angels, see Young, 1:249, 265, 373, 581, L352; also tapers, Young, 1:262, L408; or candles, Young, 1:591; or a sword, Young, 1:639, L600a.

18. See Mayer-Thurman, *Raiment for the Lord's Service,* 13, 48, which contains useful photographs with descriptions of medieval vestments.

    See also Hope and Atchley, *English Liturgical Colours.*

19. For a photographic illustration of vesting in a medieval amice, see Braun, *Gewandung,* 35, fig. 4. For the Marys "in [ad] modum Mulierum," see Young, 1:262, 294, 591, L408; or "uestibus muliebribus," Young, 1:257; or "tenentes figuram Mulierum," Young, 1:352, L545, L633, L635, L639, L691, L694, L695, L696, L698, L699, L706, L738, L756, L761, L762, L765; or "in similitudinem trium Mariarum," Young, 1:393; or "in similitudine Mulierum," L269, L453, L454. The cope is the costume most frequently mentioned.

    For the Marys wearing the cope, see Young, 1:244, 247, 249, 253, 255, 257, 258, 260, 263, 264, 266, 280, 285, 309, 312, 321, 326, 347, 385, 577, 581, 592, 596, 614, 630, 667, 668; L86, L105, L106, L190a, L190b, L308, L315, L331, L344, L352, L447, L449, L485, L545, L600a, L662, L664, L665, L673, L675, L677, L678, L679, L680, L691, L694, L695, L696, L698, L706, L756, L765.

    Once the Marys are "cum capis de pallio" (Young, 1:304). The Marys' copes designated specifically as being white (Young, 1:247, 258, 266, 285, 577, 668) and as "bonis capis" (Young, 1:253, 309). When mentioned together with the amice, (Young, 1:260, 285, 312, 385); "in superpelliceis et in capis sericis, capitibus uelatis" (Young, 1:347).

    For the text from Sion, see L746.

    Gustave Cohen says that the Marys covered their heads with amices "d'imiter le plus possible la coiffure féminine à la mode." See Cohen, *Histoire,* 36, 39.

    At Vadstena the three clerics representing the Marys wore copes (tres clerici pro mulieribus in capis), in this instance of very considerable interest for us since there is a fine pre-Reformation cope extant from the abbey which displays local Brigittine work along with embroidered orphreys of Flemish workmanship. There is no record that this cope, a gift to the abbey in 1489, was actually used in a *Visitatio,* but it does represent a type that in fact was utilized and that was essential to the costuming of the play. This cope is a rare example of an extant vestment from a church where the medieval drama flourished, in this case probably continuing until the expulsion of the Brigittine order from Sweden in 1595. See A. E.

Davidson, *Holy Week and Easter Ceremonies*, 72; Estham, "Medeltida Textilier," 110–12.

20. Young, 1:251 n. 1: "*Corbicularius* appears to be a term peculiar to Angers, and denotes a cleric vested in a certain sort of surplice."

    Eveillon, *De Processionibus Ecclesiasticis Liber*, 178.

21. Texts from Fleury (L49), Fécamp (Young, 1:264), Trier (Young, 1:280; L350), Meissen (Young, 1:330), Moosburg (Young, 1:362), Urgel (L464).

22. Over eighty of the *Visitatio* texts edited by Young and Lipphardt mention the habit of the Marys.

    For Marys carrying thuribles, see Young, 1:249, 266, 581, 595, 596, L86, L207, L256, L315, L350, L374, L447, L449, L485, L545, L602c, L694, L695, L696, L706, L745, L756, L765; gold or silver vases, Young, 1:262, 591, 594, 615, L408; simply vases, Young, 1:264, 370, 661, L455, 455a; pyxes, Young, 1:258, 347, 408, L213, L269, L600a, L796; candles or tapers, Young, 1:262, 279, 580, 594, L105, L106, L374, L408, L119, L213, L460, L485, L600a, L661, L662, L664, L665, L667, L673, L675, L677, L678, L678a, L679, L680, L681; casks, Young, 1:372, L600a.

    Texts from Metz (Young, 1:261), from Wolfenbüttel (Young, 1:668).

    That the Marys carry thuribles seems conventional in Ottonian manuscript illuminations, as they do in the *Benedictional of St. Ethelwold*. See, for example, the illumination in the Pericopes Book of Henry II in Mayr-Harting, *Ottonian Book Illumination*, 1: figs. 106–7, and also Collins, *Production*, fig. 9.

23. Max von Boehn says that at Salisbury the Marys were given furs as undergarments (fourteenth century): *Das Bühnenkostüm*, 79. This is repeated by Knoll, *Die Rolle des Maria Magdalena*, 91.

    Text from Barking (Young, 1:381).

    For examples of pyxes, see Collins, *Production*, figs. 7–8.

24. See Réau, *Iconographie de l'art chrétien*, 1:86.

    De Moléon (pseud. for Jean Baptiste le Brun des Marettes), *Voyages liturgiques de France* (Paris: Delaulne, 1718), 98; quoted in Lipphardt, 90.

25. Texts from Dublin (Young, 1:349), Meissen (Young, 1:331), Moosburg (Young, 1:362), Prague (Young, 1:345), Rheinau (Young, 1:385).

26. Chambers, *Mediaeval Stage*, 2:35 n. 2: *Labarum* "is the banner of Constantine with the Chi-Ro monogram . . . but the banner usually attached to the cross in mediaeval pictures of the Resurrection itself bears simply a large cross."

    David Bevington and J. Q. Adams suggest that "textum auro paratum" refers to a gold cloth, the "paratorium" used to cover the chalice before and after Mass. See Bevington, *Medieval Drama*, 44; Adams, *Chief Pre-Shakespearean Dramas*, 20. Also possibly a maniple: see Braun, *Gewandung*, 553–34, 538. However, at the conclusion of the Fleury *Peregrinus*, the Risen Lord carries a Gospel-book ("textum Evvangelii"). See Young, 1:474.

    In addition, "filacteria preciosa in capite" could refer to a head covering of cloth rather than to a phylactery, at St. Lambrecht (*Visitatio*, ca. 1200) used to wrap the cross. Young, 1:363, L728.

27. Texts from Rouen (Young, 1:371), St. Gall (Young, 1:667), Brixen (L542a, in Vol. 6), Fleury (Young, 1:395–97), Chiemsee (Young, 1:399, assigned to Nuremberg), Mont-St.-Michel (Young, 1:372), Nottuln (L795), Coutances (Young, 1:408–9), Vich (Donovan, *Liturgical Drama*,

87–91). See Braun, *Gewandung*, 166–67 for *planeta plicata*.

28. Chambers thinks that Christ might have had a "spade, which is exchanged . . . for the cross." See Chambers, *Mediaeval Stage*, 2:35. Wilhelm Creizenach also makes this suggestion in *Geschichte des neueren Dramas*, 1:50.

29. Texts from Klosterneuburg (Young, 1:423*ff.*), Tours (Young, 1:444*ff.*), Benediktbeuern (Young, 1:435).

30. See Young, 1:459 (Sicily), 1:461 (Rouen); Cohen, *Histoire*, 40: "sorte de pèlerines à capuchon que portaient les moines." He is probably referring to the Fleury *Peregrinus*. Contemporary iconography shows us pilgrims and travelers in general dressed in this way. See Mâle, *Religious Art in France*, 141–42. On the *Peregrinus*, see also Pächt, *Rise of Pictorial Narrative*.

31. See Dante Alighieri, *La vita nuova*, 222–23. I am grateful to Professor Mireille Madou, University of Leiden, for this reference. See also Toynbee, *Concise Dictionary of Proper Names*, 403, 412, 463.

32. See also the discussion of the angel (with the word "deinfulatus") in the Fleury *Visitatio*, earlier in the present chapter.

    See the miter, created ca. 1180–1210 by English artisans, illustrated in Staniland, *Medieval Craftsmen*, figs. 7–8.

    The display of his wounds by the Resurrected Christ was conventional, and the wounds themselves became the objects of devotion, especially in the fifteenth and early sixteenth century.

33. Christ wears a phylactery "in capite" at the conclusion of the Fleury *Visitatio*.

    Texts from Sicily (Young, 1:459), Rouen (Young, 1:461), Padua (Young, 1:482), Maastricht (L826), Rouen (Young, 1:693), Fleury (Young, 1:471–75).

    For an analogue in the visual arts, see the wayfarers in Collins, *Production*, fig. 21. See Lipphardt's note on Compostela pilgrims (8:791).

34. Inguanez, "Un dramma della Passione." For the text of the Monte Cassino Passion, see Sticca, *Latin Passion Play*, 66–78; for a translation and important discussion see Edwards, *Monte Cassino Passion*. For an analysis of theatrical values in the text see Owens, "Montecassino Passion Play."

35. Sticca, *Latin Passion Play*, 76–77. Text from Sulmona (Young, 1:701).

36. Texts from the Fleury *Lazarus* (Young, 2:200), Benediktbeuern (Young, 1:522). See Young, 1:521 for the item "Chramer, gip die varwe mier," sung by Mary Magdalen.

37. The following material derives from Wackernell, *Altdeutsche Passionsspiele*; financial records for Bozen, 1514: ccxxxv–ccxlv; for other productions in Bozen, xl–l; for Sterzing, xi.

    See also the Brixen texts and documents published by Lipphardt, L542a in Vol. 6: from Gschwend, *Die Depositio*. The following costume descriptions, dated 1553, are taken from instructions in German to the sacristan in Brixen Cathedral. They are for the staging of a German-Latin Easter play at Brixen, but whether for indoor or outdoor performance we cannot be certain. Salvator has "an alb with red apparels, a humeral veil, a stole, and a cope [ain mantl], all red, and a cingulum." St. John: also a red cope, an alb, a humeral veil with red apparels, and a cingulum. St. Peter: a white cope, an alb, a humeral veil with white apparels, a cingulum, and "the wooden key." St. Thomas: the brown cope with gold fireirons (feur eyssen) and flamcs, an alb, a humeral veil with red apparels, a cingulum, and an old breviary. Mary Magdalen: the blue damask cope. The other two Marys: the two simple blue velvet copes. The Gardener: an iron shovel from the refectory. The two Angels: two simple red stoles. The man who says the final verse at the end of the play: a red deacon's dalmatic (Leviten rockh). In the chest with various unspecified props are also crowns.

Further discussions of these productions are in Chapter 3 of the present study.

38. Wackernell, *Altdeutsche Passionsspiele,* 100, 118, 125.

39. Ibid., 476.

40. Ibid., 200–26, 501.

41. Ibid., 199.

42. Ibid., xcv.

43. D'Ancona, *Origini del teatro italiano,* 1:246–50, 251–53; Meredith and Tailby, *Staging of Religious Drama,* 243–47.

The relationship between the visual arts and the plays is a vexed one, but with regard to Ascension iconography shared by art, drama, and ceremony see Schapiro, "Image of the Disappearing Christ."

44. Texts from Padua (Young, 2:9), Montpellier (Young, 2:12), Rouen (Young, 2:14, 429, 17).

See the examples published by Collins, *Production,* figs. 26–8; to these examples a great many more could be added.

45. Donovan, *Liturgical Drama:* Pleinpied (36–37), Narbonne (35), Toledo (32–33, 44).

46. Trexler, *Journey of the Magi,* 44–75.

47. Texts from Besançon (Young, 2:38 [punctuation not Young's], 434); Limoges (Young, 2:34), Rouen (Young, 2:436), Padua (Young, 2:99), Fleury (Young, 2:87); Young (Young, 2:100) calls these "untidy tunics." The *stricta tunica* was narrow: Braun, *Gewandung,* 288.

48. Texts from Laon (Young, 2:145), Rouen (Young, 2:154–65).

For the text of the Pseudo-Augustinian sermon, see for convenience Young, 2:125–32. Mâle has called attention to the façade of Notre Dame la Grande at Poitiers which has figures with scrolls containing abbreviated texts from the Sermon. See Mâle, *Religious Art in France,* 146–47, fig. 129.

For Priests "in modum Prophetarum" see Young 2:253 (Padua).

49. Text from Rouen (Young, 1:370, 661).

50. These horns, which, if they derive from an earlier exemplar, may predate the later prevalence of horns on Moses in medieval iconography, have been the occasion for a warm debate concerning the influence of liturgical drama on iconography. See Mâle, *L'Art religieux,* 146, for an argument in favor of liturgical drama's priority. See Watson, *Early Iconography of the Tree of Jesse,* 27, for dissent; and Pächt, *Rise of the Pictorial Narrative,* for general affirmation of Mâle's point with analogies from the influence of the *Peregrinus* plays. A survey of the iconography and its possible meanings is in Mellinkoff, *Horned Moses,* especially 28–36.

51. Filipe Fernández Vallejo, *Disertación VI. sobre las Representaciones Poeticas en el Templo, y Sybila de la noche de Navidad,* as quoted by Donovan, *Liturgical Drama,* 43. An illustration in Vallejo's study is cited by Donovan, 41, but not reproduced; it contains a depiction of some significance for the potential costuming of the Sibyl as she appeared at Toledo in the eighteenth century: she wore "a kind of peaked coronet, higher in front than in the back, evidently a symbol of her prophetic powers," and also "a necklace and pendant." See Donovan, 39, 41; the picture is reproduced in Gillet, "*Memorias* of Felipe Fernández Vallejo," 273.

52. Cohen, *Histoire,* 43, assumes that she is wearing red makeup.

Texts from Benediktbeuern (Young, 2:180), Fleury (Young, 2:200), Padua (Young, 2:253).

53. Texts from Vorau (Young, 2:259), Laon (Young, 2:268–71), Beauvais (Young, 2:290–301). The *Daniel* by Hilarius (Young, 2:276–86).

For varieties of Jewish clothing see Mellinkoff, *Outcasts,* 1:59.

In the *Daniel,* Marius Sepet suggests skins or masks for the lions. See Sepet, *Les Prophètes du Christ,* 67.

Young (2:486) quotes from G. Desjardins, *Histoire de la Cathédrale de Beauvais* (Beauvais: Pineau, 1865), 119, 169–70.

54. Young, 2:227–42; Meredith and Tailby, *Staging of Religious Drama,* 207–25. See also Haller, *Figurative Representation.* Haller reprints Young's text and provides a translation.

55. Weiner, *Philippe de Mézières' Description of the "Festum Praesentationis Beatae Mariae,"* 82 n. 15, notes that Ecclesia has been mentioned earlier as a woman. Young, 2:228: "Postea erit quedam mulier pulcherrima etatis circiter XX. annorum."

56. Young, 2:479.

57. Estham, "Medeltida Textilier," 107–22.

Christie, *English Medieval Embroidery,* 3. See also Rickert, *Painting in Britain,* 138.

At a later date there were attempts to raise silkworms in France and even England; see Serres, *Perfect Use of Silk-Wormes.*

58. King and Levey, *Victoria and Albert Museum's Textile Collection,* 21, 37, figs. 8–9; Staniland, *Medieval Craftsmen,* fig. 16.

59. Fitch, "London Makers of Opus Anglicanum," 294–95.

60. Lespinasse, *Les Métiers et corporations,* 2:166–67. For a useful translation and discussion see Staniland, *Medieval Craftsmen,* 13–14. See also Depping, *Réglemens sur les arts,* 379–82.

Walton, "Textiles," 322–23.

61. Cennini, *Il libro dell'arte,* 2:105. Making designs on silk could be more complicated and might involve somewhat different techniques than for ordinary cloth; see Cennini, 106–7. For some general remarks on textiles with regard to their production for the later vernacular plays, see Davidson, *Technology, Guilds, and Early English Drama,* 57–79.

62. Wackernell, *Altdeutsche Passionsspiele,* 438. In the Michael Passion (fifteenth and sixteenth century), intended for outdoor production, Satan disguised himself three times in this episode—as a hermit, a doctor, and finally as a king. Douhet, *Dictionnaire des mystères,* 715–16.

Chapter 5: Acting

1. Migne, *Patrologia Latina,* 105:989: "Sacramenta debent habere similitudinem aliquam earum rerum quarum sacramenta sunt. Quapropter, similis sit sacerdos Christo, sicut panis et liquor similia sunt corpori Christi. Sic est immolatio sacerdotis in altari quodammodo ut Christi immolatio in cruce."

For major work relative to the present study of acting see the following: Garnier, *Le Langage de l'image au moyen âge;* Roeder, *Die Gebärde im Drama des Mittelalters;* Davidson, *Gesture.*

2. Translation from Hardison, *Christian Rite,* 39–40. Text in Migne, *Patrologia Latina,* 172:570; quote from Young, 1:83.

Sciendum quod hi qui tragoedias in theatris rectibant, actus pugnantium gestibus populo repraesentabant. Sic tragicus noster pugnam Christi populo Christiano in theatro Ecclesiae gestibus suis repraesentat, eique victoriam redemptionis suae inculcat. Itaque cum presbyter *Orate* dicit, Christum pro nobis in agonia positum exprimit, cum apostolos orare monuit. Per secretum silentium, significat Christum velut agnum sine voce ad victimam ductum. Per manuum expansionem, designat Christi in cruce extensionem. Per cantum praefationis, exprimit clamorem Christi in cruce pendentis. Decem namque psalmos, scilicet a *Deus meus respice* usque *In manus tuas commendo spiritum meum* cantavit, et sic exspiravit. Per Canonis secretum innuit Sabbati silentium. Per pacem, et communicationem designat pacem datam post Christi resurrectionem et gaudii communicationem. Confecto sacramento, pax et communio populo a sacerdote datur, quia accusatore nostro ab agonotheta nostro per duellum prostrato, pax a judica populo denuntiatur, ad convivium invitatur. Deinde ad propria redire cum gaudio per *Ite missa est* imperatur. Qui gratias Deo jubilat et gaudens domum remeat.

3. In this list of twenty-three, I include a thirteenth-century *Visitatio* from the women's convent of Wöltingerrode (L766). It is closely related to other north German convents where women did play the Marys (e.g., Gernrode), but the text does not divulge that information. Interestingly, the Wöltingerrode *Visitatio* concludes with three German hymns in the vernacular, the populus joining in.

   In addition, Walther Lipphardt published a fourteenth-century *Visitatio* fragment from the women's convent of Wienhausen, near Celle. It was found under the floor of the nuns' choir area. It consists chiefly of Magdalen's exchange with the Risen Christ. A rhymed German paraphrase follows each speech. See Lipphardt, "Die Visitatio Sepulchri."

   See also a somewhat different version of this section in Ogden, "Women Play Women."

4. Rankin, "Mary Magdalene Scene," 241, 250.

   Another indication that nuns were creating their own individual versions of the *Visitatio Sepulchri* comes from the St. Thomas convent in Andernach. There a fourteenth-century manuscript (L355a) includes two, alternative melodies to the "Surrexit Dominus," the joyous antiphon that climaxes the *Visitatio*. To the best of my knowledge, it is the only such musical choice among the manuscripts of the liturgical drama. In addition, the superscript over this drama is unique: "Ordo Ad Sepulcrum Angelorum."

5. At Origny the three Marys kneel and kiss the gravecloth held by Peter and John, a gesture no doubt linked with a relic in the treasury of the nunnery (L825). Two other texts from Origny say that at the conclusion of the *Visitatio* the townspeople (les bonnes gens) are to be allowed to kiss the reliquaries (L303, L303a).

   At Wilton, a *Visitatio* with many strong textual and musical links to Origny, the three Marys venerate (adorent) a book extended to them by a subdeacon, and the nuns and the townspeople kiss it (omnis et populus).

6. For information about the *Confiteor*, the *Misereatur*, and the *Indulgentiam* throughout this period, see Jungmann, *Mass of the Roman Rite.*

   I wish to thank Professor Joseph Duggan for his help in translating the medieval French and Richard D. McCall for his discussions of Jungmann et al. Any errors in the analysis of this purification rite are mine, not theirs.

7. Other Marys played by women who dress in white are at Barking and Troyes, as already noted, where they also say Confession before performing—to the Abbess at Barking and to a priest at Troyes—and at Wilton, where they first wash their hands. At Regensburg-Obermünster they dress in the overgarments also used for the Maundy observances (washing of feet, feeding of the poor). At Gernrode they dress in special nuns' habits.

For men's performances, the only Marys in white are at Dublin, with surplices, and Mont-St.-Michel, with boys as the women (iuveni) in white dalmatics with the hoods pulled up "in the manner of matrons [women]" (dalmaticis albis, habentes amicta super capita ad modum Matronarum).

   At Barking and at Marienberg the women prepare to perform the Mary-roles in the Mary Magdalen Chapel.

8. At Rouen Cathedral an angel points with his finger to the sepulchre (L776).

   The *Visitatio Sepulchri* at Winchester and at Rouen served as models for Barking. Barking, in turn, served as a model for Dublin. Rouen also served as a model for Origny. See, for example, Dolan, *Drame liturgique de Pâques,* 137*ff.*

9. Mary Magdalen also prostrates herself before the Risen Christ at the nunnery of Nottuln, but this is part of a little four-phase ceremony where she sings three pieces, genuflecting to Jesus at each of the first two and prostrating herself at the third, whereupon Jesus bends down and raises her up and blesses her. There is no "Noli me tangere" moment.

   Rouen provided one of the models or sources for the author-composer of the Origny *Visitatio.* However, Mary Magdalen is not further singled out there save as *medius mulierum.*

   At Wilton the three Marys approach the sepulchre and prostrate themselves "one by one" when the angel invites them, "Venite et videte."

10. Mary Magdalen at Barking points with her finger to the place "where the angel was sitting" (ubi Angelus sedebat), the only overt indication of an exit by the angel(s).

   At Sainte-Chapelle, Paris, the first two Marys point with their fingers to the sepulchre and to the angels respectively. L148–49. In the *Visitatio* at Rouen, it is the angel who points with his finger—singing "Non est hic" and indicating the sepulchre to the Marys. At Narbonne, Magdalen points with her finger to the angels. At Rheinau (a very ceremonial, late text, ca. 1600) a priest points with his finger to the angels.

   Gesturing toward the sepulchre, the angels, and the gravecloth(s) occurs somewhat more frequently. At Dublin two of the three Marys respond *quasi monstrando* to "Dic nobis, Maria?". At Tours, Mary Magdalen indicates four times with a gesture (e.g., *Maria ostendat eis Sepulchrum*)—toward the sepulchre, the angel, the sudary, and the cross—and two or three times at Maastricht. At Besançon, the second Mary shows or points to the gravecloths and the angels (ostendens sudarium et vestes et Angelos). At Padua, Magdalen gestures toward the angels and the gravecloth; in a later text, toward the sepulchre and then the angels. And in a late (1582), very ceremonial text from St. Gall four boys as angels gesture with their hands toward the sepulchre. L331.

   The Magdalen character in the Cathedral of Rouen displays and unfolds the gravecloth(s) during the Easter play of *The Wayfarer,* the *Officium Peregrinorum* (ostendat et explicet unum syndonem ex una parte loco sudarii, et alium ex altera parte loco vestium).

   The rare "Spes nostra" (Our hope) instead of "Spes mea" (My hope) in the Origny text also occurs at Barking; and at Le Mans (L113, L114), and in a body of Parisian texts (L123–49).

11. A thirteenth- and fourteenth-century text from Origny (L303, L303a) have "les bonnes gens" permitted to kiss reliquaries at the sepulchre following the performance. During the *Depositio* at Essen, an ivory-bound missal from the eleventh century, one of the treasures of the cathedral, was carried in procession and placed in the sepulchre. For other uses of texts as sacred treasures, see L9, L25, L49, L50, L74 (gold), L728, L779.

12. It is possible that at Barking the Holy Trinity Altar was at the western end of the church, a traditional locus for "Galilee." See the "Galilee" discussion in Chapter 3, regarding Fleury. See note 7 above on costume.

Note the useful English translation of the *Depositio, Elevatio* (with the Harrowing of Hell), and *Visitatio* from Barking in Meredith and Tailby, *Staging of Religious Drama*, 226–29.

13. The quotation from the Gospel of Luke appears in but one other liturgical drama: in the Mont-St.-Michel text. It is not an antiphon. Young, 1:373.

14. Jesus' reappearance to the three Marys together and their prostration—but not the holding and kissing—also occurs in the older Rouen text, a major source for Barking and Origny.

Roeder, *Die Gebärde*, 60–61: "In dieser Feier erscheinen drei Formen des Kusses: Altarkuss [richtiger: der Kuss der Stelle im Hl. Grab, wo der Herr gelegen hat—W.L.], Fusskuss und Kuss der Leintücher. Es sind liturgische Gebärden, die in dieser Feier an theatralisch-wirkungsvoller Stelle in den Darstellungszusammenhang eingegliedert sind." (Three forms of the kiss occur in this ceremony: kissing the altar [more correctly: kissing the place in the sepulchre where the Lord's body had lain—W.L. (inserted note by Walther Lipphardt)], kissing the feet, and kissing the gravecloths. In this ceremony these are liturgical gestures inserted into the framework of performance and positioned for theatrical effect.)

Also as at Origny (and at Le Mans, and in a group of Parisian texts), the Magdalen of Barking sings "Spes nostra" instead of the usual "Spes mea." L113–14; L123–49.

15. By "emphasis on Magdalen" I mean something more than her carrying a pyxe between two thurible-bearing Marys or her singing the *Dic nobis, Maria* exchange. I mean: to add at least an extra gesture, or, at the farther range, to include a scene such as her recognition of the Risen Christ. In regard to whether men or women played the Marys, four *Visitatio* texts remain especially puzzling and tantalizing. Each contains a major Mary-Magdalen role as well as elaborate and detailed stage directions for acting, particularly for the expression of emotion: manuscripts from the Cathedrals of Braunschweig and Coutances, respectively; a manuscript from the monastery of Egmond but which may derive from Rijnsberg, the nunnery linked to Egmond; and from the Municipal Library of Tours a manuscript whose ecclesiastical link we do not know. It is possible that nuns or canonesses took the roles of the Marys in all four. However, I have counted three among the twenty-one men's texts, setting aside the Tours manuscript.

16. See, e.g., Haskins, *Mary Magdalen.*

A fourteenth-century manuscript from a Strassburg Magdalen Convent includes singing the *Dic nobis, Maria* during an *Elevatio* but no *Visitatio Sepulchri* (L343).

17. The earliest *Visitatio* texts with Mary Magdalen as a character: from Vich in Spain (possibly eleventh century), and St. George Nunnery in Prague (twelfth century).

The thrice-repeated "Maria/Raboni" exchange from Wienhausen published by Lipphardt, "Visitatio Sepulchri ."

For additional scripts for performers see Aschaffenburg (L501, L503), Mainz (L260), and Verdun (L361–362a).

18. A singular situation is recorded by the 1438 *Visitatio* text from the St. Julia Convent in Brescia. It is one of the rare Italian documents linked with this drama. There two nuns as angels were led by the "cantoria" (cantoria accipiant duas dominas)—"cantoria" presumably the lead singers (male or female?)—to the high altar, and then three nuns (tres dominas) as the Marys were led to the middle of the (east) choir.

Thereupon they sang the "Quem quaeritis" exchange across the high altar. No male clergy seems to be involved. This little ceremonial observance is also singular in that it segues seamlessly into the Introit of the Mass. It does not occur at the close of Matins, just before the concluding *Te Deum*. And as a prelude to Mass, one or more priest-celebrants had to be present. Although the manuscript itself comes from a late date, it records an ancient practice, perhaps even predating our earliest secure evidence for the *Visitatio* played by women. In addition, the Brescia text documents the only *Visitatio* where women sang the roles of angels.

19. Michael, "Fahrendes Volk," 3–8.

20. Most of the following references in this chapter are to Young, Donovan, *Liturgical Drama* ("D"), and Lipphardt ("L"). References are preceded where relevant by the date of the respective manuscript. References to Young are given without author identification, and without volume number if the material is published in his first volume, and are given with "2" if the material appears in his second volume. "L" refers not to a page number but to a text number in the Lipphardt volumes.

Deacons as Marys with priests as angels: eleventh century, 241; twelfth century, 215; thirteenth century, 302.

Deacons as Marys with boys as angels: thirteenth century, 279, 293; fifteenth century, 602, 661; seventeenth century, 603.

Clerici as Marys with deacons as angels: anno 1384, L447; fifteenth century, L449.

Canons as Marys with deacons as angels: anno 1400, L762.

Priests as Marys, deacons as angels: annis 1192–96, L190a; annis 1192–96, L190b; fifteenth century, L192; fourteenth–fifteenth centuries, L352.

Presbyters as Marys, deacons as angels: fifteenth century, L485; anno 1515, L545; fifteenth century, L599a; sixteenth century, L600a; anno 1160, L694; fourteenth century, L695; anno 1439, L698; fifteenth century, L706; annis 1220–60, L756; fifteenth century, L765.

Fratres as Marys, deacons as angels: anno 1364, L633.

Oblates (*Obleiarii, Oblaiarii, Oblatarii*) as Marys, deacons as angels: fifteenth century?, L647–49, L654–55.

Deacons as Marys, priests as angels: anno 1240, L269; anno 1324, L279.

Deacons as angels: anno 1500, L795; annis 1192–98, L468; eleventh century, L472; fourteenth–fifteenth centuries, L736.

Deacons as Marys: 1480, L308; twelfth century, L315.

At Mainz (dated 1547) three senior priests carried lights and sang the Mary roles from books (614, L260).

In the *Visitatio* at St. Edith's, Wilton, a priest played both the angel and the Risen Christ. See Rankin, "New English Source of the *Visitatio Sepulchri*."

21. Players of shepherds: 2:8, 9, 12, 14, 428; D34, D35, D36, D125.
Players of Kings: 2:34, 37, 43, 50, 434, 436, 437.
Players of midwives: 2:8, 9, 12, 14, 16, 428, 435, 437, 448.
Boys as angels in *Visitatio*: 219, 244, 257, 265, 279, 293, 372, 408, 599, 602, 603, 614, 615, 632, 661; L87, L106, L373, L453, L454, L464, L492, L494, L536a, L536d, L536q, L536r, L536x, L536y, L576d, L579g, L746.

Clerici as angels: 228, 262, 580, 591, 592, 648, 649; L408, L615a, L738.

Boys as Marys: L453, L454, L464, L536k. Were the oblates boys in Passau texts? (See preceding note.)

Boys as Christ Resurrectus: L456a, L459.

Boys as shepherds: Montpellier (2:12), German text (2:448), Clermont-Ferrand (2:12).

At Troyes (thirteenth century, 603) a special instructor taught the "ij enfans" who played the angels, while at Padua (thirteenth century, 294) and Fritzlar (fifteenth century, 257) *scolares* acted all of the roles, appropriately accompanied in the former instance by the *magister scolarum.* Youths impersonated the women at Mont-St.-Michel (fourteenth century, 575) and at Worms (fifteenth century, 591); and choir boys were even cast as Peter and John at Bamberg (anno 1587, 323).

In Canon Vallejo's eighteenth-century description of a shepherds' play at Toledo, certain chanters step forward and take two of the shepherds by the hands to sing with them a vernacular song (D33).

22. Vasari, *Le vite,* 1:627–31.

23. Boys: Vorau (2:259), Cleves (592–93).

Children impersonated the twelve apostles, if not all of the characters, in the fifteenth-century *Planctus* from Regensburg (513), and in the sixteenth century they acted out the *Annunciation* at Saint-Omer (2:482) and Tournai (2:480), requiring the services of a tutor.

24. Peter and John: St. Lambrecht (364), Rheinau (385), Zurich (314), Essen (333), Augsburg (645), Meissen (331), Moosburg (362–63). For Peter's limp, see also L632 (Vorau).

25. Haller, *Figurative Representation,* 27.

26. Sulmona (701); Shrewsbury (2:514).

Orlando Furioso, actor's part, in Greg, *Dramatic Documents from the Elizabethan Playhouses.*

27. Vocal quality: Aldersbach (649), Strassburg (L344), Aschaffenburg (L503), Melk (L615a), St. Florian (355), Vienna (L762), Passau (354, 646, 652, 655; L647, L654), Tournai (2:480).

28. Marienberg bei Helmstedt (L791), Meissen (331), Moosburg (362–63), Sion (L746).

29. In regard to *voce alta* as referring to "intensity," see the discussion of vocal ideals in the Middle Ages by Vellekoop, "De klank van licht en donker."

30. Likewise, a fifteenth-century text from Urgel directs that the *Venite et videte* be sung "ter, prima vice alta, secunda alciori, tertia altissima" (L464); a text dated 1700 from Neuenherse directs that *Surrexit Dominus de sepulchro* be sung "ter semper altius" (L624).

Essen (334). The manuscripts of Haarlem (320) are now in Utrecht, Rijksmuseum Het Catharijneconvent. Dublin (349–50).

31. *Visitatio* texts showing vocal contrast, Melk (241–42), Winchester (581–82).

See also: St. Lambrecht (twelfth century, fourteenth century, 363); Zwiefalten (twelfth century, 266); Prüfening and Rheinau (twelfth century, thirteenth century, 597); Cividale (fourteenth century, 268); Hirsau (fifteenth century, 596); Magdeburg (fifteenth century, 630); Worms (fifteenth century, 591). See especially Chiemsee (cited as Nuremberg, thirteenth century, 399) and Coutances (fifteenth century, 408).

The following example from the *Peregrinus* of Fleury where the two wayfarers sing in a medium voice (modica uoce) and Christ in a grave or deep voice (graui uoce) is the only evidence known to me in this drama of Christ's voice quality. However, the medieval *Passio,* the forerunner of Bach's *Passionen,* may present an analogous situation. The four Gospel narratives of the Passion were sung during Holy Week, divided into three "singing parts": a high pitch for Synagoga (the people in the narrative),

medium pitch for the narrator-Evangelist, and low pitch for Christ. Until rather late in the Middle Ages all three parts were sung by a single deacon, completely in keeping with the intoning of the Gospel by a cantor every day of the year. There was nothing dramatic here. As John Stevens puts it, through these long narratives one should "see the three *voces* [sic] as clarifying features rather than anything more subtle." See Stevens, *Words and Music in the Middle Ages,* 321; see also Schuler, *Die Musik der Osterfeiern.*

32. Vocal contrast in rhythm of performance: Fleury (471), Sicily (480), Rouen (2:436), Fleury (2:110), Padua (2:249), Benediktbeuern (2:176–77), *Presentation* (2:233–38), Chiemsee (cited as Nuremberg, 398–400).

33. The raised voice: Hilarius' *Daniel* (2:286), *Purification* (2:254), Fleury *St. Paul* (2:221), Tours (446), *Presentation* (2:233ff.), Limoges *Officium Stellae* (2:34).

34. The raised voice, exuberance: Fleury shepherds (2:88), Beauvais *Daniel* (2:300), Rouen (660), Wilton (Rankin, "New English Source," 8, 10).

35. Sound of exclamation: Beauvais *Daniel* (2:297, 301, 292, 300), St. Lambrecht (365), Essen (334), Benediktbeuern (515, 516), Laon (2:270).

36. Sorrow and lamentation: *Visitatio* (324 querla voce, 347, 409), Wilton (Rankin, "New English Source," 6), Beauvais *Daniel* (2:300), Freising (2:119), Fleury *Lazarus* (2:207), Benediktbeuern (524, 530), Fleury *Getron* (2:353), Fleury *Tres Filiae* (2:318), Benediktbeuern (523, 529, 530).

37. Grief and consolation: Winchester (581), Fleury (394), Coutances (408), Zwiefalten (266), Barking (382).

38. I am particularly indebted to Professor Kees Vellekoop at the University of Utrecht for his judgments here as to such matters as loudness and pitch, and for guiding me to information on terminology regarding French instruments and the singing voices of the medieval *Passio.*

39. Gentle or soft voice: Rouen *Officium Stellae* (2:436, 437), Chiemsee (cited as Nuremberg, 399), Havelberg (668), Zwiefalten (267), Prüfening and Rheinau (597), Hirsau (596).

40. Moments of verisimilitude: Vorau (2:260), Fleury *Getron* (2:356), Barking (383), Coutances (409), *Antichrist* (2:378), Fleury *Lazarus* (2:207), Klosterneuburg (428), Benediktbeuern (2:176).

41. Cividale (268), Chiemsee (cited as Nuremberg, 398).

42. Münster (602), Bamberg (324), Paris (L120).

43. Winchester (249), Paris, Sainte-Chapelle (287), Winchester (249), Fleury (393), Chalon-sur-Saône (L103).

44. Fécamp (264).

45. Meissen (L612), Zurich (315); *Peregrinus,* Rouen (461).

46. Barking (383), Gandersheim (L785), Fleury (394), Chiemsee (cited as Nuremberg, 399).

47. Strassburg (L344), Rheinau (385).

48. Fécamp (264), Coutances (409), Verdun (578).

49. Silence: Nottuln (L795), Augsburg (310), St. Lambrecht (363), Prüfening and Rheinau (597), Hirsau (596), Benediktbeuern (528).

50. Text of *Adam:* Aebischer, *Le Mystère d'Adam.* Translation of *Adam* in Stone, *Adam.* For simple chant settings of the blocks of liturgical music that mark the *Adam,* see Axton and Stevens, "Le Jeu d' Adam." Text of *Planctus Mariae:* Young, 507–12.

For a discussion of staging possibilities see Muir, *Liturgy and Drama in the Anglo-Norman "Adam,"* including consideration of Willem Noomen's attempt to locate the play inside the church—"Note sur l'élément liturgique du *Jeu d'Adam,*" 635–38; and Noomen, "Le *Jeu d'Adam.*" Noomen put his case succinctly in his edition of *Le Jeu d'Adam*, 13: ". . . il est question d'une *ecclesia* (l. 252, etc.), où se retire Figura; il est permis d'hésiter s'il faut entendre par ce terme l'église devant laquelle la pièce était jouée, ou une construction se trouvant à l'intérieur du bâtiment. Dans le premier cas, la représentation aurait lieu hors de l'église, dans le second, à l'intérieur. Le sens qu'on donnera au mot *chorus* (l. 1282), qui désigne le lieu où se lit la leçon *Vos, inquam, convenio, o Judei,* dépend de la solution qu'on adoptera."

The devil also appears at this comparatively early date in the twelfth-century *Ordo Virtutum* (ca. 1155), by Hildegard von Bingen: "Strepitus Diaboli." Unlike all other dialogue in the play, his speeches have no music. Hildegard describes his delivery of his lines with *strepitus*—clamor, uproar, shrieking. See, for example, Barth, et al., *Hildegard von Bingen, Lieder;* Herwegen, *Reigen der Tugenden;* and the facsimile in Gmelch, *Die Kompositionen der heil. . . .*

Hildegard, from Rupertsberg and Eibingen (Rüdesheim), reminds one of Hrotswitha von (nearby) Gandersheim (tenth century), with her six Christian imitations of Terence's plays, perhaps intended for formal, static recital just as the morality play *Ordo Virtutum* seems intended for formal, static singing rather than as a play to be acted out with gesture and movement.

For a discussion of possibly direct links between mimes and the medieval music-drama, see Hunningher, *Origin of the Theater,* 63–83. He drew attention to the important miniatures of performers in a Troparium from St. Martial de Limoges (MS. Lat. 1118, dated 988–996, Bibliothèque Nationale, Paris), but in my view he pressed his evidence too hard when he wished to see medieval mimes as "the tropes' performers" (83). For one thing, the music of "Quem quaeritis," the *Visitatio Sepulchri,* and the received liturgy interweaves and continues to interweave so intimately that to posit an "outside," non-ecclesiastical creator and performer seems farfetched. In addition, a thousand rubrics tell us about ecclesiastical performers; none, save for some people in Mézières' *Presentation* (Young, vol. 2), about secular players. On the other hand, there may well have been later influence from the so-called mimes on works such as the Beauvais *Daniel,* while surely professional players had a strong hand in the outdoor drama—both religious and secular—which was spoken (not sung) and performed in the vernacular.

51. Body language: Rouen (370), Vorau (2:260), Moosburg (361), Meissen (331), Rouen (2:158), Laon (2:145), Benediktbeuern (2:173, 175).

52. Montpellier *Officium Stellae* (2:68).
Weiner, *Philippe de Mézières' Description of the "Festum Praesentationis Beatae Mariae,"* 36.

53. Frank, *Medieval French Drama,* 35.

54. Cividale (380).

55. Acts of awe, homage, humility, respect, reverence: Einsiedeln (391), Rouen (660), Wilton (Rankin, "New English Source," 6–11), Rheinau (387), Barking (383), Münster (664), Benediktbeuern (518), Fleury *Lazarus* (2:200); Beauvais *Peregrinus* (467), Tours (438), Benediktbeuern (465), Fleury *Peregrinus* (474), Fleury *Tres Filiae* (2:320); Montpellier (2:70), Sens (615), Fleury *Officium Stellae* (2:84), Sulmona (701), Laon (2:269); *Ascension,* Wesselofsky, "Italienische Mysterien," 437, 439; *Presentation* (2:235).

56. Special shows of reverence: Beauvais *Daniel* (2:290); Toul (263); *Annunciation,* Wesselofsky, "Italienische Mysterien," 430.

57. Running, hastening: Verdun (578), Rheinau (387), Chiemsee (cited as Nuremberg, 400), Fleury *Getron* (2:356).

58. Search steps: Winchester (581), Fleury (393), Prüfening (597), Rheinau (597), Aquileia (313), Wilton (Rankin, "New English Source," 6), Indersdorf (331), Rouen (461).

59. Grief: Tours (443), Coutances (409), Freising (2:120), Fleury *Ordo Rachelis* (2:112), Fleury *Lazarus* (2:206). At Barking, too, Magdalen sighs (suspirando concinat) when she commences the *Te suspiro* (383).
Wesselofsky, "Italienische Mysterien," 438: "Die Apostel neigen sich gegen einander, weinen und sagen wehklagend: Herr, verlasse uns nicht. . . ."; Haller, *Figurative Representation,* 23; Young, 2:238.

60. Fear, anxiety: Klosterneuberg (423), Sulmona (702), Coutances (408), Fleury *Officium Stellae* (2:84), Laon *Joseph* (2:269), *Presentation* (2:238, translation mine), Nottuln (L795), Benediktbeuern (2:175).

61. Shock and confusion: Hilarius' *Daniel* (2:278), Beauvais *Daniel* (2:292), *Antichrist* (2:381), Benediktbeuern (2:180). *Peregrinus*—Beauvais (468), Rouen (462), Fleury (472). Fleury *St. Paul* (2:220).

62. Anger: Benediktbeuern (2:184), Freising (2:95), Montpellier (2:71), Fleury *Officium Stellae* (2:87), Bilsen (2:77), Fleury *Ordo Rachelis* (2:110), Benediktbeuern (2:175), Fleury *St. Paul* (2:220), *Presentation* (2:239).
It is in an indignant mood that Thomas in the Tours *Ludus Paschalis* expresses his refusal to believe the Resurrection story (quasi indignatus, 446).

63. Affection: Laon *Joseph* (2:273), Benediktbeuern (531), Padua *Annunciation* (2:248).

64. The rubrics of the church plays contain a vocabulary of ritual. These ritualistic observances are embedded in the dramatic action: *abluo* (to cleanse, wash), *absolvo* (to absolve, pardon), *adoleo* (to make fragrant, cense), *adoro* (to adore, worship), *aspergo* (to sprinkle [with holy water]), *benedictio victualium* (blessing of the meal), *benedictio* (blessing), *communico* (to receive communion, to communicate), *communio* (communion), *confero . . . pax* (bring together . . . the kiss of peace), *deosculo* (to kiss), *divido* (to divide . . . the host), *flecto* (to bend . . . the knees), *frango* (to break . . . bread), *geniculo* (to genuflect), *humi prostrate* (bowed to the ground), *incenso* (to cense), *incensum porrigo* (to direct incense at), *lavo* (to wash . . . the altars/ . . . the feet), *offero* (to offer, donate), *osculo* (to kiss), *ostencio* (to show . . . /exhibit . . . the cross), *pax* (peace, kiss of peace), *salutatio* (greeting, adoration, kissing), *saluto* (to greet, salute, kiss), *thurifico* (to cense), *triplici ductu* (with a triple swing [of the thurible]), *tumulo* (to bury, entomb).

65. Pax: Fleury *Officium Stellae* (2:85), Compiègne (2:54), Montpellier (2:70), Tours (445), Benediktbeuern (515). Greeting, blessing: Tournai *Annunciation* (2:481), Fleury *Peregrinus* (473), *Presentation* (2:237), Fleury *Peregrinus* (472), Beauvais *Peregrinus* (468). Consecration: *Presentation* (2:237), *Antichrist* (2:377), Besançon (2:434).
Prayer: Lazarus—Hilarius (2:217), Fleury (2:208); Benediktbeuern (525), Fleury *Getron* (2:355), *Presentation* (2:240), Tournai *Annunciation* (2:481), Fleury *Officium Stellae* (2:89), Rouen (2:436, 438), Rouen (2:44, 437).

66. Additional verbs in handling props and dealing with set pieces: *aufero* (bring to), *claudo* (close), *compulsatio* (strike together), *cooperio* (to cover), *defero* (carry away . . . the cross/ . . . gifts), *denudo* (strip . . . the altar), *depono* (take off, put down), *detego* (uncover, discover), *differo* (carry away), *discooperio* (to uncover, reveal), *distributio* (to distribute . . . candles), *elevo* (lift up), *excipio* (to take out, remove), *expando* (spread out), *expendo* (spread out), *extendo* (stretch

out), *extinguo* (put out, extinguish), *extollo* (lift up), *fero* (bring, carry), *impono* (put in, place), *levo* (lift, raise), *ligo* (tie), *loco* (place), *paro* (prepare), *patefacio* (open, make open), *pono* (put, place), *praefero* (bring forth, bring forward), *pro(h)icio* (*nebulae*, throw forth clouds [of some sort]), *pulso* (pound, beat), *pulsus* (knock), *recondo* (hide, conceal), *repono* (put back, lay to rest), *subinfero* (add, subjoin), *subiungo* (add, subjoin), *sublevo* (lift up), *sumo* (take up, pick up), *teneo* (hold), *tollo* (lift, raise up), *traho* (*baculum*, draw, raise . . . their staffs), *velo* (cover, veil).

67. Daily exchange indicated by speech ascriptions: *affor* (speak to, address), *amplecto* (embrace), *audio* (hear), *considero* (contemplate, consider), *detineo* (detain), *devito* (avoid), *dico* (say), *discumbo* (recline), *existimo* (suppose, consider), *interrogo* (ask, question), *invito* (invite), *loquor* (speak, say), *ordino* (set in order), *puto* (think, suppose).

68. Action verbs in the rubrics: *accendo* (ignite, burn), *adhaereo* (cling to), *agnosco* (know, recognize), *aspicio* (look in, peer in), *compello* (force), *converto* (turn together), *corrumpo* (corrupt), *descendo* (climb down), *diverto* (turn away), *duco* (lead), *eicio* (throw away), *evanesco* (vanish, disappear), *introspicio* (look inside), *invenio* (find, come upon), *iubeo* (order, command), *nitor* (struggle), *nuncio* (announce), *peto* (seek), *pisco* (fish), *procido* (fall down), *procumbo* (lie down), *prosequor* (follow), *prospicio* (look in, peer in), *recognosco* (recognize), *remaneo* (stay behind), *respicio* (look back), *respondeo* (answer), *retineo* (hold back), *reverto* (turn back, turn around), *se associo* (fall in, around, with), *sepelio* (bury, entomb), *signo* (seal), *subsequor* (follow), *subsisto* (stand below), *subtraho* (draw away), *tango* (touch), *traho* (draw . . . back), *trudo* (knock), *verto* (turn—*alter altero*, one to another), *visito* (go and see, visit).

69. Summary catalogue, movement and gesture: Verdun (578), Fleury *Getron* (2:357), Fleury *Lazarus* (2:206), Benediktbeuern (525), Winchester (581), Fleury *Visitatio* (393), Rouen *Peregrinus* (461), Tournai *Annunciation* (2:481), Fleury *St. Paul* (2:220), Laon (2:269), Beauvais *Peregrinus* (468), Rouen *Peregrinus* (462), *Antichrist* (2:375).

   Head, eyes: Wesselofsky, "Italienische Mysterien," 430; Moosburg *Ascension* (487); Wesselofsky, 437.

   Hand, arm: Benediktbeuern (436), Tours (446), Origny (419), Rheinau (387), Rouen (371, 661), Benediktbeuern (531), Wesselofsky (p. 430), Tours (443); Fleury *Getron* (2:355), *Presentation* (2:237), Moosburg (487), Padua *Annunciation* (2:249), *Antichrist* (2:387), Benediktbeuern (516, 532), *Presentation* (2:238, 234), Tournai *Annunciation* (2:481), Rouen *Visitatio* (370, 661), Rouen *Peregrinus* (461, 693), Beauvais *Daniel* (2:291).

70. Especially mimed moments: Padua (107), St. Lambrecht (363), Chiemsee (cited as Nuremberg, 398), Rouen (461, 693), Fleury *Peregrinus* (471), Fleury *Officium Stellae* (2:87), *Presentation* (2:241), Tournai *Annunciation* (2:481) and *Presentation* (2:234), Benediktbeuern (2:181), Laon *Ordo Rachelis* (2:104), Paris, Sainte-Chapelle (288), Coutances (408), Sulmona (701), Benediktbeuern (514*ff.*, 418*ff.*), Laon *Joseph* (2:269); Wesselofsky, "Italienische Mysterien," 431.

71. Eating, sleeping, washing, dressing: Fleury *Peregrinus* (472), Fleury *Lazarus* (2:200), Fleury *Getron* (2:355), Benediktbeuern (514), Vorau *Isaac* (2:259), Fleury *Getron* (2:356), Benediktbeuern (521); Tegernsee *Antichrist* (2:378), Benediktbeuern (528); Mone, *Altteutsche Schauspiele.*

72. Extended mime or dumb show: Tegernsee *Antichrist* (2:377, 379), Fleury *Getron* (2:352), *Daniel* (2:281, 297),

Fleury *Ordo Rachelis* (2:111), Benediktbeuern (2:189), *Isaac* (2:261), Laon (2:270).

   Hunninger, *Origin of the Theater*, 63–83, discusses what he considers to be the very influential role of medieval mimes, both in the inception of the liturgical drama and in its later manifestations.

Chapter 6: The Music

1. Stevens, *Words and Music in the Middle Ages*, 345–46; transcription of the *Officium Pastorum*, Rouen, 339–44.

   The shepherds' song "Pax in terris" also appears in two contemporary collections of songs. According to musicologist Susan Rankin, this evidence may indicate that the song was composed "quite independently of the play." See Rankin, "Liturgical Drama," 2:346.

2. Wherever "Quem quaeritis" appeared as a trope prior to Mass, either at Easter or at Christmas, it remained a trope, never becoming part of a liturgical drama.

3. Crocker, "Medieval Chant," 2:283, 293–94.

4. Smoldon, "Easter Sepulchre," 17.

   Smoldon pioneered in his mastery of musical sources and his insistence that one is "dealing not with dramas, but *music*-dramas, or, in other words, *operas.*" This attention to relationships between drama and music pervades his posthumously published book, *Music of the Medieval Church Dramas*; see page v.

   Two exceptions to the single-line plainchant of these dramas are found in the *Purification* from Padua (fourteenth century), where angels twice sing in two-part harmony, and in the Shrewsbury fragments (fourteenth century), where two passages of the Easter play indicate three-part harmony. See Vecchi, *Uffici drammatici padovani*, 24–31; Waterhouse, *Non-Cycle Mystery Plays*, 1–7.

5. Rankin, "Liturgical Drama," 331.

6. Note: "crecit" should read "crescit" in the music example: see L781, and Young, 1:378–80.

   Smoldon, "Easter Sepulchre," 13. See in addition Smoldon's discussion in *Music of the Medieval Church Dramas*, 370–72.

   In this context, it is important to note that melismatic passages can also serve in the chant as rhetorical markers, demonstrative rather than expressive or even affective in the sense of mood creating.

7. Stevens, *Words and Music in the Middle Ages*, 355.

8. Transcriptions of the lament by *Judaeus*: Wagenaar-Nolthenius, "Der *Planctus Iudei*," 884 (with numbered lines, and musical phrases under discussion marked). Discussion follows this transcription.

   Collins, *Medieval Church Music-Dramas*, 348–53.

   Notation at lines 20 and 21 of *The Image of St. Nicholas* (*Iconia Sancti Nicolai*). Line 20: in his transcription Collins starts the second sweep on high *f*. Line 21: in his transcription Collins makes the high *e* both times into an *e*-flat and the finale a seven-note sweep (*Medieval Church Music-Dramas*).

   Alenu (*Olenu*), "It is our duty": the ancient Jewish hymn is still sung today.

   Marlowe, *Jew of Malta*, 90–91.

   For an incisive discussion of this play and its music, and of the other St. Nicholas plays, see the article by Kees Vellekoop, "Sint Nicolaas." The suggestion of the impact of Jewish psalm cantillation on this solo comes from Wagenaar-Nolthenius, "Der *Planctus Iudei*," 881–85. Her transcription is included. Play text quotes from Young, 2:346–47. Discussion also in

Smoldon, *Music of the Medieval Church Dramas*, 265–70. However, I cannot agree with Smoldon's judgment that "the music just drifts" and "is rather disappointing." Smoldon says that in this solo he, Smoldon, is looking for "order and balance." I have tried to demonstrate, however briefly, that the emotional state of *Judaeus* at this point in the drama is marked by anything but "order and balance," and that both words and music convey his disorder and imbalance.

9. The problem with talking about dance rhythms, as some analysts of this music do, is that one cannot see the "dance rhythms" in the source when, as is the case here, rhythm is not indicated. "Goliards" and "Goliard influences" on this music and on the poetry and music of the *Carmina Burana* from Benediktbeuern are often cited in discussions of their uncommon features. These "Goliards" seem to have been wandering priests and poets, according to their poems given to riotous living, minstrelsy, and debauchery (was this a kind of poetic guise?), but one does not know what their connection might have been with this drama. In the fourteenth century "jongleurs" came to be known also as "Goliards."

For a facsimile and new transcript of the *Daniel* manuscript (British Library, Egerton MS. 2615), words and music, together with discussions of the play in its own time and ours, see Ogden, *Play of Daniel*.

10. The manuscript, in a Montpellier library, is of unknown origin and has no music. See Young, 2:68.

11. Rankin, "Liturgical Drama," 352; 322–23 for music Examples 7, 8.

See also Audrey Ekdahl Davidson, "Music in the Beauvais *Ludus Danielis*," in Ogden, *Play of Daniel*, 77–86.

12. Binkley, "Greater Passion Play from Carmina Burana."

13. These aesthetic characteristics of modes given by Marion Bauer in *International Cyclopedia of Music and Musicians*, 1363, 1648; and Blom, *Grove's Dictionary of Music and Musicians*, 5:799.

A comparative table of qualities assigned to the modes by five theorists is included in: Wolf, "Anonymi cujusdam Codex Basiliensis," 409.

The Dorian and Hypomixolydian modes are the most frequently used modes in Gregorian chant. They both have approximately the range of *D* to *d*. The Phrygian is rarely used. The fact that the drama as distinct from the liturgy employs a variety of modes, particularly in scores other than those for the *Visitatio Sepulchri*, suggests conscious evocation of atmosphere and mood in scenes through music.

As Richard Crocker points out, beginning around the year 1000, an era of music theorists accompanied a new lyricism in the chant and "a much greater degree of definitive pitch content" in neumatic notation. See Crocker, "Medieval Chant," 281–83.

14. Modes in the Beauvais *Daniel* and *Ludus Paschalis* from the Tours manuscript are discussed by Smoldon, *Play of Daniel*, 8–9, and by Krieg, *Das lateinische Osterspiel von Tours*, 66*ff*.

15. Thomas, *Le "Sponsus*," 186.

16. Krieg, *Das lateinische Osterspiel von Tours*, 120.

17. Smoldon, *Peregrinus*, iv.

18. In his *Words and Music in the Middle Ages*, 361, John Stevens sees the musical relationship between the *planctus* and its framework in this drama as exemplary in general of the musical relationship between the liturgical drama and its liturgical settings.

See the transcription of Rachel's lament, from the Fleury Playbook, in ibid., 356–58.

19. Young, 2:117, 59, 84. van Waesberghe, "Dutch Easter Play"; Vellekoop, "Het paasspel van Egmond."

20. Organ participation, Young:

1:334, *Visitatio*, Essen (thirteenth century), *Te Deum.*

1:359, *Visitatio*, Diessen (fifteenth century), *Victimae Paschali, Te Deum.*

1:297, *Visitatio*, Regensburg (fifteenth century), *Alleluia surrexit pastor, Te Deum.*

1:617, *Visitatio*, Bamberg (sixteenth century), opening processional, *Te Deum.*

1:342, *Visitatio*, Halle (sixteenth century), *Te Deum.*

1:669, *Visitatio*, Zwickau (sixteenth century), opening processional, *Te Deum.*

2:250, *Annunciation*, Padua (fourteenth century), final *Magnificat.*

1:696, *Ascension*, Berlin (sixteenth century), opening processional with *Tempus est, Festum nunc celebre, Benedictus, Ite in orbem*, final processional.

1:490, Pentecost, Halle (sixteenth century), *Veni creator.*

2:256, *Assumption*, Halle (sixteenth century), at raising of image.

Also *Visitatio*, Nuremberg (seventeenth-century copy), *Ad tumulum venerunt*, final *Christ ist erstanden*, in van Waesberghe, "Das Nürnberger Osterspiel," 303–8: L193 *Visitatio* Bamberg. Also L533 *Visitatio* Berlin ca. 1530; L715a *Visitatio* Salzburg (sixteenth century); L716 *Ordo recipiendi Ss. Christi Corpus e sepulchro in Sancta Nocte Paschae* Salzburg ca. 1640; L785 *Visitatio* Gandersheim (sixteenth century); L793 *Visitatio* Liebfrauen ca. 1600.

One must be cautious here with *organ-* words. For example, *cantus organicus* and *organum* refer to polyphony, while *orgonye* means singing in parts. However, from the fifteenth century onward it is probable that in these rubrics an organ is really meant.

21. Bells at the conclusion of the *Visitatio Sepulchri*, Young: *Regularis Concordia* (tenth, eleventh centuries), 1:582, 250; Rheinau (thirteenth century), 1:597; South Germany (thirteenth century), 1:310; Indersdorf (fifteenth century), 1:333; Regensburg (fifteenth century), 1:297, 586. At Soissons (twelfth-thirteenth century), 1:304, bells were carried in the procession to the sepulchre and were rung as the Host was withdrawn and then at the high altar; other bells apparently sounded during and after the *Te Deum*. Prior to the *Te Deum*, bells accompanied the singing of *Christus resurgens* at Troyes (thirteenth century), 1:604, and *summe campanulae* sounded at St. Gall (sixteenth century), 1:622, as the last of the replies to *Dic nobis, Maria* was sung.

References related to other plays come from Padua, where bells sounded at the start of the *Officium Pastorum* (thirteenth century), unusual in that it preceded Matins, and the *campana magna* called the clergy to the church for the *Annunciation* (fourteenth): Young, 2:9, 248. Bells were also rung at the opening and closing processionals for the *Ascension* in Berlin (sixteenth century), 1:696, and at the beginning of the Pentecost celebration at Halle (sixteenth century), 1:490.

See Smits van Waesberghe, *Cymbala, Bells in the Middle Ages*, and Bowles, "Were Musical Instruments used in the Liturgical Service during the Middle Ages?"

22. See Ogden, *Play of Daniel*, for a facsimile of the original manuscript, British Library, Egerton. MS. 2615, and a

transcription by A. Marcel J. Zijlstra, and a translation. The stage direction mentions only "cythariste." They could be harp players, the harp a royal instrument belonging, for example, to King David. Or they could be lute players. A line in their subsequent music mentions drums and *citharae*.

See also Greenberg, *Play of Daniel*, ix. In the magnificent production of *Daniel* at the Cloisters in New York City, 1958, which occasioned this edition, the cue for using a number of instruments was taken from this passage. However, the lines are probably a matter of poetic license, and upon further investigation the adviser on this aspect of the performance, Edmund Bowles, changed his earlier position. See also Bowles, "Role of Musical Instruments in Medieval Sacred Drama"; Young, 2:290–301.

23. Young, 2:230, 233.

24. Wesselofsky, "Italienische Mysterien," 427–28, 429, 436, 438.

25. References to trumpets (and pipes), Young:

1:490, Pentecost, Halle (sixteenth century), trumpets, pipes (fistulatores ciuitatis), organ with hymn "Veni creator."

2:256, *Assumption*, Halle (sixteenth century), trumpets, pipes, organ at raising of image.

1:696, *Ascension*, Berlin (sixteenth century), trumpets at raising of image; drums as thunder at dropping down of Host.

1:643, *Visitatio*, Erlangen (sixteenth century), trumpets prior to *Te Deum*.

Pipes and trumpets played during the outdoor procession of the Magi through the streets of Milan to the Church of St. Eustorgio, 1336(?): Young, 2:451.

Trumpets and shotguns at the beginning of the *Visitatio* when the empty tomb is discovered: Donovan, *Liturgical Drama*, 60–62, *Visitatio* and *Elevatio* Granada (sixteenth century).

26. References to mode and repetition of melody from Stevens and Sage, "Medieval Drama." See also Stevens, *Words and Music in the Middle Ages*, where the author analyzes in detail ten of the sixteen different music-dramas which exist in complete score in one or more versions.

27. Rankin, "Liturgical Drama," 339.

28. Stevens, *Words and Music in the Middle Ages*, 361; transcription of the *Ordo Rachelis* in the Fleury Playbook, 356–58.

Additional transcription: Hoppin, "The Lament of Rachel."

29. Regarding the two instrumentalists in the *Presentation*, Mézières describes them: "Duo Iuuenes qui pulsabunt instrumenta dulcia induti erunt sicut Angeli" (Young, 2:230). "Two youths who will pluck sweet instruments will be dressed as angels." These stringed instruments ("pulsare" means "to pluck") could be lutes or harps. One could compare these "Pulsatores" with the "Cythariste" of the Beauvais *Daniel*. In their translations, Robert Haller and Albert Weiner mislead one in describing the two musicians as "striking their instruments." See Haller, *Figurative Representation*, 14; Weiner, *Philippe de Mézières' Description of the "Festum Praesentationis Beatae Mariae."*

In the twelfth-century *Jeu d'Adam* there is also a costume change: upon recognizing his sin, Adam exchanges his "red tunic" for "poor clothes sewn with figleaves." See Noomen, *Le Jeu d'Adam*, 17, 41; Axton and Stevens, "Le Jeu d'Adam," 7, 24—with music but omitting the final Prophet play.

30. "Philippe de Mézières, Presentation of Mary in the Temple (1372)," in Meredith and Tailby, *Staging of Religious Drama*, 207–25; Weiner, *Description*, 52, 53, 48, 56–57; Young, 2:227ff.

A twelfth-century text of the *Visitatio* performed in

Jerusalem mentions the throng of worshippers (propter astancium peregrinorum multitudinem), Young, 1:262; and a large crowd entered the Church of St. Eustorgio in Milan (1336) for the Magi play there (cum mirabili populorum), Young, 2:451.

31. Young, 1:482.

32. Wesselofsky, *Italienische Mysterien*, 429, 431, 437.

33. For the *Regularis Concordia*, see Sheingorn, *Easter Sepulchre in England*, 20–22, figs. 3–4; for the *Visitatio* in the Fleury Playbook, see Young, 1:393–97, and Campbell and Davidson, *Fleury "Playbook"*, figs. 51–56.

34. From recent research on the library of Fleury we know now that the late twelfth-century manuscript of the Fleury Playbook was copied at Fleury. Whether playtexts in it derived from elsewhere is another question. Conversation with Marco Mostert (University of Amsterdam), 27 May 1992, Wassenaar, The Netherlands.

In "Liturgical Drama," 355, Susan Rankin summarizes the palaeographical evidence: "Palaeographical characteristics suggest that the book was written somewhere in the Île-de-France, by an individual who lacked access to a well-provided scriptorium. Probably, it was in the student circles of either Paris or Orléans . . . ."

For the argument for Fleury see Collins, "Home of the Fleury *Playbook*," 26–34.

35. On the phenomenological questions which are raised here, see Flanigan, "Liturgical Context of the *Quem Queritis* Trope."

36. Young, 2:85.

See David Bevington's sensitive study of references to this audience: "The Staging of Twelfth-Century Liturgical Drama in the Fleury *Playbook*."

37. Young, 2:15, 45, 438.

In the *New Oxford History of Music* (2:320), Susan Rankin observes that of the five manuscript sources of the Magi play datable prior to 1050, four "are far enough dissociated from liturgical singing to suggest that, unlike *Quem queritis*, the Magi play did not originate within the liturgy." The origins of two are obscure; the other two belonged to communities of canons (Ste. Corneille de Compiègne, and the Frankfurt Salvatorstift). Susan Rankin puzzles over the meaning of this transmission pattern and concludes that "the new plays are quite unlike any contemporary ceremonies involving *Quem queritis*." These two communities of canons were linked to public churches, suggesting perhaps that the Magi play originated with the process of gift-giving by townspeople (as well as clergy). In the Cathedral of Rouen the contrast between the in-house shepherd play, for the monastics, and the public Magi play, for clergy and laity, implies differing performer-congregation relationships.

38. These texts have been cited from Lipphardt.

Braunschweig: L780.

Constance: L239, L241. For commentary on Constance see Lipphardt, 7:187. The 1502 rubric reads: "Ad matutinum ante compulsationem fit Processio ad sanctum Sepulchrum cum luminibus, thuribulo et aqua benedicta" (L241). This would mean that the *Surrexit Dominus de sepulcro* and the *Te Deum* were sung before Matins. The only other instances that I know where these pieces were performed just preceding Easter Matins occur in texts from Fulda, Rheinau, and St. Gall, also apparently recording very old practice. The positioning of the ceremony or drama was in flux and differed with geographical region. Lipphardt also notes that nowhere else but at Constance does one discover this particular relationship of three antiphons in performance: *Venite et videte, Et recordate,* and *Surrexit Dominus*.

As mentioned, an earlier text from Constance (fifteenth century, L239) also seems to put the procession out to the sepulchre immediately before Matins, including an antiphon (presumably the *Surrexit Dominus*) and the *Te Deum,* followed thereafter by the opening of Matins in the cathedral with "Domine labia mea" (Lord, open my lips). There the initial stage direction reads: "In die sancto Pasce ad Matutinas secundo pulsu angularis Domini ibunt ad sacrum Sepulcrum cum candelis et Sacerdos ornatus." For discussion of the staging at Constance Cathedral see Chapter 3 of the present study.

Gernrode: L786.

Magdeburg: L608-611.

Sion (Sitten): L746, L746a,b,c. For the early *Officium Stellae* from Sion as well as Easter texts, see Carlen, "Das Ordinarium Sedunense."

39. See Bjork, "On the Dissemination of *Quem quaeritis,*" esp. table 1 (52–53).

40. Where from a given church there are multiple manuscript copies of a liturgical drama containing an audience reference, we have tabulated that as a single audience reference: for example, multiple copies (usually with slight variations) of the *Visitatio Sepulchri* from a church with a rubric calling for the congregation to join in singing "Christ ist erstanden." However, if from that same church there is a variant manuscript of the same drama, for instance the *Visitatio Sepulchri,* with an additional rubric containing a different audience reference, for instance a rubric specifying that the Marys are to display the gravecloth to the populace, then we have tabulated that as a second audience reference. I wish to thank Julie Goda and Kathy Moon for their work on these audience tabulations.

41. Anke Roeder has undertaken a thorough study of gesture in the Easter plays as related to ecclesiastical ritual; see *Die Gebärde.*

Bibliography

Adams, Joseph Quincy. *Chief Pre-Shakespearean Dramas.* Boston: Houghton Mifflin, 1924.

Aebischer, Paul, ed. *Le Mystère d'Adam.* Paris: Minard, 1963.

Antonini, Alessandra, François-Olivier Dubuis, and Antoine Lugon. "Les fouilles récentes dans la cathédrale de Sion (1985 et 1988)." *Vallesia* 44 (1989): 61–78.

Arens, F., ed. *Der Liber Ordinarius der Essener Stiftskirche.* Paderborn: n.p., 1908.

Aubert, Marcel. "La Cathédrale [de Rouen]." *Congrès archéologique de France* 89 (1926): 11–71.

———. "Saint-Benoît-sur-Loire." *Congrès archéologique de France* 93 (1930): 569–656.

"AVISTA Sessions 1996: Cloth, Clothing, and Textiles." *AVISTA Forum* 10 (1996-97): 5–14.

Axton, Richard and John Stevens, trans. "Le Jeu d'Adam." In *Medieval French Plays.* Oxford: Blackwell, 1971.

Banchereau, Jules. *L'Église de Saint-Benoît-sur-Loire.* Paris: H. Laurens, 1930.

Bandmann, Günter. "Früh- und Hochmittelalterliche Altaranordnung als Darstellung." In *Das erste Jahrtausend.* Edited by Victor H. Elbern. 3 vols. Düsseldorf: L. Schwann, 1962–64. 1:371–411.

Barth, P. M. et al., eds. *Hildegard von Bingen, Lieder.* Salzburg: Otto Müller Verlag, 1969.

Bauer, Marion. *The International Cyclopedia of Music and Musicians.* Edited by Oscar Thompson. London: Dodd, Mead, 1964.

Belcari, Feo. *La Festa della annuntiatione di nostra donna.* Florence: Bartolomeo di Libri, ca. 1500.

Berthault, Pierre-Gabriel. *Collection complète des tableaux historique de la révolution française.* Paris: Auber, 1804.

Bevington, David. *Medieval Drama.* Boston: Houghton Mifflin, 1975.

———. "The Staging of Twelfth-Century Liturgical Drama in the Fleury Playbook." *Comparative Drama* 18 (1984): 97–117.

Biddle, Martin. *Excavations Near Winchester Cathedral, 1961–1968.* Winchester: Wykeham Press, 1969.

———. "Felix urbs Winthonia: Winchester in the Age of Monastic Reform." In *Tenth-Century Studies: Essays in Commemoration of the Millennium of the Council of Winchester and "Regularis Concordia".* Edited by David Parsons. London and Chichester: Phillimore, 1975.

Binkley, Thomas. "The Greater Passion Play from Carmina Burana: An Introduction." In *Alte Musik, Praxis und Reflexion.* Edited by Peter Reidemeister and Veronika Gutmann. Winterthur, Switz.: Amadeus, 1983. 144-57.

Bishop, T. A. M. *Aethici Istrici Cosmographia Vergilio Salisburgensi Rectius Adscripta.* Umbrae Codicum Occidentalium 10. Amsterdam: North-Holland, 1966.

Bjork, David A. "On the Dissemination of *Quem quaeritis* and the *Visitatio Sepulchri* and the Chronology of Their Early Sources." *Comparative Drama* 14 (1980): 46–69.

Blom, Eric, ed. *Grove's Dictionary of Music and Musicians.* London: Macmillan, 1954.

Boehn, Max von. *Das Bühnenkostüm.* Berlin: B. Cassirer, 1921.

Boor, Helmut de. *Die Textgeschichte der lateinischen Osterfeiern.* Hermaea, Germanistische Forschungen, neue Folge 12. Tübingen, 1967.

Borger, Hugo. "Die Architektur und ihre Geschichte." In *Das Essener Münster.* Essen: Fredebeul and Koenen, 1963.

Bowles, Edmund A. Letter to the editor. *The Galpin Society Journal* 11 (1958): 85–87.

———. Letter to the editor. *The Galpin Society Journal* 12 (1959): 89–92.

———. "The Role of Musical Instruments in Medieval Sacred Drama." *The Musical Quarterly* 45 (1959): 67-84.

———. "Were Musical Instruments used in the Liturgical Service during the Middle Ages?" *The Galpin Society Journal* 10 (1957): 40–57.

Braun, Joseph. *Der christliche Altar in seiner geschichtlichen Entwicklung.* 2 vols. Munich: Karl Widmann, 1924.

———. *Die liturgische Gewandung im Occident und Orient.* Freiburg im Breisgau: Herder, 1907.

Brockett, Clyde W. "A Previously Unknown *Ordo Prophetarum* in a Manuscript in Zagreb." *Comparative Drama* 27 (1993): 114–27.

———. "The Role of the Office Antiphon in the Tenth-Century Liturgical Drama." *Musica disciplina* 34 (1980).

Brooks, Neil C. "Eine liturgisch-dramatische Himmelfahrtsfeier." *Zeitschrift für deutsches Alterthum und deutsche Literatur* 62 (1925).

———. *The Sepulchre of Christ in Art and Liturgy.* University of Illinois Studies in Language and Literature 7. Urbana: University of Illinois Press, 1921.

Buechner, Frederick. *The Faces of Jesus.* New York: Simon and Schuster, 1974.

Campbell, Thomas P., and Clifford Davidson, eds. *The Fleury "Playbook": Essays and Studies.* Early Drama, Art, and Music Monograph Series 7. Kalamazoo, Mich.: Medieval Institute Publications, 1985.

Carlen, Albert. "Das Ordinarium Sedunense und die Anfänge der geistlichen Spiele im Wallis." *Blätter aus der Walliser Geschichte* 9 (1943): 349–73.

Carment-Lanfry, Anne-Marie. *La Cathédrale de Rouen.* Colmar: Saep, 1973.

Castrucci, Sebastiano Fantoni. *Istoria della città d'Avignone.* Vol. 1. Venice, 1678.

Cennini, Cennino d'Andrea. *Il libro dell'arte: The Craftsman's Handbook.* Edited and translated by Daniel V. Thompson, Jr. 2 vols. New Haven: Yale University Press, 1932–33.

Chambers, E. K. *The Mediaeval Stage.* 2 vols. Oxford: Oxford University Press, 1903.

Chenesseau, Georges. *L'Abbaye de Fleury à Saint-Benoît-sur-Loire.* Paris: G. van Oest, 1931.

Christie, A. G. I. *English Medieval Embroidery.* Oxford: Clarendon Press, 1938.

Clemens, Mellin, and Rosenthal. *Der Dom zu Magdeburg.* Magdeburg: Creutz'sche Buchhandlung, [1852].

Cohen, Gustave. *Anthologie du drame liturgique en France au moyen-âge.* Paris: Editions du Cerf, 1955.

———. *Histoire de la mise en scène dans le théâtre religieux français du moyen âge.* Paris: Champion, 1926.

Collins, Fletcher, Jr. "The Home of the Fleury *Playbook.*" In *The Fleury "Playbook": Essays and Studies.* Edited by Thomas P. Campbell and Clifford Davidson. Early Drama, Art, and Music Monograph Series 7. Kalamazoo, Mich.: Medieval Institute Publications, 1985. 26–84.

———. *Medieval Church Music-Dramas: A Repertory of Complete Plays.* Charlottesville: University of Virginia Press, 1972.

———. *The Production of Medieval Church Music-Drama.* Charlottesville: University of Virginia Press, 1972.

Corbin, Solange. "Le Manuscrit 201 d'Orléans." *Romania* 74 (1953): 1–43.

Coussemaker, E. de. ed. *Drames liturgiques du moyen-âge.* Rennes, 1860.

Craig, Hardin. *English Religious Drama of the Middle Ages.* Oxford: Oxford University Press, 1967.

Creizenach, Wilhelm. *Geschichte des neueren Dramas.* 5 vols. Halle: S. M. Niemeyer, 1893–1911.

Crocker, Richard. "Medieval Chant." In Crocker and Hiley. 225–309.

Crocker, Richard, and David Hiley, eds. *The New Oxford History of Music.* Vol. 2. *The Early Middle Ages to 1300.* Oxford: Oxford University Press, 1990.

Crombach, H. *Primitae Gentium, seu Historia SS. Trium Regum Magorum.* Cologne, 1654.

Dalman, D. Gustaf. *Das Grab Christi in Deutschland.* Leipzig: Dieterisch'sche Verlagsbuchhandlung, 1922.

D'Ancona, Alessandro. *Origini del teatro italiano.* 2 vols. Turin: E. Loescher, 1891.

Dante Alighieri. *La vita nuova.* Edited by Guglielmo Gorni. Turin: Giulio Einaudi, 1996.

Davenport, Millia. *The Book of Costume.* 2 vols. New York: Crown, 1948.

Davidson, Audrey Ekdahl. "Music in the Beauvais *Ludus Danielis.*" In Ogden, *Play of Daniel.* 77–86.

———, ed. Hildegard von Bingen, *"Ordo Virtutum."* Kalamazoo, Mich.: Medieval Institute Publications, 1985.

———, ed. *Holy Week and Easter Ceremonies and Dramas from Medieval Sweden.* Early Drama, Art, and Music Monograph Series 13. Kalamazoo, Mich.: Medieval Institute Publications, 1990.

Davidson, Audrey Ekdahl, and Clifford Davidson. *Performing Medieval Music Drama.* Kalamazoo, Mich.: Medieval Institute Publications, 1998.

Davidson, Clifford. "Ceremonies and Liturgical Plays." *Illustrations of the Stage and Acting in England to 1580.* Early Drama, Art, and Music Monograph Series 16. Kalamazoo, Mich.: Medieval Institute Publications, 1991. 7–18.

———. "Heaven's Fragrance." In *The Iconography of Heaven.* Edited by Clifford Davidson. Early Drama, Art, and Music Monograph Series 21. Kalamazoo, Mich.: Medieval Institute Publications, 1994.

———. "Saints and Angels." In *The Iconography of Heaven.* Edited by Clifford Davidson. Early Drama, Art, and Music Monograph Series 21. Kalamazoo, Mich.: Medieval Institute Publications, 1994.

———. *Technology, Guilds, and Early English Drama.* Early Drama, Art, and Music Monograph Series 23. Kalamazoo, Mich.: Medieval Institute Publications, 1996.

———, ed. *Gesture in Medieval Drama and Art.* Kalamazoo, Mich.: Medieval Institute Publications, 2001.

———, ed. *Material Culture and Medieval Drama.* Kalamazoo, Mich.: Medieval Institute Publications, 1998.

Dehio, Georg. *Der Bamberger Dom.* Munich: Piper, 1939.

———. *Handbuch der deutschen Kunstdenkmäler, Suddeutschland.* Vol. 3. Berlin: E. Wasmuth, 1920.

Delamare, René, ed. *Le De officiis ecclesiasticis de Jean D'Avranches, archevêque de Rouen (1067–79).* Paris: A. Picard, 1923.

Depping, Georges Bernard. *Réglemens sur les arts et métiers de Paris, rédigés au XIIIe siècle.* Paris: Crapelet, 1837.

Deville, Jean. *Revue des architectes de la cathédrale de Rouen.* Rouen, 1848.

Dolan, Diane. *Le Drame liturgique de Pâques en Normandie et en Angleterre au moyen-âge.* Paris: Presses universitaires de France, 1975.

Donovan, Richard B. *The Liturgical Drama in Medieval Spain.* Studies and Texts 4. Toronto: Pontifical Institute of Mediaeval Studies, 1958.

Douhet, Jules de. *Dictionnaire des mystères.* Paris, 1854.

Dresserus, Mattheus. *Sächsisch Chronicon.* Wittenburg: Johan Kraft, 1596.

Drumbl, Johann. *Fremde Texte.* Milan: Edizioni Unicopli, 1984.

Dubuis, François-Olivier, and Antoine Lugon. "La Cathédrale Notre-Dame de Sion: le contexte historique des vestiges découverts en 1985 et 1988." *Vallesia* 44 (1989): 79–114.

Du Cange, Charles du Fresne. *Glossarium Mediae et Infimae Latinitatis.* Graz: Akademische Druck- und Verlagsanstalt, 1954.

Ebert, Friedrich Adolf. *Der Dom zu Meissen.* Meissen: n.p., 1835.

Edwards, Robert. *The Montecassino Passion and the Poetics of Medieval Drama.* Berkeley and Los Angeles: University of California Press, 1977.

Eigentliche Beschreibung der welt-beruhmten primat-erzbischof-flichen Dom-kirchen zu Magdeburg. [Magdeburg], 1671.

Erdmann, Wolfgang et al. "Neue Untersuchungen an der Stiftskirche zu Gernrode." In *Bernwardinische Kunst.* Edited by

Martin Gosebruch. Göttingen: Verlag Erich Goltze, 1988. 245–85.

Erenstein, Robert L., and Dunbar H. Ogden. "At Hathui's Tomb and The Lions' Den." *Journal of Dramatic Theory and Criticism* 12 (1997): 160–174.

Estham, Inger. "Medeltida Textilier" and "Inredning." In *Vadstena Klosterkyrka.* Vol. 2. Sveriges Kyrkor 194. Edited by Aron Andersson. Stockholm: Almqvist and Wiksell International, 1983. 107–22.

Eveillon, Jacques. *De Processionibus Ecclesiasticis Liber.* Paris: P. Guillemot, 1655.

Fitch, Marc. "The London Makers of Opus Anglicanum." *Transactions of the London and Middlesex Archaeological Society* 29 (1976).

Flanigan, C. Clifford. "The Fleury Playbook and the Traditions of Medieval Latin Drama." *Comparative Drama* 18 (1984): 348–72.

———. "The Liturgical Context of the *Quem Queritis* Trope." *Comparative Drama* 8 (1974): 45–62.

Flüeler, M. Augustina. *Das sakrale Gewand.* Würzburg: Echter Verlag, 1964.

Fohlen, Claude. *Histoire de Besançon.* 2 vols. Paris: Nouvelle Librairie de France, 1964–65.

Frank, Grace. *The Medieval French Drama.* Oxford: Clarendon Press, 1954.

Garnier, François. *Le Langage de l'image au moyen âge.* Vol. 1. *Signification et symbolique.* Vol. 2. *Grammaire des gestes.* Paris: Le Léopard d'or, 1982, 1989.

Geijer, Agnes. *A History of Textile Art.* London: Pasold Research Fund and Sotheby Parke Bernet, 1979.

Gersdorf, E. G. *Urkundenbuch des Hochstifts Meissen.* Vol. 3. Leipzig: Giesecke and Devrient, 1867.

Gillet, Joseph. "The *Memorias* of Felipe Fernández Vallejo and the History of the Early Spanish Drama." In *Essays and Studies in Honor of Carleton Brown.* London: Oxford University Press, 1940. 264–80.

Girard, Joseph. *Évocation du vieil Avignon.* Paris: Les Éditions de Minuit, 1958.

Gmelch, Joseph, ed. *Die Kompositionen der heil. Hildegard.* Düsseldorf: L. Schwann, [1913?]. Facsimile.

Grant, Lindy. "Rouen Cathedral, 1200–1237." In *Medieval Art, Architecture and Archaeology at Rouen.* Edited by Jenny Stratford. British Archaeological Association, Leeds: Maney, 1993. 60–68.

Greenberg, Noah, ed. *The Play of Daniel.* New York: Oxford University Press, 1959.

Greg, W. W., ed. *Dramatic Documents from the Elizabethan Playhouses.* 2 vols. Oxford: Clarendon Press, 1931.

Grieschel, Walther. *Der Magdeburger Dom.* Berlin: Frankfurter Verlags-Anstalt, 1929.

Gschwend, Kolumban. *Die Depositio und Elevatio Crucis im Raum der alten Diözese Brixen.* Sarnen: L. Ehrli, 1965.

Haastrup, Ulla. "Medieval Props in the Liturgical Drama." *Hafnia* 11 (1987): 133–70.

Halio, Jay L., and Hugh Richmond, eds. *Shakespearean Illuminations: Essays in Honor of Marvin Rosenberg.* Newark, Del.: University of Delaware Press, 1998.

Haller, Robert S. *Figurative Representation of the Presentation of the Virgin Mary in the Temple.* Lincoln: University of Nebraska Press, 1971.

Hardison, O. B., Jr. *Christian Rite and Christian Drama in the Middle Ages.* Baltimore: Johns Hopkins University Press, 1965.

Haskins, Susan. *Mary Magdalen, Myth and Metaphor.* New York: Harcourt Brace, 1994.

Heitz, Carol. *Recherches sur les rapports entre architecture et liturgie à l'époque carolingienne.* Paris: S.E.V.P.E.N., 1963.

Herwegen, Ildefons, ed. *Reigen der Tugenden, Ordo Virtutum.* Berlin: Sankt Augustinus Verlag, 1927.

Holderegger, Hermann. "Die Kirche von Valeria bei Sitten." In *Anzeiger für Schweizer Altertumskunde,* Neue Folge 31.

Hope, William St. John. "The Plan and Arrangement of the First Cathedral Church of Canterbury." *Proceedings of the Society of Antiquaries of London.* 2nd ser. 30 (1917–18): 136–58.

Hope, William St. John, and E. G. C. F. Atchley. *English Liturgical Colours.* London: Society for Promoting Christian Knowledge, 1918.

Hoppin, Richard, ed. "The Lament of Rachel." *Anthology of Medieval Music.* New York: W. W. Norton, 1978.

Horn, Walter, and Ernest Born. *The Plan of St. Gall.* 3 vols. Berkeley: University of California Press, 1979.

Hunningher, Benjamin. *The Origin of the Theater.* New York: Hill and Wang, 1961.

Inguanez, Dom Mauro. "Un dramma della Passione del secolo XII." *Miscellanea Cassinese* 12 (1936).

Irsch, Nikolaus. *Der Dom zu Trier.* Düsseldorf: L. Schwann, 1931.

Jezler, Peter. "Gab es in Konstanz ein ottonisches Osterspiel?" In *Variorum munera florum, Latinität als prägende Kraft mittelalterlicher Kultur, Festschrift für Hans F. Haefele.* Edited by Adolf Reinle et al. Sigmaringen: Jan Thorbecke Verlag, [1985?].

Jungmann, Joseph. *The Mass of the Roman Rite.* 2 vols., 1951, 1955. Reprint, 1992. Westminster, Md.: Christian Classics.

King, Donald, and Santina Levey. *The Victoria and Albert Museum's Textile Collection: Embroidery in Britain from 1200 to 1750.* London: Victoria and Albert Museum, 1993.

Klukas, Arnold W. "Liturgy and Architecture: Deerhurst Priory as an Expression of the *Regularis Concordia.*" *Viator: Medieval and Renaissance Studies* 15 (1984): 81–98.

Knoll, Otto. *Die Rolle der Maria Magdalena im geistlichen Spiel des Mittelalters.* Leipzig, 1934.

Kobialka, Michal. *This Is My Body.* Ann Arbor: University of Michigan, 1999.

Koch, Norbert. "Der Innenraum des Braunschweiger Domes." In *Stadt im Wandel.* Edited by Cord Meckseper. Stuttgart: Cantz, 1985.

Krieg, Eduard. *Das lateinische Osterspiel von Tours.* Literarhistorisch musikwissenschaftliche Abhandlungen 13. Würzburg: n.p., 1956.

Kroos, Renate. "Quellen zur liturgischen Benutzung des Domes und zu seiner Ausstattung." In *Der Magdeburger Dom.* Edited by Ernest Ullmann. Leipzig: E.A. Seemann, 1989.

Kurzeja, A. *Der älteste Liber Ordinarius der Trierer Domkirche. Reclams Kunstführer, Deutschland.* Stuttgart: Reclam, 1959.

Labande, L. H. "Guide archéologique du congrès d'Avignon en 1909." *Congrès archéologique de France* 76 (1909).

Lanckoronski, Karl. *Der Dom von Aquileia.* Vienna: Gerlach and Wiedling, 1906.

Lange, Carl. *Die lateinischen Osterfeiern.* Munich: E. Stahl, 1887.

Larson, Orville K. "Ascension Images in Art and Theatre." *Gazette des Beaux Arts* 54 (1959): 161–76.

Latham, R. E. *Revised Medieval Latin Word-List from British and Irish Sources.* London: Oxford University Press, 1965.

Lespinasse, René de. *Les Métiers et corporations de la ville de Paris.* 3 vols. Paris: Imprimerie Nationale, 1886–97.

Le Verdier, Pierre. *Mystère de l'incarnation et nativité de Notre Sauveur et Rédempteur Jésus-Christ représenté à Rouen en 1474.* Vol. 1. Rouen, 1886.

Lippardt, Walther. *Lateinische Osterfeiern und Osterspiele.* 9 vols. Berlin and New York: Walter de Gruyter, 1975–90.

———. "Die Visitatio Sepulchri (III. Stufe) von Gernrode." *Daphnis* 1 (1972): 1–14.

———. "Die Visitatio Sepulchri in Zisterzienserinnenklöstern der Lüneburger Heide." *Daphnis* 1 (1972): 119–29.

Logeman, W. S. "De consuetudine monachorum." *Anglia* 13 (1891): 365–454.

Loisel, Armand. *La Cathédrale de Rouen.* Paris: Henri Laurens, [1913].

Loth, Julien. *La Cathédrale de Rouen.* Rouen, 1879.

Lugon, Antoine. "Documents relatifs à la cathédrale de Sion du bas Moyen Age au XXe siècle." *Vallesia* 44 (1989): 115–210.

Maas, Jon A. "Castello IV: A Study of the Technology of Filippo Brunelleschi." *AVISTA Forum* 7 (1993-94): 1–7.

Mâle, Émile. *L'Art religieux du XIIe siècle en France.* Paris: Armand Colin, 1928.

———. *Religious Art in France: The Twelfth Century.* Translated by Marthiel Mathews. Edited by Harry Bober. Bollingen Series 90. Part 1. Princeton: Princeton University Press, 1978.

Marlowe, Christopher. *The Jew of Malta.* Edited by N. W. Bawcutt. The Revels Plays. Manchester: Manchester University Press, 1979.

Massip, J. Frances. "The Cloud: A Medieval Aerial Device, Its Origins, and Its Use in Spain Today." *Early Drama, Art, and Music Review* 16 (1994): 65–77.

———. "The Staging of the Assumption in Europe." *Comparative Drama* 25 (1991): 17–28.

Mayer, Heinrich. *Bamberg als Kunststadt.* Bamberg: Bayerische Verlagsanstalt, 1955.

Mayer-Thurman, Christa C. *Raiment for the Lord's Service, A Thousand Years of Western Vestments.* Chicago: Art Institute of Chicago, 1975.

Mayr-Harting, Henry. *Ottonian Book Illumination.* 2 vols. London: Harvey Miller, 1991.

Mellinkoff, Ruth. *The Horned Moses in Medieval Art and Thought.* Berkeley and Los Angeles: University of California Press, 1970.

———. *Outcasts: Signs of Otherness in Northern European Art of the Late Middle Ages.* 2 vols. Berkeley and Los Angeles: University of California Press, 1993.

Meredith, Peter, and John F. Tailby, eds. *The Staging of Religious Drama in Europe in the Later Middle Ages.* Early Drama, Art, and Music Monograph Series 4. Kalamazoo, Mich.: Medieval Institute Publications, 1983.

Mézières, Philippe de. *The Presentation Play.* Edited and translated by Robert S. Haller. Lincoln: University of Nebraska Press, 1971.

Michael, Wolfgang. "Fahrendes Volk und mittelalteriches Drama."

Kleine Schriften der Gesellschaft für Theatergeschichte 17 (1960): 3-8.

———. *Frühformen der deutschen Bühne.* Berlin: Selbstverlag der Gesellschaft für Theatergeschichte, 1963.

———. "The Staging of the Bozen Passion Play." *The Germanic Review* 25 (1950): 178–95.

Migne, J. P., ed. *Patrologiae Cursus Completus: Patrologia Latina.* Vol. 150. Paris, 1854.

Milchsack, Gustav. "Die Oster- und Passionsspiele." *Benediktinische Monatsschrift* 5 (1923): 105–16.

———. *Die Oster- und Passionsspiele.* Wolfenbüttel: J. Zwissler, 1880.

Möbius, Helga. *Der Dom zu Magdeburg.* Dresden, 1967.

Molinari, Cesare. *Spettacoli fiorentini del quattrocento.* Venice: Neri Pozza, 1961.

Mone, F. J., ed. *Altteutsche Schauspiele.* Leipzig, 1841.

Monterosso, Rafaello. *Sacre rappresentazioni nel Manoscritto 201 della bibliothèque municipale di Orléans.* Edited by Giampiero Tintori. Instituta et Monumenta. Ser. 1. No. 2. Cremona, 1958.

Morcquereau, A., and J. Gajard, eds. *Paléographie musicale.* Ser. 2. Vol. 1. Solesmes, 1900.

Muir, Lynette R. *Liturgy and Drama in the Anglo-Norman "Adam".* Oxford: Blackwell, 1973.

Nagler, A. M. *The Medieval Religious Stage.* New Haven: Yale University Press, 1976.

———. *Sources of Theatrical History.* New York: Theatre Annual, 1952.

Nicoll, Allardyce. *The Development of the Theatre.* London: Harrap, 1959.

Noomen, Willem, ed. *Le Jeu d'Adam.* Paris: Honoré Champion, 1971.

———. "Le *Jeu d'Adam*: Étude descriptive et analytique." *Romania* 89 (1968): 145–93.

———. "Note sur l'élément liturgique de *Jeu d'Adam*." In *Omagiu lui Alexandru Rosetti.* Bucharest: Editura Academiei Repoublicii Socialiste Romania, 1965.

Nordsieck, Reinhold. "Der Bühnenplan des Vigil Raber: ein Beitrag zur Bühnengeschichte des Mittelalters." *Monatshefte für deutschen Unterricht* 37 (1945): 114–29.

Ogden, D. H. "Costume Change in the Liturgical Drama." *Early Drama, Art, and Music Review* 21 (1999): 80–88.

———. "Costumes and Vestments in the Medieval Music Drama." In Clifford Davidson, *Material Culture*, 1–57.

———. "Gesture and Characterization in the Liturgical Drama." In Clifford Davidson, *Gesture*, 26–47.

———. *The Play of Daniel: Critical Essays.* Early Drama, Art, and Music Monograph Series 24. Kalamazoo, Mich.: Medieval Institute Publications, 1996.

———. "Set Pieces and Special Effects in the Liturgical Drama." Part I. *Early Drama, Art, and Music Review* 18 (1996): 76–88. Part II. 19 (1996): 22–40.

———. "The Staging of *The Play of Daniel* in the Twelfth Century." In D. H. Ogden, *The Play of Daniel: Critical Essays*, 11–32.

———. "The Use of Architectural Space in Medieval Music-Drama." *Comparative Drama* 8 (1974): 63–76.

———. "The *Visitatio Sepulchri*: Public Enactment and Hidden Rite." *Early Drama, Art, and Music Review* 16 (1994): 95–102.

————. "Women Play Women in the Liturgical Drama of the Middle Ages." In Halio and Richmond, 336–60.

————, and Robert L. Erenstein. See Erenstein.

Owens, Melody. "The Montecassino Passion Play." Doctoral dissertation. University of California, Berkeley, 1987.

Pächt, Otto. *The Rise of Pictorial Narrative in Twelfth-Century England.* Oxford: Clarendon Press, 1962.

Petersen, Niels Holger. "Operaens liturgiske forankring." Doctoral dissertation. Institute of Church History, Copenhagen, Denmark, 1994.

————. "*Quem quaeritis* in Winchester as Authentic Roman Liturgy." Paper presented at the International Congress on Medieval Studies. Kalamazoo, Mich. 9 May 1993.

Planchart, Alejandro Enrique. *The Repertory of Tropes at Winchester.* 2 vols. Princeton: Princeton University Press, 1977.

Quirk, R. N. "Winchester Cathedral in the Tenth Century." *The Archaeological Journal* 114 (1959): 28–68.

Raine, James, ed. *The Historians of the Church of York.* Rolls Series 71. London: Longman, 1879.

Rankin, Susan. "Liturgical Drama." In Crocker and Hiley, 310–56.

————. "The Mary Magdalene Scene in the 'Visitatio Sepulchri' Ceremonies." *Early Music History.* Vol. 1. *Studies in Medieval and Early Modern Music.* Edited by Iain Fenlon. Cambridge: Cambridge University Press, 1981.

————. *The Music of the Medieval Liturgical Drama in France and England.* 2 vols. London and New York: Garland, 1989.

————. "A New English Source of the *Visitatio Sepulchri.*" *Journal of the Plainsong and Mediaeval Music Society* 4 (1981): 1–11.

Réau, Louis. *Iconographie de l'art chrétien.* 3 vols. Paris: Presses universitaires de France, 1955–59.

Reitzenstein, Alexander, Freiherr von. "Die Baugeschichte des Bamberger Domes." *Münchener Jahrbuch der bildenden Kunst* 11 (1934): 113–52.

Rickert, Margaret. *Painting in Britain: The Middle Ages.* Second edition. Harmondsworth: Penguin, 1965.

Rocher, J. N. M. *Histoire de l'abbaye royale de Saint-Benoît-sur-Loire.* Orléans, 1865.

Roeder, Anke. *Die Gebärde im Drama des Mittelalters: Osterfeiern, Osterspiele.* Münchener Texte und Untersuchungen zur dt. Lit. des Mittelalters 49. Munich: C. H. Beck'sche Verlagsbuchhandlung, 1974.

Ronig, F., ed. *Der Trier Dom.* Neuss: Verlag Gesellschaft fur Buchdruckerei, 1980.

Sachs, H., E. Badstübner, and H. Neumann. *Christliche Ikonographie in Stichworten.* Leipzig: Koehler und Amelang, 1980.

Schapiro, Meyer. "The Image of the Disappearing Christ." In *Late Antique, Early Christian and Mediaeval Art: Selected Papers.* New York: George Braziller, 1979. 266–87.

Schoettgen, Christian, and Georg Kreysig, eds. "Calendarium ecclesiae cathedralis Misnensis." In *Diplomataria et scriptores historiae germanicae medii aevi.* Vol. 3. Altenburg, 1755.

Schuler, E. *Die Musik der Osterfeiern, Osterspiele und Passionen des Mittelalters.* Kassel: Bärenreiter Verlag, 1951.

Schulze, Hans K. *Das Stift Gernrode.* Cologne: Böhlau, 1965.

Schwarzweber, Annemarie. *Das heilige Grab in der deutschen Bildnerei des Mittelalters.* Freiburg i. B.: Eberhard Albert Universitätsbuchhandlung, 1940.

Schwechten, F. W. *Der Dom zu Meissen.* Berlin: L. W. Wittich, 1826.

Sepet, Marius. *Les Prophètes du Christ.* Paris: Didier, 1878.

Serres, Olivier de. *The Perfect Use of Silk-Wormes.* London: N. Crynes, 1607. Reprint, New York: Da Capo Press, 1971.

Sheingorn, Pamela. *The Easter Sepulchre in England.* Early Drama, Art, and Music Reference Series 5. Kalamazoo, Mich.: Medieval Institute Publications, 1987.

Singer, Charles. "Epilogue: East and West in Retrospect." In *A History of Technology.* Edited by Charles Singer et al. 7 vols. Oxford: Clarendon Press, 1954–78. 2: 761–64.

"Sistema francese antico, derivato dal sistema di Carlomagno." *Enciclopedia italiana.* Vol. 23. Rome: Instituto della Enciclopedia italiana, 1934.

Smits van Waesberghe, J. *Cymbala, Bells in the Middle Ages.* Rome: American Institute of Musicology, 1951.

————. "A Dutch Easter Play." *Musica Disciplina* 7 (1953): 15–37.

————. *Muziek en drama in de middeleeuwen.* Amsterdam: Bigot and van Rossum, 1942.

————. "Das Nürnberger Osterspiel." In *Festschrift, Joseph Schmidt-Görg zum 60. Geburtstag.* Edited by Dagmar Weise. Bonn: Beethovenhaus, 1957. 303–8.

Smoldon, William. "The Easter Sepulchre Music Drama." *Music and Letters* 27 (1946): 1–17.

————. *The Music of the Medieval Church Dramas.* Edited by Cynthia Bourgeault. London: Oxford University Press, 1980.

————, ed. *Peregrinus.* London: Oxford University Press, [1965].

————, ed. *The Play of Daniel.* London: Plainsong and Medieval Music Society, 1960.

Staniland, Kay. *Medieval Craftsmen: Embroiderers.* London: British Museum Press, 1991.

Stevens, John. *Words and Music in the Middle Ages.* Cambridge: Cambridge University Press, 1986.

Stevens, John, and Jack Sage. "Medieval Drama." In *The New Grove Dictionary of Music and Musicians.* Vol. 12. London: Macmillan, 1980. 21–58.

Sticca, Sandro. *The Latin Passion Play: Its Origins and Development.* Albany: State University of New York, 1970.

Stone, Edward Noble, trans. *Adam.* University of Washington Publications in Language and Literature 4 (1929).

Symons, Thomas. *Regularis Concordia.* London: Nelson, 1953.

————. "Sources of the *Regularis Concordia.*" *The Downside Review* 59 (1941).

Thomas, Lucien-Paul. *Le "Sponsus".* Paris: Presses universitaires de France, 1951.

Toschi, Paolo. *Le origini del teatro italiano.* Turin: Einaudi, 1955.

Tournier, René. "La Cathédrale de Besançon." *Congrès archéologique de France* 118 (1960): 36–52.

————. *Les Églises comtoises.* Paris: A. et J. Picard, 1954.

Toynbee, Paget. *Concise Dictionary of Proper Names and Notable Matters in the Works of Dante.* New York: Phaeton Press, 1968.

Trexler, Richard C. *The Journey of the Magi: Meanings in History of a Christian Story.* Princeton: Princeton University Press, 1997.

Turchetti, Piero. "Brunelleschi, Filippo." In *Enciclopedia dello spettacolo.* Vol. 2. Rome: Le Maschere, 1954. 1198–9.

Ursinus, Johann F. *Die Geschichte der Domkirche zu Meissen.* Dresden, 1782.

Vale, Giuseppe. "Storia della Basilica doppo il secolo IX." *La basilica di Aquileia.* Bologna: N. Zanichelli, 1933.

Vasari, Giorgio. *Le vite dei piú eccellenti pittori, scultori e architetti.* Edited by Carlo Ragghianti. Milan: Classici Rizzoli, 1942.

Vecchi, Giuseppe. *Uffici drammatici padovani.* Florence: Leo S. Olschki, 1954.

Vellekoop, Kees. "De klank van licht en donker." In *Licht en donker in de middeleeuwen.* Edited by R. E. V. Stuip and K. Vellekoop. Utrecht: H. E. S. Uitgevers, 1992. 65–76.

———. "Het paasspel van Egmond." In *Floris V.* The Hague: Martinus Nijhoff, 1979. 51–70.

———. "'Orality versus Literacy'—and Music." Paper presented at a symposium of the Netherlands Institute for Advanced Study. 25 September 1991.

———. "Sint Nicolaas." In *Andere structuren, andere heiligen.* Edited by R. E. V. Stuip and K. Vellekoop. Utrecht: H. E. S. Uitgevers, 1983. 133–61.

Victoria and Albert Museum. *Opus Anglicanum, English Medieval Embroidery.* London: The Arts Council, 1963.

Voigtländer, Klaus. *Die Stiftskirche zu Gernrode und ihre Restaurierung, 1858–1872.* Berlin: Akademie Verlag, 1980.

Wackernell, J. E. *Altdeutsche Passionsspiele aus Tirol.* Graz: K. K. Universitäts-Buchdruckerei, 1897.

Wagenaar-Nolthenius, H. "Der *Planctus Iudei* und der Gesang jüdischer Märtyrer in Blois anno 1171." In *Mélanges offerts à René Crozet.* Poitiers: Société d'études médiévales, 1966.

Walton, Penelope. "Textiles." In *English Medieval Industries: Craftsmen, Techniques, Products.* Edited by John Blair and Nigel Ramsay. London: Hambledon Press, 1991.

Waterhouse, Osborn, ed. *The Non-Cycle Mystery Plays.* Early English Text Society, Extra Series 104. London, 1909.

Watson, Arthur. *The Early Iconography of the Tree of Jesus.* London: Oxford University Press, 1934.

Warner, George F., and Henry A. Wilson, eds. *The Benedictional of Saint Aethelwold.* Oxford: Roxburghe Club, 1910.

Weiner, Albert B., trans. of Philippe de Mézières. *Description of the "Festum Praesentationis Beatae Mariae".* New Haven: Andrew Kner, 1958.

Wentz, Gottfried, and Berent Schwineköper. *Das Erzbistum Magdeburg.* Germania Sacra 1. Berlin: Walter de Gruyter, 1972.

Wesselofsky, Alexander. "Italienische Mysterien in einem russischen Reisebericht des XV. Jahrhunderts." *Russische Revue* 10 (1877): 425–41.

Wickham, G. W. G. "The Romanesque Style in Medieval Drama." In *Tenth-Century Studies: Essays in Commemoration of the Millennium of the Council of Winchester and "Regularis Concordia".* Edited by David Parsons. London and Chichester: Phillimore, 1975.

Wolf, Johannes. "Anonymi cujusdam Codex Basiliensis." *Vierteljahrsschrift für Musikwissenschaft* 9 (1893).

Woolf, Rosemary. *The English Mystery Plays.* Berkeley and Los Angeles: University of California Press, 1972.

Young, Karl. *The Drama of the Medieval Church.* 2 vols. 1933. Reprint, Oxford: Clarendon Press, 1955.

———. *The Dramatic Associations of the Easter Sepulchre.* University of Wisconsin Studies in Language and Literature 10. Madison, 1920.

———. "The Origin of the Easter Play." *PMLA* 29 (1914): 1–58.

———. "Philippe de Mézières' Dramatic Office for the Presentation of the Virgin." *PMLA* 26 (1911): 181–234.

Zimmermann, W. *Das Münster zu Essen.* Essen: Fredebeul und Koenen, 1956.

Index

Numbers in boldface refer to illustration pages.